Anne's House of Dreams & Anne of Ingleside

Anne's House of Dreams & Anne of Ingleside

LUCY MAUD MONTGOMERY

NIMBUS PUBLISHING
NIMBUS.CA

Nimbus Publishing, 2026
Anne's House of Dreams - First published 1917
Anne of Ingleside - First published 1939

Nimbus Publishing Limited
3660 Strawberry Hill Street, Halifax, NS, B3K 5A9
(902) 455-4286 nimbus.ca

Artwork copyright Briana Corr Scott
Printed and bound in China
NB1861

Nimbus Publishing is based in Kjipuktuk, Mi'kma'ki, the traditional territory of the Mi'kmaq People.

Library and Archives Canada Cataloguing in Publication
Title: Anne's house of dreams ; & Anne of Ingleside / Lucy Maud Montgomery.
Other titles: Anne's house of dreams (Compilation)
Names: Montgomery, L. M. (Lucy Maud), 1874-1942, author | Container of (work): Montgomery, L. M. (Lucy Maud), 1874-1942. Anne's house of dreams. | Container of (work): Montgomery, L. M. (Lucy Maud), 1874-1942. Anne of Ingleside.
Description: Series statement: L.M. Montgomery kindred classics ; book 3
Identifiers: Canadiana 20260102792 | ISBN 9781774715147 (softcover)
Subjects: LCGFT: Novels.
Classification: LCC PS8526.O55 A68 2026 | DDC C813/.52—dc23

Canada Council for the Arts | Conseil des arts du Canada

Nimbus Publishing acknowledges the financial support for its publishing activities from the Government of Canada, the Canada Council for the Arts, and from the Province of Nova Scotia. We are pleased to work in partnership with the Province of Nova Scotia to develop and promote our creative industries for the benefit of all Nova Scotians.

Anne's House of Dreams

LUCY MAUD MONTGOMERY

NIMBUS
PUBLISHING
NIMBUS.CA

CONTENTS

1
In the Garret of Green Gables

"Thanks be, I'm done with geometry, learning or teaching it," said Anne Shirley, a trifle vindictively, as she thumped a somewhat battered volume of Euclid into a big chest of books, banged the lid in triumph, and sat down upon it, looking at Diana Wright across the Green Gables garret, with gray eyes that were like a morning sky.

The garret was a shadowy, suggestive, delightful place, as all garrets should be. Through the open window, by which Anne sat, blew the sweet, scented, sun-warm air of the August afternoon; outside, poplar boughs rustled and tossed in the wind; beyond them were the woods, where Lover's Lane wound its enchanted path, and the old apple orchard which still bore its rosy harvests munificently. And, over all, was a great mountain range of snowy clouds in the blue southern sky. Through the other window was glimpsed a distant, white-capped, blue sea—the beautiful St. Lawrence Gulf, on which floats, like a jewel, Abegweit, whose softer, sweeter Indian name has long been forsaken for the more prosaic one of Prince Edward Island.

Diana Wright, three years older than when we last saw her, had grown somewhat matronly in the intervening time. But her eyes were as black and brilliant, her cheeks as rosy, and her dimples as enchanting, as in the long-ago days when she and Anne Shirley had vowed eternal friendship in the garden at Orchard Slope. In her arms she held a small, sleeping, black-curled creature, who for two happy years had been known to the world of Avonlea as "Small Anne Cordelia." Avonlea folks knew why Diana had called her Anne, of course, but Avonlea folks were puzzled by the Cordelia. There had never been a Cordelia in the Wright or Barry connections. Mrs. Harmon Andrews said she supposed Diana had found the name in some trashy novel, and wondered that Fred hadn't more sense than to allow it. But Diana and Anne smiled at each other. They knew how Small Anne Cordelia had come by her name.

"You always hated geometry," said Diana with a retrospective smile. "I should think you'd be real glad to be through with teaching, anyhow."

"Oh, I've always liked teaching, apart from geometry. These past three years in Summerside have been very pleasant ones. Mrs. Harmon Andrews told me when I came home that I wouldn't likely find married life as much better than teaching as I expected. Evidently Mrs. Harmon is of Hamlet's opinion that it may be better to bear the ills that we have than fly to others that we know not of."

Anne's laugh, as blithe and irresistible as of yore, with an added note of sweetness and maturity, rang through the garret. Marilla in the kitchen below, compounding blue plum preserve, heard it and smiled; then sighed to think how seldom that dear laugh would echo through Green Gables in the years to come. Nothing in her life had ever given Marilla so much happiness as the knowledge that Anne was going to marry Gilbert Blythe; but every joy must bring with it its little shadow of sorrow. During the three Summerside years Anne had been home often for vacations and weekends; but, after this, a bi-annual visit would be as much as could be hoped for.

"You needn't let what Mrs. Harmon says worry you," said Diana, with the calm assurance of the four-years matron. "Married life has its ups and downs, of course. You mustn't expect that everything will always go smoothly. But I can assure you, Anne, that it's a happy life, when you're married to the right man."

Anne smothered a smile. Diana's airs of vast experience always amused her a little.

"I daresay I'll be putting them on too, when I've been married four years," she thought. "Surely my sense of humour will preserve me from it, though."

"Is it settled yet where you are going to live?" asked Diana, cuddling Small Cordelia with the inimitable gesture of motherhood which always sent through Anne's heart, filled with sweet, unuttered dreams and hopes, a thrill that was half pure pleasure and half a strange, ethereal pain.

"Yes. That was what I wanted to tell you when I 'phoned to you to come down today. By the way, I can't realise that we really have telephones in Avonlea now. It sounds so preposterously up-to-date and modernish for this darling, leisurely old place."

"We can thank the A. V. I. S. for them," said Diana. "We should never have got the line if they hadn't taken the matter up and carried it through. There was enough cold water thrown to discourage any society. But they stuck to it, nevertheless. You did a splendid thing for Avonlea when you founded that society, Anne. What fun we did have at our meetings! Will you ever forget the blue hall and Judson Parker's scheme for painting medicine advertisements on his fence?"

"I don't know that I'm wholly grateful to the A. V. I. S. in the matter of the telephone," said Anne. "Oh, I know it's most convenient—even more so than our old device of signalling to each other by flashes of candlelight! And, as Mrs. Rachel says, 'Avonlea must keep up with the procession, that's what.' But somehow I feel as if I didn't want Avonlea spoiled by what Mr. Harrison, when he wants to be witty, calls 'modern inconveniences.' I should like to have it kept always just as it was in the dear old years. That's foolish—and sentimental—and impossible.

So I shall immediately become wise and practical and possible. The telephone, as Mr. Harrison concedes, is 'a buster of a good thing'—even if you do know that probably half a dozen interested people are listening along the line."

"That's the worst of it," sighed Diana. "It's so annoying to hear the receivers going down whenever you ring anyone up. They say Mrs. Harmon Andrews insisted that their phone should be put in their kitchen just so that she could listen whenever it rang and keep an eye on the dinner at the same time. Today, when you called me, I distinctly heard that queer clock of the Pyes' striking. So no doubt Josie or Gertie was listening."

"Oh, so that is why you said, 'You've got a new clock at Green Gables, haven't you?' I couldn't imagine what you meant. I heard a vicious click as soon as you had spoken. I suppose it was the Pye receiver being hung up with profane energy. Well, never mind the Pyes. As Mrs. Rachel says, 'Pyes they always were and Pyes they always will be, world without end, amen.' I want to talk of pleasanter things. It's all settled as to where my new home shall be."

"Oh, Anne, where? I do hope it's near here."

"No-o-o, that's the drawback. Gilbert is going to settle at Four Winds Harbour—sixty miles from here."

"Sixty! It might as well be six hundred," sighed Diana. "I never can get further from home now than Charlottetown."

"You'll have to come to Four Winds. It's the most beautiful harbour on the Island. There's a little village called Glen St. Mary at its head, and Dr. David Blythe has been practising there for fifty years. He is Gilbert's great-uncle, you know. He is going to retire, and Gilbert is to take over his practice. Dr. Blythe is going to keep his house, though, so we shall have to find a habitation for ourselves. I don't know yet what it is, or where it will be in reality, but I have a little house o' dreams all furnished in my imagination—a tiny, delightful castle in Spain."

"Where are you going for your wedding tour?" asked Diana.

"Nowhere. Don't look horrified, Diana dearest. You suggest Mrs. Harmon Andrews. She, no doubt, will remark condescendingly that people who can't afford wedding 'towers' are real sensible not to take them; and then she'll remind me that Jane went to Europe for hers. I want to spend *my* honeymoon at Four Winds in my own dear house of dreams."

"And you've decided not to have any bridesmaid?"

"There isn't anyone to have. You and Phil and Priscilla and Jane all stole a march on me in the matter of marriage; and Stella is teaching in Vancouver. I have no other 'kindred soul' and I won't have a bridesmaid who isn't."

"But you are going to wear a veil, aren't you?" asked Diana, anxiously.

"Yes, indeedy. I shouldn't feel like a bride without one. I remember telling Matthew, that evening when he brought me to Green Gables, that I never expected to be a bride because I was so homely no one would ever want to marry me—unless some foreign missionary did. I had an idea then that foreign missionaries couldn't afford to be finicky in the matter of looks if they wanted a girl to risk her life among cannibals. You should have seen the foreign missionary Priscilla married. He was as handsome and inscrutable as those day-dreams we once planned to marry ourselves, Diana; he was the best dressed man I ever met, and he raved over Priscilla's 'ethereal, golden beauty.' But of course there are no cannibals in Japan."

"Your wedding dress is a dream, anyhow," sighed Diana rapturously. "You'll look like a perfect queen in it—you're so tall and slender. How *do* you keep so slim, Anne? I'm fatter than ever—I'll soon have no waist at all."

"Stoutness and slimness seem to be matters of predestination," said Anne. "At all events, Mrs. Harmon Andrews can't say to you what she said to me when I came home from

Summerside, 'Well, Anne, you're just about as skinny as ever.' It sounds quite romantic to be 'slender,' but 'skinny' has a very different tang."

"Mrs. Harmon has been talking about your trousseau. She admits it's as nice as Jane's, although she says Jane married a millionaire and you are only marrying a 'poor doctor without a cent to his name.' "

Anne laughed.

"My dresses *are* nice. I love pretty things. I remember the first pretty dress I ever had—the brown gloria Matthew gave me for our school concert. Before that everything I had was so ugly. It seemed to me that I stepped into a new world that night."

"That was the night Gilbert recited 'Bingen on the Rhine,' and looked at you when he said, 'There's another, *not* a sister.' And you were so furious because he put your pink tissue rose in his breast pocket! You didn't much imagine then that you would ever marry him."

"Oh, well, that's another instance of predestination," laughed Anne, as they went down the garret stairs.

2
The House of Dreams

There was more excitement in the air of Green Gables than there had ever been before in all its history. Even Marilla was so excited that she couldn't help showing it—which was little short of being phenomenal.

"There's never been a wedding in this house," she said, half apologetically, to Mrs. Rachel Lynde. "When I was a child I heard an old minister say that a house was not a real home until it had been consecrated by a birth, a wedding and a death. We've had deaths here—my father and mother died here as well as Matthew; and we've even had a birth here. Long ago, just after we moved into this house, we had a married hired man for a little while, and his wife had a baby here. But there's never been a wedding before. It does seem so strange to think of Anne being married. In a way she just seems to me the little girl Matthew brought home here fourteen years ago. I can't realise that she's grown up. I shall never forget what I felt when I saw Matthew bringing in a *girl.* I wonder what became of the boy we would have got if there hadn't been a mistake. I wonder what *his* fate was."

"Well, it was a fortunate mistake," said Mrs. Rachel Lynde, "though, mind you, there was a time I didn't think so—that evening I came up to see Anne and she treated us to such a scene. Many things have changed since then, that's what."

Mrs. Rachel sighed, and then brisked up again. When weddings were in order Mrs. Rachel was ready to let the dead past bury its dead.

"I'm going to give Anne two of my cotton warp spreads," she resumed. "A tobacco-stripe one and an apple-leaf one. She tells me they're getting to be real fashionable again. Well, fashion or no fashion, I don't believe there's anything prettier for a spare-room bed than a nice apple-leaf spread, that's what. I must see about getting them bleached. I've had them sewed up in cotton bags ever since Thomas died, and no doubt they're an awful colour. But there's a month yet, and dew-bleaching will work wonders."

Only a month! Marilla sighed and then said proudly: "I'm giving Anne that half dozen braided rugs I have in the garret. I never supposed she'd want them—they're so old-fashioned, and nobody seems to want anything but hooked mats now. But she asked me for them—said she'd rather have them than anything else for her floors. They *are* pretty. I made them of the nicest rags, and braided them in stripes. It was such company these last few winters. And I'll make her enough blue plum preserve to stock her jam closet for a year. It seems real strange. Those blue plum trees hadn't even a blossom for three years, and I thought they might as well be cut down. And this last spring they were white, and such a crop of plums I never remember at Green Gables."

"Well, thank goodness that Anne and Gilbert really are going to be married after all. It's what I've always prayed for," said Mrs. Rachel, in the tone of one who is comfortably sure that her prayers have availed much. "It was a great relief to find out that she really didn't mean to take the Kingsport man. He was rich to be sure, and Gilbert is poor—at least, to begin with; but then he's an Island boy."

"He's Gilbert Blythe," said Marilla contentedly.

Marilla would have died the death before she would have put into words the thought that was always in the background of her mind whenever she had looked at Gilbert from his childhood up—the thought that, had it not been for her own wilful pride long, long ago, he might have been *her* son. Marilla felt that, in some strange way, his marriage with Anne would put right that old mistake. Good had come out of the evil of the ancient bitterness.

As for Anne herself, she was so happy that she almost felt frightened. The gods, so says the old superstition, do not like to behold too happy mortals. It is certain, at least, that some human beings do not. Two of that ilk descended upon Anne one violet dusk and proceeded to do what in them lay to prick the rainbow bubble of her satisfaction. If she thought she was getting any particular prize in young Dr. Blythe, or if she imagined that he was still as infatuated with her as he might have been in his salad days, it was surely their duty to put the matter before her in another light. Yet these two worthy ladies were not enemies of Anne; on the contrary, they were really quite fond of her, and would have defended her as their own young had anyone else attacked her. Human nature is not obliged to be consistent.

Mrs. Inglis—*nee* Jane Andrews, to quote from the *Daily Enterprise*—came with her mother and Mrs. Jasper Bell. But in Jane the milk of human kindness had not been curdled by years of matrimonial bickerings. Her lines had fallen in pleasant places. In spite of the fact—as Mrs. Rachel Lynde would say—that she had married a millionaire, her marriage had been happy. Wealth had not spoiled her. She was still the placid, amiable, pink-cheeked Jane of the old quartette, sympathising with her old chum's happiness and as keenly interested in all the dainty details of Anne's trousseau as if it could rival her own silken and bejewelled splendours. Jane was not brilliant, and had probably never made a remark worth listening to in her life; but she never said anything that would hurt anyone's feelings—which may be a negative talent but is likewise a rare and enviable one.

"So Gilbert didn't go back on you after all," said Mrs. Harmon Andrews, contriving to convey an expression of surprise in her tone. "Well, the Blythes generally keep their word when they've once passed it, no matter what happens. Let me see—you're twenty-five, aren't you, Anne? When I was a girl twenty-five was the first corner. But you look quite young. Redheaded people always do."

"Red hair is very fashionable now," said Anne, trying to smile, but speaking rather coldly. Life had developed in her a sense of humour which helped her over many difficulties; but as yet nothing had availed to steel her against a reference to her hair.

"So it is—so it is," conceded Mrs. Harmon. "There's no telling what queer freaks fashion will take. Well, Anne, your things are very pretty, and very suitable to your position in life, aren't they, Jane? I hope you'll be very happy. You have my best wishes.

I'm sure. A long engagement doesn't often turn out well. But, of course, in your case it couldn't be helped."

"Gilbert looks very young for a doctor. I'm afraid people won't have much confidence in him," said Mrs. Jasper Bell gloomily. Then she shut her mouth tightly, as if she had said what she considered it her duty to say and held her conscience clear. She belonged to the type which always has a stringy black feather in its hat and straggling locks of hair on its neck.

Anne's surface pleasure in her pretty bridal things was temporarily shadowed; but the deeps of happiness below could not thus be disturbed; and the little stings of Mesdames Bell and Andrews were forgotten when Gilbert came later, and they wandered down to the birches of the brook, which had been saplings when Anne had come to Green Gables, but were now tall, ivory columns in a fairy palace of twilight and stars. In their shadows Anne and Gilbert talked in lover-fashion of their new home and their new life together.

"I've found a nest for us, Anne."

"Oh, where? Not right in the village, I hope. I wouldn't like that altogether."

"No. There was no house to be had in the village. This is a little white house on the harbour shore, half way between Glen St. Mary and Four Winds Point. It's a little out of the way, but when we get a 'phone in that won't matter so much. The situation is beautiful. It looks to the sunset and has the great blue harbour before it. The sand-dunes aren't very far away—the sea-winds blow over them and the sea spray drenches them."

"But the house itself, Gilbert,—*our* first home? What is it like?"

"Not very large, but large enough for us. There's a splendid living room with a fireplace in it downstairs, and a dining room that looks out on the harbour, and a little room that will do for my office. It is about sixty years old—the oldest house in

Four Winds. But it has been kept in pretty good repair, and was all done over about fifteen years ago—shingled, plastered and refloored. It was well built to begin with. I understand that there was some romantic story connected with its building, but the man I rented it from didn't know it. He said Captain Jim was the only one who could spin that old yarn now."

"Who is Captain Jim?"

"The keeper of the lighthouse on Four Winds Point. You'll love that Four Winds light, Anne. It's a revolving one, and it flashes like a magnificent star through the twilights. We can see it from our living room windows and our front door."

"Who owns the house?"

"Well, it's the property of the Glen St. Mary Presbyterian Church now, and I rented it from the trustees. But it belonged until lately to a very old lady, Miss Elizabeth Russell. She died last spring, and as she had no near relatives she left her property to the Glen St. Mary Church. Her furniture is still in the house, and I bought most of it—for a mere song you might say, because it was all so old-fashioned that the trustees despaired of selling it. Glen St. Mary folks prefer plush brocade and sideboards with mirrors and ornamentations, I fancy. But Miss Russell's furniture is very good and I feel sure you'll like it, Anne."

"So far, good," said Anne, nodding cautious approval. "But Gilbert, people cannot live by furniture alone. You haven't yet mentioned one very important thing. Are there *trees* about this house?"

"Heaps of them, oh, dryad! There is a big grove of fir trees behind it, two rows of Lombardy poplars down the lane, and a ring of white birches around a very delightful garden. Our front door opens right into the garden, but there is another entrance—a little gate hung between two firs. The hinges are on one trunk and the catch on the other. Their boughs form an arch overhead."

"Oh, I'm so glad! I couldn't live where there were no trees—something vital in me would starve. Well, after that, there's no use asking you if there's a brook anywhere near. *That* would be expecting too much."

"But there *is* a brook—and it actually cuts across one corner of the garden."

"Then," said Anne, with a long sigh of supreme satisfaction, "this house you have found *is* my house of dreams and none other."

3
The Land of Dreams Among

"Have you made up your mind who you're going to have to the wedding, Anne?" asked Mrs. Rachel Lynde, as she hemstitched table napkins industriously. "It's time your invitations were sent, even if they are to be only informal ones."

"I don't mean to have very many," said Anne. "We just want those we love best to see us married. Gilbert's people, and Mr. and Mrs. Allan, and Mr. and Mrs. Harrison."

"There was a time when you'd hardly have numbered Mr. Harrison among your dearest friends," said Marilla drily.

"Well, I wasn't *very* strongly attracted to him at our first meeting," acknowledged Anne, with a laugh over the recollection. "But Mr. Harrison has improved on acquaintance, and Mrs. Harrison is really a dear. Then, of course, there are Miss Lavendar and Paul."

"Have they decided to come to the Island this summer? I thought they were going to Europe."

"They changed their minds when I wrote them I was going to

be married. I had a letter from Paul today. He says he *must* come to my wedding, no matter what happens to Europe."

"That child always idolised you," remarked Mrs. Rachel.

"That 'child' is a young man of nineteen now, Mrs. Lynde."

"How time does fly!" was Mrs. Lynde's brilliant and original response.

"Charlotta the Fourth may come with them. She sent word by Paul that she would come if her husband would let her. I wonder if she still wears those enormous blue bows, and whether her husband calls her Charlotta or Leonora. I should love to have Charlotta at my wedding. Charlotta and I were at a wedding long syne. They expect to be at Echo Lodge next week. Then there are Phil and the Reverend Jo—"

"It sounds awful to hear you speaking of a minister like that, Anne," said Mrs. Rachel severely.

"His wife calls him that."

"She should have more respect for his holy office, then," retorted Mrs. Rachel.

"I've heard you criticise ministers pretty sharply yourself," teased Anne.

"Yes, but I do it reverently," protested Mrs. Lynde. "You never heard me *nickname* a minister."

Anne smothered a smile.

"Well, there are Diana and Fred and little Fred and Small Anne Cordelia—and Jane Andrews. I wish I could have Miss Stacey and Aunt Jamesina and Priscilla and Stella. But Stella is in Vancouver, and Pris is in Japan, and Miss Stacey is married in California, and Aunt Jamesina has gone to India to explore her daughter's mission field, in spite of her horror of snakes. It's really dreadful—the way people get scattered over the globe."

"The Lord never intended it, that's what," said Mrs. Rachel authoritatively. "In my young days people grew up and married and settled down where they were born, or pretty near it. Thank goodness you've stuck to the Island, Anne. I was afraid Gilbert would insist on rushing off to the ends of the earth when he got through college, and dragging you with him."

"If everybody stayed where he was born places would soon be filled up, Mrs. Lynde."

"Oh, I'm not going to argue with you, Anne. *I* am not a B.A. What time of the day is the ceremony to be?"

"We have decided on noon—high noon, as the society reporters say. That will give us time to catch the evening train to Glen St. Mary."

"And you'll be married in the parlour?"

"No—not unless it rains. We mean to be married in the orchard—with the blue sky over us and the sunshine around us. Do you know when and where I'd like to be married, if I could? It would be at dawn—a June dawn, with a glorious sunrise, and roses blooming in the gardens; and I would slip down and meet Gilbert and we would go together to the heart of the beech woods,—and there, under the green arches that would be like a splendid cathedral, we would be married." Marilla sniffed scornfully and Mrs. Lynde looked shocked.

"But that would be terrible queer, Anne. Why, it wouldn't really seem legal. And what would Mrs. Harmon Andrews say?"

"Ah, there's the rub," sighed Anne. "There are so many things in life we cannot do because of the fear of what Mrs. Harmon Andrews would say. "Tis true, 'tis pity, and pity 'tis, 'tis true.' What delightful things we might do were it not for Mrs. Harmon Andrews!"

"By times, Anne, I don't feel quite sure that I understand you altogether," complained Mrs. Lynde.

"Anne was always romantic, you know," said Marilla apologetically.

"Well, married life will most likely cure her of that," Mrs. Rachel responded comfortingly.

Anne laughed and slipped away to Lover's Lane, where Gilbert found her; and neither of them seemed to entertain much fear, or hope, that their married life would cure them of romance.

The Echo Lodge people came over the next week, and Green Gables buzzed with the delight of them. Miss Lavendar had changed so little that the three years since her last Island visit might have been a watch in the night; but Anne gasped with amazement over Paul. Could this splendid six feet of manhood be the little Paul of Avonlea schooldays?

"You really make me feel old, Paul," said Anne. "Why, I have to look up to you!"

"You'll never grow old, Teacher," said Paul. "You are one of the fortunate mortals who have found and drunk from the Fountain of Youth,—you and Mother Lavendar. See here! When you're married I *won't* call you Mrs. Blythe. To me you'll always be 'Teacher'—the teacher of the best lessons I ever learned. I want to show you something."

The "something" was a pocketbook full of poems. Paul had put some of his beautiful fancies into verse, and magazine editors had not been as unappreciative as they are sometimes supposed to be. Anne read Paul's poems with real delight. They were full of charm and promise.

"You'll be famous yet, Paul. I always dreamed of having one famous pupil. He was to be a college president—but a great poet would be even better. Some day I'll be able to boast that I whipped the distinguished Paul Irving. But then I never did whip you, did I Paul? What an opportunity lost! I think I kept you in at recess, however."

"You may be famous yourself, Teacher. I've seen a good deal of your work these last three years."

"No. I know what I can do. I can write pretty, fanciful little sketches that children love and editors send welcome cheques for.

But I can do nothing big. My only chance for earthly immortality is a corner in your Memoirs."

Charlotta the Fourth had discarded the blue bows but her freckles were not noticeably less.

"I never did think I'd come down to marrying a Yankee, Miss Shirley, ma'am," she said. "But you never know what's before you, and it isn't his fault. He was born that way."

"You're a Yankee yourself, Charlotta, since you've married one."

"Miss Shirley, ma'am, I'm *not!* And I wouldn't be if I was to marry a dozen Yankees! Tom's kind of nice. And besides, I thought I'd better not be too hard to please, for I mightn't get another chance. Tom don't drink and he don't growl because he has to work between meals, and when all's said and done I'm satisfied, Miss Shirley, ma'am."

"Does he call you Leonora?" asked Anne.

"Goodness, no, Miss Shirley, ma'am. I wouldn't know who he meant if he did. Of course, when we got married he had to say, 'I take thee, Leonora,' and I declare to you, Miss Shirley, ma'am, I've had the most dreadful feeling ever since that it wasn't me he was talking to and I haven't been rightly married at all. And so you're going to be married yourself, Miss Shirley, ma'am? I always thought I'd like to marry a doctor. It would be so handy when the children had measles and croup. Tom is only a bricklayer, but he's real good-tempered. When I said to him, says I, 'Tom, can I go to Miss Shirley's wedding? I mean to go anyhow, but I'd like to have your consent,' he just says, 'Suit yourself, Charlotta, and you'll suit me.' That's a real pleasant kind of husband to have, Miss Shirley, ma'am."

Philippa and her Reverend Jo arrived at Green Gables the day before the wedding. Anne and Phil had a rapturous meeting which presently simmered down to a cosy, confidential chat over all that had been and was about to be.

"Queen Anne, you're as queenly as ever. I've got fearfully thin since the babies came. I'm not half so good-looking; but I think Jo likes it. There's not such a contrast between us, you see. And oh, it's perfectly magnificent that you're going to marry Gilbert. Roy Gardner wouldn't have done at all, at all. I can see that now, though I was horribly disappointed at the time. You know, Anne, you did treat Roy very badly."

"He has recovered, I understand," smiled Anne.

"Oh, yes. He is married and his wife is a sweet little thing and they're perfectly happy. Everything works together for good. Jo and the Bible say that, and they are pretty good authorities."

"Are Alec and Alonzo married yet?"

"Alec is, but Alonzo isn't. How those dear old days at Patty's Place come back when I'm talking to you, Anne! What fun we had!"

"Have you been to Patty's Place lately?"

"Oh, yes, I go often. Miss Patty and Miss Maria still sit by the fireplace and knit. And that reminds me—we've brought you a wedding gift from them, Anne. Guess what it is."

"I never could. How did they know I was going to be married?"

"Oh, I told them. I was there last week. And they were so interested. Two days ago Miss Patty wrote me a note asking me to call; and then she asked if I would take her gift to you. What would you wish most from Patty's Place, Anne?"

"You can't mean that Miss Patty has sent me her china dogs?"

"Go up head. They're in my trunk this very moment. And I've a letter for you. Wait a moment and I'll get it."

"Dear Miss Shirley," Miss Patty had written, "Maria and I were very much interested in hearing of your approaching nuptials. We send you our best wishes. Maria and I have never married, but we have no objection to other people doing so. We are sending you the china dogs. I intended to leave them to you in my will, because you seemed to have a sincere affection for them. But Maria and I expect to live a good while yet (D.V.), so I have decided to give you the dogs while you are young. You will not have forgotten that Gog looks to the right and Magog to the left."

"Just fancy those lovely old dogs sitting by the fireplace in my house of dreams," said Anne rapturously. "I never expected anything so delightful."

That evening Green Gables hummed with preparations for the following day; but in the twilight Anne slipped away. She had a little pilgrimage to make on this last day of her girlhood and she must make it alone. She went to Matthew's grave, in the little poplar-shaded Avonlea graveyard, and there kept a silent tryst with old memories and immortal loves.

"How glad Matthew would be tomorrow if he were here," she whispered. "But I believe he does know and is glad of it—somewhere else. I've read somewhere that 'our dead are never dead until we have forgotten them.' Matthew will never be dead to me, for I can never forget him."

She left on his grave the flowers she had brought and walked slowly down the long hill. It was a gracious evening, full of delectable lights and shadows. In the west was a sky of mackerel clouds—crimson and amber-tinted, with long strips of apple-green sky between. Beyond was the glimmering radiance of a sunset sea, and the ceaseless voice of many waters came up from the tawny shore. All around her, lying in the fine, beautiful country silence, were the hills and fields and woods she had known and loved so long.

"History repeats itself," said Gilbert, joining her as she passed the Blythe gate. "Do you remember our first walk down this hill, Anne—our first walk together anywhere, for that matter?"

"I was coming home in the twilight from Matthew's grave—and you came out of the gate; and I swallowed the pride of years and spoke to you."

"And all heaven opened before me," supplemented Gilbert. "From that moment I looked forward to tomorrow. When I left you at your gate that night and walked home I was the happiest boy in the world. Anne had forgiven me."

"I think you had the most to forgive. I was an ungrateful little wretch—and after you had really saved my life that day on the pond, too. How I loathed that load of obligation at first! I don't deserve the happiness that has come to me."

Gilbert laughed and clasped tighter the girlish hand that wore his ring. Anne's engagement ring was a circlet of pearls. She had refused to wear a diamond.

"I've never really liked diamonds since I found out they weren't the lovely purple I had dreamed. They will always suggest my old disappointment."

"But pearls are for tears, the old legend says," Gilbert had objected.

"I'm not afraid of that. And tears can be happy as well as sad. My very happiest moments have been when I had tears in my eyes—when Marilla told me I might stay at Green Gables—when Matthew gave me the first pretty dress I ever had—when I heard that you were going to recover from the fever. So give me pearls for our troth ring, Gilbert, and I'll willingly accept the sorrow of life with its joy."

But tonight our lovers thought only of joy and never of sorrow. For the morrow was their wedding day, and their house of dreams awaited them on the misty, purple shore of Four Winds Harbour.

4
The First Bride of Green Gables

Anne wakened on the morning of her wedding day to find the sunshine winking in at the window of the little porch gable and a September breeze frolicking with her curtains.

"I'm so glad the sun will shine on me," she thought happily.

She recalled the first morning she had wakened in that little porch room, when the sunshine had crept in on her through the blossom-drift of the old Snow Queen. That had not been a happy wakening, for it brought with it the bitter disappointment of the preceding night. But since then the little room had been endeared and consecrated by years of happy childhood dreams and maiden visions. To it she had come back joyfully after all her absences; at its window she had knelt through that night of bitter agony when she believed Gilbert dying, and by it she had sat in speechless happiness the night of her betrothal. Many vigils of joy and some of sorrow had been kept there; and today she must leave it forever. Henceforth it would be hers no more; fifteen-year-old Dora was to inherit it when she had gone. Nor did Anne wish it otherwise; the little room was sacred to youth and girlhood—to the past that was to close today before the chapter of wifehood opened.

Green Gables was a busy and joyous house that forenoon. Diana arrived early, with little Fred and Small Anne Cordelia, to lend a hand. Davy and Dora, the Green Gables twins, whisked the babies off to the garden.

"Don't let Small Anne Cordelia spoil her clothes," warned Diana anxiously.

"You needn't be afraid to trust her with Dora," said Marilla. "That child is more sensible and careful than most of the mothers

I've known. She's really a wonder in some ways. Not much like that other harum-scarum I brought up."

Marilla smiled across her chicken salad at Anne. It might even be suspected that she liked the harum-scarum best after all.

"Those twins are real nice children," said Mrs. Rachel, when she was sure they were out of earshot. "Dora is so womanly and helpful, and Davy is developing into a very smart boy. He isn't the holy terror for mischief he used to be."

"I never was so distracted in my life as I was the first six months he was here," acknowledged Marilla. "After that I suppose I got used to him. He's taken a great notion to farming lately, and wants me to let him try running the farm next year. I may, for Mr. Barry doesn't think he'll want to rent it much longer, and some new arrangement will have to be made."

"Well, you certainly have a lovely day for your wedding, Anne," said Diana, as she slipped a voluminous apron over her silken array. "You couldn't have had a finer one if you'd ordered it from Eaton's."

"Indeed, there's too much money going out of this Island to that same Eaton's," said Mrs. Lynde indignantly. She had strong views on the subject of octopuslike department stores, and never lost an opportunity of airing them. "And as for those catalogues of theirs, they're the Avonlea girls' Bible now, that's what. They pore over them on Sundays instead of studying the Holy Scriptures."

"Well, they're splendid to amuse children with," said Diana. "Fred and Small Anne look at the pictures by the hour."

"*I* amused ten children without the aid of Eaton's catalogue," said Mrs. Rachel severely.

"Come, you two, don't quarrel over Eaton's catalogue," said Anne gaily. "This is my day of days, you know. I'm so happy I want everyone else to be happy, too."

"I'm sure I hope your happiness will last, child," sighed Mrs. Rachel. She did hope it truly, and believed it, but she was afraid it was in the nature of a challenge to Providence to flaunt your happiness too openly. Anne, for her own good, must be toned down a trifle.

But it was a happy and beautiful bride who came down the old, homespun-carpeted stairs that September noon—the first bride of Green Gables, slender and shining-eyed, in the mist of her maiden veil, with her arms full of roses. Gilbert, waiting for her in the hall below, looked up at her with adoring eyes. She was his at last, this evasive, long-sought Anne, won after years of patient waiting. It was to him she was coming in the sweet surrender of the bride. Was he worthy of her? Could he make her as happy as he hoped? If he failed her—if he could not measure up to her standard of manhood—then, as she held out her hand, their eyes met and all doubt was swept away in a glad certainty. They belonged to each other; and, no matter what life might hold for them, it could never alter that. Their happiness was in each other's keeping and both were unafraid.

They were married in the sunshine of the old orchard, circled by the loving and kindly faces of long-familiar friends. Mr. Allan married them, and the Reverend Jo made what Mrs. Rachel Lynde afterwards pronounced to be the "most beautiful wedding prayer" she had ever heard. Birds do not often sing in September, but one sang sweetly from some hidden bough while Gilbert and Anne repeated their deathless vows. Anne heard it and thrilled to it; Gilbert heard it, and wondered only that all the birds in the world had not burst into jubilant song; Paul heard it and later wrote a lyric about it which was one of the most admired in his first volume of verse; Charlotta the Fourth heard it and was blissfully sure it meant good luck for her adored Miss Shirley. The bird sang until the ceremony was ended and then it wound up with one mad little, glad little trill. Never had the old gray-green house among its enfolding orchards known a blither, merrier afternoon. All the old jests and quips that must have done duty at weddings since Eden were served up, and seemed as new and brilliant and mirth-provoking as if they had never been uttered before. Laughter and joy had their way; and when Anne and Gilbert left to catch the Carmody train, with Paul as driver, the twins were ready with rice and old shoes, in the throwing of which Charlotta the Fourth and Mr. Harrison bore a valiant part. Marilla stood at the gate and watched the carriage out of sight down the long lane with its banks of goldenrod. Anne turned at its end to wave her last good-bye. She was gone—Green Gables was her home no more; Marilla's face looked very gray and old as she turned to the house which Anne had filled for fourteen years, and even in her absence, with light and life.

But Diana and her small fry, the Echo Lodge people and the Allans, had stayed to help the two old ladies over the loneliness of the first evening; and they contrived to have a quietly pleasant little supper time, sitting long around the table and chatting over all the details of the day. While they were sitting there Anne and Gilbert were alighting from the train at Glen St. Mary.

5

The Home Coming

Dr. David Blythe had sent his horse and buggy to meet them, and the urchin who had brought it slipped away with a sympathetic grin, leaving them to the delight of driving alone to their new home through the radiant evening.

Anne never forgot the loveliness of the view that broke upon them when they had driven over the hill behind the village. Her new home could not yet be seen; but before her lay Four Winds Harbour like a great, shining mirror of rose and silver. Far down, she saw its entrance between the bar of sand-dunes on one side and a steep, high, grim, red-sandstone cliff on the other. Beyond the bar the sea, calm and austere, dreamed in the afterlight. The little fishing village, nestled in the cove where the sand-dunes met the harbour shore, looked like a great opal in the haze. The sky over them was like a jewelled cup from which the dusk was pouring; the air was crisp with the compelling tang of the sea, and the whole landscape was infused with the subtleties of a sea evening. A few dim sails drifted along the darkening, fir-clad harbour shores. A bell was ringing from the tower of a little white church on the far side; mellowly and dreamily sweet, the chime floated across the water blent with the moan of the sea. The great revolving light on the cliff at the channel flashed warm and golden against the clear northern sky, a trembling, quivering star of good hope. Far out along the horizon was the crinkled gray ribbon of a passing steamer's smoke.

"Oh, beautiful, beautiful," murmured Anne. "I shall love Four Winds, Gilbert. Where is our house?"

"We can't see it yet—the belt of birch running up from that little cove hides it. It's about two miles from Glen St. Mary, and there's another mile between it and the lighthouse. We won't have many neighbours, Anne. There's only one house near us and I don't know who lives in it. Shall you be lonely when I'm away?"

"Not with that light and that loveliness for company. Who lives in that house, Gilbert?"

"I don't know. It doesn't look—exactly—as if the occupants would be kindred spirits, Anne, does it?"

The house was a large, substantial affair, painted such a vivid green that the landscape seemed quite faded by contrast. There was an orchard behind it, and a nicely kept lawn before it, but, somehow, there was a certain bareness about it. Perhaps its neatness was responsible for this; the whole establishment, house, barns, orchard, garden, lawn and lane, was so starkly neat.

"It doesn't seem probable that anyone with that taste in paint could be *very* kindred," acknowledged Anne, "unless it were an accident—like our blue hall. I feel certain there are no children there, at least. It's even neater than the old Copp place on the Tory road, and I never expected to see anything neater than that." They had not met anybody on the moist, red road that wound along the harbour shore. But just before they came to the belt of birch which hid their home, Anne saw a girl who was driving a flock of snow-white geese along the crest of a velvety green hill on the right. Great, scattered firs grew along it. Between their trunks one saw glimpses of yellow harvest fields, gleams of golden sand-hills, and bits of blue sea. The girl was tall and wore a dress of pale blue print. She walked with a certain springiness of step and erectness of bearing. She and her geese came out of the gate at the foot of the hill as Anne and Gilbert passed. She stood with her hand on the fastening of the gate, and looked steadily at them, with an expression that hardly attained to interest, but did not descend to curiosity. It seemed to Anne, for a fleeting moment, that there was even a veiled hint of hostility in it. But it was the girl's beauty which made Anne give a little gasp—a beauty so marked that it must have attracted attention anywhere. She was hatless, but heavy braids of burnished hair, the hue of ripe wheat, were twisted about her head like a coronet; her eyes were blue and star-like; her figure, in its plain print gown, was magnificent; and her lips were as crimson as the bunch of blood-red poppies she wore at her belt.

"Gilbert, who is the girl we have just passed?" asked Anne, in a low voice.

"I didn't notice any girl," said Gilbert, who had eyes only for his bride.

"She was standing by that gate—no, don't look back. She is still watching us. I never saw such a beautiful face."

"I don't remember seeing any very handsome girls while I was here. There are some pretty girls up at the Glen, but I hardly think they could be called beautiful."

"This girl is. You can't have seen her, or you would remember her. Nobody could forget her. I never saw such a face except in pictures. And her hair! It made me think of Browning's 'cord of gold' and 'gorgeous snake'!"

"Probably she's some visitor in Four Winds—likely some one from that big summer hotel over the harbour."

"She wore a white apron and she was driving geese."

"She might do that for amusement. Look, Anne—there's our house."

Anne looked and forgot for a time the girl with the splendid, resentful eyes. The first glimpse of her new home was a delight to eye and spirit—it looked so like a big, creamy seashell stranded on the harbour shore. The rows of tall Lombardy poplars down its lane stood out in stately, purple silhouette against the sky. Behind it, sheltering its garden from the too keen breath of sea winds, was a cloudy fir wood, in which the winds might make all kinds of weird and haunting music. Like all woods, it seemed to be holding and enfolding secrets in its recesses,—secrets whose charm is only to be won by entering in and patiently seeking. Outwardly, dark green arms keep them inviolate from curious or indifferent eyes.

The night winds were beginning their wild dances beyond the bar and the fishing hamlet across the harbour was gemmed with lights as Anne and Gilbert drove up the poplar lane. The door of the little house opened, and a warm glow of firelight flickered out into the dusk. Gilbert lifted Anne from the buggy and led her into the garden, through the little gate between the ruddy-tipped firs, up the trim, red path to the sandstone step.

"Welcome home," he whispered, and hand in hand they stepped over the threshold of their house of dreams.

6
Captain Jim

"Old Doctor Dave" and "Mrs. Doctor Dave" had come down to the little house to greet the bride and groom. Doctor Dave was a big, jolly, white-whiskered old fellow, and Mrs. Doctor was a trim, rosy-cheeked, silver-haired little lady who took Anne at once to her heart, literally and figuratively.

"I'm so glad to see you, dear. You must be real tired. We've got a bite of supper ready, and Captain Jim brought up some trout for you. Captain Jim—where are you? Oh, he's slipped out to see to the horse, I suppose. Come upstairs and take your things off."

Anne looked about her with bright, appreciative eyes as she followed Mrs. Doctor Dave upstairs. She liked the appearance of her new home very much. It seemed to have the atmosphere of Green Gables and the flavour of her old traditions.

"I think I would have found Miss Elizabeth Russell a 'kindred spirit,'" she murmured when she was alone in her room. There were two windows in it; the dormer one looked out on the lower harbour and the sand-bar and the Four Winds light.

"'A magic casement opening on the foam Of perilous seas in fairy lands forlorn,'" quoted Anne softly. The gable window gave a view of a little harvest-hued valley through which a brook ran. Half a mile up the brook was the only house in sight— an old, rambling, gray one surrounded by huge willows through which its windows peered, like shy, seeking eyes, into the dusk. Anne wondered who lived there; they would be her nearest neighbours and she hoped they would be nice. She suddenly found herself thinking of the beautiful girl with the white geese.

"Gilbert thought she didn't belong here," mused Anne, "but I feel sure she does. There was something about her that made her part of the sea and the sky and the harbour. Four Winds is in her blood."

When Anne went downstairs Gilbert was standing before the fireplace talking to a stranger. Both turned as Anne entered.

"Anne, this is Captain Boyd. Captain Boyd, my wife."

It was the first time Gilbert had said "my wife" to anybody but Anne, and he narrowly escaped bursting with the pride of it. The old captain held out a sinewy hand to Anne; they smiled at each other and were friends from that moment. Kindred spirit flashed recognition to kindred spirit.

"I'm right down pleased to meet you, Mistress Blythe; and I hope you'll be as happy as the first bride was who came here. I can't wish you no better than *that.* But your husband doesn't introduce me jest exactly right. 'Captain Jim' is my week-a-day name and you might as well begin as you're sartain to end up—calling me that. You sartainly are a nice little bride, Mistress Blythe. Looking at you sorter makes me feel that I've jest been married myself."

Amid the laughter that followed Mrs. Doctor Dave urged Captain Jim to stay and have supper with them.

"Thank you kindly. 'Twill be a real treat, Mistress Doctor. I mostly has to eat my meals alone, with the reflection of my ugly old phiz in a looking-glass opposite for company. 'Tisn't often I have a chance to sit down with two such sweet, purty ladies."

Captain Jim's compliments may look very bald on paper, but he paid them with such a gracious, gentle deference of tone and look that the woman upon whom they were bestowed felt that she was being offered a queen's tribute in kingly fashion.

Captain Jim was a high-souled, simple-minded old man, with eternal youth in his eyes and heart. He had a tall, rather ungainly figure, somewhat stooped, yet suggestive of great strength and endurance; a clean-shaven face deeply lined and bronzed; a thick mane of iron-gray hair falling quite to his shoulders, and a pair of remarkably blue, deep-set eyes, which sometimes twinkled and sometimes dreamed, and sometimes looked out seaward with a wistful quest in them, as of one seeking something precious and lost. Anne was to learn one day what it was for which Captain Jim looked.

It could not be denied that Captain Jim was a homely man. His spare jaws, rugged mouth, and square brow were not fashioned on the lines of beauty; and he had passed through many hardships and sorrows which had marked his body as well as his soul; but though at first sight Anne thought him plain she never thought anything more about it—the spirit shining through that rugged tenement beautified it so wholly.

They gathered gaily around the supper table. The hearth fire banished the chill of the September evening, but the window of the dining room was open and sea breezes entered at their own sweet will. The view was magnificent, taking in the harbour and the sweep of low, purple hills beyond. The table was heaped with Mrs. Doctor's delicacies but the *piece de resistance* was undoubtedly the big platter of sea-trout.

"Thought they'd be sorter tasty after travelling," said Captain Jim. "They're fresh as trout can be. Mistress Blythe. Two hours ago they were swimming in the Glen Pond."

"Who is attending to the light tonight, Captain Jim?" asked Doctor Dave.

"Nephew Alec. He understands it as well as I do. Well, now, I'm real glad you asked me to stay to supper. I'm proper hungry—didn't have much of a dinner today."

"I believe you half starve yourself most of the time down at that light," said Mrs. Doctor Dave severely. "You won't take the trouble to get up a decent meal."

"Oh, I do, Mistress Doctor, I do," protested Captain Jim. "Why, I live like a king gen'rally. Last night I was up to the Glen and took home two pounds of steak. I meant to have a spanking good dinner today."

"And what happened to the steak?" asked Mrs. Doctor Dave. "Did you lose it on the way home?"

"No." Captain Jim looked sheepish. "Just at bedtime a poor, ornery sort of dog came along and asked for a night's lodging. Guess he belonged to some of the fishermen 'long shore. I couldn't turn the poor cur out—he had a sore foot. So I shut him in the porch, with an old bag to lie on, and went to bed. But somehow I couldn't sleep. Come to think it over, I sorter remembered that the dog looked hungry."

"And you got up and gave him that steak—*all* that steak," said Mrs. Doctor Dave, with a kind of triumphant reproof.

"Well, there wasn't anything else *to* give him," said Captain Jim deprecatingly. "Nothing a dog'd care for, that is. I reckon he *was* hungry, for he made about two bites of it. I had a fine sleep the rest of the night but my dinner had to be sorter scanty—potatoes and point, as you might say. The dog, he lit out for home this morning. I reckon *he* weren't a vegetarian."

"The idea of starving yourself for a worthless dog!" sniffed Mrs. Doctor.

"You don't know but he may be worth a lot to somebody," protested Captain Jim. "He didn't *look* of much account, but you can't go by looks in jedging a dog. Like meself, he might be a real beauty inside. The First Mate didn't approve of him, I'll allow. His language was right down forcible. But the First Mate is prejudiced. No use in taking a cat's opinion of a dog. 'Tennyrate, I lost my dinner, so this nice spread in this dee-lightful company is real pleasant. It's a great thing to have good neighbours."

"Who lives in the house among the willows up the brook?" asked Anne.

"Mrs. Dick Moore," said Captain Jim—"and her husband," he added, as if by way of an afterthought.

Anne smiled, and deduced a mental picture of Mrs. Dick Moore from Captain Jim's way of putting it; evidently a second Mrs. Rachel Lynde.

"You haven't many neighbours, Mistress Blythe," Captain Jim went on. "This side of the harbour is mighty thinly settled. Most of the land belongs to Mr. Howard up yander past the Glen, and he rents it out for pasture. The other side of the harbour, now, is thick with folks—'specially MacAllisters. There's a whole colony of MacAllisters—you can't throw a stone but you hit one. I was talking to old Leon Blacquiere the other day. He's been working on the harbour all summer. 'Dey're nearly all MacAllisters over thar,' he told me. 'Dare's Neil MacAllister and Sandy MacAllister and William MacAllister and Alec MacAllister and Angus MacAllister—and I believe dare's de Devil MacAllister.'"

"There are nearly as many Elliotts and Crawfords," said Doctor Dave, after the laughter had subsided. "You know, Gilbert, we folk on this side of Four Winds have an old saying—'From the conceit of the Elliotts, the pride of the MacAllisters, and the vain-glory of the Crawfords, good Lord deliver us.' "

"There's a plenty of fine people among them, though," said Captain Jim. "I sailed with William Crawford for many a year, and for courage and endurance and truth that man hadn't an equal. They've got brains over on that side of Four Winds. Mebbe that's why this side is sorter inclined to pick on 'em. Strange, ain't it, how folks seem to resent anyone being born a mite cleverer than they be."

Doctor Dave, who had a forty years' feud with the over-harbour people, laughed and subsided.

"Who lives in that brilliant emerald house about half a mile up the road?" asked Gilbert.

Captain Jim smiled delightedly.

"Miss Cornelia Bryant. She'll likely be over to see you soon, seeing you're Presbyterians. If you were Methodists she wouldn't come at all. Cornelia has a holy horror of Methodists."

"She's quite a character," chuckled Doctor Dave. "A most inveterate man-hater!"

"Sour grapes?" queried Gilbert, laughing.

"No, 'tisn't sour grapes," answered Captain Jim seriously. "Cornelia could have had her pick when she was young. Even yet she's only to say the word to see the old widowers jump. She jest seems to have been born with a sort of chronic spite agin men and Methodists. She's got the bitterest tongue and the kindest heart in Four Winds. Wherever there's any trouble, that woman is there, doing everything to help in the tenderest way. She never says a harsh word about another woman, and if she likes to card us poor scalawags of men down I reckon our tough old hides can stand it."

"She always speaks well of you, Captain Jim," said Mrs. Doctor.

"Yes, I'm afraid so. I don't half like it. It makes me feel as if there must be something sorter unnatural about me."

7

The Schoolmaster's Bride

"Who was the first bride who came to this house, Captain Jim?" Anne asked, as they sat around the fireplace after supper.

"Was she a part of the story I've heard was connected with this house?" asked Gilbert. "Somebody told me you could tell it, Captain Jim."

"Well, yes, I know it. I reckon I'm the only person living in Four Winds now that can remember the schoolmaster's bride as she was when she come to the Island. She's been dead this thirty year, but she was one of them women you never forget."

"Tell us the story," pleaded Anne. "I want to find out all about the women who have lived in this house before me."

"Well, there's jest been three—Elizabeth Russell, and Mrs. Ned Russell, and the schoolmaster's bride. Elizabeth Russell was a nice, clever little critter, and Mrs. Ned was a nice woman, too. But they weren't ever like the schoolmaster's bride.

"The schoolmaster's name was John Selwyn. He came out from the Old Country to teach school at the Glen when I was a boy of sixteen. He wasn't much like the usual run of derelicts who used to come out to P. E. I. to teach school in them days. Most of them were clever, drunken critters who taught the children the three R's when they were sober, and lambasted them when they wasn't. But John Selwyn was a fine, handsome young fellow. He boarded at my father's, and he and me were cronies, though he was ten years older'n me. We read and walked and talked a heap together. He knew about all the poetry that was ever written, I reckon, and he used to quote it to me along shore in the evenings. Dad thought it an awful waste of time, but he sorter endured it, hoping it'd put me off the notion of going to sea. Well, nothing could do *that*—mother come of a race of sea-going folk and it was born in me. But I loved to hear John read and recite. It's almost sixty years ago, but I could repeat yards of poetry I learned from him. Nearly sixty years!"

Captain Jim was silent for a space, gazing into the glowing fire in a quest of the bygones. Then, with a sigh, he resumed his story.

"I remember one spring evening I met him on the sand-hills. He looked sorter uplifted—jest like you did, Dr. Blythe, when you brought Mistress Blythe in tonight. I thought of him the minute I seen you. And he told me that he had a sweetheart back home and that she was coming out to him. I wasn't more'n half pleased, ornery young lump of selfishness that I was; I thought he wouldn't be as much my friend after she came. But I'd enough decency not to let him see it. He told me all about her. Her name was Persis Leigh, and she would have come out with him if it hadn't been for her old uncle. He was sick, and he'd looked after her when her parents died and she wouldn't leave him. And now he was dead and she was coming out to marry John Selwyn. 'Twasn't no easy journey for a woman in them days. There weren't no steamers, you must ricollect.

"'When do you expect her?' says I.

"'She sails on the *Royal William,* the 20th of June,' says he, 'and so she should be here by mid-July. I must set Carpenter Johnson to building me a home for her. Her letter come today. I knew before I opened it that it was good news for me. I saw her a few nights ago.'

"I didn't understand him, and then he explained—though I didn't understand *that* much better. He said he had a gift—or a curse. Them was his words, Mistress Blythe—a gift or a curse. He didn't know which it was. He said a great-great-grandmother of his had it, and they burned her for a witch on account of it. He said queer spells—trances, I think was the name he give 'em—come over him now and again. Are there such things, Doctor?"

"There are people who are certainly subject to trances," answered Gilbert. "The matter is more in the line of psychical research than medical. What were the trances of this John Selwyn like?"

"Like dreams," said the old Doctor skeptically.

"He said he could see things in them," said Captain Jim slowly. "Mind you, I'm telling you jest what *he* said—things that were happening—things that were *going* to happen. He said they were sometimes a comfort to him and sometimes a horror. Four nights before this he'd been in one—went into it while he was sitting looking at the fire. And he saw an old room he knew well in England, and Persis Leigh in it, holding out her hands to him and looking glad and happy. So he knew he was going to hear good news of her."

"A dream—a dream," scoffed the old Doctor.

"Likely—likely," conceded Captain Jim. "That's what *I* said to him at the time. It was a vast more comfortable to think so. I didn't like the idea of him seeing things like that—it was real uncanny.

"'No,' says he, 'I didn't dream it. But we won't talk of this again. You won't be so much my friend if you think much about it.'

"I told him nothing could make me any less his friend. But he jest shook his head and says, says he:

"'Lad, I know. I've lost friends before because of this. I don't blame them. There are times when I feel hardly friendly to myself because of it. Such a power has a bit of divinity in it—whether of a good or an evil divinity who shall say? And we mortals all shrink from too close contact with God or devil.'

"Them was his words. I remember them as if 'twas yesterday, though I didn't know jest what he meant. What do you s'pose he *did* mean, doctor?"

"I doubt if he knew what he meant himself," said Doctor Dave testily.

"I think I understand," whispered Anne. She was listening in her old attitude of clasped lips and shining eyes. Captain Jim treated himself to an admiring smile before he went on with his story.

"Well, purty soon all the Glen and Four Winds people knew the schoolmaster's bride was coming, and they were all glad because they thought so much of him. And everybody took an interest in his new house—*this* house. He picked this site for it, because you could see the harbour and hear the sea from it. He made the garden out there for his bride, but he didn't plant the Lombardies. Mrs. Ned Russell planted *them.* But there's a double row of rose-bushes in the garden that the little girls who went to the Glen school set out there for the schoolmaster's bride. He said they were pink for her cheeks and white for her brow and red for her lips. He'd quoted poetry so much that he sorter got into the habit of talking it, too, I reckon.

"Almost everybody sent him some little present to help out the furnishing of the house. When the Russells came into it they were well-to-do and furnished it real handsome, as you can see; but the first furniture that went into it was plain enough. This little house was rich in love, though. The women sent in quilts and tablecloths and towels, and one man made a chest for her, and another a table and so on. Even blind old Aunt Margaret Boyd wove a little basket for her out of the sweet-scented sand-hill grass. The schoolmaster's wife used it for years to keep her handkerchiefs in.

"Well, at last everything was ready—even to the logs in the big fireplace ready for lighting. 'Twasn't exactly *this* fireplace, though 'twas in the same place. Miss Elizabeth had this put in when she made the house over fifteen years ago. It was a big, old-fashioned fireplace where you could have roasted an ox. Many's the time I've sat here and spun yarns, same's I'm doing tonight."

Again there was a silence, while Captain Jim kept a passing tryst with visitants Anne and Gilbert could not see—the folks who had sat with him around that fireplace in the vanished years, with mirth and bridal joy shining in eyes long since closed forever under churchyard sod or heaving leagues of sea. Here on olden nights children had tossed laughter lightly to and fro. Here on winter evenings friends had gathered. Dance and music and jest had been here. Here youths and maidens had dreamed. For Captain Jim the little house was tenanted with shapes entreating remembrance.

"It was the first of July when the house was finished. The schoolmaster began to count the days then. We used to see him walking along the shore, and we'd say to each other, 'She'll soon be with him now.'

"She was expected the middle of July, but she didn't come then. Nobody felt anxious. Vessels were often delayed for days and mebbe weeks. The *Royal William* was a week overdue—and then two—and then three. And at last we began to be frightened, and it got worse and worse. Fin'lly I couldn't bear to look into John Selwyn's eyes. D'ye know, Mistress Blythe"—Captain Jim lowered his voice—"I used to think that they looked just like what his old great-great-grandmother's must have been when they were burning her to death. He never said much but he taught school like a man in a dream and then hurried to the shore. Many a night he walked there from dark to dawn. People said he was losing his mind. Everybody had given up hope—the *Royal William* was eight weeks overdue. It was the middle of September and the schoolmaster's bride hadn't come—never would come, we thought.

"There was a big storm then that lasted three days, and on the evening after it died away I went to the shore. I found the schoolmaster there, leaning with his arms folded against a big rock, gazing out to sea.

"I spoke to him but he didn't answer. His eyes seemed to be looking at something I couldn't see. His face was set, like a dead man's.

"'John—John,' I called out—jest like that—jest like a frightened child, 'wake up—wake up.'

"That strange, awful look seemed to sorter fade out of his eyes. He turned his head and looked at me. I've never forgot his face—never will forget it till I ships for my last voyage.

"'All is well, lad,' he says. 'I've seen the *Royal William* coming around East Point. She will be here by dawn. Tomorrow night I shall sit with my bride by my own hearth-fire.'

"Do you think he did see it?" demanded Captain Jim abruptly.

"God knows," said Gilbert softly. "Great love and great pain might compass we know not what marvels."

"I am sure he did see it," said Anne earnestly.

"Fol-de-rol," said Doctor Dave, but he spoke with less conviction than usual.

"Because, you know," said Captain Jim solemnly, "the *Royal William* came into Four Winds Harbour at daylight the next morning. Every soul in the Glen and along the shore was at the old wharf to meet her. The schoolmaster had been watching there all night. How we cheered as she sailed up the channel."

Captain Jim's eyes were shining. They were looking at the Four Winds Harbour of sixty years agone, with a battered old ship sailing through the sunrise splendour.

"And Persis Leigh was on board?" asked Anne.

"Yes—her and the captain's wife. They'd had an awful passage—storm after storm—and their provisions give out, too. But there they were at last. When Persis Leigh stepped onto the old wharf John Selwyn took her in his arms—and folks stopped cheering and begun to cry. I cried myself, though 'twas years, mind you, afore I'd admit it. Ain't it funny how ashamed boys are of tears?"

"Was Persis Leigh beautiful?" asked Anne.

"Well, I don't know that you'd call her beautiful exactly—I—don't—know," said Captain Jim slowly. "Somehow, you never got so far along as to wonder if she was handsome or not. It jest didn't matter. There was something so sweet and winsome about her that you had to love her, that was all. But she was pleasant to look at—big, clear, hazel eyes and heaps of glossy brown hair, and an English skin. John and her were married at our house that night at early candlelighting; everybody from far and near was there to see it and we all brought them down here afterwards. Mistress Selwyn lighted the fire, and we went away and left them sitting here, jest as John had seen in that vision of his. A strange thing—a strange thing! But I've seen a turrible lot of strange things in my time."

Captain Jim shook his head sagely.

"It's a dear story," said Anne, feeling that for once she had got enough romance to satisfy her. "How long did they live here?"

"Fifteen years. I ran off to sea soon after they were married, like the young scalawag I was. But every time I come back from a voyage I'd head for here, even before I went home, and tell Mistress Selwyn all about it. Fifteen happy years! They had a sort of talent for happiness, them two. Some folks are like that, if you've noticed. They *couldn't* be unhappy for long, no matter what happened. They quarrelled once or twice, for they was both high-sperrited. But Mistress Selwyn says to me once, says she, laughing in that pretty way of hers, 'I felt dreadful when John and I quarrelled, but underneath it all I was very happy because I had such a nice husband to quarrel with and make it up with.' Then they moved to Charlottetown, and Ned Russell bought this house and brought his bride here. They were a gay young pair, as I remember them. Miss Elizabeth Russell was Alec's sister. She came to live with them a year or so later, and she was a creature of mirth, too. The walls of this house must be sorter *soaked* with laughing and good times. You're the third bride I've seen come here, Mistress Blythe—and the handsomest."

Captain Jim contrived to give his sunflower compliment the delicacy of a violet, and Anne wore it proudly. She was looking her best that night, with the bridal rose on her cheeks and the love-light in her eyes; even gruff old Doctor Dave gave her an approving glance, and told his wife, as they drove home together, that that redheaded wife of the boy's was something of a beauty.

"I must be getting back to the light," announced Captain Jim. "I've enj'yed this evening something tremenjus."

"You must come often to see us," said Anne.

"I wonder if you'd give that invitation if you knew how likely I'll be to accept it," Captain Jim remarked whimsically.

"Which is another way of saying you wonder if I mean it," smiled Anne. "I do, 'cross my heart,' as we used to say at school."

"Then I'll come. You're likely to be pestered with me at any hour. And I'll be proud to have you drop down and visit me now and then, too. Gin'rally I haven't anyone to talk to but the First Mate, bless his sociable heart. He's a mighty good listener, and has forgot more'n any MacAllister of them all ever knew, but he isn't much of a conversationalist. You're young and I'm old, but our souls are about the same age, I reckon. We both belong to the race that knows Joseph, as Cornelia Bryant would say."

"'The race that knows Joseph?'" puzzled Anne.

"Yes. Cornelia divides all the folks in the world into two kinds—the race that knows Joseph and the race that don't. If a person sorter sees eye to eye with you, and has pretty much the same ideas about things, and the same taste in jokes—why, then he belongs to the race that knows Joseph."

"Oh, I understand," exclaimed Anne, light breaking in upon her. "It's what I used to call—and still call in quotation marks—'kindred spirits.'"

"Jest so—jest so," agreed Captain Jim. "We're it, whatever it is. When you come in tonight, Mistress Blythe, I says to myself, says I, 'Yes, she's of the race that knows Joseph.' And mighty glad I was, for if it wasn't so we couldn't have had any real satisfaction in each other's company. The race that knows Joseph is the salt of the airth, I reckon."

The moon had just risen when Anne and Gilbert went to the door with their guests. Four Winds Harbour was beginning to be a thing of dream and glamour and enchantment—a spellbound haven where no tempest might ever ravin. The Lombardies down the lane, tall and sombre as the priestly forms of some mystic band, were tipped with silver.

"Always liked Lombardies," said Captain Jim, waving a long arm at them. "They're the trees of princesses. They're out of fashion now. Folks complain that they die at the top and get ragged-looking. So they do—so they do, if you don't risk your neck every spring climbing up a light ladder to trim them out.

I always did it for Miss Elizabeth, so her Lombardies never got out-at-elbows. She was especially fond of them. She liked their dignity and stand-offishness. *They* don't hobnob with every Tom, Dick and Harry. If it's maples for company, Mistress Blythe, it's Lombardies for society."

"What a beautiful night," said Mrs. Doctor Dave, as she climbed into the Doctor's buggy.

"Most nights are beautiful," said Captain Jim. "But I 'low that moonlight over Four Winds makes me sorter wonder what's left for heaven. The moon's a great friend of mine, Mistress Blythe. I've loved her ever since I can remember. When I was a little chap of eight I fell asleep in the garden one evening and wasn't missed. I woke up along in the night and I was most scared to death. What shadows and queer noises there was! I dursn't move. Jest crouched there quaking, poor small mite. Seemed 'sif there wasn't anyone in the world but meself and it was mighty big. Then all at once I saw the moon looking down to me through the apple boughs, jest like an old friend. I was comforted right off. Got up and walked to the house as brave as a lion, looking at her. Many's the night I've watched her from the deck of my vessel, on seas far away from here. Why don't you folks tell me to take in the slack of my jaw and go home?"

The laughter of the goodnights died away. Anne and Gilbert walked hand in hand around their garden. The brook that ran across the corner dimpled pellucidly in the shadows of the birches. The poppies along its banks were like shallow cups of moonlight. Flowers that had been planted by the hands of the schoolmaster's bride flung their sweetness on the shadowy air, like the beauty and blessing of sacred yesterdays. Anne paused in the gloom to gather a spray.

"I love to smell flowers in the dark," she said. "You get hold of their soul then. Oh, Gilbert, this little house is all I've dreamed it. And I'm so glad that we are not the first who have kept bridal tryst here!"

8
Miss Cornelia Bryant Comes to Call

That September was a month of golden mists and purple hazes at Four Winds Harbour—a month of sun-steeped days and of nights that were swimming in moonlight, or pulsating with stars. No storm marred it, no rough wind blew. Anne and Gilbert put their nest in order, rambled on the shores, sailed on the harbour, drove about Four Winds and the Glen, or through the ferny, sequestered roads of the woods around the harbour head; in short, had such a honeymoon as any lovers in the world might have envied them.

"If life were to stop short just now it would still have been richly worth while, just for the sake of these past four weeks, wouldn't it?" said Anne. "I don't suppose we will ever have four such perfect weeks again—but we've *had* them. Everything—wind, weather, folks, house of dreams—has conspired to make our honeymoon delightful. There hasn't even been a rainy day since we came here."

"And we haven't quarrelled once," teased Gilbert.

"Well, 'that's a pleasure all the greater for being deferred,'" quoted Anne. "I'm so glad we decided to spend our honeymoon here. Our memories of it will always belong here, in our house of dreams, instead of being scattered about in strange places."

There was a certain tang of romance and adventure in the atmosphere of their new home which Anne had never found in Avonlea. There, although she had lived in sight of the sea, it had not entered intimately into her life. In Four Winds it surrounded her and called to her constantly. From every window of her new home she saw some varying aspect of it. Its haunting murmur was ever in her ears. Vessels sailed up the harbour every day to the wharf at the Glen, or sailed out again through the sunset, bound for ports that might be half way round the globe. Fishing boats went white-winged down the channel in the mornings, and returned laden in the evenings. Sailors and fisher-folk travelled the red, winding harbour roads, light-hearted and content. There was always a certain sense of things going to happen—of adventures and farings-forth. The ways of Four Winds were less staid and settled and grooved than those of Avonlea; winds of change blew over them; the sea called ever to the dwellers on shore, and even those who might not answer its call felt the thrill and unrest and mystery and possibilities of it.

"I understand now why some men must go to sea," said Anne. "That desire which comes to us all at times—'to sail beyond the bourne of sunset'—must be very imperious when it is born in you. I don't wonder Captain Jim ran away because of it. I never see a ship sailing out of the channel, or a gull soaring over the sand-bar, without wishing I were on board the ship or had wings, not like a dove 'to fly away and be at rest,' but like a gull, to sweep out into the very heart of a storm."

"You'll stay right here with me, Anne-girl," said Gilbert lazily. "I won't have you flying away from me into the hearts of storms."

They were sitting on their red sandstone doorstep in the late afternoon. Great tranquillities were all about them in land and sea and sky. Silvery gulls were soaring over them. The horizons were laced with long trails of frail, pinkish clouds. The hushed air was threaded with a murmurous refrain of minstrel winds and waves. Pale asters were blowing in the sere and misty meadows between them and the harbour.

"Doctors who have to be up all night waiting on sick folk don't feel very adventurous, I suppose," Anne said indulgently. "If you had had a good sleep last night, Gilbert, you'd be as ready as I am for a flight of imagination."

"I did good work last night, Anne," said Gilbert quietly. "Under God, I saved a life. This is the first time I could ever really claim that. In other cases I may have helped; but Anne, if I had not stayed at Allonby's last night and fought death hand to hand, that woman would have died before morning. I tried an experiment that was certainly never tried in Four Winds before. I doubt if it was ever tried anywhere before outside of a hospital. It was a new thing in Kingston hospital last winter. I could never have dared try it here if I had not been absolutely certain that there was no other chance. I risked it—and it succeeded. As a result, a good wife and mother is saved for long years of happiness and usefulness. As I drove home this morning, while the sun was rising over the harbour, I thanked God that I had chosen the profession I did. I had fought a good fight and won—think of it, Anne, *won,* against the Great Destroyer. It's what I dreamed of doing long ago when we talked together of what we wanted to do in life. That dream of mine came true this morning."

"Was that the only one of your dreams that has come true?" asked Anne, who knew perfectly well what the substance of his answer would be, but wanted to hear it again.

"*You* know, Anne-girl," said Gilbert, smiling into her eyes. At that moment there were certainly two perfectly happy people sitting on the doorstep of a little white house on the Four Winds Harbour shore.

Presently Gilbert said, with a change of tone, "Do I or do I not see a full-rigged ship sailing up our lane?"

Anne looked and sprang up.

"That must be either Miss Cornelia Bryant or Mrs. Moore coming to call," she said.

"I'm going into the office, and if it is Miss Cornelia I warn you that I'll eavesdrop," said Gilbert. "From all I've heard regarding Miss Cornelia I conclude that her conversation will not be dull, to say the least."

"It may be Mrs. Moore."

"I don't think Mrs. Moore is built on those lines. I saw her working in her garden the other day, and, though I was too far away to see clearly, I thought she was rather slender. She doesn't seem very socially inclined when she has never called on you yet, although she's your nearest neighbour."

"She can't be like Mrs. Lynde, after all, or curiosity would have brought her," said Anne. "This caller is, I think, Miss Cornelia."

Miss Cornelia it was; moreover, Miss Cornelia had not come to make any brief and fashionable wedding call. She had her work under her arm in a substantial parcel, and when Anne asked her to stay she promptly took off her capacious sun-hat, which had been held on her head, despite irreverent September breezes, by a tight elastic band under her hard little knob of fair hair. No hat pins for Miss Cornelia, an it please ye! Elastic bands had been good enough for her mother and they were good enough for *her*. She had a fresh, round, pink-and-white face, and jolly brown eyes. She did not look in the least like the traditional old maid, and there was something in her expression which won Anne instantly. With her old instinctive quickness to discern kindred spirits she knew she was going to like Miss Cornelia, in spite of uncertain oddities of opinion, and certain oddities of attire.

Nobody but Miss Cornelia would have come to make a call arrayed in a striped blue-and-white apron and a wrapper of chocolate print, with a design of huge, pink roses scattered over it.

And nobody but Miss Cornelia could have looked dignified and suitably garbed in it. Had Miss Cornelia been entering a palace to call on a prince's bride, she would have been just as dignified and just as wholly mistress of the situation. She would have trailed her rose-spattered flounce over the marble floors just as unconcernedly, and she would have proceeded just as calmly to disabuse the mind of the princess of any idea that the possession of a mere man, be he prince or peasant, was anything to brag of.

"I've brought my work, Mrs. Blythe, dearie," she remarked, unrolling some dainty material. "I'm in a hurry to get this done, and there isn't any time to lose."

Anne looked in some surprise at the white garment spread over Miss Cornelia's ample lap. It was certainly a baby's dress, and it was most beautifully made, with tiny frills and tucks. Miss Cornelia adjusted her glasses and fell to embroidering with exquisite stitches.

"This is for Mrs. Fred Proctor up at the Glen," she announced. "She's expecting her eighth baby any day now, and not a stitch has she ready for it. The other seven have wore out all she made for the first, and she's never had time or strength or spirit to make any more. That woman is a martyr, Mrs. Blythe, believe *me*. When she married Fred Proctor *I* knew how it would turn out. He was one of your wicked, fascinating men. After he got married he left off being fascinating and just kept on being wicked. He drinks and he neglects his family. Isn't that like a man? I don't know how Mrs. Proctor would ever keep her children decently clothed if her neighbours didn't help her out." As Anne was afterwards to learn, Miss Cornelia was the only neighbour who troubled herself much about the decency of the young Proctors.

"When I heard this eighth baby was coming I decided to make some things for it," Miss Cornelia went on. "This is the last and I want to finish it today."

"It's certainly very pretty," said Anne. "I'll get my sewing and we'll have a little thimble party of two. You are a beautiful sewer, Miss Bryant."

"Yes, I'm the best sewer in these parts," said Miss Cornelia in a matter-of-fact tone. "I ought to be! Lord, I've done more of it than if I'd had a hundred children of my own, believe me! I s'pose I'm a fool, to be putting hand embroidery on this dress for an eighth baby. But, Lord, Mrs. Blythe, dearie, it isn't to blame for being the eighth, and I kind of wished it to have one real pretty dress, just as if it *was* wanted. Nobody's wanting the poor mite—so I put some extra fuss on its little things just on that account."

"Any baby might be proud of that dress," said Anne, feeling still more strongly that she was going to like Miss Cornelia.

"I s'pose you've been thinking I was never coming to call on you," resumed Miss Cornelia. "But this is harvest month, you know, and I've been busy—and a lot of extra hands hanging round, eating more'n they work, just like the men. I'd have come yesterday, but I went to Mrs. Roderick MacAllister's funeral. At first I thought my head was aching so badly I couldn't enjoy myself if I did go. But she was a hundred years old, and I'd always promised myself that I'd go to her funeral."

"Was it a successful function?" asked Anne, noticing that the office door was ajar.

"What's that? Oh, yes, it was a tremendous funeral. She had a very large connection. There was over one hundred and twenty carriages in the procession. There was one or two funny things happened. I thought that die I would to see old Joe Bradshaw, who is an infidel and never darkens the door of a church, singing 'Safe in the Arms of Jesus' with great gusto and fervour. He glories in singing—that's why he never misses a funeral. Poor Mrs. Bradshaw didn't look much like singing—all wore out slaving. Old Joe starts out once in a while to buy her a present and brings home some new kind of farm machinery. Isn't that like a man? But what else would you expect of a man who never goes to church, even a Methodist one? I was real thankful to see you and the young Doctor in the Presbyterian church your first Sunday. No doctor for me who isn't a Presbyterian."

"We were in the Methodist church last Sunday evening," said Anne wickedly.

"Oh, I s'pose Dr. Blythe has to go to the Methodist church once in a while or he wouldn't get the Methodist practice."

"We liked the sermon very much," declared Anne boldly. "And I thought the Methodist minister's prayer was one of the most beautiful I ever heard."

"Oh, I've no doubt he can pray. I never heard anyone make more beautiful prayers than old Simon Bentley, who was always drunk, or hoping to be, and the drunker he was the better he prayed."

"The Methodist minister is very line looking," said Anne, for the benefit of the office door.

"Yes, he's quite ornamental," agreed Miss Cornelia. "Oh, and very ladylike. And he thinks that every girl who looks at him falls in love with him! If you and the young doctor take *my* advice, you won't have much to do with the Methodists. My motto is—if you *are* a Presbyterian, *be* a Presbyterian."

"Don't you think that Methodists go to heaven as well as Presbyterians?" asked Anne smilelessly.

"That isn't for *us* to decide. It's in higher hands than ours," said Miss Cornelia solemnly. "But I ain't going to associate with them on earth whatever I may have to do in heaven. *This* Methodist minister isn't married. The last one they had was, and his wife was the silliest, flightiest little thing I ever saw. I told her husband once that he should have waited till she was grown up before he married her. He said he wanted to have the training of her. Wasn't that like a man?"

"It's rather hard to decide just when people *are* grown up," laughed Anne.

"That's a true word, dearie. Some are grown up when they're born, and others ain't grown up when they're eighty, believe *me.* That same Mrs. Roderick I was speaking of never grew up. She was as foolish when she was a hundred as when she was ten."

"Perhaps that was why she lived so long," suggested Anne.

"Maybe 'twas. *I'd* rather live fifty sensible years than a hundred foolish ones."

"But just think what a dull world it would be if everyone was sensible," pleaded Anne.

Miss Cornelia disdained any skirmish of flippant epigram.

"Mrs. Roderick was a Milgrave, and the Milgraves never had much sense. Her nephew, Ebenezer Milgrave, used to be insane for years. He believed he was dead and used to rage at his wife because she wouldn't bury him. *I'd* a-done it."

Miss Cornelia looked so grimly determined that Anne could almost see her with a spade in her hand. "Don't you know *any* good husbands, Miss Bryant?"

"Oh, yes, lots of them—over yonder," said Miss Cornelia, waving her hand through the open window towards the little graveyard of the church across the harbour.

"But living—going about in the flesh?" persisted Anne.

"Oh, there's a few, just to show that with God all things are possible," acknowledged Miss Cornelia reluctantly. "I don't deny that an odd man here and there, if he's caught young and trained up proper, and if his mother has spanked him well beforehand, may turn out a decent being. *Your* husband, now, isn't so bad, as men go, from all I hear. I s'pose—Miss Cornelia looked sharply at Anne over her glasses—"you think there's nobody like him in the world."

"There isn't," said Anne promptly.

"Ah, well, I heard another bride say that once," sighed Miss Cornelia. "Jennie Dean thought when she married that there wasn't anybody like *her* husband in the world. And she was right—there wasn't! And a good thing, too, believe *me*! He led her an awful life— and he was courting his second wife while Jennie was dying. Wasn't that like a man? However, I hope *your* confidence will be better justified, dearie. The young doctor is taking real well. I was afraid at first he mightn't, for folks hereabouts have always thought old Doctor Dave the only doctor in the world. Doctor Dave hadn't much tact, to be sure—he was always talking of ropes in houses where someone had hanged himself. But folks forgot their hurt feelings when they had a pain in their stomachs. If he'd been a minister instead of a doctor they'd never have forgiven him. Soul-ache doesn't worry folks near as much as stomach-ache. Seeing as we're both Presbyterians and no Methodists around, will you tell me your candid opinion of *our* minister?"

"Why—really—I—well," hesitated Anne.

Miss Cornelia nodded.

"Exactly. I agree with you, dearie. We made a mistake when we called *him*. His face just looks like one of those long, narrow stones in the graveyard, doesn't it? 'Sacred to the memory' ought to be written on his forehead. I shall never forget the first sermon he preached after he came. It was on the subject of everyone doing what they were best fitted for—a very good subject, of course; but such illustrations as he used! He said, 'If you had a cow and an apple tree, and if you tied the apple tree in your stable and planted the cow in your orchard, with her legs up, how much milk would you get from the apple tree, or how many apples from the cow?' Did you ever hear the like in your born days, dearie? I was so thankful there were no Methodists there that day—they'd never have been done hooting over it. But what I dislike most in him is his habit of agreeing with everybody, no matter what is said. If you said to him, 'You're a scoundrel,' he'd say, with that smooth smile of his, 'Yes, that's so.'

A minister should have more backbone. The long and the short of it is, I consider him a reverend jackass. But, of course, this is just between you and me. When there are Methodists in hearing I praise him to the skies. Some folks think his wife dresses too gay, but *I* say when she has to live with a face like that she needs something to cheer her up. You'll never hear *me* condemning a woman for her dress. I'm only too thankful when her husband isn't too mean and miserly to allow it. Not that I bother much with dress myself. Women just dress to please the men, and I'd never stoop to *that*. I have had a real placid, comfortable life, dearie, and it's just because I never cared a cent what the men thought."

"Why do you hate the men so, Miss Bryant?"

"Lord, dearie, I don't hate them. They aren't worth it. I just sort of despise them. I think I'll like *your* husband if he keeps on as he has begun. But apart from him, about the only men in the world I've much use for are the old doctor and Captain Jim."

"Captain Jim is certainly splendid," agreed Anne cordially.

"Captain Jim is a good man, but he's kind of vexing in one way. You *can't* make him mad. I've tried for twenty years and he just keeps on being placid. It does sort of rile me. And I s'pose the woman he should have married got a man who went into tantrums twice a day."

"Who was she?"

"Oh, I don't know, dearie. I never remember of Captain Jim making up to anybody. He was edging on old as far as my memory goes. He's seventy-six, you know. I never heard any reason for his staying a bachelor, but there must be one, believe *me*. He sailed all his life till five years ago, and there's no corner of the earth he hasn't poked his nose into. He and Elizabeth Russell were great cronies, all their lives, but they never had any notion of sweet-hearting. Elizabeth never married, though she had plenty of chances. She was a great beauty when she was young.

The year the Prince of Wales came to the Island she was visiting her uncle in Charlottetown and he was a Government official, and so she got invited to the great ball. She was the prettiest girl there, and the Prince danced with her, and all the other women he didn't dance with were furious about it, because their social standing was higher than hers and they said he shouldn't have passed them over. Elizabeth was always very proud of that dance. Mean folks said that was why she never married—she shouldn't put up with an ordinary man after dancing with a prince. But that wasn't so. She told me the reason once—it was because she had such a temper that she was afraid she couldn't live peaceably with any man. She *had* an awful temper—she used to have to go upstairs and bite pieces out of her bureau to keep it down by times. But I told her that wasn't any reason for not marrying if she wanted to. There's no reason why we should let the men have a monopoly of temper, is there, Mrs. Blythe, dearie?"

"I've a bit of temper myself," sighed Anne.

"It's well you have, dearie. You won't be half so likely to be trodden on, believe me! My, how that golden glow of yours is blooming! Your garden looks fine. Poor Elizabeth always took such care of it."

"I love it," said Anne. "I'm glad it's so full of old-fashioned flowers. Speaking of gardening, we want to get a man to dig up that little lot beyond the fir grove and set it out with strawberry plants for us. Gilbert is so busy he will never get time for it this fall. Do you know anyone we can get?"

"Well, Henry Hammond up at the Glen goes out doing jobs like that. He'll do, maybe. He's always a heap more interested in his wages than in his work, just like a man, and he's so slow in the uptake that he stands still for five minutes before it dawns on him that he's stopped. His father threw a stump at him when he was small. Nice gentle missile, wasn't it? So like a man! Course, the boy never got over it. But he's the only one I can recommend at all. He painted my house for me last spring. It looks real nice now, don't you think?"

Anne was saved by the clock striking five.

"Lord, is it that late?" exclaimed Miss Cornelia. "How time does slip by when you're enjoying yourself! Well, I must betake myself home."

"No indeed! You are going to stay and have tea with us," said Anne eagerly.

"Are you asking me because you think you ought to, or because you really want to?" demanded Miss Cornelia.

"Because I really want to."

"Then I'll stay. *You* belong to the race that knows Joseph."

"I know we are going to be friends," said Anne, with the smile that only they of the household or faith ever saw.

"Yes, we are, dearie. Thank goodness, we can choose our friends. We have to take our relatives as they are, and be thankful if there are no penitentiary birds among them. Not that I've many—none nearer than second cousins. I'm a kind of lonely soul, Mrs. Blythe."

There was a wistful note in Miss Cornelia's voice.

"I wish you would call me Anne," exclaimed Anne impulsively. "It would seem more *homey*. Everyone in Four Winds, except my husband, calls me Mrs. Blythe, and it makes me feel like a stranger. Do you know that your name is very near being the one I yearned after when I was a child. I hated 'Anne' and I called myself 'Cordelia' in imagination."

"I like Anne. It was my mother's name. Old-fashioned names are the best and sweetest in my opinion. If you're going to get tea you might send the young doctor to talk to me. He's been lying on the sofa in that office ever since I came, laughing fit to kill over what I've been saying."

"How did you know?" cried Anne, too aghast at this instance of Miss Cornelia's uncanny prescience to make a polite denial.

"I saw him sitting beside you when I came up the lane, and I know men's tricks," retorted Miss Cornelia. "There, I've finished my little dress, dearie, and the eighth baby can come as soon as it pleases."

9
An Evening at Four Winds Point

It was late September when Anne and Gilbert were able to pay Four Winds light their promised visit. They had often planned to go, but something always occurred to prevent them. Captain Jim had "dropped in" several times at the little house.

"I don't stand on ceremony, Mistress Blythe," he told Anne. "It's a real pleasure to me to come here, and I'm not going to deny myself jest because you havan't got down to see me. There oughtn't to be no bargaining like that among the race that knows Joseph. I'll come when I can, and you come when you can, and so long's we have our pleasant little chat it don't matter a mite what roof's over us."

Captain Jim took a great fancy to Gog and Magog, who were presiding over the destinies of the hearth in the little house with as much dignity and aplomb as they had done at Patty's Place.

"Aren't they the cutest little cusses?" he would say delightedly; and he bade them greeting and farewell as gravely and invariably as he did his host and hostess. Captain Jim was not going to offend household deities by any lack of reverence and ceremony.

"You've made this little house just about perfect," he told Anne. "It never was so nice before. Mistress Selwyn had your taste and she did wonders; but folks in those days didn't have the pretty little curtains and pictures and nicknacks you have. As for Elizabeth, she lived in the past. You've kinder brought the future into it, so to speak. I'd be real happy even if we couldn't talk at all, when I come here—jest to sit and look at you and your pictures and your flowers would be enough of a treat. It's beautiful—beautiful."

Captain Jim was a passionate worshipper of beauty. Every lovely thing heard or seen gave him a deep, subtle, inner joy that irradiated his life. He was quite keenly aware of his own lack of outward comeliness and lamented it.

"Folks say I'm good," he remarked whimsically upon one occasion, "but I sometimes wish the Lord had made me only half as good and put the rest of it into looks. But there, I reckon He knew what He was about, as a good Captain should. Some of us have to be homely, or the purty ones—like Mistress Blythe here—wouldn't show up so well."

One evening Anne and Gilbert finally walked down to the Four Winds light. The day had begun sombrely in gray cloud and mist, but it had ended in a pomp of scarlet and gold. Over the western hills beyond the harbour were amber deeps and crystalline shallows, with the fire of sunset below. The north was a mackerel sky of little, fiery golden clouds. The red light flamed on the white sails of a vessel gliding down the channel, bound to a southern port in a land of palms. Beyond her, it smote upon and incarnadined the shining, white, grassless faces of the sand-dunes. To the right, it fell on the old house among the willows up the brook, and gave it for a fleeting space casements more splendid than those of an old cathedral. They glowed out of its quiet and grayness like the throbbing, blood-red thoughts of a vivid soul imprisoned in a dull husk of environment.

"That old house up the brook always seems so lonely," said Anne. "I never see visitors there. Of course, its lane opens on the upper road—but I don't think there's much coming and going. It seems odd we've never met the Moores yet, when they live within fifteen minutes' walk of us. I may have seen them in church, of course, but if so I didn't know them. I'm sorry they are so unsociable, when they are our only near neighbours."

"Evidently they don't belong to the race that knows Joseph," laughed Gilbert. "Have you ever found out who that girl was whom you thought so beautiful?"

"No. Somehow I have never remembered to ask about her. But I've never seen her anywhere, so I suppose she must have been a stranger. Oh, the sun has just vanished—and there's the light."

As the dusk deepened, the great beacon cut swathes of light through it, sweeping in a circle over the fields and the harbour, the sandbar and the gulf.

"I feel as if it might catch me and whisk me leagues out to sea," said Anne, as one drenched them with radiance; and she felt rather relieved when they got so near the Point that they were inside the range of those dazzling, recurrent flashes.

As they turned into the little lane that led across the fields to the Point they met a man coming out of it—a man of such extraordinary appearance that for a moment they both frankly stared. He was a decidedly fine-looking person—tall, broad-shouldered, well-featured, with a Roman nose and frank gray eyes; he was dressed in a prosperous farmer's Sunday best; in so far he might have been any inhabitant of Four Winds or the Glen. But, flowing over his breast nearly to his knees, was a river of crinkly brown beard; and adown his back, beneath his commonplace felt hat, was a corresponding cascade of thick, wavy, brown hair.

"Anne," murmured Gilbert, when they were out of earshot, "you didn't put what Uncle Dave calls 'a little of the Scott Act' in that lemonade you gave me just before we left home, did you?"

"No, I didn't," said Anne, stifling her laughter, lest the retreating enigma should hear her. "Who in the world can he be?"

"I don't know; but if Captain Jim keeps apparitions like that down at this Point I'm going to carry cold iron in my pocket when I come here. He wasn't a sailor, or one might pardon his eccentricity of appearance; he must belong to the over-harbour clans. Uncle Dave says they have several freaks over there."

"Uncle Dave is a little prejudiced, I think. You know all the over-harbour people who come to the Glen Church seem very nice. Oh, Gilbert, isn't this beautiful?"

The Four Winds light was built on a spur of red sandstone cliff jutting out into the gulf. On one side, across the channel, stretched the silvery sand shore of the bar; on the other, extended a long, curving beach of red cliffs, rising steeply from the pebbled coves. It was a shore that knew the magic and mystery of storm and star. There is a great solitude about such a shore. The woods are never solitary—they are full of whispering, beckoning, friendly life. But the sea is a mighty soul, forever moaning of some great, unshareable sorrow, which shuts it up into itself for all eternity. We can never pierce its infinite mystery—we may only wander, awed and spell-bound, on the outer fringe of it. The woods call to us with a hundred voices, but the sea has one only—a mighty voice that drowns our souls in its majestic music. The woods are human, but the sea is of the company of the archangels.

Anne and Gilbert found Uncle Jim sitting on a bench outside the lighthouse, putting the finishing touches to a wonderful, full-rigged, toy schooner. He rose and welcomed them to his abode with the gentle, unconscious courtesy that became him so well.

"This has been a purty nice day all through, Mistress Blythe, and now, right at the last, it's brought its best. Would you like to sit down here outside a bit, while the light lasts? I've just finished this bit of a plaything for my little grand-nephew, Joe, up at the Glen. After I promised to make it for him I was kinder sorry, for his mother was vexed. She's afraid he'll be wanting to go to sea later on and she doesn't want the notion encouraged in him. But what could I do, Mistress Blythe? I'd *promised* him, and I think it's sorter real dastardly to break a promise you make to a child. Come, sit down. It won't take long to stay an hour."

The wind was off shore, and only broke the sea's surface into long, silvery ripples, and sent sheeny shadows flying out across it, from every point and headland, like transparent wings. The dusk was hanging a curtain of violet gloom over the sand-dunes and the headlands where gulls were huddling. The sky was faintly filmed over with scarfs of silken vapor. Cloud fleets rode at anchor along the horizons. An evening star was watching over the bar.

"Isn't that a view worth looking at?" said Captain Jim, with a loving, proprietary pride. "Nice and far from the market-place, ain't it? No buying and selling and getting gain. You don't have to pay anything—all that sea and sky free—'without money and without price.' There's going to be a moonrise purty soon, too—I'm never tired of finding out what a moonrise can be over them rocks and sea and harbour. There's a surprise in it every time."

They had their moonrise, and watched its marvel and magic in a silence that asked nothing of the world or each other. Then they went up into the tower, and Captain Jim showed and explained the mechanism of the great light. Finally they found themselves in the dining room, where a fire of driftwood was weaving flames of wavering, elusive, sea-born hues in the open fireplace.

"I put this fireplace in myself," remarked Captain Jim. "The Government don't give lighthouse keepers such luxuries. Look at the colours that wood makes. If you'd like some driftwood for your fire, Mistress Blythe, I'll bring you up a load some day. Sit down. I'm going to make you a cup of tea."

Captain Jim placed a chair for Anne, having first removed therefrom a huge, orange-coloured cat and a newspaper.

"Get down, Matey. The sofa is your place. I must put this paper away safe till I can find time to finish the story in it. It's called *A Mad Love.* 'Tisn't my favourite brand of fiction, but I'm reading it jest to see how long she can spin it out. It's at the sixty-second chapter now, and the wedding ain't any nearer than when it begun, far's I can see. When little Joe comes I have to read him pirate yarns. Ain't it strange how innocent little creatures like children like the blood-thirstiest stories?"

"Like my lad Davy at home," said Anne. "He wants tales that reek with gore."

Captain Jim's tea proved to be nectar. He was pleased as a child with Anne's compliments, but he affected a fine indifference.

"The secret is I don't skimp the cream," he remarked airily. Captain Jim had never heard of Oliver Wendell Holmes, but he evidently agreed with that writer's dictum that "big heart never liked little cream pot."

"We met an odd-looking personage coming out of your lane," said Gilbert as they sipped. "Who was he?" Captain Jim grinned.

"That's Marshall Elliott—a mighty fine man with jest one streak of foolishness in him. I s'pose you wondered what his object was in turning himself into a sort of dime museum freak."

"Is he a modem Nazarite or a Hebrew prophet left over from olden times?" asked Anne.

"Neither of them. It's politics that's at the bottom of his freak. All those Elliotts and Crawfords and MacAllisters are dyed-in-the-wool politicians. They're born Grit or Tory, as the case may be, and they live Grit or Tory, and they die Grit or Tory; and what they're going to do in heaven, where there's probably no politics, is more than I can fathom. This Marshall Elliott was born a Grit. I'm a Grit myself in moderation, but there's no moderation about Marshall. Fifteen years ago there was a specially bitter general election. Marshall fought for his party tooth and nail. He was dead sure the Liberals would win—so sure that he got up at a public meeting and vowed that he wouldn't shave his face or cut his hair until the Grits were in power. Well, they didn't go in—and they've never got in yet—and you saw the result tonight for yourselves. Marshall stuck to his word."

"What does his wife think of it?" asked Anne.

"He's a bachelor. But if he had a wife I reckon she couldn't make him break that vow. That family of Elliotts has always been more stubborn than natteral. Marshall's brother Alexander had a dog he set great store by, and when it died the man actilly wanted to have it buried in the graveyard, 'along with the other Christians,' he said. Course, he wasn't allowed to; so he buried it just outside the graveyard fence, and never darkened the church door again. But Sundays he'd drive his family to church and sit by that dog's grave and read his Bible all the time service was going on. They say when he was dying he asked his wife to bury him beside the dog; she was a meek little soul but she fired up at *that*. She said *she* wasn't going to be buried beside no dog, and if he'd rather have his last resting place beside the dog than beside her, jest to say so. Alexander Elliott was a stubborn mule, but he was fond of his wife, so he give in and said, 'Well, durn it, bury me where you please. But when Gabriel's trump blows I expect my dog to rise with the rest of us, for he had as much soul as any durned Elliott or Crawford or MacAllister that ever strutted.' Them was *his* parting words. As for Marshall, we're all used to him, but he must strike strangers as right down peculiar-looking. I've known him ever since he was ten—he's about fifty now—and I like him. Him and me was out cod-fishing today. That's about all I'm good for now—catching trout and cod occasional. But 'tweren't always so—not by no manner of means. I used to do other things, as you'd admit if you saw my life-book."

Anne was just going to ask what his life-book was when the First Mate created a diversion by springing upon Captain Jim's knee. He was a gorgeous beastie, with a face as round as a full moon, vivid green eyes, and immense, white, double paws. Captain Jim stroked his velvet back gently.

"I never fancied cats much till I found the First Mate," he remarked, to the accompaniment of the Mate's tremendous purrs. "I saved his life, and when you've saved a creature's life you're bound to love it. It's next thing to giving life. There's some tumble thoughtless people in the world, Mistress Blythe. Some of them city folks who have summer homes over the harbour are so thoughtless that they're cruel. It's the worst kind of cruelty—the thoughtless kind. You can't cope with it. They keep cats there in the summer, and feed and pet 'em, and doll 'em up with ribbons and collars. And then in the fall they go off and leave 'em to starve or freeze. It makes my blood boil, Mistress Blythe. One day last winter I found a poor old mother cat dead on the shore, lying against the skin-and-bone bodies of her three little kittens. She'd died trying to shelter 'em. She had her poor stiff paws around 'em. Master, I cried. Then I swore. Then I carried them poor little kittens home and fed 'em up and found good homes for 'em. I knew the woman who left the cat and when she come back this summer I jest went over the harbour and told her my opinion of her. It was rank meddling, but I do love meddling in a good cause."

"How did she take it?" asked Gilbert.

"Cried and said she 'didn't think.' I says to her, says I, 'Do you s'pose that'll be held for a good excuse in the day of Jedgment, when you'll have to account for that poor old mother's life? The Lord'll ask you what He give you your brains for if it wasn't to think, I reckon.' I don't fancy she'll leave cats to starve another time."

"Was the First Mate one of the forsaken?" asked Anne, making advances to him which were responded to graciously, if condescendingly.

"Yes. I found *him* one bitter cold day in winter, caught in the branches of a tree by his dum-fool ribbon collar. He was almost starving. If you could have seen his eyes, Mistress Blythe! He was nothing but a kitten, and he'd got his living somehow since he'd been left until he got hung up. When I loosed him he give my hand a pitiful swipe with his little red tongue. He wasn't the able seaman you see now. He was meek as Moses. That was nine years ago. His life has been long in the land for a cat. He's a good old pal, the First Mate is."

"I should have expected you to have a dog," said Gilbert.

Captain Jim shook his head.

"I had a dog once. I thought so much of him that when he died I couldn't bear the thought of getting another in his place. He was a *friend*—you understand, Mistress Blythe? Matey's only a pal. I'm fond of Matey —all the fonder on account of the spice of devilment that's in him—like there is in all cats. But I *loved* my dog. I always had a sneaking sympathy for Alexander Elliott about *his* dog. There isn't any devil in a good dog. That's why they're more lovable than cats, I reckon. But I'm darned if they're as interesting. Here I am, talking too much. Why don't you check me? When I do get a chance to talk to anyone I run on turrible. If you've done your tea I've a few little things, you might like to look at—picked 'em up in the queer corners I used to be poking my nose into."

Captain Jim's "few little things" turned out to be a most interesting collection of curios, hideous, quaint and beautiful. And almost every one had some striking story attached to it.

Anne never forgot the delight with which she listened to those old tales that moonlit evening by that enchanted driftwood fire, while the silver sea called to them through the open window and sobbed against the rocks below them.

Captain Jim never said a boastful word, but it was impossible to help seeing what a hero the man had been—brave, true, resourceful, unselfish. He sat there in his little room and made those things live again for his hearers. By a lift of the eyebrow, a twist of the lip, a gesture, a word, he painted a whole scene or character so that they saw it as it was.

Some of Captain Jim's adventures had such a marvelous edge that Anne and Gilbert secretly wondered if he were not drawing a rather long bow at their credulous expense. But in this, as they found later, they did him injustice. His tales were all literally true. Captain Jim had the gift of the born story-teller, whereby "unhappy, far-off things" can be brought vividly before the hearer in all their pristine poignancy.

Anne and Gilbert laughed and shivered over his tales, and once Anne found herself crying. Captain Jim surveyed her tears with pleasure shining from his face.

"I like to see folks cry that way," he remarked. "It's a compliment. But I can't do justice to the things I've seen or helped to do. I've 'em all jotted down in my life-book, but I haven't got the knack of writing them out properly. If I could hit on jest the right words and string 'em together proper on paper I could make a great book. It would beat *A Mad Love* holler, and I believe Joe'd like it as well as the pirate yarns. Yes, I've had some adventures in my time; and, do you know, Mistress Blythe, I still lust after 'em. Yes, old and useless as I be, there's an awful longing sweeps over me at times to sail out—out—out there—forever and ever."

"Like Ulysses, you would

> *'Sail beyond the sunset and the baths*
> *Of all the western stars until you die,'"*

said Anne dreamily.

"Ulysses? I've read of him. Yes, that's jest how I feel—jest how all us old sailors feel, I reckon. I'll die on land after all, I s'pose. Well, what is to be will be. There was old William Ford at the Glen who never went on the water in his life, 'cause he was afraid of being drowned. A fortune-teller had predicted he would be. And one day he fainted and fell with his face in the barn trough and was drowned. Must you go? Well, come soon and come often. The doctor is to do the talking next time. He knows a heap of things I want to find out. I'm sorter lonesome here by times. It's been worse since Elizabeth Russell died. Her and me was such cronies."

Captain Jim spoke with the pathos of the aged, who see their old friends slipping from them one by one—friends whose place can never be quite filled by those of a younger generation, even of the race that knows Joseph. Anne and Gilbert promised to come soon and often.

"He's a rare old fellow, isn't he?" said Gilbert, as they walked home.

"Somehow, I can't reconcile his simple, kindly personality with the wild, adventurous life he has lived," mused Anne.

"You wouldn't find it so hard if you had seen him the other day down at the fishing village. One of the men of Peter Gautier's boat made a nasty remark about some girl along the shore. Captain Jim fairly scorched the wretched fellow with the lightning of his eyes. He seemed a man transformed. He didn't say much—but the way he said it! You'd have thought it would strip the flesh from the fellow's bones. I understand that Captain Jim will never allow a word against any woman to be said in his presence."

"I wonder why he never married," said Anne. "He should have sons with their ships at sea now, and grandchildren climbing over him to hear his stories—he's that kind of a man. Instead, he has nothing but a magnificent cat."

But Anne was mistaken. Captain Jim had more than that. He had a memory.

10
Leslie Moore

"I'm going for a walk to the outside shore tonight," Anne told Gog and Magog one October evening. There was no one else to tell, for Gilbert had gone over the harbour. Anne had her little domain in the speckless order one would expect of anyone brought up by Marilla Cuthbert, and felt that she could gad shoreward with a clear conscience. Many and delightful had been her shore rambles, sometimes with Gilbert, sometimes with Captain Jim, sometimes alone with her own thoughts and new, poignantly-sweet dreams that were beginning to span life with their rainbows. She loved the gentle, misty harbour shore and the silvery, wind-haunted sand shore, but best of all she loved the rock shore, with its cliffs and caves and piles of surf-worn boulders, and its coves where the pebbles glittered under the pools; and it was to this shore she hied herself tonight.

There had been an autumn storm of wind and rain, lasting for three days. Thunderous had been the crash of billows on the rocks, wild the white spray and spume that blew over the bar, troubled and misty and tempest-torn the erstwhile blue peace of Four Winds Harbour. Now it was over, and the shore lay clean-washed after the storm; not a wind stirred, but there was still a fine surf on, dashing on sand and rock in a splendid white turmoil—the only restless thing in the great, pervading stillness and peace.

"Oh, this is a moment worth living through weeks of storm and stress for," Anne exclaimed, delightedly sending her far gaze across the tossing waters from the top of the cliff where she stood. Presently she scrambled down the steep path to the little cove below, where she seemed shut in with rocks and sea and sky.

"I'm going to dance and sing," she said. "There's no one here to see me—the sea-gulls won't carry tales of the matter. I may be as crazy as I like."

She caught up her skirt and pirouetted along the hard strip of sand just out of reach of the waves that almost lapped her feet with their spent foam. Whirling round and round, laughing like a child, she reached the little headland that ran out to the east of the cove; then she stopped suddenly, blushing crimson; she was not alone; there had been a witness to her dance and laughter.

The girl of the golden hair and sea-blue eyes was sitting on a boulder of the headland, half-hidden by a jutting rock. She was looking straight at Anne with a strange expression—part wonder, part sympathy, part—could it be?—envy. She was bareheaded, and her splendid hair, more than ever like Browning's "gorgeous snake," was bound about her head with a crimson ribbon. She wore a dress of some dark material, very plainly made; but swathed about her waist, outlining its fine curves, was a vivid girdle of red silk. Her hands, clasped over her knee, were brown and somewhat work-hardened; but the skin of her throat and cheeks was as white as cream. A flying gleam of sunset broke through a low-lying western cloud and fell across her hair. For a moment she seemed the spirit of the sea personified—all its mystery, all its passion, all its elusive charm.

"You—you must think me crazy," stammered Anne, trying to recover her self-possession. To be seen by this stately girl in such an abandon of childishness she, Mrs. Dr. Blythe, with all the dignity of the matron to keep up—it was too bad!

"No," said the girl, "I don't."

She said nothing more; her voice was expressionless; her manner slightly repellent; but there was something in her eyes—eager yet shy, defiant yet pleading—which turned Anne from her purpose of walking away. Instead, she sat down on the boulder beside the girl.

"Let's introduce ourselves," she said, with the smile that had never yet failed to win confidence and friendliness. "I am Mrs. Blythe—and I live in that little white house up the harbour shore."

"Yes, I know," said the girl. "I am Leslie Moore— Mrs. Dick Moore," she added stiffly.

Anne was silent for a moment from sheer amazement. It had not occurred to her that this girl was married—there seemed nothing of the wife about her. And that she should be the neighbour whom Anne had pictured as a commonplace Four Winds housewife! Anne could not quickly adjust her mental focus to this astonishing change.

"Then—then you live in that gray house up the brook," she stammered.

"Yes. I should have gone over to call on you long ago," said the other. She did not offer any explanation or excuse for not having gone.

"I wish you *would* come," said Anne, recovering herself somewhat. "We're such near neighbours we ought to be friends. That is the sole fault of Four Winds—there aren't quite enough neighbours. Otherwise it is perfection."

"You like it?"

"*Like* it! I love it. It is the most beautiful place I ever saw."

"I've never seen many places," said Leslie Moore, slowly, "but I've always thought it was very lovely here. I—I love it, too."

She spoke, as she looked, shyly, yet eagerly. Anne had an odd impression that this strange girl—the word "girl" would persist—could say a good deal if she chose.

"I often come to the shore," she added.

"So do I," said Anne. "It's a wonder we haven't met here before."

"Probably you come earlier in the evening than I do. It is generally late—almost dark—when I come. And I love to come just after a storm—like this. I don't like the sea so well when it's calm and quiet. I like the struggle—and the crash—and the noise."

"I love it in all its moods," declared Anne. "The sea at Four Winds is to me what Lover's Lane was at home. Tonight it seemed so free—so untamed—something broke loose in me, too, out of sympathy. That was why I danced along the shore in that wild way. I didn't suppose anybody was looking, of course. If Miss Cornelia Bryant had seen me she would have foreboded a gloomy prospect for poor young Dr. Blythe."

"You know Miss Cornelia?" said Leslie, laughing. She had an exquisite laugh; it bubbled up suddenly and unexpectedly with something of the delicious quality of a baby's. Anne laughed, too.

"Oh, yes. She has been down to my house of dreams several times."

"Your house of dreams?"

"Oh, that's a dear, foolish little name Gilbert and I have for our home. We just call it that between ourselves. It slipped out before I thought."

"So Miss Russell's little white house is *your* house of dreams," said Leslie wonderingly. "*I* had a house of dreams once—but it was a palace," she added, with a laugh, the sweetness of which was marred by a little note of derision.

"Oh, I once dreamed of a palace, too," said Anne. "I suppose all girls do. And then we settle down contentedly in eight-room houses that seem to fulfill all the desires of our hearts—because our prince is there. *You* should have had your palace really, though—you are so beautiful. You *must* let me say it—it *has* to be said—I'm nearly bursting with admiration. You are the loveliest thing I ever saw, Mrs. Moore."

"If we are to be friends you must call me Leslie," said the other with an odd passion.

"Of course I will. And *my* friends call me Anne."

"I suppose I am beautiful," Leslie went on, looking stormily out to sea. "I hate my beauty. I wish I had always been as brown and plain as the brownest and plainest girl at the fishing village over there. Well, what do you think of Miss Cornelia?"

The abrupt change of subject shut the door on any further confidences.

"Miss Cornelia is a darling, isn't she?" said Anne. "Gilbert and I were invited to her house to a state tea last week. You've heard of groaning tables."

"I seem to recall seeing the expression in the newspaper reports of weddings," said Leslie, smiling.

"Well, Miss Cornelia's groaned—at least, it creaked—positively. You couldn't have believed she would have cooked so much for two ordinary people. She had every kind of pie you could name, I think,—except lemon pie. She said she had taken the prize for lemon pies at the Charlottetown Exhibition ten years ago and had never made any since for fear of losing her reputation for them."

"Were you able to eat enough pie to please her?"

"*I* wasn't. Gilbert won her heart by eating—I won't tell you how much. She said she never knew a man who didn't like pie better than his Bible. Do you know, I love Miss Cornelia."

"So do I," said Leslie. "She is the best friend I have in the world."

Anne wondered secretly why, if this were so, Miss Cornelia had never mentioned Mrs. Dick Moore to her. Miss Cornelia had certainly talked freely about every other individual in or near Four Winds.

"Isn't that beautiful?" said Leslie, after a brief silence, pointing to the exquisite effect of a shaft of light falling through a cleft in the rock behind them, across a dark green pool at its base. "If I had come here—and seen nothing but just that—I would go home satisfied."

"The effects of light and shadow all along these shores are wonderful," agreed Anne. "My little sewing room looks out on the harbour, and I sit at its window and feast my eyes. The colours and shadows are never the same two minutes together."

"And you are never lonely?" asked Leslie abruptly. "Never—when you are alone?"

"No. I don't think I've ever been lonely in my life," answered Anne. "Even when I'm alone I have real good company—dreams and imaginations and pretendings. I *like* to be alone now and then, just to think over things and *taste* them. But I love friendship—and nice, jolly little times with people. Oh, *won't* you come to see me—often? Please do. I believe," Anne added, laughing, "that you'd like me if you knew me."

"I wonder if *you* would like *me*," said Leslie seriously. She was not fishing for a compliment. She looked out across the waves that were beginning to be garlanded with blossoms of moonlit foam, and her eyes filled with shadows.

"I'm sure I would," said Anne. "And please don't think I'm utterly irresponsible because you saw me dancing on the shore at sunset. No doubt I shall be dignified after a time. You see, I haven't been married very long. I feel like a girl, and sometimes like a child, yet."

"I have been married twelve years," said Leslie.

Here was another unbelievable thing.

"Why, you can't be as old as I am!" exclaimed Anne. "You must have been a child when you were married."

"I was sixteen," said Leslie, rising, and picking up the cap and jacket lying beside her. "I am twenty-eight now. Well, I must go back."

"So must I. Gilbert will probably be home. But I'm so glad we both came to the shore tonight and met each other."

Leslie said nothing, and Anne was a little chilled. She had offered friendship frankly but it had not been accepted very graciously, if it had not been absolutely repelled. In silence they climbed the cliffs and walked across a pasture-field of which the feathery, bleached, wild grasses were like a carpet of creamy velvet in the moonlight. When they reached the shore lane Leslie turned.

"I go this way, Mrs. Blythe. You will come over and see me some time, won't you?"

Anne felt as if the invitation had been thrown at her. She got the impression that Leslie Moore gave it reluctantly.

"I will come if you really want me to," she said a little coldly.

"Oh, I do—I do," exclaimed Leslie, with an eagerness which seemed to burst forth and beat down some restraint that had been imposed on it.

"Then I'll come. Good-night—Leslie."

"Good-night, Mrs. Blythe."

Anne walked home in a brown study and poured out her tale to Gilbert.

"So Mrs. Dick Moore isn't one of the race that knows Joseph?" said Gilbert teasingly.

"No—o—o, not exactly. And yet—I think she *was* one of them once, but has gone or got into exile," said Anne musingly. "She is certainly very different from the other women about here. You can't talk about eggs and butter to her. To think I've been imagining her a second Mrs. Rachel Lynde! Have you ever seen Dick Moore, Gilbert?"

"No. I've seen several men working about the fields of the farm, but I don't know which was Moore."

"She never mentioned him. I *know* she isn't happy."

"From what you tell me I suppose she was married before she was old enough to know her own mind or heart, and found out too late that she had made a mistake. It's a common tragedy enough, Anne. A fine woman would have made the best of it. Mrs. Moore has evidently let it make her bitter and resentful."

"Don't let us judge her till we know," pleaded Anne. "I don't believe her case is so ordinary. You will understand her fascination when you meet her, Gilbert. It is a thing quite apart from her beauty. I feel that she possesses a rich nature, into which a friend might enter as into a kingdom; but for some reason she bars everyone out and shuts all her possibilities up in herself, so that they cannot develop and blossom. There, I've been struggling to define her to myself ever since I left her, and that is the nearest I can get to it. I'm going to ask Miss Cornelia about her."

11

The Story of Leslie Moore

"Yes, the eighth baby arrived a fortnight ago," said Miss Cornelia, from a rocker before the fire of the little house one chilly October afternoon. "It's a girl. Fred was ranting mad—said he wanted a boy—when the truth is he didn't want it at all. If it had been a boy he'd have ranted because it wasn't a girl. They had four girls and three boys before, so I can't see that it made much difference what this one was, but of course he'd have to be cantankerous, just like a man. The baby is real pretty, dressed up in its nice little clothes. It has black eyes and the dearest, tiny hands."

"I must go and see it. I just love babies," said Anne, smiling to herself over a thought too dear and sacred to be put into words.

"I don't say but what they're nice," admitted Miss Cornelia. "But some folks seem to have more than they really need, believe *me*. My poor cousin Flora up at the Glen had eleven, and such a slave as she is! Her husband suicided three years ago. Just like a man!"

"What made him do that?" asked Anne, rather shocked.

"Couldn't get his way over something, so he jumped into the well. A good riddance! He was a born tyrant. But of course it spoiled the well. Flora could never abide the thought of using it again, poor thing! So she had another dug and a frightful expense it was, and the water as hard as nails. If he *had* to drown himself there was plenty of water in the harbour, wasn't there? I've no patience with a man like that. We've only had two suicides in Four Winds in my recollection. The other was Frank West—Leslie Moore's father. By the way, has Leslie ever been over to call on you yet?"

"No, but I met her on the shore a few nights ago and we scraped an acquaintance," said Anne, pricking up her ears.

Miss Cornelia nodded.

"I'm glad, dearie. I was hoping you'd foregather with her. What do you think of her?"

"I thought her very beautiful."

"Oh, of course. There was never anybody about Four Winds could touch her for looks. Did you ever see her hair? It reaches to her feet when she lets it down. But I meant how did you like her?"

"I think I could like her very much if she'd let me," said Anne slowly.

"But she wouldn't let you—she pushed you off and kept you at arm's length. Poor Leslie! You wouldn't be much surprised if you knew what her life has been. It's been a tragedy—a tragedy!" repeated Miss Cornelia emphatically.

"I wish you would tell me all about her—that is, if you can do so without betraying any confidence."

"Lord, dearie, everybody in Four Winds knows poor Leslie's story. It's no secret—the *outside*, that is. Nobody knows the *inside* but Leslie herself, and she doesn't take folks into her confidence. I'm about the best friend she has on earth, I reckon, and she's never uttered a word of complaint to me. Have you ever seen Dick Moore?"

"No."

"Well, I may as well begin at the beginning and tell you everything straight through, so you'll understand it. As I said, Leslie's father was Frank West. He was clever and shiftless—just like a man. Oh, he had heaps of brains—and much good they did him! He started to go to college, and he went for two years, and then his health broke down. The Wests were all inclined to be consumptive. So Frank came home and started farming. He married Rose Elliott from over harbour. Rose was reckoned the beauty of Four Winds—Leslie takes her looks from her mother, but she has ten times the spirit and go that Rose had, and a far better figure. Now you know, Anne, I always take the ground that us women ought to stand by each other. We've got enough to endure at the hands of the men, the Lord knows, so I hold we hadn't ought to clapper-claw one another, and it isn't often you'll find me running down another woman. But I never had much use for Rose Elliott. She was spoiled to begin with, believe *me*, and she was nothing but a lazy, selfish, whining creature. Frank was no hand to work, so they were poor as Job's turkey. Poor! They lived on potatoes and point, believe *me.* They had two children—Leslie and Kenneth. Leslie had her mother's looks and her father's brains, and something she didn't get from either of them. She took after her Grandmother West—a splendid old lady. She was the brightest, friendliest, merriest thing when she was a child, Anne. Everybody liked her. She was her father's favourite and she was awful fond of him. They were 'chums,' as she used to say. She couldn't see any of his faults—and he *was* a taking sort of man in some ways.

"Well, when Leslie was twelve years old, the first dreadful thing happened. She worshipped little Kenneth—he was four years younger than her, and he *was* a dear little chap. And he was killed one day—fell off a big load of hay just as it was going into the barn, and the wheel went right over his little body and crushed the life out of it. And mind you, Anne, Leslie saw it. She was looking down from the loft. She gave one screech—the hired man said he never heard such a sound in all his life—he said it would ring in his ears till Gabriel's trump drove it out. But she never screeched or cried again about it. She jumped from the loft onto the load and from the load to the floor, and caught up the little bleeding, warm, dead body, Anne—they had to tear it from her before she would let it go. They sent for me—I can't talk of it."

Miss Cornelia wiped the tears from her kindly brown eyes and sewed in bitter silence for a few minutes.

"Well," she resumed, "it was all over—they buried little Kenneth in that graveyard over the harbour, and after a while Leslie went back to her school and her studies. She never mentioned Kenneth's name—I've never heard it cross her lips from that day to this. I reckon that old hurt still aches and burns at times; but she was only a child and time is real kind to children, Anne, dearie. After a while she began to laugh again—she had the prettiest laugh. You don't often hear it now."

"I heard it once the other night," said Anne. "It *is* a beautiful laugh."

"Frank West began to go down after Kenneth's death. He wasn't strong and it was a shock to him, because he was real fond of the child, though, as I've said, Leslie was his favourite. He got mopey and melancholy, and couldn't or wouldn't work. And one day, when Leslie was fourteen years of age, he hanged himself—and in the parlour, too, mind you, Anne, right in the middle of the parlour from the lamp hook in the ceiling. Wasn't that like a man? It was the anniversary of his wedding day, too. Nice, tasty time to pick for it, wasn't it? And, of course, that poor Leslie had to be the one to find him. She went into the parlour that morning, singing, with some fresh flowers for the vases, and there she saw her father hanging from the ceiling, his face as black as a coal. It was something awful, believe me!"

"Oh, how horrible!" said Anne, shuddering. "The poor, poor child!"

"Leslie didn't cry at her father's funeral any more than she had cried at Kenneth's. Rose whooped and howled for two, however, and Leslie had all she could do trying to calm and comfort her mother. I was disgusted with Rose and so was everyone else, but Leslie never got out of patience. She loved her mother. Leslie is clannish—her own could never do wrong in her eyes. Well, they buried Frank West beside Kenneth, and Rose put up a great big monument to him. It was bigger than his character, believe *me*! Anyhow, it was bigger than Rose could afford, for the farm was mortgaged for more than its value. But not long after Leslie's old grandmother West died and she left Leslie a little money—enough to give her a year at Queen's Academy. Leslie had made up her mind to pass for a teacher if she could, and then earn enough to put herself through Redmond College. That had been her father's pet scheme—he wanted her to have what he had lost. Leslie was full of ambition and her head was chock full of brains. She went to Queen's, and she took two years' work in one year and got her First; and when she came home she got the Glen school. She was so happy and hopeful and full of life and eagerness. When I think of what she was then and what she is now, I say—drat the men!"

Miss Cornelia snipped her thread off as viciously as if, Nero-like, she was severing the neck of mankind by the stroke.

"Dick Moore came into her life that summer. His father, Abner Moore, kept store at the Glen, but Dick had a sea-going streak in him from his mother; he used to sail in summer and clerk in his father's store in winter. He was a big, handsome fellow, with a little ugly soul. He was always wanting something till he got it, and then he stopped wanting it—just like a man. Oh, he didn't growl at the weather when it was fine, and he was mostly real pleasant and agreeable when everything went right. But he drank a good deal, and there were some nasty stories told of him and a girl down at the fishing village. He wasn't fit for Leslie to wipe her feet on, that's the long and short of it. And he was a Methodist! But he was clean mad about her—because of her good looks in the first place, and because she wouldn't have anything to say to him in the second. He vowed he'd have her—and he got her!"

"How did he bring it about?"

"Oh, it was an iniquitous thing! I'll never forgive Rose West. You see, dearie, Abner Moore held the mortgage on the West farm, and the interest was overdue some years, and Dick just went and told Mrs. West that if Leslie wouldn't marry him he'd get his father to foreclose the mortgage. Rose carried on terrible—fainted and wept, and pleaded with Leslie not to let her be turned out of her home. She said it would break her heart to leave the home she'd come to as a bride. I wouldn't have blamed her for feeling dreadful bad over it—but you wouldn't have thought she'd be so selfish as to sacrifice her own flesh and blood because of it, would you? Well, she was. And Leslie gave in—she loved her mother so much she would have done anything to save her pain. She married Dick Moore. None of us knew why at the time. It wasn't till long afterward that I found out how her mother had worried her into it. I was sure there was something wrong, though, because I knew how she had snubbed him time and again, and it wasn't like Leslie to turn face-about like that. Besides, I knew that Dick Moore wasn't the kind of man Leslie could ever fancy, in spite of his good looks and dashing ways. Of course, there was no wedding, but Rose asked me to go and see them married. I went, but I was sorry I did. I'd seen Leslie's face at her brother's funeral and at her father's funeral—and now it seemed to me I was seeing it at her own funeral. But Rose was smiling as a basket of chips, believe *me*!

"Leslie and Dick settled down on the West place—Rose couldn't bear to part with her dear daughter!—and lived there for the winter. In the spring Rose took pneumonia and died—a year too late! Leslie was heartbroken enough over it. Isn't it terrible the way some unworthy folks are loved, while others that deserve it far more, you'd think, never get much affection? As for Dick, he'd had enough of quiet married life—just like a man. He was for up and off. He went over to Nova Scotia to visit his relations—his father had come from Nova Scotia—and he wrote back to Leslie that his cousin, George Moore, was going on a voyage to Havana and he was going too. The name of the vessel was the *Four Sisters* and they were to be gone about nine weeks.

"It must have been a relief to Leslie. But she never said anything. From the day of her marriage she was just what she is now—cold and proud, and keeping everyone but me at a distance. I won't *be* kept at a distance, believe *me*! I've just stuck to Leslie as close as I knew how in spite of everything."

"She told me you were the best friend she had," said Anne.

"Did she?" exclaimed Miss Cornelia delightedly. "Well, I'm real thankful to hear it. Sometimes I've wondered if she really did want me around at all—she never let me think so. You must have thawed her out more than you think, or she wouldn't have said that much itself to you. Oh, that poor, heart-broken girl! I never see Dick Moore but I want to run a knife clean through him."

Miss Cornelia wiped her eyes again and having relieved her feelings by her blood-thirsty wish, took up her tale.

"Well, Leslie was left over there alone. Dick had put in the crop before he went, and old Abner looked after it. The summer went by and the *Four Sisters* didn't come back. The Nova Scotia Moores investigated, and found she had got to Havana and discharged her cargo and took on another and left for home; and that was all they ever found out about her. By degrees people began to talk of Dick Moore as one that was dead. Almost everyone believed that he was, though no one felt certain, for men have turned up here at the harbour after they'd been gone for years. Leslie never thought he was dead—and she was right. A thousand pities too! The next summer Captain Jim was in Havana—that was before he gave up the sea, of course. He thought he'd poke round a bit—Captain Jim was always meddlesome, just like a man—and he went to inquiring round among the sailors' boarding houses and places like that, to see if he could find out anything about the crew of the *Four Sisters.* He'd better have let sleeping dogs lie, in my opinion! Well, he went to one out-of- the-way place, and there he found a man and he knew at first sight it was Dick Moore, though he had a big beard. Captain Jim got it shaved off and then there was no doubt—Dick Moore it was—his body at least. His mind wasn't there—as for his soul, in my opinion he never had one!"

"What had happened to him?"

"Nobody knows the rights of it. All the folks who kept the boarding house could tell was that about a year before they had found him lying on their doorstep one morning in an awful condition—his head battered to a jelly almost. They supposed he'd got hurt in some drunken row, and likely that's the truth of it. They took him in, never thinking he could live. But he did—and he was just like a child when he got well. He hadn't memory or intellect or reason. They tried to find out who he was but they never could. He couldn't even tell them his name—he could only say a few simple words. He had a letter on him beginning 'Dear Dick' and signed 'Leslie,' but there was no address on it and the envelope was gone. They let him stay on—he learned to do a few odd jobs about the place—and there Captain Jim found him. He brought him home—and I've always said it was a bad day's work, though I s'pose there was nothing else he could do. He thought maybe when Dick got home and saw his old surroundings and familiar faces his memory would wake up. But it hadn't any effect. There he's been at the house up the brook ever since. He's just like a child, no more nor less. Takes fractious spells occasionally, but mostly he's just vacant and good humoured and harmless. He's apt to run away if he isn't watched. That's the burden Leslie has had to carry for eleven years—and all alone. Old Abner Moore died soon after Dick was brought home and it was found he was almost bankrupt. When things were settled up there was nothing for Leslie and Dick but the old West farm. Leslie rented it to John Ward, and the rent is all she has to live on. Sometimes in summer she takes a boarder to help out. But most visitors prefer the other side of the harbour where the hotels and summer cottages are. Leslie's house is too far from the bathing shore. She's taken care of Dick and she's never been away from him for eleven years—she's tied to that imbecile for life. And after all the dreams and hopes she once had! You can imagine what it has been like for her, Anne, dearie—with her beauty and spirit and pride and cleverness. It's just been a living death."

"Poor, poor girl!" said Anne again. Her own happiness seemed to reproach her. What right had she to be so happy when another human soul must be so miserable?

"Will you tell me just what Leslie said and how she acted the night you met her on the shore?" asked Miss Cornelia.

She listened intently and nodded her satisfaction.

"*You* thought she was stiff and cold, Anne dearie, but I can tell you she thawed out wonderful for her. She must have taken to you real strong. I'm so glad. You may be able to help her a good deal. I was thankful when I heard that a young couple was coming to this house, for I hoped it would mean some friends for Leslie; especially if you belonged to the race that knows Joseph. You *will* be her friend, won't you, Anne, dearie?"

"Indeed I will, if she'll let me," said Anne, with all her own sweet, impulsive earnestness.

"No, you must be her friend, whether she'll let you or not," said Miss Cornelia resolutely. "Don't you mind if she's stiff by times—don't notice it. Remember what her life has been—and is—and must always be, I suppose, for creatures like Dick Moore live forever, I understand. You should see how fat he's got since he came home. He used to be lean enough. Just *make* her be friends—you can do it—you're one of those who have the knack. Only you mustn't be sensitive. And don't mind if she doesn't seem to want you to go over there much. She knows that some women don't like to be where Dick is—they complain he gives them the creeps. Just get her to come over here as often as she can. She can't get away so very much—she can't leave Dick long, for the Lord knows what he'd do—burn the house down most likely. At nights, after he's in bed and asleep, is about the only time she's free. He always goes to bed early and sleeps like the dead till next morning. That is how you came to meet her at the shore likely. She wanders there considerable."

"I will do everything I can for her," said Anne. Her interest in Leslie Moore, which had been vivid ever since she had seen her driving her geese down the hill, was intensified a thousand fold by Miss Cornelia's narration. The girl's beauty and sorrow and loneliness drew her with an irresistible fascination. She had never known anyone like her; her friends had hitherto been wholesome, normal, merry girls like herself, with only the average trials of human care and bereavement to shadow their girlish dreams. Leslie Moore stood apart, a tragic appealing figure of thwarted womanhood. Anne resolved that she would win entrance into the kingdom of that lonely soul and find there the comradeship it could so richly give, were it not for the cruel fetters that held it in a prison not of its own making.

"And mind you this, Anne, dearie," said Miss Cornelia, who had not yet wholly relieved her mind. "You mustn't think Leslie is an infidel because she hardly ever goes to church—or even that she's a Methodist. She can't take Dick to church, of course—not that he ever troubled church much in his best days. But you just remember that she's a real strong Presbyterian at heart, Anne, dearie."

12
Leslie Comes Over

Leslie came over to the house of dreams one frosty October night, when moonlit mists were hanging over the harbour and curling like silver ribbons along the seaward glens. She looked as if she repented coming when Gilbert answered her knock; but Anne flew past him, pounced on her, and drew her in.

"I'm so glad you picked tonight for a call," she said gaily. "I made up a lot of extra good fudge this afternoon and we want someone to help us eat it—before the fire—while we tell stories. Perhaps Captain Jim will drop in, too. This is his night."

"No. Captain Jim is over home," said Leslie. "He—he made me come here," she added, half defiantly.

"I'll say a thank-you to him for that when I see him," said Anne, pulling easy chairs before the fire.

"Oh, I don't mean that I didn't want to come," protested Leslie, flushing a little. "I—I've been thinking of coming—but it isn't always easy for me to get away."

"Of course it must be hard for you to leave Mr. Moore," said Anne, in a matter-of-fact tone. She had decided that it would be best to mention Dick Moore occasionally as an accepted fact, and not give undue morbidness to the subject by avoiding it. She was right, for Leslie's air of constraint suddenly vanished. Evidently she had been wondering how much Anne knew of the conditions of her life and was relieved that no explanations were needed. She allowed her cap and jacket to be taken, and sat down with a girlish snuggle in the big armchair by Magog. She was dressed prettily and carefully, with the customary touch of colour in the scarlet geranium at her white throat. Her beautiful hair gleamed like molten gold in the warm firelight. Her sea-blue eyes were full of soft laughter and allurement. For the moment, under the influence of the little house of dreams, she was a girl again—a girl forgetful of the past and its bitterness. The atmosphere of the many loves that had sanctified the little house was all about her; the companionship of two healthy, happy, young folks of her own generation encircled her; she felt and yielded to the magic of her surroundings—Miss Cornelia and Captain Jim would scarcely have recognized her; Anne found it hard to believe that this was the cold, unresponsive woman she had met on the shore—this animated girl who talked and listened with the eagerness of a starved soul. And how hungrily Leslie's eyes looked at the bookcases between the windows!

"Our library isn't very extensive," said Anne, "but every book in it is a *friend.* We've picked our books up through the years, here and there, never buying one until we had first read it and knew that it belonged to the race of Joseph."

Leslie laughed—beautiful laughter that seemed akin to all the mirth that had echoed through the little house in the vanished years.

"I have a few books of father's—not many," she said. "I've read them until I know them almost by heart. I don't get many books. There's a circulating library at the Glen store—but I don't think the committee who pick the books for Mr. Parker know what books are of Joseph's race—or perhaps they don't care. It was so seldom I got one I really liked that I gave up getting any."

"I hope you'll look on our bookshelves as your own," said Anne. "You are entirely and wholeheartedly welcome to the loan of any book on them."

"You are setting a feast of fat things before me," said Leslie, joyously. Then, as the clock struck ten, she rose, half unwillingly.

"I must go. I didn't realise it was so late. Captain Jim is always saying it doesn't take long to stay an hour. But I stayed two—and oh, but I've enjoyed them," she added frankly.

"Come often," said Anne and Gilbert. They had risen and stood together in the firelight's glow. Leslie looked at them—youthful, hopeful, happy, typifying all she had missed and must forever miss. The light went out of her face and eyes; the girl vanished; it was the sorrowful, cheated woman who answered the invitation almost coldly and got herself away with a pitiful haste.

Anne watched her until she was lost in the shadows of the chill and misty night. Then she turned slowly back to the glow of her own radiant hearthstone.

"Isn't she lovely, Gilbert? Her hair fascinates me. Miss Cornelia says it reaches to her feet. Ruby Gillis had beautiful hair—but Leslie's is *alive*—every thread of it is living gold."

"She is very beautiful," agreed Gilbert, so heartily that Anne almost wished he was a *little* less enthusiastic.

"Gilbert, would you like my hair better if it were like Leslie's?" she asked wistfully.

"I wouldn't have your hair any colour but just what it is for the world," said Gilbert, with one or two convincing accompaniments. "You wouldn't be *Anne* if you had golden hair—or hair of any colour but"—

"Red," said Anne, with gloomy satisfaction.

"Yes, red—to give warmth to that milk-white skin and those shining gray-green eyes of yours. Golden hair wouldn't suit you at all, Queen Anne—*my* Queen Anne—queen of my heart and life and home."

"Then you may admire Leslie's all you like," said Anne magnanimously.

13
A Ghostly Evening

One evening, a week later, Anne decided to run over the fields to the house up the brook for an informal call. It was an evening of gray fog that had crept in from the gulf, swathed the harbour, filled the glens and valleys, and clung heavily to the autumnal meadows. Through it the sea sobbed and shuddered. Anne saw Four Winds in a new aspect, and found it weird and mysterious and fascinating; but it also gave her a little feeling of loneliness. Gilbert was away and would be away until the morrow, attending a medical pow-wow in Charlottetown. Anne longed for an hour of fellowship with some girl friend. Captain Jim and Miss Cornelia were "good fellows" each, in their own way; but youth yearned to youth.

"If only Diana or Phil or Pris or Stella could drop in for a chat," she said to herself, "how delightful it would be! This is such a *ghostly* night. I'm sure all the ships that ever sailed out of Four Winds to their doom could be seen tonight sailing up the harbour with their drowned crews on their decks, if that shrouding fog could suddenly be drawn aside. I feel as if it concealed innumerable mysteries—as if I were surrounded by the wraiths of old generations of Four Winds people peering at me through that gray veil. If ever the dear dead ladies of this little house came back to revisit it they would come on just such a night as this. If I sit here any longer I'll see one of them there opposite me in Gilbert's chair. This place isn't exactly canny tonight. Even Gog and Magog have an air of pricking up their ears to hear the footsteps of unseen guests. I'll run over to see Leslie before I frighten myself with my own fancies, as I did long ago in the matter of the Haunted Wood. I'll leave my house of dreams to welcome back its old inhabitants. My fire will give them my good-will and greeting—they will be gone before I come back, and my house will be mine once more. Tonight I am sure it is keeping a tryst with the past."

Laughing a little over her fancy, yet with something of a creepy sensation in the region of her spine, Anne kissed her hand to Gog and Magog and slipped out into the fog, with some of the new magazines under her arm for Leslie.

"Leslie's wild for books and magazines," Miss Cornelia had told her, "and she hardly ever sees one. She can't afford to buy them or subscribe for them. She's really pitifully poor, Anne. I don't see how she makes out to live at all on the little rent the farm brings in. She never even hints a complaint on the score of poverty, but I know what it must be. She's been handicapped by it all her life. She didn't mind it when she was free and ambitious, but it must gall now, believe *me*. I'm glad she seemed so bright and merry the evening she spent with you. Captain Jim told me he had fairly to put her cap and coat on and push her out of the door. Don't be too long going to see her either. If you are she'll think it's because you don't like the sight of Dick, and she'll crawl into her shell again. Dick's a great, big, harmless baby, but that silly grin and chuckle of his do get on some people's nerves. Thank goodness, I've no nerves myself. I like Dick Moore better now than I ever did when he was in his right senses—though the Lord knows that isn't saying much. I was down there one day in housecleaning time helping Leslie a bit, and I was frying doughnuts. Dick was hanging round to get one, as usual, and all at once he picked up a scalding hot one I'd just fished out and dropped it on the back of my neck when I was bending over. Then he laughed and laughed. Believe *me*, Anne, it took all the grace of God in my heart to keep me from just whisking up that stew-pan of boiling fat and pouring it over his head."

Anne laughed over Miss Cornelia's wrath as she sped through the darkness. But laughter accorded ill with that night. She was sober enough when she reached the house among the willows. Everything was very silent. The front part of the house seemed dark and deserted, so Anne slipped round the side door, which opened from the veranda into a little sitting room. There she halted noiselessly.

The door was open. Beyond, in the dimly lighted room, sat Leslie Moore, with her arms flung out on the table and her head bent upon them. She was weeping horribly—with low, fierce, choking sobs, as if some agony in her soul were trying to tear itself out. An old black dog was sitting by her, his nose resting on her lap, his big doggish eyes full of mute, imploring sympathy and devotion. Anne drew back in dismay. She felt that she could not intermeddle with this bitterness. Her heart ached with a sympathy she might not utter. To go in now would be to shut the door forever on any possible help or friendship. Some instinct warned Anne that the proud, bitter girl would never forgive the one who thus surprised her in her abandonment of despair.

Anne slipped noiselessly from the veranda and found her way across the yard. Beyond, she heard voices in the gloom and saw the dim glow of a light. At the gate she met two men—Captain Jim with a lantern, and another who she knew must be Dick Moore—a big man, badly gone to fat, with a broad, round, red face, and vacant eyes. Even in the dull light Anne got the impression that there was something unusual about his eyes.

"Is this you, Mistress Blythe?" said Captain Jim. "Now, now, you hadn't oughter be roaming about alone on a night like this. You could get lost in this fog easier than not. Jest you wait till I see Dick safe inside the door and I'll come back and light you over the fields. I ain't going to have Dr. Blythe coming home and finding that you walked clean over Cape Leforce in the fog. A woman did that once, forty years ago."

"So you've been over to see Leslie," he said, when he rejoined her.

"I didn't go in," said Anne, and told what she had seen. Captain Jim sighed.

"Poor, poor, little girl! She don't cry often, Mistress Blythe—she's too brave for that. She must feel terrible when she does cry. A night like this is hard on poor women who have sorrows. There's something about it that kinder brings up all we've suffered—or feared."

"It's full of ghosts," said Anne, with a shiver. "That was why I came over—I wanted to clasp a human hand and hear a human voice. There seem to be so many *inhuman* presences about tonight. Even my own dear house was full of them. They fairly elbowed me out. So I fled over here for companionship of my kind."

"You were right not to go in, though, Mistress Blythe. Leslie wouldn't have liked it. She wouldn't have liked me going in with Dick, as I'd have done if I hadn't met you. I had Dick down with me all day. I keep him with me as much as I can to help Leslie a bit."

"Isn't there something odd about his eyes?" asked Anne.

"You noticed that? Yes, one is blue and t'other is hazel—his father had the same. It's a Moore peculiarity. That was what told me he was Dick Moore when I saw him first down in Cuby. If it hadn't a-bin for his eyes I mightn't a-known him, what with his beard and fat. You know, I reckon, that it was me found him and brought him home. Miss Cornelia always says I shouldn't have done it, but I can't agree with her. It was the *right* thing to do—and so 'twas the only thing. There ain't no question in my mind about *that*. But my old heart aches for Leslie. She's only twenty-eight and she's eaten more bread with sorrow than most women do in eighty years."

They walked on in silence for a little while. Presently Anne said, "Do you know, Captain Jim, I never like walking with a lantern. I have always the strangest feeling that just outside the circle of light, just over its edge in the darkness, I am surrounded by a ring of furtive, sinister things, watching me from the shadows with hostile eyes. I've had that feeling from childhood. What is the reason? I never feel like that when I'm really in the darkness—when it is close all around me—I'm not the least frightened."

"I've something of that feeling myself," admitted Captain Jim. "I reckon when the darkness is close to us it is a friend. But when we sorter push it away from us—divorce ourselves from it, so to speak, with lantern light—it becomes an enemy. But the fog is lifting. There's a smart west wind rising, if you notice. The stars will be out when you get home."

They were out; and when Anne re-entered her house of dreams the red embers were still glowing on the hearth, and all the haunting presences were gone.

14
November Days

The splendour of colour which had glowed for weeks along the shores of Four Winds Harbour had faded out into the soft gray-blue of late autumnal hills. There came many days when fields and shores were dim with misty rain, or shivering before the breath of a melancholy sea-wind—nights, too, of storm and tempest, when Anne sometimes wakened to pray that no ship might be beating up the grim north shore, for if it were so not even the great, faithful light, whirling through the darkness unafraid, could avail to guide it into safe haven.

"In November I sometimes feel as if spring could never come again," she sighed, grieving over the hopeless unsightliness of her frosted and bedraggled flower-plots. The gay little garden of the schoolmaster's bride was rather a forlorn place now, and the Lombardies and birches were under bare poles, as Captain Jim said. But the fir-wood behind the little house was forever green and staunch; and even in November and December there came gracious days of sunshine and purple hazes, when the harbour danced and sparkled as blithely as in midsummer, and the gulf was so softly blue and tender that the storm and the wild wind seemed only things of a long-past dream.

Anne and Gilbert spent many an autumn evening at the lighthouse. It was always a cheery place. Even when the east wind sang in minor and the sea was dead and gray, hints of sunshine seemed to be lurking all about it. Perhaps this was because the First Mate always paraded it in panoply of gold. He was so large and effulgent that one hardly missed the sun, and his resounding purrs formed a pleasant accompaniment to the laughter and conversation which went on around Captain Jim's fireplace. Captain Jim and Gilbert had many long discussions and high converse on matters beyond the ken of cat or king.

"I like to ponder on all kinds of problems, though I can't solve 'em," said Captain Jim. "My father held that we should never talk of things we couldn't understand, but if we didn't, doctor, the subjects for conversation would be mighty few. I reckon the gods laugh many a time to hear us, but what matters so long as we remember that we're only men and don't take to fancying that we're gods ourselves, really, knowing good and evil. I reckon our pow-pows won't do us or anyone much harm, so let's have another whack at the whence, why and whither this evening, doctor."

While they "whacked," Anne listened or dreamed. Sometimes Leslie went to the lighthouse with them, and she and Anne wandered along the shore in the eerie twilight, or sat on the rocks below the lighthouse until the darkness drove them back to the cheer of the driftwood fire. Then Captain Jim would brew them tea and tell them

> "*tales of land and sea*
> *And whatsoever might betide*
> *The great forgotten world outside.*"

Leslie seemed always to enjoy those lighthouse carousals very much, and bloomed out for the time being into ready wit and beautiful laughter, or glowing-eyed silence. There was a certain tang and savour in the conversation when Leslie was present which they missed when she was absent. Even when she did not talk she seemed to inspire others to brilliancy. Captain Jim told his stories better, Gilbert was quicker in argument and repartee, Anne felt little gushes and trickles of fancy and imagination bubbling to her lips under the influence of Leslie's personality.

"That girl was born to be a leader in social and intellectual circles, far away from Four Winds," she said to Gilbert as they walked home one night. "She's just wasted here—wasted."

"Weren't you listening to Captain Jim and yours truly the other night when we discussed that subject generally? We came to the comforting conclusion that the Creator probably knew how to run His universe quite as well as we do, and that, after all, there are no such things as 'wasted' lives, saving and except when an individual wilfully squanders and wastes his own life—which Leslie Moore certainly hasn't done. And some people might think that a Redmond B.A., whom editors were beginning to honour, was 'wasted' as the wife of a struggling country doctor in the rural community of Four Winds."

"Gilbert!"

"If you had married Roy Gardner, now," continued Gilbert mercilessly, "*you* could have been 'a leader in social and intellectual circles far away from Four Winds.' "

"Gilbert *Blythe*!"

"You *know* you were in love with him at one time, Anne."

"Gilbert, that's mean—'pisen mean, just like all the men,' as Miss Cornelia says. I *never* was in love with him. I only imagined I was. *You* know that. You *know* I'd rather be your wife in our house of dreams and fulfilment than a queen in a palace."

Gilbert's answer was not in words; but I am afraid that both of them forgot poor Leslie speeding her lonely way across the fields to a house that was neither a palace nor the fulfilment of a dream.

The moon was rising over the sad, dark sea behind them and transfiguring it. Her light had not yet reached the harbour, the further side of which was shadowy and suggestive, with dim coves and rich glooms and jewelling lights.

"How the homelights shine out to-night through the dark!" said Anne. "That string of them over the harbour looks like a necklace. And what a coruscation there is up at the Glen! Oh, look, Gilbert, there is ours. I'm so glad we left it burning. I hate to come home to a dark house. *Our* homelight, Gilbert! Isn't it lovely to see?"

"Just one of earth's many millions of homes, Anne-girl—but ours—*ours*—our beacon in 'a naughty world.' When a fellow has a home and a dear, little, red-haired wife in it what more need he ask of life?"

"Well, he might ask *one* thing more," whispered Anne happily. "Oh, Gilbert, it seems as if I just *couldn't* wait for the spring."

15
Christmas at Four Winds

At first Anne and Gilbert talked of going home to Avonlea for Christmas; but eventually they decided to stay in Four Winds. "I want to spend the first Christmas of our life together in our own home," decreed Anne.

So it fell out that Marilla and Mrs. Rachel Lynde and the twins came to Four Winds for Christmas. Marilla had the face of a woman who had circumnavigated the globe. She had never been sixty miles away from home before; and had never eaten a Christmas dinner anywhere save at Green Gables.

Mrs. Rachel had made and brought with her an enormous plum pudding. Nothing could have convinced Mrs. Rachel that a college graduate of the younger generation could make a Christmas plum pudding properly; but she bestowed approval on Anne's house.

"Anne's a good housekeeper," she said to Marilla in the spare room the night of their arrival. "I've looked into her bread box and her scrap pail. I always judge a housekeeper by those, that's what. There's nothing in the pail that shouldn't have been thrown away, and no stale pieces in the bread box. Of course, she was trained up with you—but, then, she went to college afterwards.

I notice she's got my tobacco stripe quilt on the bed here, and that big round braided mat of yours before her living-room fire. It makes me feel right at home."

Anne's first Christmas in her own house was as delightful as she could have wished. The day was fine and bright; the first skim of snow had fallen on Christmas Eve and made the world beautiful; the harbour was still open and glittering.

Captain Jim and Miss Cornelia came to dinner. Leslie and Dick had been invited, but Leslie made excuse; they always went to her Uncle Isaac West's for Christmas, she said.

"She'd rather have it so," Miss Cornelia told Anne. "She can't bear taking Dick where there are strangers. Christmas is always a hard time for Leslie. She and her father used to make a lot of it."

Miss Cornelia and Mrs. Rachel did not take a very violent fancy to each other. "Two suns hold not their courses in one sphere." But they did not clash at all, for Mrs. Rachel was in the kitchen helping Anne and Marilla with the dinner, and it fell to Gilbert to entertain Captain Jim and Miss Cornelia,—or rather to be entertained by them, for a dialogue between those two old friends and antagonists was assuredly never dull.

"It's many a year since there was a Christmas dinner here, Mistress Blythe," said Captain Jim. "Miss Russell always went to her friends in town for Christmas. But I was here to the first Christmas dinner that was ever eaten in this house—and the schoolmaster's bride cooked it. That was sixty years ago today, Mistress Blythe—and a day very like this—just enough snow to make the hills white, and the harbour as blue as June. I was only a lad, and I'd never been invited out to dinner before, and I was too shy to eat enough. I've got all over *that*."

"Most men do," said Miss Cornelia, sewing furiously. Miss Cornelia was not going to sit with idle hands, even on Christmas. Babies come without any consideration for holidays, and there was some expected in a poverty-stricken household at

Glen St. Mary. Miss Cornelia had sent that household a substantial dinner for its little swarm, and so meant to eat her own with a comfortable conscience.

"Well, you know, the way to a man's heart is through his stomach, Cornelia," explained Captain Jim.

"I believe you—when he *has* a heart," retorted Miss Cornelia. "I suppose that's why so many women kill themselves cooking—just as poor Amelia Baxter did. She died last Christmas morning, and she said it was the first Christmas since she was married that she didn't have to cook a big, twenty-plate dinner. It must have been a real pleasant change for her. Well, she's been dead a year, so you'll soon hear of Horace Baxter taking notice."

"I heard he was taking notice already," said Captain Jim, winking at Gilbert. "Wasn't he up to your place one Sunday lately, with his funeral blacks on, and a boiled collar?"

"No, he wasn't. And he needn't come neither. I could have had him long ago when he was fresh. I don't want any second-hand goods, believe *me*. As for Horace Baxter, he was in financial difficulties a year ago last summer, and he prayed to the Lord for help; and when his wife died and he got her life insurance he said he believed it was the answer to his prayer. Wasn't that like a man?"

"Have you really proof that he said that, Cornelia?"

"I have the Methodist minister's word for it—if you call that proof. Robert Baxter told me the same thing too, but I admit *that* isn't evidence. Robert Baxter isn't often known to tell the truth."

"Come, come, Cornelia, I think he generally tells the truth, but he changes his opinion so often it sometimes sounds as if he didn't."

"It sounds like it mighty often, believe *me*. But trust one man to excuse another. I have no use for Robert Baxter. He turned Methodist just because the Presbyterian choir happened to be singing 'Behold the bridegroom cometh' for a collection piece when him and Margaret walked up the aisle the Sunday after they were married. Served him right for being late! He always insisted the choir did it on purpose to insult him, as if he was of that much importance. But that family always thought they were much bigger potatoes than they really were. His brother Eliphalet imagined the devil was always at his elbow—but *I* never believed the devil wasted that much time on him."

"I—don't—know," said Captain Jim thoughtfully. "Eliphalet Baxter lived too much alone—hadn't even a cat or dog to keep him human. When a man is alone he's mighty apt to be with the devil—if he ain't with God. He has to choose which company he'll keep, I reckon. If the devil always was at Life Baxter's elbow it must have been because Life liked to have him there."

"Man-like," said Miss Cornelia, and subsided into silence over a complicated arrangement of tucks until Captain Jim deliberately stirred her up again by remarking in a casual way:

"I was up to the Methodist church last Sunday morning."

"You'd better have been home reading your Bible," was Miss Cornelia's retort.

"Come now, Cornelia, *I* can't see any harm in going to the Methodist church when there's no preaching in your own. I've been a Presbyterian for seventy-six years, and it isn't likely my theology will hoist anchor at this late day."

"It's setting a bad example," said Miss Cornelia grimly.

"Besides," continued wicked Captain Jim, "I wanted to hear some good singing. The Methodists have a good choir; and you can't deny, Cornelia, that the singing in our church is awful since the split in the choir."

"What if the singing isn't good? They're doing their best, and God sees no difference between the voice of a crow and the voice of a nightingale."

"Come, come, Cornelia," said Captain Jim mildly, "I've a better opinion of the Almighty's ear for music than *that*."

"What caused the trouble in our choir?" asked Gilbert, who was suffering from suppressed laughter.

"It dates back to the new church, three years ago," answered Captain Jim. "We had a fearful time over the building of that church—fell out over the question of a new site. The two sites wasn't more'n two hundred yards apart, but you'd have thought they was a thousand by the bitterness of that fight. We was split up into three factions—one wanted the east site and one the south, and one held to the old. It was fought out in bed and at board, and in church and at market. All the old scandals of three generations were dragged out of their graves and aired. Three matches was broken up by it. And the meetings we had to try to settle the question! Cornelia, will you ever forget the one when old Luther Burns got up and made a speech? *He* stated his opinions forcibly."

"Call a spade a spade, Captain. You mean he got red-mad and raked them all, fore and aft. They deserved it too—a pack of incapables. But what would you expect of a committee of men? That building committee held twenty-seven meetings, and at the end of the twenty-seventh weren't no nearer having a church than when they begun—not so near, for a fact, for in one fit of hurrying things along they'd gone to work and tore the old church down, so there we were, without a church, and no place but the hall to worship in."

"The Methodists offered us their church, Cornelia."

"The Glen St. Mary church wouldn't have been built to this day," went on Miss Cornelia, ignoring Captain Jim, "if we women hadn't just started in and took charge. We said *we* meant to have a church, if the men meant to quarrel till doomsday, and we were tired of being a laughing-stock for the Methodists. We held *one* meeting and elected a committee and canvassed for subscriptions. We got them, too. When any of the men tried to sass us we told them they'd tried for two years to build a church and it was our turn now. We shut them up close, believe *me*, and in six months we had our church. Of course when the men saw we were determined they stopped fighting and went to work, manlike, as soon as they saw they had to, or quit bossing. Oh, women can't preach or be elders; but they can build churches and scare up the money for them."

"The Methodists allow women to preach," said Captain Jim.

Miss Cornelia glared at him.

"I never said the Methodists hadn't common sense, Captain. What I say is, I doubt if they have much religion."

"I suppose you are in favor of votes for women, Miss Cornelia," said Gilbert.

"I'm not hankering after the vote, believe *me*," said Miss Cornelia scornfully, "*I* know what it is to clean up after the men. But some of these days, when the men realise they've got the world into a mess they can't get it out of, they'll be glad to give us the vote, and shoulder their troubles over on us. That's *their* scheme. Oh, it's well that women are patient, believe me!"

"What about Job?" suggested Captain Jim.

"Job! It was such a rare thing to find a patient man that when one was really discovered they were determined he shouldn't be forgotten," retorted Miss Cornelia triumphantly. "Anyhow, the virtue doesn't go with the name. There never was such an impatient man born as old Job Taylor over harbour."

"Well, you know, he had a good deal to try him, Cornelia. Even you can't defend his wife. I always remember what old William MacAllister said of her at her funeral, 'There's nae doot she was a Chreestian wumman, but she had the de'il's own temper.'"

"I suppose she *was* trying," admitted Miss Cornelia reluctantly, "but that didn't justify what Job said when she died. He rode home from the graveyard the day of the funeral with my father. He never said a word till they got near home. Then he heaved a big sigh and said, 'You may not believe it, Stephen, but this is the happiest day of my life!' Wasn't that like a man?"

"I s'pose poor old Mrs. Job did make life kinder uneasy for him," reflected Captain Jim.

"Well, there's such a thing as decency, isn't there? Even if a man is rejoicing in his heart over his wife being dead, he needn't proclaim it to the four winds of heaven. And happy day or not, Job Taylor wasn't long in marrying again, you might notice. His second wife could manage him. She made him walk Spanish, believe me! The first thing she did was to make him hustle round and put up a tombstone to the first Mrs. Job—and she had a place left on it for her own name. She said there'd be nobody to make Job put up a monument to *her*."

"Speaking of Taylors, how is Mrs. Lewis Taylor up at the Glen, doctor?" asked Captain Jim.

"She's getting better slowly—but she has to work too hard," replied Gilbert.

"Her husband works hard too—raising prize pigs," said Miss Cornelia. "He's noted for his beautiful pigs. He's a heap prouder of his pigs than of his children. But then, to be sure, his pigs are the best pigs possible, while his children don't amount to much. He picked a poor mother for them, and starved her while she was bearing and rearing them. His pigs got the cream and his children got the skim milk."

"There are times, Cornelia, when I have to agree with you, though it hurts me," said Captain Jim. "That's just exactly the truth about Lewis Taylor. When I see those poor, miserable children of his, robbed of all children ought to have, it p'isens my own bite and sup for days afterwards."

Gilbert went out to the kitchen in response to Anne's beckoning. Anne shut the door and gave him a connubial lecture.

"Gilbert, you and Captain Jim must stop baiting Miss Cornelia. Oh, I've been listening to you—and I just won't allow it."

"Anne, Miss Cornelia is enjoying herself hugely. You know she is."

"Well, never mind. You two needn't egg her on like that. Dinner is ready now, and Gilbert, *don't* let Mrs. Rachel carve the geese. I know she means to offer to do it because she doesn't think you can do it properly. Show her you can."

"I ought to be able to. I've been studying A-B-C-D diagrams of carving for the past month," said Gilbert. "Only don't talk to me while I'm doing it, Anne, for if you drive the letters out of my head I'll be in a worse predicament than you were in old geometry days when the teacher changed them."

Gilbert carved the geese beautifully. Even Mrs. Rachel had to admit that. And everybody ate of them and enjoyed them. Anne's first Christmas dinner was a great success and she beamed with housewifely pride. Merry was the feast and long; and when it was over they gathered around the cheer of the red hearth flame and Captain Jim told them stories until the red sun swung low over Four Winds Harbour, and the long shadows of the Lombardies fell across the snow in the lane.

"I must be getting back to the light," he said finally. "I'll jest have time to walk home before sun-down. Thank you for a beautiful Christmas, Mistress Blythe. Bring Master Davy down to the light some night before he goes home."

"I want to see those stone gods," said Davy with a relish.

16

New Year's Eve at the Light

The Green Gables folk went home after Christmas, Marilla under solemn covenant to return for a month in the spring.

More snow came before New Year's, and the harbour froze over, but the gulf still was free, beyond the white, imprisoned fields. The last day of the old year was one of those bright, cold dazzling winter days, which bombard us with their brilliancy, and command our admiration but never our love. The sky was sharp and blue; the snow diamonds sparkled insistently; the stark trees were bare and shameless, with a kind of brazen beauty; the hills shot assaulting lances of crystal. Even the shadows were sharp and stiff and clear-cut, as no proper shadows should be. Everything that was handsome seemed ten times handsomer and less attractive in the glaring splendour; and everything that was ugly seemed ten times uglier, and everything was either handsome or ugly. There was no soft blending, or kind obscurity, or elusive mistiness in that searching glitter. The only things that held their own individuality were the firs—for the fir is the tree of mystery and shadows, and yields never to the encroachments of crude radiance.

But finally the day began to realise that she was growing old. Then a certain pensiveness fell over her beauty which dimmed yet intensified it; sharp angles, glittering points, melted away into curves and enticing gleams. The white harbour put on soft grays and pinks; the far-away hills turned amethyst.

"The old year is going away beautifully," said Anne. She and Leslie and Gilbert were on their way to the Four Winds Point, having plotted with Captain Jim to watch the New Year in at the light. The sun had set and in the southwestern sky hung Venus, glorious and golden, having drawn as near to her earth-sister as is possible for her. For the first time Anne and Gilbert saw the shadow cast by that brilliant star of evening, that faint, mysterious shadow, never seen save when there is white snow to reveal it, and then only with averted vision, vanishing when you gaze at it directly.

"It's like the spirit of a shadow, isn't it?" whispered Anne. "You can see it so plainly haunting your side when you look ahead; but when you turn and look at it—it's gone."

"I have heard that you can see the shadow of Venus only once in a lifetime, and that within a year of seeing it your life's most wonderful gift will come to you," said Leslie. But she spoke rather hardly; perhaps she thought that even the shadow of Venus could bring her no gift of life. Anne smiled in the soft twilight; she felt quite sure what the mystic shadow promised her.

They found Marshall Elliott at the lighthouse. At first Anne felt inclined to resent the intrusion of this long-haired, long-bearded eccentric into the familiar little circle. But Marshall Elliott soon proved his legitimate claim to membership in the household of Joseph. He was a witty, intelligent, well-read man, rivalling Captain Jim himself in the knack of telling a good story. They were all glad when he agreed to watch the old year out with them.

Captain Jim's small nephew Joe had come down to spend New Year's with his great-uncle, and had fallen asleep on the sofa with the First Mate curled up in a huge golden ball at his feet.

"Ain't he a dear little man?" said Captain Jim gloatingly. "I do love to watch a little child asleep, Mistress Blythe. It's the most beautiful sight in the world, I reckon. Joe does love to get down here for a night, because I have him sleep with me. At home he has to sleep with the other two boys, and he doesn't like it. 'Why can't I sleep with father, Uncle Jim?' say he. 'Everybody in the Bible sleep with their fathers.' As for the questions he asks, the minister himself couldn't answer them. They fair swamp me. 'Uncle Jim, if I wasn't *me* who'd I be?' and, 'Uncle Jim, what would happen if God died?' He fired them two off at me tonight, afore he went to sleep. As for his imagination, it sails away from everything. He makes up the most remarkable yarns—and then his mother shuts him up in the closet for telling stories. And he sits down and makes up another one, and has it ready to relate to her when she lets him out. He had one for me when he come down tonight. 'Uncle Jim,' says he, solemn as a tombstone, 'I had a 'venture in the Glen today.' 'Yes, what was it?' says I, expecting something quite startling, but nowise prepared for what I really got. 'I met a wolf in the street,' says he, 'a 'normous wolf with a big, red mouf and *awful* long teeth, Uncle Jim.' 'I didn't know there was any wolves up at the Glen,' says I. 'Oh, he comed there from far, far away,' says Joe, 'and I fought he was going to eat me up, Uncle Jim.' 'Were you scared?' says I. 'No, 'cause I had a big gun,' says Joe, 'and I shot the wolf dead, Uncle Jim,—solid dead—and then he went up to heaven and bit God,' says he. Well, I was fair staggered, Mistress Blythe."

The hours bloomed into mirth around the driftwood fire. Captain Jim told tales, and Marshall Elliott sang old Scotch ballads in a fine tenor voice; finally Captain Jim took down his old brown fiddle from the wall and began to play. He had a tolerable knack of fiddling, which all appreciated save the First Mate, who sprang from the sofa as if he had been shot, emitted a shriek of protest, and fled wildly up the stairs.

"Can't cultivate an ear for music in that cat nohow," said Captain Jim. "He won't stay long enough to learn to like it. When we got the organ up at the Glen church old Elder Richards bounced up from his seat the minute the organist began to play and scuttled down the aisle and out of the church at the rate of no-man's-business. It reminded me so strong of the First Mate tearing loose as soon as I begin to fiddle that I come nearer to laughing out loud in church than I ever did before or since."

There was something so infectious in the rollicking tunes which Captain Jim played that very soon Marshall Elliott's feet began to twitch. He had been a noted dancer in his youth. Presently he started up and held out his hands to Leslie. Instantly she responded. Round and round the firelit room they circled with a rhythmic grace that was wonderful. Leslie danced like one inspired; the wild, sweet abandon of the music seemed to have entered into and possessed her. Anne watched her in fascinated admiration. She had never seen her like this. All the innate richness and colour and charm of her nature seemed to have broken loose and overflowed in crimson cheek and glowing eye and grace of motion. Even the aspect of Marshall Elliott, with his long beard and hair, could not spoil the picture. On the contrary, it seemed to enhance it. Marshall Elliott looked like a Viking of elder days, dancing with one of the blue-eyed golden-haired daughters of the Northland.

"The purtiest dancing I ever saw, and I've seen some in my time," declared Captain Jim, when at last the bow fell from his tired hand. Leslie dropped into her chair, laughing, breathless.

"I love dancing," she said apart to Anne. "I haven't danced since I was sixteen—but I love it. The music seems to run through my veins like quicksilver and I forget everything—everything—except the delight of keeping time to it. There isn't any floor beneath me, or roof over me—I'm floating amid the stars."

Captain Jim hung his fiddle up in its place, beside a large frame enclosing several banknotes.

"Is there anybody else of your acquaintance who can afford to hang his walls with banknotes for pictures?" he asked. "There's twenty ten-dollar notes there, not worth the glass over them. They're old Bank of P. E. Island notes. Had them by me when the bank faded, and I had 'em framed and hung up, partly as a reminder not to put your trust in banks, and partly to give me a real luxurious, millionairy feeling. Hullo, Matey, don't be scared. You can come back now. The music and revelry is over for tonight. The old year has just another hour to stay with us. I've seen seventy-six New Years come in over that gulf yonder, Mistress Blythe."

"You'll see a hundred," said Marshall Elliott.

Captain Jim shook his head.

"No; and I don't want to—at least, I think I don't. Death grows friendlier as we grow older. Not that one of us really wants to die though, Marshall. Tennyson spoke truth when he said that. There's old Mrs. Wallace up at the Glen. She's had heaps of trouble all her life, poor soul, and she's lost almost everyone she cared about. She's always saying that she'll be glad when her time comes, and she doesn't want to sojourn any longer in this vale of tears. But when she takes a sick spell there's a fuss! Doctors from town, and a trained nurse, and enough medicine to kill a dog. Life may be a vale of tears, all right, but there are some folks who enjoy weeping, I reckon."

They spent the old year's last hour quietly around the fire. A few minutes before twelve Captain Jim rose and opened the door.

"We must let the New Year in," he said.

Outside was a fine blue night. A sparkling ribbon of moonlight garlanded the gulf. Inside the bar the harbour shone like a pavement of pearl. They stood before the door and waited—Captain Jim with his ripe, full experience, Marshall Elliott in his vigorous but empty middle life, Gilbert and Anne with their precious memories and exquisite hopes, Leslie with her record of starved years and her hopeless future. The clock on the little shelf above the fireplace struck twelve.

"Welcome, New Year," said Captain Jim, bowing low as the last stroke died away. "I wish you all the best year of your lives, mates. I reckon that whatever the New Year brings us will be the best the Great Captain has for us—and somehow or other we'll all make port in a good harbour."

17
A Four Winds Winter

Winter set in vigorously after New Year's. Big, white drifts heaped themselves about the little house, and palms of frost covered its windows. The harbour ice grew harder and thicker, until the Four Winds people began their usual winter travelling over it. The safe ways were "bushed" by a benevolent Government, and night and day the gay tinkle of the sleighbells sounded on it. On moonlit nights Anne heard them in her house of dreams like fairy chimes. The gulf froze over, and the Four Winds light flashed no more. During the months when navigation was closed Captain Jim's office was a sinecure.

"The First Mate and I will have nothing to do till spring except keep warm and amuse ourselves. The last lighthouse keeper used always to move up to the Glen in winter; but I'd rather stay at the Point. The First Mate might get poisoned or chewed up by dogs at the Glen. It's a mite lonely, to be sure, with neither the light nor the water for company, but if our friends come to see us often we'll weather it through."

Captain Jim had an ice boat, and many a wild, glorious spin Gilbert and Anne and Leslie had over the glib harbour ice with him. Anne and Leslie took long snow-shoe tramps together, too, over the fields, or across the harbour after storms, or through the woods beyond the Glen. They were very good comrades in their rambles and their fireside communings. Each had something to give the other—each felt life the richer for friendly exchange of thought and friendly silence; each looked across the white fields between their homes with a pleasant consciousness of a friend beyond. But, in spite of all this, Anne felt that there was always a barrier between Leslie and herself—a constraint that never wholly vanished.

"I don't know why I can't get closer to her," Anne said one evening to Captain Jim. "I like her so much—I admire her so much—I *want* to take her right into my heart and creep right into hers. But I can never cross the barrier."

"You've been too happy all your life, Mistress Blythe," said Captain Jim thoughtfully. "I reckon that's why you and Leslie can't get real close together in your souls. The barrier between you is her experience of sorrow and trouble. She ain't responsible for it and you ain't; but it's there and neither of you can cross it."

"My childhood wasn't very happy before I came to Green Gables," said Anne, gazing soberly out of the window at the still, sad, dead beauty of the leafless tree-shadows on the moonlit snow.

"Mebbe not—but it was just the usual unhappiness of a child who hasn't anyone to look after it properly. There hasn't been any *tragedy* in your life, Mistress Blythe. And poor Leslie's has been almost *all* tragedy. She feels, I reckon, though mebbe she hardly knows she feels it, that there's a vast deal in her life you can't enter nor understand—and so she has to keep you back from it—hold you off, so to speak, from hurting her. You know if we've got anything about us that hurts we shrink from anyone's touch on or near it. It holds good with our souls as well as our bodies, I reckon. Leslie's soul must be near raw—it's no wonder she hides it away."

"If that were really all, I wouldn't mind, Captain Jim. I would understand. But there are times—not always, but now and again—when I almost have to believe that Leslie doesn't—doesn't like me. Sometimes I surprise a look in her eyes that seems to show resentment and dislike—it goes so quickly—but I've seen it, I'm sure of that. And it hurts me, Captain Jim. I'm not used to being disliked—and I've tried so hard to win Leslie's friendship."

"You have won it, Mistress Blythe. Don't you go cherishing any foolish notion that Leslie don't like you. If she didn't she wouldn't have anything to do with you, much less chumming with you as she does. I know Leslie Moore too well not to be sure of that."

"The first time I ever saw her, driving her geese down the hill on the day I came to Four Winds, she looked at me with the same expression," persisted Anne. "I felt it, even in the midst of my admiration of her beauty. She looked at me resentfully—she did, indeed, Captain Jim."

"The resentment must have been about something else, Mistress Blythe, and you jest come in for a share of it because you happened past. Leslie *does* take sullen spells now and again, poor girl. I can't blame her, when I know what she has to put up with. I don't know why it's permitted. The doctor and I have talked a lot about the origin of evil, but we haven't quite found out all about it yet. There's a vast of onunderstandable things in life, ain't there, Mistress Blythe? Sometimes things seem to work out real proper-like, same as with you and the doctor. And then again they all seem to go catawampus. There's Leslie, so clever and beautiful you'd think she was meant for a queen, and instead she's cooped up over there, robbed of almost everything a woman'd value, with no prospect except waiting on Dick Moore all her life. Though, mind you, Mistress Blythe, I daresay she'd choose her life now, such as it is, rather than the life she lived with Dick before he went away. *That's* something a clumsy old sailor's tongue mustn't meddle with. But you've helped Leslie a lot—she's a different creature since you come to Four Winds. Us old friends see the difference in her, as you can't. Miss Cornelia and me was talking it over the other day, and it's one of the mighty few p'ints that we see eye to eye on. So jest you throw overboard any idea of her not liking you."

Anne could hardly discard it completely, for there were undoubtedly times when she felt, with an instinct that was not to be combated by reason, that Leslie harboured a queer, indefinable resentment towards her. At times, this secret consciousness marred the delight of their comradeship; at others it was almost forgotten; but Anne always felt the hidden thorn was there, and might prick her at any moment. She felt a cruel sting from it on the day when she told Leslie of what she hoped the spring would bring to the little house of dreams. Leslie looked at her with hard, bitter, unfriendly eyes.

"So you are to have *that*, too," she said in a choked voice. And without another word she had turned and gone across the fields homeward. Anne was deeply hurt; for the moment she felt as if she could never like Leslie again. But when Leslie came over a few evenings later she was so pleasant, so friendly, so frank, and witty, and winsome, that Anne was charmed into forgiveness and forgetfulness. Only, she never mentioned her darling hope to Leslie again; nor did Leslie ever refer to it. But one evening, when late winter was listening for the word of spring, she came over to the little house for a twilight chat; and when she went away she left a small, white box on the table. Anne found it after she was gone and opened it wonderingly. In it was a tiny white dress of exquisite workmanship—delicate embroidery, wonderful tucking, sheer loveliness. Every stitch in it was handwork; and the little frills of lace at neck and sleeves were of real Valenciennes. Lying on it was a card—"with Leslie's love."

"What hours of work she must have put on it," said Anne. "And the material must have cost more than she could really afford. It is very sweet of her."

But Leslie was brusque and curt when Anne thanked her, and again the latter felt thrown back upon herself.

Leslie's gift was not alone in the little house. Miss Cornelia had, for the time being, given up sewing for unwanted, unwelcome eighth babies, and fallen to sewing for a very much wanted first one, whose welcome would leave nothing to be desired. Philippa Blake and Diana Wright each sent a marvellous garment; and Mrs. Rachel Lynde sent several, in which good material and honest stitches took the place of embroidery and frills. Anne herself made many, desecrated by no touch of machinery, spending over them the happiest hours of that happy winter.

Captain Jim was the most frequent guest of the little house, and none was more welcome. Everyday Anne loved the simple-souled, true-hearted old sailor more and more. He was as refreshing as a sea-breeze, as interesting as some ancient chronicle. She was never tired of listening to his stories, and his quaint remarks and comments were a continual delight to her. Captain Jim was one of those rare and interesting people who "never speak but they say something." The milk of human kindness and the wisdom of the serpent were mingled in his composition in delightful proportions.

Nothing ever seemed to put Captain Jim out or depress him in any way.

"I've kind of contracted a habit of enj'ying things," he remarked once, when Anne had commented on his invariable cheerfulness. "It's got so chronic that I believe I even enj'y the disagreeable things. It's great fun thinking they can't last. 'Old rheumatiz,' says I, when it grips me hard, 'you've *got* to stop aching sometime. The worse you are the sooner you'll stop, mebbe. I'm bound to get the better of you in the long run whether in the body or out of the body.' "

One night, by the fireside at the light Anne saw Captain Jim's "life-book." He needed no coaxing to show it and proudly gave it to her to read.

"I writ it to leave to little Joe," he said. "I don't like the idea of everything I've done and seen being clean forgot after I've shipped for my last v'yage. Joe, he'll remember it, and tell the yarns to his children."

It was an old leather-bound book filled with the record of his voyages and adventures. Anne thought what a treasure trove it would be to a writer. Every sentence was a nugget. In itself the book had no literary merit; Captain Jim's charm of story-telling failed him when he came to pen and ink; he could only jot down the outline of his famous tales, and both spelling and grammar were sadly askew. But Anne felt that if anyone possessed of the gift could take that simple record of a brave, adventurous life, reading between the bald lines the tales of dangers staunchly faced and duty manfully done, a wonderful story might be made from it. Rich comedy and thrilling tragedy were both lying hidden in Captain Jim's "life-book," waiting for the touch of the master hand to waken the laughter and grief and horror of thousands.

Anne said something of this to Gilbert as they walked home.

"Why don't you try your hand at it yourself, Anne?" Anne shook her head.

"No. I only wish I could. But it's not in the power of my gift. You know what my forte is, Gilbert—the fanciful, the fairylike, the pretty. To write Captain Jim's life-book as it should be written one should be a master of vigorous yet subtle style, a keen psychologist, a born humourist and a born tragedian. A rare combination of gifts is needed. Paul might do it if he were older. Anyhow, I'm going to ask him to come down next summer and meet Captain Jim."

"Come to this shore," wrote Anne to Paul. "I'm afraid you cannot find here Nora or the Golden Lady or the Twin Sailors; but you will find one old sailor who can tell you wonderful stories."

Paul, however, wrote back, saying regretfully that he could not come that year. He was going abroad for two years' study.

"When I return I'll come to Four Winds, dear Teacher," he wrote.

"But meanwhile, Captain Jim is growing old," said Anne, sorrowfully, "and there is nobody to write his life-book."

18
Spring Days

The ice in the harbour grew black and rotten in the March suns; in April there were blue waters and a windy, white-capped gulf and again the Four Winds light begemmed the twilights.

"I'm so glad to see it once more," said Anne, on the first evening of its reappearance. "I've missed it so all winter. The north-western sky has seemed blank and lonely without it."

The land was tender with brand-new, golden-green, baby leaves. There was an emerald mist on the woods beyond the Glen. The seaward valleys were full of fairy mists at dawn.

Vibrant winds came and went with salt foam in their breath. The sea laughed and flashed and preened and allured, like a beautiful, coquettish woman. The herring schooled and the fishing village woke to life. The harbour was alive with white sails making for the channel. The ships began to sail outward and inward again.

"On a spring day like this," said Anne, "I know exactly what my soul will feel like on the resurrection morning."

"There are times in spring when I sorter feel that I might have been a poet if I'd been caught young," remarked Captain Jim. "I catch myself conning over old lines and verses I heard the schoolmaster reciting sixty years ago. They don't trouble me at other times. Now I feel as if I had to get out on the rocks or the fields or the water and spout them."

Captain Jim had come up that afternoon to bring Anne a load of shells for the garden, and a little bunch of sweet-grass which he had found in a ramble over the sand-dunes.

"It's getting real scarce along this shore now," he said. "When I was a boy there was a-plenty of it. But now it's only once in a while you'll find a plot—and never when you're looking for it. You jest have to stumble on it—you're walking along on the sand-hills, never thinking of sweet-grass—and all at once the air is full of sweetness—and there's the grass under your feet. I favour the smell of sweet-grass. It always makes me think of my mother."

"She was fond of it?" asked Anne.

"Not that I knows on. Dunno's she ever saw any sweet-grass. No, it's because it has a kind of motherly perfume—not too young, you understand—something kind of seasoned and wholesome and dependable—jest like a mother. The schoolmaster's bride always kept it among her handkerchiefs. You might put that little bunch among yours, Mistress Blythe. I don't like these boughten scents—but a whiff of sweet-grass belongs anywhere a lady does."

Anne had not been especially enthusiastic over the idea of surrounding her flower beds with quahog shells; as a decoration they did not appeal to her on first thought. But she would not have hurt Captain Jim's feelings for anything; so she assumed a virtue she did not at first feel, and thanked him heartily. And when Captain Jim had proudly encircled every bed with a rim of the big, milk-white shells, Anne found to her surprise that she liked the effect. On a town lawn, or even up at the Glen, they would not have been in keeping, but here, in the old-fashioned, seabound garden of the little house of dreams, they *belonged.*

"They *do* look nice," she said sincerely.

"The schoolmaster's bride always had cow-hawks round her beds," said Captain Jim. "She was a master hand with flowers. She *looked* at 'em—and touched 'em—and touched 'em—*so*—and they grew like mad. Some folks have that knack—I reckon you have it, too, Mistress Blythe."

"Oh, I don't know—but I love my garden, and I love working in it. To potter with green, growing things, watching each day to see the dear, new sprouts come up, is like taking a hand in creation, I think. Just now my garden is like faith—the substance of things hoped for. But bide a wee."

"It always amazes me to look at the little, wrinkled brown seeds and think of the rainbows in 'em," said Captain Jim. "When I ponder on them seeds I don't find it nowise hard to believe that we've got souls that'll live in other worlds. You couldn't hardly believe there was life in them tiny things, some no bigger than grains of dust, let alone colour and scent, if you hadn't seen the miracle, could you?"

Anne, who was counting her days like silver beads on a rosary, could not now take the long walk to the lighthouse or up the Glen road. But Miss Cornelia and Captain Jim came very often to the little house. Miss Cornelia was the joy of Anne's and Gilbert's existence. They laughed side-splittingly over her speeches after every visit. When Captain Jim and she happened to visit the little house at the same time there was much sport for the listening. They waged wordy warfare, she attacking, he defending. Anne once reproached the Captain for his baiting of Miss Cornelia.

"Oh, I do love to set her going, Mistress Blythe," chuckled the unrepentant sinner. "It's the greatest amusement I have in life. That tongue of hers would blister a stone. And you and that young dog of a doctor enj'y listening to her as much as I do."

Captain Jim came along another evening to bring Anne some mayflowers. The garden was full of the moist, scented air of a maritime spring evening. There was a milk-white mist on the edge of the sea, with a young moon kissing it, and a silver gladness of stars over the Glen. The bell of the church across the harbour was ringing dreamily sweet. The mellow chime drifted through the dusk to mingle with the soft spring-moan of the sea. Captain Jim's mayflowers added the last completing touch to the charm of the night.

"I haven't seen any this spring, and I've missed them," said Anne, burying her face in them.

"They ain't to be found around Four Winds, only in the barrens away behind the Glen up yander. I took a little trip today to the Land-of-nothing-to-do, and hunted these up for you. I reckon they're the last you'll see this spring, for they're nearly done."

"How kind and thoughtful you are, Captain Jim. Nobody else—not even Gilbert"—with a shake of her head at him—"remembered that I always long for mayflowers in spring."

"Well, I had another errand, too—I wanted to take Mr. Howard back yander a mess of trout. He likes one occasional, and it's all I can do for a kindness he did me once. I stayed all the afternoon and talked to him. He likes to talk to me, though he's a highly eddicated man and I'm only an ignorant old sailor, because he's one of the folks that's *got* to talk or they're miserable, and he finds listeners scarce around here. The Glen folks fight shy of him because they think he's an infidel. He ain't that far gone exactly—few men is, I reckon— but he's what you might call a heretic. Heretics are wicked, but they're mighty interesting. It's jest that they've got sorter lost looking for God, being under the impression that He's hard to find—which He ain't never. Most of 'em blunder to Him after awhile, I guess. I don't think listening to Mr. Howard's arguments is likely to do *me* much harm. Mind you, I believe what I was brought up to believe. It saves a vast of bother—and back of it all, God is good. The trouble with Mr. Howard is that he's a leetle too clever. He thinks that he's bound to live up to his cleverness, and that it's smarter to thrash out some new way of getting to heaven than to go by the old track the common, ignorant folks is travelling. But he'll get there sometime all right, and then he'll laugh at himself."

"Mr. Howard was a Methodist to begin with," said Miss Cornelia, as if she thought he had not far to go from that to heresy.

"Do you know, Cornelia," said Captain Jim gravely, "I've often thought that if I wasn't a Presbyterian I'd be a Methodist."

"Oh, well," conceded Miss Cornelia, "if you weren't a Presbyterian it wouldn't matter much what you were. Speaking of heresy, reminds me, doctor—I've brought back that book you lent me—that *Natural Law in the Spiritual World*—I didn't read more'n a third of it. I can read sense, and I can read non-sense, but that book is neither the one nor the other."

"It *is* considered rather heretical in some quarters," admitted Gilbert, "but I told you that before you took it. Miss Cornelia."

"Oh, I wouldn't have minded its being heretical. I can stand wickedness, but I can't stand foolishness," said Miss Cornelia calmly, and with the air of having said the last thing there was to say about *Natural Law*.

"Speaking of books, *A Mad Love* come to an end at last two weeks ago," remarked Captain Jim musingly.

"It run to one hundred and three chapters. When they got married the book stopped right off, so I reckon their troubles were all over. It's real nice that that's the way in books anyhow, isn't it, even if 'tisn't so anywhere else?"

"I never read novels," said Miss Cornelia. "Did you hear how Geordie Russell was today, Captain Jim?"

"Yes, I called in on my way home to see him. He's getting round all right—but stewing in a broth of trouble, as usual, poor man. 'Course he brews up most of it for himself, but I reckon that don't make it any easier to bear."

"He's an awful pessimist," said Miss Cornelia.

"Well, no he ain't a pessimist exactly, Cornelia. He only jest never finds anything that suits him."

"And isn't that a pessimist?"

"No, no. A pessimist is one who never expects to find anything to suit him. Geordie hain't got *that* far yet."

"You'd find something good to say of the devil himself, Jim Boyd."

"Well, you've heard the story of the old lady who said he

was persevering. But no, Cornelia, I've nothing good to say of the devil."

"Do you believe in him at all?" asked Miss Cornelia seriously.

"How can you ask that when you know what a good Presbyterian I am, Cornelia? How could a Presbyterian get along without a devil?"

"*Do* you?" persisted Miss Cornelia.

Captain Jim suddenly became grave.

"I believe in what I heard a minister once call 'a mighty and malignant and *intelligent* power of evil working in the universe,'" he said solemnly. "I do *that*, Cornelia. You can call it the devil, or the 'principle of evil,' or the Old Scratch, or any name you like. It's *there*, and all the infidels and heretics in the world can't argue it away, any more'n they can argue God away. It's there, and it's working. But, mind you, Cornelia, I believe it's going to get the worst of it in the long run."

"I am sure I hope so," said Miss Cornelia, none too hopefully. "But speaking of the devil, I am positive that Billy Booth is possessed by him now. Have you heard of Billy's latest performance?"

"No, what was that?"

"He's gone and burned up his wife's new, brown broadcloth suit, that she paid twenty-five dollars for in Charlottetown, because he declares the men looked too admiring at her when she wore it to church the first time. Wasn't that like a man?"

"Mistress Booth *is* mighty pretty, and brown's her colour," said Captain Jim reflectively.

"Is that any good reason why he should poke her new suit into the kitchen stove? Billy Booth is a jealous fool, and he makes his wife's life miserable. She's cried all the week about her suit. Oh, Anne, I wish I could write like you, believe *me*. Wouldn't I score some of the men round here!"

"Those Booths are all a mite queer," said Captain Jim. "Billy seemed the sanest of the lot till he got married and then this queer jealous streak cropped out in him. His brother Daniel, now, was always odd."

"Took tantrums every few days or so and wouldn't get out of bed," said Miss Cornelia with a relish. "His wife would have to do all the barn work till he got over his spell. When he died people wrote her letters of condolence; if I'd written anything it would have been one of congratulation. Their father, old Abram Booth, was a disgusting old sot. He was drunk at his wife's funeral, and kept reefing round and hiccuping 'I didn't dri—i—i—nk much but I feel a—a—awfully que—e—e —r.' I gave him a good jab in the back with my umbrella when he came near me, and it sobered him up until they got the casket out of the house. Young Johnny Booth was to have been married yesterday, but he couldn't be because he's gone and got the mumps. Wasn't that like a man?"

"How could he help getting the mumps, poor fellow?"

"I'd poor fellow him, believe *me,* if I was Kate Sterns. I don't know how he could help getting the mumps, but I *do* know the wedding supper was all prepared and everything will be spoiled before he's well again. Such a waste! He should have had the mumps when he was a boy."

"Come, come, Cornelia, don't you think you're a mite unreasonable?"

Miss Cornelia disdained to reply and turned instead to Susan Baker, a grim-faced, kind-hearted elderly spinster of the Glen, who had been installed as maid-of-all-work at the little house for some weeks. Susan had been up to the Glen to make a sick call, and had just returned.

"How is poor old Aunt Mandy tonight?" asked Miss Cornelia.

Susan sighed.

"Very poorly—very poorly, Cornelia. I am afraid she will soon be in heaven, poor thing!"

"Oh, surely, it's not so bad as that!" exclaimed Miss Cornelia, sympathetically.

Captain Jim and Gilbert looked at each other. Then they suddenly rose and went out.

"There are times," said Captain Jim, between spasms, "when it would be a sin *not* to laugh. Them two excellent women!"

19
Dawn and Dusk

In early June, when the sand-hills were a great glory of pink wild roses, and the Glen was smothered in apple-blossoms, Marilla arrived at the little house, accompanied by a black horse-hair trunk, patterned with brass nails, which had reposed undisturbed in the Green Gables garret for half a century. Susan Baker, who, during her few weeks' sojourn in the little house, had come to worship "young Mrs. Doctor," as she called Anne, with blind fervour, looked rather jealously askance at Marilla at first. But as Marilla did not try to interfere in kitchen matters, and showed no desire to interrupt Susan's ministrations to young Mrs. Doctor, the good handmaiden became reconciled to her presence, and told her cronies at the Glen that Miss Cuthbert was a fine old lady and knew her place.

One evening, when the sky's limpid bowl was filled with a red glory, and the robins were thrilling the golden twilight with jubilant hymns to the stars of evening, there was a sudden commotion in the little house of dreams. Telephone messages were sent up to the Glen, Doctor Dave and a white-capped nurse came hastily down, Marilla paced the garden walks between the quahog shells, murmuring prayers between her set lips, and

Susan sat in the kitchen with cotton wool in her ears and her apron over her head.

Leslie, looking out from the house up the brook, saw that every window of the little house was alight, and did not sleep that night.

The June night was short; but it seemed an eternity to those who waited and watched.

"Oh, will it *never* end?" said Marilla; then she saw how grave the nurse and Doctor Dave looked, and she dared ask no more questions. Suppose Anne—but Marilla could not suppose it.

"Do not tell me," said Susan fiercely, answering the anguish in Marilla's eyes, "that God could be so cruel as to take that darling lamb from us when we all love her so much."

"He has taken others as well beloved," said Marilla hoarsely.

But at dawn, when the rising sun rent apart the mists hanging over the sand-bar, and made rainbows of them, joy came to the little house. Anne was safe, and a wee, white lady, with her mother's big eyes, was lying beside her. Gilbert, his face gray and haggard from his night's agony, came down to tell Marilla and Susan.

"Thank God," shuddered Marilla.

Susan got up and took the cotton wool out of her ears.

"Now for breakfast," she said briskly. "I am of the opinion that we will all be glad of a bite and sup. You tell young Mrs. Doctor not to worry about a single thing—Susan is at the helm. You tell her just to think of her baby."

Gilbert smiled sadly as he went away. Anne, her pale face blanched with its baptism of pain, her eyes aglow with the holy passion of motherhood, did not need to be told to think of her baby. She thought of nothing else. For a few hours she tasted of happiness so rare and exquisite that she wondered if the angels in heaven did not envy her.

"Little Joyce," she murmured, when Marilla came in to see the baby. "We planned to call her that if she were a girlie. There were so many we would have liked to name her for; we couldn't choose between them, so we decided on Joyce—we can call her Joy for short—Joy—it suits so well. Oh, Marilla, I thought I was happy before. Now I know that I just dreamed a pleasant dream of happiness. *This* is the reality."

"You mustn't talk, Anne—wait till you're stronger," said Marilla warningly.

"You know how hard it is for me *not* to talk," smiled Anne.

At first she was too weak and too happy to notice that Gilbert and the nurse looked grave and Marilla sorrowful. Then, as subtly, and coldly, and remorselessly as a sea-fog stealing landward, fear crept into her heart. Why was not Gilbert gladder? Why would he not talk about the baby? Why would they not let her have it with her after that first heavenly-happy hour? Was—was there anything wrong?

"Gilbert," whispered Anne imploringly, "the baby—is all right—isn't she? Tell me—tell me."

Gilbert was a long while in turning round; then he bent over Anne and looked in her eyes. Marilla, listening fearfully outside the door, heard a pitiful, heartbroken moan, and fled to the kitchen where Susan was weeping.

"Oh, the poor lamb—the poor lamb! How can she bear it, Miss Cuthbert? I am afraid it will kill her. She has been that built up and happy, longing for that baby, and planning for it. Cannot anything be done nohow, Miss Cuthbert?"

"I'm afraid not, Susan. Gilbert says there is no hope. He knew from the first the little thing couldn't live."

"And it is such a sweet baby," sobbed Susan. "I never saw one so white—they are mostly red or yallow. And it opened its big eyes as if it was months old. The little, little thing! Oh, the poor, young Mrs. Doctor!' At sunset the little soul that had come with the dawning went away, leaving heartbreak behind it. Miss Cornelia took the wee, white lady from the kindly but stranger hands of the nurse, and dressed the tiny waxen form in the beautiful dress Leslie had made for it. Leslie had asked her to do that. Then she took it back and laid it beside the poor, broken, tear-blinded little mother.

"The Lord has given and the Lord has taken away, dearie," she said through her own tears. "Blessed be the name of the Lord."

Then she went away, leaving Anne and Gilbert alone together with their dead.

The next day, the small white Joy was laid in a velvet casket which Leslie had lined with apple-blossoms, and taken to the graveyard of the church across the harbour. Miss Cornelia and Marilla put all the little love-made garments away, together with the ruffled basket which had been befrilled and belaced for dimpled limbs and downy head. Little Joy was never to sleep there; she had found a colder, narrower bed.

"This has been an awful disappointment to me," sighed Miss Cornelia. "I've looked forward to this baby—and I did want it to be a girl, too."

"I can only be thankful that Anne's life was spared," said Marilla, with a shiver, recalling those hours of darkness when the girl she loved was passing through the valley of the shadow.

"Poor, poor lamb! Her heart is broken," said Susan.

"I *envy* Anne," said Leslie suddenly and fiercely, "and I'd envy her even if she had died! She was a mother for one beautiful day. I'd gladly give my life for *that*!"

"I wouldn't talk like that, Leslie, dearie," said Miss Cornelia deprecatingly. She was afraid that the dignified Miss Cuthbert would think Leslie quite terrible.

Anne's convalescence was long, and made bitter for her by many things. The bloom and sunshine of the Four Winds world grated harshly on her; and yet, when the rain fell heavily, she pictured it beating so mercilessly down on that little grave across the harbour; and when the wind blew around the eaves she heard sad voices in it she had never heard before.

Kindly callers hurt her, too, with the well-meant platitudes with which they strove to cover the nakedness of bereavement. A letter from Phil Blake was an added sting. Phil had heard of the baby's birth, but not of its death, and she wrote Anne a congratulatory letter of sweet mirth which hurt her horribly.

"I would have laughed over it so happily if I had my baby," she sobbed to Marilla. "But when I haven't it just seems like wanton cruelty—though I know Phil wouldn't hurt me for the world. Oh, Marilla, I don't see how I can *ever* be happy again—*everything* will hurt me all the rest of my life."

"Time will help you," said Marilla, who was racked with sympathy but could never learn to express it in other than age-worn formulas.

"It doesn't seem *fair,* " said Anne rebelliously. "Babies are born and live where they are not wanted—where they will be neglected—where they will have no chance. I would have loved my baby so—and cared for it so tenderly—and tried to give her every chance for good. And yet I wasn't allowed to keep her."

"It was God's will, Anne," said Marilla, helpless before the riddle of the universe—the *why* of undeserved pain. "And little Joy is better off."

"I can't believe *that,* " cried Anne bitterly. Then, seeing that Marilla looked shocked, she added passionately, "Why should she be born at all—why should anyone be born at all—if she's better off dead? I *don't* believe it is better for a child to die at birth than to live its life out—and love and be loved—and enjoy and suffer—and do its work—and develop a character that would give it a personality in eternity. And how do you know it was God's will? Perhaps it was just a thwarting of His purpose by the Power of Evil. We can't be expected to be resigned to *that*."

"Oh, Anne, don't talk so," said Marilla, genuinely alarmed lest Anne were drifting into deep and dangerous waters. "We can't understand—but we must have faith—we *must* believe that all is for the best. I know you find it hard to think so, just now. But try to be brave—for Gilbert's sake. He's so worried about you. You aren't getting strong as fast as you should."

"Oh, I know I've been very selfish," sighed Anne. "I love Gilbert more than ever—and I want to live for his sake. But it seems as if part of me was buried over there in that little harbour graveyard—and it hurts so much that I'm afraid of life."

"It won't hurt so much always, Anne."

"The thought that it may stop hurting sometimes hurts me worse than all else, Marilla."

"Yes, I know, I've felt that too, about other things. But we all love you, Anne. Captain Jim has been up every day to ask for you—and Mrs. Moore haunts the place—and Miss Bryant spends most of her time, I think, cooking up nice things for you. Susan doesn't like it very well. She thinks she can cook as well as Miss Bryant."

"Dear Susan! Oh, everybody has been so dear and good and lovely to me, Marilla. I'm not ungrateful—and perhaps—when this horrible ache grows a little less—I'll find that I can go on living."

20
Lost Margaret

Anne found that she could go on living; the day came when she even smiled again over one of Miss Cornelia's speeches. But there was something in the smile that had never been in Anne's smile before and would never be absent from it again.

On the first day she was able to go for a drive Gilbert took her down to Four Winds Point, and left her there while he rowed over the channel to see a patient at the fishing village. A rollicking wind was scudding across the harbour and the dunes, whipping the water into white-caps and washing the sandshore with long lines of silvery breakers.

"I'm real proud to see you here again, Mistress Blythe," said Captain Jim. "Sit down—sit down. I'm afeared it's mighty dusty here today—but there's no need of looking at dust when you can look at such scenery, is there?"

"I don't mind the dust," said Anne, "but Gilbert says I must keep in the open air. I think I'll go and sit on the rocks down there."

"Would you like company or would you rather be alone?"

"If by company you mean yours I'd much rather have it than be alone," said Anne, smiling. Then she sighed. She had never before minded being alone. Now she dreaded it. When she was alone now she felt so dreadfully alone.

"Here's a nice little spot where the wind can't get at you," said Captain Jim, when they reached the rocks. "I often sit here. It's a great place jest to sit and dream."

"Oh—dreams," sighed Anne. "I can't dream now, Captain Jim—I'm done with dreams."

"Oh, no, you're not, Mistress Blythe—oh, no, you're not," said Captain Jim meditatively. "I know how you feel jest now—but if you keep on living you'll get glad again and the first thing you know you'll be dreaming again—-thank the good Lord for it! If it wasn't for our dreams they might as well bury us. How'd we stand living if it wasn't for our dream of immortality? And that's a dream that's *bound* to come true, Mistress Blythe. You'll see your little Joyce again some day."

"But she won't be my baby," said Anne, with trembling lips. "Oh, she may be, as Longfellow says, 'a fair maiden clothed with celestial grace'—but she'll be a stranger to me."

"God will manage better'n *that*, I believe," said Captain Jim.

They were both silent for a little time. Then Captain Jim said very softly:

"Mistress Blythe, may I tell you about lost Margaret?"

"Of course," said Anne gently. She did not know who "lost Margaret" was, but she felt that she was going to hear the romance of Captain Jim's life.

"I've often wanted to tell you about her," Captain Jim went on. "Do you know why, Mistress Blythe? It's because I want somebody to remember and think of her sometime after I'm gone. I can't bear that her name should be forgotten by all living souls. And now nobody remembers lost Margaret but me."

Then Captain Jim told the story—an old, old forgotten story, for it was over fifty years since Margaret had fallen asleep one day in her father's dory and drifted—or so it was supposed, for nothing was ever certainly known as to her fate—out of the channel, beyond the bar, to perish in the black thunder-squall which had come up so suddenly that long-ago summer afternoon. But to Captain Jim those fifty years were but as yesterday when it is past.

"I walked the shore for months after that," he said sadly, "Looking to find her dear, sweet little body; but the sea never give her back to me. But I'll find her sometime. Mistress Blythe—I'll find her sometime. She's waiting for me. I wish I could tell you jest how she looked, but I can't. I've seen a fine, silvery mist hanging over the bar at sunrise that seemed like her—and then again I've seen a white birch in the woods back yander that made me think of her. She had pale, brown hair and a little white, sweet face, and long slender fingers like yours, Mistress Blythe, only browner, for she was a shore girl.

Sometimes I wake up in the night and hear the sea calling to me in the old way, and it seems as if lost Margaret called in it. And when there's a storm and the waves are sobbing and moaning I hear her lamenting among them. And when they laugh on a gay day it's *her* laugh—lost Margaret's sweet, roguish, little laugh. The sea took her from me, but some day I'll find her, Mistress Blythe. It can't keep us apart forever."

"I am glad you have told me about her," said Anne. "I have often wondered why you had lived all your life alone."

"I couldn't ever care for anyone else. Lost Margaret took my heart with her—out there," said the old lover, who had been faithful for fifty years to his drowned sweetheart. "You won't mind if I talk a good deal about her, will you, Mistress Blythe? It's a pleasure to me—for all the pain went out of her memory years ago and jest left its blessing. I know you'll never forget her, Mistress Blythe. And if the years, as I hope, bring other little folks to your home, I want you to promise me that you'll tell *them* the story of lost Margaret, so that her name won't be forgotten among humankind."

21
Barriers Swept Away

"Anne," said Leslie, breaking abruptly a short silence, "you don't know how *good* it is to be sitting here with you again—working—and talking—and being silent together."

They were sitting among the blue-eyed grasses on the bank of the brook in Anne's garden. The water sparkled and crooned past them; the birches threw dappled shadows over them; roses bloomed along the walks. The sun was beginning to be low, and the air was full of woven music. There was one music of the wind in the firs behind the house, and another of the waves on the bar, and still another from the distant bell of the church near which the wee, white lady slept.

Anne loved that bell, though it brought sorrowful thoughts now.

She looked curiously at Leslie, who had thrown down her sewing and spoken with a lack of restraint that was very unusual with her.

"On that horrible night when you were so ill," Leslie went on, "I kept thinking that perhaps we'd have no more talks and walks and *works* together. And I realised just what your friendship had come to mean to me—just what *you* meant—and just what a hateful little beast I had been."

"Leslie! Leslie! I never allow anyone to call my friends names."

"It's true. That's exactly what I am—a hateful little beast. There's something I've *got* to tell you, Anne. I suppose it will make you despise me, but I *must* confess it. Anne, there have been times this past winter and spring when I have *hated* you."

"I knew it," said Anne calmly.

"You *knew* it?"

"Yes, I saw it in your eyes."

"And yet you went on liking me and being my friend."

"Well, it was only now and then you hated me, Leslie. Between times you loved me, I think."

"I certainly did. But that other horrid feeling was always there, spoiling it, back in my heart. I kept it down—sometimes I forgot it—but sometimes it would surge up and take possession of me. I hated you because I *envied* you—oh, I was sick with envy of you at times. You had a dear little home—and love—and happiness—and glad dreams—everything I wanted—and never had—and never could have. Oh, never could have! *That* was what stung. I wouldn't have envied you, if I had had any *hope* that life would ever be different for me. But I hadn't—I hadn't—and it didn't seem *fair*. It made me rebellious—and it hurt me—and so I hated you at times. Oh, I was so ashamed of it—I'm dying of shame now—but I couldn't conquer it. That night, when I was afraid you mightn't live—I thought I was going to be punished for my wickedness—and I loved you so then. Anne, Anne, I never had anything to love since my mother died, except Dick's old dog—and it's so dreadful to have nothing to love—life is so *empty*— and there's *nothing* worse than emptiness—and I might have loved you so much—and that horrible thing had spoiled it—"

Leslie was trembling and growing almost incoherent with the violence of her emotion.

"Don't, Leslie," implored Anne, "oh, don't. I understand—don't talk of it any more."

"I must—I must. When I knew you were going to live I vowed that I would tell you as soon as you were well—that I wouldn't go on accepting your friendship and companionship without telling you how unworthy I was of it. And I've been so afraid—it would turn you against me."

"You needn't fear that, Leslie."

"Oh, I'm so glad—so glad, Anne." Leslie clasped her brown, work-hardened hands tightly together to still their shaking. "But I want to tell you everything, now I've begun. You don't remember the first time I saw you, I suppose—it wasn't that night on the shore—"

"No, it was the night Gilbert and I came home. You were driving your geese down the hill. I should think I *do* remember it! I thought you were so beautiful—I longed for weeks after to find out who you were."

"I knew who *you* were, although I had never seen either of you before. I had heard of the new doctor and his bride who were coming to live in Miss Russell's little house. I—I hated you that very moment, Anne."

"I felt the resentment in your eyes—then I doubted—I thought I must be mistaken—because *why* should it be?"

"It was because you looked so happy. Oh, you'll agree with me now that I *am* a hateful beast—to hate another woman just because she was happy,—and when her happiness didn't take anything from me! That was why I never went to see you. I knew quite well I ought to go—even our simple Four Winds customs demanded that. But I couldn't. I used to watch you from my window—I could see you and your husband strolling about your garden in the evening—or you running down the poplar lane to meet him. And it hurt me. And yet in another way I wanted to go over. I felt that, if I were not so miserable, I could have liked you and found in you what I've never had in my life— an intimate, *real* friend of my own age. And then you remember that night at the shore? You were afraid I would think you crazy. You must have thought *I* was."

"No, but I couldn't understand you, Leslie. One moment you drew me to you—the next you pushed me back."

"I was very unhappy that evening. I had had a hard day. Dick had been very—very hard to manage that day. Generally he is quite good-natured and easily controlled, you know, Anne. But some days he is very different. I was so heartsick—I ran away to the shore as soon as he went to sleep. It was my only refuge. I sat there thinking of how my poor father had ended his life, and wondering if I wouldn't be driven to it some day. Oh, my heart was full of black thoughts! And then you came dancing along the cove like a glad, light-hearted child. I—I hated you more then than I've ever done since. And yet I craved your friendship. The one feeling swayed me one moment; the other feeling the next. When I got home that night I cried for shame of what you must think of me. But it's always been just the same when

I came over here. Sometimes I'd be happy and enjoy my visit. And at other times that hideous feeling would mar it all. There were times when everything about you and your house hurt me. You had so many dear little things I couldn't have. Do you know—it's ridiculous—but I had an especial spite at those china dogs of yours. There were times when I wanted to catch up Gog and Magog and bang their pert black noses together! Oh, you smile, Anne—but it was never funny to me. I would come here and see you and Gilbert with your books and your flowers, and your household gods, and your little family jokes—and your love for each other showing in every look and word, even when you didn't know it—and I would go home to—you know what I went home to! Oh, Anne, I don't believe I'm jealous and envious by nature. When I was a girl I lacked many things my schoolmates had, but I never cared—I never disliked them for it. But I seem to have grown so hateful—"

"Leslie, dearest, stop blaming yourself. You are *not* hateful or jealous or envious. The life you have to live has warped you a little, perhaps—but it would have ruined a nature less fine and noble than yours. I'm letting you tell me all this because I believe it's better for you to talk it out and rid your soul of it. But don't blame yourself any more."

"Well, I won't. I just wanted you to know me as I am. That time you told me of your darling hope for the spring was the worst of all, Anne. I shall never forgive myself for the way I behaved then. I repented it with tears. And I *did* put many a tender and loving thought of you into the little dress I made. But I might have known that anything I made could only be a shroud in the end."

"Now, Leslie, that *is* bitter and morbid—put such thoughts away. I was so glad when you brought the little dress; and since I had to lose little Joyce I like to think that the dress she wore was the one you made for her when you let yourself love me."

"Anne, do you know, I believe I shall always love you after this. I don't think I'll ever feel that dreadful way about you again. Talking it all out seems to have done away with it, somehow. It's very strange—and I thought it so real and bitter. It's like opening the door of a dark room to show some hideous creature you've believed to be there—and when the light streams in your monster turns out to have been just a shadow, vanishing when the light comes. It will never come between us again."

"No, we are real friends now, Leslie, and I am very glad."

"I hope you won't misunderstand me if I say something else. Anne, I was grieved to the core of my heart when you lost your baby; and if I could have saved her for you by cutting off one of my hands I would have done it. But your sorrow has brought us closer together. Your perfect happiness isn't a barrier any longer. Oh, don't misunderstand, dearest—I'm *not* glad that your happiness isn't perfect any longer—I can say that sincerely; but since it isn't, there isn't such a gulf between us."

"I *do* understand that, too, Leslie. Now, we'll just shut up the past and forget what was unpleasant in it. It's all going to be different. We're both of the race of Joseph now. I think you've been wonderful—wonderful. And, Leslie, I can't help believing that life has something good and beautiful for you yet."

Leslie shook her head.

"No," she said dully. "There isn't any hope. Dick will never be better—and even if his memory were to come back—oh, Anne, it would be worse, even worse, than it is now. *This* is something you can't understand, you happy bride. Anne, did Miss Cornelia ever tell you how I came to marry Dick?"

"Yes."

"I'm glad—I wanted you to know—but I couldn't bring myself to talk of it if you hadn't known. Anne, it seems to me that ever since I was twelve years old life has been bitter. Before that I had a happy childhood. We were very poor—but we didn't mind. Father was so splendid—so clever and loving and sympathetic. We were chums as far back as I can remember. And mother was so sweet. She was very, very beautiful. I look like her, but I am not so beautiful as she was."

"Miss Cornelia says you are far more beautiful."

"She is mistaken—or prejudiced. I think my figure *is* better—mother was slight and bent by hard work—but she had the face of an angel. I used just to look up at her in worship. We all worshipped her,—father and Kenneth and I."

Anne remembered that Miss Cornelia had given her a very different impression of Leslie's mother. But had not love the truer vision? Still, it *was* selfish of Rose West to make her daughter marry Dick Moore.

"Kenneth was my brother," went on Leslie. "Oh, I can't tell you how I loved him. And he was cruelly killed. Do you know how?"

"Yes."

"Anne, I saw his little face as the wheel went over him. He fell on his back. Anne—Anne—I can see it now. I shall always see it. Anne, all I ask of heaven is that that recollection shall be blotted out of my memory. O my God!"

"Leslie, don't speak of it. I know the story—don't go into details that only harrow your soul up unavailingly. It *will* be blotted out."

After a moment's struggle, Leslie regained a measure of self-control.

"Then father's health got worse and he grew despondent—his mind became unbalanced—you've heard all that, too?"

"Yes."

"After that I had just mother to live for. But I was very ambitious. I meant to teach and earn my way through college. I meant to climb to the very top—oh, I won't talk of that either. It's no use. You know what happened. I couldn't see my dear little heart-broken mother, who had been such a slave all her life, turned out of her home. Of course, I could have earned enough for us to live on. But mother *couldn't* leave her home. She had come there as a bride—and she had loved father so—and all her memories were there. Even yet, Anne, when I think that I made her last year happy I'm not sorry for what I did. As for Dick—I didn't hate him when I married him—I just felt for him the indifferent, friendly feeling I had for most of my schoolmates. I knew he drank some—but I had never heard the story of the girl down at the fishing cove. If I had, I *couldn't* have married him, even for mother's sake. Afterwards—I *did* hate him—but mother never knew. She died—and then I was alone. I was only seventeen and I was alone. Dick had gone off in the *Four Sisters*. I hoped he wouldn't be home very much more. The sea had always been in his blood. I had no other hope. Well, Captain Jim brought him home, as you know—and that's all there is to say. You know me now, Anne—the worst of me—the barriers are all down. And you still want to be my friend?"

Anne looked up through the birches, at the white paper-lantern of a half moon drifting downwards to the gulf of sunset. Her face was very sweet.

"I am your friend and you are mine, for always," she said. "Such a friend as I never had before. I have had many dear and beloved friends—but there is a something in you, Leslie, that I never found in anyone else. You have more to offer me in that rich nature of yours, and I have more to give you than I had in my careless girlhood. We are both women—and friends forever." They clasped hands and smiled at each other through the tears that filled the gray eyes and the blue.

22
Miss Cornelia Arranges Matters

Gilbert insisted that Susan should be kept on at the little house for the summer. Anne protested at first.

"Life here with just the two of us is so sweet, Gilbert. It spoils it a little to have anyone else. Susan is a dear soul, but she is an outsider. It won't hurt me to do the work here."

"You must take your doctor's advice," said Gilbert. "There's an old proverb to the effect that shoemakers' wives go barefoot and doctors' wives die young. I don't mean that it shall be true in my household. You will keep Susan until the old spring comes back into your step, and those little hollows on your cheeks fill out."

"You just take it easy, Mrs. Doctor, dear," said Susan, coming abruptly in. "Have a good time and do not worry about the pantry. Susan is at the helm. There is no use in keeping a dog and doing your own barking. I am going to take your breakfast up to you every morning."

"Indeed you are not," laughed Anne. "I agree with Miss Cornelia that it's a scandal for a woman who isn't sick to eat her breakfast in bed, and almost justifies the men in any enormities."

"Oh, Cornelia!" said Susan, with ineffable contempt. "I think you have better sense, Mrs. Doctor, dear, than to heed what Cornelia Bryant says. I cannot see why she must be always running down the men, even if she is an old maid. *I* am an old maid, but you never hear *me* abusing the men. I like 'em. I would have married one if I could. Is it not funny nobody ever asked me to marry him, Mrs. Doctor, dear? I am no beauty, but I am as good-looking as most of the married women you see. But I never had a beau. What do you suppose is the reason?"

"It may be predestination," suggested Anne, with unearthly solemnity.

Susan nodded.

"That is what I have often thought, Mrs. Doctor, dear, and a great comfort it is. I do not mind nobody wanting me if the Almighty decreed it so for His own wise purposes. But sometimes doubt creeps in, Mrs. Doctor, dear, and I wonder if maybe the Old Scratch has not more to do with it than anyone else. I cannot feel resigned *then*. But maybe," added Susan, brightening up, "I will have a chance to get married yet. I often and often think of the old verse my aunt used to repeat:

'There never was a goose so gray but sometime soon or late
Some honest gander came her way and took her for his mate!'

A woman cannot ever be sure of not being married till she is buried, Mrs. Doctor, dear, and meanwhile I will make a batch of cherry pies. I notice the doctor favours 'em, and I *do* like cooking for a man who appreciates his victuals."

Miss Cornelia dropped in that afternoon, puffing a little.

"I don't mind the world or the devil much, but the flesh *does* rather bother me," she admitted. "You always look as cool as a cucumber, Anne, dearie. Do I smell cherry pie? If I do, ask me to stay for tea. Haven't tasted a cherry pie this summer. My cherries have all been stolen by those scamps of Gilman boys from the Glen."

"Now, now, Cornelia," remonstrated Captain Jim, who had been reading a sea novel in a corner of the living room, "you shouldn't say that about those two poor, motherless little Gilman boys, unless you've got certain proof. Jest because their father ain't none too honest isn't any reason for calling them thieves. It's more likely it's been the robins took your cherries. They're turrible thick this year."

"Robins!" said Miss Cornelia disdainfully. "Humph! Two-legged robins, believe me!"

"Well, most of the Four Winds robins *are* constructed on that principle," said Captain Jim gravely.

Miss Cornelia stared at him for a moment. Then she leaned back in her rocker and laughed long and ungrudgingly.

"Well, you *have* got one on me at last, Jim Boyd, I'll admit. Just look how pleased he is, Anne, dearie, grinning like a Chessy-cat. As for the robins' legs, if robins have great, big, bare, sunburned legs, with ragged trousers hanging on 'em, such as I saw up in my cherry tree one morning at sunrise last week, I'll beg the Gilman boys' pardon. By the time I got down they were gone. I couldn't understand how they had disappeared so quick, but Captain Jim has enlightened me. They flew away, of course."

Captain Jim laughed and went away, regretfully declining an invitation to stay to supper and partake of cherry pie.

"I'm on my way to see Leslie and ask her if she'll take a boarder," Miss Cornelia resumed. "I'd a letter yesterday from a Mrs. Daly in Toronto, who boarded a spell with me two years ago. She wanted me to take a friend of hers for the summer. His name is Owen Ford, and he's a newspaper man, and it seems he's a grandson of the schoolmaster who built this house. John Selwyn's oldest daughter married an Ontario man named Ford, and this is her son. He wants to see the old place his grandparents lived in. He had a bad spell of typhoid in the spring and hasn't got rightly over it, so his doctor has ordered him to the sea. He doesn't want to go to the hotel—he just wants a quiet home place. I can't take him, for I have to be away in August. I've been appointed a delegate to the W.F.M.S. convention in Kingsport and I'm going. I don't know whether Leslie'll want to be bothered with him, either, but there's no one else. If she can't take him he'll have to go over the harbour."

"When you've seen her come back and help us eat our cherry pies," said Anne. "Bring Leslie and Dick, too, if they can come. And so you're going to Kingsport? What a nice time you will have. I must give you a letter to a friend of mine there—Mrs. Jonas Blake."

"I've prevailed on Mrs. Thomas Holt to go with me," said Miss Cornelia complacently. "It's time she had a little holiday, believe *me*. She has just about worked herself to death. Tom Holt can crochet beautifully, but he can't make a living for his family. He never seems to be able to get up early enough to do any work, but I notice he can always get up early to go fishing. Isn't that like a man?"

Anne smiled. She had learned to discount largely Miss Cornelia's opinions of the Four Winds men. Otherwise she must have believed them the most hopeless assortment of reprobates and ne'er-do-wells in the world, with veritable slaves and martyrs for wives. This particular Tom Holt, for example, she knew to be a kind husband, a much loved father, and an excellent neighbour. If he were rather inclined to be lazy, liking better the fishing he had been born for than the farming he had not, and if he had a harmless eccentricity for doing fancy work, nobody save Miss Cornelia seemed to hold it against him. His wife was a "hustler," who gloried in hustling; his family got a comfortable living off the farm; and his strapping sons and daughters, inheriting their mother's energy, were all in a fair way to do well in the world. There was not a happier household in Glen St. Mary than the Holts'.

Miss Cornelia returned satisfied from the house up the brook.

"Leslie's going to take him," she announced. "She jumped at the chance. She wants to make a little money to shingle the roof of her house this fall, and she didn't know how she was going to manage it. I expect Captain Jim'll be more than interested when he hears that a grandson of the Selwyns is coming here. Leslie said to tell you she hankered after cherry pie, but she couldn't come to tea because she has to go and hunt up her turkeys. They've strayed away. But she said, if there was a piece left, for you to put it in the pantry and she'd run over in the cat's light, when prowling's in order, to get it. You don't know, Anne, dearie, what good it did my heart to hear Leslie send you a message like that, laughing like she used to long ago. There's a great change come over her lately. She laughs and jokes like a girl, and from her talk I gather she's here real often."

"Every day—or else I'm over there," said Anne. "I don't know what I'd do without Leslie, especially just now when Gilbert is so busy. He's hardly ever home except for a few hours in the wee sma's. He's really working himself to death. So many of the over-harbour people send for him now."

"They might better be content with their own doctor," said Miss Cornelia. "Though to be sure I can't blame them, for he's a Methodist. Ever since Dr. Blythe brought Mrs. Allonby round folks think he can raise the dead. I believe Dr. Dave is a mite jealous—just like a man. He thinks Dr. Blythe has too many new-fangled notions! 'Well,' I says to him, 'it was a new-fangled notion saved Rhoda Allonby. If *you'd* been attending her she'd have died, and had a tombstone saying it had pleased God to take her away.' Oh, I *do* like to speak my mind to Dr. Dave! He's bossed the Glen for years, and he thinks he's forgotten more than other people ever knew. Speaking of doctors, I wish Dr. Blythe'd run over and see to that boil on Dick Moore's neck. It's getting past Leslie's skill. I'm sure I don't know what Dick Moore wants to start in having boils for—as if he wasn't enough trouble without that!"

"Do you know, Dick has taken quite a fancy to me," said Anne. "He follows me round like a dog, and smiles like a pleased child when I notice him."

"Does it make you creepy?"

"Not at all. I rather like poor Dick Moore. He seems so pitiful and appealing, somehow."

"You wouldn't think him very appealing if you'd see him on his cantankerous days, believe *me*. But I'm glad you don't mind him—it's all the nicer for Leslie. She'll have more to do when her boarder comes. I hope he'll be a decent creature. You'll probably like him—he's a writer."

"I wonder why people so commonly suppose that if two individuals are both writers they must therefore be hugely congenial," said Anne, rather scornfully. "Nobody would expect two blacksmiths to be violently attracted towards each other merely because they were both blacksmiths."

Nevertheless, she looked forward to the advent of Owen Ford with a pleasant sense of expectation. If he were young and likeable he might prove a very pleasant addition to society in Four Winds. The latch-string of the little house was always out for the race of Joseph.

23

Owen Ford Comes

One evening Miss Cornelia telephoned down to Anne.

"The writer man has just arrived here. I'm going to drive him down to your place, and you can show him the way to Leslie's. It's shorter than driving round by the other road, and I'm in a mortal hurry. The Reese baby has gone and fallen into a pail of hot water at the Glen, and got nearly scalded to death and they want me right off—to put a new skin on the child, I presume. Mrs. Reese is always so careless, and then expects other people to mend her mistakes. You won't mind, will you, dearie? His trunk can go down tomorrow."

"Very well," said Anne. "What is he like, Miss Cornelia?"

"You'll see what he's like outside when I take him down. As for what he's like inside only the Lord who made him knows *that*. I'm not going to say another word, for every receiver in the Glen is down."

"Miss Cornelia evidently can't find much fault with Mr. Ford's looks, or she would find it in spite of the receivers," said Anne. "I conclude therefore, Susan, that Mr. Ford is rather handsome than otherwise."

"Well, Mrs. Doctor, dear, I *do* enjoy seeing a well-looking man," said Susan candidly. "Had I not better get up a snack for him? There is a strawberry pie that would melt in your mouth."

"No, Leslie is expecting him and has his supper ready. Besides, I want that strawberry pie for my own poor man. He won't be home till late, so leave the pie and a glass of milk for him, Susan."

"That I will, Mrs. Doctor, dear. Susan is at the helm. After all, it is better to give pie to your own men than to strangers, who may be only seeking to devour, and the doctor himself is as well-looking a man as you often come across."

When Owen Ford came Anne secretly admitted, as Miss Cornelia towed him in, that he was very "well-looking" indeed. He was tall and broad-shouldered, with thick, brown hair, finely-cut nose and chin, large and brilliant dark-gray eyes.

"And did you notice his ears and his teeth, Mrs. Doctor, dear?" queried Susan later on. "He has got the nicest-shaped ears I ever saw on a man's head. I am choice about ears. When I was young I was scared that I might have to marry a man with ears like flaps. But I need not have worried, for never a chance did I have with any kind of ears."

Anne had not noticed Owen Ford's ears, but she did see his teeth, as his lips parted over them in a frank and friendly smile:

Unsmiling, his face was rather sad and absent in expression, not unlike the melancholy, inscrutable hero of Anne's own early dreams; but mirth and humour and charm lighted it up when he smiled. Certainly, on the outside, as Miss Cornelia said, Owen Ford was a very presentable fellow.

"You cannot realise how delighted I am to be here, Mrs. Blythe," he said, looking around him with eager, interested eyes. "I have an odd feeling of coming home. My mother was born and spent her childhood here, you know. She used to talk a great deal to me of her old home. I know the geography of it as well as of the one I lived in, and of course, she told me the story of the building of the house, and of my grandfather's agonised watch for the *Royal William*. I had thought that so old a house must have vanished years ago, or I should have come to see it before this."

"Old houses don't vanish easily on this enchanted coast," smiled Anne. "This is a 'land where all things always seem the same'—nearly always, at least. John Selwvn's house hasn't even been much changed, and outside the rose-bushes your grandfather planted for his bride are blooming this very minute."

"How the thought links me with them! With your leave I must explore the whole place soon."

"Our latch-string will always be out for you," promised Anne. "And do you know that the old sea captain who keeps the Four Winds light knew John Selwyn and his bride well in his boyhood? He told me their story the night I came here—the third bride of the old house."

"Can it be possible? This *is* a discovery. I must hunt him up."

"It won't be difficult; we are all cronies of Captain Jim. He will be as eager to see you as you could be to see him. Your grandmother shines like a star in his memory. But I think Mrs. Moore is expecting you. I'll show you our 'cross-lots' road."

Anne walked with him to the house up the brook, over a field that was as white as snow with daisies. A boat-load of people were singing far across the harbour. The sound drifted over the water like faint, unearthly music, wind-blown across a starlit sea. The big light flashed and beaconed. Owen Ford looked around him with satisfaction.

"And so this is Four Winds," he said. "I wasn't prepared to find it quite so beautiful, in spite of all mother's praises. What colours—what scenery—what charm! I shall get as strong as a horse in no time. And if inspiration comes from beauty, I should certainly be able to begin my great Canadian novel here."

"You haven't begun it yet?" asked Anne.

"Alack-a-day, no. I've never been able to get the right central idea for it. It lurks beyond me—it allures—and beckons—and recedes—I almost grasp it and it is gone. Perhaps amid this peace and loveliness, I shall be able to capture it. Miss Bryant tells me that you write."

"Oh, I do little things for children. I haven't done much since I was married. And I have no designs on a great Canadian novel," laughed Anne. "That is quite beyond me."

Owen Ford laughed too.

"I dare say it is beyond me as well. All the same I mean to have a try at it some day, if I can ever get time. A newspaper man doesn't have much chance for that sort of thing. I've done a good deal of short story writing for the magazines, but I've never had the leisure that seems to be necessary for the writing of a book. With three months of liberty I ought to make a start, though—if I could only get the necessary *motif* for it—the *soul* of the book."

An idea whisked through Anne's brain with a suddenness that made her jump. But she did not utter it, for they had reached the Moore house. As they entered the yard Leslie came out on the veranda from the side door, peering through the gloom for some sign of her expected guest. She stood just where the warm yellow light flooded her from the open door. She wore a plain dress of cheap, cream-tinted cotton voile, with the usual girdle of crimson. Leslie was never without her touch of crimson. She had told Anne that she never felt satisfied without a gleam of red somewhere about her, if it were only a flower. To Anne, it always seemed to symbolise Leslie's glowing, pent-up personality, denied all expression save in that flaming glint. Leslie's dress was cut a little away at the neck and had short sleeves. Her arms gleamed like ivory-tinted marble. Every exquisite curve of her form was outlined in soft darkness against the light. Her hair shone in it like flame. Beyond her was a purple sky, flowering with stars over the harbour.

Anne heard her companion give a gasp. Even in the dusk she could see the amazement and admiration on his face.

"Who is that beautiful creature?" he asked.

"That is Mrs. Moore," said Anne. "She is very lovely, isn't she?"

"I—I never saw anything like her," he answered, rather dazedly. "I wasn't prepared—I didn't expect— good heavens, one *doesn't* expect a goddess for a landlady! Why, if she were clothed in a gown of sea-purple, with a rope of amethysts in her hair, she would be a veritable sea-queen. And she takes in boarders!"

"Even goddesses must live," said Anne. "And Leslie isn't a goddess. She's just a very beautiful woman, as human as the rest of us. Did Miss Bryant tell you about Mr. Moore?"

"Yes,—he's mentally deficient, or something of the sort, isn't he? But she said nothing about Mrs. Moore, and I supposed she'd be the usual hustling country housewife who takes in boarders to earn an honest penny."

"Well, that's just what Leslie is doing," said Anne crisply. "And it isn't altogether pleasant for her, either. I hope you won't mind Dick. If you do, please don't let Leslie see it. It would hurt her horribly. He's just a big baby, and sometimes a rather annoying one."

"Oh, I won't mind him. I don't suppose I'll be much in the

house anyhow, except for meals. But what a shame it all is! Her life must be a hard one."

"It is. But she doesn't like to be pitied."

Leslie had gone back into the house and now met them at the front door. She greeted Owen Ford with cold civility, and told him in a business-like tone that his room and his supper were ready for him. Dick, with a pleased grin, shambled upstairs with the valise, and Owen Ford was installed as an inmate of the old house among the willows.

24

The Life-Book of Captain Jim

"I have a little brown cocoon of an idea that may possibly expand into a magnificent moth of fulfilment," Anne told Gilbert when she reached home. He had returned earlier than she had expected, and was enjoying Susan's strawberry pie. Susan herself hovered in the background, like a rather grim but beneficent guardian spirit, and found as much pleasure in watching Gilbert eat pie as he did in eating it.

"What is your idea?" he asked.

"I sha'n't tell you just yet—not till I see if I can bring the thing about."

"What sort of a chap is Ford?"

"Oh, very nice, and quite good-looking."

"Such beautiful ears, doctor, dear," interjected Susan with a relish.

"He is about thirty or thirty-five, I think, and he meditates writing a novel. His voice is pleasant and his smile delightful, and he knows how to dress. He looks as if life hadn't been altogether easy for him, somehow."

Owen Ford came over the next evening with a note to Anne from Leslie; they spent the sunset-time in the garden and then went for a moonlit sail on the harbour, in the little boat Gilbert had set up for summer outings. They liked Owen immensely and had that feeling of having known him for many years which distinguishes the freemasonry of the house of Joseph. "He is as nice as his ears, Mrs. Doctor, dear," said Susan, when he had gone. He had told Susan that he had never tasted anything like her strawberry shortcake and Susan's susceptible heart was his forever.

"He has got a way with him," she reflected, as she cleared up the relics of the supper. "It is real queer he is not married, for a man like that could have anybody for the asking. Well, maybe he is like me, and has not met the right one yet."

Susan really grew quite romantic in her musings as she washed the supper dishes.

Two nights later Anne took Owen Ford down to Four Winds Point to introduce him to Captain Jim. The clover fields along the harbour shore were whitening in the western wind, and Captain Jim had one of his finest sunsets on exhibition. He himself had just returned from a trip over the harbour.

"I had to go over and tell Henry Pollock he was dying. Everybody else was afraid to tell him. They expected he'd take on turrible, for he's been dreadful determined to live, and been making no end of plans for the fall. His wife thought he oughter be told and that I'd be the best one to break it to him that he couldn't get better. Henry and me are old cronies—we sailed in the *Gray Gull* for years together. Well, I went over and sat down by Henry's bed and I says to him, says I, jest right out plain and simple, for if a thing's got to be told it may as well be told first as last, says I, 'Mate, I reckon you've got your sailing orders this time.' I was sorter quaking inside, for it's an awful thing to have to tell a man who hain't any idea he's dying that he is. But lo and behold, Mistress Blythe, Henry looks up at me, with those bright old black eyes of his in his wizened face and says, says he, 'Tell me something I don't know, Jim Boyd, if you want to give me information. I've known *that* for a week.' I was too astonished to speak, and Henry, he chuckled. 'To see you coming in here,' says he, 'with your face as solemn as a tombstone and sitting down there with your hands clasped over your stomach, and passing me out a blue-mouldy old item of news like that! It'd make a cat laugh, Jim Boyd,' says he. 'Who told you?' says I, stupid like. 'Nobody,' says he. 'A week ago Tuesday night I was lying here awake—and I jest knew. I'd suspicioned it before, but then I *knew*. I've been keeping up for the wife's sake. And I'd *like* to have got that barn built, for Eben'll never get it right. But anyhow, now that you've eased your mind, Jim, put on a smile and tell me something interesting.' Well, there it was. They'd been so scared to tell him and he knew it all the time. Strange how nature looks out for us, ain't it, and lets us know what we should know when the time comes? Did I never tell you the yarn about Henry getting the fish hook in his nose, Mistress Blythe?"

"No."

"Well, him and me had a laugh over it today. It happened nigh unto thirty years ago. Him and me and several more was out mackerel fishing one day. It was a great day—never saw such a school of mackerel in the gulf—and in the general excitement Henry got quite wild and contrived to stick a fish hook clean through one side of his nose. Well, there he was; there was barb on one end and a big piece of lead on the other, so it couldn't be pulled out. We wanted to take him ashore at once, but Henry was game; he said he'd be jiggered if he'd leave a school like that for anything short of lockjaw; then he kept fishing away, hauling in hand over fist and groaning between times. Fin'lly the school passed and we come in with a load; I got a file and begun to try to file through that hook. I tried to be as easy as I could, but you should have heard Henry—no, you shouldn't either. It was well no ladies were around. Henry wasn't a swearing man, but he'd heard some few matters of that sort along shore in his time, and he fished 'em all out of his recollection and hurled 'em at me. Fin'lly he declared he couldn't stand it and I had no bowels of compassion. So we hitched up and I drove him to a doctor in Charlottetown, thirty-five miles—there weren't none nearer in them days—with that blessed hook still hanging from his nose. When we got there old Dr. Crabb jest took a file and filed that hook jest the same as I'd tried to do, only he weren't a mite particular about doing it easy!"

Captain Jim's visit to his old friend had revived many recollections and he was now in the full tide of reminiscences.

"Henry was asking me today if I remembered the time old Father Chiniquy blessed Alexander MacAllister's boat. Another odd yarn—and true as gospel. I was in the boat myself. We went out, him and me, in Alexander MacAllister's boat one morning at sunrise. Besides, there was a French boy in the boat—Catholic of course. You know old Father Chiniquy had turned Protestant, so the Catholics hadn't much use for him. Well, we sat out in the gulf in the broiling sun till noon, and not a bite did we get. When we went ashore old Father Chiniquy had to go, so he said in that polite way of his, 'I'm very sorry I cannot go out with you dis afternoon, Mr. MacAllister, but I leave you my blessing. You will catch a t'ousand dis afternoon.' Well, we did not catch a thousand, but we caught exactly nine hundred and ninety-nine—the biggest catch for a small boat on the whole north shore that summer. Curious, wasn't it? Alexander MacAllister, he says to Andrew Peters, 'Well, and what do you think of Father Chiniquy now?' 'Vell,' growled Andrew, 'I t'ink de old devil has got a blessing left yet.' Laws, how Henry did laugh over that today!"

"Do you know who Mr. Ford is, Captain Jim?" asked Anne, seeing that Captain Jim's fountain of reminiscence had ran out for the present. "I want you to guess."

Captain Jim shook his head.

"I never was any hand at guessing, Mistress Blythe, and yet I seen them eyes before?—for I *have* seen 'em."

"Think of a September morning many years ago," said Anne, softly. "Think of a ship sailing up the harbour—a ship long waited for and despaired of. Think of the day the *Royal William* came in and the first look you had at the schoolmaster's bride."

Captain Jim sprang up.

"They're Persis Selwyn's eyes," he almost shouted. "You can't be her son—you must be her—"

"Grandson; yes, I am Alice Selwyn's son."

Captain Jim swooped down on Owen Ford and shook his hand over again.

"Alice Selwyn's son! Lord, but you're welcome! Many's the time I've wondered where the descendants of the schoolmaster were living. I knew there was none on the Island. Alice—Alice—the first baby ever born in that little house. No baby ever brought more joy! I've dandled her a hundred times. It was from my knee she took her first steps alone. Can't I see her mother's face watching her—and it was near sixty years ago. Is she living yet?"

"No, she died when I was only a boy."

"Oh, it doesn't seem right that I should be living to hear that," sighed Captain Jim. "But I'm heart-glad to see you. It's brought back my youth for a little while. You won't know yet what boon *that* is. Mistress Blythe here has the trick—she does it quite often for me." Captain Jim was still more excited when he discovered that Owen Ford was what he called a "real writing man." He gazed at him as at a superior being. Captain Jim knew that Anne wrote, but he had never taken that fact very seriously. Captain Jim thought women were delightful creatures, who ought to have the vote, and everything else they wanted, bless their hearts; but he did not believe they could write.

"Jest look at *A Mad Lov*e," he would protest. "A woman wrote that and jest look at it—one hundred and three chapters when it could all have been told in ten. A writing woman never knows when to stop; that's the trouble. The p'int of good writing is to know when to stop."

"Mr. Ford wants to hear some of your stories, Captain Jim," said Anne. "Tell him the one about the captain who went crazy and imagined he was the Flying Dutchman."

This was Captain Jim's best story. It was a compound of horror and humour, and though Anne had heard it several times she laughed as heartily and shivered as fearsomely over it as Mr. Ford did. Other tales followed, for Captain Jim had an audience after his own heart. He told how his vessel had been run down by a steamer; how he had been boarded by Malay pirates; how his ship had caught fire; how he helped a political prisoner escape from a South African republic; how he had been wrecked one fall on the Magdalens and stranded there for the winter; how a tiger had broken loose on board ship; how his crew had mutinied and marooned him on a barren island—these and many other tales, tragic or humorous or grotesque, did Captain Jim relate. The mystery of the sea, the fascination of far lands, the lure of adventure, the laughter of the world—his hearers felt and realised them all. Owen Ford listened, with his head on his hand, and the First Mate purring on his knee, his brilliant eyes fastened on Captain Jim's rugged, eloquent face.

"Won't you let Mr. Ford see your life-book, Captain Jim?" asked Anne, when Captain Jim finally declared that yarn-spinning must end for the time.

"Oh, he won't want to be bothered with *that*," protested Captain Jim, who was secretly dying to show it.

"I should like nothing better than to see it, Captain Boyd," said Owen. "If it is half as wonderful as your tales it will be worth seeing."

With pretended reluctance Captain Jim dug his life-book out of his old chest and handed it to Owen.

"I reckon you won't care to wrastle long with my old hand o' write. I never had much schooling," he observed carelessly. "Just wrote that there to amuse my nephew Joe. He's always wanting stories. Comes here yesterday and says to me, reproachful-like, as I was lifting a twenty-pound codfish out of my boat, 'Uncle Jim, ain't a codfish a dumb animal?' I'd been a-telling him, you see, that he must be real kind to dumb animals, and never hurt 'em in any way. I got out of the scrape by saying a codfish was dumb enough but it wasn't an animal, but Joe didn't look satisfied, and I wasn't satisfied myself. You've got to be mighty careful what you tell them little critters. *They* can see through you."

While talking, Captain Jim watched Owen Ford from the corner of his eyes as the latter examined the life-book; and presently observing that his guest was lost in its pages, he turned smilingly to his cupboard and proceeded to make a pot of tea. Owen Ford separated himself from the life-book, with as much reluctance as a miser wrenches himself from his gold, long enough to drink his tea, and then returned to it hungrily.

"Oh, you can take that thing home with you if you want to," said Captain Jim, as if the "thing" were not his most treasured possession. "I must go down and pull my boat up a bit on the skids. There's a wind coming. Did you notice the sky tonight?

'Mackerel skies and mares' tails
Make tall ships carry short sails.'"

Owen Ford accepted the offer of the life-book gladly. On their way home Anne told him the story of lost Margaret.

"That old captain is a wonderful old fellow," he said. "What a life he has led! Why, the man had more adventures in one week of his life than most of us have in a lifetime. Do you really think his tales are all true?"

"I certainly do. I am sure Captain Jim could not tell a lie; and besides, all the people about here say that everything happened as he relates it. There used to be plenty of his old shipmates alive to corroborate him. He's one of the last of the old type of P. E. Island sea-captains. They are almost extinct now."

25

The Writing of the Book

Owen Ford came over to the little house the next morning in a state of great excitement.

"Mrs. Blythe, this is a wonderful book—absolutely wonderful. If I could take it and use the material for a book 1 feel certain I could make the novel of the year out of it. Do you suppose Captain Jim would let me do it?"

"Let you! I'm sure he would be delighted," cried Anne. "I admit that it was what was in my head when I took you down last night. Captain Jim has always been wishing he could get somebody to write his life-book properly for him."

"Will you go down to the Point with me this evening, Mrs. Blythe? I'll ask him about the life-book myself, but I want you to tell him that you told me the story of lost Margaret and ask him if he will let me use it as a thread of romance with which to weave the stories of the life-book into a harmonious whole."

Captain Jim was more excited than ever when Owen Ford told him of his plan. At last his cherished dream was to be realised and his "life-book" given to the world. He was also pleased that the story of lost Margaret should be woven into it.

"It will keep her name from being forgotten," he said wistfully. "That's why I want it put in."

"We'll collaborate," cried Owen delightedly. "You will give the soul and I the body. Oh, we'll write a famous book between us, Captain Jim. And we'll get right to work."

"And to think my book is to be writ by the schoolmaster's grandson!" exclaimed Captain Jim. "Lad, your grandfather was my dearest friend. I thought there was nobody like him. I see now why I had to wait so long. It couldn't be writ till the right man come. You *belong* here—you've got the soul of this old north shore in you—you're the only one who *could* write it."

It was arranged that the tiny room off the living room at the lighthouse should be given over to Owen for a workshop. It was necessary that Captain Jim should be near him as he wrote, for consultation upon many matters of sea-faring and gulf lore of which Owen was quite ignorant.

He began work on the book the very next morning, and flung himself into it heart and soul. As for Captain Jim, he was a happy man that summer. He looked upon the little room where Owen worked as a sacred shrine. Owen talked everything over with Captain Jim, but he would not let him see the manuscript.

"You must wait until it is published," he said. "Then you'll get it all at once in its best shape."

He delved into the treasures of the life-book and used them freely. He dreamed and brooded over lost Margaret until she became a vivid reality to him and, lived in his pages. As the book progressed it took possession of him and he worked at it with feverish eagerness. He let Anne and Leslie read the manuscript and criticise it; and the concluding chapter of the book, which the critics, later on, were pleased to call idyllic, was modelled upon a suggestion of Leslie's.

Anne fairly hugged herself with delight over the success of her idea.

"I knew when I looked at Owen Ford that was the very man for it," she told Gilbert. "Both humour and passion were in his face, and that, together with the art of expression, was just what was necessary for the writing of such a book. As Mrs. Rachel would say, he was predestined for the part."

Owen Ford wrote in the mornings. The afternoons were generally spent in some merry outing with the Blythes. Leslie often went, too, for Captain Jim took charge of Dick frequently, in order to set her free. They went boating on the harbour and up the three pretty rivers that flowed into it; they had clam-bakes on the bar and mussel-bakes on the rocks; they picked strawberries on the sand-dunes; they went out cod-fishing with Captain Jim; they shot plover in the shore fields and wild ducks in the cove—at least, the men did. In the evenings they rambled in the low-lying, daisied, shore fields under a golden moon, or they sat in the living room at the little house where often the coolness of the sea breeze justified a drift-wood fire, and talked of the thousand and one things which happy, eager, clever young people can find to talk about.

Ever since the day on which she had made her confession to Anne, Leslie had been a changed creature. There was no trace of her old coldness and reserve, no shadow of her old bitterness. The girlhood of which she had been cheated seemed to come back to her with the ripeness of womanhood; she expanded like a flower of flame and perfume; no laugh was readier than hers, no wit quicker, in the twilight circles of that enchanted summer. When she could not be with them, all felt that some exquisite savour was lacking in their intercourse. Her beauty was illumined by the awakened soul within, as some rosy lamp might shine through a flawless vase of alabaster. There were hours when Anne's eyes seemed to ache with the splendour of her. As for Owen Ford, the "Margaret" of his book, although she had the soft brown hair and elfin face of the real girl who had vanished so long ago, "pillowed where lost Atlantis sleeps," had the personality of Leslie Moore, as it was revealed to him in those halcyon days at Four Winds Harbour.

All in all, it was a never-to-be-forgotten summer—one of those summers which come seldom into any life, but leave a rich heritage of beautiful memories in their going—one of those summers which, in a fortunate combination of delightful weather, delightful friends and delightful doings, come as near to perfection as anything can come in this world.

"Too good to last," Anne told herself with a little sigh, on the September day when a certain nip in the wind and a certain shade of intense blue on the gulf water said that autumn was hard by.

That evening Owen Ford told them that he had finished his book and that his vacation must come to an end.

"I have a good deal to do to it yet—revising and pruning and so forth," he said, "but in the main it's done. I wrote the last sentence this morning. If I can find a publisher for it it will probably be out next summer or fall."

Owen had not much doubt that he would find a publisher. He knew that he had written a great book—a book that would score a wonderful success—a book that would *live*. He knew that it would bring him both fame and fortune; but when he had written the last line of it he had bowed his head on the manuscript and so sat for a long time. And his thoughts were not of the good work he had done.

26
Owen Ford's Confession

"I'm so sorry Gilbert is away," said Anne. "He had to go—Allan Lyons at the Glen has met with a serious accident. He will not likely be home till very late. But he told me to tell you he'd be up and over early enough in the morning to see you before you left. It's too provoking. Susan and I had planned such a nice little jamboree for your last night here."

She was sitting beside the garden brook on the little rustic seat Gilbert had built. Owen Ford stood before her, leaning against the bronze column of a yellow birch. He was very pale and his face bore the marks of the preceding sleepless night. Anne glancing up at him, wondered if, after all, his summer had brought him the strength it should. Had he worked too hard over his book? She remembered that for a week he had not been looking well.

"I'm rather glad the doctor is away," said Owen slowly. "I wanted to see you alone, Mrs. Blythe. There is something I must tell somebody, or I think it will drive me mad. I've been trying for a week to look it in the face—and I can't. I know I can trust you—and, besides, you will understand. A woman with eyes like yours always understands. You are one of the folks people instinctively tell things to. Mrs. Blythe, I love Leslie. *Love* her! That seems too weak a word!"

His voice suddenly broke with the suppressed passion of his utterance. He turned his head away and hid his face on his arm. His whole form shook. Anne sat looking at him, pale and aghast. She had never thought of this! And yet—how was it she had never thought of it? It now seemed a natural and inevitable thing. She wondered at her own blindness. But—but—things like this did not happen in Four Winds. Elsewhere in the world human passions might set at defiance human conventions and laws—but not *here*, surely. Leslie had kept summer boarders off and on for ten years, and nothing like this had happened. But perhaps they had not been like Owen Ford; and the vivid, *living* Leslie of this summer was not the cold, sullen girl of other years. Oh, *somebody* should have thought of this! Why hadn't Miss Cornelia thought of it? Miss Cornelia was always ready enough to sound the alarm where men were concerned. Anne felt an unreasonable resentment against Miss Cornelia. Then she gave a little inward groan. No matter who was to blame the mischief was done. And Leslie—what of Leslie? It was for Leslie Anne felt most concerned.

"Does Leslie know this, Mr. Ford?" she asked quietly.

"No—no,—unless she has guessed it. You surely don't think I'd be cad and scoundrel enough to tell her, Mrs. Blythe. I couldn't help loving her—that's all—and my misery is greater than I can bear."

"Does *she* care?" asked Anne. The moment the question crossed her lips she felt that she should not have asked it. Owen Ford answered it with over-eager protest.

"No—no, of course not. But I could make her care if she were free—I know I could."

"She does care—and he knows it," thought Anne. Aloud she said, sympathetically but decidedly:

"But she is not free, Mr. Ford. And the only thing you can do is to go away in silence and leave her to her own life."

"I know—I know," groaned Owen. He sat down on the grassy bank and stared moodily into the amber water beneath him. "I know there's nothing to do—nothing but to say conventionally, 'Good-bye, Mrs. Moore. Thank you for all your kindness to me this summer,' just as I would have said it to the sonsy, bustling, keen-eyed housewife I expected her to be when I came. Then I'll pay my board money like any honest boarder and go! Oh, it's very simple. No doubt—no perplexity —a straight road to the end of the world! And I'll walk it—you needn't fear that I won't, Mrs. Blythe. But it would be easier to walk over red-hot ploughshares."

Anne flinched with the pain of his voice. And there was so little she could say that would be adequate to the situation. Blame was out of the question—advice was not needed—sympathy was mocked by the man's stark agony. She could only feel with him in a maze of compassion and regret. Her heart ached for Leslie! Had not that poor girl suffered enough without this?

"It wouldn't be so hard to go and leave her if she were only happy," resumed Owen passionately. "But to think of her living death—to realise what it is to which I do leave her! *That* is the worst of all. I would give my life to make her happy—and I can do nothing even to help her—nothing. She is bound forever to that poor wretch—with nothing to look forward to but growing old in a succession of empty, meaningless, barren years. It drives me mad to think of it. But I must go through my life, never seeing her, but always knowing what she is enduring. It's hideous—hideous!"

"It is very hard," said Anne sorrowfully. "We—her friends here—all know how hard it is for her."

"And she is so richly fitted for life," said Owen rebelliously. "Her beauty is the least of her dower—and she is the most beautiful woman I've ever known. That laugh of hers! I've angled all summer to evoke that laugh, just for the delight of hearing it. And her eyes— they are as deep and blue as the gulf out there. I never saw such blueness—and gold! Did you ever see her hair down, Mrs. Blythe?"

"No."

"I did—once. I had gone down to the Point to go fishing with Captain Jim but it was too rough to go out, so I came back. She had taken the opportunity of what she expected to be an afternoon alone to wash her hair, and she was standing on the veranda in the sunshine to dry it. It fell all about her to her feet in a fountain of living gold. When she saw me she hurried in, and the wind caught her hair and swirled it all around her—Danae in her cloud. Somehow, just then the knowledge that I loved her came home to me—and I realised that I had loved her from the moment I first saw her standing against the darkness in that glow of light. And she must live on here—petting and soothing Dick, pinching and saving for a mere existence, while I spend my life longing vainly for her, and debarred, by that very fact, from even giving her the little help a friend might. I walked the shore last night, almost till dawn, and thrashed it all out over and over again. And yet, in spite of everything, I can't find it in my heart to be sorry that I came to Four Winds. It seems to me that, bad as everything is, it would be still worse never to have known Leslie. It's burning, searing pain to love her and leave her—but not to have loved her is unthinkable. I suppose all this sounds very crazy—all these terrible emotions always do sound foolish when we put them into our inadequate words. They are not meant to be spoken—only felt and endured. I shouldn't have spoken—but it has helped—some. At least, it has given me strength to go away respectably to-morrow morning, without making a scene. You'll write me now and then, won't you, Mrs. Blythe, and give me what news there is to give of her?"

"Yes," said Anne. "Oh, I'm so sorry you are going—we'll miss you so—we've all been such friends! If it were not for this you could come back other summers. Perhaps, even yet—by-and-by—when you've forgotten, perhaps—"

"I shall never forget—and I shall never come back to Four Winds," said Owen briefly.

Silence and twilight fell over the garden. Far away the sea was lapping gently and monotonously on the bar. The wind of evening in the poplars sounded like some sad, weird, old rune—some broken dream of old memories. A slender shapely young aspen rose up before them against the fine maize and emerald and paling rose of the western sky, which brought out every leaf and twig in dark, tremulous, elfin loveliness.

"Isn't that beautiful?" said Owen, pointing to it with the air of a man who puts a certain conversation behind him.

"It's so beautiful that it hurts me," said Anne softly. "Perfect things like that always did hurt me—I remember I called it 'the queer ache' when I was a child. What is the reason that pain like this seems inseparable from perfection? Is it the pain of finality—when we realise that there can be nothing beyond but retrogression?"

"Perhaps," said Owen dreamily, "it is the prisoned infinite in us calling out to its kindred infinite as expressed in that visible perfection."

"You seem to have a cold in the head. Better rub some tallow on your nose when you go to bed," said Miss Cornelia, who had come in through the little gate between the firs in time to catch Owen's last remark. Miss Cornelia liked Owen; but it was a matter of principle with her to visit any "high falutin" language from a man with a snub.

Miss Cornelia personated the comedy that ever peeps around the corner at the tragedy of life. Anne, whose nerves had been rather strained, laughed hysterically, and even Owen smiled. Certainly, sentiment and passion had a way of shrinking out of sight in Miss Cornelia's presence. And yet to Anne nothing seemed quite as hopeless and dark and painful as it had seemed a few moments before. But sleep was far from her eyes that night.

27
On the Sand-Bar

Owen Ford left Four Winds the next morning. In the evening Anne went over to see Leslie, but found nobody. The house was locked and there was no light in any window. It looked like a home left soulless. Leslie did not run over on the following day—-which Anne thought a bad sign.

Gilbert having occasion to go in the evening to the fishing cove, Anne drove with him to the Point, intending to stay awhile with Captain Jim. But the great light, cutting its swathes through the fog of the autumn evening, was in care of Alec Boyd and Captain Jim was away.

"What will you do?" asked Gilbert. "Come with me?"

"I don't want to go to the cove—but I'll go over the channel with you, and roam about on the sandshore till you come back. The rock shore is too slippery and grim to-night."

Alone on the sands of the bar Anne gave herself up to the eerie charm of the night. It was warm for September, and the late afternoon had been very foggy; but a full moon had in part lessened the fog and transformed the harbour and the gulf and the surrounding shores into a strange, fantastic, unreal world of pale silver mist, through which everything loomed phantom-like. Captain Josiah Crawford's black schooner sailing down the channel, laden with potatoes for Bluenose ports, was a spectral ship bound for a far unchartered land, ever receding, never to be reached. The calls of unseen gulls overhead were the cries of the souls of doomed seamen. The little curls of foam that blew across the sand were elfin things stealing up from the sea-caves. The big, round-shouldered sand-dunes were the sleeping giants of some old northern tale. The lights that glimmered palely across the harbour were the delusive beacons on some coast of fairyland.

Anne pleased herself with a hundred fancies as she wandered through the mist. It was delightful—romantic—mysterious to be roaming here alone on this enchanted shore.

But was she alone? Something loomed in the mist before her—took shape and form—suddenly moved towards her across the wave-rippled sand.

"Leslie!" exclaimed Anne in amazement. "Whatever are you doing—*here*—to-night?"

"If it comes to that, whatever are *you* doing here?" said Leslie, trying to laugh. The effort was a failure. She looked very pale and tired; but the love locks under her scarlet cap were curling about her face and eyes like little sparkling rings of gold.

"I'm waiting for Gilbert—he's over at the cove. I intended to stay at the light, but Captain Jim is away."

"Well, *I* came here because I wanted to walk—and walk—and *walk*," said Leslie restlessly. "I couldn't on the rock shore—the tide was too high and the rocks prisoned me. I had to come here—or I should have gone mad, I think. I rowed myself over the channel in Captain Jim's flat. I've been here for an hour. Come—come—let us walk. I can't stand still. Oh, Anne!"

"Leslie, dearest, what is the trouble?" asked Anne, though she knew too well already.

"I can't tell you—don't ask me. I wouldn't mind your knowing—I wish you did know—but I can't tell you—I can't tell anyone. I've been such a fool, Anne—and oh, it hurts so terribly to be a fool. There's nothing so painful in the world."

She laughed bitterly. Anne slipped her arm around her.

"Leslie, is it that you have learned to care for Mr. Ford?"

Leslie turned herself about passionately.

"How did you know?" she cried. "Anne, how did you know? Oh, is it written in my face for everyone to see? Is it as plain as that?"

"No, no. I—1 can't tell you how I knew. It just came into my mind, somehow. Leslie, don't look at me like that!"

"Do you despise me?" demanded Leslie in a fierce, low tone. "Do you think I'm wicked—unwomanly? Or do you think I'm just plain fool?"

"I don't think you any of those things. Come, dear, let's just talk it over sensibly, as we might talk over any other of the great crises of life. You've been brooding over it and let yourself drift into a morbid view of it. You know you have a little tendency to do that about everything that goes wrong, and you promised me that you would fight against it."

"But—oh, it's so—so shameful," murmured Leslie. "To love him—unsought—and when I'm not free to love anybody."

"There's nothing shameful about it. But I'm very sorry that you have learned to care for Owen, because, as things are, it will only make you more unhappy."

"I didn't *learn* to care," said Leslie, walking on and speaking passionately. "If it had been like that I could have prevented it. I never dreamed of such a thing until that day, a week ago, when he told me he had finished his book and must soon go away. Then—then I knew. I felt as if someone had struck me a terrible blow. I didn't say anything—I couldn't speak—but I don't know what I looked like. I'm so afraid my face betrayed me. Oh, I would die of shame if I thought he knew—or suspected."

Anne was miserably silent, hampered by her deductions from her conversation with Owen. Leslie went on feverishly, as if she found relief in speech.

"I was so happy all this summer, Anne—happier than I ever was in my life. I thought it was because everything had been made clear between you and me, and that it was our friendship which made life seem so beautiful and full once more. And it *was*, in part—but not all—oh, not nearly all. I know now why everything was so different. And now it's all over—and he has gone. How can I live, Anne? When I turned back into the house this morning after he had gone the solitude struck me like a blow in the face."

"It won't seem so hard by-and-by, dear," said Anne, who always felt the pain of her friends so keenly that she could not speak easy, fluent words of comforting. Besides, she remembered how well-meant speeches had hurt her in her own sorrow and was afraid.

"Oh, it seems to me it will grow harder all the time," said Leslie miserably. "I've nothing to look forward to. Morning will come after morning—and he will not come back—he will never come back. Oh, when I think that I will never see him again I feel as if a great brutal hand had twisted itself among my heart-strings, and was wrenching them. Once, long ago, I dreamed of love—and I thought it must be beautiful—and *now*—it's like *this*. When he went away yesterday morning he was so cold and indifferent. He said 'Good-bye, Mrs. Moore' in the coldest tone in the world—as if we had not even been friends—as if I meant absolutely nothing to him. I know I don't—I didn't want him to care—but he *might* have been a little kinder."

"Oh, I wish Gilbert would come," thought Anne. She was racked between her sympathy for Leslie and the necessity of avoiding anything that would betray Owen's confidence. She knew why his good-bye had been so cold—why it could not have the cordiality that their good-comradeship demanded—but she could not tell Leslie.

"I couldn't help it, Anne—I couldn't help it," said poor Leslie.

"I know that."

"Do you blame me so very much?"

"I don't blame you at all."

"And you won't—you won't tell Gilbert?"

"Leslie! Do you think I would do such a thing?"

"Oh, I don't know—you and Gilbert are such *chums*. I don't see how you could help telling him everything."

"Everything about my own concerns—yes. But not my friends' secrets."

"I couldn't have *him* know. But I'm glad *you* know. I would feel guilty if there were anything I was ashamed to tell you. I hope Miss Cornelia won't find out. Sometimes I feel as if those terrible, kind brown eyes of hers read my very soul. Oh, I wish this mist would never lift—I wish I could just stay in it forever, hidden away from every living being. I don't see how I can go on with life. This summer has been so full. I never was lonely for a moment. Before Owen came there used to be horrible moments—when I had been with you and Gilbert—and then had to leave you. You two would walk away together and I would walk away *alone*. After Owen came he was always there to walk home with me—we would laugh and talk as you and Gilbert were doing—there were no more lonely, envious moments for me. And *now!* Oh, yes, I've been a fool. Let's have done talking about my folly. I'll never bore you with it again."

"Here is Gilbert, and you are coming back with us," said Anne, who had no intention of leaving Leslie to wander alone on the sand-bar on such a night and in such a mood. "There's plenty of room in our boat for three, and we'll tie the flat on behind."

"Oh, I suppose, I must reconcile myself to being the odd one again," said poor Leslie with another bitter laugh. "Forgive me, Anne—that was hateful. I ought to be thankful—and I *am*—that I have two good friends who are glad to count me in as a third. Don't mind my hateful speeches. I just seem to be one great pain all over and everything hurts me."

"Leslie seemed very quiet tonight, didn't she?" said Gilbert, when he and Anne reached home. "What in the world was she doing over there on the bar alone?"

"Oh, she was tired—and you know she likes to go to the shore after one of Dick's bad days."

"What a pity she hadn't met and married a fellow like Ford long ago," ruminated Gilbert. "They'd have made an ideal couple, wouldn't they?"

"For pity's sake, Gilbert, don't develop into a matchmaker. It's an abominable profession for a man," cried Anne rather sharply, afraid that Gilbert might blunder on the truth if he kept on in this strain.

"Bless us, Anne-girl, I'm not matchmaking," protested Gilbert, rather surprised at her tone. "I was only thinking of one of the might-have-beens."

"Well, don't. It's a waste of time," said Anne. Then she added suddenly:

"Oh, Gilbert, I wish everybody could be as happy as we are."

28
Odds and Ends

"I've been reading obituary notices," said Miss Cornelia, laying down the *Daily Enterprise* and taking up her sewing.

The harbour was lying black and sullen under a dour November sky; the wet, dead leaves clung drenched and sodden to the window sills; but the little house was gay with firelight and spring-like with Anne's ferns and geraniums.

"It's always summer here, Anne," Leslie had said one day; and all who were the guests of that house of dreams felt the same.

"The *Enterprise* seems to run to obituaries these days," quoth Miss Cornelia. "It always has a couple of columns of them, and I read every line. It's one of my forms of recreation, especially when there's some original poetry attached to them. Here's a choice sample for you:

'*She's gone to be with her Maker,*
Never more to roam.

She used to play and sing with joy
The song of Home, Sweet Home.'

Who says we haven't any poetical talent on the Island! Have you ever noticed what heaps of good people die, Anne, dearie? It's kind of pitiful. Here's ten obituaries, and every one of them saints and models, even the men. Here's old Peter Stimson, who has 'left a large circle of friends to mourn his untimely loss.' Lord, Anne, dearie, that man was eighty, and everybody who knew him had been wishing him dead these thirty years. Read obituaries when you're blue, Anne, dearie—especially the ones of folks you know. If you've any sense of humour at all they'll cheer you up, believe *me*. I just wish *I* had the writing of the obituaries of some people. Isn't 'obituary' an awful ugly word? This very Peter I've been speaking of had a face exactly like one. I never saw it but I thought of the word *obituary* then and there. There's only one uglier word that I know of, and that's *relict*. Lord, Anne, dearie, I may be an old maid, but there's this comfort in it—I'll never be any man's 'relict.' "

"It *is* an ugly word," said Anne, laughing. "Avonlea graveyard was full of old tombstones 'sacred to the memory of So-and-So, *relict* of the late So-and-So.' It always made me think of something wornout and moth-eaten. Why is it that so many of the words connected with death are so disagreeable? I do wish that the custom of calling a dead body 'the remains' could be abolished. I positively shiver when I hear the undertaker say at a funeral, 'All who wish to see the remains please step this way.' It always gives me the horrible impression that I am about to view the scene of a cannibal feast."

"Well, all I hope," said Miss Cornelia calmly, "is that when I'm dead nobody will call me 'our departed sister.' I took a scunner at this sistering-and-brothering business five years ago when there was a travelling evangelist holding meetings at the Glen.

I hadn't any use for him from the start. I felt in my bones that there was something wrong with him. And there was. Mind you, he was pretending to be a Presbyterian—Presbyterian, *he* called it—and all the time he was a Methodist. He brothered and sistered everybody. He had a large circle of relations, that man had. He clutched my hand fervently one night, and said imploringly, 'My *dear* sister Bryant, are you a Christian?' I just looked him over a bit, and then I said calmly, 'The only brother I ever had, Mr. Fiske, was buried fifteen years ago, I haven't adopted any since. As for being a Christian, I was that, I hope and believe, when you were crawling about the floor in petticoats.' *That* squelched him, believe *me*. Mind you, Anne, dearie, I'm not down on all evangelists. We've had some real fine, earnest men, who did a lot of good and made the old sinners squirm. But this Fiske-man wasn't one of them. I had a good laugh all to myself one evening. Fiske had asked all who were Christians to stand up. *I* didn't, believe *me*! I never had any use for that sort of thing. But most of them did, and then he asked all who wanted to be Christians to stand up. Nobody stirred for a spell, so Fiske started up a hymn at the top of his voice. Just in front of me poor little Ikey Baker was sitting in the Millison pew. He was a home boy, ten years old, and Millison just about worked him to death. The poor little creature was always so tired he fell asleep right off whenever he went to church or anywhere he could sit still for a few minutes. He'd been sleeping all through the meeting, and I was thankful to see the poor child getting a rest, believe *me*. Well, when Fiske's voice went soaring skyward and the rest joined in, poor Ikey wakened with a start. He thought it was just an ordinary singing and that everybody ought to stand up, so he scrambled to his feet mighty quick knowing he'd get a combing down from Maria Millison for sleeping in meeting. Fiske saw him, stopped and shouted, 'Another soul saved! Glory Hallelujah!' And there was poor, frightened Ikey, only half awake and yawning, never thinking about his soul at all. Poor child, he never had time to think of anything but his tired, overworked little body.

"Leslie went one night and the Fiske-man got right after her—oh, he was especially anxious about the souls of the nice-looking girls, believe me!—and he hurt her feelings so she never went again. And then he prayed every night after that, right in public that the Lord would soften her hard heart. Finally I went to Mr. Leavitt, our minister then, and told him if he didn't make Fiske stop that I'd just rise up the next night and throw my hymn book at him when he mentioned that 'beautiful but unrepentant young woman.' I'd have done it too, believe *me*. Mr. Leavitt did put a stop to it, but Fiske kept on with his meetings until Charley Douglas put an end to his career in the Glen. Mrs. Charley had been out in California all winter. She'd been real melancholy in the fall—religious melancholy—it ran in her family. Her father worried so much over believing that he had committed the unpardonable sin that he died in the asylum. So when Rose Douglas got that way Charley packed her off to visit her sister in Los Angeles. She got perfectly well and came home just when the Fiske revival was in full swing. She stepped off the train at the Glen, real smiling and chipper, and the first thing she saw staring her in the face on the black, gable-end of the freight shed, was the question, in big white letters, two feet high, 'Wither goest thou—to heaven or hell?' That had been one of Fiske's ideas, and he had got Henry Hammond to paint it. Rose just gave a shriek and fainted; and when they got her home she was worse than ever. Charley Douglas went to Mr. Leavitt and told him that every Douglas would leave the church if Fiske was kept there any longer. Mr. Leavitt had to give in, for the Douglases paid half his salary, so Fiske departed, and we had to depend on our Bibles once more for instructions on how to get to heaven. After he was gone Mr. Leavitt found out he was just a masquerading Methodist, and he felt pretty sick, believe *me*.

Mr. Leavitt fell short in some ways, but he was a good, sound Presbyterian."

"By the way, I had a letter from Mr. Ford yesterday," said Anne. "He asked me to remember him kindly to you."

"I don't want his remembrances," said Miss Cornelia, curtly.

"Why?" said Anne, in astonishment. "I thought you liked him."

"Well, so I did, in a kind of way. But I'll never forgive him for what he done to Leslie. There's that poor child eating her heart out about him—as if she hadn't had trouble enough—and him ranting round Toronto, I've no doubt, enjoying himself same as ever. Just like a man."

"Oh, Miss Cornelia, how did you find out?"

"Lord, Anne, dearie, I've got eyes, haven't I? And I've known Leslie since she was a baby. There's been a new kind of heartbreak in her eyes all the fall, and I know that writer-man was behind it somehow. I'll never forgive myself for being the means of bringing him here. But I never expected he'd be like he was. I thought he'd just be like the other men Leslie had boarded—conceited young asses, every one of them, that she never had any use for. One of them did try to flirt with her once and she froze him out—so bad, I feel sure he's never got himself thawed since. So I never thought of any danger."

"Don't let Leslie suspect you know her secret," said Anne hurriedly. "I think it would hurt her."

"Trust me, Anne, dearie. *I* wasn't born yesterday. Oh, a plague on all the men! One of them ruined Leslie's life to begin with, and now another of the tribe comes and makes her still more wretched. Anne, this world is an awful place, believe *me*."

"'*There's something in the world amiss*
Will be unriddled by and by.'"

quoted Anne dreamily.

"If it is, it'll be in a world where there aren't any men," said Miss Cornelia gloomily.

"What have the men been doing now?" asked Gilbert entering.

"Mischief—mischief! What else did they ever do?"

"It was Eve ate the apple, Miss Cornelia."

"'Twas a he-creature tempted her," retorted Miss Cornelia triumphantly.

Leslie, after her first anguish was over, found it possible to go on with life after all, as most of us do, no matter what our particular form of torment has been. It is even possible that she enjoyed moments of it, when she was one of the gay circle in the little house of dreams. But if Anne ever hoped that she was forgetting Owen Ford she would have been undeceived by the furtive hunger in Leslie's eyes whenever his name was mentioned. Pitiful to that hunger, Anne always contrived to tell Captain Jim or Gilbert bits of news from Owen's letters when Leslie was with them. The girl's flush and pallor at such moments spoke all too eloquently of the emotion that filled her being. But she never spoke of him to Anne, or mentioned that night on the sand-bar.

One day her old dog died and she grieved bitterly over him.

"He's been my friend so long," she said sorrowfully to Anne. "He was Dick's old dog, you know—Dick had him for a year or so before we were married. He left him with me when he sailed on the *Four Sisters*. Carlo got very fond of me—and his dog-love helped me through that first dreadful year after mother died, when I was all alone. When I heard that Dick was coming back I was afraid Carlo wouldn't be so much mine. But he never seemed to care for Dick, though he had been so fond of him once. He would snap and growl at him as if he were a stranger. I was glad. It was nice to have one thing whose love was all mine. That old dog has been such a comfort to me, Anne. He got so feeble in the fall that I was afraid he couldn't live long—but I hoped I could nurse him through the winter. He seemed pretty well this morning. He was lying on the rug before the fire; then, all at once, he got up and crept over to me; he put his head on my lap and gave me one loving look out of his big, soft, dog eyes—and then he just shivered and died. I shall miss him so."

"Let me give you another dog, Leslie," said Anne. "I'm getting a lovely Gordon setter for a Christmas present for Gilbert. Let me give you one too."

Leslie shook her head.

"Not just now, thank you, Anne. I don't feel like having another dog yet. I don't seem to have any affection left for another. Perhaps—in time—I'll let you give me one. I really need one as a kind of protection. But there was something almost human about Carlo—it wouldn't be *decent* to fill his place too hurriedly, dear old fellow."

Anne went to Avonlea a week before Christmas and stayed until after the holidays. Gilbert came up for her, and there was a glad New Year celebration at Green Gables, when Barrys and Blythes and Wrights assembled to devour a dinner which had cost Mrs. Rachel and Marilla much careful thought and preparation. When they went back to Four Winds the little house was almost drifted over, for the third storm of a winter that was to prove phenomenally stormy had whirled up the harbour and heaped huge snow mountains about everything it encountered. But Captain Jim had shovelled out doors and paths, and Miss Cornelia had come down and kindled the hearth-fire.

"It's good to see you back Anne, dearie! But did you ever see such drifts? You can't see the Moore place at all unless you go upstairs. Leslie'll be so glad you're back. She's almost buried alive over there. Fortunately Dick can shovel snow, and thinks it's great fun. Susan sent me word to tell you she would be on hand tomorrow. Where are you off to now, Captain?"

"I reckon I'll plough up to the Glen and sit a bit with old Martin Strong. He's not far from his end and he's lonesome. He hasn't many friends—been too busy all his life to make any. He's made heaps of money, though."

"Well, he thought that since he couldn't serve God and Mammon he'd better stick to Mammon," said Miss Cornelia crisply. "So he shouldn't complain if he doesn't find Mammon very good company now."

Captain Jim went out, but remembered something in the yard and turned back for a moment.

"I'd a letter from Mr. Ford, Mistress Blythe, and he says the life-book is accepted and is going to be published next fall. I felt fair uplifted when I got the news. To think that I'm to see it in print at last."

"That man is clean crazy on the subject of his life- book," said Miss Cornelia compassionately. "For my part, I think there's far too many books in the world now."

29

Gilbert and Anne Disagree

Gilbert laid down the ponderous medical tome over which he had been poring until the increasing dusk of the March evening made him desist. He leaned back in his chair and gazed meditatively out of the window. It was early spring—probably the ugliest time of the year. Not even the sunset could redeem the dead, sodden landscape and rotten-black harbour ice upon which he looked. No sign of life was visible, save a big black crow winging his solitary way across a leaden field. Gilbert speculated idly concerning that crow. Was he a family crow, with a black but comely crow wife awaiting him in the woods beyond the Glen? Or was he a glossy young buck of a crow on courting thoughts intent? Or was he a cynical bachelor crow, believing that he travels the fastest who travels alone? Whatever he was, he soon disappeared in congenial gloom and Gilbert turned to the cheerier view indoors.

The firelight flickered from point to point, gleaming on the white and green coats of Gog and Magog, on the sleek, brown head of the beautiful setter basking on the rug, on the picture frames on the walls, on the vaseful of daffodils from the window garden, on Anne herself, sitting by her little table, with her sewing beside her and her hands clasped over her knee while she traced out pictures in the fire—Castles in Spain whose airy turrets pierced moonlit cloud and sunset bar—ships sailing from the Haven of Good Hopes straight to Four Winds Harbour with precious burthen. For Anne was again a dreamer of dreams, albeit a grim shape of fear went with her night and day to shadow and darken her visions.

Gilbert was accustomed to refer to himself as "an old married man." But he still looked upon Anne with the incredulous eyes of a lover. He couldn't wholly believe yet that she was really his. It *might* be only a dream after all, part and parcel of this magic house of dreams. His soul still went on tip-toe before her, lest the charm be shattered and the dream dispelled.

"Anne," he said slowly, "lend me your ears. I want to talk with you about something."

Anne looked across at him through the fire-lit gloom.

"What is it?" she asked, gaily. "You look fearfully solemn, Gilbert. I really haven't done anything naughty to-day. Ask Susan."

"It's not of you—or ourselves—I want to talk. It's about Dick Moore."

"Dick Moore?" echoed Anne, sitting up alertly. "Why, what in the world have you to say about Dick Moore?"

"I've been thinking a great deal about him lately. Do you

remember that time last summer I treated him for those carbuncles on his neck?"

"Yes—yes."

"I took the opportunity to examine the scars on his head thoroughly. I've always thought Dick was a very interesting case from a medical point of view. Lately I've been studying the history of trephining and the cases where it has been employed. Anne, I have come to the conclusion that if Dick Moore were taken to a good hospital and the operation of trephining performed on several places in his skull, his memory and faculties might be restored."

"Gilbert!" Anne's voice was full of protest. "Surely you don't mean it!"

"I do, indeed. And I have decided that it is my duty to broach the subject to Leslie."

"Gilbert Blythe, you shall *not* do any such thing," cried Anne vehemently. "Oh, Gilbert, you won't—you won't. You couldn't be so cruel. Promise me you won't."

"Why, Anne-girl, I didn't suppose you would take it like this. Be reasonable—"

"I won't be reasonable—I can't be reasonable—I *am* reasonable. It is you who are unreasonable. Gilbert, have you ever once thought what it would mean for Leslie if Dick Moore were to be restored to his right senses? Just stop and think! She's unhappy enough now; but life as Dick's nurse and attendant is a thousand times easier for her than life as Dick's wife. I know—I *know*! It's unthinkable. Don't you meddle with the matter. Leave well enough alone."

"I *have* thought over that aspect of the case thoroughly, Anne. But I believe that a doctor is bound to set the sanctity of a patient's mind and body above all other considerations, no matter what the consequences may be. I believe it his duty to endeavour to restore health and sanity, if there is any hope whatever of it."

"But Dick isn't your patient in that respect," cried Anne, taking another tack. "If Leslie had asked you if anything could be done for him, *then* it might be your duty to tell her what you really thought. But you've no right to meddle."

"I don't call it meddling. Uncle Dave told Leslie twelve years ago that nothing could be done for Dick. She believes that, of course."

"And why did Uncle Dave tell her that, if it wasn't true?" cried Anne, triumphantly. "Doesn't he know as much about it as you?"

"I think not—though it may sound conceited and presumptuous to say it. And you know as well as I that he is rather prejudiced against what he calls 'these newfangled notions of cutting and carving.' He's even opposed to operating for appendicitis."

"He's right," exclaimed Anne, with a complete change of front. "I believe myself that you modem doctors are entirely too fond of making experiments with human flesh and blood."

"Rhoda Allonby would not be a living woman today if I had been afraid of making a certain experiment," argued Gilbert. "I took the risk—and saved her life."

"I'm sick and tired of hearing about Rhoda Allonby," cried Anne—most unjustly, for Gilbert had never mentioned Mrs. Allonby's name since the day he had told Anne of his success in regard to her. And he could not be blamed for other people's discussion of it.

Gilbert felt rather hurt.

"I had not expected you to look at the matter as you do, Anne," he said a little stiffly, getting up and moving towards the office door. It was their first approach to a quarrel.

But Anne flew after him and dragged him back.

"Now Gilbert, you are not 'going off mad.' Sit down here and I'll apologise bee-yew-ti-fully. I shouldn't have said that. But—oh, if you knew—"

Anne checked herself just in time. She had been on the very verge of betraying Leslie's secret.

"Knew what a woman feels about it," she concluded lamely.

"I think I do know. I've looked at the matter from every point of view—and I've been driven to the conclusion that it is my duty to tell Leslie that I believe it is possible that Dick can be restored to himself; there my responsibility ends. It will be for her to decide what she will do."

"I don't think you've any right to put such a responsibility on her. She has enough to bear. She is poor—how could she afford such an operation?"

"That is for her to decide," persisted Gilbert stubbornly.

"You say you think that Dick can be cured. But are you *sure* of it?"

"Certainly not. Nobody could be sure of such a thing. There may have been lesions of the brain itself, the effect of which can never be removed. But if, as I believe, his loss of memory and other faculties is due merely to the pressure on the brain centres of certain depressed areas of bone, then he can be cured."

"But it's only a possibility!" insisted Anne. "Now, suppose you tell Leslie and she decides to have the operation. It will cost a great deal. She will have to borrow the money, or sell her little property. And suppose the operation is a failure and Dick remains the same. How will she be able to pay back the money she borrows, or make a living for herself and that big helpless creature if she sells the farm?"

"Oh, I know—I know. But it is my duty to tell her. 1 can't get away from that conviction."

"Oh, I know the Blythe stubbornness," groaned Anne. "But don't do this solely on your own responsibility. Consult Doctor Dave."

"I *have* done so," said Gilbert reluctantly.

"And what did he say?"

"In brief—as you say—leave well enough alone. Apart from his prejudice against newfangled surgery, I'm afraid he looks at the case from your point of view—don't do it, for Leslie's sake."

"There now," cried Anne triumphantly. "I do think, Gilbert, that you ought to abide by the judgment of a man nearly eighty, who has seen a great deal and saved scores of lives himself—surely his opinion ought to weigh more than a mere boy's."

"Thank you."

"Don't laugh. It's too serious."

"That's just my point. It *is* serious. Here is a man who is a helpless burden. He may be restored to reason and usefulness—"

"He was so very useful before," interjected Anne witheringly.

"He may be given a chance to make good and redeem the past. His wife doesn't know this. I do. It is therefore my duty to tell her that there is such a possibility. That, boiled down, is my decision."

"Don't say 'decision' yet, Gilbert. Consult somebody else. Ask Captain Jim what he thinks about it."

"Very well. But I'll not promise to abide by his opinion, Anne. This is something a man must decide for himself. My conscience would never be easy if I kept silent on the subject."

"Oh, your conscience!" moaned Anne. "I suppose that Uncle Dave has a conscience too, hasn't he?"

"Yes. But I am not the keeper of his conscience. Come Anne, if this affair did not concern Leslie—if it were a purely abstract case, you would agree with me,—you know you would."

"I wouldn't," vowed Anne, trying to believe it herself. "Oh, you can argue all night, Gilbert, but you won't convince me. Just you ask Miss Cornelia what she thinks of it."

"You're driven to the last ditch, Anne, when you bring up Miss Cornelia as a reinforcement. She will say, 'Just like a man,' and rage furiously. No matter. This is no affair for Miss Cornelia to settle. Leslie alone must decide it."

"You know very well how she will decide it," said Anne, almost in tears. "She has ideals of duty, too. I don't see how you can take such a responsibility on your shoulders. *I* couldn't."

"'*Because right is right to follow right*
Were wisdom in the scorn of consequence,'"

quoted Gilbert.

"Oh, you think a couplet of poetry a convincing argument!" scoffed Anne. "That is so like a man."

And then she laughed in spite of herself. It sounded so like an echo of Miss Cornelia.

"Well, if you won't accept Tennyson as an authority, perhaps you will believe the words of a Greater than he," said Gilbert seriously. "'Ye shall know the truth and the truth shall make you free.' I believe that, Anne, with all my heart. It's the greatest and grandest verse in the Bible—or in any literature—and the *truest*, if there are comparative degrees of trueness. And it's the first duty of a man to tell the truth, as he sees it and believes it."

"In this case the truth won't make poor Leslie free," sighed Anne. "It will probably end in still more bitter bondage for her. Oh, Gilbert, I *can't* think you are right."

30
Leslie Decides

A sudden outbreak of a virulent type of influenza at the Glen and down at the fishing village kept Gilbert so busy for the next fortnight that he had no time to pay the promised visit to Captain Jim. Anne hoped against hope that he had abandoned the idea about Dick Moore, and, resolving to let sleeping dogs lie, she said no more about the subject. But she thought of it incessantly.

"I wonder if it would be right for me to tell him that Leslie cares for Owen," she thought. "He would never let her suspect that he knew, so her pride would not suffer, and it *might* convince him that he should let Dick Moore alone. Shall I—shall I? No, after all, I cannot. A promise is sacred, and I've no right to betray Leslie's secret. But oh, I never felt so worried over anything in my life as I do over this. It's spoiling the spring—it's spoiling everything."

One evening Gilbert abruptly proposed that they go down and see Captain Jim. With a sinking heart Anne agreed, and they set forth. Two weeks of kind sunshine had wrought a miracle in the bleak landscape over which Gilbert's crow had flown. The hills and fields were dry and brown and warm, ready to break into bud and blossom; the harbour was laughter-shaken again; the long harbour road was like a gleaming red ribbon; down on the dunes a crowd of boys, who were out smelt fishing, were burning the thick, dry sand-hill grass of the preceding summer. The flames swept over the dunes rosily, flinging their cardinal banners against the dark gulf beyond, and illuminating the channel and the fishing village. It was a picturesque scene which would at other times have delighted Anne's eyes; but she was not enjoying this walk. Neither was Gilbert. Their usual good-comradeship and Josephian community of taste and view-point were sadly lacking. Anne's disapproval of the whole project showed itself in the haughty uplift of her head and the studied politeness of her remarks. Gilbert's mouth was set in all the Blythe obstinacy, but his eyes were troubled. He meant to do what he believed to be his duty; but to be at outs with Anne was a high price to pay. Altogether, both were glad when they reached the light—and remorseful that they should be glad.

Captain Jim put away the fishing net upon which he was working, and welcomed them joyfully. In the searching light of the spring evening he looked older than Anne had ever seen him. His hair had grown much grayer, and the strong old hand shook a little. But his blue eyes were clear and steady, and the staunch soul looked out through them gallant and unafraid.

Captain Jim listened in amazed silence while Gilbert said what he had come to say. Anne, who knew how the old man worshipped Leslie, felt quite sure that he would side with her, although she had not much hope that this would influence Gilbert. She was therefore surprised beyond measure when Captain Jim, slowly and sorrowfully, but unhesitatingly, gave it as his opinion that Leslie should be told.

"Oh, Captain Jim, I didn't think you'd say that," she exclaimed reproachfully. "I thought you wouldn't want to make more trouble for her."

Captain Jim shook his head.

"I don't want to. I know how you feel about it, Mistress Blythe—just as I feel meself. But it ain't our feelings we have to steer by through life—no, no we'd make shipwreck mighty often if we did that. There's only the one safe compass and we've got to set our course by that—what it's right to do. I agree with the doctor. If there's a chance for Dick, Leslie should be told of it. There's no two sides to that, in my opinion."

"Well," said Anne, giving up in despair, "wait until Miss Cornelia gets after you two men."

"Cornelia'll rake us fore and aft, no doubt," assented Captain Jim. "You women are lovely critters, Mistress Blythe, but you're just a mite illogical. You're a highly eddicated lady and Cornelia isn't, but you're like as two peas when it comes to that. I dunno's you're any the worse for it. Logic is a sort of hard, merciless thing, I reckon. Now, I'll brew a cup of tea and we'll drink it and talk of pleasant things, jest to calm our minds a bit."

At least, Captain Jim's tea and conversation calmed Anne's mind to such an extent that she did not make Gilbert suffer so acutely on the way home as she had deliberately intended to do. She did not refer to the burning question at all, but she chatted amiably of other matters, and Gilbert understood that he was forgiven under protest.

"Captain Jim seems very frail and bent this spring. The winter has aged him," said Anne sadly. "I am afraid that he will soon be going to seek lost Margaret. I can't bear to think of it."

"Four Winds won't be the same place when Captain Jim 'sets out to sea,'" agreed Gilbert.

The following evening he went to the house up the brook. Anne wandered dismally around until his return.

"Well, what did Leslie say?" she demanded when he came in.

"Very little. I think she felt rather dazed."

"And is she going to have the operation?"

"She is going to think it over and decide very soon."

Gilbert flung himself wearily into the easy chair before the fire. He looked tired. It had not been an easy thing for him to tell Leslie. And the terror that had sprung into her eyes when the meaning of what he told her came home to her was not a pleasant thing to remember. Now, when the die was cast, he was beset with doubts of his own wisdom.

Anne looked at him remorsefully; then she slipped down on the rug beside him and laid her glossy red head on his arm.

"Gilbert, I've been rather hateful over this. I won't be any more. Please just call me red-headed and forgive me."

By which Gilbert understood that, no matter what came of it, there would be no I-told-you-so's. But he was not wholly comforted. Duty in the abstract is one thing; duty in the concrete is quite another, especially when the doer is confronted by a woman's stricken eyes.

Some instinct made Anne keep away from Leslie for the next three days. On the third evening Leslie came down to the little house and told Gilbert that she had made up her mind; she would take Dick to Montreal and have the operation.

She was very pale and seemed to have wrapped herself in her old mantle of aloofness. But her eyes had lost the look which had haunted Gilbert; they were cold and bright; and she proceeded to discuss details with him in a crisp, business-like way. There were plans to be made and many things to be thought over. When Leslie had got the information she wanted she went home. Anne wanted to walk part of the way with her.

"Better not," said Leslie curtly. "To-day's rain has made the ground damp. Good-night."

"Have I lost my friend?" said Anne with a sigh. "If the operation is successful and Dick Moore finds himself again Leslie will retreat into some remote fastness of her soul where none of us can ever find her."

"Perhaps she will leave him," said Gilbert.

"Leslie would never do that, Gilbert. Her sense of duty is very strong. She told me once that her Grandmother West always impressed upon her the fact that when she assumed any responsibility she must never shirk it, no matter what the consequences might be. That is one of her cardinal rules. I suppose it's very old-fashioned."

"Don't be bitter, Anne-girl. You know you don't think it old-fashioned—you know you have the very same idea of the sacredness of assumed responsibilities yourself. And you are right. Shirking responsibilities is the curse of our modern life—the secret of all the unrest and discontent that is seething in the world."

"Thus saith the preacher," mocked Anne. But under the mockery she felt that he was right; and she was very sick at heart for Leslie.

A week later Miss Cornelia descended like an avalanche upon the little house. Gilbert was away and Anne was compelled to bear the shock of the impact alone.

Miss Cornelia hardly waited to get her hat off before she began.

"Anne, do you mean to tell me it's true what I've heard—that Dr. Blythe has told Leslie Dick can be cured, and that she is going to take him to Montreal to have him operated on?"

"Yes, it is quite true, Miss Cornelia," said Anne bravely.

"Well, it's inhuman cruelty, that's what it is," said Miss Cornelia, violently agitated. "I did think Dr. Blythe was a decent man. I didn't think he could have been guilty of this."

"Dr. Blythe thought it was his duty to tell Leslie that there was a chance for Dick," said Anne with spirit, "and," she added, loyalty to Gilbert getting the better of her, "I agree with him."

"Oh, no, you don't, dearie," said Miss Cornelia. "No person with any bowels of compassion could."

"Captain Jim does."

"Don't quote that old ninny to me," cried Miss Cornelia. "And I don't care who agrees with him. Think—*think* what it means to that poor hunted, harried girl."

"We *do* think of it. But Gilbert believes that a doctor should put the welfare of a patient's mind and body before all other considerations."

"That's just like a man. But I expected better things of you, Anne," said Miss Cornelia, more in sorrow than in wrath; then she proceeded to bombard Anne with precisely the same arguments with which the latter had attacked Gilbert; and Anne valiantly defended her husband with the weapons he had used for his own protection. Long was the fray, but Miss Cornelia made an end at last.

"It's an iniquitous shame," she declared, almost in tears. "That's just what it is—an iniquitous shame. Poor, poor Leslie!"

"Don't you think Dick should be considered a little, too?" pleaded Anne.

"Dick! Dick Moore! *He's* happy enough. He's a better-behaved and more reputable member of society now than he ever was before. Why, he was a drunkard and perhaps worse. Are you going to set him loose again to roar and to devour?"

"He may reform," said poor Anne, beset by foe without and traitor within.

"Reform your grandmother!" retorted Miss Cornelia. "Dick Moore got the injuries that left him as he is in a drunken brawl. He *deserves* his fate. It was sent on him for a punishment. I don't believe the doctor has any business to tamper with the visitations of God."

"Nobody knows how Dick was hurt, Miss Cornelia. It may not have been in a drunken brawl at all. He may have been waylaid and robbed."

"Pigs *may* whistle, but they've poor mouths for it," said Miss Cornelia. "Well, the gist of what you tell me is that the thing is settled and there's no use in talking. If that's so I'll hold my tongue. I don't propose to wear *my* teeth out gnawing files. When a thing has to be I give in to it. But I like to make mighty sure first that it *has* to be. Now, I'll devote *my* energies to comforting and sustaining Leslie. And after all," added Miss Cornelia, brightening up hopefully, "perhaps nothing can be done for Dick."

31
The Truth Makes Free

Leslie, having once made up her mind what to do, proceeded to do it with characteristic resolution and speed. House-cleaning must be finished with first, whatever issues of life and death might await beyond.

The gray house up the brook was put into flawless order and cleanliness, with Miss Cornelia's ready assistance. Miss Cornelia, having said her say to Anne, and later on to Gilbert and Captain Jim—sparing neither of them, let it be assured—never spoke of the matter to Leslie. She accepted the fact of Dick's operation, referred to it when necessary in a business-like way, and ignored it when it was not. Leslie never attempted to discuss it. She was very cold and quiet during these beautiful spring days. She seldom visited Anne, and though she was invariably courteous and friendly, that very courtesy was as an icy barrier between her and the people of the little house. The old jokes and laughter and chumminess of common things could not reach her over it. Anne refused to feel hurt. She knew that Leslie was in the grip of a hideous dread—a dread that wrapped her away from all little glimpses of happiness and hours of pleasure. When one great passion seizes possession of the soul all other feelings are crowded aside. Never in all her life had Leslie Moore shuddered away from the future with more intolerable terror. But she went forward as unswervingly in the path she had elected as the martyrs of old walked their chosen way, knowing the end of it to be the fiery agony of the stake.

The financial question was settled with greater ease than Anne had feared. Leslie borrowed the necessary money from Captain Jim, and, at her insistence, he took a mortgage on the little farm.

"So that is one thing off the poor girl's mind," Miss Cornelia told Anne, "and off mine too. Now, if Dick gets well enough to work again he'll be able to earn enough to pay the interest on it; and if he doesn't I know Captain Jim'll manage someway that Leslie won't have to. He said as much to me. 'I'm getting old, Cornelia,' he said, 'and I've no chick or child of my own. Leslie won't take a gift from a living man, but mebbe she will from a dead one.' So it will be all right as far as *that* goes. I wish everything else might be settled as satisfactorily. As for that wretch of a Dick, he's been awful these last few days. The devil was in him, believe *me*! Leslie and I couldn't get on with our work for the tricks he'd play. He chased all her ducks one day around the yard till most of them died. And not one thing would he do for us. Sometimes, you know, he'll make himself quite handy, bringing in pails of water and wood. But this week if we sent him to the well he'd try to climb down into it. I thought once, 'If you'd only shoot down there head-first everything would be nicely settled.' "

"Oh, Miss Cornelia!"

"Now, you needn't Miss Cornelia me, Anne, dearie. *Anybody* would have thought the same. If the Montreal doctors can make a rational creature out of Dick Moore they're wonders."

Leslie took Dick to Montreal early in May. Gilbert went with her, to help her, and make the necessary arrangements for her. He came home with the report that the Montreal surgeon whom they had consulted agreed with him that there was a good chance of Dick's restoration.

"Very comforting," was Miss Cornelia's sarcastic comment.

Anne only sighed. Leslie had been very distant at their parting. But she had promised to write. Ten days after Gilbert's return the letter came. Leslie wrote that the operation had been successfully performed and that Dick was making a good recovery.

"What does she mean by 'successfully?'" asked Anne. "Does she mean that Dick's memory is really restored?"

"Not likely—since she says nothing of it," said Gilbert. "She uses the word 'successfully' from the surgeon's point of view. The operation has been performed and followed by normal results. But it is too soon to know whether Dick's faculties will be eventually restored, wholly or in part. His memory would not be likely to return to him all at once. The process will be gradual, if it occurs at all. Is that all she says?"

"Yes—there's her letter. It's very short. Poor girl, she must be under a terrible strain. Gilbert Blythe, there are heaps of things I long to say to you, only it would be mean."

"Miss Cornelia says them for you," said Gilbert with a rueful smile. "She combs me down every time I encounter her. She makes it plain to me that she regards me as little better than a murderer, and that she thinks it a great pity that Dr. Dave ever let me step into his shoes. She even told me that the Methodist doctor over the harbour was to be preferred before me. With Miss Cornelia the force of condemnation can no further go."

"If Cornelia Bryant was sick, it would not be Doctor Dave or the Methodist doctor she would send for," sniffed Susan. "She would have you out of your hard-earned bed in the middle of the night, doctor, dear, if she took a spell of misery, that she would. And then she would likely say your bill was past all reason. But do not you mind her, doctor, dear. It takes all kinds of people to make a world."

No further word came from Leslie for some time. The May days crept away in a sweet succession and the shores of Four Winds Harbour greened and bloomed and purpled. One day in late May Gilbert came home to be met by Susan in the stable yard.

"I am afraid something has upset Mrs. Doctor, doctor, dear," she said mysteriously. "She got a letter this afternoon and since then she has just been walking round the garden and talking to herself. You know it is not good for her to be on her feet so much, doctor, dear. She did not see fit to tell me what her news was, and I am no pry, doctor, dear, and never was, but it is plain something has upset her. And it is not good for her to be upset."

Gilbert hurried rather anxiously to the garden. Had anything happened at Green Gables? But Anne, sitting on the rustic seat by the brook, did not look troubled, though she was certainly much excited. Her eyes were their grayest, and scarlet spots burned on her cheeks. "What has happened, Anne?"

Anne gave a queer little laugh.

"I think you'll hardly believe it when I tell you, Gilbert. *I* can't believe it yet. As Susan said the other day, 'I feel like a fly coming to life in the sun—dazed-like.' It's all so incredible. I've read the letter a score of times and every time it's just the same—I can't believe my own eyes. Oh, Gilbert, you were right—so right. I can see that clearly enough now—and I'm so ashamed of myself—and will you ever really forgive me?"

"Anne, I'll shake you if you don't grow coherent. Redmond would be ashamed of you. *What* has happened?"

"You won't believe it—you won't believe it—"

"I'm going in to 'phone for Uncle Dave," said Gilbert, pretending to start for the house.

"Sit down, Gilbert. I'll try to tell you. I've had a letter, and oh, Gilbert, it's all so amazing—so incredibly amazing—we never thought—not one of us ever dreamed—"

"I suppose," said Gilbert, sitting down with a resigned air, "the only thing to do in a case of this kind is to have patience and go at the matter categorically. Whom is your letter from?"

"Leslie—and, oh, Gilbert—"

"Leslie! Whew! What has she to say? What's the news about Dick?"

Anne lifted the letter and held it out, calmly dramatic in a moment.

"There is *no* Dick! The man we have thought Dick Moore—whom everybody in Four Winds has believed for twelve years to be Dick Moore—is his cousin, George Moore, of Nova Scotia, who, it seems, always resembled him very strikingly. Dick Moore died of yellow fever thirteen years ago in Cuba."

32
Miss Cornelia Discusses the Affair

"And do you mean to tell me, Anne, dearie, that Dick Moore has turned out not to be Dick Moore at all but somebody else? Is *that* what you 'phoned up to me today?"

"Yes, Miss Cornelia. It is very amazing, isn't it?"

"It's—it's—just like a man," said Miss Cornelia helplessly. She took off her hat with trembling fingers. For once in her life Miss Cornelia was undeniably staggered.

"I can't seem to sense it, Anne," she said. "I've heard you say it—and I believe you—but I can't take it in. Dick Moore is dead—has been dead all these years —and Leslie is free?"

"Yes. The truth has made her free. Gilbert was right when he said that verse was the grandest in the Bible."

"Tell me everything, Anne, dearie. Since I got your 'phone I've been in a regular muddle, believe *me*. Cornelia Bryant was never so kerflummuxed before."

"There isn't a very great deal to tell. Leslie's letter was short. She didn't go into particulars. This man— George Moore—has recovered his memory and knows who he is. He says Dick took yellow fever in Cuba, and the *Four Sisters* had to sail without him. George stayed behind to nurse him. But he died very shortly afterwards. George did not write Leslie because he intended to come right home and tell her himself."

"And why didn't he?"

"I suppose his accident must have intervened. Gilbert says it is quite likely that George Moore remembers nothing of his accident, or what led to it, and may never remember it. It probably happened very soon after Dick's death. We may find out more particulars when Leslie writes again."

"Does she say what she is going to do? When is she coming home?"

"She says she will stay with George Moore until he can leave the hospital. She has written to his people in Nova Scotia. It seems that George's only near relative is a married sister much older than himself. She was living when George sailed on the *Four Sisters*, but of course we do not know what may have happened since. Did you ever see George Moore, Miss Cornelia?"

"I did. It is all coming back to me. He was here visiting his Uncle Abner eighteen years ago, when he and Dick would be about seventeen. They were double cousins, you see. Their fathers were brothers and their mothers were twin sisters, and they did look a terrible lot alike. Of course," added Miss Cornelia scornfully, "it wasn't one of those freak resemblances you read of in novels where two people are so much alike that they can fill each other's places and their nearest and dearest can't tell between them. In those days you could tell easy enough which was George and which was Dick, if you saw them together and near at hand. Apart, or some distance away, it wasn't so easy. They played lots of tricks on people and thought it great fun, the two scamps. George Moore was a little taller and a good deal fatter than Dick—though neither of them was what you would call fat—they were both of the lean kind. Dick had higher colour than George, and his hair was a shade lighter. But their features were just alike, and they both had that queer freak of eyes—-one blue and one hazel. They weren't much alike in any other way, though. George was a real nice fellow, though he was a scalawag for mischief, and some said he had a liking for a glass even then. But everybody liked him better than Dick. He spent about a month here. Leslie never saw him; she was only about eight or nine then and I remember now that she spent that whole winter over harbour with her grandmother West. Captain Jim was away, too—that was the winter he was wrecked on the Magdalens. I don't suppose either he or Leslie had ever heard about the Nova Scotia cousin looking so much like Dick. Nobody ever thought of him when Captain Jim brought Dick—George, I should say—home. Of course, we all thought Dick had changed considerable—he'd got so lumpish and fat. But we put that down to what had happened to him, and no doubt that was the reason, for, as I've said, George wasn't fat to begin with either. And there was no other way we could have guessed, for the man's senses were clean gone. I can't see that it is any wonder we were all deceived. But it's a staggering thing. And Leslie has sacrificed the best years of her life to nursing a man who hadn't any claim on her! Oh, drat the men! No matter what they do, it's the wrong thing. And no matter who they are, it's somebody they shouldn't be. They do exasperate me."

"Gilbert and Captain Jim are men, and it is through them that the truth has been discovered at last," said Anne.

"Well, I admit that," conceded Miss Cornelia reluctantly. "I'm sorry I raked the doctor off so. It's the first time in my life I've ever felt ashamed of anything I said to a man. I don't know as I shall tell him so, though. He'll just have to take it for granted. Well, Anne, dearie, it's a mercy the Lord doesn't answer all our prayers. I've been praying hard right along that the operation wouldn't cure Dick. Of course I didn't put it just quite so plain. But that was what was in the back of my mind, and I have no doubt the Lord knew it."

"Well, He has answered the spirit of your prayer. You really wished that things shouldn't be made any harder for Leslie. I'm afraid that in my secret heart I've been hoping the operation wouldn't succeed, and I am wholesomely ashamed of it."

"How does Leslie seem to take it?"

"She writes like one dazed. I think that, like ourselves, she hardly realises it yet. She says, 'It all seems like a strange dream to me, Anne.' That is the only reference she makes to herself."

"Poor child! I suppose when the chains are struck off a prisoner he'd feel queer and lost without them for a while. Anne, dearie, there's a thought keeps coming into my mind. What about Owen Ford? We both know Leslie was fond of him. Did it ever occur to you that he was fond of her?"

"It—did—once," admitted Anne, feeling that she might say so much.

"Well, I hadn't any reason to think he was, but it just appeared to me he *must* be. Now, Anne, dearie, the Lord knows I'm not a match-maker, and I scorn all such doings. But if I were you and writing to that Ford man I'd just mention, casual-like, what has happened. That is what *I'd* do."

"Of course I will mention it when I write him," said Anne, a trifle distantly. Somehow, this was a thing she could not discuss with Miss Cornelia. And yet, she had to admit that the same thought had been lurking in her mind ever since she had heard of Leslie's freedom. But she would not desecrate it by free speech.

"Of course there is no great rush, dearie. But Dick Moore's been dead for thirteen years and Leslie has wasted enough of her life for him. We'll just see what comes of it. As for this George Moore, who's gone and come back to life when everyone thought he was dead and done for, just like a man, I'm real sorry for him. He won't seem to fit in anywhere."

"He is still a young man, and if he recovers completely, as seems likely, he will be able to make a place for himself again. It must be very strange for him, poor fellow. I suppose all these years since his accident will not exist for him."

33
Leslie Returns

A fortnight later Leslie Moore came home alone to the old house where she had spent so many bitter years. In the June twilight she went over the fields to Anne's, and appeared with ghost-like suddenness in the scented garden.

"Leslie!" cried Anne in amazement. "Where have you sprung from? We never knew you were coming. Why didn't you write? We would have met you."

"I couldn't write somehow, Anne. It seemed so futile to try to say anything with pen and ink. And I wanted to get back quietly and unobserved."

Anne put her arms about Leslie and kissed her. Leslie returned the kiss warmly. She looked pale and tired, and she gave a little sigh as she dropped down on the grasses beside a great bed of daffodils that were gleaming through the pale, silvery, twilight like golden stars. "And you have come home alone, Leslie?"

"Yes. George Moore's sister came to Montreal and took him home with her. Poor fellow, he was sorry to part with me—though I was a stranger to him when his memory first came back. He clung to me in those first hard days when he was trying to realise that Dick's death was not the thing of yesterday that it seemed to him. It was all very hard for him. I helped him all I could. When his sister came it was easier for him, because it seemed to him only the other day that he had seen her last. Fortunately she had not changed much, and that helped him, too."

"It is all so strange and wonderful, Leslie. I think we none of us realise it yet."

"I cannot. When I went into the house over there an hour ago, I felt that it *must* be a dream—that Dick must be there, with his childish smile, as he had been for so long. Anne, I seem stunned yet. I'm not glad or sorry—or *anything*. I feel as if something had been torn suddenly out of my life and left a terrible hole. I feel as if I couldn't be *I*—as if I must have changed into somebody else and couldn't get used to it. It gives me a horrible lonely, dazed, helpless feeling. It's good to see you again—it seems as if you were a sort of anchor for my drifting soul. Oh, Anne, I dread it all—the gossip and wonderment and questioning. When I think of that, I wish that I need not have come home at all. Dr. Dave was at the station when I came off the train—he brought me home. Poor old man, he feels very badly because he told me years ago that nothing could be done for Dick. 'I honestly thought so, Leslie,' he said to me today. 'But I should have told you not to depend on my opinion—I should have told you to go to a specialist. If I had, you would have been saved many bitter years, and poor George Moore many wasted ones. I blame myself very much, Leslie.' I told him not to do that—he had done what he thought right. He has always been so kind to me—I couldn't bear to see him worrying over it."

"And Dick—George, I mean? Is his memory fully restored?"

"Practically. Of course, there are a great many details he can't recall yet—but he remembers more and more every day. He went out for a walk on the evening after Dick was buried. He had Dick's money and watch on him; he meant to bring them home to me, along with my letter. He admits he went to a place where the sailors resorted—and he remembers drinking—and nothing else. Anne, I shall never forget the moment he remembered his own name. I saw him looking at me with an intelligent but puzzled expression. I said, 'Do you know me, Dick?' He answered, 'I never saw you before. Who are you? And my name is not Dick. I am George Moore, and Dick died of yellow fever yesterday! Where am I? What has happened to me?' I—I fainted, Anne. And ever since I have felt as if I were in a dream."

"You will soon adjust yourself to this new state of things, Leslie. And you are young—life is before you—you will have many beautiful years yet."

"Perhaps I shall be able to look at it in that way after awhile, Anne. Just now I feel too tired and indifferent to think about the future. I'm—I'm—Anne, I'm lonely. I miss Dick. Isn't it all very strange? Do you know, I was really fond of poor Dick—George, I suppose I should say—just as I would have been fond of a helpless child who depended on me for everything. I would never have admitted it—I was really ashamed of it—because, you see, I had hated and despised Dick so much before he went away. When I heard that Captain Jim was bringing him home I expected I would just feel the same to him. But I never did—although I continued to loathe him as I remembered him before. From the time he came home I felt only pity—a pity that hurt and wrung me. I supposed then that it was just because his accident had made him so helpless and changed. But now I believe it was because there was really a different personality there. Carlo knew it, Anne—I know now that Carlo knew it. I always thought it strange that Carlo shouldn't have known Dick. Dogs are usually so faithful. But *he* knew it was not his master who had come back, although none of the rest of us did. I had never seen George Moore, you know. I remember now that Dick once mentioned casually that he had a cousin in Nova Scotia who looked as much like him as a twin; but the thing had gone out of my memory, and in any case I would never have thought it of any importance. You see, it never occurred to me to question Dick's identity. Any change in him seemed to me just the result of the accident.

"Oh, Anne, that night in April when Gilbert told me he thought Dick might be cured! I can never forget it. It seemed to me that I had once been a prisoner in a hideous cage of torture, and then the door had been opened and I could get out. I was still chained to the cage but I was not in it. And that night I felt that a merciless hand was drawing me back into the cage—back to a torture even more terrible than it had once been. I didn't blame Gilbert. I felt he was right. And he had been very good—he said that if, in view of the expense and uncertainty of the operation, I should decide not to risk it, he would not blame me in the least. But I knew how I ought to decide—and I couldn't face it. All night I walked the floor like a mad woman, trying to compel myself to face it. I couldn't, Anne—I thought I couldn't—and when morning broke I set my teeth and resolved that I *wouldn't*. I would let things remain as they were. It was very wicked, I know. It would have been a just punishment for such wickedness if I had just been left to abide by that decision. I kept to it all day. That afternoon I had to go up to the Glen to do some shopping. It was one of Dick's quiet, drowsy days, so I left him alone. I was gone a little longer than I had expected, and he missed me. He felt lonely. And when I got home, he ran to meet me just like a child, with such a pleased smile on his face. Somehow, Anne, I just gave way then. That smile on his poor vacant face was more than I could endure. I felt as if I were denying a child the chance to grow and develop. I knew that I must give him his chance, no matter what the consequences might be. So I came over and told Gilbert. Oh, Anne, you must have thought me hateful in those weeks before I went away. I didn't mean to be—but I couldn't think of anything except what I had to do, and everything and everybody about me were like shadows."

"I know—I understood, Leslie. And now it is all over—your chain is broken—there is no cage."

"There is no cage," repeated Leslie absently, plucking at the fringing grasses with her slender, brown hands. "But—it doesn't seem as if there were anything else, Anne. You—you remember what I told you of my folly that night on the sand-bar? I find one doesn't get over being a fool very quickly. Sometimes I think there are people who are fools forever. And to be a fool—of that kind—is almost as bad as being a—a dog on a chain."

"You will feel very differently after you get over being tired and bewildered," said Anne, who, knowing a certain thing that Leslie did not know, did not feel herself called upon to waste overmuch sympathy.

Leslie laid her splendid golden head against Anne's knee.

"Anyhow, I have *you*," she said. "Life can't be altogether empty with such a friend. Anne, pat my head—just as if I were a little girl—*mother* me a bit—and let me tell you while my stubborn tongue is loosed a little just what you and your comradeship have meant to me since that night I met you on the rock shore."

34
The Ship o' Dreams Comes to Harbour

One morning, when a windy golden sunrise was billowing over the gulf in waves of light, a certain weary stork flew over the bar of Four Winds Harbour on his way from the Land of Evening Stars. Under his wing was tucked a sleepy, starry-eyed, little creature. The stork was tired, and he looked wistfully about him. He knew he was somewhere near his destination, but he could not yet see it. The big, white lighthouse on the red sandstone cliff had its good points; but no stork possessed of any gumption would leave a new, velvet baby there. An old gray house, surrounded by willows, in a blossomy brook valley, looked more promising, but did not seem quite the thing either. The staring green abode further on was manifestly out of the question. Then the stork brightened up. He had caught sight of the very place—a little white house nestled against a big, whispering fir-wood, with a spiral of blue smoke winding up from its kitchen chimney—a house which just looked as if it were meant for babies. The stork gave a sigh of satisfaction, and softly alighted on the ridge-pole.

Half an hour later Gilbert ran down the hall and tapped on the spare-room door. A drowsy voice answered him and in a moment Marilla's pale, scared face peeped out from behind the door.

"Marilla, Anne has sent me to tell you that a certain young gentleman has arrived here. He hasn't brought much luggage with him, but he evidently means to stay."

"For pity's sake!" said Marilla blankly. "You don't mean to tell me, Gilbert, that it's all over. Why wasn't I called?"

"Anne wouldn't let us disturb you when there was no need. Nobody was called until about two hours ago. There was no 'passage perilous' this time."

"And—and—Gilbert—will this baby live?"

"He certainly will. He weighs ten pounds and—why, listen to him. Nothing wrong with his lungs, is there? The nurse says his hair will be red. Anne is furious with her, and I'm tickled to death."

That was a wonderful day in the little house of dreams.

"The best dream of all has come true," said Anne, pale and rapturous. "Oh, Marilla, I hardly dare believe it, after that horrible day last summer. I have had a heartache ever since then—but it is gone now."

"This baby will take Joy's place," said Marilla.

"Oh, no, no, *no*, Marilla. He can't—nothing can ever do that. He has his own place, my dear, wee man-child. But little Joy has hers, and always will have it. If she had lived she would have been over a year old. She would have been toddling around on her tiny feet and lisping a few words. I can see her so plainly, Marilla. Oh, I know now that Captain Jim was right when he said God would manage better than that my baby would seem a stranger to me when I found her Beyond. I've learned *that* this past year. I've followed her development day by day and week by week—I always shall. I shall know just how she grows from year to year—and when I meet her again I'll know her—she won't be a stranger. Oh, Marilla, *look* at his dear, darling toes! Isn't it strange they should be so perfect?"

"It would be stranger if they weren't," said Marilla crisply. Now that all was safely over, Marilla was herself again.

"Oh, I know—but it seems as if they couldn't be quite *finished*, you know—and they are, even to the tiny nails. And his hands—*just* look at his hands, Marilla."

"They appear to be a good deal like hands," Marilla conceded.

"See how he clings to my finger. I'm sure he knows me already. He cries when the nurse takes him away. Oh, Marilla, do you think—you don't think, do you— that his hair is going to be red?"

"I don't see much hair of any colour," said Marilla. "I wouldn't worry about it, if I were you, until it becomes visible."

"Marilla, he *has* hair—look at that fine little down all over his head. Anyway, nurse says his eyes will be hazel and his forehead is exactly like Gilbert's."

"And he has the nicest little ears, Mrs. Doctor, dear." said Susan. "The first thing I did was to look at his ears. Hair is deceitful and noses and eyes change, and you cannot tell what is going to come of them, but ears is ears from start to finish, and you always know where you are with them. Just look at their shape—and they are set right back against his precious head. You will never need to be ashamed of his ears, Mrs. Doctor, dear."

Anne's convalescence was rapid and happy. Folks came and worshipped the baby, as people have bowed before the kingship of the new-born since long before the Wise Men of the East knelt in homage to the Royal Babe of the Bethlehem manger. Leslie, slowly finding herself amid the new conditions of her life, hovered over it, like a beautiful, golden-crowned Madonna. Miss Cornelia nursed it as knackily as could any mother in Israel. Captain Jim held the small creature in his big brown hands and gazed tenderly at it, with eyes that saw the children who had never been born to him.

"What are you going to call him?" asked Miss Cornelia.

"Anne has settled his name," answered Gilbert.

"James Matthew—after the two finest gentlemen I've ever known—not even saving your presence," said Anne with a saucy glance at Gilbert.

Gilbert smiled.

"I never knew Matthew very well; he was so shy we boys couldn't get acquainted with him—but I quite agree with you that Captain Jim is one of the rarest and finest souls God ever clothed in clay. He is so delighted over the fact that we have given his name to our small lad. It seems he has no other namesake."

"Well, James Matthew is a name that will wear well and not fade in the washing," said Miss Cornelia. "I'm glad you didn't load him down with some high-falutin, romantic name that he'd be ashamed of when he gets to be a grandfather. Mrs. William Drew at the Glen has called her baby Bertie Shakespeare. Quite a combination, isn't it? And I'm glad you haven't had much trouble picking on a name. Some folks have an awful time. When the Stanley Flaggs' first boy was born there was so much rivalry as to who the child should be named for that the poor little soul had to go for two years without a name. Then a brother came along and there it was—'Big Baby' and 'Little Baby.' Finally they called Big Baby Peter and Little Baby Isaac, after the two grandfathers, and had them both christened together. And each tried to see if it couldn't howl the other down. You know that Highland Scotch family of MacNabs back of the Glen? They've got twelve boys and the oldest and the youngest are both called Neil—Big Neil and Little Neil in the same family. Well, I s'pose they ran out of names."

"I have read somewhere," laughed Anne, "that the first child is a poem but the tenth is very prosy prose. Perhaps Mrs. MacNab thought that the twelfth was merely an old tale re-told."

"Well, there's something to be said for large families," said Miss Cornelia, with a sigh. "I was an only child for eight years and I did long for a brother and sister. Mother told me to pray for one—and pray I did, believe *me*. Well, one day Aunt Nellie came to me and said, 'Cornelia, there is a little brother for you upstairs in your ma's room. You can go up and see him.' I was so excited and delighted I just flew upstairs. And old Mrs. Flagg lifted up the baby for me to see. Lord, Anne, dearie, I never was so disappointed in my life. You see, I'd been praying for a *brother two years older than myself*."

"How long did it take you to get over your disappointment?" asked Anne, amid her laughter.

"Well, I had a spite at Providence for a good spell, and for weeks I wouldn't even look at the baby. Nobody knew why, for I never told. Then he began to get real cute, and held out his wee hands to me and I began to get fond of him. But I didn't get really reconciled to him until one day a school chum came to see him and said she thought he was awful small for his age. I just got boiling mad, and I sailed right into her, and told her she didn't know a nice baby when she saw one, and ours was the nicest baby in the world. And after that I just worshipped him. Mother died before he was three years old and I was sister and mother to him both. Poor little lad, he was never strong, and he died when he wasn't much over twenty. Seems to me I'd have given anything on earth, Anne, dearie, if he'd only lived."

Miss Cornelia sighed. Gilbert had gone down and Leslie, who had been crooning over the small James Matthew in the dormer window, laid him asleep in his basket and went her way. As soon as she was safely out of earshot, Miss Cornelia bent forward and said in a conspirator's whisper:

"Anne, dearie, I'd a letter from Owen Ford yesterday. He's in Vancouver just now, but he wants to know if I can board him for a month later on. *You* know what that means. Well, I hope we're doing right."

"We've nothing to do with it—we couldn't prevent him from coming to Four Winds if he wanted to," said Anne quickly. She did not like the feeling of match-making Miss Cornelia's whispers gave her; and then she weakly succumbed herself.

"Don't let Leslie know he is coming until he is here," she said. "If she found out I feel sure she would go away at once. She intends to go in the fall anyhow—she told me so the other day. She is going to Montreal to take up nursing and make what she can of her life."

'Oh, well, Anne, dearie," said Miss Cornelia, nodding sagely, "that is all as it may be. You and I have done our part. We must leave the rest to Higher Hands."

35
Politics at Four Winds

When Anne came downstairs again, the Island, as well as all Canada, was in the throes of a campaign preceding a general election. Gilbert, who was an ardent Conservative, found himself caught in the vortex, being much in demand for speech-making at the various country rallies. Miss Cornelia did not approve of his mixing up in politics and told Anne so.

"Dr. Dave never did it. Dr. Blythe will find he is making a mistake, believe *me*. Politics is something no decent man should meddle with."

"Is the government of the country to be left solely to the rogues then?" asked Anne.

"Yes—so long as it's Conservative rogues," said Miss Cornelia, marching off with the honours of war. "Men and politicians are all tarred with the same brush. The Grits have it laid on thicker than the Conservatives, that's all—*considerably* thicker. But Grit or Tory, my advice to Dr. Blythe is to steer clear of politics. First thing you know, he'll be running an election himself, and going off to Ottawa for half the year and leaving his practice to go to the dogs."

"Ah, well, let's not borrow trouble," said Anne. "The rate of interest is too high. Instead, let's look at Little Jem. It should be spelled with a G. Isn't he perfectly beautiful? Just see the dimples in his elbows. We'll bring him up to be a good Conservative, you and I, Miss Cornelia."

"Bring him up to be a good man," said Miss Cornelia. "They're scarce and valuable; though, mind you, I wouldn't like to see him a Grit. As for the election, you and I may be thankful we don't live over harbour. The air there is blue these days. Every Elliott and Crawford and MacAllister is on the warpath, loaded for bear. This side is peaceful and calm, seeing there's so few men. Captain Jim's a Grit, but it's my opinion he's ashamed of it, for he never talks politics. There isn't any earthly doubt that the Conservatives will be returned with a big majority again."

Miss Cornelia was mistaken. On the morning after the election Captain Jim dropped in at the little house to tell the news. So virulent is the microbe of party politics, even in a peaceable old man, that Captain Jim's cheeks were flushed and his eyes were flashing with all his old-time fire.

"Mistress Blythe, the Liberals are in with a sweeping majority. After eighteen years of Tory mismanagement this down-trodden country is going to have a chance at last."

"I never heard you make such a bitter partisan speech before, Captain Jim. I didn't think you had so much political venom in you," laughed Anne, who was not much excited over the tidings. Little Jem had said "Wow-ga" that morning. What were principalities and powers, the rise and fall of dynasties, the overthrow of Grit or Tory, compared with that miraculous occurrence?

"It's been accumulating for a long while," said Captain Jim, with a deprecating smile. "I thought I was only a moderate Grit, but when the news came that we were in I found out how Gritty I really was."

"You know the doctor and I are Conservatives."

"Ah, well, it's the only bad thing I know of either of you, Mistress Blythe. Cornelia is a Tory, too. I called in on my way from the Glen to tell her the news."

"Didn't you know you took your life in your hands?"

"Yes, but I couldn't resist the temptation."

"How did she take it?"

"Comparatively calm, Mistress Blythe, comparatively calm. She says, says she, 'Well, Providence sends seasons of humiliation to a country, same as to individuals. You Grits have been cold and hungry for many a year. Make haste to get warmed and fed, for you won't be in long.' 'Well, now, Cornelia,' I says, 'mebbe Providence thinks Canada needs a real long spell of humiliation.' Ah, Susan, have *you* heard the news? The Liberals are in."

Susan had just come in from the kitchen, attended by the odour of delectable dishes which always seemed to hover around her.

"Now, are they?" she said, with beautiful unconcern. "Well, I never could see but that my bread rose just as light when Grits were in as when they were not. And if any party, Mrs. Doctor, dear, will make it rain before the week is out, and save our kitchen garden from entire ruination, that is the party Susan will vote for. In the meantime, will you just step out and give me your opinion on the meat for dinner? I am fearing that it is very tough, and I think that we had better change our butcher as well as our government."

One evening, a week later, Anne walked down to the Point, to see if she could get some fresh fish from Captain Jim, leaving Little Jem for the first time. It was quite a tragedy. Suppose he cried? Suppose Susan did not know just exactly what to do for him? Susan was calm and serene.

"I have had as much experience with him as you, Mrs. Doctor, dear, have I not?"

"Yes, with him—but not with other babies. Why, I looked after three pairs of twins, when I was a child, Susan. When they cried, I gave them peppermint or castor oil quite coolly. It's quite curious now to recall how lightly I took all those babies and their woes."

"Oh, well, if Little Jem cries, I will just clap a hot water bag on his little stomach," said Susan.

"Not too hot, you know," said Anne anxiously. Oh, was it really wise to go?

"Do not you fret, Mrs. Doctor, dear. Susan is not the woman to burn a wee man. Bless him, he has no notion of crying."

Anne tore herself away finally and enjoyed her walk to the Point after all, through the long shadows of the sun-setting. Captain Jim was not in the living room of the lighthouse, but another man was—a handsome, middle-aged man, with a strong, clean-shaven chin, who was unknown to Anne. Nevertheless, when she sat down, he began to talk to her with all the assurance of an old acquaintance. There was nothing amiss in what he said or the way he said it, but Anne rather resented such a cool taking-for-granted in a complete stranger. Her replies were frosty, and as few as decency required. Nothing daunted, her companion talked on for several minutes, then excused himself and went away. Anne could have sworn there was a twinkle in his eye and it annoyed her. Who was the creature? There was something vaguely familiar about him but she was certain she had never seen him before.

"Captain Jim, who was that who just went out?" she asked, as Captain Jim came in.

"Marshall Elliott," answered the captain.

"Marshall Elliott!" cried Anne. "Oh, Captain Jim—it wasn't—yes, it *was* his voice—oh, Captain Jim, I didn't know him—and I was quite insulting to him! *Why* didn't he tell me? He must have seen I didn't know him."

"He wouldn't say a word about it—he'd just enjoy the joke. Don't worry over snubbing him—he'll think it fun. Yes, Marshall's shaved off his beard at last and cut his hair. His party is in, you know. I didn't know him myself first time I saw him. He was up in Carter Flagg's store at the Glen the night after election day, along with a crowd of others, waiting for the news. About twelve the 'phone came through—the Liberals were in. Marshall just got up and walked out—he didn't cheer or shout—he left the others to do that, and they nearly lifted the roof off Carter's store, I reckon. Of course, all the Tories were over in Raymond Russell's store. Not much cheering *there*. Marshall went straight down the street to the side door of Augustus Palmer's barber shop. Augustus was in bed asleep, but Marshall hammered on the door until he got up and come down, wanting to know what all the racket was about.

"'Come into your shop and do the best job you ever did in your life, Gus,' said Marshall. "The Liberals are in and you're going to barber a good Grit before the sun rises.'

"Gus was mad as hops—partly because he'd been dragged out of bed, but more because he's a Tory. He vowed he wouldn't shave any man after twelve at night.

"'You'll do what I want you to do, sonny,' said Marshall, 'or I'll jest turn you over my knee and give you one of those spankings your mother forgot.'

"He'd have done it, too, and Gus knew it, for Marshall is as strong as an ox and Gus is only a midget of a man. So he gave in and towed Marshall in to the shop and went to work. 'Now,' says he, 'I'll barber you up, but if you say one word to me about the Grits getting in while I'm doing it I'll cut your throat with this razor,' says he. You wouldn't have thought mild little Gus could be so bloodthirsty, would you? Shows what party politics will do for a man. Marshall kept quiet and got his hair and beard disposed of and went home. When his old housekeeper heard him come upstairs she peeked out of her bedroom door to see whether 'twas him or the hired boy. And when she saw a strange man striding down the hall with a candle in his hand she screamed blue murder and fainted dead away. They had to send for the doctor before they could bring her to, and it was several days before she could look at Marshall without shaking all over."

Captain Jim had no fish. He seldom went out in his boat that summer, and his long tramping expeditions were over. He spent a great deal of his time sitting by his seaward window, looking out over the gulf, with his swiftly-whitening head leaning on his hand. He sat there to-night for many silent minutes, keeping some trysts with the past which Anne would not disturb. Presently he pointed to the iris of the West:

"That's beautiful, isn't it, Mistress Blythe? But I wish you could have seen the sunrise this morning. It was a wonderful thing—wonderful. I've seen all kinds of sunrises come over that gulf. I've been all over the world, Mistress Blythe, and take it all in all, I've never seen a finer sight than a summer sunrise over the gulf. A man can't pick his time for dying, Mistress Blythe—jest got to go when the Great Captain gives His sailing orders. But if I could I'd go out when the morning comes across that water.

I've watched it many a time and thought what a thing it would be to pass out through that great white glory to whatever was waiting beyant, on a sea that ain't mapped out on any airthly chart. I think, Mistress Blythe, that I'd find lost Margaret there."

Captain Jim had often talked to Anne of lost Margaret since he had told her the old story. His love for her trembled in every tone—-that love that had never grown faint or forgetful.

"Anyway, I hope when my time comes I'll go quick and easy. I don't think I'm a coward, Mistress Blythe—I've looked an ugly death in the face more than once without blenching. But the thought of a lingering death does give me a queer, sick feeling of horror."

"Don't talk about leaving us, dear, *dear* Captain Jim," pleaded Anne, in a choked voice, patting the old brown hand, once so strong, but now grown very feeble. "What would we do without you?"

Captain Jim smiled beautifully.

"Oh, you'd get along nicely—nicely—but you wouldn't forget the old man altogether, Mistress Blythe—no, I don't think you'll ever quite forget him. The race of Joseph always remembers one another. But it'll be a memory that won't hurt—I like to think that my memory won't hurt my friends—it'll always be kind of pleasant to them, I hope and believe. It won't be very long now before lost Margaret calls me, for the last time. I'll be all ready to answer. I jest spoke of this because there's a little favour I want to ask of you. Here's the poor old Matey of mine"—Captain Him reached out a hand and poked the big, warm, velvety, golden ball of the sofa. The First Mate uncoiled himself like a spring with a nice, throaty, comfortable sound, half purr, half meow, stretched his paws in the air, turned over and coiled himself up again.He'l miss me when I start on the Long V'yage. I can't bear to hink of leaving the poor critter to starve, like he was left before. If anything happens to me will you give Matey a bite and a corner, Mistress Blythe?"

"Indeed I will."

"Then that is all I had on my mind. Your little Jem is to have a few curious things I picked up—I've seen to that. And now I don't like to seee tears in those pretty eyes, Mistress Blythe. I'll mebbe hang on for a quite a spell yet. I heard you reading a piece of petry one day last winter—one of Tennyson's pieces. I'd sorter like to hear it again, if you could recite it for me."

Softly and clearly, while the seawind blew in on them, Anne repeated the beautiful lines of Tennyson's wonderful swan song—"Crossing the Bar." The old captain kept time gently with his sinewy hand.

"Yes, yes, Mistress Blythe," he said, when she had finished, "that's it, that's it. He wasn't a sailor, you tell me—I dunno how he could have put an old sailor's feelings into words like that, if he wasn't one. He didn't want any 'sadness o' farewells' and neither do I Mistress Blythe—for all will be well with me and mine beyant the bar."

36
Beauty for Ashes

"Any news from Green Gables, Anne?"

"Nothing very especial," replied Anne, folding up Marilla's letter. "Jack Donnell has been there shingling the roof. He is a full-fledged carpenter now, so it seems he has had his own way in regard to the choice of a life-work. You remember his mother wanted him to be a college professor. I shall never forget the day she came to the school and rated me for failing to call him St. Clair."

"Does anyone ever call him that now?"

"Evidently not. It seems that he has completely lived it down. Even his mother has succumbed. I always thought that a boy with Jake's chin and mouth would get his own way in the end. Diana writes me that Dora has a beau. Just think of it—that child!"

"Dora is seventeen," said Gilbert. "Charlie Sloane and I were both mad about you when you were seventeen, Anne."

"Really, Gilbert, we must be getting on in years," said Anne, with a half-rueful smile, "when children who were six when we thought ourselves grown up are old enough now to have beaux. Dora's is Ralph Andrews—Jane's brother. I remember him as a little, round, fat, white-headed fellow who was always at the foot of his class. But I understand he is quite a fine-looking young man now."

"Dora will probably marry young. She's of the same type as Charlotta the Fourth—she'll never miss her first chance for fear she might not get another."

"Well, if she marries Ralph I hope he will be a little more up-and-coming than his brother Billy," mused Anne.

"For instance," said Gilbert, laughing, "let us hope he will be able to propose on his own account. Anne, would you have married Billy if he had asked you himself, instead of getting Jane to do it for him?"

"I might have." Anne went off into a shriek of laughter over the recollection of her first proposal. "The shock of the whole thing might have hypnotised me into some rash and foolish act. Let us be thankful he did it by proxy."

"I had a letter from George Moore yesterday," said Leslie, from the corner where she was reading.

"Oh, how is he?" asked Anne interestedly, yet with an unreal feeling that she was inquiring about some one whom she did not know.

"He is well, but he finds it very hard to adapt himself to all the changes in his old home and friends. He is going to sea again in the spring. It's in his blood, he says, and he longs for it. But he told me something that made me glad for him, poor fellow. Before he sailed on the *Four Sisters* he was engaged to a girl at home. He did not tell me anything about her in Montreal, because he said he supposed she would have forgotten him and married someone else long ago, and with him, you see, his engagement and love was still a thing of the present. It was pretty hard on him, but when he got home he found she had never married and still cared for him. They are to be married this fall. I'm going to ask him to bring her over here for a little trip; he says he wants to come and see the place where he lived so many years without knowing it."

"What a nice little romance," said Anne, whose love for the romantic was immortal. "And to think," she added with a sigh of self-reproach, "that if I had had my way George Moore would never have come up from the grave in which his identity was buried. How I did fight against Gilbert's suggestion! Well, I am punished: I shall never be able to have a different opinion from Gilbert's again! If I try to have, he will squelch me by casting George Moore's case up to me!"

"As if even that would squelch a woman!" mocked Gilbert. "At least do not become my echo, Anne. A little opposition gives spice to life. I do not want a wife like John MacAllister's over the harbour. No matter what he says, she at once remarks in that drab, lifeless little voice of hers, 'That is very true, John, dear me!'"

Anne and Leslie laughed. Anne's laughter was silver and Leslie's golden, and the combination of the two was as satisfactory as a perfect chord in music.

Susan, coming in on the heels of the laughter, echoed it with a resounding sigh.

"Why, Susan, what is the matter?" asked Gilbert.

"There's nothing wrong with Little Jem, is there, Susan?" cried Anne, starting up in alarm.

"No, no, calm yourself, Mrs. Doctor, dear. Something has happened, though. Dear me, everything has gone catawampus with me this week. I spoiled the bread as you know too well—and I scorched the doctor's best shirt bosom—and I broke your big platter. And now, on the top of all this, comes word that my sister Matilda has broken her leg and wants me to go and stay with her for a spell."

"Oh, I'm very sorry—sorry that your sister has met with such an accident, I mean," exclaimed Anne.

"Ah, well, man was made to mourn, Mrs. Doctor, dear. That sounds as if it ought to be in the Bible, but they tell me a person named Burns wrote it. And there is no doubt that we are born to trouble as the sparks fly upward. As for Matilda, I do not know what to think of her. None of our family ever broke their legs before. But whatever she has done she is still my sister, and I feel that it is my duty to go and wait on her, if you can spare me for a few weeks, Mrs. Doctor, dear."

"Of course, Susan, of course. I can get someone to help me while you are gone."

"If you cannot I will not go, Mrs. Doctor, dear, Matilda's leg to the contrary notwithstanding. I will not have you worried, and that blessed child upset in consequence, for any number of legs."

"Oh, you must go to your sister at once, Susan. I can get a girl from the cove, who will do for a time."

"Anne, will you let me come and stay with you while Susan is away?" exclaimed Leslie. "Do! I'd love to—and it would be an act of charity on your part. I'm so horribly lonely over there in that big barn of a house. There's so little to do—and at night I'm worse than lonely—I'm frightened and nervous in spite of locked doors. There was a tramp around two days ago."

Anne joyfully agreed, and next day Leslie was installed as an inmate of the little house of dreams. Miss Cornelia warmly approved of the arrangement.

"It seems Providential," she told Anne in confidence. "I'm sorry for Matilda Clow, but since she had to break her leg it couldn't have happened at a better time. Leslie will be here while Owen Ford is in Four Winds, and those old cats up at the Glen won't get the chance to meow, as they would if she was living over there alone and Owen going to see her. They are doing enough of it as it is, because she doesn't put on mourning. I said to one of them, 'If you mean she should put on mourning for George Moore, it seems to me more like his resurrection than his funeral; and if it's Dick you mean, I confess *I* can't see the propriety of going into weeds for a man who died thirteen years ago and good riddance then!' And when old Louisa Baldwin remarked to me that she thought it very strange that Leslie should never have suspected it wasn't her own husband *I* said, '*You* never suspected it wasn't Dick Moore, and you were next-door neighbour to him all his life, and by nature you're ten times as suspicious as Leslie.' But you can't stop people's tongues, Anne, dearie, and I'm real thankful Leslie will be under your roof while Owen is courting her."

Owen Ford came to the little house one August evening when Leslie and Anne were absorbed in worshipping the baby. He paused at the open door of the living room, unseen by the two within, gazing with greedy eyes at the beautiful picture. Leslie sat on the floor with the baby in her lap, making ecstatic dabs at his fat little hands as he fluttered them in the air.

"Oh, you dear, beautiful beloved baby," she mumbled, catching one wee hand and covering it with kisses.

"Isn't him ze darlingest itty sing," crooned Anne, hanging over the arm of her chair adoringly. "Dem itty wee pads are ze very tweetest handies in ze whole big world, isn't dey, you darling itty man."

Anne, in the months before Little Jem's coming, had pored diligently over several wise volumes, and pinned her faith to one in especial, "Sir Oracle on the Care and Training of Children." Sir Oracle implored parents by all they held sacred never to talk "baby talk" to their children. Infants should invariably be addressed in classical language from the moment of their birth. So should they learn to speak English undefiled from their earliest utterance. "How," demanded Sir Oracle, "can a mother reasonably expect her child to learn correct speech, when she continually accustoms its impressionable gray matter to such absurd expressions and distortions of our noble tongue as thoughtless mothers inflict every day on the helpless creatures committed to their care? Can a child who is constantly called 'tweet itty wee singie' ever attain to any proper conception of his own being and possibilities and destiny?"

Anne was vastly impressed with this, and informed Gilbert that she meant to make it an inflexible rule never, under any circumstances, to talk "baby talk" to her children. Gilbert agreed with her, and they made a solemn compact on the subject—a compact which Anne shamelessly violated the very first moment Little Jem was laid in her arms. "Oh, the darling itty wee sing!" she had exclaimed. And she had continued to violate it ever since. When Gilbert teased her she laughed Sir Oracle to scorn.

"He never had any children of his own, Gilbert—I am positive he hadn't or he would never have written such rubbish. You just can't help talking baby talk to a baby. It comes natural—and it's *right*. It would be inhuman to talk to those tiny, soft, velvety little creatures as we do to great big boys and girls. Babies want love and cuddling and all the sweet baby talk they can get, and Little Jem is going to have it, bless his dear itty heartums."

"But you're the worst I ever heard, Anne," protested Gilbert, who, not being a mother but only a father, was not wholly convinced yet that Sir Oracle was wrong. "I never heard anything like the way you talk to that child."

"Very likely you never did. Go away—go away. Didn't I bring up three pairs of Hammond twins before I was eleven? You and

Sir Oracle are nothing but coldblooded theorists. Gilbert, *just* look at him! He's smiling at me—he knows what we're talking about. And oo dest agwees wif evy word muzzer says, don't oo, angel-lover?"

Gilbert put his arm about them. "Oh, you mothers!" he said. "You mothers! God knew what He was about when He made you."

So Little Jem was talked to and loved and cuddled: and he throve as became a child of the house of dreams. Leslie was quite as foolish over him as Anne was. When their work was done and Gilbert was out of the way, they gave themselves over to shameless orgies of lovemaking and ecstasies of adoration, such as that in which Owen Ford had surprised them.

Leslie was the first to become aware of him. Even in the twilight Anne could see the sudden whiteness that swept over her beautiful face, blotting out the crimson of lip and cheeks.

Owen came forward, eagerly, blind for a moment to Anne.

"Leslie!" he said, holding out his hand. It was the first time he had ever called her by her name; but the hand Leslie gave him was cold; and she was very quiet all the evening, while Anne and Gilbert and Owen laughed and talked together. Before his call ended she excused herself and went upstairs. Owen's gay spirits flagged and he went away soon after with a downcast air.

Gilbert looked at Anne.

"Anne, what are you up to? There's something going on that I don't understand. The whole air here to-night has been charged with electricity. Leslie sits like the muse of tragedy; Owen Ford jokes and laughs on the surface, and watches Leslie with the eyes of his soul. You seem all the time to be bursting with some suppressed excitement. Own up. What secret have you been keeping from your deceived husband?"

"Don't be a goose, Gilbert," was Anne's conjugal reply. "As for Leslie, she is absurd and I'm going up to tell her so."

Anne found Leslie at the dormer window of her room. The little place was filled with the rhythmic thunder of the sea. Leslie sat with locked hands in the misty moonshine—a beautiful, accusing presence.

"Anne," she said in a low, reproachful voice, "did you know Owen Ford was coming to Four Winds?"

"I did," said Anne brazenly.

"Oh, you should have told me, Anne," Leslie cried passionately. "If I had known I would have gone away—I wouldn't have stayed here to meet him. You should have told me. It wasn't fair of you, Anne—oh, it wasn't fair!"

Leslie's lips were trembling and her whole form was tense with emotion. But Anne laughed heartlessly. She bent over and kissed Leslie's upturned, reproachful face.

"Leslie, you are an adorable goose. Owen Ford didn't rush from the Pacific to the Atlantic from a burning desire to see *me*. Neither do I believe that he was inspired by any wild and frenzied passion for Miss Cornelia. Take off your tragic airs, my dear friend, and fold them up and put them away in lavender. You'll never need them again. There are some people who can see through a grindstone when there is a hole in it, even if you cannot. I am not a prophetess, but I shall venture on a prediction. The bitterness of life is over for you. After this you are going to have the joys and hopes—and I daresay the sorrows, too—of a happy woman. The omen of the shadow of Venus did come true for you, Leslie. The year in which you saw it brought your life's best gift for you—your love for Owen Ford. Now, go right to bed and have a good sleep."

Leslie obeyed orders in so far that she went to bed: but it may be questioned if she slept much. I do not think she dared to dream wakingly; life had been so hard for this poor Leslie, the path on which she had had to walk had been so straight, that she could not whisper to her own heart the hopes that might wait on the future. But she watched the great revolving light bestarring the short hours of the summer night, and her eyes grew soft and bright and young once more. Nor, when Owen Ford came next day, to ask her to go with him to the shore, did she say him nay.

37

Miss Cornelia Makes a Startling Announcement

Miss Cornelia sailed down to the little house one drowsy afternoon, when the gulf was the faint, bleached blue of hot August seas, and the orange lilies at the gate of Anne's garden held up their imperial cups to be filled with the molten gold of August sunshine. Not that Miss Cornelia concerned herself with painted oceans or sun-thirsty lilies. She sat in her favourite rocker in unusual idleness. She sewed not, neither did she spin. Nor did she say a single derogatory word concerning any portion of mankind. In short, Miss Cornelia's conversation was singularly devoid of spice that day, and Gilbert, who had stayed home to listen to her, instead of going a-fishing, as he had intended, felt himself aggrieved. What had come over Miss Cornelia? She did not look cast down or worried. On the contrary, there was a certain air of nervous exultation about her.

"Where is Leslie?" she asked—not as if it mattered much either.

"Owen and she went raspberrying in the woods back of her farm," answered Anne. "They won't be back before supper time—if then."

"They don't seem to have any idea that there is such a thing as a clock," said Gilbert. "I can't get to the bottom of that affair. I'm certain you women pulled strings. But Anne, undutiful wife, won't tell me. Will you, Miss Cornelia?"

"No, I shall not. But," said Miss Cornelia, with the air of one determined to take the plunge and have it over, "I will tell you something else. I came today on purpose to tell it. I am going to be married."

Anne and Gilbert were silent. If Miss Cornelia had announced her intention of going out to the channel and drowning herself the thing might have been believable. This was not. So they waited. Of course Miss Cornelia had made a mistake.

"Well, you both look sort of kerflummexed," said Miss Cornelia, with a twinkle in her eyes. Now that the awkward moment of revelation was over, Miss Cornelia was her own woman again. "Do you think I'm too young and inexperienced for matrimony?"

"You know—it *is* rather staggering," said Gilbert, trying to gather his wits together. "I've heard you say a score of times that you wouldn't marry the best man in the world."

"I'm not going to marry the best man in the world," retorted Miss Cornelia. "Marshall Elliott is a long way from being the best."

"Are you going to marry Marshall Elliott?" exclaimed Anne, recovering her power of speech under this second shock.

"Yes. I could have had him any time these twenty years if I'd lifted my finger. But do you suppose I was going to walk into church beside a perambulating haystack like that?"

"I am sure we are very glad—and we wish you all possible happiness," said Anne, very flatly and inadequately, as she felt. She was not prepared for such an occasion. She had never imagined herself offering betrothal felicitations to Miss Cornelia.

"Thanks, I knew you would," said Miss Cornelia. "You are the first of my friends to know it."

"We shall be so sorry to lose you, though, dear Miss Cornelia," said Anne, beginning to be a little sad and sentimental.

"Oh, you won't lose me," said Miss Cornelia unsentimentally. "You don't suppose I would live over harbour with all those MacAllisters and Elliotts and Crawfords, do you? 'From the conceit of the Elliotts, the pride of the MacAllisters and the vain-glory of the Crawfords, good Lord deliver us.' Marshall is coming to live at my place. I'm sick and tired of hired men. That Jim Hastings I've got this summer is positively the worst of the species. He would drive anyone to getting married. What do you think? He upset the churn yesterday and spilled a big churning of cream over the yard. And not one whit concerned about it was he! Just gave a foolish laugh and said cream was good for the land. Wasn't that like a man? I told him I wasn't in the habit of fertilising my back yard with cream."

"Well, I wish you all manner of happiness too, Miss Cornelia," said Gilbert, solemnly; "but," he added, unable to resist the temptation to tease Miss Cornelia, despite Anne's imploring eyes, "I fear your day of independence is done. As you know, Marshall Elliott is a very determined man."

"I like a man who can stick to a thing," retorted Miss Cornelia. "Amos Grant, who used to be after me long ago, couldn't. You never saw such a weather-vane. He jumped into the pond to drown himself once and then changed his mind and swum out again. Wasn't that like a man? Marshall would have stuck to it and drowned."

"And he has a bit of a temper, they tell me," persisted Gilbert.

"He wouldn't be an Elliott if he hadn't. I'm thankful he has. It will be real fun to make him mad. And you can generally do something with a tempery man when it comes to repenting time. But you can't do anything with a man who just keeps placid and aggravating."

"You know he's a Grit, Miss Cornelia."

"Yes, he *is*," admitted Miss Cornelia rather sadly. "And of course there is no hope of making a Conservative of him. But at least he is a Presbyterian. So I suppose I shall have to be satisfied with that."

"Would you marry him if he were a Methodist, Miss Cornelia?"

"No, I would not. Politics is for this world, but religion is for both."

"And you may be a 'relict' after all, Miss Cornelia."

"Not I. Marshall will live me out. The Elliotts are long-lived, and the Bryants are not."

"When are you to be married?" asked Anne.

"In about a month's time. My wedding dress is to be navy blue silk. And I want to ask you, Anne, dearie, if you think it would be all right to wear a veil with a navy blue dress. I've always thought I'd like to wear a veil if I ever got married. Marshall says to have it if I want to. Isn't that like a man?"

"Why shouldn't you wear it if you want to?" asked Anne.

"Well, one doesn't want to be different from other people," said Miss Cornelia, who was not noticeably like anyone else on the face of the earth. "As I say, I do fancy a veil. But maybe it shouldn't be worn with any dress but a white one. Please tell me, Anne, dearie, what you really think. I'll go by your advice."

"I don't think veils are usually worn with any but white dresses," admitted Anne, "but that is merely a convention; and I am like Mr. Elliott, Miss Cornelia. I don't see any good reason why you shouldn't have a veil if you want one."

But Miss Cornelia, who made her calls in calico wrappers, shook her head.

"If it isn't the proper thing I won't wear it," she said, with a sigh of regret for a lost dream.

"Since you are determined to be married, Miss Cornelia," said Gilbert solemnly, "I shall give you the excellent rules for the management of a husband which my grandmother gave my mother when she married my father."

"Well, I reckon I can manage Marshall Elliott," said Miss Cornelia placidly. "But let us hear your rules."

"The first one is, catch him."

"He's caught. Go on."

"The second one is, feed him well."

"With enough pie. What next?"

"The third and fourth are—keep your eye on him."

"I believe you," said Miss Cornelia emphatically.

38
Red Roses

The garden of the little house was a haunt beloved of bees and reddened by late roses that August. The little house folk lived much in it, and were given to taking picnic suppers in the grassy corner beyond the brook and sitting about in it through the twilights when great night moths sailed athwart the velvet gloom. One evening Owen Ford found Leslie alone in it. Anne and Gilbert were away, and Susan, who was expected back that night, had not yet returned.

The northern sky was amber and pale green over the fir tops. The air was cool, for August was nearing September, and Leslie wore a crimson scarf over her white dress. Together they wandered through the little, friendly, flower-crowded paths in silence. Owen must go soon. His holiday was nearly over. Leslie found her heart beating wildly. She knew that this beloved garden was to be the scene of the binding words that must seal their as yet unworded understanding.

"Some evenings a strange odour blows down the air of this garden, like a phantom perfume," said Owen. "I have never been able to discover from just what flower it comes. It is elusive and haunting and wonderfully sweet. I like to fancy it is the soul of Grandmother Selwyn passing on a little visit to the old spot she loved so well. There should be a lot of friendly ghosts about this little old house."

"I have lived under its roof only a month," said Leslie, "but I love it as I never loved the house over there where I have lived all my life."

"This house was builded and consecrated by love," said Owen. "Such houses *must* exert an influence over those who live in them. And this garden—it is over sixty years old and the history of a thousand hopes and joys is written in its blossoms. Some of those flowers were actually set out by the schoolmaster's bride, and she has been dead for thirty years. Yet they bloom on every summer. Look at those red roses, Leslie—how they queen it over everything else!"

"I love the red roses," said Leslie. "Anne likes the pink ones best, and Gilbert likes the white. But I want the crimson ones. They satisfy some craving in me as no other flower does."

"These roses are very late—they bloom after all the others have gone—and they hold all the warmth and soul of the summer come to fruition," said Owen, plucking some of the glowing, half-opened buds. "The rose is the flower of love—the world has acclaimed it so for centuries. The pink roses are love hopeful and expectant—the white roses are love dead or forsaken—but the red roses—ah, Leslie, what are the red roses?"

"Love triumphant," said Leslie in a low voice.

"Yes—love triumphant and perfect. Leslie, you know—you understand. I have loved you from the first. And I *know* you love me—I don't need to ask you. But I want to hear you say it—my darling—my darling!"

Leslie said something in a very low and tremulous voice. Their hands and lips met; it was life's supreme moment for them and as they stood there in the old garden, with its many years of love and delight and sorrow and glory, he crowned her shining hair with the red, red rose of a love triumphant.

Anne and Gilbert returned presently, accompanied by Captain Jim. Anne lighted a few sticks of driftwood in the fireplace, for love of the pixy flames, and they sat around it for an hour of good fellowship.

"When I sit looking at a driftwood fire it's easy to believe I'm young again," said Captain Jim.

"Can you read futures in the fire, Captain Jim?" asked Owen.

Captain Jim looked at them all affectionately, and then back again at Leslie's vivid face and glowing eyes.

"I don't need the fire to read your futures," he said. "I see happiness for all of you—all of you—for Leslie and Mr. Ford—and the Doctor here and Mistress Blythe—and Little Jem—and children that ain't born yet but will be. Happiness for you all—though, mind you, I reckon, you'll have your troubles and worries and sorrows, too. They're bound to come—and no house, whether it's a palace or a little house of dreams, can bar 'em out. But they won't get the better of you if you face 'em *together* with love and trust. You can weather any storm with them two for compass and pilot."

The old man rose suddenly and placed one hand on Leslie's head and one on Anne's.

"Two good, sweet women," he said. "True and faithful and to be depended on. Your husbands will have honour in the gates because of you—your children will rise up and call you blessed in the years to come."

There was a strange solemnity about the little scene. Anne and Leslie bowed as those receiving a benediction. Gilbert suddenly brushed his hand over his eyes; Owen Ford was rapt as one who can see visions. All were silent for a space. The little house of dreams added another poignant and unforgettable moment to its store of memories.

"I must be going now," said Captain Jim slowly at last. He took up his hat and looked lingeringly about the room.

"Good night, all of you," he said, as he went out.

Anne, pierced by the unusual wistfulness of his farewell, walked through the little gate hung between the firs.

"Ay, ay," he called cheerily back to her. But Captain Jim had sat by the old fireside of the house of dreams for the last time.

Anne went slowly back to the others.

"It's so—so pitiful to think of him going all alone down to that lonely Point," she said. "And there is no one to welcome him there."

"Captain Jim is such good company for others that one can't imagine him being anything but good company for himself," said Owen. "But he must often be lonely. There was a touch of the seer about him tonight—he spoke as one to whom it had been given to speak. Well, I must be going, too."

Anne and Gilbert discreetly melted away; but when Owen had gone Anne returned, to find Leslie standing by the hearth.

"Oh, Leslie—I know—and I'm so glad, dear," she said, putting her arms about her.

"Anne, my happiness frightens me," whispered Leslie. "It seems too great to be real—I'm afraid to speak of it—to think of it. It seems to me that it must just be another dream of this house of dreams and it will vanish when I leave here."

"Well, you are not going to leave here—until Owen takes you. You are going to stay with me until that time comes. Do you think I'd let you go over to that lonely, sad place again?"

"Thank you, dear. I meant to ask you if I might stay with you. I didn't want to go back there—it would seem like going back into the chill and dreariness of the old life again.

Anne, Anne, what a friend you've been to me—'a good, sweet woman—true and faithful and to be depended on'—Captain Jim summed you up."

"He said 'women,' not 'woman,'" smiled Anne. "Perhaps Captain Jim sees us both through the rose-coloured spectacles of his love for us. But we can try to live up to his belief in us, at least."

"Do you remember, Anne," said Leslie slowly, "that I once said—that night we met on the shore—that I hated my good looks? I did—then. It's always seemed to me that if I had been homely Dick would never have thought of me. I hated my beauty because it had attracted him, but now—oh, I'm glad that I have it. It's all I have to offer Owen,—his artist soul delights in it. I feel as if I do not come to him quite empty-handed."

"Owen loves your beauty, Leslie. Who would not? But it's foolish of you to say or think that that is all you bring him. *He* will tell you that—I needn't. And now I must lock up. I expected Susan back tonight, but she has not come."

"Oh, yes, here I am, Mrs. Doctor, dear," said Susan, entering unexpectedly from the kitchen, "and puffing like a hen drawing rails at that! It's quite a walk from the Glen down here."

"I'm glad to see you back, Susan. How is your sister?"

"She is able to sit up, but of course she cannot walk yet. However, she is very well able to get on without me now, for her daughter has come home for her vacation. And I am thankful to be back, Mrs. Doctor, dear. Matilda's leg was broken and no mistake, but her tongue was not. She would talk the legs off an iron pot, that she would, Mrs. Doctor, dear, though I grieve to say it of my own sister. She was always a great talker and yet she was the first of our family to get married. She really did not care much about marrying James Clow, but she could not bear to disoblige him. Not but what James is a good man—the only fault I have to find with him is that he always starts in to say grace with such an unearthly groan, Mrs. Doctor, dear. It always frightens my appetite clear away. And speaking of getting married, Mrs. Doctor, dear, is it true that Cornelia Bryant is going to be married to Marshall Elliott?"

"Yes, quite true, Susan."

"Well, Mrs. Doctor, dear, it does *not* seem to me fair. Here is me, who never said a word against the men, and I cannot get married nohow. And there is Cornelia Bryant, who is never done abusing them, and all she has to do is to reach out her hand and pick one up, as it were. It is a very strange world, Mrs. Doctor, dear."

"There's another world, you know, Susan."

"Yes," said Susan with a heavy sigh, "but Mrs. Doctor, dear, there is neither marrying nor giving in marriage there."

39

Captain Jim Crosses the Bar

One day in late September Owen Ford's book came at last. Captain Jim had gone faithfully to the Glen post-office every day for a month, expecting it. This day he had not gone, and Leslie brought his copy home with hers and Anne's.

"We'll take it down to him this evening," said Anne, excited as a schoolgirl.

The walk to the Point on that clear, beguiling evening along the red harbour road was very pleasant. Then the sun dropped down behind the western hills into some valley that must have been full of lost sunsets, and at the same instant the big light flashed out on the white tower of the point.

"Captain Jim is never late by the fraction of a second," said Leslie.

Neither Anne nor Leslie ever forgot Captain Jim's face when they gave him the book—*his* book, transfigured and glorified. The cheeks that had been blanched of late suddenly flamed with the colour of boyhood; his eyes glowed with all the fire of youth; but his hands trembled as he opened it.

It was called simply *The Life-Book of Captain Jim*, and on the title page the names of Owen Ford and James Boyd were printed as collaborators. The frontispiece was a photograph of Captain Jim himself, standing at the door of the lighthouse, looking across the gulf. Owen Ford had "snapped" him one day while the book was being written. Captain Jim had known this, but he had not known that the picture was to be in the book.

"Just think of it," he said, "the old sailor right there in a real printed book. This is the proudest day of my life. I'm like to bust, girls. There'll be no sleep for me to-night. I'll read my book clean through before sunup."

"We'll go right away and leave you free to begin it," said Anne.

Captain Jim had been handling the book in a kind of reverent rapture. Now he closed it decidedly and laid it aside.

"No, no, you're not going away before you take a cup of tea with the old man," he protested. "I couldn't hear to that—could you, Matey? The life-book will keep, I reckon. I've waited for it this many a year. I can wait a little longer while I'm enjoying my friends."

Captain Jim moved about getting his kettle on to boil, and setting out his bread and butter. Despite his excitement he did not move with his old briskness. His movements were slow and halting. But the girls did not offer to help him. They knew it would hurt his feelings.

"You just picked the right evening to visit me," he said, producing a cake from his cupboard. "Leetle Joe's mother sent me down a big basket full of cakes and pies today. A blessing on all good cooks, says I. Look at this purty cake, all frosting and nuts. 'Tain't often I can entertain in such style. Set in, girls, set in! We'll 'tak a cup o' kindness yet for auld lang syne.'"

The girls "set in" right merrily. The tea was up to Captain Jim's best brewing. Little Joe's mother's cake was the last word in cakes; Captain Jim was the prince of gracious hosts, never even permitting his eyes to wander to the corner where the life-book lay, in all its bravery of green and gold. But when his door finally closed behind Anne and Leslie they knew that he went straight to it, and as they walked home they pictured the delight of the old man poring over the printed pages wherein his own life was portrayed with all the charm and colour of reality itself.

"I wonder how he will like the ending—the ending I suggested," said Leslie.

She was never to know. Early the next morning Anne awakened to find Gilbert bending over her, fully dressed, and with an expression of anxiety on his face.

"Are you called out?" she asked drowsily.

"No. Anne, I'm afraid there's something wrong at the Point. It's an hour after sunrise now, and the light is still burning. You know it has always been a matter of pride with Captain Jim to start the light the moment the sun sets, and put it out the moment it rises." Anne sat up in dismay. Through her window she saw the light blinking palely against the blue skies of dawn.

"Perhaps he has fallen asleep over his life-book," she said anxiously, "or become so absorbed in it that he has forgotten the light."

Gilbert shook his head.

"That wouldn't be like Captain Jim. Anyway, I'm going down to see."

"Wait a minute and I'll go with you," exclaimed Anne. "Oh, yes, I must—Little Jem will sleep for an hour yet, and I'll call Susan. You may need a woman's help if Captain Jim is ill."

It was an exquisite morning, full of tints and sounds at once ripe and delicate. The harbour was sparkling and dimpling like a girl; white gulls were soaring over the dunes; beyond the bar was a shining, wonderful sea. The long fields by the shore were dewy and fresh in that first fine, purely-tinted light. The wind came dancing and whistling up the channel to replace the beautiful silence with a music more beautiful still. Had it not been for the baleful star on the white tower that early walk would have been a delight to Anne and Gilbert. But they went softly with fear.

Their knock was not responded to. Gilbert opened the door and they went in.

The old room was very quiet. On the table were the remnants of the little evening feast. The lamp still burning on the corner stand. The First Mate was asleep in a square of sunshine by the sofa.

Captain Jim lay on the sofa, with his hands clasped over the life-book, open at the last page, lying on his breast. His eyes were closed and on his face was a look of the most perfect peace and happiness—the look of one who has long sought and found at last.

"He is asleep?" whispered Anne tremulously.

Gilbert went to the sofa and bent over him for a few moments. Then he straightened up.

"Yes, he sleeps—well," he said quietly. "Anne, Captain Jim has crossed the bar."

They could not know precisely at what hour he had died, but Anne always believed that he had had his wish, and went out when the morning came across the gulf. Out on that shining tide his spirit drifted, over the sunrise sea of pearl and silver, to the haven where lost Margaret waited, beyond the storms and calms.

40
Farewell to the House of Dreams

Captain Jim was buried in the little over-harbour graveyard, very near to the spot where the wee white lady slept. His relatives put up a very expensive, very ugly "monument"—a monument at which he would have poked sly fun had he seen it in life. But his real monument was in the hearts of those who knew him, and in the book that was to live for generations.

Leslie mourned that Captain Jim had not lived to see the amazing success of it.

"How he would have delighted in the reviews—they are almost all so kindly. And to have seen his life-book heading the lists of the best sellers—oh, if he could just have lived to see it, Anne!"

But Anne, despite her grief, was wiser.

"It was the book itself he cared for, Leslie—not what might be said of it—and he had it. He had read it all through. That last night must have been one of the greatest happiness for him—with the quick, painless ending he had hoped for in the morning. I am glad for Owen's sake and yours that the book is such a success—but Captain Jim was satisfied—I *know*."

The lighthouse star still kept its nightly vigil; a substitute keeper had been sent to the Point, until such time as an all-wise government could decide which of many applicants was best fitted for the place—or had the strongest pull. The First Mate was at home in the little house, beloved by Anne and Gilbert and Leslie, and tolerated by a Susan who had small liking for cats.

"I can put up with him for the sake of Captain Jim, Mrs. Doctor, dear, for I liked the old man. And I will see that he gets bite and sup, and every mouse the traps account for. But do not ask me to do more than that, Mrs. Doctor, dear. Cats is cats, and take my word for it, they will never be anything else. And at least, Mrs. Doctor, dear, do keep him away from the blessed wee man. Picture to yourself how awful it would be if he was to suck the darling's breath."

"That might be fitly called a *cat*-astrophe," said Gilbert.

"Oh, you may laugh, doctor, dear, but it would be no laughing matter."

"Cats never suck babies' breaths," said Gilbert. "That is only an old superstition, Susan."

"Oh, well, it may be a superstition or it may not, doctor, dear. All that I know is, it has happened. My sister's husband's nephew's wife's cat sucked their baby's breath, and the poor innocent was all but gone when they found it. And superstition or not, if I find that yellow beast lurking near our baby I will whack him with the poker, Mrs. Doctor, dear."

Mr. and Mrs. Marshall Elliott were living comfortably and harmoniously in the green house. Leslie was busy with sewing, for she and Owen were to be married at Christmas. Anne wondered what she would do when Leslie was gone.

"Changes come all the time. Just as soon as things get really nice they change," she said with a sigh.

"The old Morgan place up at the Glen is for sale," said Gilbert, apropos of nothing in especial.

"Is it?" asked Anne indifferently.

"Yes. Now that Mr. Morgan has gone, Mrs. Morgan wants to go to live with her children in Vancouver. She will sell cheaply, for a big place like that in a small village like the Glen will not be very easy to dispose of."

"Well, it's certainly a beautiful place, so it is likely she will find a purchaser," said Anne, absently, wondering whether she should hemstitch or feather-stitch Little Jem's "short" dresses.

He was to be shortened the next week, and Anne felt ready to cry at the thought of it.

"Suppose we buy it, Anne?" remarked Gilbert quietly.

Anne dropped her sewing and stared at him. "You're not in earnest, Gilbert?"

"Indeed I am, dear."

"And leave this darling spot—our house of dreams?" said Anne incredulously. "Oh, Gilbert, it's—it's unthinkable!"

"Listen patiently to me, dear. I know just how you feel about it. I feel the same. But we've always known we would have to move some day."

"Oh, but not so soon, Gilbert—not just yet."

"We may never get such a chance again. If we don't buy the Morgan place someone else will—and there is no other house in the Glen we would care to have, and no other really good site on which to build. This little house is—well, it is and has been what no other house can ever be to us, I admit, but you know it is out-of- the-way down here for a doctor. We have felt the inconvenience, though we've made the best of it. And it's a tight fit for us now. Perhaps, in a few years, when Jem wants a room of his own, it will be entirely too small."

"Oh, I know—I know," said Anne, tears filling her eyes. "I know all that can be said against it, but I love it so—and it's so beautiful here."

"You would find it very lonely here after Leslie goes—and Captain Jim has gone too. The Morgan place is beautiful, and in time we would love it. You know you have always admired it, Anne."

"Oh, yes, but—but—this has all seemed to come up so suddenly, Gilbert. I'm dizzy. Ten minutes ago I had no thought of leaving this dear spot. I was planning what I meant to do for it in the spring—what I meant to do in the garden. And if we leave this place who will get it? It *is* out-of-the-way, so it's likely some poor, shiftless, wandering family will rent it—and over-run it—and oh, that would be desecration. It would hurt me horribly."

"I know. But we cannot sacrifice our own interests to such considerations, Anne-girl. The Morgan place will suit us in every essential particular—we really can't afford to miss such a chance. Think of that big lawn with those magnificent old trees; and of that splendid hardwood grove behind it—twelve acres of it. What a play place for our children! There's a fine orchard, too, and you've always admired that high brick wall around the garden with the door in it—you've thought it was so like a story-book garden. And there is almost as fine a view of the harbour and the dunes from the Morgan place as from here."

"You can't see the lighthouse star from it."

"Yes. You can see it from the attic window. *There's* another advantage, Anne-girl—you love big garrets."

"There's no brook in the garden."

"Well, no, but there is one running through the maple grove into the Glen pond. And the pond itself isn't far away. You'll be able to fancy you have your own Lake of Shining Waters again."

"Well, don't say anything more about it just now, Gilbert. Give me time to think—to get used to the idea."

"All right. There is no great hurry, of course. Only—if we decide to buy, it would be well to be moved in and settled before winter."

Gilbert went out, and Anne put away Little Jem's short dresses with trembling hands. She could not sew any more that day. With tear-wet eyes she wandered over the little domain where she had reigned so happy a queen. The Morgan place was all that Gilbert claimed. The grounds were beautiful, the house old enough to have dignity and repose and traditions, and new enough to be comfortable and up-to-date. Anne had always admired it; but admiring is not loving; and she loved this little house of dreams so much. She loved *everything* about it—the garden she had tended, and which so many women had tended before her—the gleam and sparkle of the little brook that crept so roguishly across the corner—the gate between the creaking fir trees—the old red sandstone step—the stately Lombardies—the two tiny quaint glass cupboards over the chimney-piece in the living room—the crooked windows upstairs—the little jog in the staircase—why, these things were a part of her! How could she leave them?

And how this little house, consecrated aforetime by love and joy, had been re-consecrated for her by her happiness and sorrow! Here she had spent her bridal moon; here wee Joyce had lived her one brief day; here the sweetness of motherhood had come again with Little Jem; here she had heard the exquisite music of her baby's cooing laughter; here beloved friends had sat by her fireside. Joy and grief, birth and death, had made sacred forever this little house of dreams.

And now she must leave it. She knew that, even while she had contended against the idea to Gilbert. The little house was out-grown. Gilbert's interests made the change necessary; his work, successful though it had been, was hampered by his location. Anne realised that the end of their life in this dear place drew nigh, and that she must face the fact bravely. But how her heart ached!

"It will just be like tearing something out of my life," she sobbed. "And oh, if I could hope that some nice folk would come here in our place—or even that it would be left vacant. That itself would be better than having it over-run with some horde who know nothing of the geography of dreamland, and nothing of the history that has given this house its soul and its identity. And if such a tribe come here the place will go to rack and ruin in no time—an old place goes down so quickly if it is not carefully attended to. They'll tear up my garden—and let the Lombardies get ragged—and the paling will come to look like a mouth with half the teeth missing—and the roof will leak—and the plaster fall—and they'll stuff pillows and rags in broken window panes—and everything will be out-at-elbows."

Anne's imagination pictured forth so vividly the coming degeneration of her dear little house that it hurt her as severely as if it had already been an accomplished fact. She sat down on the stairs and had a long, bitter cry. Susan found her there and enquired with much concern what the trouble was.

"You have not quarrelled with the doctor, have you now, Mrs. Doctor, dear? But if you have, do not worry. It is a thing quite likely to happen with married couples, I am told, although I have had no experience that way myself. He will be sorry, and you can soon make it up."

"No, no, Susan, we haven't quarrelled. It's only—Gilbert is going to buy the Morgan place, and we'll have to go and live at the Glen. And it will break my heart."

Susan did not enter into Anne's feelings at all. She was, indeed, quite rejoiced over the prospect of living at the Glen. Her one grievance against her place in the little house was its lonesome location.

"Why, Mrs. Doctor, dear, it will be splendid. The Morgan house is such a fine, big one."

"I hate big houses," sobbed Anne.

"Oh, well, you will not hate them by the time you have half a dozen children," remarked Susan calmly. "And this house is too small already for us. We have no spare room, since Mrs. Moore is here, and that pantry is the most aggravating place I ever tried to work in. There is a corner every way you turn. Besides, it is out-of-the-world down here. There is really nothing at all but scenery."

"Out of your world perhaps, Susan—but not out of mine," said Anne with a faint smile.

"I do not quite understand you, Mrs. Doctor, dear, but of course I am not well educated. But if Dr. Blythe buys the

Morgan place he will make no mistake, and that you may tie to. They have water in it, and the pantries and closets are beautiful, and there is not another such cellar in P. E. Island, so I have been told. Why, the cellar here, Mrs. Doctor, dear, has been a heartbreak to me, as well you know."

"Oh, go away, Susan, go away," said Anne forlornly. "Cellars and pantries and closets don't make a *home*. Why don't you weep with those who weep?"

"Well, I never was much hand for weeping, Mrs. Doctor, dear. I would rather fall to and cheer people up than weep with them. Now, do not you cry and spoil your pretty eyes. This house is very well and has served your turn, but it is high time you had a better." Susan's point of view seemed to be that of most people. Leslie was the only one who sympathised understandingly with Anne. She had a good cry, too, when she heard the news. Then they both dried their tears and went to work at the preparations for moving.

"Since we must go let us go as soon as we can and have it over," said poor Anne with bitter resignation.

"You know you will like that lovely old place at the Glen after you have lived in it long enough to have dear memories woven about it," said Leslie. "Friends will come there, as they have come here—happiness will glorify it for you. Now, it's just a house to you—but the years will make it a home."

Anne and Leslie had another cry the next week when they shortened Little Jem. Anne felt the tragedy of it until evening when in his long nightie she found her own dear baby again.

"But it will be rompers next—and then trousers—and in no time he will be grown-up," she sighed.

"Well, you would not want him to stay a baby always, Mrs. Doctor, dear, would you?" said Susan. "Bless his innocent heart, he looks too sweet for anything in his little short dresses, with his dear feet sticking out. And think of the saving in the ironing, Mrs. Doctor, dear."

"Anne, I have just had a letter from Owen," said Leslie, entering with a bright face. "And, oh! I have such good news. He writes me that he is going to buy this place from the church trustees and keep it to spend our summer vacations in. Anne, are you not glad?"

"Oh, Leslie, 'glad' isn't the word for it! It seems almost too good to be true. I sha'n't feel half so badly now that I know this dear spot will never be desecrated by a vandal tribe, or left to tumble down in decay. Why, it's lovely! It's lovely!"

One October morning Anne wakened to the realisation that she had slept for the last time under the roof of her little house. The day was too busy to indulge regret and when evening came the house was stripped and bare. Anne and Gilbert were alone in it to say farewell. Leslie and Susan and Little Jem had gone to the Glen with the last load of furniture. The sunset light streamed in through the curtainless windows.

"It has all such a heart-broken, reproachful look, hasn't it?" said Anne. "Oh, I shall be so homesick at the Glen tonight!"

"We have been very happy here, haven't we, Anne- girl?" said Gilbert, his voice full of feeling.

Anne choked, unable to answer. Gilbert waited for her at the fir-tree gate, while she went over the house and said farewell to every room. She was going away; but the old house would still be there, looking seaward through its quaint windows. The autumn winds would blow around it mournfully, and the gray rain would beat upon it and the white mists would come in from the sea to enfold it; and the moonlight would fall over it and light up the old paths where the schoolmaster and his bride had walked. There on that old harbour shore the charm of story would linger; the wind would still whistle alluringly over the silver sand-dunes; the waves would still call from the red rock-coves.

"But we will be gone," said Anne through her tears. She went out, closing and locking the door behind her. Gilbert was waiting for her with a smile. The lighthouse star was gleaming northward. The little garden, where only marigolds still bloomed, was already hooding itself in shadows.

Anne knelt down and kissed the worn old step which she had crossed as a bride.

"Good-bye, dear little house of dreams," she said.

Anne of Ingleside

LUCY MAUD MONTGOMERY

NIMBUS
PUBLISHING
NIMBUS.CA

1

"How white the moonlight is tonight!" said Anne Blythe to herself, as she went up the walk of the Wright garden to Diana Wright's front door, where little cherry-blossom petals were coming down on the salty, breeze-stirred air.

She paused for a moment to look about her on hills and woods she had loved in olden days and still loved. Dear Avonlea! Glen St. Mary was home to her now and had been home for many years but Avonlea had something that Glen St. Mary could never have. Ghosts of herself met her at every turn...the fields she had roamed in welcomed her...unfading echoes of the old sweet life were all about her...every spot she looked upon had some lovely memory. There were haunted gardens here and there where bloomed all the roses of yesteryear. Anne always loved to come home to Avonlea even when, as now, the reason for her visit had been a sad one. She and Gilbert had come up for the funeral of his father and Anne had stayed for a week. Marilla and Mrs. Lynde could not bear to have her go away too soon.

Her old porch gable room was always kept for her and when Anne had gone to it the night of her arrival she found that Mrs. Lynde had put a big, homey bouquet of spring flowers in it for her...a bouquet that, when Anne buried her face in it, seemed to hold all the fragrance of unforgotten years. The Anne-who-used-to-be was waiting there for her. Deep, dear old gladnesses stirred in her heart. The gable room was putting its arms around her...enclosing her...enveloping her. She looked lovingly at her old bed with the apple-leaf spread Mrs. Lynde had knitted and the spotless pillows trimmed with deep lace Mrs. Lynde had crocheted...at Marilla's braided rugs on the floor...at the mirror that had reflected the face of the little orphan, with her unwritten child's forehead, who had cried herself to sleep there that first night so long ago. Anne forgot that she was the joyful mother of five children...with Susan Baker again knitting mysterious bootees at Ingleside. She was Anne of Green Gables once more.

Mrs. Lynde found her still staring dreamily in the mirror when she came in, bringing clean towels.

"It's real good to have you home again, Anne, that's what. It's nine years since you went away, but Marilla and I can't seem to get over missing you. It's not so lonesome now since Davy got married...Millie is a real nice little thing...such pies!...though she's curious as a chipmunk about everything. But I've always said and always will say that there's nobody like you."

"Ah, but this mirror can't be tricked, Mrs. Lynde. It's telling me plainly, 'You're not as young as you once were,'" said Anne whimsically.

"You've kept your complexion very well," said Mrs. Lynde consolingly. "Of course you never had much colour to lose."

"At any rate, I've never a hint of a second chin yet," said Anne gaily. "And my old room remembers me, Mrs. Lynde. I'm glad...it would hurt me so if I ever came back and found it had forgotten me. And it's wonderful to see the moon rising over the Haunted Wood again."

"It looks like a great big piece of gold in the sky, doesn't it?" said Mrs. Lynde, feeling that she was taking a wild, poetical flight and thankful that Marilla wasn't there to hear.

"Look at those pointed firs coming out against it...and the birches in the hollow still holding their arms up to the silver sky. They're big trees now...they were just baby things when I came here...that *does* make me feel a bit old."

"Trees are like children," said Mrs. Lynde. "It's dreadful the way they grow up the minute you turn your back on them. Look at Fred Wright...he's only thirteen but he's nearly as tall as his father. There's a hot chicken pie for supper and I made some of my lemon biscuits for you. You needn't be a mite afraid to sleep in that bed. I aired the sheets today...and Marilla didn't know I did it and gave them another airing...and Millie didn't know either of us did and gave them a third. I hope Mary Maria Blythe will get out tomorrow...she always enjoys a funeral so."

"Aunt Mary Maria...Gilbert always calls her that although she is only his father's cousin...always calls me 'Annie,'" shuddered Anne. "And the first time she saw me after I was married she said, 'It's so strange Gilbert picked you. He could have had so many nice girls.' Perhaps that's why I've never liked her...and I know Gilbert doesn't either, though he's too clannish to admit it."

"Will Gilbert be staying up long?"

"No. He has to go back tomorrow night. He left a patient in a very critical condition."

"Oh, well, I suppose there isn't much to keep him in Avonlea now, since his mother went last year. Old Mr. Blythe never held up his head after her death...just hadn't anything left to live for. The Blythes were always like that...always set their affections too much on earthly things. It's real sad to think there are none of them left in Avonlea. They were a fine old stock. But then... there's any amount of Sloanes. The Sloanes are still Sloanes, Anne, and will be for ever and ever, world without end, amen."

"Let there be as many Sloanes as there will, I'm going out after supper to walk all over the old orchard by moonlight. I suppose I'll have to go to bed finally...though I've always thought sleeping on moonlight nights a waste of time...but I'm going to wake early to see the first faint morning light steal over the Haunted Wood. The sky will turn to coral and the robins will be strutting around...perhaps a little grey sparrow will light on the windowsill...and there'll be gold and purple pansies to look at..."

"But the rabbits has et up all the June lily bed," said Mrs. Lynde sadly, as she waddled downstairs, feeling secretly relieved that there need be no more talk about the moon. Anne had always been a bit queer that way. And there did not any longer seem to be much use in hoping she would outgrow it.

Diana came down the walk to meet Anne. Even in the moonlight you saw that her hair was still black and her cheeks rosy and her eyes bright. But the moonlight could not hide that she was something stouter than in years agone...and Diana had never been what Avonlea folks called "skinny."

"Don't worry, darling...I haven't come to stay..."

"As if I'd worry over *that,*" said Diana reproachfully. "You know I'd far rather spend the evening with you than go to the reception. I feel I haven't seen half enough of you and now you're going back day after tomorrow. But Fred's brother, you know... we've just got to go."

"Of course you have. And I just ran up for a moment. I came the old way, Di...past the Dryad's Bubble...through the Haunted Wood...past your bowery old garden...and along by Willowmere. I even stopped to watch the willows upside down in the water as we always used to do. They've grown so."

"Everything has," said Diana with a sigh. "When I look at young Fred! We've all changed so...except you. You never change, Anne. How *do* you keep so slim? Look at me!"

"A bit matronish of course," laughed Anne. "But you've escaped the middle-aged spread so far, Di. As for my not changing...well, Mrs. H. B. Donnell agrees with you. She told me at the funeral that I didn't look a day older. But Mrs. Harmon Andrews doesn't. *She* said, 'Dear me, Anne, how you've failed!' It's all in the beholder's eye...or conscience. The only time I feel I'm getting along a bit is when I look at the pictures in the magazines. The heroes and heroines in them are beginning to look *too young* to me. But never mind, Di...we're going to be girls again tomorrow. That's what I've come up to tell you. We're going to take an afternoon and evening off and visit all our old haunts... every one of them. We'll walk over the spring fields and through those ferny old woods. We'll see all the old familiar things we loved and hills where we'll find our youth again. Nothing ever seems impossible in spring, you know. We'll stop feeling parental and responsible and be as giddy as Mrs. Lynde really thinks me still in her heart of hearts. There's really no fun in being sensible *all* the time, Diana."

"My, how like you that sounds! And I'd love to. But..."

"There aren't any buts. I know you're thinking, 'Who'll get the men's supper?'"

"Not exactly. Anne Cordelia can get the men's supper as well as I can, if she is only eleven," said Diana proudly. "She was going to, anyway. I was going to the Ladies' Aid. But I won't. I'll go with you. It will be like having a dream come true. You know, Anne, lots of evenings I sit down and just pretend we're little girls again. I'll take our supper with us..."

"And we'll eat it back in Hester Gray's garden...I suppose Hester Gray's garden is still there?"

"I suppose so," said Diana doubtfully. "I've never been there since I was married. Anne Cordelia explores a lot...but I always tell her she mustn't go too far from home. She loves prowling about the woods...and one day when I scolded her for talking to herself in the garden she said she wasn't talking to herself... she was talking to the spirit of the flowers. You know that dolls' tea-set with the tiny pink rosebuds you sent her for her ninth birthday. There isn't a piece broken...she's so careful. She only uses it when the Three Green People come to tea with her. I can't get out of her who she thinks *they* are. I declare in some ways, Anne, she's far more like you than she is like me."

"Perhaps there's more in a name than Shakespeare allowed. Don't grudge Anne Cordelia her fancies, Diana. I'm always sorry for children who don't spend a few years in fairyland."

"Olivia Sloane is our teacher now," said Diana doubtfully. "She's a B.A., you know, and just took the school for a year to be near her mother. *She* says children should be made to face realities."

"Have I lived to hear *you* taking up with Sloanishness, Diana Wright?"

"No...*no*...NO! I don't like her a bit...She has such round staring blue eyes like all that clan. And I don't mind Anne Cordelia's fancies. They're pretty...just like yours used to be. I guess she'll get enough 'reality' as life goes on."

"Well, it's settled then. Come down to Green Gables about two and we'll have a drink of Marilla's red currant wine...she makes it now and then in spite of the minister and Mrs. Lynde... just to make us feel real devilish."

"Do you remember the day you set me drunk on it?" giggled Diana, who did not mind "devilish" as she would if anybody but Anne used it. Everybody knew Anne didn't really mean things like that. It was just her way.

"We'll have a real do-you-remember day tomorrow, Diana. I won't keep you any longer...there's Fred coming with the buggy. Your dress is lovely."

"Fred made me get a new one for the wedding. I didn't feel we could afford it since we built the new barn, but he said he wasn't going to have *his* wife looking like someone that was sent for and couldn't go when everybody else would be dressed within an inch of her life. Wasn't that just like a man?"

"Oh, you sound just like Mrs. Elliott at the Glen," said Anne severely. "You want to watch that tendency. Would you like to live in a world where there were no men?"

"It would be horrible," admitted Diana. "Yes, yes, Fred, I'm coming. Oh, *all* right! Till tomorrow then, Anne."

Anne paused by the Dryad's Bubble on her way back. She loved that old brook so. Every trill of her childhood's laughter that it had ever caught, it had held and now seemed to give out again to her listening ears. Her old dreams...she could see them reflected in the clear Bubble...old vows...old whispers...the brook kept them all and murmured of them...but there was no one to listen save the wise old spruces in the Haunted Wood that had been listening so long.

2

"Such a lovely day...made for us," said Diana. "I'm afraid it's a pet day, though...there'll be rain tomorrow."

"Never mind. We'll drink its beauty today, even if its sunshine is gone tomorrow. We'll enjoy each other's friendship today even if we are to be parted tomorrow. Look at those long, golden-green hills...those mist-blue valleys. They're *ours,* Diana...I don't care if that furthest hill is registered in Abner Sloan's name...it's *ours* today. There's a west wind blowing...I always feel adventurous when a west wind blows...and we're going to have a perfect ramble."

They had. All the old dear spots were revisited: Lover's Lane, the Haunted Wood, Idlewild, Violet Vale, the Birch Path, Crystal Lake. There were some changes. The little ring of birch saplings in Idlewild, where they had had a playhouse long ago, had grown into big trees; the Birch Path, long untrodden, was matted with bracken; the Crystal Lake had entirely disappeared, leaving only a damp mossy hollow. But Violet Vale was purple with violets and the seedling apple tree Gilbert had once found far back in the woods was a huge tree peppered over with tiny, crimson-tipped blossom-buds.

They walked bareheaded. Annie's hair still gleamed like polished mahogany in the sunlight and Diana's was still glossy black.

They exchanged gay and understanding, warm and friendly, glances. Sometimes they walked in silence...Anne always maintained that two people as sympathetic as she and Diana could *feel* each other's thoughts. Sometimes they peppered their conversation with do-you-remembers. "Do you remember the day you fell through the Cobb duckhouse on the Tory Road?"..."Do you remember when we jumped on Aunt Josephine?"..."Do you remember our Story Club?"..."Do you remember Mrs. Morgan's visit when you stained your nose red?"..."Do you remember how we signalled to each other from our windows with candles?"..."Do you remember the fun we had at Miss Lavender's wedding and Charlotta's blue bows?"..."Do you remember the Improvement Society?" It almost seemed to them they could hear their old peals of laughter echoing down the years.

The A. V. I. S. was, it seemed, dead. It had petered out soon after Anne's marriage.

"They just couldn't keep it up, Anne. The young people in Avonlea now are not what they were in *our* day."

"Don't talk as if 'our day' were ended, Diana. We're only fifteen years old and kindred spirits. The air isn't just full of light... it *is* light. I'm not sure that I haven't sprouted wings."

"I feel just that way, too," said Diana, forgetting that she had tipped the scale at one hundred and fifty-five that morning. "I often feel that I'd love to be turned into a bird for a little while. It must be wonderful to fly."

Beauty was all around them. Unsuspected tintings glimmered in the dark demesnes of the woods and glowed in their alluring by-ways. The spring sunshine sifted through the young green leaves. Gay trills of song were everywhere. There were little hollows where you felt as if you were bathing in a pool of liquid gold. At every turn some fresh spring scent struck their faces... spice ferns...fir balsam...the wholesome odour of newly ploughed fields. There was a lane curtained with wild-cherry blossoms...a grassy old field full of tiny spruce trees just starting in life and looking like elvish things that had squatted down among the grasses...brooks not yet "too broad for leaping"...star-flowers under the firs...sheets of curly young ferns...and a birch tree whence some vandal had torn away the white-skin wrapper in several places, exposing the tints of the bark below. Anne looked at it so long that Diana wondered. She did not see what Anne did...tints ranging from purest creamy white, through exquisite golden tones, growing deeper and deeper until the inmost layer revealed the deepest richest brown as if to tell that all birches, so maiden-like and cool exteriorly, had yet warm-hued feelings.

"The primeval fire of earth at their hearts," murmured Anne.

And finally, after traversing a little wood glen full of toadstools, they found Hester Gray's garden. Not so much changed. It was still very sweet with dear flowers. There were still plenty of June lilies, as Diana called the narcissi. The row of cherry trees had grown older but was a drift of snowy bloom. You could still find the central rose walk, and the old dyke was white with strawberry blossoms and blue with violets and green with baby fern. They ate their picnic supper in a corner of it, sitting on some old mossy stones, with a lilac tree behind them flinging purple banners against a low-hanging sun. Both were hungry and both did justice to their own good cooking.

"How nice things taste out of doors!" sighed Diana comfortably. "That chocolate cake of yours, Anne...well, words fail me, but I must get the recipe. Fred would adore it. *He* can eat anything and stay thin. I'm always saying I'm *not* going to eat any more cake...because I'm getting fatter every year. I've such a horror of getting like great-aunt Sarah...she was so fat she always had to be pulled up when she had sat down. But when I see a cake like that...and last night at the reception...well, they would all have been so offended if I didn't eat."

"Did you have a nice time?"

"Oh, yes, in a way. But I fell into Fred's Cousin Henrietta's clutches...and it's *such* a delight to her to tell all about her operations and her sensations while going through them and how soon her appendix would have burst if she hadn't had it out. 'I had fifteen stitches put in it. Oh, Diana, the agony I suffered!' Well, she enjoyed it if I didn't. And she *has* suffered, so why shouldn't she have the fun of talking about it now? Jim was so funny...I don't know if Mary Alice liked it altogether...Well, just one teeny piece...may as well be hung for a sheep as a lamb, I suppose...a mere sliver can't make much difference...One thing he said...that the very night before the wedding he was so scared he felt he'd have to take the boat-train. He said all grooms felt just the same if they'd be honest about it. You don't suppose Gilbert and Fred felt like that, do you, Anne?"

"I'm sure they didn't."

"That's what Fred said when I asked him. He said all he was scared of was that I'd change my mind at the last moment like Rose Spencer. But you can never really tell what a man may be thinking. Well, there's no use worrying over it now. What a lovely time we've had this afternoon! We seem to have lived so many old happinesses over. I wish you didn't have to go tomorrow, Anne."

"Can't you come down for a visit to Ingleside sometime this summer, Diana? Before...well, before I'll not be wanting visitors for a while."

"I'd love to. But it seems impossible to get away from home in the summer. There's always so much to do."

"Rebecca Dew is coming at long last, of which I'm glad... and I'm afraid Aunt Mary Maria is, too. She hinted as much to Gilbert. He doesn't want her any more than I do...but she is 'a relation' and so his latchstring must be always out for her."

"Perhaps I'll get down in the winter. I'd love to see Ingleside again. You have a lovely home, Anne...and a lovely family."

"Ingleside *is* nice...and I do love it now. I once thought I would never love it. I hated it when we went there first...hated it for its very virtues. They were an insult to my dear House of Dreams. I remember saying piteously to Gilbert when we left it, 'We've been so happy here. We'll never be so happy anywhere else.' I revelled in a luxury of homesickness for a while. Then...I found little rootlets of affection for Ingleside beginning to sprout out. I fought against it...I really did...but at last I had to give in and admit I loved it. And I've loved it better every year since. It isn't too old a house...too old houses are sad. And it isn't too young...too young houses are crude. It's just mellow. I love every room in it. Every one has some fault but also some virtue... something that distinguishes it from all the others...gives it a personality. I love all those magnificent trees on the lawn. I don't know who planted them but every time I go upstairs I stop on the landing...you know that quaint window on the landing with the broad deep seat...and sit there looking out for a moment and say, 'God bless the man who planted those trees whoever he was.' We've really too many trees about the house but we wouldn't give up one."

"That's just like Fred. He worships that big willow south of the house. It spoils the view from the parlour windows, as I've told him again and again, but he only says, 'Would you cut a lovely thing like that down even if it does shut out the view?' So the willow stays...and it *is* lovely. That's why we've called our place Lone Willow Farm. I love the name Ingleside. It's such a nice, homey name."

"That's what Gilbert said. We had quite a time deciding on a name. We tried out several but they didn't seem to *belong.* But when we thought of Ingleside we knew it was the right one. I'm glad we have a nice big roomy house...we need it with our family. The children love it, too, small as they are."

"They're such darlings." Diana slyly cut herself another "sliver" of the chocolate cake. "I think my own are pretty nice...

but there's really something about yours...and your twins! *That* I do envy you. I've always wanted twins."

"Oh, I couldn't get away from twins...they're my destiny. But I'm disappointed mine don't look alike...not one bit alike. Nan's pretty, though, with her brown hair and eyes and her lovely complexion. Di is her father's favourite, because she has green eyes and red hair...red hair with a swirl to it. Shirley is the apple of Susan's eye...I was ill so long after he was born and she looked after him till I really believe she thinks he is her own. She calls him her 'little brown boy' and spoils him shamefully."

"And he's still so small you can creep in to find if he has kicked off the clothes and tuck him in again," said Diana enviously. "Jack's nine, you know, and he doesn't want me to do that now. He says he's too big. And I loved so to do it! Oh, I wish children didn't grow up so soon."

"None of mine have got to that stage yet...though I've noticed that since Jem began to go to school he doesn't want to hold my hand any more when we walk through the village," said Anne with a sigh. "But he and Walter and Shirley all want me to tuck them in yet. Walter sometimes makes quite a ritual of it."

"And you don't have to worry yet over what they're going to be. Now, Jack is crazy to be a soldier when he grows up...a soldier! Just fancy!"

"I wouldn't worry over that. He'll forget about it when another fancy seizes him. War is a thing of the past. Jem imagines he is going to be a sailor...like Captain Jim...and Walter is by way of being a poet. He isn't like any of the others. But they all love trees and they all love playing in 'the Hollow,' as it's called—a little valley just below Ingleside with fairy paths and a brook. A very ordinary place...just 'the Hollow' to others but to them fairyland. They've all got their faults...but they're not such a bad little gang...and luckily there's always enough love to go round. Oh, I'm glad to think that this time tomorrow night

I'll be back at Ingleside, telling my babies stories at bedtime and giving Susan's calceolarias and ferns their meed of praise. Susan has 'luck' with ferns. No one can grow them like her. I can praise her ferns honestly...but the calceolarias, Diana! They don't look like flowers to me at all. But I never hurt Susan's feeling by telling her so. I always get around it somehow. Providence has never failed yet. Susan is such a duck...I can't imagine what I'd do without her. And I remember once calling her 'an outsider.' Yes, it's lovely to think of going home and yet I'm sad to leave Green Gables, too. It's so beautiful here...with Marilla...and *you.* Our friendship has always been a very lovely thing, Diana."

"Yes...and we've always...I mean...I never could say things like you, Anne...but we *have* kept our old 'solemn vow and promise,' haven't we?"

"Always...and always will."

Anne's hand found its way into Diana's. They sat for a long time in a silence too sweet for words. Long, still evening shadows fell over the grasses and the flowers and the green reaches of the meadows beyond. The sun went down...grey-pink shades of sky deepened and paled behind the pensive trees...the spring twilight took possession of Hester Gray's garden where nobody ever walked now. Robins were sprinkling the evening air with flute-like whistles. A great star came out over the white cherry trees.

"The first star is always a miracle," said Anne dreamily.

"I could sit here forever," said Diana. "I hate the thought of leaving it."

"So do I...but after all we've only been pretending to be fifteen. We've got to remember our family cares. How those lilacs smell! Has it ever occurred to you, Diana, that there is something not quite...chaste...in the scent of lilac blossoms? Gilbert laughs at such a notion...he loves them...but to me they always seem to be remembering some secret, *too*-sweet thing."

"They're too heavy for the house, I always think," said Diana. She picked up the plate which held the remainder of the chocolate cake...looked at it longingly...shook her head and packed it in the basket with an expression of great nobility and self-denial on her face.

"Wouldn't it be fun, Diana, if now, as we went home, we were to meet our old selves running along Lover's Lane?"

Diana gave a little shiver.

"No-o-o, I don't think that would be funny, Anne. I hadn't noticed it was getting so dark. It's all right to fancy things in daylight, but..."

They went quietly, silently, lovingly home together, with the sunset glory burning on the old hills behind them and their old unforgotten love burning in their hearts.

3

Anne ended a week that had been full of pleasant days by taking flowers to Matthew's grave the next morning and in the afternoon she took the train from Carmody home. For a time she thought of all the old loved things behind her and then her thoughts ran ahead of her to the loved things before her. Her heart sang all the way because she was going home to a joyous house...a house where every one who crossed its threshold knew it was a *home*... a house that was filled all the time with laughter and silver mugs and snapshots and babies...precious things with curls and chubby knees...and rooms that would welcome her... where the chairs waited patiently and the dresses in her closet were expecting her...where little anniversaries were always being celebrated and little secrets were always being whispered.

"It's lovely to feel you like going home," thought Anne, fishing out of her purse a certain letter from a small son over which she had laughed gaily the night before, reading it proudly to the Green Gables folks...the first letter she had ever received from any of her children. It was quite a nice little letter for a seven-year-old who had been going to school only a year to write, even though Jem's spelling was a bit uncertain and there was a big blob of ink in one corner.

"Di cryed and cryed all night because Tommy Drew told her he was going to burn her doll at the steak. Susan tells us nice tails at night but she isn't you, mummy. She let me help her sow the beats last night."

"*How* could I have been happy for a whole week away from them all?" thought the chatelaine of Ingleside self-reproachfully.

"How nice to have someone meet you at the end of a journey!" she cried, as she stepped off the train at Glen St. Mary into Gilbert's waiting arms. She could never be sure Gilbert would meet her...somebody was always dying or being born...but no homecoming ever seemed just right to Anne unless he did. And he had on such a nice new light-grey suit! *(How glad I am I put on this frilly eggshell blouse with my brown suit, even if Mrs. Lynde thought I was crazy to wear it travelling. If I hadn't I wouldn't have looked so nice for Gilbert.)*

Ingleside was all lighted up, with gay Japanese lanterns hanging on the veranda. Anne ran gaily along the walk bordered by daffodils.

"Ingleside, I'm here!" she called.

They were all around her...laughing, exclaiming, jesting... with Susan Baker smiling properly in the background. Everyone of the children had a bouquet picked specially for her, even the two-year-old Shirley.

"Oh, this *is* a nice welcome home! Everything about Ingleside looks so happy. It's splendid to think my family are so glad to see me."

"If you ever go away from home again, Mummy," said Jem solemnly, "I'll go and take appensitis."

"How do you go about taking it?" asked Walter.

"S-s-sh!" Jem nudged Walter secretly and whispered, "There's a pain somewhere, I know...but I just want to scare Mummy so she *won't* go away."

Anne wanted to do a hundred things first...hug everybody... run out in the twilight and gather some of her pansies...you found pansies everywhere at Ingleside...pick up the little well-worn doll lying on the rug...hear all the juicy tidbits of gossip and news, everyone contributing something. How Nan had got the top off a tube of vaseline up her nose when the doctor was out on a case and Susan had all but gone distracted..."I assure you it was an anxious time, Mrs. Dr. dear"...how Mrs. Jud Palmer's cow had eaten fifty-seven wire nails and had to have a vet from Charlottetown...how absent-minded Mrs. Fenner Douglas had gone to church *bare-headed*...how Dad had dug all the dandelions out of the lawn..."between babies, Mrs. Dr. dear...he's had eight while you were away"...how Mr. Tom Flagg had dyed his moustache..."and his wife only dead two years"... how Rose Maxwell of the Harbour Head had jilted Jim Hudson of the Upper Glen and he had sent her a bill for all he had spent on her...what a splendid turn-out there had been at Mrs. Amasa Warren's funeral...how Carter Flagg's cat had had a piece bitten right out of the root of its tail...how Shirley had been found in a stable standing right under one of the horses..."Mrs. Dr. dear, never shall I be the same woman again"...how there was sadly too much reason to fear that the blue plum trees were developing black knot...how Di had gone about the whole day singing, "Mummy's coming home today, home today, home today" to the tune of "Merrily We Roll Along"...how the Joe Reeses had a kitten that was cross-eyed because it had been born with its eyes open...how Jem had inadvertently sat on some fly-paper before he had put his little trousers on...and how the Shrimp had fallen into the soft-water puncheon.

"He was nearly drowned, Mrs. Dr. dear, but luckily the doctor heard his howls in the nick of time and pulled him out by his hind-legs." (What is the nick of time, Mummy?)

"He seems to have recovered nicely from it," said Anne, stroking the glossy black-and-white curves of a contented pussy with huge jowls, purring on a chair in the firelight. It was never quite safe to sit down on a chair at Ingleside without first making sure there wasn't a cat in it. Susan, who had not cared much for cats to begin with, vowed she had to learn to like them in self-defense. As for the Shrimp, Gilbert had called him that a year ago when Nan had brought the miserable, scrawny kitten home from the village where some boys had been torturing it, and the name clung, though it was very inappropriate now.

"But...Susan! What has become of Gog and Magog? Oh... they haven't been broken, have they?"

"No, no, Mrs. Dr. dear," exclaimed Susan, turning a deep brick-red from shame and dashing out of the room. She returned shortly with the two china dogs which always presided at the hearth of Ingleside. "I do not see how I could have forgotten to put them back before you came. You see, Mrs. Dr. dear, Mrs. Charles Day from Charlottetown called here the day after you left...and you know how very precise and proper she is. Walter thought he ought to entertain her and he started in by pointing out the dogs to her. 'This one is God and this is My God,' he said, poor innocent child. I was horrified...though I thought that die I would to see Mrs. Day's face. I explained as best I could, for I did not want her to think us a profane family, but I decided I would just put the dogs away in the china closet, out of sight, till you got back."

"Mummy, can't we have supper soon?" said Jem pathetically. "I've got a gnawful feeling in the pit of my stomach. And oh, Mummy, we've made everybody's favourite dish!"

"We, as the flea said to the elephant, have done that very thing," said Susan with a grin. "We thought that your return should be suitably celebrated, Mrs. Dr. dear. And now where is Walter? It is his week to ring the gong for meals, bless his heart."

Supper was a gala meal...and putting all the babies to bed afterwards was a delight. Susan even allowed her to put Shirley to bed, seeing what a very special occasion it was.

"This is no common day, Mrs. Dr. dear," she said solemnly.

"Oh, Susan, there is no such thing as a common day. *Every* day has something about it no other day has. Haven't you noticed?"

"How true that is, Mrs. Dr. dear. Even last Friday now, when it rained all day, and was so dull, my big pink geranium showed buds at last after refusing to bloom for three long years. And have you noticed the calceolarias, Mrs. Dr. dear?"

"Noticed them! I never saw such calceolarias in my life, Susan. How *do* you manage it?" *(There, I've made Susan happy and haven't told a fib. I never did see such calceolarias...thank heaven!)*

"It is the result of constant care and attention, Mrs. Dr. dear. But there is something I think I ought to speak of. I think Walter *suspects something.* No doubt some of the Glen children have said things to him. So many children nowadays know so much more than is fitting. Walter said to me the other day, very thoughtful-like, 'Susan,' he said, 'are babies *very* expensive?' I was a bit dumfounded, Mrs. Dr. dear, but I kept my head. 'Some folks think they are luxuries,' I said, 'but at Ingleside we think they are necessities.' And I reproached myself with having complained aloud about the shameful price of things in all the Glen stores. I am afraid it worried the child. But if he says anything to you, Mrs. Dr. dear, you will be prepared."

"I'm sure you handled the situation beautifully, Susan," said Anne gravely. "And I think it is time they all knew what we are hoping for."

But the best of all was when Gilbert came to her, as she stood at her window, watching a fog creeping in from the sea, over the moonlit dunes and the harbour, right into the long narrow valley upon which Ingleside looked down and in which nestled the village of Glen St. Mary.

"To come back at the end of a hard day and find you! Are you happy, Annest of Annes?"

"Happy!" Anne bent to sniff a vaseful of apple blossoms Jem had set on her dressing-table. She felt surrounded and encompassed by love. "Gilbert dear, it's been lovely to be Anne of Green Gables again for a week, but it's a hundred times lovelier to come back and be Anne of Ingleside."

4

"Absolutely not," said Dr. Blythe, in a tone Jem understood.

Jem knew there was no hope of Dad's changing his mind or that Mother would try to change it for him. It was plain to be seen that on this point Mother and Dad were as one. Jem's hazel eyes darkened with anger and disappointment as he looked at his cruel parents...*glared* at them...all the more glaringly that they were so maddeningly indifferent to his glares and went on eating their supper as if nothing at all were wrong and out of joint. Of course Aunt Mary Maria noticed his glares...nothing ever escaped Aunt Mary Maria's mournful, pale-blue eyes...but she only seemed amused at them.

Bertie Shakespeare Drew had been up playing with Jem all the afternoon...Walter having gone down to the old House of Dreams to play with Kenneth and Persis Ford...and Bertie Shakespeare had told Jem that all the Glen boys were going down to the Harbour Mouth that evening to see Captain Bill Taylor tatoo a snake on his cousin Joe Drew's arm. He, Bertie Shakespeare, was going and wouldn't Jem come too? It would be such fun. Jem was at once crazy to go; and now he had been told that it was utterly out of the question.

"For one reason among many," said Dad, "it's much too far for you to go down to the Harbour Mouth with those boys. They won't get back till late and your bedtime is supposed to be at eight, son."

"*I* was sent to bed at seven every night of my life when I was a child," said Aunt Mary Maria.

"You must wait till you are older, Jem, before you go so far away in the evenings," said Mother.

"You said that last week," cried Jem indignantly, "and I *am* older now. You'd think I was a baby! Bertie's going and I'm just as old as him."

"There's measles around," said Aunt Mary Maria darkly. "You might catch measles, James."

Jem hated to be called James. And she always did it.

"I *want* to catch measles," he muttered rebelliously. Then, catching Dad's eye instead, subsided. Dad would never let anyone "talk back" to Aunt Mary Maria. Jem hated Aunt Mary Maria. Aunt Diana and Aunt Marilla were such ducks of aunts but an aunt like Aunt Mary Maria was something wholly new in Jem's experience.

"All right," he said defiantly, looking at Mother so that nobody could suppose he was talking to Aunt Mary Maria, "if you don't *want* to love me you don't *have* to. But will you like it if I just go away 'n' shoot tigers in Africa?"

"There are no tigers in Africa, dear," said Mother gently.

"Lions, then!" shouted Jem. They were determined to put him in the wrong, were they? They were bound to laugh at him, were they? He'd show them! "You can't say there's no lions in Africa. There's *millions* of lions in Africa. Africa's just *full* of lions!"

Mother and Father only smiled again, much to Aunt Mary Maria's disapproval. Impatience in children should never be condoned.

"Meanwhile," said Susan, torn between her love for and sympathy with Little Jem and her conviction that Dr. and Mrs. Dr. were perfectly right in refusing to let him go away down to the Harbour Mouth with that village gang to that disreputable, drunken old Captain Bill Taylor's place, "here is your gingerbread and whipped cream, Jem dear."

Gingerbread and whipped cream was Jem's favourite dessert. But tonight it had no charm to soothe his stormy soul.

"I don't want any!" he said sulkily. He got up and marched away from the table, turning at the door to hurl a final defiance.

"I ain't going to bed till nine o'clock, anyhow. And when I'm grown up I'm *never* going to bed. I'm going to stay up all night... every night...and get tattooed *all over.* I'm just going to be as bad as bad can be. You'll see."

"'I'm not' would be so much better than 'ain't,' dear," said Mother.

Could *nothing* make them feel?

"I suppose nobody wants *my* opinion, Annie, but if I had talked to my parents like that when I was a child I would have been whipped within an inch of my life," said Aunt Mary Maria. "I think it is a great pity the birch rod is so neglected now in some homes."

"Little Jem is not to blame," snapped Susan, seeing that Dr. and Mrs. Dr. were not going to say anything. But if Mary Maria

Blythe was going to get away with that, she, Susan would know the reason why. "Bertie Shakespeare Drew put him up to it, filling him up with what fun it would be to see Joe Drew tatooed. He was here all the afternoon and sneaked into the kitchen and took the best aluminum saucepan to use as a helmet. Said they were playing soldiers. Then they made boats out of shingles and got soaked to the bone sailing them in the Hollow brook. And after that they went hopping about the yard for a solid hour, making the weirdest noises, pretending they were frogs. Frogs! No wonder Little Jem is tired out and not himself. He is the best-behaved child that ever lived when he is not worn to a frazzle, and that you may tie to."

Aunt Mary Maria said nothing aggravatingly. She never talked to Susan Baker at meal-times, thus expressing her disapproval over Susan being allowed to "sit with the family" at all.

Anne and Susan had thrashed that out before Aunt Mary Maria had come. Susan, who "knew her place," never sat or expected to sit with the family when there was company at Ingleside.

"But Aunt Mary Maria isn't company," said Anne. "She's just one of the family...and so are you, Susan."

In the end Susan gave in, not without a secret satisfaction that Mary Maria Blythe would see that she was no common hired girl. Susan had never met Aunt Mary Maria, but a niece of Susan's, the daughter of her sister Matilda, had worked for her in Charlottetown and had told Susan all about her.

"I am not going to pretend to you, Susan, that I'm overjoyed at the prospect of a visit from Aunt Mary Maria, especially just now," said Anne frankly. "But she has written Gilbert asking if she may come for a few weeks...and you know how the doctor is about such things..."

"As he has a perfect right to be," said Susan staunchly. "What is a man to do but stand by his own flesh and blood? But as for a few weeks...well, Mrs. Dr. dear, I do not want to look on the dark side of things...but my sister Matilda's sister-in-law came to visit *her* for a few weeks and stayed for twenty years."

"I don't think we need dread anything like that, Susan," smiled Anne. "Aunt Mary Maria has a very nice home of her own in Charlottetown. But she is finding it very big and lonely. Her mother died two years ago, you know...she was eighty-five and Aunt Mary Maria was very good to her and misses her very much. Let's make her visit as pleasant as we can, Susan."

"I will do what in me lies, Mrs. Dr. dear. Of course we must put another board in the table, but after all is said and done it is better to be lengthening the table than shortening it down."

"We mustn't have flowers on the table, Susan, because I understand they give her asthma. And pepper makes her sneeze, so we'd better not have it. She is subject to frequent bad headaches, too, so we must really try not to be noisy."

"Good grief! Well, I have never noticed you and the doctor making much noise. And if I want to yell I can go to the middle of the maple bush; but if our poor children have to keep quiet *all* the time because of Mary Maria Blythe's headaches...you will excuse me for saying I think it is going a little too far, Mrs. Dr. dear."

"It's just for a few weeks, Susan."

"Let us hope so. Oh, well, Mrs. Dr. dear, we just have to take the lean streaks with the fat in this world," was Susan's final word.

So Aunt Mary Maria came, demanding immediately upon her arrival if they had had the chimneys cleaned recently. She had, it appeared, a great dread of fire. "And I've always said that the chimneys of this house aren't nearly tall enough. I hope my bed has been well aired, Annie. Damp bed linen is terrible."

She took possession of the Ingleside guest-room...and incidentally of all the other rooms in the house except Susan's.

Nobody hailed her arrival with frantic delight. Jem, after one look at her, slipped out to the kitchen and whispered to Susan, "Can we laugh while she's here, Susan?" Walter's eyes brimmed with tears at sight of her and he had to be hustled ignominiously out of the room. The twins did not wait to be hustled but ran of their own accord. Even the Shrimp, Susan averred went and had a fit in the back yard. Only Shirley stood his ground, gazing fearlessly at her out of his round brown eyes from the safe anchorage of Susan's lap and arm. Aunt Mary Maria thought the Ingleside children had very bad manners. But what could you expect when they had a mother who "wrote for the papers" and a father who thought they were perfection just because they were *his* children, and a hired girl like Susan Baker who never knew her place? But she, Mary Maria Blythe, would do her best for poor Cousin John's grandchildren as long as she was at Ingleside.

"Your grace is much too short, Gilbert," she said disapprovingly at her first meal. "Would you like me to say grace for you while I am here? It will be a better example to your family."

Much to Susan's horror Gilbert said he would and Aunt Mary Maria said grace at supper. "More like a prayer than a grace," Susan sniffed over her dishes. Susan privately agreed with her niece's description of Mary Maria Blythe. "She always seems to be smelling a bad smell, Aunt Susan. Not an unpleasant odour... just a bad smell." Gladys had a way of putting things, Susan reflected. And yet, to anyone less prejudiced than Susan Miss Mary Maria Blythe was not ill-looking for a lady of fifty-five. She had what she believed were "aristocratic features," framed by always sleek grey crimps which seemed to insult daily Susan's spiky little knob of grey hair. She dressed very nicely, wore long jet earrings in her ears and fashionably high-boned net collars on her lean throat.

"At least, we do not need to be ashamed of her appearance," reflected Susan. But what Aunt Mary Maria would have thought if she had known Susan was consoling herself on such grounds must be left to the imagination.

5

Anne was cutting a vaseful of June lilies for her room and another of Susan's peonies for Gilbert's desk in the library...the milky-white peonies with the blood-red flecks at their hearts, like a god's kiss. The air was coming alive after the unusually hot June day and one could hardly tell whether the harbour were silver or gold.

"There's going to be a wonderful sunset tonight, Susan," she said, looking in at the kitchen window as she passed it.

"I cannot admire the sunset until I have got my dishes washed, Mrs. Dr. dear," protested Susan.

"It will be gone by that time, Susan. Look at that enormous white cloud towering up over the Hollow, with its rosy-pink top. Wouldn't you like to fly up and light on it?"

Susan had a vision of herself flying up over the glen, dishcloth in hand, to that cloud. It did not appeal to her. But allowances must be made for Mrs. Dr. just now.

"There's a new, vicious kind of bug eating the rose-bushes," went on Anne. "I must spray them tomorrow. I'd like to do it tonight...this is just the kind of evening I love to work in the garden. Things are growing tonight. I hope there'll be gardens in heaven, Susan...gardens we can work in, I mean, and help things to grow."

"But not bugs surely," protested Susan.

"No-o-o, I suppose not. But a *completed* garden wouldn't really be any fun, Susan. You have to work in a garden yourself or you miss its meaning. I want to weed and dig and transplant and change and plan and prune. And I want the flowers I love in heaven...I'd rather my own pansies than the asphodel, Susan."

"Why cannot you put in the evening as you want to?" broke in Susan, who thought Mrs. Dr. was really going a little wild.

"Because the doctor wants me to go for a drive with him. He is going to see poor old Mrs. John Paxton. She is dying...he can't do her any good...he has done everything he can...but she does like to have him drop in."

"Oh, well, Mrs. Dr. dear, we all know that nobody can die or be born without him hereabouts and it is a nice evening for a drive. I think I will take a walk down to the village myself and replenish our pantry after I put the twins and Shirley to bed and manure Mrs. Aaron Ward. She isn't blooming as she ought to. Miss Blythe has just gone upstairs, sighing at every step, saying one of her headaches is coming on, so there will be a little peace and quiet for the evening at least."

"See that Jem goes to bed in good time, will you, Susan?" said Anne as she went away through the evening that was like a cup of fragrance that has spilled over. "He's really much tireder than he thinks he is. And he never wants to go to bed. Walter is not coming home tonight, Leslie asked if he might stay there."

Jem was sitting on the steps of the side door, one bare foot hooked over his knee, scowling viciously at things in general and at an enormous moon behind the Glen church spire in particular. Jem didn't like such big moons.

"Take care your face doesn't freeze like that," Aunt Mary Maria had said as she passed him on her way into the house.

Jem scowled more blackly than ever. He didn't care if his face did freeze like that. He hoped it would. "Go 'way and don't come tagging after me all the time," he told Nan, who had crept out to him after Father and Mother had driven away.

"Cross-patch!" said Nan. But before she trotted off she laid down on the step beside him the red candy lion she had brought out to him.

Jem ignored it. He felt more abused than ever. He wasn't being used right. Everybody picked on him. Hadn't Nan that very morning said, "*You* weren't born at Ingleside like the rest of us." Di had et his chocolate rabbit that forenoon though she *knew* it was his rabbit. Even Walter had deserted him, going away to dig wells in the sand with Ken and Persis Ford. Great fun that! And he wanted so much to go with Bertie to see the tattooing. Jem was sure he had never wanted anything so much in his life before. He wanted to see the wonderful, full-rigged ship that Bertie said was always on Captain Bill's mantelpiece. It was a mean shame, that's what it was.

Susan brought him out a big slice of cake covered with maple frosting and nuts, but, "No, thank you," said Jem stonily. Why hadn't she saved some of the gingerbread and cream for him? S'pose the rest of them had et it all. Pigs! He plunged into a deeper gulf of gloom. The gang would be on their way to the Harbour Mouth by now. He just couldn't bear the thought. He'd *got* to do something to get square with folks. S'posin' he sliced Di's sawdust giraffe open on the living-room rug? That would make old Susan mad...Susan with her nuts, when she knew he hated nuts in frosting. S'posin' he went and drew a moustache on that picture of the cherub on the calendar in her room? He had always hated that fat, pink, smiling cherub because it looked just like Sissy Flagg who had told round school that Jem Blythe was her beau. Hers! Sissy Flagg! But Susan thought that cherub lovely.

S'posin' he scalped Nan's doll? S'posin' he whacked the nose off Gog or Magog...or both of them? Maybe that would make Mother see he wasn't a baby any longer. Just wait till next spring!

He had brought her mayflowers for years and years and years... ever since he was four...but he wouldn't do it next spring. No, sir!

S'posin' he et a lot of the little green apples on the early tree and got nice and sick? Maybe *that* would scare them. S'posin' he never washed behind his ears again? S'posin' he made faces at everybody in church next Sunday? S'posin' he put a caterpillar on Aunt Mary Maria...a big, striped, woolly caterpillar? S'posin' he ran away to the harbour and hid in Captain David Reese's ship and sailed out of the harbour in the morning on his way to South America? Would they be sorry *then?* S'posin' he never came back? S'posin' he went hunting jaggers in Brazil? Would they be sorry *then?* No, he bet they wouldn't. Nobody loved him. There was a hole in his pants pocket. Nobody had mended it. Well, *he* didn't care. He'd just show that hole to everybody in the Glen and let people see how neglected he was. His wrongs surged up and overwhelmed him.

Tick-tack...tick-tack...tick-tack...went the old grandfather clock in the hall that had been brought to Ingleside after Grandfather Blythe's death...a deliberate old clock dating from the days when there was such a thing as time. Generally Jem loved it...now he hated it. It seemed to be laughing at him. "Ha, ha, bedtime is coming. The other fellows can go to the Harbour Mouth but you go to bed. Ha, ha...ha, ha...ha, ha!"

Why did he have to go to bed every night? Yes, why?

Susan came out on her way to the Glen and looked tenderly at the small, rebellious figure.

"You needn't go to bed till I get back, Little Jem," she said indulgently.

"I ain't going to bed tonight!" said Jem fiercely. *"I'm* going to run away, that's what I'm going to do, old Susan Baker. I'm going to go and jump into the pond, old Susan Baker."

Susan did not enjoy being called old, even by Little Jem. She stalked away in a grim silence. He *did* need a bit of disciplining.

The Shrimp, who had followed her out, feeling a yearning for companionship, squatted down on his black haunches before Jem, but got only a glare for his pains. "Clear out! Sitting there on your bottom, staring like Aunt Mary Maria! Scat! Oh, you won't, won't you! Then take that!"

Jem shied Shirley's little tin wheelbarrow that was lying handily near, and the Shrimp fled with a plaintive yowl to the sanctuary of the sweetbriar hedge. Look at that! Even the family cat hated him! What was the use of going on living?

He picked up the candy lion. Nan had eaten the tail and most of the hindquarters but it was still quite a lion. Might as well eat it. It might be the last lion he'd ever eat. By the time Jem had finished the lion and licked his fingers he had made up his mind what he was going to do. It was the only thing a fellow *could* do when a fellow wasn't allowed to do *anything*.

6

"Why in the world is the house lighted up like that?" exclaimed Anne, when she and Gilbert turned in at the gate at eleven o'clock. "Company must have come."

But there was no company visible when Anne hurried into the house. Nor was anyone else visible. There was a light in the kitchen...in the living-room...in the library...in the dining-room...in Susan's room and the upstairs hall...but no sign of an occupant.

"What do you suppose," began Anne...but she was interrupted by the ringing of the telephone. Gilbert answered...

listened for a moment,...uttered an ejaculation of horror...and tore out without even a glance at Anne. Evidently something dreadful had happened and there was no time to be wasted in explanations.

Anne was used to this...as the wife of a man who waits on life and death must be. With a philosophical shrug she removed her hat and coat. She felt a trifle annoyed with Susan, who really shouldn't have gone out and left all the lights blazing and all the doors wide open.

"Mrs...Dr...dear," said a voice that could not possibly be Susan's...but was.

Anne stared at Susan. Such as Susan...hatless...her grey hair full of bits of hay...her print dress shockingly stained and discoloured. And her face!

"Susan! What has happened? Susan!"

"Little Jem has disappeared."

"Disappeared!" Anne stared stupidly. "What do you mean? He can't have disappeared!"

"He has," gasped Susan, wringing her hands. "He was on the side steps when I went to the Glen. I was back before dark...and he was not there. At first...I was not scared...but I could not find him anywhere. I have searched every room in the house...he said he was going to run away..."

"Nonsense! He wouldn't do that, Susan. You have worked yourself up unnecessarily. He must be somewhere about...he has fallen asleep...he *must* be somewhere around."

"I have looked everywhere...everywhere. I have combed the grounds and the outhouses. Look at my dress...I remembered he always said it would be such fun to sleep in the hay-loft. So I went there...and fell through that hole in the corner into one of the mangers in the stable...and lit on a nest of eggs. It is a mercy I did not break a leg...if anything can be a mercy when Little Jem is lost."

Annie still refused to feel perturbed.

"Do you think he could have gone to the Harbour Mouth with the boys, after all, Susan? He has never disobeyed a command before, but..."

"No, he did not, Mrs. Dr. dear...the blessed lamb did not disobey. I rushed down to Drews' after I had searched everywhere and Bertie Shakespeare had just got home. He said Jem had not gone with them. The pit seemed to drop out of my stomach. You had trusted him to me and...I phoned Paxtons' and they said you had been there and gone they did not know where."

"We drove to Lowbridge to call on the Parkers..."

"I phoned everywhere I thought you could be. Then I went back to the village...the men have started out to search..."

"Oh, Susan, was that necessary?"

"Mrs. Dr. dear, I had looked everywhere...everywhere that child could be. Oh, what I have gone through this night! And he *said* he was going to jump into the pond..."

In spite of herself a queer little shiver ran over Anne. Of course Jem wouldn't jump into the pond...that was nonsense... but there was an old dory on it which Carter Flagg used for trouting and Jem might, in his defiant mood of the earlier evening, have tried to row about the pond in it...he had often wanted to...he might even have fallen into the pond trying to untie the dory. All at once her fear took terrible shape.

"And I haven't the slightest idea where Gilbert has gone," she thought wildly.

"What's all this fuss about?" demanded Aunt Mary Maria, suddenly appearing on the stairs, her head surrounded by a halo of crimpers and her body encased in a dragon-embroidered dressing-gown. "Can't a body *ever* get a quiet night's sleep in this house?"

"Little Jem has disappeared," said Susan again, too much in the grip of terror to resent Miss Blythe's tone. "His mother trusted me..."

Anne had gone to search the house for herself. Jem must be somewhere! He was not in his room...the bed was undisturbed....He was not in the twins' room...in hers...He was...he was nowhere in the house. Anne, after a pilgrimage from garret to cellar, returned to the living-room in a condition that was suddenly akin to panic.

"I don't want to make you nervous, Annie," said Aunt Mary Marie, lowering her voice creepily, "but have you looked in the rainwater hogshead? Little Jack MacGregor was drowned in a rainwater hogshead in town last year."

"I...I looked there," said Susan, with another wring of her hands. "I...I took a stick...and poked..."

Anne's heart, which had stood still at Aunt Mary Maria's question, resumed operations. Susan gathered herself together and stopped wringing her hands. She had remembered too late that Mrs. Dr. dear should not be upset.

"Let us calm down and pull together," she said in a trembling voice. "As you say, Mrs. Dr. dear, he *must* be somewhere about. He *cannot* have dissolved into thin air."

"Have you looked in the coal-bin? And the clock?" asked Aunt Mary Maria.

Susan *had* looked in the coal-bin but nobody had thought of the clock. It *was* quite big enough for a small boy to hide in. Anne, not considering the absurdity of supposing that Jem would crouch there for four hours, rushed to it. But Jem was not in the clock.

"I had a *feeling* something was going to happen when I went to bed tonight," said Aunt Mary Maria, pressing both hands to her temples. "When I read my nightly chapter in the Bible the words, 'Ye know not what a day may bring forth,' seemed to stand out from the page as it were. It was a sign. You'd better nerve yourself to bear the worst, Annie. He may have wandered into the marsh. It's a pity we haven't a few bloodhounds."

With a dreadful effort Anne managed a laugh.

"I'm afraid there aren't any on the Island, Aunty. If we had Gilbert's old setter Rex, who got poisoned, he would soon find Jem. I feel sure we are all alarming ourselves for nothing..."

"Tommy Spencer in Carmody disappeared mysteriously forty years ago and was never found...or was he? Well, if he was, it was only his skeleton. This is no laughing matter, Annie. I don't know how you can take it so calmly."

The telephone rang. Anne and Susan looked at each other.

"I can't...I *can't* go to the phone, Susan," said Anne in a whisper.

"I cannot either," said Susan flatly. She was to hate herself all her days for showing such weakness before Mary Maria Blythe, but she could not help it. Two hours of terrified searching and distorted imaginations had made Susan a wreck.

Aunt Mary Maria stalked to the telephone and took down the receiver, her crimpers making a horned silhouette on the wall which, Susan reflected, in spite of her anguish, looked like the old Nick himself.

"Carter Flagg says they have searched everywhere but found no sign of him yet," reported Aunt Mary Maria coolly. "But he says the dory is out in the middle of the pond with no one in it as far as they can ascertain. They are going to drag the pond."

Susan caught Anne just in time.

"No...no...I'm not going to faint, Susan," said Anne through white lips. "Help me to a chair...thanks. We *must* find Gilbert..."

"If James is drowned, Annie, you must remind yourself that he has been spared a lot of trouble in this wretched world," said Aunt Mary Marie by way of administering further consolation.

"I'm going to get the lantern and search the grounds again," said Anne, as soon as she could stand up. "Yes, I know you did, Susan...but let me...let me. I *cannot* sit still and wait."

"You must put on a sweater then, Mrs. Dr. dear. There is a heavy dew and the air is damp. I will get your red one...it is hanging on a chair in the boys' room. Wait you here till I bring it."

Susan hurried upstairs. A few moments later something that could only be described as a shriek echoed through Ingleside. Anne and Aunt Mary Maria rushed upstairs, where they found Susan laughing and crying in the hall, nearer to hysterics than Susan Baker had ever been in her life or ever would be again.

"Mrs. Dr. dear...he's there! Little Jem is there...asleep on the window-seat behind the door. I never looked there...the door hid it...and when he wasn't in his bed..."

Anne, weak with relief and joy, got herself into the room and dropped on her knees by the window-seat. In a little while she and Susan would be laughing over their own foolishness, but now there could be only tears of thankfulness. Little Jem was sound asleep on the window-seat, with an afghan pulled over him, his battered Teddy Bear in his little sunburned hands, and a forgiving Shrimp stretched across his legs. His red curls fell over the cushion. He seemed to be having a pleasant dream and Anne did not mean to waken him. But suddenly he opened his eyes that were like hazel stars and looked at her.

"Jem, darling, why aren't you in your bed? We've...we've been a little alarmed...we couldn't find you...and we never thought of looking here..."

"I wanted to lie here 'cause I could see you and Daddy drive in at the gate when you got home. It was so lonesome I just had to go to bed."

Mother was lifting him in her arms...carrying him to his own bed. It was so nice to be kissed...to feel her tucking the sheets about him with those caressing little pats that gave him such a sense of being loved. Who cared about seeing an old snake tattooed, anyhow? Mother was so nice...the nicest mother anybody ever had. Everybody in the Glen called Bertie Shakespeare's mother "Mrs. Second Skimmings" because she was so mean, and he knew...for he'd seen it...that she slapped Bertie's face for every little thing.

"Mummy," he said sleepily, "of course I'll bring you mayflowers next spring...every spring. You can depend on me."

"Of course I can, darling," said Mother.

"Well, since everyone is over their fit of the fidgets, I suppose we can draw a peaceful breath and go back to our beds," said Aunt Mary Maria. But there was some shrewish relief in her tone.

"It was very silly of me not to remember the window-seat," said Anne. "The joke is on us and the doctor will not let us forget it, you may be certain. Susan, please phone Mr. Flagg that we've found Jem."

"And a nice laugh he will have on me," said Susan happily. "Not that I care...he can laugh all he likes since Little Jem is safe."

"I could do with a cup of tea," sighed Aunt Mary Maria plaintively, gathering her dragons about her spare form.

"I will get it in a jiffy," said Susan briskly. "We will all feel the sprightlier for one. Mrs. Dr. dear, when Carter Flagg heard Little Jem was safe he said, 'Thank God.' I shall never say a word against that man again, no matter what his prices are. And don't you think we might have a chicken dinner tomorrow, Mrs. Dr. dear? Just by way of a little celebration, so to speak. And Little Jem shall have his favourite muffins for breakfast."

There was another telephone call...this time from Gilbert to say that he was taking a badly burned baby from the Harbour Head to the hospital in town and not to look for him till morning.

Anne bent from her window for a thankful goodnight look at the world before going to bed. A cool wind was blowing in from the sea. A sort of moonlit rapture was running through the trees in the Hollow. Anne could even laugh...with a quiver behind the laughter...over their panic of an hour ago and Aunt Mary Maria's absurd suggestions and ghoulish memories. Her child was safe... Gilbert was somewhere battling to save another child's life...*Dear God, help him and help the mother...help all mothers everywhere. We need so much help, with the little sensitive, loving hearts and minds that look to us for guidance and love and understanding.*

The friendly enfolding night took possession of Ingleside, and everybody, even Susan...who rather felt that she would like to crawl into some nice quiet hole and pull it in after her...fell on sleep under its sheltering roof.

7

"He'll have plenty of company...he won't be lonesome...our four...and my niece and nephew from Montreal are visiting us. What one doesn't think of the others do."

Big, sonsy, jolly Mrs. Dr. Parker smiled expansively at Walter...who returned the smile somewhat aloofly. He wasn't altogether sure he liked Mrs. Parker in spite of her smiles and jollity. There was too much of her, somehow. Dr. Parker he did like. As for "our four" and the niece and nephew from Montreal, Walter had never seen any of them. Lowbridge, where the Parkers lived, was six miles from the Glen and Walter had never been there, though Dr. and Mrs. Parker and Dr. and Mrs. Blythe visited back and forth frequently. Dr. Parker and Dad were great friends, though Walter had a feeling now and again that Mother could have got along very well without Mrs. Parker. Even at six, Walter, as Anne realized, could see things that other children could not.

Walter was not sure, either, that he really wanted to go to Lowbridge. Some visits were splendid. A trip to Avonlea now... ah, there was fun for you! And a night spent with Kenneth Ford at the old House of Dreams was more fun still...though *that* couldn't really be called visiting, for the House of Dreams always seemed like a second home to the small fry of Ingleside. But to go to Lowbridge for two whole weeks, among strangers, was a very different matter. However, it seemed to be a settled thing. For some reason, which Walter felt but could not understand, Dad and Mummy were pleased over the arrangement. Did they want to get rid of *all* their children, Walter wondered, rather sadly and uneasily. Jem was away, having been taken to Avonlea two days ago, and he had heard Susan making mysterious remarks about "sending the twins to Mrs. Marshall Elliott when the time came." What time? Aunt Mary Maria seemed very gloomy over something and had been known to say that she "wished it was all well over." What was it she wished over? Walter had no idea. But there was something strange in the air at Ingleside.

"I'll take him over tomorrow," said Gilbert.

"The youngsters will be looking forward to it," said Mrs. Parker.

"It's very kind of you, I'm sure," said Anne.

"It's all for the best, no doubt," Susan told the Shrimp darkly in the kitchen.

"It is very obliging of Mrs. Parker to take Walter off our hands, Annie," said Aunt Mary Maria, when the Parkers had gone. "She told me she had taken quite a fancy to him. People *do* take such odd fancies, don't they? Well, perhaps now for at least two weeks I'll be able to go into the bathroom without tramping on a dead fish."

"A dead fish, Aunty! You don't mean..."

"I mean exactly what I say, Annie. I always do. A dead fish! Did *you* ever step on a dead fish with your bare feet?"

"No-o...but how..."

"Walter caught a trout last night and put it in the bathtub to keep it alive, Mrs. Dr. dear," said Susan airily. "If it had stayed there it would have been all right, but somehow it got out and died in the night. Of course, if people *will* go about on bare feet..."

"I make it a rule never to quarrel with anyone," said Aunt Mary Maria, getting up and leaving the room.

"*I* am determined she shall not vex *me,* Mrs. Dr. dear," said Susan.

"Oh, Susan, she *is* getting on my nerves a bit...but of course I won't mind so much when all this is over...and it *must* be nasty to tramp on a dead fish..."

"Isn't a dead fish better than a live one, Mummy? A dead fish wouldn't squirm," said Di.

Since the truth must be told at all costs it must be admitted that the mistress and maid of Ingleside both giggled.

So that was that. But Anne wondered to Gilbert that night if Walter would be quite happy at Lowbridge.

"He's so very sensitive and imaginative," she said wistfully.

"Too much so," said Gilbert, who was tired after having had, to quote Susan, three babies that day. "Why, Anne, I believe that child is afraid to go upstairs in the dark. It will do him worlds of good to give and take with the Parker fry for a few days. He'll come home a different child."

Anne said nothing more. No doubt Gilbert was quite right. Walter was lonesome without Jem; and in view of what had happened when Shirley was born it would be just as well for Susan to have as little on her hands as possible beyond running the house and enduring Aunt Mary Maria...whose two weeks had already stretched to four.

Walter was lying awake in his bed trying to escape from the haunting thought that he was to go away next day by giving free rein to fancy. Walter had a very vivid imagination. It was to him a great white charger, like the one in the picture on the wall, on which he could gallop backward or forward in time and space. The Night was coming down...Night, like a tall, dark, bat-winged angel who lived in Mr. Andrew Taylor's woods on the south hill. Sometimes Walter welcomed her...sometimes he pictured her so vividly that he grew afraid of her. Walter dramatized and personified everything in his small world...the Wind who told him stories at night...the Frost that nipped the flowers in the garden...the Dew that fell so silverly and silently... the Moon which he felt sure he could catch if he could only go to the top of that faraway purple hill...the Mist that came in from the sea...the great Sea itself that was always changing and never changed...the dark, mysterious Tide. They were all entities to Walter. Ingleside and the Hollow and the maple grove and the Marsh and the harbour shore were full of elves and kelpies and dryads and mermaids and goblins. The black plaster-of-Paris cat on the library mantelpiece was a fairy witch. It came alive at night and prowled about the house, grown to enormous size. Walter ducked his head under the bedclothes and shivered. He was always scaring himself with his own fancies.

Perhaps Aunt Mary Maria was right when she said he was "far too nervous and high-strung," though Susan would never forgive her for it. Perhaps Aunt Kitty MacGregor of the Upper Glen, who was reported to have "the second sight," was right when, having once taken a deep look into Walter's long-lashed, smoky grey eyes, she said he "did be having an old soul in a young body." It might be that the old soul knew too much for the young brain to understand always.

Walter was told in the morning that Dad would take him to Lowbridge after dinner. He said nothing, but during dinner a choky sensation came over him and he dropped his eyes quickly to hide a sudden mist of tears. Not quickly enough, however.

"You're not going to *cry,* Walter?" said Aunt Mary Maria, as if a six-year-old mite would be disgraced forever if he cried. "If there's anything I *do* despise it's a cry-baby. And you haven't eaten your meat."

"All but the fat," said Walter, blinking valiantly but not yet daring to look up. "I don't like fat."

"When *I* was a child," said Aunt Mary Maria, "I was not allowed to have likes and dislikes. Well, Mrs. Dr. Parker will probably cure you of some of your notions. She was a Winter, I think...or was she a Clark?...no, she must have been a Campbell. But the Winters and the Campbells are all tarred with the same brush and they don't put up with any nonsense."

"Oh, please, Aunt Mary Maria, don't frighten Walter about his visit to Lowbridge," said Anne, a little spark kindling far down in her eyes.

"I'm sorry, Annie," said Aunt Mary Maria with great humility. "I should of course have remembered that *I* have no right to try to teach your children *anything.*"

"Drat her hide," muttered Susan as she went out for the dessert...Walter's favourite Queen pudding.

Anne felt miserably guilty. Gilbert had shot her a slightly reproachful glance as if to imply she might have been more patient with a poor lonely old lady.

Gilbert himself was feeling a bit seedy. The truth, as everyone knew, was that he had been terribly overworked all summer; and perhaps Aunt Mary Maria was more of a strain than he would admit. Anne made up her mind that in the fall, if all was well, she would pack him off willy-nilly for a month's snipe-shooting in Nova Scotia.

"How is your tea?" she asked Aunt Mary Maria repentantly.

Aunt Mary Maria pursed her lips.

"Too weak. But it doesn't matter. Who cares whether a poor old woman gets her tea to her liking or not? Some folks, however, think I'm real good company."

Whatever the connexion between Aunt Mary Maria's two sentences was, Anne felt she was beyond ferreting it out just then. She had turned very pale.

"I think I'll go upstairs and lie down," she said, a trifle faintly, as she rose from the table. "And I think, Gilbert...perhaps you'd better not stay long in Lowbridge...and suppose you give Miss Carson a ring."

She kissed Walter good-bye rather casually and hurriedly... very much as if she were not thinking about him at all. Walter *would not* cry. Aunt Mary Maria kissed him on the forehead... Walter hated to be moistly kissed on the forehead...and said:

"Mind your table manners at Lowbridge, Walter. Mind you ain't greedy. If you are, a Big Black Man will come along with a big black bag to pop naughty children into."

It was perhaps as well that Gilbert had gone out to harness Grey Tom and did not hear this. He and Anne had always made a point of never frightening their children with such ideas or allowing anyone else to do it. Susan did hear it as she cleared the table and Aunt Mary Maria never knew what a narrow escape she had of having the gravy boat and its contents flung at her head.

8

Generally Walter enjoyed a drive with Dad. He loved beauty, and the roads around Glen St. Mary were beautiful. The road to Lowbridge was a double ribbon of dancing buttercups, with here and there the ferny green rim of an inviting grove. But today Dad didn't seem to want to talk much and he drove Grey Tom as Walter never remembered seeing him driven before. When they reached Lowbridge he said a few hurried words aside to

Mrs. Parker and rushed out without bidding Walter good-bye. Walter had again hard work to keep from crying. It was only too plain that nobody loved him. Mother and Father used to, but they didn't any longer.

The big, untidy Parker house at Lowbridge did not seem friendly to Walter. But perhaps no house would have seemed that just then. Mrs. Parker took him out to the back yard, where shrieks of noisy mirth were resounding, and introduced him to the children who seemed to fill it. Then she promptly went back to her sewing, leaving them to "get acquainted by themselves"...a proceeding that worked very well in nine cases out of ten. Perhaps she could not be blamed for failing to see that little Walter Blythe was the tenth. She liked him...her own children were jolly little tads...Fred and Opal were inclined to put on Montreal airs, but she felt quite sure they wouldn't be unkind to anyone. Everything would go swimmingly. She was so glad she could help "poor Anne Blythe" out, even if it was only by taking one of her children off her hands. Mrs. Parker hoped "all would go well." Anne's friends were a good deal more worried over her than she was over herself, reminding each other of Shirley's birth.

A sudden hush had fallen over the back yard...a yard which ran off into a big, bowery apple orchard. Walter stood looking gravely and shyly at the Parker children and their Johnson cousins from Montreal. Bill Parker was ten...a ruddy, round-faced urchin who "took after" his mother and seemed very old and big in Walter's eyes. Andy Parker was nine and Lowbridge children could have told you that he was "the nasty Parker one" and was nicknamed "Pig" for reasons good. Walter did not like his looks from the first...his short-cropped fair bristles, his impish freckled face, his bulging blue eyes. Fred Johnson was Bill's age and Walter didn't like him either, though he was a good-looking chap with tawny curls and black eyes. His nine-year-old sister, Opal, had curls and black eyes, too...snapping black eyes. She stood with her arm about tow-headed, eight-year-old Cora Parker and they both looked Walter over condescendingly. If it had not been for Alice Parker Walter might very conceivably have turned and fled.

Alice was seven; Alice had the loveliest little ripples of golden curls all over her head; Alice had eyes as blue and soft as the violets in the Hollow; Alice had pink, dimpled cheeks; Alice wore a little frilled yellow dress in which she looked like a dancing buttercup; Alice smiled at him as if she had known him all her life; Alice was a friend.

Fred opened the conversation.

"Hello, sonny," he said condescendingly.

Walter felt the condescension at once and retreated into himself.

"My name is Walter," he said distinctly.

Fred turned to the others with a well-done air of amazement. *He'd* show this country lad!

"He says his name is *Walter*," he told Bill with a comical twist of his mouth.

"He says his name is *Walter*," Bill told Opal in turn.

"He says his name is *Walter*," Opal told the delighted Andy.

"He says his name is *Walter*," Andy told Cora.

"He says his name is *Walter*," Cora giggled to Alice.

Alice said nothing. She just looked admiringly at Walter and her look enabled him to bear up when all the rest chanted together, "He says his name is *Walter*," and then burst into shrieks of derisive laughter.

"What fun the dear little folks are having!" thought Mrs. Parker complacently over her shining.

"I heard Mom say you believed in fairies," Andy said, leering impudently.

Walter gazed levelly at him. He was not going to be downed before Alice.

"There *are* fairies," he said stoutly.

"There ain't," said Andy.

"There *are*," said Walter.

"He says there are *fairies*," Andy told Fred.

"He says there are *fairies*," Fred told Bill...and they went through the whole performance again.

It was torture to Walter, who had never been made fun of before and couldn't take it. He bit his lips to keep the tears back. He must not cry before Alice.

"How would you like to be pinched black and blue?" demanded Andy, who had made up his mind that Walter was a sissy and that it would be good fun to tease him.

"Pig, hush!" ordered Alice terribly...very terribly, although very quietly and sweetly and gently. There was something in her tone that even Andy dared not flout.

"'Course I didn't mean it," he muttered shamefacedly.

The wind veered a bit in Walter's favour and they had a fairly amiable game of tag in the orchard. But when they trouped noisily in to supper Walter was again overwhelmed with homesickness. It was so terrible that for one awful moment he was afraid he was going to cry before them all...even Alice, who, however, gave his arm such a friendly little nudge as they sat down that it helped him. But he could not eat anything...he simply could not. Mrs. Parker, for whose methods there was certainly something to be said, did not worry him about it, comfortably concluding that his appetite would be better in the morning, and the others were too much occupied in eating and talking to take much notice of him.

Walter wondered why the whole family shouted so at each other, ignorant of the fact that they had not yet had time to get out of the habit since the recent death of a very deaf and sensitive old grandmother. The noise made his head ache. Oh, at home now they would be eating supper, too. Mother would be smiling from the head of the table, Father would be joking with the twins, Susan would be pouring cream into Shirley's mug of milk, Nan would be sneaking tidbits to the Shrimp. Even Aunt Mary Maria, as part of the home circle, seemed suddenly invested with a soft, tender radiance. Who would have rung the Chinese gong for supper? It was his week to do it and Jem was away. If he could only find a place to cry in! But there seemed to be no place where you could indulge in tears at Lowbridge. Besides...there was Alice. Walter gulped down a whole glassful of ice-water and found that it helped.

"Our cat takes fits," Andy said suddenly, kicking him under the table.

"So does ours," said Walter. The Shrimp had had two fits. And he wasn't going to have the Lowbridge cats rated higher than the Ingleside cats.

"I'll bet our cat takes fittier fits than yours," taunted Andy.

"I'll bet she doesn't," retorted Walter.

"Now, now, don't let's have any arguments over your cats," said Mrs. Parker, who wanted a quiet evening to write her Institute paper on "Misunderstood Children." "Run out and play. It won't be long before your bedtime."

Bedtime! Walter suddenly realized that he had to stay here all night...many nights...two weeks of nights. It was dreadful. He went out to the orchard with clenched fists, to find Bill and Andy in a furious clinch on the grass, kicking, clawing, yelling.

"You give me the wormy apple, Bill Parker!" Andy was howling. "I'll teach you to give me wormy apples! I'll bite off your ears!"

Fights of this sort were an everyday occurrence with the Parkers. Mrs. Parker held that it didn't hurt boys to fight. She said they got a lot of devilment out of their systems that way and were as good friends as ever afterwards. But Walter had never seen anyone fighting before and was aghast.

Fred was cheering them on, Opal and Cora were laughing, but there were tears in Alice's eyes. Walter could not endure that.

He hurled himself between the combatants, who had drawn apart for a moment to snatch breath before joining battle again.

"You stop fighting," said Walter. "You're scaring Alice."

Bill and Andy stared at him in amazement for a moment, until the funny side of this baby interfering in their fight struck them. Both burst into laughter and Bill slapped him on the back.

"It's got spunk, kids," he said. "It's going to be a real boy sometime if you let it grow. Here's an apple for it...and no worms either."

Alice wiped the tears away from her soft pink cheeks and looked so adoringly at Walter that Fred didn't like it. Of course Alice was only a baby but even babies had no business to be looking adoringly at other boys when he, Fred Johnson of Montreal, was around. This must be dealt with. Fred had been into the house and had heard Aunt Jen, who had been talking over the telephone, say something to Uncle Dick.

"Your mother's awful sick," he told Walter.

"She...she isn't!" cried Walter.

"She is, too. I heard Aunt Jen telling Uncle Dick..." Fred had heard his aunt say, "Anne Blythe is sick," and it was fun to tack in the "awful."

"She'll likely be dead before you get home."

Walter looked around with tormented eyes. Again Alice ranged herself by him...and again the rest gathered around the standard of Fred. They felt something alien about this dark, handsome child...they felt an urge to tease him.

"If she is sick," said Walter, "Father will cure her."

He would...he must!

"I'm afraid that will be impossible," said Fred, pulling a long face but winking at Andy.

"Nothing is impossible for Father," insisted Walter loyally.

"Why, Russ Carter went to Charlottetown just for a day last summer and when he came home his mother was dead as a door-nail," said Bill.

"*And* buried," said Andy, thinking to add an extra dramatic touch—whether a fact or not didn't matter. "Russ was awful mad he'd missed the funeral...funerals are so jolly."

"And I've never seen a single funeral," said Opal sadly.

"Well, there'll be lots of chances for you yet," said Andy. "But you see even Dad couldn't keep Mrs. Carter alive and he's a lot better doctor than *your* father."

"He isn't..."

"Yes, he is, and a lot better-looking, too..."

"He isn't..."

"Something *always* happens when you go away from home," said Opal. "What will you feel like if you find Ingleside burned down when you go home?"

"If your mother dies, likely you children will all be sep'rated," said Cora cheerfully. "Maybe you'll come and live here."

"Yes...do," said Alice sweetly.

"Oh, his father would want to keep them," said Bill. "He'd soon be marrying again. But maybe his father will die too. I heard Dad say Dr. Blythe was working himself to death. Look at him staring. You've got girls' eyes, sonny...girls' eyes...girls' eyes."

"Aw, shut up," said Opal, suddenly tiring of the sport. "You ain't fooling him. He knows you're only teasing. Let's go down to the Park and watch the baseball game. Walter and Alice can stay here. We can't have kids tagging after us everywhere."

Walter was not sorry to see them go. Neither apparently was Alice. They sat down on an apple log and looked shyly and contentedly at each other.

"I'll show you how to play jackstones," said Alice, "and lend you my plush kangaroo."

When bedtime came Walter found himself put into the little hall bedroom alone. Mrs. Parker considerately left a candle with him and a warm puff, for the July night was unreasonably cold as even a summer night in the Maritimes sometimes is. It almost seemed as if there might be a frost.

But Walter could not sleep, not even with Alice's plush kangaroo cuddled to his cheek. Oh, if he were only home in his own room, where the big window looked out on the Glen and the little window, with a tiny roof all its own, looked out into the Scotch pine! Mother would come in and read poetry to him in her lovely voice...

"I'm a big boy...I won't cry...I wo-o-o-n't..." The tears came in spite of himself. What good were plush kangaroos? It seemed years since he had left home.

Presently the other children came back from the Park and crowded amiably into the room to sit on the bed and eat apples.

"You've been crying, baby," jeered Andy. "You're nothing but a sweet little girl. Momma's Pet!"

"Have a bite, kid," said Bill proffering a half-gnawed apple. "And cheer up. I wouldn't be surprised if your mother got better...if she's got a constitution, that is. Dad says Mrs. Stephen Flagg would-a died years ago if she hadn't a constitution. Has your mother got one?"

"Of course she has," said Walter. He had no idea what a constitution was, but if Mrs. Stephen Flagg had one Mother must.

"Mrs. Ab Sawyer died last week and Sam Clark's mother died the week before," said Andy.

"They died in the night," said Cora. "Mother says people mostly die in the night. I hope *I* won't. Fancy going to Heaven in your nightdress!"

"Children! Children! Get off to your beds," called Mrs. Parker.

The boys went, after pretending to smother Walter with a towel. After all, they rather liked the kid. Walter caught Opal's hand as she turned away.

"Opal, it isn't true Mother's sick, is it?" he whispered imploringly. He could not face being left alone with his fear.

Opal was "not a bad-hearted child," as Mrs. Parker said, but she could not resist the thrill one got out of telling bad news.

"She *is* sick. Aunt Jen says so...she said I wasn't to tell you. But I think you ought to know. Maybe she has a cancer."

"Does *everybody* have to die, Opal?" This was a new and dreadful idea to Walter, who had never thought about death before.

"Of course, silly. Only they don't die really...they go to Heaven," said Opal cheerfully.

"Not all of them," said Andy...who was listening outside the door...in a pig's whisper.

"Is...is Heaven farther away than Charlottetown?" asked Walter.

Opal shrilled with laugher.

"Well, you *are* queer! Heaven's millions of miles away. But I'll tell you what to do. You pray. Praying's good. I lost a dime once and I prayed and I found a quarter. That's how I know."

"Opal Johnson, did you hear what I said? And put out that candle in Walter's room. I'm afraid of fire," called Mrs. Parker from her room. "He should have been asleep long ago."

Opal blew out the candle and flew. Aunt Jen was easy-going, but when she *did* get riled! Andy stuck his head in at the door for a good-night benediction.

"Likely them birds in the wallpaper will come alive and pick your eyes out," he hissed.

After which everybody did really go to bed, feeling that it was the end of a perfect day and Walt Blythe wasn't a bad little kid and they'd have some more fun teasing him tomorrow.

"Dear little souls," thought Mrs. Parker sentimentally.

An unwonted quiet descended upon the Parker house and six miles away at Ingleside little Bertha Marilla Blythe was blinking round hazel eyes at the happy faces around her and the world into which she had been ushered on the coldest July night the Maritimes had experienced in eighty-seven years!

9

Walter, alone in the darkness, still found it impossible to sleep. He had never slept alone before in his short life. Always Jem or Ken near him, warm and comforting. The little room became dimly visible as the pale moonlight crept into it, but it was almost worse than darkness. A picture on the wall at the foot of his bed seemed to leer at him...pictures always looked so *different* by moonlight. You saw things in them you never suspected by daylight. The long lace curtains looked like tall thin women, one on each side of the window, weeping. There were noises about the house...creaks, sighs, whisperings. Suppose the birds in the wallpaper *were* coming to life and getting ready to pick out his eyes? A creepy fear suddenly possessed Walter...and then one great fear banished all the others. *Mother was sick.* He had to believe it since Opal had said it was true. Perhaps Mother was dying! *Perhaps mother was dead!* There would be no Mother to go home to. Walter saw Ingleside without Mother!

Suddenly Walter knew he could not bear it. He must go home. Right away—at once. He must see Mother before she... before she...died. *This* was what Aunt Mary Maria had meant. *She* had known Mother was going to die. It was no use to think of waking anyone and asking to be taken home. They wouldn't take him...they would only laugh at him. It was an awful long road home but he would walk all night.

Very quietly he slipped out of bed and put on his clothes. He took his shoes in his hand. He did not know where Mrs. Parker had put his cap, but that did not matter. He must not make any noise...he must just escape and get to Mother. He was sorry he could not say good-bye to Alice...she would have understood. Through the dark hall...down the stairs...step by step...hold your breath...was there no end to the steps?...the very furniture was listening...oh, oh!

Walter had dropped one of his shoes! Down the stairs it clattered, bumping from step to step, shot across the hall and brought up against the front door with what seemed to Walter a deafening crash.

Walter huddled in despair against the rail. *Everybody* must have heard that noise...they would come rushing out...he wouldn't be let go home...a sob of despair choked in his throat.

It seemed hours before he dared believe that nobody had wakened up...before he dared resume his careful passage down the stairs. But it was accomplished at last; he found his shoe and cautiously turned the handle of the front door...doors were never locked at the Parker place. Mrs. Parker said they hadn't anything worth stealing except children and nobody wanted *them.*

Walter was out...the door closed behind him. He slipped on his shoes and stole down the street: the house was on the edge of the village and he was soon on the open road. A moment of panic overwhelmed him. The fear of being caught and prevented was past and all his old fears of darkness and solitude returned. He had never been out *alone* in the night before. He was afraid of the *world.* It was such a huge world and he was so terribly small in it. Even the cold raw wind that was coming up from the east seemed blowing in his face as if to push him back.

Mother was going to die! Walter took a gulp and set his face towards home. On and on he went, fighting fear gallantly. It was moonlight but the moonlight let you *see* things...and nothing looked familiar. Once when he had been out with Dad he had thought he had never seen anything so pretty as a moonlit road crossed by tree shadows. But now the shadows were so black and sharp they might fly up at you. The fields had put on a strangeness. The trees were no longer friendly. They seemed to be watching him...crowding in before and behind him. Two blazing eyes looked out at him from the ditch and a black cat of unbelievable size ran across the road. *Was it a cat?* Or...? The night was cold: he shivered in his thin blouse, but he would not mind the cold if he could only stop being afraid of everything... of the shadows and the furtive sounds and the nameless things that might be prowling in the strips of woodland he passed through. He wondered what it would be like not to be afraid of anything...like Jem.

"I'll...I'll just pretend I'm not afraid," he said aloud...and then shuddered with terror over the *lost* sound of his own voice in the great night.

But he went on...one had to go on when Mother was going to die. Once he fell and bruised and skinned his knee badly on a stone. Once he heard a buggy coming along behind him and hid behind a tree till it passed, terrified lest Dr. Parker had discovered he had gone and was coming after him. Once he stopped in sheer terror of something black and furry sitting on the side of the road. He could not pass it...he could *not*... but he did. It was a big black dog... *Was* it a dog?...but he was past it. He dared not run lest it chase him. He stole a desperate glance over his shoulder...it had got up and was loping away in the opposite direction. Walter put his little brown hand up to his face and found it wet with sweat.

A star fell in the sky before him, scattering sparks of flame. Walter remembered hearing old Aunt Kitty say that when a star fell someone died. *Was it mother?* He had just been feeling that his legs would not carry him another step, but at the thought he marched on again. He was so cold now that he had almost ceased to feel afraid. Would he never get home? It must be hours and hours since he had left Lowbridge.

It *was* three hours. He had stolen out of the Parker house at eleven and it was now two. When Walter found himself on the road that dipped down into the Glen he gave a sob of relief. But as he stumbled through the village the sleeping houses seemed remote and far away. They had forgotten him. A cow suddenly bawled at him over a fence and Walter remembered that Mr. Joe Reese kept a savage bull. He broke into a run of sheer panic that carried him up the hill to the gate of Ingleside. He was home... oh, he was home!

Then he stopped short, trembling, overcome by a dreadful feeling of desolation. He had been expecting to see the warm, friendly lights of home. And there was not a light at Ingleside!

There really was a light, if he could have seen it, in a back bedroom where the nurse slept with the baby's basket beside her bed. But to all intents and purposes Ingleside was as dark as a deserted house and it broke Walter's spirit. He had never seen, never imagined, Ingleside dark at night.

It meant that mother was dead!

Walter stumbled up the drive, across the grim black shadow of the house on the lawn, to the front door. It was locked. He gave a feeble knock...he could not reach to the knocker...but there was no response, nor did he expect any. He listened...there was not a sound of *living* in the house. He knew Mother was dead and everybody had gone away.

He was by now too chilled and exhausted to cry: but he crept around to the barn and climbed the ladder to the hay-mow. He was past being frightened; he only wanted to get somewhere out of that wind and lie down till morning. Perhaps somebody would come back then after they had buried Mother.

A sleek little tiger kitten someone had given the doctor purred up to him, smelling nicely of clover hay. Walter clutched it gladly...it was warm and *alive.* But it heard the little mice scampering over the floor and would not stay. The moon looked at him through the cobwebby window but there was no comfort in that far, cold, unsympathetic moon. A light burning in a house down in the Glen was more like a friend. As long as that light shone he could bear up.

He could not sleep. His knee hurt too much and he was cold...with such a funny feeling in his stomach. Perhaps he was dying, too. He hoped he was, since everyone else was dead or gone away. Did nights ever end? Other nights had always ended but maybe this one wouldn't. He remembered a dreadful story he had heard to the effect that Captain Jack Flagg at the Harbour Mouth had said he wouldn't let the sun come up some morning when he got real mad. Suppose Captain Jack had got real mad at last.

Then the Glen light went out...and he couldn't bear it. But as the little cry of despair left his lips he realized that it was day.

10

Walter climbed down the ladder and went out. Ingleside lay in the strange, timeless light of first dawn. The sky over the birches in the Hollow was showing a faint, silvery-pink radiance. Perhaps he could get in at the side door. Susan sometimes left it open for Dad.

The side door was unlocked. With a sob of thankfulness Walter slipped into the hall. It was still dark in the house and he began stealing softly upstairs. He would go to bed...his own bed...and if nobody ever came back he could die there and go to Heaven and find Mother. Only...Walter remembered what Opal had said...Heaven was millions of miles away. In the fresh wave of desolation that swept over him Walter forgot to step carefully and set his foot heavily down on the tail of the Shrimp, who was sleeping at the curve of the stairs. The Shrimp's yowl of anguish resounded through the house.

Susan, just dropping off to sleep, was dragged back from slumber by the horrible sound. Susan had gone to bed at twelve, somewhat exhausted after her strenuous afternoon and evening, to which Mary Maria Blythe had contributed by taking "a stitch in her side" just when the tension was greatest. She had to have a hot-water bottle and a rub with liniment, and finished up with a wet cloth over her eyes because "one of her headaches" had come on.

Susan had wakened at three with a very strange feeling that somebody wanted her very badly. She had risen and tiptoed down the hall to the door of Mrs. Blythe's room. All was silence there...she could hear Anne's soft regular breathing. Susan made the rounds of the house and returned to her bed, convinced that that strange feeling was only the hangover of a nightmare. But for the rest of her life Susan believed she had had what she had always scoffed at and what Abby Flagg, who "went in" for spiritualism, called "a physic experience."

"Walter was calling me and I heard him," she averred.

Susan got up and went out again, thinking that Ingleside was really possessed that night. She was attired only in a flannel nightdress, which had shrunk in repeated washing till it was well above her bony ankles: but she seemed the most beautiful thing in the world to the white-faced, trembling little creature whose frantic grey eyes stared up at her from the landing.

"Walter Blythe!"

In two steps Susan had him in her arms...her strong, tender arms.

"Susan...is Mother dead?" said Walter.

In a very brief time everything had changed. Walter was in bed, warm, fed, comforted. Susan had whisked on a fire, got him a hot cup of milk, a slice of golden-brown toast and a big plateful of his favourite "monkey face" cookies, and then tucked him away with a hot-water bottle at his feet. She had kissed and anointed his little bruised knee. It was such a nice feeling to know that someone was looking after you...that someone wanted you...that you were important to someone.

"And you're *sure,* Susan, that Mother isn't dead?"

"Your mother is sound asleep and well and happy, my lamb."

"And wasn't she sick at all? Opal said..."

"Well, lamb, she did not feel very well for a while yesterday, but that is all over and she was never in any danger of dying this time. You just wait till you have had a sleep and you will see her...and something else. If I had hold of those young Satans at Lowbridge! I just cannot believe that you walked all the way home from Lowbridge. Six miles! On such a night!"

"I suffered awful agony of mind, Susan," said Walter gravely. But it was all over; he was safe and happy; he was...home...he was...

He was asleep.

It was nearly midday before he woke, to see sunshine billowing in through his own windows, and limped in to see Mother. He had begun to think he had been very foolish and maybe Mother would not be pleased with him for running away from Lowbridge. But Mother only put an arm around him and drew him close to her. She had heard the whole story from Susan and had thought of a few things she intended to say to Jen Parker.

"Oh, Mummy, you're not going to die...and you still love me, don't you?"

"Darling, I've no notion of dying...and I love you so much it hurts. To think that you walked all the way from Lowbridge in the night!"

"And on an empty stomach," shuddered Susan. "The wonder is he is alive to tell it. The days of miracles are not yet over and that you may tie to."

"A spunky little lad," laughed Dad, who had come in with Shirley on his shoulder. He patted Walter's head and Walter caught his hand and hugged it. There was no one like Dad in the world. But nobody must ever know how scared he had really been.

"I needn't ever go away from home again, need I, Mummy?"

"Not till you want to," promised Mother.

"I'll never," began Walter...and then stopped. After all, he wouldn't mind seeing Alice again.

"Look you here, lamb," said Susan, ushering in a rosy young lady in a white apron and cap who carried a basket.

Walter looked. A baby! A plump, roly-poly baby, with silky damp curls all over her head and such tiny cunning hands.

"Is she not a beauty?" said Susan proudly. "Look at her eyelashes...never did I see such long eyelashes on a baby. And her pretty little ears. I always look at their ears first."

Walter hesitated.

"She's sweet, Susan...oh, look at her darling little curly toes!... but...isn't she rather small?"

Susan laughed.

"Eight pounds is not small, lamb. And she has begun to take notice already. That child was not an hour old when she raised her head and *Looked* at the doctor. I have never seen the like of it in all my life."

"She's going to have red hair," said the doctor in a tone of satisfaction. "Lovely red-gold hair like her mother's."

"And hazel eyes like her father's," said the doctor's wife jubilantly.

"I don't see why one of us can't have yellow hair," said Walter dreamily, thinking of Alice.

"Yellow hair! Like the Drews!" said Susan in measureless contempt.

"She looks so cunning when she is asleep," crooned the nurse. "I never saw a baby that crinkled its eyes like that when it went to sleep."

"She is a miracle. All our babies were sweet, Gilbert, but she is the sweetest of them all."

"Lord love you," said Aunt Mary Maria with a sniff, "there's been a few babies in the world before, you know, Annie."

"*Our* baby has never been in the world before, Aunt Mary Maria," said Walter proudly. "Susan, may I kiss her...just once... please?"

"That you may," said Susan, glaring after Aunt Mary Maria's retreating back. "And now I'm going down to make a cherry pie for dinner. Mary Maria Blythe made one yesterday afternoon...I wish you could see it, Mrs. Dr. dear. It looks like something the cat dragged in. I shall eat as much of it myself as I can, rather than waste it, but such a pie shall never be set before the doctor as long as I have my health and strength and that you may tie to."

"It isn't everybody that has your knack with pastry, you know," said Anne.

"Mummy," said Walter, as the door closed behind a gratified Susan, "I think we are a very nice family, don't you?"

A very nice family, Anne reflected happily as she lay in her bed, with the baby beside her. Soon she would be about with them again, light-footed as of yore, loving them, teaching them, comforting them. They would be coming to her with their little joys and sorrows, their budding hopes, their new fears, their little problems that seemed so big to them and their little heart-breaks that seemed so bitter. She would hold all the threads of the Ingleside life in her hands again to weave into a tapestry of beauty. And Aunt Mary Maria should have no cause to say, as Anne had heard her say two days ago, "You look dreadful tired, Gilbert. Does *anybody* ever look after you?"

Downstairs Aunt Mary Maria was shaking her head despondently and saying, "All newborn infants' legs are crooked, I know, but, Susan, that child's legs are much *too* crooked. Of course we must not say so to poor Annie. Be sure you don't mention it to Annie, Susan."

Susan, for once, was beyond speech.

11

By the end of August Anne was herself again, looking forward to a happy autumn. Small Bertha Marilla grew in beauty day by day and was a centre of worship to adoring brothers and sisters.

"I thought a baby would be something that yelled all the time," said Jem, rapturously letting the tiny fingers cling around his. "Bertie Shakespeare Drew told me so."

"I am not doubting that the Drew babies yell all the time, Jem dear," said Susan. "Yell at the thought of having to be Drews, I presume. But Bertha Marilla is an *Ingleside* baby, Jem dear."

"I wish I had been born at Ingleside, Susan," said Jem wistfully. He always felt sorry he hadn't been. Di cast it up to him at times.

"Don't you find life here rather dull?" an old Queen's classmate from Charlottetown had asked Anne rather patronizingly one day.

Dull! Anne almost laughed in her caller's face. Ingleside dull! With a delicious baby bringing new wonders every day... with visits from Diana and Little Elizabeth and Rebecca Dew to be planned for...with Mrs. Sam Ellison of the Upper Glen on Gilbert's hands with a disease only three people in the world had ever been known to have before...with Walter starting to school... with Nan drinking a whole bottle of perfume from Mother's dressing-table...they thought it would kill her but she was never a whit the worse...with a strange black cat having the unheard-of number of ten kittens in the back porch...with Shirley locking himself in the bathroom and forgetting how to unlock it...with the Shrimp getting rolled up in a sheet of fly-paper...with Aunt Mary Maria setting the curtains of her room on fire in the dead of night while prowling with a candle, and rousing the household with appalling screams. Life dull!

For Aunt Mary Maria was still at Ingleside. Occasionally she would say pathetically, "Whenever you are tired of me just let me know...I'm used to looking after myself." There was only one thing to say to that and of course Gilbert always said it. Though he did not say it quite as heartily as at first. Even Gilbert's "clannishness" was beginning to wear a little thin; he was realizing rather helplessly..."man-like" as Miss Cornelia sniffed...that Aunt Mary Maria was by way of becoming a bit of a problem in his household. He *had* ventured one day to give a slight hint as to how houses suffered if left too long without inhabitants; and Aunt Mary Maria agreed with him, calmly remarking that she was thinking of selling her Charlottetown house.

"Not a bad idea," encouraged Gilbert. "And I know a very nice little cottage in town for sale...a friend of mine is going to California...it's very like that one you admired so much where Mrs. Sarah Newman lives..."

"But lives *alone,*" sighed Aunt Mary Maria.

"She likes it," said Anne hopefully.

"There's something wrong with anyone who likes living alone, Anne," said Aunt Mary Maria.

Susan repressed a groan with difficulty.

Diana came for a week in September. Then Little Elizabeth came...Little Elizabeth no longer...tall, slender, beautiful Elizabeth now. But still with the golden hair and wistful smile. Her father was returning to his office in Paris and Elizabeth was going with him to keep his house. She and Anne took long walks around the storied shores of the old harbour, coming home beneath silent, watchful autumn stars. They relived the old Windy Poplars life and retraced their steps in the map of fairyland which Elizabeth still had and meant to keep forever.

"Hanging on the wall of my room wherever I go," she said.

One day a wind blew through the Ingleside garden...the first wind of autumn. That night the rose of the sunset was a trifle austere. All at once the summer had grown old. The turn of the season had come.

"It's early for fall," said Aunt Mary Maria in a tone that implied the fall had insulted her.

But the fall was beautiful, too. There was the joy of winds blowing in from a darkly blue gulf and the splendour of harvest moons. There were lyric asters in the Hollow and children laughing in an apple-laden orchard, clear serene evenings on the high hill pastures of the Upper Glen and silvery mackerel skies with dank birds flying across them; and, as the days shortened, little grey mists stealing over the dunes and up the harbour.

With the falling leaves Rebecca Dew came to Ingleside to make a visit promised for years. She came for a week but was prevailed upon to stay two...none being so urgent as Susan. Susan and Rebecca Dew seemed to discover at first sight that they were kindred spirits...perhaps because they both loved Anne...perhaps because they both hated Aunt Mary Maria.

There came an evening in the kitchen when, as the rain dripped down on the dead leaves outside and the wind cried around the eaves and corners of Ingleside, Susan poured out all her woes to sympathetic Rebecca Dew. The doctor and his wife had gone out to make a call, the small fry were all cosy in their beds, and Aunt Mary Maria fortunately out of the way with a headache..."just like a band of iron round my brain," she had moaned.

"Anyone," remarked Rebecca Dew, opening the oven door and depositing her feet comfortably in the oven, "who eats as much fried mackerel as that woman did for supper *deserves* to have a headache. I do not deny I ate my share...for I will say, Miss Baker, I never knew anyone who could fry mackerel like you...but I did *not* eat four pieces."

"Miss Dew dear," said Susan earnestly, laying down her knitting and gazing imploringly into Rebecca's little black eyes, "you have seen something of what Mary Maria Blythe is like in the time you have been here. But you do not know the half...no, nor yet the quarter. Miss Dew dear, I feel that I can trust you. May I open my heart to you in strict confidence?"

"You may, Miss Baker."

"That woman came here in June and it is my opinion she means to stay here the rest of her life. Everyone in this house detests her...even the doctor has no use for her now, hide it as he will and does. But he is clannish and says his father's cousin must not be made to feel unwelcome in his house. I have begged," said Susan, in a tone which seemed to imply she had done it on her knees, "I have begged Mrs. Dr. to put her foot down and say Mary Maria Blythe must go. But Mrs. Dr. is too softhearted... and so we are helpless, Miss Dew...completely helpless."

"I wish *I* had the handling of her," said Rebecca Dew, who had smarted considerably herself under some of Aunt Mary Maria's remarks. "I know as well as anyone, Miss Baker, that we must not violate the sacred proprieties of hospitality, but I assure you, Miss Baker, that I would let her have it straight."

"*I* could handle her if I did not know my place, Miss Dew. *I* never forget that I am not mistress here. Sometimes, Miss Dew, I say solemnly to myself, 'Susan Baker, are you or are you not a door-mat?' But you know how my hands are tied. I *cannot* desert Mrs. Dr. and I *must not* add to her troubles by fighting with Mary Maria Blythe. I shall continue to endeavour to do my duty. Because, Miss Dew dear," said Susan solemnly, "I could cheerfully die for either the doctor or his wife. We were such a happy family before she came here, Miss Dew. But she is making our lives miserable and what is to be the outcome I cannot tell, being no prophetess, Miss Dew. Or rather, I *can* tell. We will all be driven into lunatic asylums. It is not any one thing, Miss Dew...it is scores of them, Miss Dew...hundreds of them, Miss Dew. You can endure one mosquito, Miss Dew...but think of millions of them!"

Rebecca Dew thought of them with a mournful shake of her head.

"She is always telling Mrs. Dr. how to run her house and what clothes she should wear. She is always watching me...and she says she never saw such quarrelsome children. Miss Dew dear, you have seen for yourself that our children *never* quarrel... well, hardly ever..."

"They are among the most admirable children I have ever seen, Miss Baker."

"She snoops and pries..."

"I have caught her at it myself, Miss Baker."

"She's always getting offended and heart-broken over something but never offended enough to up and leave. She just sits around looking lonely and neglected until poor Mrs. Dr. is almost distracted. Nothing suits her. If a window is open she complains of draughts. If they are all shut she says she *does* like a little fresh air once in a while. She cannot bear onions...she cannot even bear the smell of them. She says they make her sick. So Mrs. Dr. says we must not use any. Now," said Susan grandly, "it may be a common taste to like onions, Miss Dew dear, but we all plead guilty to it at Ingleside."

"I am very partial to onions myself," admitted Rebecca Dew.

"She cannot bear cats. She says cats give her the creeps. It does not make any difference whether she sees them or not. Just to know there is one about the place is enough for her. So that poor Shrimp hardly dare show his face in the house. I have never altogether liked cats myself, Miss Dew, but I maintain they have a right to wave their own tails. And it is, 'Susan, never forget that I cannot eat eggs, please,' or 'Susan, how often must I tell you I cannot eat cold toast?' or 'Susan, *some* people may be able to drink stewed tea but I am not in that fortunate class.' Stewed tea, Miss Dew! As if I ever offered anyone stewed tea!"

"Nobody could ever suppose it of you, Miss Baker."

"If there is a question that should not be asked she will ask it. She is jealous because the doctor tells things to his wife before he tells them to her...and she is always trying to pick news out of him about his patients. Nothing aggravates him so much, Miss Dew. A doctor must know how to hold his tongue, as you are well aware. And her tantrums about fire! 'Susan Baker,' she says to me, 'I hope you never light a fire with coal-oil. Or leave oily rags lying around, Susan. They have been known to cause spontaneous combustion in less than an hour. How would you like to stand and watch this house burn down, Susan, knowing it was your fault?' Well, Miss Dew dear, I had my laugh on her over *that.* It was that very night she set her curtains on fire and the yells of her are ringing in my ears yet. And just when the poor doctor had got to sleep after having been up for two nights! What infuriates me most, Miss Dew, is that before she goes anywhere she goes into my pantry and *counts the eggs*. It takes all my philosophy to refrain from saying, 'Why not count the spoons, too?' Of course the children hate her. Mrs. Dr. is just about worn out keeping them from showing it. She actually slapped Nan one day when the doctor and Mrs. Dr. were both away...*slapped* her... just because Nan called her 'Mrs. Mefusaleh'...having heard that imp of a Ken Ford saying it."

"I'd have slapped *her*," said Rebecca Dew viciously.

"I told her if she ever did the like again I *would* slap her. 'An occasional spanking we do have at Ingleside,' I told her, 'but slapping never, so put that in pickle.' She was sulky and offended for a week but at least she has never dared to lay a finger on one of them since. She loves it when their parents punish them, though. 'If *I* was your mother,' she says to Little Jem one evening. 'Oh ho, you won't ever be anybody's mother,' said the poor child...driven to it, Miss Dew, absolutely driven to it. The doctor sent him to bed without his supper, but who would you suppose, Miss Dew, saw that some was smuggled up to him later on?"

"Ah, now, *who*?" chortled Rebecca Dew, entering into the spirit of the tale.

"It would have broken your heart, Miss Dew, to hear the prayer he put up afterwards...all off his own bat, 'O God, please forgive me for being impertinent to Aunt Mary Maria. And O God, please help me to be always very polite to Aunt Mary Maria.' It brought the tears into my eyes, the poor lamb. I do *not* hold with irreverence or impertinence from youth to age, Miss Dew dear, but I must admit that when Bertie Shakespeare Drew threw a spit-ball at her one day...it just missed her nose by an inch, Miss Dew...I waylaid him at the gate on his way home and gave him a bag of doughnuts. Of course I did not tell him why. He was tickled over it...for doughnuts do not grow on trees, Miss Dew, and Mrs. Second Skimmings never makes them. Nan and Di...I would not breathe this to a soul but you, Miss Dew... the doctor and his wife never dream of it or they would put a stop to it...Nan and Di have named their old china doll with the split head after Aunt Mary Maria and whenever she scolds them they go out and drown her...the doll I mean...in the rainwater hogshead. Many's the jolly drowning we have had, I can assure you. But you could not believe what that woman did the other night, Miss Dew."

"I'd believe anything of her, Miss Baker."

"She would not eat a bite of supper because her feelings had been hurt over something, but she went into the pantry before she went to bed and *ate up a lunch I had left for the poor doctor*... every crumb, Miss Dew dear. I hope you will not think me an infidel, Miss Dew, but I cannot understand why the Good Lord does not get tired of some people."

"You must not allow yourself to lose your sense of humour, Miss Baker," said Rebecca Dew firmly.

"Oh, I am very well aware that there is a comical side to a toad under a harrow, Miss Dew. But the question is, does the toad see it? I am sorry to have bothered you with all this, Miss Dew dear, but it has been a great relief. I cannot say these things to Mrs. Dr. and I have been feeling lately that if I did not find an outlet I would *burst.*"

"How well I know that feeling, Miss Baker."

"And now, Miss Dew dear," said Susan, getting up briskly, "what do you say to a cup of tea before bed? And a cold chicken leg, Miss Dew?"

"I have never denied," said Rebecca Dew, taking her well-baked feet out of the oven, "that while we should not forget the Higher Things of Life good food is a pleasant thing in moderation."

12

Gilbert had his two weeks' snipe shooting in Nova Scotia...not even Anne could persuade him to take a month...and November closed in on Ingleside. The dark hills, with the darker spruces marching over them, looked grim on early falling nights, but Ingleside bloomed with firelight and laughter, though the winds come in from the Atlantic singing of mournful things.

"Why isn't the wind happy, Mummy?" asked Walter one night.

"Because it is remembering all the sorrow of the world since time began," answered Anne.

"It is moaning just because there is so much dampness in the air," sniffed Aunt Mary Maria, "and my back is killing me."

But some days even the wind blew cheerfully through the silvery grey maple wood and some days there was no wind at all, only mellow Indian summer sunshine and the quiet shadows of the bare trees all over the lawn and frosty stillness at sunset.

"Look at that white evening star over the lombardy in the corner," said Anne. "Whenever I see anything like that I am minded to be just glad I am alive."

"You do say such funny things, Annie. Stars are quite common in P. E. Island," said Aunt Mary Maria...and thought: "Stars indeed! As if no one ever saw a star before! Didn't Annie know of the terrible waste that was going on in the kitchen every day? Didn't she know of the reckless way Susan Baker threw eggs about and used lard where dripping would do quite as well? Or didn't she care? Poor Gilbert! No wonder he had to keep his nose to the grindstone!"

November went out in greys and browns: but by morning the snow had woven its old white spell and Jem shouted with delight as he rushed down to breakfast.

"Oh, Mummy, it will soon be Christmas now and Santa Claus will be coming!"

"You surely don't believe in Santa Claus *still?*" said Aunt Mary Maria.

Anne shot a glance of alarm at Gilbert, who said gravely: "We want the children to possess their heritage of fairyland as long as they can, Aunty."

Luckily Jem had paid no attention to Aunt Mary Maria. He and Walter were too eager to get out into the new wonderful world to which winter had brought its own loveliness. Anne always hated to see the beauty of the untrodden snow marred by footprints; but that couldn't be helped and there was still beauty and to spare at eventide when the west was aflame over all the whitened hollows in the violet hills and Anne was sitting in the living-room before a fire of rock maple. Firelight, she thought, was always so lovely. It did such tricksy, unexpected things. Parts of the room flashed into being and then out again. Pictures came and went. Shadows lurked and sprang. Outside, through the big unshaded window, the whole scene was elvishly reflected on the lawn with Aunt Mary Maria apparently sitting stark upright...Aunt Mary Maria never allowed herself to "loll"... under the Scotch pine.

Gilbert was "lolling" on the couch, trying to forget that he had lost a patient from pneumonia that day. Small Rilla was trying to eat her pink fists in her basket; even the Shrimp, with his white paws curled in under his breast, was daring to purr on the hearth-rug, much to Aunt Mary Maria's disapproval.

"Speaking of cats," said Aunt Mary Maria pathetically... though nobody *had* been speaking of them..."do *all* the cats in the Glen visit us at night? How anyone could have slept through the caterwauling last night *I* really am at a loss to understand. Of course, my room being at the back I suppose I get the full benefit of the free concert."

Before anyone had to reply Susan entered, saying that she had seen Mrs. Marshall Elliott in Carter Flagg's store and she was coming up when she had finished her shopping. Susan did not add that Mrs. Elliott had said anxiously, "*What* is the matter with Mrs. Blythe, Susan? I thought last Sunday in church she looked so tired and worried. I never saw her look like that before."

"*I* can tell you what is the matter with Mrs. Blythe," Susan had answered grimly. "She had got a bad attack of Aunt Mary

Maria. And the doctor cannot seem to see it, even though he does worship the ground she walks on."

"Isn't that like a man?" said Mrs. Elliott.

"I am glad," said Anne, springing up to light a lamp. "I haven't seen Miss Cornelia for so long. Now we'll catch up with the news."

"Won't we!" said Gilbert dryly.

"That woman is an evil-minded gossip," said Aunt Mary Maria severely.

For the first time in her life, perhaps, Susan bristled up in defence of Miss Cornelia.

"That she is not, Miss Blythe, and Susan Baker will never stand by and hear her so miscalled. Evil-minded, indeed! Did you ever hear, Miss Blythe, of the pot calling the kettle black?"

"Susan...Susan," said Anne imploringly.

"I beg your pardon, Mrs. Dr. dear. I admit I have forgotten my place. But there are *some* things not to be endured."

Whereupon a door was banged as doors were seldom banged at Ingleside.

"You see, Annie?" said Aunt Mary Maria significantly. "But I suppose as long as you are willing to overlook that sort of thing in a servant there is nothing anyone can do."

Gilbert got up and went to the library where a tired man might count on some peace. And Aunt Mary Maria, who didn't like Miss Cornelia, betook herself to bed. So that when Miss Cornelia came in she found Anne alone, drooping rather limply over the baby's basket. Miss Cornelia did not, as usual, start in unloading a budget of gossip. Instead, when she had laid aside her wraps, she sat down beside Anne and took her hand.

"Anne dearie, what is the matter? I know there's something. Is that jolly old soul of a Mary Maria just tormenting you to death?"

Anne tried to smile.

"Oh, Miss Cornelia...I know I'm foolish to mind it so much...but this has been one of the days when it seems I just *cannot* go on enduring her. She...she's simply poisoning our life here..."

"Why don't you just tell her to go?"

"Oh, we can't do that, Miss Cornelia. At least, *I* can't and Gilbert won't. He says he could never look himself in the face again if he turned his own flesh and blood out of doors."

"Cat's hindfoot!" said Miss Cornelia eloquently. "She's got plenty of money and a good home of her own. How would it be turning her out of doors to tell her she'd better go and live in it?"

"I know...but Gilbert...I don't think he quite realises everything. He's away so much...and really...everything is so little in itself...I'm ashamed..."

"I know, dearie. Just those little things that are horribly big. Of course a *man* wouldn't understand. I know a woman in Charlottetown who knows her well. She says Mary Maria Blythe never had a friend in her life. She says her name should be Blight not Blythe. What you need, dearie, is just enough backbone to say you won't put up with it any longer."

"I feel as you do in dreams when you're trying to run and can only drag your feet," said Anne drearily. "If it were only now and then...but it's every day. Meal times are perfect horrors now. Gilbert says he can't carve roasts any more."

"He'd notice *that*," sniffed Miss Cornelia.

"We can never have any real conversations at meals because she is sure to say something disagreeable every time anyone speaks. She corrects the children for their manners continually and always calls attention to their faults before company. We used to have such pleasant meals...and now! She resents laughter...and you know what we are for laughing. Somebody is always seeing a joke...or used to be. She can't let anything pass. Today she said, 'Gilbert, don't sulk. Have you and Annie quarrelled?' Just because we were quiet. You know Gilbert is always a little depressed when he loses a patient he thinks ought to have lived. And then she lectured us on our folly and warned us not to let the sun go down on our wrath. Oh, we laughed at it afterwards...but just at the time! She and Susan don't get along. And we *can't* keep Susan from muttering asides that are the reverse of polite. She more than muttered when Aunt Mary Maria told her she had never seen such a liar as Walter...because she heard him telling Di a long tale about meeting the man in the moon and what they said to each other. She wanted to scour his mouth out with soap and water. She and Susan had a battle royal that time. And she is filling the children's minds with all sorts of gruesome ideas. She told Nan about a child who was naughty and died in its sleep and Nan is afraid to go to sleep now. She told Di that if she were always a good girl her parents would come to love her as well as they loved Nan, even if she did have red hair. Gilbert really was very angry when he heard that and spoke to her sharply. I couldn't help hoping she'd take offence and go... even though I would hate to have anyone leave my home because she was offended. But she just let those big blue eyes of her fill with tears and said she didn't mean any harm. She'd always heard that twins were never loved equally and she'd been thinking we favoured Nan and that poor Di felt it! She cried all night about it and Gilbert felt that he had been a brute...and *apologized*."

"He would!" said Miss Cornelia.

"Oh, I shouldn't be talking like this, Miss Cornelia. When I 'count my mercies' I feel it's very petty of me to mind these things...even if they do rub a little bloom off life. And she isn't always hateful...she is quite nice by spells..."

"Do you tell me so?" said Miss Cornelia sarcastically.

"Yes...and kind. She heard me say I wanted an afternoon tea-set and she went to Toronto and got me one...by mail order! And, oh, Miss Cornelia, it's so ugly!"

Anne gave a laugh that ended in a sob. Then she laughed again.

"Now we won't talk of her any more...it doesn't seem so bad now that I've blurted this all out...like a baby. Look at wee Rilla, Miss Cornelia. Aren't her lashes darling when she is asleep? Now let's have a good gab-fest."

Anne was herself again by the time Miss Cornelia had gone. Nevertheless she sat thoughtfully before her fire for some time. She had not told Miss Cornelia all of it. She had never told Gilbert any of it. There were so many little things...

"So little I can't complain of them," thought Anne. "And yet...it's the little things that fret the holes in life...like moths...and ruin it."

Aunt Mary Maria with her trick of acting the hostess...Aunt Mary Maria inviting guests and never saying a word about it till they came..."*She makes me feel as if I didn't belong in my own home.*" Aunt Mary Maria moving the furniture around when Anne was out. "I hope you don't mind, Annie; I thought we need the table so much more here than in the library." Aunt Mary Maria's insatiable childish curiosity about everything...her point-blank questions about intimate matters..."*always coming into my room without knocking...always smelling smoke...always plumping up the cushions I've crushed...always implying that I gossip too much with Susan...always picking at the children.... We have to be at them all the time to make them behave and then we can't manage it always.*"

"Ugly old Aunt Maywia," Shirley had said distinctly one dreadful day. Gilbert had been going to spank him for it, but Susan had risen up in outraged majesty and forbade it.

"We're cowed," thought Anne. "This household is beginning to revolve around the question, 'Will Aunt Mary Maria like it?' We won't admit it but it's true. Anything rather than have her wiping tears nobly away. It just can't go on."

Then Anne remembered what Miss Cornelia had said...that Mary Maria Blythe had never had a friend. How terrible! Out of her own richness of friendships Anne felt a sudden rush of compassion for this woman who had never had a friend...who had nothing before her but a lonely, restless old age with no one coming to her for shelter or healing, for hope and help, for warmth and love. Surely they could have patience with her. These annoyances were only superficial, after all. They could not poison the deep springs of life.

"I've just had a terrible spasm of being sorry for myself, that's all," said Anne, picking Rilla out of her basket and thrilling to the little round satin cheek against hers. "It's over now and I'm wholesomely ashamed of it."

13

"We never seem to have old-fashioned winters nowadays, do we, Mummy?" said Walter gloomily.

For the November snow had gone long ago and all through December Glen St. Mary had been a black and sombre land, rimmed in by a grey gulf dotted with curling crests of ice-white foam. There had been only a few sunny days, when the harbour sparkled in the golden arms of the hills: the rest had been dour and hard-bitten. In vain had the Ingleside folks hoped for snow for Christmas: but preparations went steadily on and as the last week drew to a close Ingleside was full of mystery and secrets and whispers and delicious smells. Now on the very day before Christmas everything was ready. The fir tree Walter and Jem had brought up from the Hollow was in the corner of the living-room, the doors and windows were hung with big green wreaths tied with huge bows of red ribbon. The banisters were twined with creeping spruce and Susan's pantry was crammed to overflowing. Then, late in the afternoon, when they all had resigned themselves to a dingy "green" Christmas somebody looked out of a window and saw white flakes as big as feathers falling thickly.

"Snow! Snow!! Snow!!!" shouted Jem. "A white Christmas after all, Mummy!"

The Ingleside children went to bed happy. It was so nice to snuggle down warm and cosy and listen to the storm howling outside through the grey snowy night. Anne and Susan went to work to deck the Christmas tree..."acting like two children themselves," thought Aunt Mary Maria scornfully. She did not approve of candles on a tree..."suppose the house caught fire from them." She did not approve of coloured balls... "suppose the twins ate them." But nobody paid any attention to her. They had learned that that was the only condition on which life with Aunt Mary Maria was livable.

"Finished!" cried Anne, as she fastened the great silver star to the top of the proud little fir. "And, oh, Susan, doesn't it look pretty! Isn't it nice we can all be children again at Christmas without being ashamed of it! I'm so glad the snow came...but I hope the storm won't outlast the night."

"It's going to storm all day tomorrow," said Aunt Mary Maria positively. "I can tell by my poor back."

Anne went through the hall, opened the big front door, and peered out. The world was lost in a white passion of snowstorm. The window-panes were grey with drifted snow. The Scotch pine was an enormous sheeted ghost.

"It doesn't look very promising," Anne admitted ruefully.

"God manages the weather yet, Mrs. Dr. dear, and not Miss Mary Maria Blythe," said Susan over her shoulder.

"I hope there won't be a sick call tonight at least," said Anne as she turned away. Susan took one parting look into the gloom before she locked out the stormy night.

"Don't *you* go and have a baby tonight," she warned darkly in the direction of the Upper Glen where Mrs. George Drew was expecting her fourth.

In spite of Aunt Mary Maria's back the storm spent itself in the night and morning filled the secret hollow of snow among the hills with the red wine of winter sunrise. All the small fry were up early, looking starry and expectant.

"*Did* Santa get through the storm, Mummy?"

"No. He was sick and didn't dare try," said Aunt Mary Maria, who was in a good humour...for her...and felt joky.

"Santa Claus got here all right," said Susan before their eyes had time to blur, "and after you've had your breakfast you'll see what he did to your tree."

After breakfast Dad mysteriously disappeared, but nobody missed him because they were so taken up with the tree...the lively tree, all gold and silver bubbles and lighted candles in the still dark room, with parcels in all colours and tied with the loveliest ribbons piled about it. Then Santa appeared, a gorgeous Santa, all crimson and white fur, with a long white beard and *such* a jolly big stomach...Susan had stuffed three cushions into the red velveteen cassock Anne had made for Gilbert. Shirley screamed with terror at first, but refused to be taken out, for all that. Santa distributed all the gifts with a funny little speech for everyone in a voice that sounded oddly familiar even through the mask; and then just at the end his beard caught fire from a candle and Aunt Mary Maria had some slight satisfaction out of the incident though not enough to prevent her from sighing mournfully.

"Ah me, Christmas isn't what it was when I was a child." She looked with disapproval at the present Little Elizabeth had sent Anne from Paris...a beautiful little bronze reproduction of Artemis of the Silver Bow.

"What shameless hussy is that?" she inquired sternly.

"The goddess Diana," said Anne, exchanging a grin with Gilbert.

"Oh, a heathen! Well, that's different, I suppose. But if I were you, Annie, I wouldn't leave it where the children can see it. Sometimes I am beginning to think there is no such thing as modesty left in the world. My grandmother," concluded Aunt Mary Maria, with the delightful inconsequence that characterized so many of her remarks, "never wore less than three petticoats, winter and summer."

Aunt Mary Maria had knitted "wristers" for all the children out of a dreadful shade of magenta yarn, also a sweater for Anne; Gilbert received a bilious necktie and Susan got a red flannel petticoat. Even Susan considered red flannel petticoats out of date, but she thanked Aunt Mary Maria gallantly.

"Some poor home missionary may be the better of it," she thought. "Three petticoats, indeed! I flatter myself I am a decent woman and I like that Silver Bow person. She may not have much in the way of clothes on, but if I had a figure like that I do not know that I would want to hide it. But now to see about the turkey stuffing...not that it will amount to much with no onion in it."

Ingleside was full of happiness that day, just plain, old-fashioned happiness, in spite of Aunt Mary Maria, who certainly did not like to see people too happy.

"White meat only, please. (James, eat your soup quietly.) Ah, you are not the carver your father was, Gilbert. *He* could give everyone the bit she liked best. (Twins, older people would like a chance now and then to get a word in edgewise. *I* was brought up by the rule that children should be seen and not heard.) No, thank you, Gilbert, no salad for me. I don't eat raw food. Yes, Annie, I'll take a *little* pudding. Mince pies are entirely too indigestible."

"Susan's mince pies are poems, just as her apple pies are lyrics," said the doctor. "Give *me* a piece of both, Anne-girl."

"Do you really like to be called 'girl' at your age, Annie? Walter, you haven't eaten all your bread and butter. Plenty of poor children would be glad to have it. James dear, blow your nose and have it over with, I *cannot* endure sniffling."

But it was a gay and lovely Christmas. Even Aunt Mary Maria thawed out a little after dinner, said almost graciously that the presents given her had been quite nice, and even endured the Shrimp with an air of patient martyrdom that made them all feel a little ashamed of loving him.

"I think our little folks have had a nice time," said Anne happily that night, as she looked at the pattern of trees woven against the white hills and sunset sky, and the children out on the lawn busily scattering crumbs for birds over the snow. The wind was sighing softly in the boughs, sending flurries over the lawn and promising more storm for the morrow, but Ingleside had had its day.

"I suppose they had," agreed Aunt Mary Maria. "I'm sure they did enough squealing, anyhow. As for what they have eaten...ah well, you're only young once and I suppose you have plenty of castor-oil in the house."

14

It was what Susan called a streaky winter...all thaws and freezes that kept Ingleside decorated with fantastic fringes of icicles. The children fed seven blue-jays who came regularly to the orchard for their rations and let Jem pick them up, though they flew from everybody else. Anne sat up o' nights to pore over seed catalogues in January and February. Then the winds of March swirled over the dunes and up the harbors and over the hills. Rabbits, said Susan, were laying Easter eggs.

"Isn't March an INciting month, Mummy?" cried Jem, who was a little brother to all the winds that blew.

They could have spared the "incitement" of Jem scratching his hand on a rusty nail and having a nasty time of it for some days, while Aunt Mary Maria told all the stories of blood-poisoning she had ever heard. But that, Anne reflected when the danger was over, was what you must expect with a small son who was always trying experiments.

And lo, it was April! With the laughter of April rain...the whisper of April rain...the trickle, the sweep, the drive, the lash, the dance, the splash of April rain. "Oh, Mummy, hasn't the world got its face washed nice and clean?" cried Di, on the morning sunshine returned.

There were pale spring stars shining over fields of mist, there were pussywillows in the marsh. Even the little twigs on the trees seemed all at once to have lost their clear cold quality and to have become soft and languorous. The first robin was an event; the Hollow was once more a place full of wild free delight; Jem brought his mother the first mayflowers...rather to Aunt Mary Maria's offence, since she thought they should have been offered to *her*; Susan began sorting over the attic shelves, and Anne, who had hardly had a minute to herself all winter, put on spring gladness as a garment and literally lived in her garden, while the Shrimp showed his spring raptures by writhing all over the paths.

"You care more for that garden than you do for your husband, Annie," said Aunt Mary Maria.

"My garden is so kind to me," answered Anne dreamily... then, realizing the implications that might be taken out of her remark, began to laugh.

"You do say the most extraordinary things, Annie. Of course *I* know you don't mean that Gilbert isn't kind...but what if a stranger heard you say such a thing?"

"Dear Aunt Mary Maria," said Anne gaily, "I'm really not responsible for the things I say this time of the year. Everybody around here knows that. I'm always a little mad in spring. But it's such a divine madness. Do you notice those mists over the dunes like dancing witches? And the daffodils? We've never had such a show of daffodils at Ingleside before."

"I don't care much for daffodils. They are such flaunting things," said Aunt Mary Maria, drawing her shawl around her and going indoors to protect her back.

"Do you know, Mrs. Dr. dear," said Susan ominously, "what has become of those new irises you wanted to plant in that shady corner? *She* planted them this afternoon when you were out right in the sunniest part of the back yard."

"Oh, Susan! And we can't move them because she'd be so hurt!"

"If you will just give *me* the word, Mrs. Dr. dear..."

"No, no, Susan, we'll leave them there for the time being. She cried, you remember, when I hinted that she shouldn't have pruned the spirea *before* blooming."

"But sneering at our daffodils, Mrs. Dr. dear...and them famous all around the harbour..."

"And deserve to be. Look at them laughing at you for minding Aunt Mary Maria. Susan, the nasturtiums are coming up in this corner, after all. It's such fun when you've given up hope of a thing to find it has suddenly popped up. I'm going to have a little rose garden made in the southwest corner. The very name of rose garden thrills to my toes. Did you ever see such a *blue* blueness of sky before, Susan? And if you listen very carefully now at night you can hear all the little brooks of the countryside gossiping. I've half a notion to sleep in the Hollow tonight with a pillow of wild violets."

"You would find it very damp," said Susan patiently. Mrs. Dr. was always like this in the spring. It would pass.

"Susan," said Anne coaxingly, "I want to have a birthday party next week."

"Well, and why should you not?' asked Susan. To be sure, none of the family had a birthday the last week in May, but if Mrs. Dr. wanted a birthday party why boggle over that?

"For Aunt Mary Maria," went on Anne, as one determined to get the worst over. "Her birthday is next week. Gilbert says she is fifty-five and I've been thinking."

"Mrs. Dr. dear, do you really mean to get up a party for that..."

"Count a hundred, Susan...count a hundred, Susan dear. It would please her so. What has she in life, after all?"

"That is her own fault..."

"Perhaps so. But, Susan, I really want to do this for her."

"Mrs. Dr. dear," said Susan ominously, "you have always been kind enough to give me a week's vacation whenever I felt I needed it. Perhaps I had better take it next week! I will ask my niece Gladys to come and help you out. And then Miss Mary Maria Blythe can have a dozen birthday parties, for all of me."

"If you feel like that about it, Susan, I'll give up the idea, of course," said Anne slowly.

"Mrs. Dr. dear, that woman has foisted herself upon you and means to stay here forever. She has worried you...and henpecked the doctor...and made the children's lives miserable. I say nothing about myself, for who am I? She has scolded and nagged and insinuated and whined...and now you want to get up a birthday party for her! Well, all I can say is, if you want to do that...we'll just have to go ahead and have it!"

"Susan, you old duck!"

Plotting and planning followed. Susan, having yielded, was determined that for the honour of Ingleside the party must be something that even Mary Maria Blythe could not find fault with.

"I think we'll have a luncheon, Susan. Then they'll be away early enough for me to go to the concert at Lowbridge with the doctor. We'll keep it a secret and surprise her. She shan't know a thing about it till the last minute. I'll invite all the people in the Glen she likes..."

"And who may *they* be, Mrs. Dr. dear?"

"Well, tolerates, then. And her cousin, Adella Carey from Lowbridge, and some people from town. We'll have a big plummy birthday cake with fifty-five candles on it..."

"Which *I* am to make, of course..."

"Susan, you *know* you make the best fruit-cake in P. E. Island..."

"I know that I am as wax in your hands, Mrs. Dr. dear."

A mysterious week followed. An air of hush-hush pervaded Ingleside. Everybody was sworn not to give the secret away to Aunt Mary Maria. But Anne and Susan had reckoned without gossip. The night before the party Aunt Mary Maria came home from a call in the Glen to find them sitting rather wearily in the unlighted sun-room.

"All in the dark, Annie? It beats me how anyone can like sitting in the dark. It gives me the blues."

"It isn't dark...it's twilight...there has been a love-match between light and dark and beautiful exceedingly is the offspring thereof," said Anne, more to herself than anybody else.

"I suppose you know what you mean yourself, Annie. And so you're having a party tomorrow?"

Anne suddenly sat bolt upright. Susan, already sitting so, could not sit any uprighter.

"Why...why...Aunty..."

"You always leave me to hear things from outsiders," said Aunt Mary Maria, but seemingly more in sorrow than in anger.

"We...we meant it for a surprise, Aunty..."

"I don't know what you want of a party this time of year when you can't depend on the weather, Annie."

Anne drew a breath of relief. Evidently Aunt Mary Maria knew only that there was to be a party, not that it had any connexion with her.

"I...I wanted to have it before the spring flowers were done, Aunty."

"I shall wear my garnet taffeta. I suppose, Annie, if I had not heard of this in the village I should have been caught by all your fine friends tomorrow in a cotton dress."

"Oh, no, Aunty. We meant to tell you in time to dress, of course..."

"Well, if *my* advice means anything to you, Annie...and sometimes I am almost compelled to think it does not...I would say that in future it would be better for you not to be *quite so secretive* about things. By the way, are you aware that they are saying in the village that it was Jem who threw the stone through the window of the Methodist church?"

"He did not," said Anne quietly. "He told me he did not."

"Are you sure, Annie dear, that he was not fibbing?"

"Annie dear" still spoke quietly.

"Quite sure, Aunt Mary Maria. Jem has never told me an untruth in his life."

"Well, I thought you ought to know what was being said."

Aunt Mary Maria stalked off in her usual gracious manner, ostentatiously avoiding the Shrimp, who was lying on his back on the floor entreating someone to tickle his stomach.

Susan and Anne drew a long breath.

"I think I'll go to bed, Susan. And I do hope it is going to be fine tomorrow. I don't like the look of that dark cloud over the harbour."

"It will be fine, Mrs. Dr. dear," reassured Susan. "The almanack says so."

Susan had an almanack which foretold the whole year's weather and was right often enough to keep up its credit.

"Leave the side door unlocked for the doctor, Susan. He may be late getting home from town. He went in for the roses... fifty-five golden roses, Susan...I've heard Aunt Mary Maria say that yellow roses were the only flowers she liked."

Half an hour later, Susan, reading her nightly chapter in her Bible, came across the verse, "Withdraw thy foot from thy neighbour's house lest he weary of thee and hate thee." She put a sprig of southernwood in it to mark the spot. "Even in those days," she reflected.

Anne and Susan were both up early, desiring to complete certain last preparations before Aunt Mary Maria should be about. Anne always liked to get up early and catch that mystical half-hour before sunrise when the world belongs to the fairies and the old gods. She liked to see the morning sky of pale rose and gold behind the church spire, the thin, translucent glow of sunrise spreading over the dunes, the first violet spirals of smoke floating up from the village roofs.

"It's as if we had had a day made to order, Mrs. Dr. dear," said Susan complacently, as she feathered an orange-frosted cake with cocoanut. "I will try my hand at them new-fangled butterballs after breakfast and I will phone Carter Flagg every half-hour to make sure that he will not forget the ice-cream. And there will be time to scrub the verandah steps."

"Is that necessary, Susan?"

"Mrs. Dr. dear, you have invited Mrs. Marshall Elliott, have you not? *She* shall not see *our* verandah steps otherwise than spotless. But you will see to the decorations, Mrs. Dr. dear? I was not born with the gift of arranging flowers."

"Four cakes! Gee!" said Jem.

"When we give a party," said Susan grandly, "we *give* a party."

The guests came in due time and were received by Aunt Mary Maria in garnet taffeta and by Anne in biscuit-coloured voile. Anne thought of putting on her white muslin, for the day was summer-warm, but decided otherwise.

"Very sensible of you, Annie," commented Aunt Mary Maria. "White, I always say, is only for the young."

Everything went according to schedule. The table looked beautiful with Anne's prettiest dishes and the exotic beauty of white and purple iris. Susan's butterballs made a sensation, nothing like them having been seen in the Glen before; her cream soup was the last word in soups; the chicken salad had been made of Ingleside "chickens that *are* chickens"; the badgered Carter Flagg sent up the ice-cream on the tick of the dot. Finally Susan, bearing the birthday cake with its fifty-five lighted candles as if it were the Baptist's head on a charger, marched in and set it down before Aunt Mary Maria.

Anne, outwardly the smiling serene hostess, had been feeling very uncomfortable for some time. In spite of all outward smoothness she had an ever-deepening conviction that something had gone terribly wrong. On the guests' arrival she had been too much occupied to notice the change that came over Aunt Mary Maria's face when Mrs. Marshall Elliott cordially wished her many happy returns of the day. But when they were all finally seated around the table Anne wakened up to the fact that Aunt Mary Maria was looking anything but pleased. She was actually white...it *couldn't* be with fury!...and not one word did she say as the meal progressed, save curt replies to remarks addressed to her. She took only two spoonfuls of soup and three mouthfuls of salad; as for the ice-cream, she behaved to it as if it wasn't there.

When Susan set the birthday cake, with its flickering candles, down before her, Aunt Mary Maria gave a fearful gulp which was not quite successful in swallowing a sob and consequently issued as a strangled whoop.

"Aunty, aren't you feeling well?" cried Anne.

Aunt Mary Maria stared at her icily.

"*Quite* well, Annie. Remarkably well, indeed, for *such an aged person* as myself."

At this auspicious moment the twins popped in, carrying between them the basketful of fifty-five yellow roses, and, amid a suddenly frozen silence, presented it to Aunt Mary Maria, with lisped congratulations and good wishes. A chorus of admiration went up from the table, but Aunt Mary Maria did not join in it.

"The...the twins will blow out the candles for you, Aunty," faltered Anne nervously, "and then...will you cut the birthday cake?"

"Not being quite senile...yet...Annie, I can blow the candles out myself."

Aunt Mary Maria proceeded to blow them out, painstakingly and deliberately. With equal painstaking and deliberation she cut the cake. Then she laid the knife down.

"And now perhaps I may be excused, Annie. *Such an old woman* as I am needs rest after so much excitement."

Swish went Aunt Mary Maria's taffeta skirt. Crash went the basket of roses as she swept past it. Click went Aunt Mary Maria's high heels up the stairs. Bang went Aunt Mary Maria's door in the distance.

The dumfounded guests ate their slices of birthday cake with such appetite as they could muster, in a strained silence broken only by a story Mrs. Amos Martin told desperately of a doctor in Nova Scotia who had poisoned several patients by injecting diphtheria germs into them. The others, feeling that this might not be in the best of taste, did not back up her laudable effort to "liven things up" and all went away as soon as they decently could.

A distracted Anne rushed to Aunt Mary Maria's room.

"Aunty, *what* is the matter?..."

"Was it necessary to advertise my age in public, Annie? And to ask Adella Carey here...to have her find out how old I am... she's been dying to know for years!"

"Aunty, we meant...we meant..."

"I don't know what your purpose was, Annie. That there is something back of all this I know very well...oh, I can read your mind, dear Annie...but I shall not try to ferret it out...I shall leave it between you and your conscience."

"Aunt Mary Maria, my only intention was to give you a happy birthday. I'm dreadfully sorry..."

Aunt Mary Maria put her handkerchief to her eyes and smiled bravely.

"Of course I forgive you, Annie. But you must realize that after such a deliberate attempt to injure my feelings I cannot stay here any longer."

"Amity, won't you believe..."

Aunt Mary Maria lifted a long, thin, knobby hand.

"Don't let us discuss it, Annie. I want peace...just peace. 'A wounded spirit who can bear?'"

Anne went to the concert with Gilbert that night, but it could not be said she enjoyed it. Gilbert took the whole matter "just like a man," as Miss Cornelia might have said.

"I remember she was always a little touchy about her age. Dad used to rag her. I should have warned you...but it had slipped my memory. If she goes, don't try to stop her"...and refrained through clannishness from adding "good riddance!"

"She will not go. No such good luck, Mrs. Dr. dear," said Susan incredulously.

But for once Susan was wrong. Aunt Mary Maria went away the very next day, forgiving everybody with her parting breath.

"Don't blame Annie, Gilbert," she said magnanimously. "I acquit her of all intentional insult. I never minded her having secrets from me...though to a sensitive mind like mine...but in spite of everything I've always liked poor Annie"...this with the air of one confessing a weakness. "But Susan Baker is a cat of another colour. My last word to you, Gilbert, is...put Susan Baker in her place and keep her there."

Nobody could believe in their good luck at first. Then they woke up to the fact that Aunt Mary Maria had really gone... that it was possible to laugh again without hurting anyone's feelings...open all the windows without anyone complaining of draughts...eat a meal without anyone telling you that something you specially liked was liable to produce cancer of the stomach.

"I've never sped a parting guest so willingly," thought Anne, half guiltily. "It *is* nice to call your soul your own again."

The Shrimp groomed himself meticulously, feeling that, after all, there was some fun in being a cat. The first peony burst into bloom in the garden.

"The world is just full of poetry, isn't it, Mummy?" said Walter.

"It is going to be a real nice June," foretold Susan. "The almanack says so. There are going to be a few brides and most likely at least two funerals. Does it not seem strange to be able to draw a free breath again? When I think that I did all that in me lay to prevent you giving that party, Mrs. Dr. dear, I realize afresh that there *is* an overruling Providence. And don't you think, Mrs. Dr. dear, that the doctor would relish some onions with his fried steak today?"

15

"I felt I had to come up, dearie," said Miss Cornelia, "and explain about that telephone. It was all a mistake...I'm so sorry...Cousin Sarah isn't dead, after all." Anne, smothering a smile, offered Miss Cornelia a chair on the verandah, and Susan, looking up from the collar of Irish-crochet lace she was making for her niece Gladys, uttered a scrupulously polite, "Good-evening, *Mrs.* Marshall Elliott."

"The word came out from the hospital this morning that she had passed away in the night, and I felt I ought to inform you, since she was the doctor's patient. But it was another Sarah Chase and Cousin Sarah is living and likely to live, I'm thankful to say. It's real nice and cool here, Anne. I always say if there's a breeze to be had anywhere it's at Ingleside."

"Susan and I have been enjoying the charm of this starlit evening," said Anne, laying aside the dress of pink, smocked muslin she was making for Nan and clasping her hands over her knees. An excuse to be idle for a little while was not unwelcome. Neither she nor Susan had many idle moments nowadays.

There was going to be a moonrise and the prophecy of it was even lovelier than the moonrise itself would be. Tiger lilies were "burning bright" along the walk and whiffs of honeysuckle went and came on the wings of the dreaming wind.

"Look at that wave of poppies breaking against the garden wall, Miss Cornelia. Susan and I are very proud of our poppies this year, though we hadn't a single thing to do with them. Walter spilt a packet of seed there by accident in the spring and this is the result. Every year we have some delightful surprise like that."

"I'm partial to poppies," said Miss Cornelia, "though they don't last long."

"They have only a day to live," admitted Anne, "but how imperially, how gorgeous they live it! Isn't that better than being a stiff horrible zinnia that lasts practically for ever? We have no zinnias at Ingleside. They're the only flowers we are not friends with. Susan won't even speak to them."

"Anybody being murdered in the Hollow?" asked Miss Cornelia. Indeed, the sounds that came drifting up would seem to indicate that someone was being burned at the stake. But Anne and Susan were too accustomed to that to be disturbed.

"Persis and Kenneth have been here all day and they wound up by a banquet in the Hollow. As for Mrs. Chase, Gilbert went to town this morning, so he would know the truth about her. I am glad for everyone's sake she is doing so well...the other doctors did not agree with Gilbert's diagnosis and he was a little worried."

"Sarah warned us when she went to the hospital that we were not to bury her unless we were sure she was dead," said Miss Cornelia, fanning herself majestically and wondering how the doctor's wife always managed to look so cool. "You see, we were always a little afraid her husband was buried alive...he looked so life-like. But nobody thought of it until it was too late. He was a brother of this Richard Chase who bought the old Moorside farm and moved there from Lowbridge in the spring. *He's* a card. Said he came to the country to get some peace...he had to spend all his time in Lowbridge dodging widows"..."and old maids," Miss Cornelia might have added but did not, out of regard for Susan's feelings.

"I've met his daughter Stella...she comes to choir practice. We've taken quite a fancy to each other."

"Stella *is* a sweet girl...one of the few girls left that can blush. I've always loved her. Her mother and I used to be great cronies. Poor Lisette!"

"She died young?"

"Yes, when Stella was only eight. Richard brought Stella up himself. And him an infidel if he's anything! He says women are only important biologically...whatever that may mean. He's always shooting off some big talk like that."

"He doesn't seem to have made such a bad job of bringing her up," said Anne, who thought Stella Chase one of the most charming girls she had ever met.

"Oh, you couldn't spoil Stella. And I'm not denying Richard has got a good deal in his head-piece. But he's a crank about young men...he has never let poor Stella have a single beau in her life! All the young men who tried to go with her he simply terrified out of their senses with sarcasm. He is the most sarcastic creature you ever heard of. Stella can't manage him...her mother before her couldn't manage him. They didn't know how. He goes by contraries but neither of them ever seemed to catch on to that."

"I thought Stella seemed very devoted to her father."

"Oh, she is. She adores him. He is a most agreeable man when he gets his own way about everything. But he should have more sense about Stella's marrying. He must know he can't live forever...though to hear him talk you'd think he meant to. He isn't an old man, of course...he was very young when he was married. But strokes run in that family. And what is Stella to do after he's gone? Just shrivel up, I suppose."

Susan looked up from the intricate rose of her Irish crochet long enough to say decidedly:

"I do not hold with old folks spoiling young ones lives in that fashion."

"Perhaps if Stella really cared for anyone her father's objections might not weight much with her."

"That's where you're mistaken, Anne dearie. Stella would never marry anyone her father didn't like. And I can tell you another whose life is going to be spoiled, and that's Marshall's nephew, Alden Churchill. Mary is *determined* he shan't marry as long as she can keep him from it. She's even more contrary than Richard...if she was a weather-vane she'd point north when the wind was south. The property is hers till Alden marries and then it goes to him, you know. Every time he's gone about with a girl she has contrived to put a stop to it somehow."

"Indeed, is it *all* her doings, *Mrs.* Marshall Elliott?" queried Susan dryly. "Some folks think that Alden is very changeable. I have heard him called a flirt."

"Alden is handsome and the girls chase him," retorted Miss Cornelia. "*I* don't blame him for stringing them along a bit and dropping them when he's taught them a lesson. But there's been one or two nice girls he really liked and Mary just blocked it every time. She told me so herself...told me she went to the Bible...she's always 'going to the Bible'...and turned up a verse and every time it was a warning against Alden getting married. I've no patience with her and her odd ways. Why can't she go to church and be a decent creature like the rest of us around Four Winds? But no, she must set up a religion for herself, consisting of 'going to the Bible.' Last fall, when that valuable horse took sick...worth four hundred if a dollar...instead of sending for the Lowbridge vet she 'went to the Bible' and turned up a verse...'The Lord giveth and the Lord taketh away. Blessed be the name of the Lord.' So send for the vet she would not and the horse died. Fancy applying that verse in such a way, Anne dearie. I call it irreverent. I told her so flat but all the answer I got was a dirty look. And she won't have the phone put in. 'Do you think I'm going to talk into a box on the wall?' she says when anyone broaches it."

Miss Cornelia paused, rather out of breath. Her sister-in-law's vagaries always made her impatient.

"Alden isn't at all like his mother," said Anne.

"Alden's like his father...a finer man never stepped...as men go. Why he ever married Mary was something the Elliotts could never fathom. Though they were more than glad to get her married off so well...she always had a screw loose and such a beanpole of a girl. Of course she had lots of money...her Aunt Mary left her everything...but that wasn't the reason, George Churchill was really in love with her. I don't know how Alden stands his mother's whims; but he's been a good son."

"Do you know what has just occurred to me, Miss Cornelia?" said Anne with an impish smile. "Wouldn't it be a nice thing if Alden and Stella should fall in love with each other?"

"There isn't much chance of that and they wouldn't get anywhere if they did. Mary would tear up the turf and Richard would show a plain farmer the door in a minute, even if he is a farmer himself now. But Stella isn't the kind of a girl Alden fancies...he likes the high-coloured laughing ones. And Stella wouldn't care for *his* type. I did hear the new minister at Lowbridge was making sheep's eyes at her."

"Isn't he rather anemic and short-sighted?" asked Anne.

"And his eyes bulge," said Susan. "They must be dreadful when he tries to look sentimental."

"At least he's a Presbyterian," said Miss Cornelia, as if that atoned for much. "Well, I must be going. I find if I'm out in the dew much my neuralgia troubles me."

"I'll walk down to the gate with you."

"You always looked like a queen in that dress, Anne dearie," said Miss Cornelia, admiringly and irrelevantly.

Anne met Owen and Leslie Ford at the gate and brought them back to the verandah. Susan had vanished to get lemonade for the doctor, who had just arrived home, and the children came swarming up from the Hollow sleepy and happy.

"You were making dreadful noise as I drove in," said Gilbert. "The whole countryside must have heard you."

Persis Ford, shaking back her thick honey-tinted curls, stuck out her tongue at him. Persis was a great favourite with "Uncle Gil."

"We were just imitating howling dervishes, so of course we had to howl," explained Kenneth.

"Look at the state your blouse is in," said Leslie rather severely.

"I fell in Di's mud-pie," said Kenneth, with decided satisfaction in his tone. He loathed those starched, spotless blouses Mother made him wear when he came up to the Glen.

"Mother dearwums," said Jem, "can I have those old ostrich feathers in the garret to sew in the back of my pants for a tail?

We're going to have a circus tomorrow and I'm to be the ostrich. And we're going to get an elephant."

"Do you know that it costs six hundred dollars a year to feed an elephant?" said Gilbert solemnly.

"An imaginary elephant doesn't cost anything," explained Jem patiently.

Anne laughed. "We never need to be economical in our imaginations, thank heaven."

Walter said nothing. He was a little tired and quite content to sit down beside Mother on the steps and lean his black head against her shoulder. Leslie Ford, looking at him, thought that he had the face of a genius...the remote, detached look of a soul from another star. Earth was not his habitat.

Everybody was very happy in this golden hour of a golden day. A bell in a church across the harbour rang faintly and sweetly. The moon was making patterns on the water. The dunes shimmered in hazy silver. There was a tang of mint in the air and some unseen roses were unbearably sweet. And Anne, looking dreamily over the lawn with eyes that, in spite of six children, were still very young, thought there was nothing in the world so slim and elfin as a very young lombardy poplar by moonlight.

Then she began to think about Stella Chase and Alden Churchill, until Gilbert offered her a penny for her thoughts.

"I'm thinking seriously of trying my hand at matchmaking," retorted Anne.

Gilbert looked at the others in mock despair.

"I was afraid it would break out again some day. I've done my best, but you can't reform a born matchmaker. She has a positive passion for it. The number of matches she has made is incredible. I couldn't sleep o' nights if I had such responsibilities on my conscience."

"But they're all happy," protested Anne. "I'm really an adept. Think of all the matches I've made...or been accused of making...

Theodora Dix and Ludovic Speed...Stephen Clark and Prissie Gardner...Janet Sweet and John Douglas...Professor Carter and Esme Taylor...Nora and Jim...and Dovie and Jarvis..."

"Oh, I admit it. This wife of mine, Owen, has never lost her sense of expectation. Thistles may, for her, bear figs at any time. I suppose she'll keep on trying to marry people off until she grows up."

"I think she had something to do with another match yet," said Owen, smiling at his wife.

"Not I," said Anne promptly. "Blame Gilbert for that. I did my best to persuade him not to have that operation performed on George Moore. Talk about sleeping o' nights...there are nights when *I* wake up in a cold perspiration dreaming that I succeeded."

"Well, they say it is only happy women who match-make, so that is one up for me," said Gilbert complacently. "What new victims have you in mind now, Anne?"

Anne only grinned at him. Matchmaking is something requiring subtlety and discretion and there are things you do not tell even to your husband.

16

Anne lay awake for hours that night and several nights thereafter, thinking about Alden and Stella. She had a feeling that Stella thought longingly about marriage...a home...babies. She had begged one night to be allowed to give Rilla her bath..."It's so delightful to bathe her plump, dimpled little body"...and again, shyly, "It's so lovely, Mrs. Blythe, to have little darling velvet arms stretched out to you. Babies are so *right*, aren't they?" It would be a shame if a grouchy father should prevent the blossoming of those secret hopes.

It would be an ideal marriage. But how could it be brought about, with everybody concerned a bit stubborn and contrary? For the stubbornness and contrariness were not all on the old folks' side. Anne suspected that both Alden and Stella had a streak of it. This required an entirely different technique from any previous affair. In the nick of time Anne remembered Dovie's father.

Anne tilted her chin and went at it. Alden and Stella, she considered, were as good as married from that hour.

There was no time to be lost. Alden, who lived at the Harbour Head and went to the Anglican church over the harbour, had not even met Stella Chase as yet...perhaps had not even seen her. He had not been dangling after any girl for some months, but he might begin at any moment. Mrs. Janet Swift, of the Upper Glen, had a very handsome niece visiting her and Alden was always after the new girls. The first thing to do, then, was to have Alden and Stella meet. How was this to be managed? It must be brought about in some way absolutely innocent in appearance. Anne racked her brains but could think of nothing more original than giving a party and inviting them both. She did not altogether like the idea. It was hot weather for a party...and the Four Winds young people were such romps. Anne knew Susan would never consent to a party without practically housecleaning Ingleside from attic to cellar...and Susan was feeling the heat this summer. But a good cause demands sacrifices. Jen Pringle, B.A., had written that she was coming for a long-promised visit to Ingleside and that would be the very excuse for a party. Luck seemed to be on her side. Jen came...the invitations were sent out...Susan gave Ingleside its overhauling...she and Anne did all the cooking for the party themselves in the heart of a heat-wave.

Anne was woefully tired the night before the party. The heat had been terrible...Jem was sick in bed with an attack of what

Anne secretly feared was appendicitis though Gilbert lightly dismissed it as only green apples...and the Shrimp had been nearly scalded to death when Jen Pringle, trying to help Susan, knocked a pan of hot water off the stove on him. Every bone in Anne's body ached, her head ached, her feet ached, her eyes ached. Jen had gone with a group of young fry to see the lighthouse, telling Anne to go right to bed; but instead of going to bed she sat out on the verandah in the dampness that followed the afternoon's thunderstorm and talked to Alden Churchill, who had called to get some medicine for his mother's bronchitis but would not go into the house. Anne thought it was a heaven-sent opportunity, for she wanted very much to have a talk with him. They were quite good friends, since Alden often called on a similar errand.

Alden sat on the verandah step with his bare head thrown back against the post. He was, as Anne always thought, a very handsome fellow...tall and broad-shouldered, with a marble-white face that never tanned, vivid blue eyes, and a stiff, upstanding brush of inky black hair. He had a laughing voice and a nice, deferential way which women of all ages liked. He had gone to Queen's for three years and had thought of going to Redmond, but his mother refused to let him go, alleging Biblical reasons, and Alden had settled down contentedly enough on the farm. He liked farming, he had told Anne; it was free, out-of-doors, independent work: he had his mother's knack of making money and his father's attractive personality. It was no wonder he was considered something of a matrimonial prize.

"Alden, I want to ask a favour of you," said Anne winningly. "Will you do it for me?"

"Sure, Mrs. Blythe," he answered heartily. "Just name it. You know I'd do anything for you."

Alden was really very fond of Mrs. Blythe and would really have done a good deal for her.

"I'm afraid it will bore you," said Anne anxiously. "But it's just this...I want you to see that Stella Chase has a good time at my party tomorrow night. I'm so afraid she won't. She doesn't know many young people around here yet...most of them are younger than she is...at least the boys are. Ask her to dance and see that she isn't left alone and out of things. She's so shy with strangers. I do want her to have a good time."

"Oh, I'll do my best," said Alden readily.

"But you mustn't fall in love with her, you know," warned Anne, laughing carefully.

"Have a heart, Mrs. Blythe. Why not?"

"Well," confidentially, "I think Mr. Paxton of Lowbridge has taken quite a fancy to her."

"That conceited young coxcomb?" exploded Alden, with unexpected warmth.

Anne looked mild rebuke.

"Why, Alden, I'm told he is a very nice young man. It's only that kind of a man who would have any chance with Stella's father, you know."

"That so?" said Alden, relapsing into his indifference.

"Yes...and I don't know if even he would. I understand Mr. Chase thinks there is nobody good enough for Stella. I'm afraid a plain farmer wouldn't have a look-in. So I don't want you to make trouble for yourself falling in love with a girl you could never get. I'm just dropping a friendly warning. I'm sure your mother would think as I do."

"Oh, thanks...What sort of a girl is she, anyhow. Looks good?"

"Well, I admit she isn't a beauty. I like Stella very much...but she's a little pale and retiring. Not overly strong...but I'm told Mr. Paxton has money of his own. To my thinking it should be an ideal match and I don't want anyone to spoil it."

"Why didn't you invite Mr. Paxton to your spree and tell *him* to give your Stella a good time?" demanded Alden rather truculently.

"You know a minister wouldn't come to a dance, Alden. Now, don't be cranky...and do see that Stella has a nice time."

"Oh, I'll see that she has a rip-roaring time. Good-night, Mrs. Blythe."

Alden swung off abruptly. Left alone, Anne laughed. "Now, if I know anything of human nature that boy will sail right in to show the world he can get Stella if he wants her in spite of anybody. He rose right to my bait about the minister. But I suppose I'm in for a bad night with this headache."

She had a bad night, complicated by what Susan called "a crick in the neck," and felt about as brilliant as grey flannel in the morning; but in the evening she was a gay and gallant hostess. The party was a success. Everybody seemed to have a good time. Stella certainly had. Alden saw to that almost too zealously for good form, Anne thought. It was going a bit strong for a first meeting that Alden should whisk Stella off to a dim corner of the verandah after supper and keep her there for an hour. But on the whole Anne was satisfied when she thought things over the next morning. To be sure, the dining-room carpet has been practically ruined by two spilled saucerfuls of ice-cream and a plateful of cake being ground into it; Gilbert's grandmother's Bristol glass candlesticks had been smashed to smithereens; somebody had upset a pitcherful of rainwater in the spare room which had soaked down and discoloured the library ceiling in a tragic fashion; the tassels were half torn off the chesterfield; Susan's big Boston fern, the pride of her heart, had apparently been sat upon by some large and heavy person. But on the credit side of the ledger was the fact that, unless all signs failed, Alden had fallen for Stella. Anne thought the balance was in her favour.

Local gossip within the next few weeks confirmed this view. It became increasingly evident that Alden was hooked. But what about Stella? Anne did not think Stella was the sort of girl to fall too ripely into any man's outstretched hand. She had a spice of her father's "contrariness," which in her worked out as a charming independence.

Again luck befriended a worried matchmaker. Stella came to see the Ingleside delphiniums one evening and afterwards they sat on the verandah and talked. Stella Chase was a pale, slender thing, rather shy but intensely sweet. She had a soft cloud of pale gold hair and wood-brown eyes. Anne thought it was her eyelashes did the trick, for she was not really pretty. They were unbelievably long and when she lifted them and dropped them it did things to masculine hearts. She had a certain distinction of manner which made her seem a little older than her twenty-four years and a nose that might be decidedly aquiline in later life.

"I've been hearing things about you, Stella," said Anne, shaking a finger at her. "And...I...don't...know...if...I...liked...them. Will you forgive me for saying that I wonder if Alden Churchill is just the right beau for you?"

Stella turned a startled face.

"Why...I thought you liked Alden, Mrs. Blythe."

"I do like him. But...well, you see...he has the reputation of being very fickle. I'm told no girl can hold him long. A good many have tried...and failed. I'd hate to see you left like that if his fancy veered."

"I think you are mistaken about Alden, Mrs. Blythe," said Stella slowly.

"I hope so, Stella. If you were a different type now...bouncing and jolly, like Eileen Swift..."

"Oh, well...I must be going home," said Stella vaguely. "Father will be lonely."

When she had gone Anne laughed again.

"I rather think Stella has gone away secretly vowing that she will show meddlesome friends that she can hold Alden and that no Eileen Swift shall ever get her claws on him. That little toss of her head and that sudden flush on her cheeks told me that.

So much for the young folks. I'm afraid the older ones will be tougher nuts to crack."

17

Anne's luck held. The Women's Missionary Auxiliary asked her if she would call on Mrs. George Churchill for her yearly contribution to the society. Mrs. Churchill seldom went to church and was not a member of the Auxiliary, but she "believed in missions" and always gave a generous sum if anyone called and asked her for it. People enjoyed doing this so little that the members had to take their turn at it and this year the turn was Anne's.

She walked down one evening, taking a daisied trail across lots which led over the sweet, cool loveliness of a hill-top to the road where the Churchill farm lay, a mile from the Glen. It was rather a dull road, with grey snake fences running up steep little slopes...yet it had homelights...a brook...the smell of hayfields that run down to the sea...gardens. Anne stopped to look at every garden she passed. Her interest in gardens was perennial. Gilbert was wont to say that Anne *had* to buy a book if the word "garden" were in the title.

A lazy boat idled down the harbour and far out a vessel was becalmed. Anne always watched an outward bound ship with a little quickening of her pulses. She understood Captain Franklin Drew when she heard him say once, as he went on board his vessel at the wharf, "God, how sorry I am for the folks we leave on shore!"

The big Churchill house, with the grim iron lacework around its flat mansard roof, looked down on the harbour and the dunes. Mrs. Churchill greeted her politely, if none too effusively, and ushered her into a gloomy and splendid parlour, the dark, brown-papered walls of which were hung with innumerable crayons of departed Churchills and Elliotts. Mrs. Churchill sat down on a green plush sofa, folded her long thin hands, and gazed steadily at her caller.

Mary Churchill was tall and gaunt and austere. She had a prominent chin, deep-set blue eyes like Alden's, and a wide, compressed mouth. She never wasted words and she never gossipped. So Anne found it rather difficult to work up to her objective naturally, but she managed it through the medium of the new minister across the harbour whom Mrs. Churchill did not like.

"He is not a spiritual man," said Mrs. Churchill coldly.

"I have heard that his sermons are remarkable," said Anne.

"I heard one and do not wish to hear more. My soul sought food and was given a lecture. He believes the Kingdom of Heaven can be taken by brains. It cannot."

"Speaking of ministers...they have a very clever one at Lowbridge now. I think he is interested in my young friend, Stella Chase. Gossip says it will be a match."

"Do you mean a marriage?" said Mrs. Churchill.

Anne felt snubbed but reflected that you had to swallow things like that when you were interfering in what didn't concern you.

"I think it would be a very suitable one, Mrs. Churchill. Stella is especially fitted for a minister's wife. I've been telling Alden he mustn't try to spoil it."

"Why?" asked Mrs. Churchill, without the flicker of an eyelid.

"Well...really...you know...I'm afraid Alden would stand no chance whatever. Mr. Chase doesn't think anyone good enough for Stella. All Alden's friends would hate to see him dropped suddenly like an old glove. He's too nice a boy for that."

"No girl ever dropped my son," said Mrs. Churchill, compressing her thin lips. "It was always the other way about. He found them out, for all their curls and giggles, their wrigglings and mincings. My son can marry any woman he chooses, Mrs. Blythe...*any* woman."

"Oh?" said Anne's tongue. Her tone said, "Of course I am too polite to contradict you but you have not changed my opinion." Mary Churchill understood and her white, shrivelled face warmed a little as she went out of the room to get her missionary contribution.

"You have the most wonderful view here," said Anne, when Mrs. Churchill ushered her to the door.

Mrs. Churchill gave the gulf a glance of disapproval.

"If you felt the bite of the east wind in winter, Mrs. Blythe, you might not think so much of the view. It's cool enough tonight. I should think you'd be afraid of catching cold in that thin dress. Not but what it's a pretty one. You are young enough still to care for gauds and vanities. I have ceased to feel any interest in such transitory things."

Anne felt fairly well satisfied with the interview as she went home through the dim green twilight.

"Of course one can't count on Mrs. Churchill," she told a flock of starlings who were holding a parliament in a little field scooped out of the woods, "but I think I worried her a little. I could see she didn't like having people think Alden *could* be jilted. Well, I've done what in me lies with all concerned except Mr. Chase and I don't see what I can do with him when I don't even know him. I wonder if he has the slightest notion that Alden and Stella are sweethearting. Not likely. Stella would never dare take Alden to the house, of course. Now, what *am* I to do about Mr. Chase?"

It was really uncanny...the way things helped her out. One evening Miss Cornelia came along and asked Anne to accompany her to the Chase home.

"I'm going down to ask Richard Chase for a contribution to the new church kitchen stove. Will you come with me, dearie, just as a moral support? I hate to tackle him alone."

They found Mr. Chase standing on his front steps, looking, with his long legs and his long nose, rather like a meditative crane. He had a few shining strands of hair brushed over the top of his bald head and his little grey eyes twinkled at them. He happened to be thinking that if that was the doctor's wife with old Cornelia she had a mighty good figure. As for Cousin Cornelia, twice removed, she was a bit too solidly built and had about as much intellect as a grasshopper, but she wasn't a bad old cat at all if you always rubbed her the right way.

He invited them courteously into his small library, where Miss Cornelia settled into a chair with a little grunt.

"It's dreadful hot tonight. I'm afraid we'll have a thunderstorm. Mercy on us, Richard, that cat is bigger than ever!"

Richard Chase had a familiar in the shape of a yellow cat of abnormal size which now climbed up on his knee. He stroked it tenderly.

"Thomas the Rhymer gives the world assurance of a cat," he said. "Don't you, Thomas? Look at your Aunt Cornelia, Rhymer. Observe the baleful glances she is casting at you out of orbs created to express only kindness and affection."

"Don't you call me that beast's Aunt Cornelia!" protested Mrs. Elliott sharply. "A joke is a joke but that is carrying things too far."

"Wouldn't you rather be the Rhymer's aunt than Neddy Churchill's aunt?" queried Richard Chase plaintively. "Neddy is a glutton and a wine-bibber, isn't he? I've heard you giving a catalogue of his sins. Wouldn't you rather be aunt to a fine upstanding cat like Thomas with a blameless record where whiskey and tabbies are concerned?"

"Poor Ned is a human being," retorted Miss Cornelia. "I don't like cats. That is the only fault I have to find with Alden

Churchill. He has got the strangest liking for cats, too. Lord knows where he got it...both his father and mother loathed them."

"What a sensible young man he must be!"

"Sensible! Well, he's sensible enough...except in the matter of cats and his hankering after evolution...another thing he didn't inherit from his mother."

"Do you know, Mrs. Elliott," said Richard Chase solemnly, "I have a secret leaning towards evolution myself."

"So you've told me before. Well, believe what you want to, Dick Chase...just like a man. Thank God, nobody could ever make *me* believe that I descended from a monkey."

"You don't look it, I confess, you comely woman. I see no simian resemblances in your rosy, comfortable, eminently gracious physiognomy. Still, your great-grandmother a million times removed swung herself from branch to branch by her tail. Science proves that, Cornelia...take it or leave it."

"I'll leave it, then. I'm not going to argue with you on that or any point. I've got my own religion and no ape-ancestors figure in it. By the way, Richard, Stella doesn't look so well this summer as I'd like to see her."

"She always feels the hot weather a good deal. She'll pick up when it's cooler."

"I hope so. Lisette picked up every summer but the last, Richard...don't forget that. Stella has her mother's constitution. It's just as well she isn't likely to marry."

"Why isn't she likely to marry? I ask from curiosity, Cornelia...rank curiosity. The processes of feminine thought are intensely interesting to me. From what premises or data do you draw the conclusion, in your own delightful offhand way, that Stella is not likely to marry?"

"Well, Richard, to put it plainly, she isn't the kind of girl that is very popular with men. She's a good, sweet girl, but she doesn't take with men."

"She has had admirers. I have spent much of my substance in the purchase and maintenance of shotguns and bulldogs."

"They admired your money-bags, I fancy. They were easily discouraged, weren't they? Just one broadside of sarcasm from you and off they went. If they had really wanted Stella they wouldn't have wilted for that any more than for your imaginary bulldog. No, Richard, you might as well admit the fact that Stella isn't the girl to win desirable beaus. Lisette wasn't, you know. She never had a beau till you came along."

"But wasn't I worth waiting for? Surely Lisette was a wise young woman. You would not have me give my daughter to any Tom, Dick or Harry, would you? My star, who, in spite of your disparaging remarks, is fit to shine in the palaces of kings?"

"We have no kings in Canada," retorted Miss Cornelia. "I'm not saying Stella isn't a lovely girl. I'm only saying the men don't seem to see it and, considering her constitution, I think it is just as well. A good thing for you, too. You could never get on without her...you'd be as helpless as a baby. Well, promise us a contribution to the church stove range and we'll be off. I know you're dying to pick up that book of yours."

"Admirable, clear-sighted woman! What a treasure you are for a cousin-in-law! I admit it...I *am* dying. But no other than yourself would have been perspicacious enough to see it or amiable enough to save my life by acting upon it. How much are you holding me up for?"

"You can afford five dollars."

"I never argue with a lady. Five dollars it is. Ah, going? She never loses time, this unique woman! Once her object is attained she straightway leaves you in peace. They don't hatch her breed of cats nowadays. Good-evening pearl of in-laws."

During the whole call Anne had not uttered one word. Why should she when Mrs. Elliott was doing her work for her so cleverly and unconsciously? But as Richard Chase bowed them out he suddenly bent forward confidentially.

"You've got the finest pair of ankles I've ever seen, Mrs. Blythe, and I've been about a bit in my time."

"Isn't he dreadful?" gasped Miss Cornelia as they went down the lane. "He's always saying outrageous things like that to women. You mustn't mind him, Anne dearie."

Anne didn't. She rather liked Richard Chase.

"I don't think," she reflected, "that he quite liked the idea of Stella not being popular with the men, in spite of the fact that their grandfathers were monkeys. I think he'd like to 'show folks,' too. Well I have done all I can do. I have interested Alden and Stella in each other; and, between us, Miss Cornelia and I have, I think, made Mrs. Churchill and Mr. Chase rather for the match than against it. Now I must just sit tight and see how it turns out."

A month later Stella Chase came to Ingleside and again sat down by Anne on the verandah steps...thinking, as she did so, that she hoped she would look like Mrs. Blythe some day...with that *ripened* look...the look of a woman who has lived fully and graciously.

The cool smoky evening had followed a cool, yellowish-grey day in early September. It was threaded with the gentle moan of the sea.

"The sea is unhappy tonight," Walter would say when he heard that sound.

Stella seemed absent-minded and quiet. Presently she said abruptly, looking up at a sorcery of stars that was being woven in the purple night, "Mrs. Blythe, I want to tell you something."

"Yes, dear?"

"I'm engaged to Alden Churchill," said Stella desperately. "We've been engaged ever since last Christmas. We told Father and Mrs. Churchill right away but we've kept it a secret from everyone else just because it was so sweet to have such a secret. We hated to share it with the world. But we are going to be married next month."

Anne gave an excellent imitation of a woman who had been turned to stone. Stella was still staring at the stars, so she did not see the expression on Mrs. Blythe's face. She went on, a little more easily:

"Alden and I met at a party in Lowbridge last November. We...loved each other from the very first moment. He said he had always dreamed of me...had always been looking for me. He said to himself, 'There is my wife,' when he saw me come in at the door. And I...felt just the same. Oh, we are so happy, Mrs. Blythe!"

Still Anne said nothing, several times over.

"The only cloud on my happiness is your attitude about the matter, Mrs. Blythe. Won't you try to approve? You've been such a dear friend to me since I came to Glen St. Mary...I've felt as if you were an older sister. And I'll feel so badly if I think my marriage is against your wish."

There was a sound of tears in Stella's voice. Anne recovered her powers of speech.

"Dearest, your happiness is all I've wanted. I like Alden...he's a splendid fellow...only he *had* the reputation of being a flirt..."

"But he isn't. He was just looking for the right one, don't you see, Mrs. Blythe? And he couldn't find her."

"How does your father regard it?"

"Oh, Father is greatly pleased. He took to Alden from the start. They used to argue for hours about evolution. Father said he always meant to let me marry when the right man came along. I feel dreadfully about leaving him, but he says young birds have a right to their own nest. Cousin Delia Chase is coming to keep house for him and Father likes her very much."

"And Alden's mother?"

"She is quite willing, too. When Alden told her last Christmas that we were engaged she went to the Bible and the very first verse she turned up was, 'A man shall leave father and mother and cleave unto his wife.' She said it was perfectly clear then what she ought to do and she consented at once. She is going to go to that little house of hers in Lowbridge."

"I am glad you won't have to live with that green plush sofa," said Anne.

"The sofa? Oh, yes, the furniture is very old-fashioned, isn't it? But she is taking it with her and Alden is going to refurnish completely. So you see everyone is pleased, Mrs. Blythe, and won't you give us your good wishes, too?"

Anne leaned forward and kissed Stella's cool satin cheek.

"I am *very* glad for you. God bless the days that are coming for you, my dear."

When Stella had gone Anne flew up to her own room to avoid seeing anyone for a few moments. A cynical, lopsided old moon was coming out from behind some shaggy clouds in the east and the fields beyond seemed to wink slyly and impishly at her.

She took stock of all the preceding weeks. She had ruined her dining-room carpet, destroyed two treasured heirlooms and spoiled her library ceiling; she had been trying to use Mrs. Churchill as a cat's-paw and Mrs. Churchill must have been laughing in her sleeve all the time.

"Who," asked Anne of the moon, "has been made the biggest fool of in this affair? I know what Gilbert's opinion will be. All the trouble I've gone to, to bring about a marriage between two people who were already engaged? I'm cured of matchmaking then...absolutely cured. Never will I lift a finger to promote a marriage if nobody in the world ever gets married again. Well, there is one consolation...Jen Pringle's letter today saying she is going to marry Lewis Stedman whom she met at my party. The Bristol candlesticks were not sacrificed entirely in vain. Boys... boys! *Must* you make such unearthly noises down there?"

"We're owls...we *have* to hoot," Jem's injured voice proclaimed from the dark shrubbery. He knew he was making a very good job of hooting. Jem could mimic the voice of any little wild thing out in the woods. Walter was not so good at it and he presently ceased being an owl and became a rather disillusioned little boy, creeping to Mother for comfort.

"Mummy, I thought crickets *sang*... and Mr. Carter Flagg said today they don't...they just make that noise scraping their hind-legs. *Do* they, Mummy?"

"Something like that...I'm not quite sure of the process. But *that* is their way of singing, you know."

"I don't like it. I'll never like to hear them singing again."

"Oh, yes, you will. You'll forget about the hind-legs in time and just think of their fairy chorus all over the harvest meadows and the autumn hills. Isn't it bedtime, small son?"

"Mummy, will you tell me a bedtime story that will send a cold chill down my spine? And sit beside me afterwards till I go to sleep?"

"What else are mothers for, darling?"

18

"'The time has come the Walrus said to talk of'...having a dog," said Gilbert.

They had not had a dog at Ingleside since old Rex had been poisoned; but boys should have a dog and the doctor decided he would get them one. But he was so busy that fall that he kept putting it off; and finally one November day Jem arrived home from an afternoon spent with a school pal carrying a dog...a little "yaller" dog with two black ears sticking cockily up.

"Joe Reese gave it to me, Mother. His name is Gyp. Hasn't he got the cutest tail? I can keep him, can't I, Mother?"

"What kind of a dog is he, darling?" asked Anne dubiously.

"I...I think he's a lot of kinds," said Jem. "That makes him more int'resting, don't you think, Mother? More exciting than if he was just one kind. *Please,* Mother."

"Oh, if your father says yes..."

Gilbert said "yes" and Jem entered into his heritage. Everybody at Ingleside welcomed Gyp into the family, except the Shrimp, who expressed his opinion without circumlocution. Even Susan took a liking to him and when she spun in the garret on rainy days Gyp, in his master's absence at school, stayed with her, gloriously hunting imaginary rats in dark corners and uttering a yelp of terror whenever his eagerness brought him too close to the little spinning-wheel. It was never used...the Morgans had left it there when they moved out...and sat in its dark corner like a little bent old woman. Nobody could understand Gyp's fear of it. He did not mind the big wheel at all but sat quite close to it while Susan sent it whirling around with her wheel-pin, and raced back and forward beside her as she paced the length of the garret, twirling the long thread of wool. Susan admitted that a dog could be real company and thought his trick of lying on his back, waving his fore-paws in the air, when he wanted a bone, the cleverest ever. She was as angry as Jem when Bertie Shakespeare sneeringly remarked, "Call that a dog?"

"We *do* call it a dog," said Susan with ominous calm. "Perhaps *you* would call it a hippopotamus." And Bertie had to go home that day without getting a piece of a wonderful concoction Susan called "apple crunch pie" and made regularly for the two boys and their pals. She was not around when Mac Reese asked, "Did the tide bring that in?" but Jem was able to stand up for his own dog and when Nat Flagg said that Gypsy's legs were too long for his size Jem retorted that a dog's legs had to be long enough to reach the ground. Natty was not overbright and that floored him.

November was stingy of its sunshine that year: raw winds blew through the bare, silver-branched maple grove and the Hollow was almost constantly filled with mist...not a gracious, eerie thing like a fog but what Dad called "dank, dark, depressing, dripping, drizzly mist." The Ingleside fry had to spend most of their play-time in the garret, but they made delightful friends of two partridges that came every evening to a certain huge old apple tree, and five of their gorgeous jays were still faithful, clucking impishly as they ate the food the children put out for them. Only they were greedy and selfish and kept all the other birds away.

Winter set in with December and it snowed ceaselessly for three weeks. The fields beyond Ingleside were unbroken silver pastures, fence and gate-posts wore tall white caps, windows whitened with fairy patterns and Ingleside lights bloomed out through the dim, snowy twilights, welcoming all wanderers home. It seemed to Susan that there had never been so many winter babies as there were that year; and when she left "the doctor's bite" in the pantry for him night after night she darkly opined that it would be a miracle if he toughed it out till spring.

"*The* ninth Drew baby! As if there weren't enough Drews in the world already!"

"I suppose Mrs. Drew will think it just the wonder we think Rilla, Susan."

"You *will* have your joke, Mrs. Dr. dear."

But in the library or the big kitchen the children planned out their summer playhouse in the Hollow while storms howled outside, or fluffy white clouds were blown over frosty stars. For blow it high or blow it low there was always at Ingleside glowing fires, comfort, shelter from storm, odours of good cheer, beds for tired little creatures.

Christmas came and went undarkened this year by any shadow of Aunt Mary Maria. There were rabbit trails in the snow to follow and great crusted fields over which you raced with your shadows and glistening hills for coasting and new skates to be tried out on the pond in the chill, rosy world of winter sunset. And always a yellow dog with black ears to run with you or meet you with ecstatic yelps of welcome when you came home, to sleep at the foot of your bed when you slept and lie at your feet while you learned your spellings, to sit close to you at meals and give you occasional reminding nudges with his little paw.

"Mother dearwums, I don't know how I lived before Gyp came. He can talk, Mother...he can really...with his eyes, you know."

Then...tragedy! One day Gyp seemed a little dull. He would not eat though Susan tempted him with the spare-rib bone he loved; the next day the Lowbridge vet was sent for and shook his head. It was hard to say...the dog might have found something poisonous in the woods...he might recover and he might not. The little dog lay very quietly, taking no notice of anyone except Jem; almost to the last he tried to wag his tail when Jem touched him.

"Mother dearwums, would it be wrong to pray for Gyp?"

"Of course not, dear. We can pray always for anything we love. But I am afraid...Gyppy is a very sick little dog."

"Mother, you don't think Gyppy is going to die!"

Gyp died the next morning. It was the first time death had entered into Jem's world. No one of us ever forgets the experience of watching something we love die, even if it is "only a little dog." Nobody at weeping Ingleside used that expression, not even Susan, who wiped a very red nose and muttered:

"I never took up with a dog before...and I never will again. It hurts too much."

Susan was not acquainted with Kipling's poem on the folly of giving your heart to a dog to tear; but if she had been she would, in spite of her contempt for poetry, have thought that for once a poet had uttered sense.

Night was hard for poor Jem. Mother and Father had to be away. Walter had cried himself to sleep and he was alone...with not even a dog to talk to. The dear brown eyes that had always been lifted to him so trustingly were glazed in death.

"Dear God," prayed Jem, "please look after my little dog who died today. You'll know him by the two black ears. Don't let him be lonesome for me..."

Jem buried his face in the bedspread to smother a sob. When he put out the light the dark night would be looking through the window at him and there would be no Gyp. The cold winter morning would come and there would be no Gyp. Day would follow day for years and years and there would be no Gyp. He just couldn't bear it.

Then a tender arm was slipped around him and he was held close in a warm embrace. Oh, there was love left yet in the world, even if Gyppy had gone.

"Mother, will it always be like this?"

"Not always." Anne did not tell him he would soon forget... that before long Gyppy would only be a dear memory. "Not always, little Jem. This will heal sometime...as your burned hand healed though it hurt so much at first."

"Dad said he would get me another dog. I don't have to have it, do I? I don't want another dog, Mother...not ever."

"I know, darling."

Mother knew everything. Nobody had a mother like his. He wanted to do something for her...and all at once it came to him what he would do. He would get her one of those pearl necklaces in Mr. Flagg's store. He had heard her say once that she really would like to have a pearl necklace and Dad had said, "When our ship comes in I'll get you one, Anne-girl."

Ways and means must be considered: He had an allowance but it was all needed for necessary things and pearl necklaces were not among the items budgeted for. Besides, he wanted to earn the money for it himself. It would be really his gift then. Mother's birthday was in March...only six weeks away. And the necklace would cost fifty cents!

19

It was not easy to earn money in the Glen but Jem went at it determinedly. He made tops out of old reels for the boys in school for two cents apiece. He sold three treasured milk teeth for three cents. He sold his slice of apple crunch pie every Saturday afternoon to Bertie Shakespeare Drew. Every night he put what he had earned into the little brass pig Nan had given him for Christmas. Such a nice shiny brass pig with a slit in his back wherein to drop coins. When you had put in fifty coppers the pig would open neatly of his own accord if you twisted his tail and yield you back your wealth. Finally to make up the last eight cents he sold his string of birds' eggs to Mac Reese. It was the finest string in the Glen and it hurt a little to let it go. But the birthday was drawing nearer and the money must be come by. Jem dropped the eight cents into the pig as soon as Mac had paid him and gloated over it.

"Twist his tail and see if he will really open up," said Mac, who didn't believe he would. But Jem refused; he was not going to open it until he was ready to go for the necklace.

The Missionary Auxiliary met at Ingleside the next afternoon and never forgot it. Right in the middle of Mrs. Norman Taylor's prayer...and Mrs. Norman Taylor was credited with being very proud of her prayers...a frantic small boy burst into the living-room.

"My brass pig's gone, Mother...my brass pig's gone!"

Anne hustled him out but Mrs. Norman always considered that her prayer was spoiled and, as she had especially wanted to impress a visiting minister's wife, it was long years before she forgave Jem or would have his father as a doctor again. After the ladies had gone home Ingleside was ransacked from top to bottom for the pig, without result. Jem, between the scolding he had got for his behaviour and his anguish over his loss, could remember just when he had seen it last or where. Mac Reese, telephoned to, responded that the last he had seen of the pig it was standing on Jem's bureau.

"You don't suppose, Susan, that Mac Reese..."

"No, Mrs. Dr. dear, I feel quite sure he didn't. The Reeses have their faults...terrible keen after the money they are, but it has to be honestly come by. *Where* can that blessed pig be?"

"Maybe the rats et it?" said Di. Jem scoffed at the idea but it worried him. Of course rats couldn't eat a brass pig with fifty coppers inside of him. But *could* they?

"No, no, dear. Your pig will turn up," assured Mother.

It hadn't turned up when Jem went to school the next day. News of his loss had reached school before him and many things were said to him, not exactly comforting. But at recess Sissy Flagg sidled up to him ingratiatingly. Sissy Flagg liked Jem and Jem did not like her, in spite of—or perhaps because of—her thick yellow curls and huge brown eyes. Even at eight one may have problems concerning the opposite sex.

"I can tell you who's got your pig."

"Who?"

"You've got to pick me for Clap-in and Clap-out and I'll tell you."

It was a bitter pill but Jem swallowed it. Anything to find that pig! He sat in an agony of blushes beside the triumphant

Sissy while they clapped in and clapped out, and when the bell rang he demanded his reward.

"Alice Palmer says Willy Drew told her Bob Russell told him Fred Elliott said he knew where your pig was. Go and ask Fred."

"Cheat!" cried Jem, glaring at her. *"Cheat!"*

Sissy laughed arrogantly. *She* didn't care. Jem Blythe had had to sit with her for once anyhow.

Jem went to Fred Elliott, who at first declared he knew nothing about the old pig and didn't want to. Jem was in despair. Fred Elliott was three years older than he was and a noted bully. Suddenly he had an inspiration. He pointed a grimy forefinger sternly at big, red-faced Fred Elliott.

"You are a transubstantiationalist," he said distinctly.

"Here, you, don't you call me names, young Blythe."

"That is more than a name," said Jem. "That is a hoodoo word. If I say it again and point my finger at you...*so*... you may have bad luck for a week. Maybe your toes will drop off. I'll count ten and if you haven't told me before I get to ten I'll hoodoo you."

Fred didn't believe it. But the skating race came off that night and he wasn't taking chances. Besides, toes were toes. At six he surrendered.

"All right...all right. Don't bust your jaws saying that a second time. Mac knows where your pig is...he said he did."

Mac was not in school, but when Anne heard Jem's story she telephoned his mother. Mrs. Reese came up a little later, flushed and apologetic.

"Mac didn't take the pig, Mrs. Blythe. He just wanted to see if it would open, so when Jem was out of the room he twisted the tail. It fell apart in two pieces and he couldn't get it together again. So he put the two halves of the pig and the money in one of Jem's Sunday boots in the closet. He hadn't ought to have touched it...and his father has whaled the stuffing out of him... but he didn't *steal* it, Mrs. Blythe."

"What was that word you said to Fred Elliott, Little Jem dear?" asked Susan, when the dismembered pig had been found and the money counted.

"Transubstantiationalist," said Jem proudly. "Walter found it in the dictionary last week...you know he likes great big *full* words, Susan...and...and we both learned how to pronounce it. We said it over to each other twenty-one times in bed before we went to sleep so that we'd remember it."

Now that the necklace was bought and stowed away in the third box from the top in the middle drawer of Susan's bureau... Susan having been privy to the plan all along...Jem thought the birthday would never come. He gloated over his unconscious mother. Little *she* knew what was hidden in Susan's bureau drawer...little *she* knew what her birthday would bring her...little *she* knew when she sang the twins to sleep with,

"I saw a ship a-sailing, a-sailing on the sea
And oh, it was all laden with pretty things for me,"

what the ship would bring her.

Gilbert had an attack of influenza in early March which almost ran to pneumonia. There were a few anxious days at Ingleside. Anne went about as usual, smoothing out tangles, administering consolation, bending over moonlit beds to see if dear little bodies were warm; but the children missed her laughter.

"What will the world do if Father dies?" whispered Walter, white-lipped.

"He isn't going to die, darling. He is out of danger now."

Anne wondered herself what their small world of Four Winds and the Glens and the Harbour Head would do if...if...anything had happened to Gilbert. They were all coming to depend on him so. The Upper Glen people especially seemed really to believe that he could raise the dead and only refrained because it would be crossing the purposes of the Almighty. He *had* done it once, they averred...old Uncle Archibald MacGregor had solemnly assured Susan that Samuel Hewett was dead as a doornail when Dr. Blythe brought him to. However that might be, when living people saw Gilbert's lean brown face and friendly hazel eyes by their bedside and heard his cheery, "Why, there's nothing the matter with *you*,"... well, they believed it until it came true. As for namesakes, he had more than he could count. The whole Four Winds district was peppered with young Gilberts. There was even a tiny Gilbertine.

So Dad was about again and Mother was laughing again, and...at last, it was the night before the birthday.

"If you go to bed early, Little Jem, tomorrow will come quicker," assured Susan.

Jem tried it but it didn't seem to work. Walter fell asleep promptly, but Jem squirmed about. He was afraid to go sleep. Suppose he didn't waken in time and everybody else had given their presents to Mother? He wanted to be the very first. Why hadn't he asked Susan to be sure and call him? She had gone out to make a visit somewhere but he would ask her when she came in. If he were sure of hearing her! Well, he'd just go down and lie on the living-room sofa and then he couldn't miss her.

Jem crept down and curled up on the chesterfield. He could see over the Glen. The moon was filling the hollows among the white, snowy dunes with magic. The great trees that were so mysterious at night held out their arms about Ingleside. He heard all the night sounds of a house...a floor creaking...someone turning in bed...the crumble and fall of coals in the fireplace... the scurrying of a little mouse in the china-closet. Was that an avalanche? No, only snow sliding off the roof. It was a little lonesome...why didn't Susan come?...if he only had Gyp now... dear Gyppy. Had he forgotten Gyp? No, not forgotten exactly.

But it didn't hurt so much now to think of him...one *did* think of other things a good deal of the time. Sleep well, dearest of dogs. Perhaps sometime he *would* have another dog, after all. It would be nice if he had one right now...or Shrimp. But the Shrimp wasn't round. Selfish old cat! Thinking of nothing but his own affairs!

No sign of Susan yet, coming along the long road that wound endlessly on through that strange white moonlit distance that was his own familiar Glen in daytime. Well, he would just have to imagine things to pass the time. Some day he would go to Baffin Land and live with Eskimos. Some day he would sail to far seas and cook a shark for Christmas dinner like Captain Jim. He would go on an expedition to the Congo in search of gorillas. He would be a diver and wander through radiant crystal halls under the sea. He would get Uncle Davy to teach him how to milk into the cat's mouth the next time he went up to Avonlea. Uncle Davy did that so expertly. Perhaps he would be a pirate. Susan wanted him to be a minister. The minister could do the most good but wouldn't a pirate have the most fun? Suppose the little wooden soldier hopped off the mantelpiece and shot off his gun! Suppose the chairs began walking about the room! Suppose the tiger rug came alive! Suppose the "quack beas" which he and Walter "pretended" all over the house when they were very young, really were about! Jem was suddenly frightened. In daytime he did not often forget the difference between romance and reality, but it was different in this endless night. Tick-tack went the clock...tick-tack...and for every tick there was a quack bear sitting on a step of the stairs. The stairs were just *black* with quack bears. They would sit there till daylight...*gibbering.*

Suppose God forgot to let the sun rise! The thought was so terrible that Jem buried his face in the afghan to shut it out, and there Susan found him sound asleep, when she came home in the fiery orange of a winter sunrise.

"Little Jem!"

Jem uncoiled himself and sat up, yawning. It had been a busy night for Silversmith Frost and the woods were fairyland. A far-off hill was touched with a crimson spear. All the white fields beyond the Glen were a lovely rose-colour. It was Mother's birthday morning.

"I was waiting for you, Susan...to tell you to call me...and you never came..."

"I went down to see the John Warrens, because their aunt had died, and they asked me to stay and sit up with the corpse," explained Susan cheerfully. "I didn't suppose you'd be trying to catch pneumonia, too, the minute my back was turned. Scamper off to your bed and I'll call you when I hear your mother stirring."

"Susan, how do you stab sharks?" Jem wanted to know before he went upstairs.

"I do not stab them," answered Susan.

Mother was up when he went into her room, brushing her long shining hair before the glass. Her eyes when she saw the necklace!

"Jem darling! For me!"

"*Now* you won't have to wait till Dad's ship comes in," said Jem with a fine nonchalance. What was that gleaming greenly on Mother's hand? A ring...Dad's present. All very well, but rings were common things...even Sissy Flagg had one. But a pearl necklace!

"A necklace is such a nice birthdayish thing," said Mother.

20

When Gilbert and Anne went to dinner with friends in Charlottetown one evening in late March Anne put on a new dress of ice-green encrusted with silver around neck and arms; and she wore Gilbert's emerald ring and Jem's necklace.

"Haven't I got a handsome wife, Jem?" asked Dad proudly.

Jem thought Mother was very handsome and her dress very lovely. How pretty the pearls looked on her white throat! He always liked to see Mother dressed up, but he liked it still better when she took off a splendid dress. It had transformed her into an alien. She was not really Mother in it.

After supper Jem went to the village to do an errand for Susan and it was while he was waiting in Mr. Flagg's store... rather afraid that Sissy might come in as she sometimes did and be entirely too friendly...that the blow fell...the shattering blow of disillusionment which is so terrible to a child because so unexpected and so seemingly inescapable.

Two girls were standing before the glass show case where Mr. Carter Flagg kept necklaces and chain bracelets and hair barettes.

"Aren't those pearl strings pretty?" said Abbie Russell.

"You'd almost think they were real," said Leona Reese.

They passed on then, quite unwitting of what they had done to the small boy sitting on the nail-keg. Jem continued to sit there for some time longer. He was incapable of movement.

"What's the matter, sonny?" inquired Mr. Flagg. "You seem kind of low in your mind."

Jem looked at Mr. Flagg with tragic eyes. His mouth was strangely dry.

"Please, Mr. Flagg...are those...those necklaces...they *are* real pearls, aren't they?"

Mr. Flagg laughed.

"No, Jem. I'm afraid you can't get real pearls for fifty cents, you know. A real pearl necklace like that would cost hundreds of dollars. They're just pearl beads...very good ones for the price, too. I got 'em at a bankrupt sale...that's why I can sell 'em so cheap. Ordin'rily they run to a dollar. Only one left...they went like hot cakes."

Jem slid off the keg and went out, totally forgetting what Susan had sent him for. He walked blindly up the frozen road home. Overhead was a hard dark wintry sky; there was what Susan called "a feel" of snow in the air, and a skim of ice over the puddles. The harbour lay black and sullen between its bare banks. Before Jem reached home a snow-squall was whitening over them. He wished it would snow...and snow...and snow...till he was buried and everybody was buried fathoms deep. There was no justice anywhere in the world.

Jem was heartbroken. And let no one scoff at his heartbreak for scorn of its cause. His humiliation was utter and complete. He had given Mother what he and she had supposed was a pearl necklace...and it was only an old imitation. What would she say...what would she feel like...when she knew? For of course she must be told. It never occurred to Jem to think for a moment that she need not be told. Mother must not be "fooled" any longer. She must know that her pearls weren't real. Poor Mother! She had been so proud of them...had he not seen the pride shining in her eyes when she had kissed him and thanked him for them?

Jem slipped in by the side door and went straight to bed, where Walter was already sound asleep. But Jem could not sleep; he was awake when Mother came home and slipped in to see that Walter and he were warm.

"Jem, dear, are you awake at this hour? You're not sick?"

"No, but I'm very unhappy *here*, Mother dearwums," said Jem, putting his hand on his stomach, fondly believing it to be his heart.

"What is the matter, dear?"

"I…I…there is something I must tell you, Mother. You'll be awfully disappointed, Mother…but I didn't mean to deceive you, Mother…truly I didn't."

"I'm sure you didn't, dear. What is it? Don't be afraid."

"Oh, Mother dearwums, those pearls aren't real pearls…I thought they were…I *did* think they were…*did*…"

Jem's eyes were full of tears. He couldn't go on.

If Anne wanted to smile there was no sign of it on her face. Shirley had bumped his head that day, Nan had sprained her ankle, Di had lost her voice with a cold. Anne had kissed and bandaged and soothed; but this was different…this needed all the secret wisdom of mothers.

"Jem, I never thought you supposed they were real pearls. I knew they weren't…at least in one sense of real. In another, they are the most real things I've ever had given me. Because there was love and work and self-sacrifice in them…and *that* makes them more precious to me than all the gems that divers have fished up from the sea for queens to wear. Darling, I wouldn't exchange my pretty beads for the necklace I read of last night which some millionaire gave his bride and which cost half a million. So *that* shows you what your gift is worth to me, dearest of dear little sons. Do you feel better now?"

Jem was so happy he was ashamed of it. He was afraid it was babyish to be so happy. "Oh, life is *bearable* again," he said cautiously.

The tears had vanished from his sparkling eyes. All was well. Mother's arms were about him…Mother *did* like her necklace… nothing else mattered. Some day he would give her one that would cost no mere half but a whole million. Meanwhile, he was tired…his bed was very warm and cosy…Mother's hands smelled like roses…and he didn't hate Leona Reese any more.

"Mother dearwums, you do look so sweet in that dress," he said sleepily. "Sweet and pure…pure as Epps' cocoa."

Anne smiled as she hugged him and thought of a ridiculous thing she had read in a medical journal that day, signed Dr. V. Z. Tomachowsky. "*You must never kiss your little son lest you set up a Jocasta complex.*" She had laughed over it at the time and been a little angry as well. Now she only felt pity for the writer of it. Poor, poor man! For of course V. Z. Tomachowsky was a man. No woman would ever write anything so silly and wicked.

21

April came tiptoeing in beautifully that year with sunshine and soft winds for a few days; and then a driving northeast snowstorm dropped a white blanket over the world again. "Snow in April is abominable," said Anne. "Like a slap in the face when you expected a kiss." Ingleside was fringed with icicles and for two long weeks the days were raw and the nights hard-bitten. Then the snow grudgingly disappeared and when the news went round that the first robin had been seen in the Hollow Ingleside plucked up heart and ventured to believe that the miracle of spring was really going to happen again.

"Oh, Mummy, it *smells* like spring today," cried Nan, delightedly snuffing the fresh moist air. "Mummy, isn't spring an exciting time!"

Spring was trying out her paces that day...like an adorable baby just learning to walk. The winter pattern of trees and fields was beginning to be overlaid with hints of green and Jem had again brought in the first mayflowers. But an enormously fat lady, sinking puffingly into one of the Ingleside easy-chairs, sighed and said sadly that the springs weren't so nice as they were when she was young.

"Don't you think perhaps the change is in us...not in the springs, Mrs. Mitchell?" smiled Anne.

"Mebbe so. I know *I* am changed, all too well. I don't suppose to look at me now you'd think I was once the prettiest girl in these parts."

Anne reflected that she certainly wouldn't. The thin, stringy, mouse-coloured hair under Mrs. Mitchell's crape bonnet and long sweeping "widow's veil" was streaked with grey; her blue, expressionless eyes were faded and hollow; and to call her double chin chinned erred on the side of charity. But Mrs. Anthony Mitchell was feeling quite contented with herself just then for nobody in Four Winds had finer weeds. Her voluminous black dress was crape to the knees. One wore mourning in those days with a vengeance.

Anne was spared the necessity of saying anything, for Mrs. Mitchell gave her no chance.

"My soft water system went dry this week...there's a leak in it...so I kem down to the village this morning to get Raymond Russell to come and fix it. And thinks I to myself, 'Now that I'm here I'll just run up to Ingleside and ask Mrs. Dr. Blythe to write an obitchery for Anthony."

"An obituary?" said Anne blankly.

"Yes...them things they put in the papers about dead people, you know," explained Mrs. Anthony. "I want Anthony should have a real good one...something out of the common. You write things, don't you?"

"Occasionally I do write a little story," admitted Anne. "But a busy mother hasn't much time for that. I had wonderful dreams once but now I'm afraid I'll never be in Who's Who, Mrs. Mitchell. And I never wrote an obituary in my life."

"Oh, they can't be hard to write. Old Uncle Charlie Bates over our way writes most of them for the Lower Glen, but he ain't a bit poetical and I've set my heart on a piece of poetry for Anthony. My, but he was always so fond of poetry. I was up to hear you give that talk on bandages to the Glen Institute last week and thinks I to myself, 'Anyone who can talk as glib as that can likely write a real poetical obitchery.' You will do it for me, won't you, Mrs. Blythe? Anthony would have liked it. He always admired you. He said once that when you come into a room you made all the other women look 'common and undistinguished.' He sometimes talked real poetical but he meant well. I've been reading a lot of obitcheries...I have a big scrapbook full of them... but it didn't seem to me he'd have liked any of them. He used to laugh at them so much. And it's time it was done. He's been dead two months. He died lingering but painless. Coming on spring's an inconvenient time for anyone to die, Mrs. Blythe, but I've made the best of it. I s'pose Uncle Charlie will be hopping mad if I get anyone else to write Anthony's obitchery but I don't care. Uncle Charlie has a wonderful flow of language but him and Anthony never hit it off any too well and the long and short of it is I'm *not* going to have him write Anthony's obitchery. I've been Anthony's wife...his faithful and loving wife for thirty-five years... thirty-five years, Mrs. Blythe,"...as if she were afraid Anne might think of only thirty-four..."and I'm going to have an obitchery he'd like if it takes a leg. That was what my daughter Seraphine said to me—she's married at Lowbridge, you know...nice name, Seraphine, isn't it?...I got it off a gravestone. Anthony didn't like it...he wanted to call her Judith after his mother. But I said it was too solemn a name and he give in real kindly. He weren't no hand for arguing...though he always called her Seraph...where was I?"

"Your daughter was saying..."

"Oh, yes, Seraphine said to me, 'Mother, whatever else you have or don't have, have a real nice obitchery for Father.' Her and her father were always real thick, though he poked a bit of fun at her now and then, just as he did at me. Now, won't you, Mrs. Blythe?"

"I really don't know a great deal about your husband, Mrs. Mitchell."

"Oh, I can tell you all about him...if you don't want to know the colour of his eyes. Do you know, Mrs. Blythe, when Seraphine and me was talking things over after the funeral I couldn't tell the colour of his eyes, after living with him thirty-five years. They was kind of soft and dreamy anyhow. He used to look so pleading with them when he was courting me. He had a real hard time to get me, Mrs. Blythe. He was mad about me for years. I was full of bounce then and meant to pick and choose. My life story would be real thrilling if you ever get short of material, Mrs. Blythe. Ah well, them days are gone. I had more beaus than you could shake a stick at. But they kept coming and going...and Anthony just kept coming. He was kind of good-looking, too... such a nice lean man. I never could abide pudgy men...and he was a cut or two above me...I'd be the last one to deny that. 'It'll be a step up for a Plummer if you marry a Mitchell,' Ma said...I was a Plummer, Mrs. Blythe...John A. Plummer's daughter. And he paid me such nice romantic compliments, Mrs. Blythe. Once he told me I had the ethereal charm of moonlight. I knew it meant something nice though I don't know yet what 'ethereal' means. I've always been meaning to look it up in the dictionary but I never get around to it. Well, anyway, in the end I passed my word of honour that I would be his bride. That is...I mean...I said I'd take him. My, but I wish you could have seen me in my wedding-dress, Mrs. Blythe. They all said I was a picture. Slim as a trout with hair yaller as gold, and such a complexion. Ah, time makes turrible changes in us. *You* haven't come to that yet, Mrs. Blythe. You're real pretty still...and a highly eddicated woman into the bargain. Ah well, we can't all be clever...some of us have to do the cooking. That dress you've got on is real handsome,

Mrs. Blythe. You never wear black, I notice...you're right...you'll have to wear it soon enough. Put it off till you have to, I say. Well, where was I?"

"You were...trying to tell me something about Mr. Mitchell."

"Oh, yes. Well, we were married. There was a big comet that night...I remember seeing it as we drove home. It's a real pity you couldn't have seen that comet, Mrs. Blythe. It was simply pretty. I don't suppose you could work it into the obitchery, could you?"

"It...might be rather difficult..."

"Well," Mrs. Mitchell surrendered the comet with a sigh, "you'll have to do the best you can. He hadn't a very exciting life. He got drunk once...he said he just wanted to see what it was like for once...he was always of an inquiring turn of mind. But of course you couldn't put that in an obitchery. Nothing much else ever happened to him. Not to complain, but just to state facts he was a bit shiftless and easy-going. He would sit for an hour looking into a hollyhock. My, but he was fond of flowers... hated to mow down the buttercups. No matter if the wheat crop failed as long as there was farewell-summers and goldenrod. And trees...that orchard of his...I always told him, joking like, that he cared more for his trees than for me. And his farm...my, but he loved his bit of land. He seemed to think it was a human being. Many's the time I've heard him say, 'I think I'll go out and have a little talk to my farm.' When we got old I wanted him to sell, seeing as we had no boys, and retire to Lowbridge, but he would say, 'I can't sell my farm...I can't sell my heart.' Ain't men funny? Not long before he died he took a notion to have a boiled hen for dinner, 'cooked in that way you have,' says he. He was always partial to my cooking, if I do say it. The only thing he couldn't abide was my lettuce salad with nuts in it. He said the nuts was so durned unexpected. But there wasn't a hen to spare...they was all laying good...and there was only one rooster left and of course I couldn't kill him. My, but I like to see the roosters strutting round. Ain't anything much handsomer than a fine rooster, do you think, Mrs. Blythe? Well, where was I?"

"You were saying your husband wanted you to cook a hen for him."

"Oh, yes. And I've been so sorry ever since I didn't. I wake up in the night and think of it. But I didn't know he was going to die, Mrs. Blythe. He never complained much and always said he was better. And interested in things to the last. If I'd a-known he was going to die, Mrs. Blythe, I'd have cooked a hen for him, eggs or no eggs."

Mrs. Mitchell removed her rusty black lace mitts and wiped her eyes with a handkerchief, black-bordered a full two inches.

"He'd have enjoyed it," she sobbed. "He had his own teeth to the last, poor dear. Well, anyway"...folding the handkerchief and putting on the mitts, "he was sixty-five, so he weren't far from the allotted span. And I've got another coffin-plate. Mary Martha Plummer and me started collecting coffin-plates at the same time but she soon got ahead of me...so many of her relation died, not to speak of her three children. She's got more coffin-plates than anyone in these parts. I didn't seem to have much luck but I've got a full mantelpiece at last. My cousin, Thomas Bates, was buried last week and I wanted his wife to give me the coffin-plate, but she had it buried with him. Said collecting coffin-plates was a relic of barbarism. She was a Hampson and the Hampsons were always odd. Well, where was I?"

Anne really could not tell Mrs. Mitchell where she was this time. The coffin-plates had dazed her.

"Oh, well, anyway poor Anthony died. 'I go gladly and in quietness,' was all that he said but he smiled just at the last...at the ceiling, not at me nor Seraphine. I'm so glad he was so happy just afore he died. There were times I used to think perhaps he wasn't quite happy, Mrs. Blythe...he was so terrible high-strung and sensitive. But he looked real noble and sublime in his coffin.

We had a grand funeral. It was just a lovely day. He was buried with loads of flowers. I took a sinking spell at the last but otherwise everything went off very well. We buried him in the Lower Glen graveyard though all his family were buried in Lowbridge. But he picked out his graveyard long ago...said he wanted to be buried near his farm and where he could hear the sea and the wind in the trees...there's trees around three sides of that graveyard, you know. I was glad, too...I always thought it was such a cosy little graveyard and we can keep geraniums growing on his grave. He was a good man...he's likely in Heaven now, so that needn't trouble you. I always think it must be some chore to write an obichery when you *don't* know where the departed is. I can depend on you, then, Mrs. Blythe?"

Anne consented, feeling that Mrs. Mitchell would stay there and talk until she did consent. Mrs. Mitchell, with another sigh of relief, heaved herself out of her chair.

"I must be stepping. I'm expecting a hatching of turkey poults today. I've enjoyed my conversation with you and I wish I could have stayed longer. It's lonesome being a widow woman. A man mayn't amount to an awful lot but you sort of miss him when he goes."

Anne politely saw her down the walk. The children were stalking robins on the lawn and daffodil tips were poking up everywhere.

"You've got a nice proud house here...a real nice proud house, Mrs. Blythe. I've always felt I'd like a big house. But with only us and Seraphine...and where was the money to come from?...and, anyway, Anthony'd never hear of it. He had an awful affection for that old house. I'm meaning to sell if I get a fair offer and live either in Lowbridge or Mowbray Narrows, whichever I decide would be the best place to be a widow in. Anthony's insurance will come in handy. Say what you like it's easier to bear a full sorrow than an empty one. You'll find that out when you're a widow yourself...though I hope that'll be a good few years yet. How is the doctor getting on? It's been a real sickly winter so he ought to have done pretty well. My, what a nice little family you've got! Three girls! Nice now, but wait you till they come to the boy-crazy age. Not that I'd much trouble with Seraphine. She was quiet...like her father...and stubborn like him. When she fell in love with John Whitaker, have him she would in spite of all I could say. A rowan tree? Whyn't you have it planted by the front door? It would keep the fairies out."

"But who would want to keep the fairies out, Mrs. Mitchell?"

"Now you're talking like Anthony. I was only joking. O' course I don't believe in fairies...but if they did happen to exist I've heard they were pesky mischievous. Well, good-bye, Mrs. Blythe. I'll call round next week for the obitchery."

22

"You've let yourself in for it, Mrs. Dr. dear," said Susan, who had overheard most of the conversation as she polished her silver in the pantry.

"Haven't I? But, Susan, I really do want to write that 'obituary.' I liked Anthony Mitchell...what little I've seen of him... and I feel sure that he'd turn over in his grave if his obituary was like the run of the mill in the *Daily Enterprise.* Anthony had an inconvenient sense of humour."

"Anthony Mitchell was a real nice fellow when he was young, Mrs. Dr. dear. Though a bit dreamy they said. He didn't hustle enough to suit Bessy Plummer, but he made a decent living and paid his debts. Of course he married the last girl he should have. But although Bessy Plummer looks like a comic valentine now she was pretty as a picture then. Some of us, Mrs. Dr. dear," concluded Susan with a sigh, "haven't even that much to remember."

"Mummy," said Walter, "the snack-dragons are coming up thick all around the back porch. And a pair of robins are beginning to build a nest on the pantry window-sill. You'll let them, won't you, Mummy? You won't open the window and scare them away?"

Anne had met Anthony Mitchell once or twice, though the little grey house between the spruce woods and the sea, with the great big willow tree over it like a huge umbrella, where he lived, was in the Lower Glen and the doctor from Mowbray Narrows attended most of the people there. But Gilbert had bought hay from him now and then and once when he had brought a load Anne had taken him all over her garden and they had found out that they talked the same language. She had liked him...his lean, lined, friendly face, his brave, shrewd, yellowish-hazel eyes that had never faltered or been hoodwinked...save once, perhaps, when Bessy Plummer's shallow and fleeting beauty had tricked him into a foolish marriage. Yet he never seemed unhappy or unsatisfied. As long as he could plough and garden and reap he was as contented as a sunny old pasture. His black hair was but lightly frosted with silver and a ripe, serene spirit revealed itself in his rare but sweet smiles. His old fields had given him bread and delight, joy of conquest and comfort in sorrow. Anne was satisfied because he was buried near them. He might have "gone gladly" but he had lived gladly, too. The Mowbray Narrows doctor had said that when he told Anthony Mitchell he could hold out to him no hope of recovery Anthony had smiled and replied, "Well, life is a trifle monotonous at times now I'm getting old. Death will be something of a change. I'm real curious about it, doctor." Even Mrs. Anthony, among all her rambling absurdities, had dropped a few things that revealed the real Anthony. Anne wrote "The Old Man's Grave" a few evenings later by her room window and read it over with a sense of satisfaction.

"Make it where the winds may sweep
Through the pine boughs soft and deep,
And the murmur of the sea
Come across the orient lea,
And the falling raindrops sing
Gently to his slumbering.

"Make it where the meadows wide
Greenly lie on every side,
Harvest fields he reaped and trod,
Westering slopes of clover sod,
Orchard lands where bloom and blow
Trees he planted long ago.

"Make it where the starshine dim
May be always close to him,
And the sunrise glory spread
Lavishly around his bed,
And the dewy grasses creep
Tenderly above his sleep.

"Since these things to him were dear
Through full many a well-spent year,
It is surely meet their grace
Should be on his resting place,
And the murmur of the sea
Be his dirge eternally."

"I think Anthony Mitchell would have liked that," said Anne, flinging her window open to lean out to the spring. Already there were crooked little rows of young lettuce in the children's garden; the sunset was soft and pink behind the maple grove; the Hollow rang with the faint, sweet laughter of children.

"Spring is so lovely I hate to go to sleep and miss any of it," said Anne.

Mrs. Anthony Mitchell came up to get her "obitchery" one afternoon the next week. Anne read it to her with a secret bit of pride; but Mrs. Anthony's face did not express unmixed satisfaction.

"My, I call that real sprightly. You do put things so well. But...but...you didn't say a word about him being in heaven. Weren't you *sure* he is there?"

"So sure that it wasn't necessary to mention it, Mrs. Mitchell."

"Well, *some* people might doubt. He...he didn't go to church as often as he might...though he was a member in good standing. And it doesn't tell his age...nor mention the flowers. Why, you just couldn't count the wreaths on the coffin. Flowers are poetical enough, I should think!"

"I'm sorry..."

"Oh, I don't blame you...not a mite do I blame you. You've done your best and it sounds beautiful. What do I owe you?"

"Why...why...*nothing*, Mrs. Mitchell. I couldn't think of such a thing."

"Well, I thought likely you'd say that, so I brung you up a bottle of my dandelion wine. It sweetens the stomach if you're ever bothered with gas. I'd have brung a bottle of my yarb tea, too, only I was afraid the doctor mightn't approve. But if you'd like some and think you can smuggle it in unbeknownst to him you've only to say the word."

"No, no, thank you," said Anne rather flatly. She had not yet quite recovered from "sprightly."

"Just as you like. You'd be welcome to it. I'll not be needing any more medicine myself this spring. When my second cousin, Malachi Plummer, died in the winter I asked his widow to give me the three bottles of medicine there was left over... they got it by the dozen. She was going to throw them out but I was always one that could never bear to waste anything. I couldn't take more than one bottle myself but I made our hired man take the other two. 'If it doesn't do you any good it won't do you any harm,' I told him. I won't say I'm not rather relieved you didn't want any cash for the obitchery for I'm rather short of ready money just now. A funeral is so expensive though D. B. Martin is about the cheapest undertaker in these parts. I haven't even got my black paid for yet. I won't feel I'm really in mourning till it is. Luckily I hadn't to get a new bunnit. This was the bunnit I had made for Mother's funeral ten years ago. It's kind of fortunate black becomes me, ain't it? If you'd see Malachi Plummer's widow now, with her sailer face! Well, I must be stepping. And I'm much obliged to you, Mrs. Blythe, even if...but I feel sure you did your best and it's lovely poetry."

"Won't you stay and have supper with us?" asked Anne. "Susan and I are all alone...the doctor is away and the children are having their first picnic supper in the Hollow."

"I don't mind," said Mrs. Anthony, slipping willingly back into her chair. "I'll be glad to set a spell longer. Somehow it takes so long to get rested when you get old. And," she added, with a smile of dreamy beatitude on her pink face, "didn't I smell fried parsnips?"

Anne almost grudged the fried parsnips when the *Daily Enterprise* came out the next week. There, in the obituary column, was "The Old Man's Grave"...with five verses instead of the original four! And the fifth verse was:

"A wonderful husband, companion and aid,
One who was better the Lord never made,
A wonderful husband, tender and true,
One in a million, dear Anthony, was you."

"! ! !" said Ingleside.

"I hope you didn't mind me tacking on another verse," said Mrs. Mitchell to Anne at the next Institute meeting. "I just wanted to praise Anthony a little more...and my nephew, Johnny Plummer, writ it. He just sot down and scribbled it off quick as a wink. He's like you...he doesn't look clever but he can poetize. He got it through his mother...she was a Wickford. The Plummers haven't a speck of poetry in them...not a speck."

"What a pity you didn't think of getting him to write Mr. Mitchell's 'obitchery' in the first place," said Anne coldly.

"Yes, isn't it? But I didn't know he could write poetry and I'd set my heart on it for Anthony's send-off. Then his mother showed me a poem he'd writ on a squirrel drowned in a pail of maple syrup...a really touching thing. But yours was real nice, too, Mrs. Blythe. I think the two combined together made something out of the common, don't you?"

"I do," said Anne.

23

The Ingleside children were having bad luck with pets. The wriggly curly little black pup Dad brought home from Charlottetown one day just walked out the next week and disappeared into the blue. Nothing was ever seen or heard of him again, and though there were whispers of a sailor from the Harbour Head having been seen taking a small black pup on board his ship the night she sailed, his fate remained one of the deep and dark unsolved mysteries of the Ingleside chronicles. Walter took it harder than Jem, who had not yet quite forgotten his anguish over Gyp's death and was not ever again going to let himself love a dog not wisely but too well. Then Tiger Tom, who lived in the barn and was never allowed in the house because of his thievish propensities but got a good deal of petting for all that, was found stark and stiff on the barn floor and had to be buried with pomp and circumstance in the Hollow. Finally Jem's rabbit, Bun, which he had bought from Joe Russell for a quarter, sickened and died. Perhaps its death was hastened by a dose of patent medicine Jem gave him, perhaps not. Joe had advised it and Joe ought to know. But Jem felt as if he had murdered Bun.

"*Is* there a curse on Ingleside?" he demanded gloomily, when Bun had been laid to rest beside Tiger Tom. Walter wrote an epitaph for him and he and Jem and the twins wore black ribbons tied round their arms for a week, to the horror of Susan who deemed it sacrilege. Susan was not inconsolable for the loss of Bun, who had got out once and worked havoc in her garden. Still less did she approve of two toads Walter brought in and put in the cellar. She put one of them out when evening came but could not find the other and Walter lay awake and worried.

"Maybe they were husband and wife," he thought. "Maybe they're awful lonely and unhappy now they're separated. It was the little one Susan put out, so I guess she was the lady toad and maybe she's frightened to death all alone in that big yard without anyone to protect her...just like a widow."

Walter couldn't endure thinking about the widow's woes, so he slipped down to the cellar to hunt for the gentleman toad, but only succeeded in knocking down a pile of Susan's discarded tinware with a resulting racket that might have wakened the dead. It woke only Susan, however, who came marching down with a candle, the fluttering flame of which cast the weirdest shadows on her gaunt face.

"Walter Blythe, whatever are you doing?"

"Susan, I've got to find that toad," said Walter desperately. "Susan, just think how you would feel without your husband, if you had one."

"What on earth are you talking about?" demanded the justifiably mystified Susan.

At this point the gentleman toad, who had evidently given himself up for lost when Susan appeared on the scene, hopped out into the open from behind Susan's cask of dill pickles. Walter pounced on him and slipped him out through the window, where it is to be hoped he rejoined his supposed love and lived happily ever afterwards.

"You know you shouldn't have brought those creatures into the cellar," said Susan sternly. "What would they live on?"

"Of course I meant to catch insects for them," said Walter, aggrieved. "I wanted to *study* them."

"There is simply no being up to them," moaned Susan, as she followed an indignant young Blythe up the stairs. And did not mean the toads.

They had better luck with their robin. They had found him, little more than a baby, on the doorstep after a June night storm of wind and rain. He had a grey back and a mottled breast and bright eyes, and from the first he seemed to have complete confidence in all the Ingleside people, not even excepting the Shrimp, who never attempted to molest him, not even when Cock Robin hopped saucily up to his plate and helped himself. They fed him on worms at first and he had such an appetite that Shirley spent most of his time digging them. He stored the worms in cans and left them around the house, much to Susan's disgust, but she would have endured more than that for Cock Robin, who lighted so fearlessly on her work-worn finger and chirrupped in her very face. Susan had taken a great fancy to Cock Robin and thought it worth mentioning in a letter to Rebecca Dew that his breast was beginning to change to a beautiful rusty red.

"Do not think that my intellect is weakening I beg of you, Miss Dew dear," she wrote. "I suppose it is very silly to be so fond of a bird but the human heart has its weaknesses. He is not imprisoned like a canary...something I could never abide, Miss Dew dear...but ranges at will through house and garden and sleeps on a bow by Walter's study platform up in the apple tree looking into Rilla's window. Once when they took him to the Hollow he flew away but returned at eventide to their great joy and I must in all cander add to my own."

The Hollow was "the Hollow" no longer. Walter had begun to feel that such a delightful spot deserved a name more in keeping with its romantic possibilities. One rainy afternoon they had to play in the garret but the sun broke out in the early evening and flooded the Glen with splendor. "Oh, look at the nithe wainbow!" cried Rilla, who always talked with a charming little lisp.

It was the most magnificent rainbow they had ever seen. One end seemed to rest on the very spire of the Presbyterian church while the other dropped down into the reedy corner of the pond that ran into the upper end of the valley. And Walter then and there named it Rainbow Valley.

Rainbow Valley had become a world in itself to the children of Ingleside. Little winds played there ceaselessly and bird-songs re-echoed from dawn to dark. White birches glimmered all over it and from one of them...the White Lady...Walter pretended that a little dryad came out every night to talk to them. A maple tree and a spruce tree, growing so closely together that their boughs intertwined, he named "The Tree Lovers" and an old string of sleigh-bells he had hung upon them made chimes elfin and aerial when the wind shook them. A dragon guarded the stone bridge they had built across the brook. The trees that met over it could be swart Paynims at need and the rich green mosses along the banks were carpets, none finer, from Samarkand. Robin Hood and his merry men lurked on all sides; three water sprites dwelt in the spring; the deserted old Barclay house at the Glen end, with its grass-grown dyke and its garden overgrown with caraway, was easily transformed into a beleaguered castle. The Crusader's sword had long been rust but the Ingleside butcher-knife was a blade forged in fairyland and whenever Susan missed the cover of her roasting pan she knew that it was serving as a shield for a plumed and glittering knight on high adventure bent in Rainbow Valley.

Sometimes they played pirates, to please Jem, who at ten years was beginning to like a tang of gore in his amusements, but Walter always balked at walking the plank, which Jem thought the best of the performance. Sometimes he wondered if Walter really was enough of a stalwart to be a buccaneer, though he smothered the thought loyally and had more than one pitched and successful battle with boys in school who called Walter "Sissy Blythe"...or had called him that until they found out it meant a set-to with Jem who had a most disconcerting knack with his fists.

Jem was sometimes allowed now to go down to the Harbour Mouth of an evening to buy fish. It was an errand he delighted in, for it meant that he could sit in Captain Malachi Russell's cabin at the foot of a bent-covered field close to the harbour, and listen to Captain Malachi and his cronies, who had once been daredevil young sea captains, spinning yarns. Every one of them had something to tell when tales were going round. Old Oliver Reese...who was actually suspected of being a pirate in his youth...had been taken captive by a cannibal king...Sam Elliott had been through the San Francisco earthquake..."Bold

William" Macdougall had had a lurid fight with a shark...Andy Baker had been caught in a waterspout. Moreover, Andy could spit straighter, as he averred, than any man in Four Winds. Hook-nosed, lean-jawed Captain Malachi, with his bristly grey moustache, was Jem's favourite. He had been captain of a brigantine when he was only seventeen, sailing to Buenos Aires with cargoes of lumber. He had an anchor tattooed on each cheek and he had a wonderful old watch you wound with a key. When he was in good humour he let Jem wind it and when he was in very good humour he would take Jem out cod-fishing or digging clams at low tide, and when he was in his best humour he would show Jem the many ship models he had carved. Jem thought they were romance itself. Among them was a Viking boat, with a striped square sail and a fearsome dragon in front...a caravel of Columbus...the *Mayflower*...a rakish craft called *The Flying Dutchman*...and no end of beautiful brigantines and schooners and barques and clipper-ships and timber droghers.

"Will you teach me how to carve ships like that, Captain Malachi?" pleaded Jem.

Captain Malachi shook his head and spat reflectively into the gulf.

"It doesn't come by teaching, son. Ye'd have to sail the seas for thirty or forty years and then maybe ye'd have enough understanding of ships to do it...understanding *and* love. Ships are like weemen, son...they've got to be understood and loved or they'll never give up their secrets. And even at that ye may think ye know a ship from stem to stern, inside *and* out, and ye'll find she's still hanging out on ye and keeping her soul shut on you. She'd fly from you like a bird if ye let go your grip on her. There's one ship I sailed on that I've never been able to whittle a model of, times out of mind as I've tried. A dour, stubborn vessel she was! And there was one woman...but it's time I took in the slack of my jaw. I've got a ship all ready to go into a bottle and I'll let ye into the secret of that, son."

So Jem never heard anything more of the "woman" and didn't care, for he was not interested in the sex, apart from Mother and Susan. *They* were not "weemen." They were just Mother and Susan.

When Gyp had died Jem had felt he never wanted another dog; but time heals amazingly and Jem was beginning to feel doggish again. The puppy wasn't really a dog...he was only an incident. Jem had a procession of dogs marching around the walls of his attic den where he kept Captain Jim's collection of curios...dogs clipped from magazines...a lordly mastiff...a nice jowly bulldog...a dachshund that looked as if somebody had taken a dog by his head and heels and pulled him out like elastic...a shaven poodle with a tassel on the end of his tail...a fox-terrier...a Russian wolfhound...Jem wondered if Russian wolf-hounds ever got anything to eat...a saucy Pom...a spotted Dalmatian...a spaniel with appealing eyes. All dogs of high degree but all lacking something in Jem's eyes...he didn't just know what.

Then the advertisement came out in the *Daily Enterprise.* "For sale, a dog. Apply Roddy Crawford, Harbour Head." Nothing more. Jem could not have told why the advertisement stuck in his mind or why he felt there was a sadness in its very brevity. He found out from Craig Russell who Roddy Crawford was.

"Roddy's father died a month ago and he has to go to live with his aunt in town. His mother died years ago. And Jake Millison has bought the farm. But the house is going to be torn down. Maybe his aunt won't let him keep his dog. It's no great shakes of a dog but Roddy has always had an awful notion of it."

"I wonder how much he wants for it. I've only got a dollar," said Jem.

"I guess what he wants most is a good home for it," said Craig. "But your dad would give you the money for it, wouldn't he?"

"Yes. But I want to buy a dog with my own money," said Jem. "It would feel more like *my* dog then."

Craig shrugged. Those Ingleside kids *were* funny. What did it matter who put up the cash for an old dog?

That evening Dad drove Jem down to the old, thin, run-down Crawford farm, where they found Roddy Crawford and his dog. Roddy was a boy of about Jem's age...a pale lad, with straight, reddish-brown hair and a crop of freckles; his dog had silky brown ears, a brown nose and tail and the most beautiful soft brown eyes ever seen in a dog's head. The moment Jem saw that darling dog, with the white stripe down his forehead that parted in two between his eyes and framed his nose, he knew he must have him.

"You want to sell your dog?" he asked eagerly.

"I *don't* want to sell him," said Roddy dully. "But Jake says I'll have to or he'll drown him. He says Aunt Vinnie won't have a dog about."

"What do you want for him?" asked Jem, scared that some prohibitive price would be named.

Roddy gave a great gulp. He held out his dog.

"Here, take him," he said hoarsely. "I ain't going to sell him...I ain't. Money would never pay for Bruno. If you'll give him a good home...and be kind to him..."

"Oh, I'll be kind to him," said Jem eagerly. "But you must take my dollar. I wouldn't feel he was *my* dog if you didn't. I won't *take* him if you don't."

He forced the dollar into Roddy's reluctant hand...he took Bruno and held him close to his breast. The little dog looked back at his master. Jem could not see his eyes but he could see Roddy's.

"If you want him so much..."

"I want him but I can't have him," snapped Roddy. "There's been five people here after him and I wouldn't let one of them have him...Jake was awful mad but I don't care. They weren't *right.* But you...I want *you* to have him since *I* can't...and take him out of my sight quick!"

Jem obeyed. The little dog was trembling in his arms but he made no protest. Jem held him lovingly all the way back to Ingleside.

"Dad, how did Adam know that a dog was a *dog*?"

"Because a dog couldn't be anything but a dog," grinned Dad. "Could he now?"

Jem was too excited to sleep for ever so long that night. He had never seen a dog he liked so much as Bruno. No wonder Roddy hated parting with him. But Bruno would soon forget Roddy and love *him.* They would be pals. He must remember to ask Mother to make sure the butcher sent up the bones.

"I love everybody and everything in the world," said Jem. "Dear God, bless every cat and dog in the world but specially Bruno."

Jem fell asleep at last. Perhaps a little dog lying at the foot of the bed with his chin upon his outstretched paws slept, too: and perhaps he did not.

24

Cock Robin had ceased to subsist solely on worms and ate rice, corn, lettuce and nasturtium seeds. He had grown to be a huge size...the "big robin" at Ingleside was becoming locally famous... and his breast had turned to a beautiful red. He would perch on Susan's shoulder and watch her knit. He would fly to meet Anne when she returned after an absence and hop before her into the house: he came to Walter's windowsill every morning for crumbs. He took his daily bath in a basin in the back yard, in the corner of the sweet-briar hedge, and would raise the most unholy fuss if he found no water in it. The doctor complained that his pens and matches were always strewn all over the library, but found nobody to sympathize with him, and even he surrendered when Cock Robin lit fearlessly on his hand one day to pick up a flower seed. Everybody was bewitched by Cock Robin...except perhaps Jem, who had set his heart on Bruno and was slowly but all too surely learning a bitter lesson...that you can buy a dog's body but you cannot buy his love.

At first Jem never suspected this. Of course Bruno would be a bit homesick and lonesome for a time, but that would soon wear off. Jem found it did not. Bruno was the most obedient little dog in the world; he did exactly what he was told and even Susan admitted that a better-behaved animal couldn't be found. But there was no life in him. When Jem took him out Bruno's eyes would gleam alertly at first, his tail would wag and he would start off cockily. But after a little while the glow would leave his eyes and he would trot meekly beside Jem with drooping crest. Kindness was showered upon him by all...the juciest and meatiest of bones were at his disposal...not the slightest objection was made to his sleeping at the foot of Jem's bed every night. But Bruno remained remote...inaccessible...a stranger. Sometimes in the night Jem woke and reached down to pat the sturdy little body; but there was never any answering lick of tongue or thump of tail. Bruno permitted caresses but he would not respond to them.

Jem set his teeth. There was a good bit of determination in James Matthew Blythe and he was not going to be beaten by a dog...*His* dog whom he had bought fairly and squarely with money hardly saved from his allowance. Bruno would just *have* to get over being homesick for Roddy...*have* to give up looking at you with the pathetic eyes of a lost creature...*have* to learn to love him.

Jem had to stand up for Bruno, for the other boys in school, suspecting how he loved the dog, were always trying to "pick on" him.

"Your dog has fleas...Great Big fleas," taunted Perry Reese. Jem had to trounce him before Perry would take it back and say Bruno hadn't a single flea...not one.

"*My* pup takes fits once a week," boasted Rob Russell. "I'll bet your old pup never had a fit in his life. If I had a dog like that I'd run him through the meat-grinder."

"We *had* a dog like that once," said Mike Drew, "but we drowned him."

"My dog's an *awful* dog," said Sam Warren proudly. "He kills the chickens and chews up all the clothes on wash-day. Bet your old dog hasn't spunk enough for that."

Jem sorrowfully admitted to himself, if not to Sam, that Bruno hadn't. He almost wished he had. And it stung when Watty Flagg shouted, "Your dog's a *good* dog...he never barks on Sunday," because Bruno didn't bark any day.

But with it all he was such a dear, adorable little dog.

"Bruno, *why* won't you love me?" almost sobbed Jem. "There's nothing I wouldn't do for you...we could have *such* fun together." But he would not admit defeat to anyone.

Jem hurried home one evening from a mussel-bake at the Harbour Mouth because he knew a storm was coming. The sea moaned so. Things had a sinister, lonely look. There was a long rip and tear of thunder as Jem dashed into Ingleside.

"Where's Bruno?" he shouted.

It was the first time he had gone anywhere without Bruno. He had thought the long walk to the Harbour Mouth would be too much for a little dog. Jem would not admit to himself that such a long walk with a dog whose heart was not in it would be a little too much for him as well.

It developed that nobody knew where Bruno was. He had not been seen since Jem left after supper. Jem hunted everywhere but he was not to be found. The rain was coming down in floods, the world was drowned in lightning. Was Bruno out in that black night...*lost?* Bruno was afraid of thunderstorms. The only times he had ever seemed to come near Jem in spirit was when he crept close to him while the sky was riven asunder.

Jem worried so that when the storm was spent Gilbert said:

"I ought to go up to the Head anyway to see how Roy Westcott is getting on. You can come, too, Jem, and we'll drive round by the old Crawford place on our way home. I've an idea Bruno has gone back there."

"Six miles? He'd never!" said Jem.

But he had. When they got to the old, deserted, lightless Crawford house a shivering bedraggled little creature was huddled forlornly on the wet doorstep, looking at them with tired, unsatisfied eyes. He made no objection when Jem gathered him up in his arms and carried him out to the buggy through the knee-high, tangled grass.

Jem was happy. How the moon was rushing through the sky as the clouds tore past her! How delicious were the smells of the rain-wet woods as they drove along! What a world it was!

"I guess Bruno will be contented at Ingleside after this, Dad."

"Perhaps," was all Dad said. He hated to throw cold water but he suspected that a little dog's heart, losing its last home, was finally broken.

Bruno had never eaten very much but after that night he ate less and less. Came a day when he would not eat at all. The vet was sent for but could find nothing wrong.

"I knew one dog in my experience who died of grief and I think this is another," he told the doctor aside.

He left a "tonic" which Bruno took obediently and then lay down again, his head on his paws, staring into vacancy. Jem stood looking at him for a long while, his hands in his pockets; then he went into the library to have a talk with Dad.

Gilbert went to town the next day, made some inquiries, and brought Roddy Crawford out to Ingleside. When Roddy came up the verandah steps Bruno, hearing his footfall from the living-room, lifted his head and cocked his ears. The next moment his emaciated little body hurled itself across the rug towards the pale, brown-eyed lad.

"Mrs. Dr. dear," Susan said in an awed tone that night, "the dog was *crying*... he *was*. The tears actually rolled down his nose. I do not blame you if you do not believe it. Never would I have believed it if I had not seen it with my own eyes."

Roddy held Bruno against his heart and looked half defiantly, half pleadingly at Jem.

"You bought him, I know...but he belongs to me. Jake told me a lie. Aunt Vinnie says she wouldn't mind a dog a bit, but I thought I mustn't ask for him back. Here's your dollar...I never spent a cent of it...I couldn't."

For just a moment Jem hesitated. Then he saw Bruno's eyes. "What a little pig I am!" he thought in disgust with himself. He took the dollar.

Roddy suddenly smiled. The smile changed his sulky face completely but all he could say was a gruff, "Thanks."

Roddy slept with Jem that night, a replete Bruno stretched between them. But before he went to bed Roddy knelt to say his prayers and Bruno squatted on his haunches beside him, laying his forepaws on the bed. If ever a dog prayed Bruno prayed then...a prayer of thanksgiving and renewed joy in life.

When Roddy brought him food Bruno ate it eagerly, keeping an eye on Roddy all the time. He pranced friskily after Jem and Roddy when they went down to the Glen. "Such a perked-up dog you never saw," declared Susan.

But the next evening, after Roddy and Bruno had gone back, Jem sat on the side-door steps in the owl light for a long time. He refused to go digging for pirate hoards in Rainbow Valley with Walter...Jem felt no longer splendidly bold and buccaneering. He wouldn't even look at the Shrimp who was humped in the mint, lashing his tail like a fierce mountain lion crouching to spring. What business had cats to go on being happy at Ingleside when dogs broke their hearts!

He was even grumpy with Rilla when she brought him her blue velvet elephant. Velvet elephants when Bruno had gone! Nan got as short shrift when she came and suggested they should say what they thought of God in a whisper.

"You don't s'pose I'm blaming God for THIS?" said Jem sternly. "You haven't any sense of proportion, Nan Blythe."

Nan went away quite crushed through she hadn't the least glimmering what Jem meant, and Jem scowled at the embers of the smouldering sunset. Dogs were barking all over the Glen. The Jenkins down the road were out calling theirs...all of them took turns at it. Everyone, even the Jenkins tribe, could have a dog...everyone but him. Life stretched before him like a desert where there would be no dogs.

Anne came and sat down on a lower step, carefully not looking at him. Jem *felt* her sympathy.

"Motherest," he said in a choked voice, "*Why* wouldn't Bruno love me when I loved him so much? Am I...do you think I am the kind of boy dogs don't like?"

"No, darling. Remember how Gyp loved you. It was just that Bruno had only so much love to give...and he had given it all. There are dogs like that...one-man dogs."

"Anyhow, Bruno and Roddy are happy," said Jem with grim satisfaction, as he bent over and kissed the top of Mother's smooth ripply head. "But I'll never have another dog."

Anne thought this would pass; he had felt the same when Gyppy died. But it did not. The iron had bitten deeply into Jem's soul. Dogs were to come and go at Ingleside...dogs that belonged just to the family and were nice dogs, whom Jem petted and played with as the others did. But there was to be no "Jem's dog" until a certain "Little Dog Monday" was to take possession of his heart and love him with a devotion passing Bruno's love...a devotion that was to make history in the Glen. But that was still many a long year away; and a very lonely boy climbed into Jem's bed that night.

"I wish I was a girl," he thought fiercely, "so's I could cry *and* cry!"

25

Nan and Di were going to school. They started the last week in August.

"Will we know *everything* by night, Mummy?" asked Di solemnly the first morning.

Now, in early September, Anne and Susan had got used to it, and even took pleasure in seeing the two mites trip off every morning, so tiny and carefree and neat, thinking going to school quite an adventure. They always took an apple in their basket for teacher and they wore frocks of pink and blue ruffled gingham. Since they did not look in the least alike they were never dressed alike. Diana, with her red hair, could not wear pink, but it suited Nan, who was much the prettier of the Ingleside twins. She had brown eyes, brown hair and a lovely complexion, of which she was quite aware even at seven. A certain starriness had gone to the fashioning of her. She held her head proudly, with her little saucy chin a wee bit in evidence, and so was already thought rather "stuck-up."

"She'll imitate all her mother's tricks and poses," said Mrs. Alec Davies. "She has all her airs and graces already, if you ask me."

The twins were dissimilar in more than looks. Di, in spite of her physical resemblance to her mother, was very much her father's child, so far as disposition and qualities went. She had the beginnings of his practical bent, his plain common sense, his twinkling sense of humour. Nan had inherited in full her mother's gift of imagination and was already making life interesting for herself in her own way. For example, she had had no end of excitement this summer making bargains with God, the gist of the matter being, "If you'll do such-and-such a thing I'll do such-and-such a thing."

All the Ingleside children had been started in life with the old classic, "Now I lay me"...then promoted to "Our Father"...then encouraged to make their own small petitions also in whatever language they chose. What gave Nan the idea that God might be induced to grant her petitions by promises of good behaviour or displays of fortitude would be hard to say. Perhaps a certain rather young and pretty Sunday School teacher was indirectly responsible for it by her frequent admonitions that if they were not good girls God would not do this or that for them. It was easy to turn this idea inside out and come to the conclusion that if you *were* this or that, *did* this or that, you had a right to expect that God would do the things you wanted. Nan's first "bargain" in the spring had been so successful that it outweighed some failures and she had gone on all summer. Nobody knew of it, not even Di. Nan hugged her secret and took to praying at sundry times and in divers places, instead of only at night. Di did not approve of this and said so.

"Don't mix God up with *everything*," she told Nan severely. "You make Him too *common*."

Anne, overhearing this, rebuked her and said, "God *is* in everything, dear. He is the Friend who is always near us to give strength and courage. And Nan is quite right in praying to Him and where she wants to." Though, if Anne had known the truth about her small daughter's devotions, she would have been rather horrified.

Nan had said one night in May, "If you'll make my tooth grow in before Amy Taylor's party next week, dear God, I'll take every dose of castor-oil Susan gives me without a bit of fuss."

The very next day the tooth, whose absence had made such an unsightly and too prolonged gap in Nan's pretty mouth, had appeared and by the day of the party was fully through. What more certain sign could you want than that? Nan kept her side of the compact faithfully and Susan was amazed and delighted whenever she administered castor-oil after that. Nan took it without a grimace or protest, though she sometimes wished she had set a time limit...say for three months.

God did not always respond. But when she asked Him to send her a special button for her button-string...collecting buttons had broken out everywhere among the Glen small girls like the measles...assuring Him that if He did she would never make a fuss when Susan set the chipped plate for her...the button came the very next day, Susan having found one on an old dress in the attic. A beautiful red button set with tiny diamonds, or what Nan believed to be diamonds. She was the envied of all because of that elegant button and when Di refused the chipped plate that night Nan said virtuously, "Give it to me, Susan. I'll *always* take it after this." Susan thought she was angelically unselfish and said so. Whereupon Nan both looked and felt smug. She got a fine day for the Sunday School picnic, when everyone predicted rain the night before, by promising to brush her teeth every morning without being told. Her lost ring was restored on the condition that she kept her fingernails scrupulously clean; and when Walter handed over his picture of a flying angel which Nan had long coveted she ate the fat with the lean uncomplainingly at dinner thereafter.

When, however, she asked God to make her battered and patched Teddy Bear young again, promising to keep her bureau drawer tidy, something struck a snag. Teddy did not grow young though Nan looked for the miracle anxiously every morning and wished God would hurry. Finally she resigned herself to Teddy's age. After all, he was a nice old bear and it would be awfully hard to keep that old bureau drawer tidy. When Dad brought her home a new Teddy Bear she didn't really like it and, though with sundry misgivings of her small conscience, decided she need not take any special pains with the bureau drawer. Her faith returned when, having prayed that the missing eye of her china cat would be restored, the eye was in its place next morning, though somewhat askew, giving the cat a rather cross-eyed aspect. Susan had found it when sweeping and stuck it in with glue, but Nan did not know this and cheerfully carried out her promise of walking fourteen times around the barn on all fours. What good walking fourteen times around the barn on all fours could do God or anybody else Nan did not stop to consider. But she hated doing it...the boys were always wanting her and Di to pretend they were some kind of animals in Rainbow Valley...and perhaps there was some vague thought in her budding mind that penance might be pleasing to the mysterious Being who gave or withheld at pleasure. At any rate, she thought out several weird stunts that summer, causing Susan to wonder frequently where on earth children got the notions they did.

"Why do you suppose, Mrs. Dr. dear, that Nan must go twice around the living-room every day without walking on the floor?"

"Without walking on the floor! How does she manage it, Susan?"

"By jumping from one piece of furniture to the other, including the fender. She slipped on that yesterday and pitched head-first into the coal-scuttle. Mrs. Dr. dear, do you suppose she needs a dose of worm medicine?"

That year was always referred to in the Ingleside chronicles as the one in which Dad *almost* had pneumonia and Mother *had* it. One night, Anne, who already had a nasty cold, went with Gilbert to a party in Charlottetown...wearing a new and very becoming dress and Jem's string of pearls. She looked so well in it that all the children who had come in to see her before she left thought it was wonderful to have a mother you could be so proud of.

"Such a nice swishy pettycoat," sighed Nan. "When I grow up will I have tafty petticoats like that, Mummy?"

"I doubt if girls will be wearing petticoats at all by that time," said Dad. "I'll back water, Anne, and admit that dress is a stunner even if I didn't approve of the sequins. Now, don't try to vamp me, woman. I've paid you all the compliments I'm going to tonight. Remember what we read in the *Medical Journal* today...'Life is nothing more than delicately balanced organic chemistry,' and let it make you humble and modest. Sequins, indeed! Taffeta petticoat, forsooth. We're nothing but 'a fortuitous concatenation of atoms.' The great Dr. Von Bemburg says so."

"Don't quote that horrible Von Bemburg to me. He must have a bad case of chronic indigestion. *He* may be a concatenation of atoms, but *I* am not."

In a few days thereafter Anne was a very sick "concatenation of atoms" and Gilbert a very anxious one. Susan went about looking harassed and tired, and the trained nurse came and went with an anxious face, and a nameless shadow suddenly swooped and spread and darkened at Ingleside. The children were not told of the seriousness of their mother's illness and even Jem did not realize it fully. But they all felt the chill and the fear and went softly and unhappily. For once there was no laughter in the maple grove and no games in Rainbow Valley. But the worst of all was that they were not allowed to see Mother. No Mother meeting them with smiles when they came home, no Mother slipping in to kiss them goodnight, no Mother to soothe and sympathize and understand, no Mother to laugh over jokes with...nobody ever laughed like Mother. It was far worse than when she was away, because then you knew she was coming back...and now you knew...just *nothing*. Nobody would tell you anything...they just put you off.

Nan came home from school very pale over something Amy Taylor had told her.

"Susan, is Mother...Mother isn't...she isn't going to *die*, Susan?"

"Of course not," said Susan, too sharply and quickly. Her hands trembled as she poured out Nan's glass of milk. "Who has been talking to you?"

"Amy. She said...oh, Susan, she said she thought Mother would make such a sweet-looking corpse!"

"Never you mind what she said, my pet. The Taylors all have wagging tongues. Your blessed Mother is sick enough but she is going to pull through and that you may tie to. Do you not know that your father is at the helm?"

"God wouldn't let Mother die, would he, Susan?" asked a white-lipped Walter, looking at her with the grave intentness that made it very hard for Susan to utter her comforting lies. She was terribly afraid they *were* lies. Susan was a badly frightened woman. The nurse had shaken her head that afternoon. The doctor had refused to come down to supper.

"I suppose the Almighty knows what He's about," muttered Susan as she washed the supper dishes...and broke three of them...but for the first time in her honest, simple life she doubted it.

Nan wandered unhappily around. Dad was sitting by the library table with his head in his hands. The nurse went in and Nan heard her say she thought the crisis would come that night.

"What is a crisis?" she asked Di.

"I think it is what a butterfly hatches out of," said Di cautiously. "Let's ask Jem."

Jem knew, and told them before he went upstairs to shut himself in his room. Walter had disappeared...he was lying face downward under the White Lady in Rainbow Valley...and Susan had taken Shirley and Rilla off to bed. Nan went out alone and sat down on the steps. Behind her in the house was a terrible unaccustomed quiet. Before her the Glen was brimming with evening sunshine, but the long red road was misty with dust and the bent grasses in the harbour fields were burned white in the drouth. It had not rained for weeks and the flowers drooped in the garden...the flowers Mother had loved.

Nan was thinking deeply. Now, if ever, was the time to bargain with God. What would she promise to do if He made Mother well? It must be something tremendous...something that would make it worth His while. Nan remembered what Dicky Drew had said to Stanley Reese in school one day, "I dare you to walk through the graveyard after night." Nan had shuddered at the time. How could *anybody* walk through the graveyard after night...how could anyone even *think* of it? Nan had a horror of the graveyard not a soul in Ingleside suspected. Amy Taylor had once told her it was full of dead people..."and they don't always *stay* dead," said Amy darkly and mysteriously. Nan could hardly bring herself to walk past it alone in broad daylight.

Far away the trees on a misty golden hill were touching the sky. Nan had often though if she could get to that hill she could touch the sky, too. God lived just on the other side of it...He might hear you better there. But she could not get to that hill... she must just do the best she could here at Ingleside.

She clasped her little sunburned paws and lifted her tear-stained face to the sky.

"Dear God," she whispered, "if you make Mother get well I'll *walk through the graveyard after night.* O dear God, *please, please.* And if You do this I won't bother You for ever so long again."

26

It was life, not death, that came at the ghostliest hour of the night to Ingleside. The children, sleeping at last, must have felt even in their sleep that the Shadow had withdrawn as silently and swiftly as it had come. For when they woke, to a day dark with welcome rain, there was sunshine in their eyes. They hardly needed to be told the good news by a Susan who had grown ten years younger. The crisis was past and Mother was going to live.

It was Saturday, so there was no school. They could not stir outside...even though they loved to be out in the rain. This downpour was too much for them...and they had to be very quiet inside. But they had never felt happier. Dad, almost sleepless for a week, had flung himself on the spare-room bed for a long deep slumber...but not before he had sent a long-distance message to a green-gabled house in Avonlea where two old ladies had been trembling every time the telephone rang.

Susan, whose heart of late had not been in her desserts, concocted a glorious "orange shuffle" for dinner, promised a jam roly-poly for supper, and baked a double batch of butterscotch cookies. Cock Robin chirped all over the place. The very chairs looked as if they wanted to dance. The flowers in the garden lifted up their faces bravely again as the dry earth welcomed the rain. And Nan, amid all her happiness, was trying to face the consequences of her bargain with God.

She had no thought of trying to back out of it, but she kept putting it off, hoping she could get a little more courage for it. The very thought of it "made her blood curdle," as Amy Taylor was so found of saying. Susan knew there was something the matter with the child and administered castor-oil, with no visible improvement. Nan took the dose quietly, though she could not help thinking that Susan gave her castor-oil much oftener since that earlier bargain. But what was castor-oil compared to walking through the graveyard after dark? Nan simply did not see how she could ever do it. But she must.

Mother was still so weak that nobody was allowed to see her save for a brief peep. And then she looked so white and thin. Was it because she, Nan, was not keeping her bargain?

"We must give her time," said Susan.

How could you give anyone time, Nan wondered. But *she* knew why Mother was not getting well faster. Nan set her little pearly teeth. Tomorrow was Saturday again and tomorrow night she would do what she had promised to do.

It rained again all the next forenoon and Nan could not help a feeling of relief. If it was going to be a rainy night, nobody, not even God, could expect her to go prowling about graveyards. By noon the rain had stopped but there came a fog creeping up the harbour and over the Glen, surrounding Ingleside with its eerie magic. So still Nan hoped. If it was foggy she couldn't go either. But at supper time a wind sprang up and the dream-like landscape of the fog vanished.

"There'll be no moon tonight," said Susan.

"Oh, Susan, can't you *make* a moon?" cried Nan despairingly. If she had to walk through the graveyard there *must* be a moon.

"Bless the child, nobody can make moons," said Susan. "I only meant it was going to be cloudy and you could not see the moon. And what difference can it make to you whether there is a moon or not?"

That was just what Nan could not explain and Susan was more worried than ever. *Something* must ail the child...she had been acting so strangely all the week. She did not eat half enough and she moped. Was she worrying about her mother? She needn't...Mrs. Dr. dear was coming on nicely.

Yes, but Nan knew that Mother would soon stop coming on nicely if she didn't keep her bargain. At sunset the clouds rolled away and the moon rose. But such a strange moon...such a huge, blood-red moon. Nan had never seen such a moon. It terrified her. Almost would she have preferred the dark.

The twins went to bed at eight and Nan had to wait until Di had gone to sleep. Di took her time about it. She was feeling too sad and disillusioned to sleep readily. Her chum, Elsie Palmer, had walked home from school with another girl and Di believed that life was practically ended for her. It was nine o'clock before Nan felt it safe to slip out of bed and dress with fingers that trembled so she could hardly cope with her buttons. Then she crept down and out of the side door while Susan set the bread in the kitchen and reflected comfortably that all under her charge were safe in bed except the poor doctor, who had been summoned post-haste to a Harbour Mouth household where a baby had swallowed a tack.

Nan went out and down to Rainbow Valley. She must take the short-cut through it and up the hill pasture. She knew that the sight of an Ingleside twin prowling along the road and through the village would cause wonderment and somebody would likely insist on bringing her home. How cold the late September night was! She had not thought about that and had not put on her jacket. Rainbow Valley by night was not the friendly haunt of daytime. The moon had shrunk to a reasonable size and was no longer red but it cast sinister black shadows. Nan had always been rather frightened of shadows. Was that paddy feet in the darkness of the withered bracken by the brook?

Nan held up her head and stuck out her chin. "I'm not frightened," she said aloud valiantly. "It's only my stomach feels a little queer. I'm being a *heroine*."

The pleasant idea of being a heroine carried her halfway up the hill. Then a strange shadow swept over the world...a cloud was crossing the moon...and Nan thought of the Bird. Amy Taylor had once told her such a terrifying tale of a Great Black Bird that swooped down on you in the night and carried you off. Was it the Bird's shadow that had crossed over her? But Mother had said there was no Big Black Bird. "I don't believe Mother could tell me a lie...not *mother*," said Nan...and went on until she reached the fence. Beyond was the road...and across it the graveyard. Nan stopped to get her breath.

Another cloud was over the moon. All around her lay a strange, dim, unknown land. "Oh, the world is too big!" shivered Nan, crowding against the fence. If she were only back in Ingleside! But..."God is watching me," said the seven-year-old scrap...and climbed the fence.

She fell off on the other side, skinning her knee and tearing her dress. As she got to her feet a sharp weed-stub pierced completely through her slipper and cut her foot. But she limped across the road to the graveyard gate.

The old graveyard lay in the shadow of the firs at its eastern end. On one side was the Methodist church, on the other the Presbyterian manse, now dark and silent during the minister's absence. The moon broke out suddenly from the cloud and the graveyard was full of shadows...shadows that shifted and danced...shadows that would grasp at you if you trusted yourself among them. A newspaper someone had discarded blew along the road, like a dancing old witch, and though Nan knew it for what it was, it was all part and parcel of the uncanniness of the night. Swish, swish, went the night-winds in the firs. A long leaf on the willow by the gate suddenly flicked her cheek like the touch of an elfin hand. For a moment her heart stood still...yet she put her hand on the hook of the gate.

Suppose a long arm reached out of a grave and dragged you down!

Nan turned. She knew now that, bargain or no bargain, she could *never* walk through that graveyard by night. The grisliest groan suddenly sounded quite close to her. It was only Mrs. Ben Baker's old cow, which she pastured on the road, getting up from behind a clump of spruces. But Nan did not wait to see what it was. In a spasm of uncontrollable panic she tore down the hill, through the village and up the road to Ingleside. Outside of the gate she dashed headlong through what Rilla called a "pud-muddle." But there was home, with the soft, glowing lights in the windows and a moment later she stumbled into Susan's kitchen, mud-spattered, with wet, bleeding feet.

"Good grief!" said Susan blankly.

"I couldn't walk through the graveyard Susan...I couldn't!" gasped Nan.

Susan asked no questions at first. She picked the chilled, distraught Nan up and peeled off her wet slippers and socks. She undressed her and put on her nightgown and carried her to bed. Then she went down to get a "bite" for her. No matter what the child had been up to she couldn't be let go to bed on an empty stomach.

Nan ate her lunch and sipped her glass of hot milk. How lovely it was to be back in a warm, lighted room, safe in her nice warm bed! But she would not tell Susan one thing about it. "It's a secret between me and God, Susan." Susan went to bed vowing she would be a happy woman when Mrs. Dr. dear was up and about again.

"They're getting beyond *me*," sighed Susan helplessly.

Mother would certainly die now. Nan woke up with that terrible conviction in her mind. She had not kept her bargain and she could not expect God would. Life was very dreadful for Nan that following week. She could take no pleasure in anything, not even in watching Susan spin in the garret...something she had always found so fascinating. She would never be able to laugh again. It wouldn't matter what she did. She gave her sawdust dog, off which Ken Ford had pulled the ears and which she loved even better than old Teddy...Nan always loved old things best... to Shirley because Shirley had always wanted it, and she gave her prized house made of shells, which Captain Malachi had brought her all the way from the West Indies, to Rilla, hoping that it would satisfy God: but she feared it would not, and when her new kitten, which she had given to Amy Taylor because Amy wanted it, came back home and persisted in coming back home Nan knew God was not satisfied. Nothing would do Him but walking through the graveyard; and poor haunted Nan knew now she could never do *that.* She was a coward and a sneak. Only sneaks, Jem had said once, tried to get out of bargains.

Anne was allowed to sit up in bed. She was nearly well again after being ill. She would soon be able to keep her house again...read her books...lie easily on her pillows...eat everything she wanted...sit by her fireplace...look to her garden...see her friends...listen to juicy bits of gossip...welcome the days shining like jewels on the necklace of the year...be again a part of the colourful pageantry of life.

She had had such a nice dinner...Susan's stuffed leg of lamb had been done to a turn. It was delightful to feel hungry again. She looked about her room at all the things she loved. She must get new curtains for it...something between spring green and pale gold; and certainly those new cupboards for towels must be put in the bathroom. Then she looked out of the window. There was some magic in the air. She could catch a blue glimpse of the harbour through the maples; the weeping birch on the lawn was a soft rain of falling gold. Vast sky-gardens arched over an opulent land holding autumn in fee...a land of unbelievable colours, mellow light and lengthening shadows. Cock Robin was tilting crazily on a fir-top; the children were laughing in the orchard as they picked apples. Laughter had come back to Ingleside. "Life *is* something more than 'delicately balanced organic chemistry,'" she thought happily.

Into the room crept Nan, eyes and nose crimson from crying.

"Mummy, I *have* to tell you...I can't wait any longer. Mummy, *I've cheated God.*"

Anne thrilled again to the soft touch of a child's little clinging hand...a child seeking help, and comfort in its bitter little problem. She listened while Nan sobbed out the whole story and managed to keep a straight face. Anne always had contrived to keep a straight face when a straight face was indicated, no matter how crazily she might laugh it over with Gilbert afterwards. She knew Nan's worry was real and dreadful to her; and she also realized that this small daughter's theology needed attention.

"Darling, you're terribly mistaken about it all. God doesn't make bargains. He *gives*...gives without asking anything from us in return except love. When you ask Father or me for something you want, *we* don't make bargains with you...and God is ever and ever so much kinder than we are. And He knows so much better than we do what is good to give."

"And He won't...He won't make you die, Mummy, because I didn't keep my promise?"

"Certainly not, darling."

"Mummy, even if I was mistooken about God...oughtn't I to keep my bargain when I made it? I *said* I would, you know. Daddy says we should always keep our promises. Won't I be *disgraced forever* if I don't?"

"When I get quite well, dear, I'll go with you some night...

and stay outside the gate...and I don't think you'll be a bit afraid to go through the graveyard then. That will relieve your poor little conscience...and you won't make any more foolish bargains with God?"

"No," promised Nan, with a rather regretful feeling that she was giving up something that, with all its drawbacks, had been pleasantly exciting. But the sparkle had come back to her eyes and a bit of the old ginger to her voice.

"I'll go and wash my face and then I'll come back and kiss you, Mummy. And I'll pick you all the snack-dragons I can find. It's been *dreadful* without you, Mummy."

"Oh, Susan," said Anne when Susan brought in her supper, "what a world it is! What a beautiful, interesting, wonderful world! Isn't it, Susan?"

"I will go so far," admitted Susan, recalling the beautiful row of pies she had just left in the pantry, "as to say that it is very tolerable."

27

October was a very happy month at Ingleside that year, full of days when you just *had* to run and sing and whistle. Mother was about again, refusing to be treated as a convalescent any longer, making garden plans, laughing again...Jem always thought Mother had such a beautiful, joyous laugh...answering innumerable questions. "Mummy, how far is it from here to the sunset?...Mummy, why can't we gather up the spilled moonlight?...Mummy, do the souls of dead people *really* come back on Hallowe'en?...Mummy, what causes the cause?...Mummy, wouldn't you rather be killed by a rattlesnake than a tiger, because the tiger would mess you up and eat you?...Mummy, what is a cubby?...Mummy, is a widow really a woman whose dreams have come true? Wally Taylor said she was...Mummy, what do little birds do when it rains *hard*?... Mummy, are we *really* a too romantic family?"

The last from Jem, who had heard in school that Mrs. Alec Davies had said so. Jem did not like Mrs. Alec Davies, because whenever she met him with Mother or Father she invariably dabbed her long forefinger at him and demanded, "Is Jemmy a good boy in school?" Jemmy! Perhaps they *were* a bit romantic. Susan must certainly have thought so when she discovered the boardwalk to the barn lavishly decorated with splotches of crimson paint. "We *had* to have them for our sham battle, Susan," explained Jem. "They represent gobs of gore."

At night there might be a line of wild geese flying across a low red moon and Jem when he saw them ached mysteriously to fly far away with them, too...to unknown shores and bring back monkeys...leopards...parrots...things like that...to explore the Spanish Main.

Some phrases, like "the Spanish Main," always sounded irresistibly alluring to Jem..."secrets of the sea" was another. To be caught in the deadly coils of a python and have a combat with a wounded rhinoceros was all in the day's work with Jem. And the very word "dragon" gave him a tremendous thrill. His favourite picture, tacked on the wall at the foot of his bed, was of a knight in armour on a beautiful plump white horse, standing on its hind legs while its rider speared a dragon who had a lovely tail flowing behind him in kinks and loops, ending with a fork. A lady in a pink robe knelt peacefully and composedly in the background with clasped hands. There was no doubt in the world that the lady looked a good deal like Maybelle Reese for whose nine-year-old favour lances were already being shattered in the Glen school. Even Susan noticed the resemblance and teased the furiously blushing Jem about it. But the dragon was really a little disappointing...it looked so small and insignificant under the huge horse. There didn't seem to be any special valour about spearing it. The dragons from which Jem rescued Maybelle in secret dreams were much more dragonish. He *had* rescued her last Monday from old Sarah Palmer's gander. Peradventure...ah, "peradventure" had a good smack!...she had noticed the lordly air with which he had caught the hissing creature by its snaky neck and flung it over the fence. But a gander was somehow not nearly so romantic as a dragon.

It was an October of winds...small winds that purred in the valley and big ones that lashed the mapletops...winds that howled along the sandshore but crouched when they came to the rocks...crouched and sprang. The nights, with their sleepy red hunter's moon, were cool enough to make the thought of a warm bed pleasant, the blueberry bushes turned scarlet, the dead ferns were a rich red-brown, sumacs burned behind the barn, green pastures lay here and there like patches on the sere harvest fields of the Upper Glen and there were gold and russet chrysanthemums in the spruce corner of the lawn. There were squirrels chattering joyfully everywhere and cricket fiddlers for fairy dances on a thousand hills. There were apples to be picked, carrots to be dug. Sometimes the boys went digging "cow-hawks" with Captain Malachi when the mysterious "tides" permitted... tides that came in to caress the land but slipped back to their own deep sea. There was a reek of leaf fires all through the Glen, a heap of big yellow pumpkins in the barn, and Susan made the first cranberry pies.

Ingleside rang with laughter from dawn to sunset. Even when the older children were in school Shirley and Rilla were big enough now to keep up the tradition of laughter. Even Gilbert laughed more than usual this fall. "I like a dad who can laugh,"

Jem reflected. Dr. Bronson of Mowbray Narrows never laughed. He was said to have built up his practice entirely on his owlish look of wisdom; but Dad had a better practice still and people were pretty far gone when they couldn't laugh over one of his jokes.

Anne was busy in her garden every warm day, drinking in colour like wine, where the late sunshine fell on crimson maples, revelling in the exquisite sadness of fleeting beauty. One gold-grey smoky afternoon she and Jem planted all the tulip bulbs, that would have a resurrection of rose and scarlet and purple and gold in June. "Isn't it nice to be preparing for spring when you know you've got to face winter, Jem?"

"And it's nice to be making the garden beautiful," said Jem. "Susan says it is God who makes everything beautiful but we can help Him out a bit, can't we, Mums?"

"Always...always, Jem. He shares that privilege with us."

Still, nothing is ever quite perfect. The Ingleside folks were worried over Cock Robin. They had been told that when the robins went away he would want to go too.

"Keep him shut up till all the rest are gone and the snow comes," advised Captain Malachi. "Then he'll kind of forget about it and be all right till spring."

So Cock Robin was a sort of prisoner. He grew very restless. He flew aimlessly about the house or sat on the window-sill and looked wistfully out at his fellows who were preparing to follow who knew what mysterious call. His appetite failed and even worms and Susan's nuttiest nuts would not tempt him. The children pointed out to him all the dangers he might encounter... cold, hunger, friendlessness, storms, black nights, cats. But Cock Robin had felt or heard the summons and all his being yearned to answer.

Susan was the last to give in. She was very grim for several days. But finally, "Let him go," she said. "It is against nature to hold him."

They set him free the last day of October, after he had been mewed up for a month. The children kissed him good-bye with tears. He flew joyfully off, returning next morning to Susan's sill for crumbs and then spreading his wings for the long flight. "He may come back to us in the spring, darling," Anne said to the sobbing Rilla. But Rilla was not to be comforted.

"That ith too far away," she sobbed.

Anne smiled and sighed. The seasons that seemed so long to Baby Rilla were beginning to pass all too quickly for her. Another summer was ended, lighted out of life by the ageless gold of Lombardy torches. Soon...all too soon...the children of Ingleside would be children no longer. But they were still hers... hers to welcome when they came home at night...hers to fill life with wonder and delight...hers to love and cheer and scold...a little. For sometimes they were very naughty, even though they hardly deserved to be called by Mrs. Alec Davies "that pack of Ingleside demons" when she heard that Bertie Shakespeare Drew had been slightly scorched while playing the part of a Red Indian burned at the stake in Rainbow Valley. It had taken Jem and Walter a little longer to untie him than they had bargained for. They got slightly singed, too, but nobody pitied *them.*

November was a dismal month that year...a month of east wind and fog. Some days there was nothing but cold mist driving past or drifting over the grey sea beyond the bar. The shivering poplar trees dropped their last leaves. The garden was dead and all its colour and personality had gone from it...except the asparagus-bed, which was still a fascinating golden jungle. Walter had to desert his study roost in the maple tree and learn his lessons in the house. It rained...and rained...and rained. "Will the world *ever* be dry again?" moaned Di despairingly. Then there was a week steeped in the magic of Indian summer sunshine, and in the cold sharp evenings Mother would touch a match to the kindling in the grate and Susan would have baked potatoes with supper.

The big fireplace was the centre of the home those evenings. It was the high spot of the day when they gathered around it after supper. Anne sewed and planned little winter wardrobes..."Nan must have a red dress, since she is so set on it"...and sometimes thought of Hannah, weaving her little coat every year for the small Samuel. Mothers were the same all through the centuries...a great sisterhood of love and service...the remembered and the unremembered alike.

Susan heard the children's spellings and then they amused themselves as they liked. Walter, living in his world of imagination and beautiful dreams, was absorbed in writing a series of letters from the chipmunk who lived in Rainbow Valley to the chipmunk who lived behind the barn. Susan pretended to scoff at them when he read them to her, but she secretly made copies of them and sent them to Rebecca Dew.

"I found these readable, Miss Dew dear, though you may consider them too trivial to peruse. In that case I know you will pardon a *doting old woman* for troubling you with them. He is considered very clever in school and at least these compositions are not poetry. I might also add that Little Jem made *ninety-nine* in his arithmetic examination last week and nobody can understand why the other mark was cut off. Perhaps I should not say so, Miss Dew dear, but it is my conviction that that child is *born for greatness.* We may not live to see it but he may yet be Premier of Canada."

The Shrimp basked in the glow and Nan's kitten, Pussywillow, which always suggested some dainty exquisite little lady in black and silver, climbed everybody's legs impartially. "Two cats, and mouse tracks everywhere in the pantry," was Susan's disapproving parenthesis. The children talked over their little adventures together and the wail of the distant ocean came through the cold autumn night.

Sometimes Miss Cornelia dropped in for a short call while her husband exchanged opinions in Carter Flagg's store. Little pitchers pricked up their long ears then, for Miss Cornelia always had the latest gossip and they always heard the most interesting things about people. It would be such fun next Sunday to sit in church and look at the said people, savouring what you knew about them, prim and proper as they looked.

"My, but you're cosy here, Anne dearie. It's a real keen night and starting to snow. Is the doctor out?"

"Yes. I hated to see him go...but they telephoned from the Harbour Head that Mrs. Brooker Shaw insisted on seeing him," said Anne, while Susan swiftly and stealthily removed from the hearth-rug a huge fishbone the Shrimp had brought in, praying that Miss Cornelia had not noticed it.

"She's no more sick than I am," said Susan bitterly. "But I hear she has got a *new lace nightgown* and no doubt she wants her doctor to see her in it. Lace nightgowns!"

"Her daughter Leona brought it home from Boston for her. She came Friday evening, with *four trunks*," said Miss Cornelia. "I can remember her starting off to the States nine years ago, lugging a broken old Gladstone bag with things oozing out of it. That was when she was feeling pretty blue over Phil Turner's jilting her. She tried to hide it but everyone *knew.* Now she's back to 'nurse her mother,' so she says. She'll be trying to flirt with the doctor, I warn you, Anne dearie. But I don't suppose it will matter to him even if he is a man. And you're not like Mrs. Dr. Bronson at Mowbray Narrows. She is very jealous of her husband's female patients, I am told."

"*And* of the trained nurses," said Susan.

"Well, some of those trained nurses *are* far too pretty for their job," said Miss Cornelia. "There's Janie Arthur now; she's taking a rest between cases and trying to keep her two young men from finding out about each other."

"Pretty as she is, she is no spring chicken now," said Susan firmly, "and it would be far better for her to make a choice and settle down. Look at her Aunt Eudora...*She* said she didn't intend to marry till she got through flirting, and behold the result. Even yet she tries to flirt with every man in sight though she is forty-five if she is a day. That is what comes of forming a habit. Did you every hear, Mrs. Dr. dear, what she said to her cousin Fanny when *she* got married? 'You're taking my leavings,' she said. I am informed there was a shower of sparks and they have never spoken since."

"Life and death are in the power of the tongue," murmured Anne absently.

"A true word, dear. Speaking of that, I wish Mr. Stanley would be a little more judicious in his sermons. He has offended Wallace Young and Wallace is going to leave the church. Everyone says the sermon last Sunday was preached at him."

"If a minister preaches a sermon that hits home to some particular individual people always suppose he meant it for that very person," said Anne. "A hand-me-down cap is bound to fit somebody's head but it doesn't follow that it was made for him."

"Sound sense," approved Susan. "And I have no use for Wallace Young. He let a firm paint ads on his cows three years ago. That is *too* economical, in my opinion."

"His brother David is going to be married at last," said Miss Cornelia. "He's been a long time making up his mind which was cheaper—marrying or hiring. 'Ye *can* keep a house without a woman but it's hard sledding, Cornelia,' he said to me once after his mother died. I had an idea that he was feeling his way but he got no encouragement from *me.* And at last he's going to marry Jessie King."

"Jessie King! But I thought he was supposed to be courting Mary North."

"*He* says he wasn't going to marry any woman who eats cabbage. But there's a story going around that he proposed to her and she boxed his ears. And Jessie King is reported to have said that she would have liked a better looking man but that he'd have to do. Well, of course it is any port in a storm for some folks."

"I do not think, Mrs. Marshall Elliott, that people in these parts say half the things they are reported to have said," rebuked Susan. "It is my opinion that Jessie King will make David Young a far better wife than he deserves...though as far as outward seeming goes I will admit he looks like something that washed in with the tide."

"Do you know that Alden and Stella have a little daughter?" asked Anne.

"So I understand. I hope Stella will be a little more sensible over it than Lisette was over *her*. Would you believe it, Anne dear, Lisette positively cried because her cousin Dora's baby walked before Stella did?"

"We mothers are a foolish race," smiled Anne. "I remember that I felt perfectly murderous when little Bob Taylor, who was the same age as Jem to a day, cut three teeth before Jem cut one."

"Bob Taylor's got to have an operation on his tonsils," said Miss Cornelia.

"Why don't *we* ever have operations, Mother?" demanded Walter and Di together in injured tones. They so often said the same thing together. Then they linked their fingers and made a wish. "We think and feel the same about *everything*," Di was wont to explain earnestly.

"Shall I ever forget Elsie Taylor's marriage?" said Miss Cornelia reminiscently. "Her best friend, Maisie Millison, was to play the wedding march. She played the Dead March in *Saul* in place of it. Of course she always said she made a mistake because she was so flustered but people had their own opinion. *She* wanted Mac Moorside for herself. A good-looking rogue with a silver tongue...always saying to women just what he thought they'd like to hear. He made Elsie's life miserable. Ah well, Anne dearie, they've both passed long since into the Silent Land and

Maisie's been married to Harley Russell for years and everybody has forgotten that he proposed to her expecting her to say 'No' and she said 'Yes' instead. Harley has forgotten it himself...just like a man. He thinks he has got the best wife in the world and congratulates himself on being clever enough to get her."

"Why did he propose to her if he wanted her to say no? It seems to me a very strange proceeding," said Susan...immediately adding with crushing humility, "But of course *I* would not be expected to know anything about *that*."

"His father ordered him to. He didn't want to, but he thought it was quite safe...There's the doctor now."

As Gilbert came in, a little flurry of snow blew in with him. He threw off his coat and sat gladly down to his own fireside.

"I'm later than I expected to be..."

"No doubt the new lace nightgown was very attractive," said Anne, with an impish grin at Miss Cornelia.

"What are you talking about? Some feminine joke beyond my coarse masculine perception, I suppose. I went on to the Upper Glen to see Walter Cooper."

"It's a mystery how that man does hang on," said Miss Cornelia.

"I've no patience with him," smiled Gilbert. "He ought to have been dead long ago. A year ago I gave him two months and here he is ruining my reputation by keeping on living."

"If you knew the Coopers as well as I do you wouldn't risk predictions on them. Don't you know his grandfather came back to life after they'd dug the grave and got the coffin? The undertaker wouldn't take it back either. However, I understand Walter Cooper is having lots of fun rehearsing his own funeral...just like a man. Well, there's Marshall's bells...and this jar of pickled pears is for you, Anne dearie."

They all went to the door to see Miss Cornelia off. Walter's dark grey eyes peered out into the stormy night.

"I wonder where Cock Robin is tonight and if he misses us," he said wistfully. Perhaps Cock Robin had gone to that mysterious place Mrs. Elliott was always referring to as the Silent Land.

"Cock Robin is in a southern land of sunshine," said Anne. "He'll be back in the spring, I feel quite sure, and that's only five months away. Chickabids, you should all have been in bed along ago."

"Susan," Di was saying in the pantry, "would you like to have a baby? I know where you could get one...brand-new."

"Ah now, where?"

"They have a new one at Amy's. Amy says the angels brought it and she thinks they might have had more sense. They've eight children now, not counting it. I heard you say yesterday that it made you lonesome to see Rilla getting so big...you'd no baby now. I'm sure Mrs. Taylor would give you hers."

"The things children think of! It runs in the Taylors to have big families. Andrew Taylor's father never could tell offhand how many children he had...always had to stop and reckon them up. But I do not think I will take any outside babies on just yet."

"Susan, Amy Taylor says you are an old maid. Are you, Susan?"

"Such has been the lot an all-wise Providence has ordained for me," said Susan unflinchingly.

"Do you *like* being an old maid, Susan?"

"I cannot truthfully say I do, my pet. But," added Susan, remembering the lot of some wives she knew, "I have learned that there are compensations. Now take your father's apple pie to him and I'll bring his tea. The poor man must be faint from hunger."

"Mother, we've got the loveliest home in the world, haven't we?" said Walter as he went sleepily upstairs. "Only...don't you think it would improve it if we had a few ghosts?"

"Ghosts?"

"Yes. Jerry Palmer's house is full of ghosts. He saw one...a tall lady in white with a skeleton hand. I told Susan about it and she said he was either fibbing or there was something the matter with his stomach."

"Susan was right. As for Ingleside, nobody but happy people have ever lived here...so you see we're not ghostable. Now say your prayers and go to sleep."

"Mother, I guess I was naughty last night. I said, 'Give us *tomorrow* our daily bread,' instead of *today.* It seemed more *logical.* Do you think God minded, Mother?"

28

Cock Robin did come back when Ingleside and Rainbow Valley burned again with the green, evasive flames of spring, and brought a bride with him. The two built a nest in Walter's apple tree and Cock Robin resumed all his old habits, but his bride was shyer or less venturesome and would never let anyone come very near her. Susan thought Cock Robin's return a positive miracle and wrote Rebecca Dew about it that very night.

The spotlight in the little drama of life at Ingleside shifted from time to time, now falling on this one, now on that. They had got through the winter without anything very much out of the way happening to anyone and in June it was Di's turn to have an adventure.

A new girl had begun coming to school...a girl who said, when the teacher asked her her name, "I am Jenny Penny," as one might say, "I am Queen Elizabeth," or "I am Helen of Troy." You felt the minute she said it that not to know Jenny Penny argued yourself unknown, and not to be condescended to by Jenny Penny meant you didn't exist at all. At least, that was how Diana Blythe felt about it, even if she couldn't have put it into those exact words.

Jenny Penny had nine years to Di's eight but from the first she took rank with the "big girls" of ten and eleven. They found they could not snub or ignore her. She was not pretty but her appearance was striking...everybody looked at her twice. She had a round creamy face with a soft glossless cloud of soot-black hair about it and enormous dusky blue eyes with long tangled black lashes. When she slowly raised those lashes and looked at you with those scornful eyes you felt that you were a worm honoured in not being stepped on. You liked better to be snubbed by her than courted by any other: and to be selected as a temporary confidante of Jenny Penny's was an honour almost too great to be borne. For Jenny Penny's confidences were exciting. Evidently the Pennys were no common people. Jenny's Aunt Lina, it appeared, possessed a wonderful gold and garnet necklace which had been given her by an uncle who was a millionaire. One of her cousins had a diamond ring that cost a thousand dollars and another cousin had won a prize in elocution over seventeen hundred competitors. She had an aunt who was a missionary and worked among the leopards in India. In short, the Glen schoolgirls, for a time at least, accepted Jenny Penny at her own valuation, looked up to her with mingled admiration and envy, and talked so much about her at their supper tables that their elders were finally constrained to take notice.

"*Who* is this little girl Di seems so taken up with, Susan?" asked Anne one evening, after Di had been telling of "the mansion" Jenny lived in, with white wooden lace around its roof, five bay-windows, a wonderful birch grove behind it, and a red marble mantelpiece in the parlor. "Penny is a name I've never heard in Four Winds. Do you know anything about them?"

"They are a new family that have moved to the old Conway farm on the Base Line, Mrs. Dr. dear. Mr. Penny is said to be a carpenter who couldn't make a living carpentering...being too busy, as I understand, trying to prove there is no God...and has decided to try farming. From all I can make out they are a queer lot. The young ones do just as they like. He says he was bossed to death when he was a kid and his children are not going to be. That is why this Jenny one is coming to the Glen school. They are nearer the Mowbray Narrows school and the other children go there, but Jenny made up her mind to come to the Glen. Half the Conway farm is in this district, so Mr. Penny pays rates to both schools and, of course, he can send his children to both if he likes. Though it seems this Jenny is his niece, not his daughter. Her father and mother are dead. They say it was George Andrew Penny who put the sheep in the basement of the Baptist church at Mowbray Narrows. I do not say they are not respectable, but they are all so *unkempt,* Mrs. Dr. dear...and the house is topsy-turvy...and, if I may presume to advise, you do not want Diana mixed up with a monkey tribe like that."

"I can't exactly prevent her from associating with Jenny in school, Susan. I don't really know anything against the child, though I feel sure she draws a long bow in telling of her relatives and adventures. However, Di will probably soon get over this 'crush' and we'll hear no more of Jenny Penny."

They continued to hear of her, however. Jenny told Di she liked her best of all the girls in the Glen school and Di, feeling that a queen had stooped to her, responded adoringly. They became inseparable at recesses; they wrote notes to each other over the weekends; they gave and received "chews" of gum: they traded buttons and cooperated in dust piles; and finally Jenny asked Di to go home with her from school and stay all night with her.

Mother said, "No," very decidedly and Di wept copiously.

"You've let me stay all night with Persis Ford," she sobbed.

"That was...different," said Anne, a little vaguely. She did not want to make a snob of Di, but all she had heard about the Penny family had made her realize that as friends for the Ingleside children they were quite out of the question and she had been considerably worried of late over the fascination Jenny so evidently possessed for Diana.

"I don't see any difference," wailed Di. "Jenny is just as much of a lady as Persis, so there! She *never* chews bought gum. She has a cousin who knows all the rules of etiquette and Jenny has learned them all from her. Jenny says *we* don't know what etiquette is. And she has had the most exciting adventures."

"Who says she has?" demanded Susan.

"She told me herself. Her folks aren't rich but they have got very rich and respectable relatives. Jenny has an uncle who is a judge and a cousin of her mother's is captain of the biggest vessel in the world. Jenny christened the ship for him when it was launched. *We* haven't got an uncle who is a judge or an aunt who is a missionary to leopards either."

"Lepers, dear, not leopards."

"Jenny *said* leopards. I guess she ought to know since it is her aunt. And there are so many things at her house I want to see... her room is papered with *parrots*... and their parlour is *full* of stuffed owls...and they have a hooked rug with a house on it in the hall...and window blinds just covered with roses...and a *real house* to play in...her uncle built it for them...and her Gammy lives with them and is the oldest person in the world. Jenny says she lived before the flood. I may never have another chance to see a person who lived before the flood."

"The grandmother is close on a hundred, I am told," said Susan, "but if your Jenny said she lived before the flood she is fibbing. You would be likely to catch goodness knows what if you went to a place like that."

"They've had everything they could have long ago," protested Di. "Jenny says they've had mumps and measles and whooping-cough and scarlet fever all in one year."

"I wouldn't put it past them having the smallpox," muttered Susan. "Talk of people being bewitched!"

"Jenny has to have her tonsils out," sobbed Di. "But *that* isn't catching, is it? Jenny had a cousin who died when she had her tonsils out...she bled to death without gaining conscious. So it is likely Jenny will too, if it runs in the family. She is delicate... she fainted three times last week. But she is *quite prepared.* And that is partly why she is so anxious to have me spend a night with her...so that I'd have it to remember after she passed away. *Please,* Mother. I'll go without the new hat with ribbon streamers you promise me if you'll let me."

But Mother was adamant and Di betook herself to a tearful pillow. Nan had no sympathy for her...Nan "had no use" for Jenny Penny.

"I don't know what has got into the child," said Anne worriedly. "She has never behaved like this before. As you say, that Penny girl seems to have bewitched her."

"You were quite right in refusing to let her go to a place so far beneath her, Mrs. Dr. dear."

"Oh, Susan, I don't want her to feel that anyone is 'beneath' her. But we must draw the line somewhere. It's not Jenny so much...I think she's harmless enough apart from her habit of exaggeration...but I'm told the boys are really dreadful. The Mowbray Narrows teacher is at her wits'-end with them."

"Do they TRYannize over you like that?" asked Jenny loftily when Di told her she was not to be allowed to go. "*I* wouldn't let anyone use *me* like that. I have too much spirit. Why, I sleep out of doors all night whenever I take the notion. I s'pose you'd never dream of doing that?"

Di looked wistfully at this mysterious girl who had "often slept out all night." How wonderful!

"You don't blame me for not going, Jenny? You know I want to go?"

"Of course I don't blame you. *Some* girls wouldn't put up with it, of course, but I s'pose you just can't help it. We could have had fun. I'd planned we'd go fishing by moonlight in our back brook. We often do. I've caught trout *that* long. And we have the dearest little pigs and a new foal that's just sweet and a litter of puppies. Well, I guess I must ask Sadie Taylor. *Her* father and mother let her call her soul her own."

"My father and mother are very good to me," protested Di loyally. "And my father is the best doctor in P. E. Island. Everyone says so."

"Putting on airs because you have a father and mother and I have none," said Jenny disdainfully. "Why, *my* father has wings and always wears a golden crown. But *I* don't go about with my head in the air on that account, do I? Now, Di, I don't want to quarrel with you but I hate to hear anyone bragging about their folks. It's not etiket. And I have made up my mind to be a lady. When that Persis Ford you're always talking of comes to Four Winds this summer *I* am not going to 'sociate with her. There's something queer about her ma, Aunt Lina says. She was married to a dead man and he come alive."

"Oh, it wasn't like that at all, Jenny. I know...Mother told me...Aunt Leslie..."

"*I* don't want to hear about her. Whatever it is, it's something that'd better not be talked of, Di. There's the bell."

"Are you really going to ask Sadie?" choked Di, her eyes widening with hurt.

"Well, not right at once. I'll wait and see. Maybe I'll give you one more chance. But if I do it will be the last."

A few days later Jenny Penny came to Di at recess.

"I heard Jem saying your pa and ma went away yesterday and wouldn't be back till tomorrow night?"

"Yes, they went up to Avonlea to see Aunt Marilla."

"Then it's *your chance*."

"My chance?"

"To stay all night with me."

"Oh, Jenny...but I couldn't."

"Of course you can. Don't be a ninny. They'll never know."

"But Susan wouldn't let me..."

"You don't have to ask her. Just come home with me from school. Nan can tell her where you've gone so she won't be worried. And she won't tell on you when your pa and ma come back. She'll be too scared they'd blame her."

Di stood in an agony of indecision. She knew perfectly well she should not go with Jenny, but the temptation was irresistible. Jenny turned the full battery of her extraordinary eyes upon Di.

"This is your *last chance*," she said dramatically. "I can't go on 'sociating with anyone who thinks herself too good to visit me. If you don't come we *part forever*."

That settled it. Di, still in the thrall of Jenny Penny's fascination, couldn't face the thought of parting forever. Nan went home alone that afternoon to tell Susan that Di had gone to stay all night with that Jenny Penny.

Had Susan been her usual active self she would have gone straight to the Pennys and brought Di home. But Susan had strained her ankle that morning and while she could make shift to hobble around and get the children's meals she knew she could never walk a mile down the Base Line road. The Pennys had no telephone and Jem and Walter flatly refused to go. They were invited to a mussel-bake at the lighthouse and nobody would eat Di at the Pennys'. Susan had to resign herself to the inevitable.

Di and Jenny went home across the fields, which made it little more than a quarter of a mile. Di, in spite of her prodding conscience, was happy. They went through so much beauty... little bays of bracken, elfin haunted, in the bays of deep-green woods, a rustling windy hollow where you waded knee-deep in butter-cups, a winding lane under young maples, a brook that was a rainbow scarf of blossom, a sunny pasture field full of strawberries. Di, just wakening to a perception of the loveliness of the world, was enraptured and almost wished Jenny wouldn't talk so much. That was all right at school but here Di wasn't sure she wanted to hear about the time Jenny poisoned herself...'zackzidentally of course...by taking the wrong kind of medicine. Jenny painted her dying agonies finely but was somewhat vague as to the reason she hadn't died after all. She had "lost conscious" but the doctor had managed to pull her back from the brink of the grave.

"Though I've never been the same since. Di Blythe, what *are* you staring at? I don't believe you've been listening at all."

"Oh, yes, I have," said Di guiltily. "I do think you've had the most wonderful life, Jenny. But look at the view."

"The view? What's a view?"

"Why...why...something you're looking at. *That*..." waving her hand at the panorama of meadow and woodland and cloud-smitten hill before them, with that sapphire dent of sea between the hills.

Jenny sniffed.

"Just a lot of old trees and cows. I've seen it a hundred times. You're awful funny by spells, Di Blythe. I don't want to hurt your feelings, but sometimes I think you're not all there. I really do. But I s'pose you can't help it. They say your ma is always raving like that. Well, there's our place."

Di gazed at the Penny house and lived through her first shock of disillusionment. Was *this* the "mansion" Jenny had talked of? It was big enough, certainly, and had the five bay-windows; but it was wofully in need of painting and much of the "wooden lace" was missing. The verandah had sagged badly and the once lovely old fanlight over the front door was broken. The blinds were crooked, there were several brown-paper panes and the "beautiful birch grove" behind the house was represented by a few lean sinewy old trees. The barns were in a very tumbledown condition, the yard was full of old rusty machinery and the garden was a perfect jungle of weeds. Di had never seen such a looking place in her life and for the first time it occurred to her to wonder if *all* Jenny's tales were true. *Could* anyone have so many narrow escapes of her life, even in nine years, as she had claimed to have?

Inside it was not much better. The parlour into which Jenny ushered her was musty and dusty. The ceiling was discoloured and covered with cracks. The famous marble mantelpiece was only painted...even Di could see that...and draped with a hideous Japanese scarf, held in place by a row of "moustache" cups. The stringy lace curtains were a bad colour and full of holes. The blinds were of blue paper, much cracked and torn, with a huge basketful of roses depicted on them. As for the parlour being full of stuffed owls, there was a small glass case in one corner containing three rather dishevelled birds, one with its eyes missing entirely. To Di, accustomed to the beauty and dignity of Ingleside, the room looked like something you had seen in a bad dream. The odd thing, however, was that Jenny seemed quite unconscious of any discrepancy between her descriptions and reality. Di wondered if she had just dreamed that Jenny had told her such and such.

It was not so bad outside. The little playhouse Mr. Penny had built in the spruce corner, looking like a real house in miniature, *was* a very interesting place and the little pigs and the new foal were "just sweet." As for the litter of mongrel puppies they were as woolly and delightful as if they had belonged to the dog caste of Vere de Vere. One was especially adorable, with long brown ears and a white spot on its forehead, a wee pink tongue and white paws. Di was bitterly disappointed to learn that they had all been promised.

'Though I don't know as we could give you one even if they weren't," said Jenny. "Uncle's awful particular where he puts his dogs. We've heard you can't get a dog to stay at Ingleside *at all.* There must be something queer about you. Uncle says dogs *know* things people don't."

"I'm sure they can't know anything nasty about *us!*" cried Di.

"Well, I *hope* not. Is your pa cruel to your ma?"

"No, of course he isn't!"

"Well, I heard that he beat her...beat her till she *screamed.* But of course I didn't believe *that.* Ain't it awful the lies people tell? Anyway, I've always liked you, Di, and I'll always stand up for you."

Di felt she ought to be very grateful for this, but somehow she was not. She was beginning to feel very much out of place and the glamour with which Jenny had been invested in her eyes was suddenly and irrevocably gone. She did not feel the old thrill when Jenny told her about the time she had been almost drowned falling in a millpond. She *did not believe it*...Jenny just *imagined* those things. And likely the millionaire uncle and the thousand-dollar diamond ring and the missionary to the leopards had just been imagined too. Di felt as flat as a pricked balloon.

But there was Gammy yet. Surely Gammy was real. When Di and Jenny returned to the house Aunt Lina, a full-breasted, red-cheeked lady in a none-too-fresh cotton print, told them Gammy wanted to see the visitor.

"Gammy's bed-rid," explained Jenny. "We always take everybody who comes in to see her. She gets mad if we don't."

"Mind you don't forget to ask her how her backache is," cautioned Aunt Lina. "She doesn't like it if folks don't remember her back."

"And Uncle John," said Jenny. "Don't forget to ask her how Uncle John is."

"Who is Uncle John?" asked Di.

"A son of hers who died fifty years ago," explained Aunt Lina. "He was sick for years afore he died and Gammy kind of got accustomed to hearing folks ask how he was. She misses it."

At the door of Gammy's room Di suddenly hung back. All at once she was terribly frightened of this incredibly old woman.

"What's the matter?" demanded Jenny. "Nobody's going to bite you!"

"Is she...did she really live before the flood, Jenny?"

"Of course not. Whoever said she did? She'll be a hundred, though, if she lives till her next birthday. Come on!"

Di went, gingerly. In a small, badly cluttered bedroom Gammy lay in a huge bed. Her face, unbelievably wrinkled and shrunken, looked like an old monkey's. She peered at Di with sunken, red-rimmed eyes and said testily:

"Stop staring. Who are you?"

"This is Diana Blythe, Gammy," said Jenny...a rather subdued Jenny.

"Humph! A nice high-sounding name! They tell me you've got a proud sister."

"Nan isn't proud," cried Di, with a flash of spirit. Had Jenny been running down Nan?

"A little saucy, ain't you? *I* wasn't brought up to speak like that to my betters. She *is* proud. Anyone who walks with her head in the air, like Young Jenny tells me she does, *is* proud. One of your hoity-toitys! Don't contradict *me*."

Gammy looked so angry that Di hastily enquired how her back was.

"Who says I've got a back? Such presumption! My back's my own business. Come here...come close to my bed!"

Di went, wishing herself a thousand miles away. What was this dreadful old woman going to do to her?

Gammy hitched herself alertly to the edge of the bed and put a clawlike hand on Di's hair.

"Sort of carroty but real slick. That's a pretty dress. Turn it up and show me your petticoat."

Di obeyed, thankful that she had on her white petticoat with its trimming of Susan's crocheted lace. But what sort of a family was it where you were made to show your petticoat?

"I always judge a girl by her petticoats," said Gammy. "Yours'll pass. Now your drawers."

Di dared not refuse. She lifted her petticoat.

"Humph! Lace on them too! That's extravagance. And you've never asked after John!"

"How is he?" gasped Di.

"How is he, says she, bold as brass. He might be dead, for all you know. Tell me this. Is it true your mother has a gold thimble...a solid gold thimble?"

"Yes. Daddy gave it to her her last birthday."

"Well, I'd never have believed it. Young Jenny told me she had, but you can't never believe a word Young Jenny says. A solid gold thimble! I never heard the beat of that. Well, you'd better go out and get your suppers. Eating never goes out of fashion. Jenny, pull up your pants. One leg's hanging below your dress. Let us have decency at least."

"My pant—drawer leg isn't hanging down," said Jenny indignantly.

"Pants for Pennys and drawers for Blythes. That's the distinction between you and always will be. Don't contradict *me*."

The whole Penny family were assembled around the supper table in the big kitchen. Di had not seen any of them before except Aunt Lina, but as she shot a glance around the board she understood why Mother and Susan had not wanted her to come here. The tablecloth was ragged and daubed with ancient gravy stains. The dishes were a nondescript assortment. As for the Pennys...Di had never sat at table with such company before and she wished herself safely back at Ingleside. But she must go through with it now.

Uncle Ben, as Jenny called him, sat at the head of the table; he had a flaming red beard and a bald, grey-fringed head. His bachelor brother, Parker, lank and unshaven, had arranged himself at an angle convenient for spitting in the wood-box, which he did at frequent intervals. The boys, Curt, twelve, and George Andrew, thirteen, had pale-blue, fishy eyes with a bold stare and bare skin showing through the holes in their ragged shirts. Curt had his hand, which he had cut on a broken bottle, tied up with a blood-stained rag. Annabel Penny, eleven, and "Gert" Penny, ten, were two rather pretty girls with round brown eyes. "Tuppy," aged two, had delightful curls and rosy cheeks, and the baby, with roguish black eyes, on Aunt Lina's lap would have been adorable if it had been *clean.*

"Curt, why didn't you clean your nails when you knew company was coming?" demanded Jenny. "Annabel, don't speak with your mouth full. I'm the only one who ever tries to teach this family any manners," she explained aside to Di.

"Shut up," said Uncle Ben in a great booming voice.

"I won't shut up...you can't make me shut up!" cried Jenny.

"Don't sass your uncle," said Aunt Lina placidly. "Come now, girls, behave like ladies. Curt, pass the potatoes to Miss Blythe."

"Oh, ho, *Miss* Blythe," sniggered Curt.

But Diana had got at least one thrill. For the first time in her life she had been called Miss Blythe.

For a wonder the food was good and abundant. Di, who was hungry, would have enjoyed the meal...though she hated drinking out of a chipped cup...if she had only been sure it was clean... and if everybody hadn't quarrelled so. Private fights were going on all the time...between George Andrew and Curt...between Curt and Annabel...between Gert and Jen...even between Uncle Ben and Aunt Lina. *They* had a terrible fight and hurled the bitterest accusations at each other. Aunt Lina cast up to Uncle Ben all the fine men she might have married and Uncle Ben said he only wished she had married anybody but him.

"Wouldn't it be dreadful if my father and mother fought like that?" thought Di. "Oh, if I were only back home! Don't suck your thumb, Tuppy."

She said that before she thought. They had had *such* a time breaking Rilla of sucking her thumb.

Instantly Curt was red with rage.

"Let him alone!" he shouted. "He can suck his thumb if he likes! *We* ain't bossed to death like you Ingleside kids are. Who do you think you are?"

"Curt, Curt! Miss Blythe will think you haven't any manners," said Aunt Lina. She was quite calm and smiling again and put two teaspoons of sugar in Uncle Ben's tea. "Don't mind him, dear. Have another piece of pie."

Di did not want another piece of pie. She only wanted to go home...and she did not see how it could be brought about.

"Well," boomed Uncle Ben, as he drained the last of his tea noisily from the saucer, "that's so much over. Get up in the morning...work all day...eat three meals and go to bed. What a life!"

"Pa loves his little joke," smiled Aunt Lina.

"Talking of jokes...I saw the Methodist minister in Flagg's store today. He tried to contradict me when I said there was no God. 'You talk on Sunday,' I told him. 'It's my turn now. Prove to me there's a God,' I told him. 'It's you that's doing the talking,' says he. They all laughed like ninnies. Thought he was smart."

No God! The bottom seemed falling out of Di's world. She wanted to cry.

29

It was worse after supper. Before that she and Jenny had been alone at least. Now there was a mob. George Andrew grabbed her hand and galloped her through a mud-puddle before she could escape him. Di had never been treated like this in her life. Jem and Walter teased her, as did Ken Ford, but she did not know anything about boys like these.

Curt offered her a chew of gum, fresh from his mouth, and was mad when she refused it.

"I'll put a live mouse on you!" he yelled. "Smartycat! Stuckupitty! Got a sissy for a brother!"

"Walter isn't a sissy!" said Di. She was half sick from fright but she would not hear Walter called names.

"He is—he writes po'try. Do you know what I'd do if I'd a brother that writ po'try? I'd drown him...like they do kittens."

"Talking of kittens, there's a lot of wild ones in the barn," said Jen. "Let's go and hunt them out."

Di simply would not go hunting kittens with those boys, and said so.

"We've got plenty of kittens at home. We've got eleven," she said proudly.

"I don't believe it!" cried Jen. "You haven't! Nobody ever had eleven kittens. It wouldn't be *right* to have eleven kittens."

"One cat has five and the other six. And I'm not going to the barn anyhow. I fell down off the loft in Amy Taylor's barn last winter. I'd have been killed if I hadn't lit on a pile of chaff."

"Well, I'd have fell off our loft once if Curt hadn't caught me," said Jen sulkily. Nobody had any right to be falling off lofts but her. Di Blythe having adventures! The impudence of her!

"You should say 'I'd *have fallen*,'" said Di; and from that moment everything was over between her and Jenny.

But the night had to be got through somehow. They did not go to bed till late because none of the Pennys ever went to bed early. The big bedroom where Jenny took her at half-past ten had two beds in it. Annabel and Gert were getting ready for theirs. Di looked at the others. The pillows were very frowsy. The quilt needed washing very badly. The paper...the famous "parrot" paper...had been leaked on and even the parrots did not look very parroty. On the stand by the bed were a granite pitcher and a tin wash-basin half full of dirty water. She could never wash her face in *that.* Well, for once she must go to bed without washing her face. At least the nightgown Aunt Lina had left for her was clean.

When Di got up from saying her prayers Jenny laughed.

"My, but you're old-fashioned. You looked so funny and holy saying your prayers. I didn't know anybody said prayers now. Prayers ain't any good. What do you say them for?"

"I've got to save my soul," said Di, quoting Susan.

"I haven't any soul," mocked Jenny.

"Perhaps not, but *I have,*" said Di, drawing herself up.

Jenny looked at her. But the spell of Jenny's eyes was broken. Never again would Di succumb to its magic.

"You're not the girl I thought you were, Diana Blythe," said Jennie sadly, as one much deceived.

Before Di could reply George Andrew and Curt rushed into the room. George Andrew wore a mask...a hideous thing with an enormous nose. Di screamed.

"Stop squealing like a pig under a gate!" ordered George Andrew. "You've got to kiss us good-night."

"If you don't we'll lock you up in that closet...and it's full of rats," said Curt.

George Andrew advanced towards Di, who shrieked again and retreated before him. The mask paralyzed her with terror. She knew quite well it was only George Andrew behind it and she was not afraid of *him;* but she would die if that awful mask came near her...she knew she would. Just as it seemed that the dreadful nose was touching her face she tripped over a stool and fell backward on the floor, striking her head on the sharp edge of Annabel's bed as she fell. For a moment she was dazed and lay with her eyes shut.

"She's gone dead...she's gone dead!" sniffled Curt, beginning to cry.

"Oh, won't you get a licking if you've killed her, George Andrew!" said Annabel.

"Maybe she's only pretending," said Curt. "Put a worm on her. I've some in this can. If she's only foxing that will bring her to."

Di heard this but was too frightened to open her eyes. *(Perhaps they would go away and leave her alone if they thought her dead. But if they put a worm on her...)*

"Prick her with a pin. If she bleeds she ain't dead," said Curt.

(She could stand a pin but not a worm.)

"She ain't dead...she *can't* be dead," whispered Jenny. "You've just scared her into a fit. But if she comes to she'll be screeching all over the place and Uncle Ben'll come in and lambast the daylights out of us. I wish I'd never asked her here, the fraid-cat!"

"Do you s'pose we could carry her home before she comes to?" suggested George Andrew.

(Oh, if they only would!)

"We couldn't...not that far," said Jenny.

"It's only a quarter of a mile 'cross lots. We'll each take an arm or leg...you and Curt and me and Annabel."

Nobody but the Pennys could have conceived such an idea or carried it out if they had. But they were used to doing anything they took it into their heads to do and a "lambasting" from the head of the household was something to be avoided if possible. Dad didn't bother about them up to a certain point but beyond that...*good-night!*

"If she comes to while we're carrying her we'll just cut and run," said George Andrew.

There wasn't the least danger of Di coming to. She trembled with thankfulness when she felt herself being hoisted up between the four of them. They crept downstairs and out of the house, across the yard and over the long clover field...past the woods... down the hill. Twice they had to lay her down while they rested. They were quite sure now she was dead and all they wanted was to get her home without being seen. If Jenny Penny never prayed in her life before she was praying now...that nobody in the village would be up. If they could get Di Blythe home they would all swear she had got so homesick at bedtime that she had insisted on going home. What happened after that would be no concern of theirs.

Di ventured to open her eyes once as they plotted this. The sleeping world around looked very strange to her. The fir trees were dark and alien. The stars were laughing at her. *("I don't like such a big sky. But if I can just hold on a little spell longer I'll be home. If they find out that I'm not dead they'll just leave me here and I'll never get home in the dark alone.")*

When the Pennys dropped Di on the verandah of Ingleside they ran like mad. Di did not dare come back to life too soon, but at last she ventured to open her eyes. Yes, she was home. It seemed almost too good to be true. She had been a very, very naughty girl but she was quite sure she would never be naughty again. She sat up and the Shrimp came stealthily up the steps and rubbed against her, purring. She hugged him to her. How nice and warm and friendly he was! She did not think she would be able to get in...she knew Susan would have all the doors locked when Dad was away and she dared not wake Susan up at this hour. But she did not mind. The June night was cold enough but she would get into the hammock and cuddle down with the Shrimp, knowing that, near to her, behind those locked doors, were Susan and the boys and Nan...and *home.*

How strange the world was after dark! Was everyone in it asleep but her? The large white roses on the bush by the steps looked like small human faces in the night. The smell of the mint was like a friend. There was a glint of firefly in the orchard. After all, she would be able to brag that she had "slept out all night."

But it was not to be. Two dark figures came through the gate and up the driveway. Gilbert went around by the back way to force open a kitchen window but Anne came up the steps and stood looking in amazement at the poor mite who sat there, with her armful of cat.

"Mummy...oh, Mummy!" She was safe in Mother's arms.

"Di, darling! What does this mean?"

"Oh, Mummy, I was bad...but I'm so sorry...and you were right...and Gammy was so dreadful—but I thought you wouldn't be back till tomorrow."

"Daddy got a telephone from Lowbridge...they have to operate on Mrs. Parker tomorrow and Dr. Parker wanted him to be there. So we caught the evening train and walked up from the station. Now tell me..."

The whole story was sobbed out by the time Gilbert had got in and opened the front door. He thought he had effected a very silent entrance, but Susan had ears that could hear a bat squeak when the safety of Ingleside was concerned, and she came limping downstairs with a wrapper over her nightgown.

There were exclamations and explanations, but Anne cut them short.

"Nobody is blaming you, Susan dear. Di has been very naughty but she knows it and I think she has had her punishment. I'm sorry we've disturbed you...you must go straight back to bed and the doctor will see to your ankle."

"I was not asleep, Mrs. Dr. dear. Do you think I could sleep, knowing where that blessed child was? And ankle or no ankle I am going to get you both a cup of tea."

"Mummy," said Di, from her own white pillow, "is Daddy ever cruel to you?"

"Cruel! To me? Why, Di..."

"The Pennys said he was...said he beat you..."

"Dear, you know what the Pennys are now, so you know better than to worry your small head over anything they said. There is always a bit of malicious gossip floating round in any place...people like that *invent* it. You must never bother about it."

"Are you going to scold me in the morning, Mummy?"

"No. I think you've learned your lesson. Now go to sleep, precious."

"Mummy is so *sensible*," was Di's last conscious thought. But Susan, as she stretched out peacefully in bed, with her ankle expertly and comfortably bandaged, was saying to herself:

"I must hunt up the fine-tooth comb in the morning...and when I see my fine Miss Jenny Penny I shall give her a ticking off she will not forget."

Jenny Penny never got the promised ticking off, for she came no more to the Glen school. Instead, she went with the other Pennys to Mowbray Narrows school, whence rumours drifted back of her yarns, among them being one of how Di Blythe, who lived in the "big house" at Glen St. Mary but was always coming down to sleep with her, had fainted one night and had been carried home at midnight pick-a-back, by her, Jenny Penny, alone and unassisted. The Ingleside people had knelt and kissed her hands out of gratitude and the doctor himself had got out his fringed-top buggy and his famous dappled grey span and driven her home. "And if there is ever *anything* I can do for you, Miss Penny, for your kindness to my beloved child you have only to name it. My best heart's blood would not be enough to repay you. I would go to Equatorial Africa to reward you for what you have done," the doctor had vowed.

30

"*I* know something you don't know...something *you* don't know... something *you* don't know," chanted Dovie Johnson, as she teetered back and forth on the very edge of the wharf.

It was Nan's turn for the spotlight...Nan's turn to add a tale to the do-you-remembers of after Ingleside years. Though Nan to the day of her death would blush to be reminded of it. She *had* been so silly.

Nan shuddered to see Dovie teetering...and yet it had a fascination. She was so sure Dovie would fall off sometime and then what? But Dovie never fell. Her luck always held.

Everything Dovie did, or said she did...which were, perhaps, two very different things, although Nan, brought up at Ingleside where nobody ever told anything but the truth even as a joke, was too innocent and credulous to know that...had a fascination for Nan. Dovie, who was eleven and had lived in Charlottetown all her life knew so much more than Nan, who was only eight. Charlottetown, Dovie said, was the only place where people knew anything. What could you know, shut off in a one-horse place like Glen St. Mary?

Dovie was spending part of her vacation with her Aunt Ella in the Glen and she and Nan had struck up a very intimate friendship in spite of the difference in their ages. Perhaps because Nan looked up to Dovie, who seemed to her to be almost grown up, with the adoration we needs must give the highest when we see it...or think we see it. Dovie liked her humble and adoring little satellite.

"There's no harm in Nan Blythe...she's only a bit soft," she told Aunt Ella.

The watchful folks at Ingleside could not see anything out of the way about Dovie...even if, as Anne reflected, her mother was a cousin of the Avonlea Pyes...and made no objection to Nan's chumming with her, though Susan from the first mistrusted those gooseberry-green eyes with their pale golden lashes. But what would you? Dovie was "nice-mannered," well-dressed, lady-like, and did not talk too much. Susan could not give any reason for her mistrust and held her peace. Dovie would be going home when school opened and in the meantime there was certainly no need of fine-tooth combs in this case.

So Nan and Dovie spent most of their spare time together at the wharf, where there was generally a ship or two with their folded wings, and Rainbow Valley hardly knew Nan that August. The other Ingleside children did not care greatly for Dovie and no love was lost. She had played a practical joke on Walter and Di had been furious and "said things." Dovie was, it seemed, fond of playing practical jokes. Perhaps that was why none of the Glen girls ever tried to lure her from Nan.

"Oh, please tell me," pleaded Nan.

But Dovie only winked a wicked eye and said that Nan was far too young to be told such a thing. This was just maddening.

"*Please* tell me, Dovie."

"Can't. It was told me as a secret by Aunt Kate and she's dead. I'm the only person in the world that knows it now. I promised when I heard it that I'd never tell a soul. You'd tell somebody... you couldn't help it."

"I wouldn't...I could so!" cried Nan.

"People say you folks at Ingleside tell each other everything. Susan'd pick it out of you in no time."

"She wouldn't. I know lots of things I've never told Susan. Secrets. I'll tell mine to you if you'll tell me yours."

"Oh, I'm not int'rested in the secrets of a little girl like you," said Dovie.

A nice insult that! Nan thought her little secrets were lovely... that one wild cherry trees she had found blooming in the spruce wood away back behind Mr. Taylor's hay barn...her dream of a tiny white fairy lying on a lily pad in the marsh...her fancy of a boat coming up the harbour drawn by swans attached to silver chains...the romance she was beginning to weave about the beautiful lady at the old MacAllister place. They were all very wonderful and magical to Nan and she felt glad, when she thought it over, that she did not have to tell them to Dovie after all.

But what *did* Dovie know about *her* that *she* didn't know? The query haunted Nan like a mosquito.

The next day Dovie again referred to her secret knowledge.

"I've been thinking it over, Nan...perhaps you *ought* to know it since it's about you. Of course what Aunt Kate meant was that I mustn't tell anyone but the person concerned. Look here. If you'll give me that china stag of yours I'll tell you what I know about you."

"Oh, I couldn't give you *that,* Dovie. Susan gave it to me my last birthday. It would hurt her feelings dreadfully."

"*All* right, then. If you'd rather have your old stag than know an important thing about yourself you can keep him. *I* don't care. I'd rather keep it. I always like to know things other girls don't. It makes you *important.* I'll look at you next Sunday in church and I'll think to myself, 'if *you* just knew what *I* know about you, Nan Blythe.' It'll be fun."

"Is what you know about me *nice*?" queried Nan.

"Oh, it's *very* romantic...just like something you'd read in a story-book. But never mind, *you* ain't interested and *I* know what I know."

By this time Nan was crazy with curiosity. Life wouldn't be worth living if she couldn't find out what Dovie's mysterious knowledge was. She had a sudden inspiration.

"Dovie, I can't give you my stag, but if you'll tell me what you know about me I'll give you my red parasol."

Dovie's gooseberry eyes gleamed. She had been eaten up by envy of that parasol.

"The new red parasol your mother brought you from town last week?" she bargained.

Nan nodded. Her breath came quickly. Was it...oh, was it possible that Dovie would really tell her?

"Will your mother let you?" demanded Dovie.

Nan nodded again, but a little uncertainly. She was none too sure of it. Dovie scented the uncertainty.

"You'll have to have that parasol right here," she said firmly, "before I can tell you. No parasol, no secret."

"I'll bring it tomorrow," promised Nan hastily. She just *had* to know what Dovie knew about her, that was all there was to it.

"Well, I'll think it over," said Dovie doubtfully. "Don't get your hopes up. I don't expect I'll tell you after all. You're too young...I've told you so often enough."

"I'm older than I was yesterday," pleaded Nan. "Oh, come, Dovie, don't be mean."

"I guess I've got a right to my own knowledge," said Dovie crushingly. "You'd tell Anne...that's your mother..."

"Of course I know my own mother's name," said Nan, a trifle on her dignity. Secrets or no secrets, there were limits. "I told you I wouldn't tell *anybody* at Ingleside."

"Will you swear it?"

"*Swear* it?"

"Don't be a poll-parrot. Of course I mean just promising solemnly."

"I promise solemnly."

"Solemner than that."

Nan didn't see how she could be any solemner. Her face would set if she was.

"'*Clasp your hands, look at the sky,*
Cross your heart and hope to die,'"

said Dovie.

Nan went through the ritual.

"You'll bring the parasol tomorrow and we'll see," said Dovie. "What did your mother do before she was married, Nan?"

"She taught school...and taught it well," said Nan.

"Well, I was just wondering. Mother thinks it was a mistake for your Dad to marry her. Nobody knew anything about her *family.* And the girls he might have had, Mother says. I must be going now. O revor."

Nan knew that meant "till tomorrow." She was very proud of having a chum who could talk French. She continued to sit on the wharf long after Dovie had gone home. She liked to sit on the wharf and watch the fishing boats going out and coming in, and sometimes a ship drifting down the harbour, bound to fair lands far away. Like Jem, she often wished she could sail away in a ship...down the blue harbour, past the bar of shadowy dunes, past the lighthouse point where at night the revolving Four Winds Light became an outpost of mystery, out, out, to the blue mist that was the summer gulf, on, on, to enchanted islands in golden morning seas. Nan flew on the wings of her imagination all over the world as she squatted there on the old sagging wharf.

But this afternoon she was all keyed up over Dovie's secret. Would Dovie really tell her? What would it be...what *could* it be? And what about those girls Father might have married? Nan liked to speculate about those girls. One of them might have been her mother. But that was horrible. Nobody could be her mother except Mother. The thing was simply unthinkable.

"I *think* Dovie Johnson is going to tell me a secret," Nan confided to Mother that night when she was being kissed bye-bye. "Of course I won't be able to tell even you, Mummy, because I've promised I wouldn't. You won't mind, will you, Mummy?"

"Not at all," said Anne, much amused.

When Nan went down to the wharf the next day she took the parasol. It was her parasol, she told herself. It had been given to her, so she had a perfect right to do what she liked with it. Having quieted her conscience with this sophistry she slipped away when nobody could see her. It gave her a pang to think of giving up her dear, gay little parasol, but by this time the craze to find out what Dovie knew had become too strong to be resisted.

"Here's the parasol, Dovie," she said breathlessly. "And now tell me the secret."

Dovie was really taken aback. She had never meant matters to go as far as this...she had never believed Nan Blythe's mother would *let* her give away her red parasol. She pursed her lips.

"I don't know as that shade of red will suit my complexion, after all. It's rather *gaudy.* I guess I won't tell." Nan had a spirit of her own and Dovie had not yet quite charmed it into blind submission. Nothing roused it more quickly than injustice.

"A bargain is a bargain, Dovie Johnson! You *said* the parasol for the secret. Here is the parasol and you've *got* to keep your promise."

"Oh, very well," said Dovie in a bored way.

Everything grew very still. The gusts of wind had died away. The water stopped glug-glugging round the piles of the wharf. Nan shivered with delicious ecstasy. She was going to find out at last what Dovie knew.

"You know the Jimmy Thomases down at the Harbour Mouth," said Dovie. "Six-toed Jimmy Thomas?"

Nan nodded. Of course she knew the Thomases...at least, knew of them. Six-toed Jimmy sometimes called at Ingleside selling fish. Susan said you never could be sure of getting good ones from him. Nan did not like the look of him. He had a bald head, with a fluff of curly white hair on either side of it, and a red, hooked nose. But what could the Thomases possibly have to do with the matter?

"And you know Cassie Thomas?" went on Dovie.

Nan had seen Cassie Thomas once when Six-toed Jimmy had brought her round with him in his fishwagon. Cassie was just about her own age, with a mop of red curls and bold, greenish-grey eyes. She had stuck her tongue out at Nan.

"Well..." Dovie drew a long breath..."this is the *truth* about you. *You* are Cassie Thomas and *she* is Nan Blythe."

Nan stared at Dovie. She hadn't the faintest glimmer of Dovie's meaning. What she had said made no sense.

"I...I...what do you mean?"

"It's plain enough, I should think," said Dovie with a pitying smile. Since she had been *forced* to tell this she was going to make it worth the telling. "You and her were born the same night. It was when the Thomases lived in the Glen. The nurse took Di's twin down to Thomas's and put her in the cradle and took you back to Di's mother. She didn't dare take Di, too, or she would have. She hated your mother and she took that way of getting even. And that is why you are really Cassie Thomas and you ought to be living down there at the Harbour Mouth and poor Cass ought to be up at Ingleside instead of being banged about by that old stepmother of hers. I feel so sorry for her many's the time."

Nan believed every word of this preposterous yarn. She had never been lied to in her life and not for one moment did she doubt the truth of Dovie's tale. It never occurred to her that anyone, much less her beloved Dovie, would or could make up such a story. She gazed at Dovie with anguished, disillusioned eyes.

"How...how did your Aunt Kate find it out?" she gasped through dry lips.

"The nurse told her on her death-bed," said Dovie solemnly. "I s'pose her conscience troubled her. Aunt Kate never told anyone but me. When I came to the Glen and saw Cassie Thomas... Nan Blythe, I mean...I took a good look at her. She's got red hair and eyes the same colour as your mother's. You've got brown eyes and brown hair. That's why you don't look like Di...twins *always* look exactly alike. And Cass has just the same kind of ears as your father...lying so nice and flat against her head. I don't s'pose anything can be done about it now. But I've often thought it wasn't fair, you having such an easy time and being kept like a doll and poor Cass—Nan—in rags, and not even getting enough to eat, many's the time. And old Six-toed beating her when he comes home drunk!...Why, what are you looking at me like that for?"

Nan's pain was greater than she could bear. All was horribly clear to her now. Folks had always thought it funny she and Di didn't look one bit alike. *This* was why.

"I *hate* you for telling me this, Dovie Johnson!"

Dovie shrugged her fat shoulders.

"I didn't tell you you'd like it, did I? You *made* me tell. Where are you going?"

For Nan, white and dizzy, had risen to her feet.

"Home...to tell Mother," she said miserably.

"You mustn't...you dassn't! Remember you swore you wouldn't tell!" cried Dovie.

Nan stared at her. It was true she had promised not to tell. And Mother always said you mustn't break a promise.

"I guess I'll be getting home myself," said Dovie, not altogether liking the look of Nan.

She snatched up the parasol and ran off, her plump bare legs twinkling along the old wharf. Behind her she left a broken-hearted child, sitting amid the ruins of her small universe. Dovie didn't care. Soft was no name for Nan. It really wasn't much fun to fool her. Of course she would tell her mother as soon as she got home and find out she had been hoaxed.

"Just as well I'm going home Sunday," reflected Dovie.

Nan sat on the wharf for what seemed hours...blind, crushed, despairing. She wasn't Mother's child! She was Six-toed Jimmy's child...Six-toed Jimmy of whom she had always had a secret dread simply because of his six toes. She had no business to be living at Ingleside, loved by Mother and Dad. "Oh!" Nan gave a piteous little moan. Mother and Dad wouldn't love her any more if they knew. All their love would go to Cassie Thomas.

Nan put her hand to her head. "It makes me dizzy," she said.

31

"What is the reason you are not eating anything, pet?" asked Susan at the supper table.

"Were you out in the sun too long, dear?" asked Mother anxiously. "Does your head ache?"

"Ye-e-s," said Nan. But it wasn't her head that ached. Was she telling a lie to Mother? And if so, how many more would she have to tell? For Nan knew she would never be able to eat again...never so long as this horrible knowledge was hers. And she knew she could never tell Mother. Not so much because of the promise...hadn't Susan said once that a bad promise was better broken than kept?...but because it would hurt Mother. Somehow, Nan knew beyond any doubt that it would hurt Mother horribly. And Mother mustn't...shouldn't...be hurt. Nor Dad.

And yet...there was Cassie Thomas. She *wouldn't* call her Nan Blythe. It made Nan feel awful beyond description to think of Cassie Thomas as being Nan Blythe. She felt as if it blotted *her* out altogether. If she wasn't Nan Blythe she wasn't anybody! She would *not* be Cassie Thomas.

But Cassie Thomas haunted her. For a week Nan was beset by her...a wretched week during which Anne and Susan were really worried over the child, who wouldn't eat and wouldn't play and, as Susan said, "just moped around." Was it because Dovie Johnson had gone home? Nan said it wasn't. Nan said it wasn't *anything.* She just felt tired. Dad looked her over and prescribed a dose which Nan took meekly. It was not so bad as castor-oil but even castor-oil meant nothing now. Nothing meant anything except Cassie Thomas...and the awful question which had emerged from her confusion of mind and taken possession of her.

Shouldn't Cassie Thomas have her rights?

Was it fair that she, Nan Blythe...Nan clung to her identity frantically...should have all the things Cassie Thomas was denied and which were hers by rights? No, it wasn't fair. Nan was despairingly sure it wasn't fair. Somewhere in Nan there was a very strong sense of justice and fair play. And it became increasingly borne in upon her that it was only fair that Cassie Thomas should be told.

After all, perhaps nobody would care very much. Mother and Dad would be a little upset at first, of course, but as soon as they knew that Cassie Thomas was their own child all their love would go to Cassie and, she, Nan, would be of no account to them. Mother would kiss Cassie Thomas and sing to her in the summer twilights...sing the song Nan liked best...

"*I saw a ship a-sailing, a-sailing on the sea,*
"*And oh, it was all laden with pretty things for me.*"

Nan and Di had often talked about the day their ship would come in. But now the pretty things...her share of them anyhow... would belong to Cassie Thomas. Cassie Thomas would take her part as fairy queen in the forthcoming Sunday School concert and wear *her* dazzling band of tinsel. How Nan had looked forward to that! Susan would make fruit puffs for Cassie Thomas and Pussywillow would purr for her. She would play with Nan's dolls in Nan's moss-carpeted play-house in the maple grove, and sleep in her bed. Would Di like that? Would Di like Casssie Thomas for a sister?

There came a day when Nan knew she could bear it no longer. She must do what was fair. She would go down to the Harbour Mouth and tell the Thomases the truth. *They* could tell Mother and Dad. Nan felt that she simply could not do *that.*

Nan felt a little better when she had come to this decision, but very, very sad. She tried to eat a little supper because it would be the last meal she would ever eat at Ingleside.

"I'll always call Mother 'Mother,'" thought Nan desperately. "And I *won't* call Six-toed Jimmy 'Father.' I'll just say 'Mr. Thomas' very respectfully. Surely he won't mind *that.*"

But something choked her. Looking up she read castor-oil in Susan's eye. Little Susan thought she wouldn't be here at bedtime to take it. Cassie Thomas would have to swallow it. That was the one thing Nan didn't envy Cassie Thomas.

Nan went off immediately after supper. She must go before it was dark or her courage would fail her. She went in her checked gingham play-dress, not daring to change it, lest Susan or Mother ask why. Besides, all her nice dresses really belonged to Cassie Thomas. But she did put on the new apron Susan had made for her...such a smart little scalloped apron, the scallops bound in turkey red. Nan loved that apron. Surely Cassie Thomas wouldn't grudge her that much.

She walked down to the village, through the village, past the wharf road, and down the harbour road, a gallant, indomitable little figure. Nan had no idea that she was a heroine. On the contrary she felt very much ashamed of herself because it was so hard to do what was right and fair, so hard to keep from hating Cassie Thomas, so hard to keep from fearing Six-toed Jimmy, so hard to keep from turning round and running back to Ingleside.

It was a lowering evening. Out to sea hung a heavy black cloud, like a great dark bat. Fitful lightning played over the harbour and the wooded hills beyond. The cluster of fishermen's houses at the Harbour Mouth lay flooded in a red light that escaped from under the cloud. Pools of water here and there glowed like great rubies. A ship, silent, white-sailed, was drifting past the dim, misty dunes to the mysterious calling ocean; the gulls were crying strangely.

Nan did not like the smell of the fishing houses or the groups of dirty children who were playing and fighting and yelling on the sands. They looked curiously at Nan when she stopped to ask them which was Six-toed Jimmy's house.

"That one over there," said a boy, pointing. "What's your business with him?"

"Thank you," said Nan, turning away.

"Have ye got no more manners than that?" yelled a girl. "Too stuck-up to answer a civil question!"

The boy got in front of her.

"See that house back of Thomases?" he said. "It's got a sea-serpent in it and I'll lock you up in it if you don't tell me what you want with Six-toed Jimmy."

"Come now, Miss Proudy," taunted a big girl. "You're from the Glen and the glenners all think they're the cheese. Answer Bill's question!"

"If you don't look out," said another boy, "I'm going to drown some kittens and I'll quite likely pop you in, too."

"If you've got a dime about you I'll sell you a tooth," said a black-browed girl, grinning. "I had one pulled yesterday."

"I haven't got a dime and your tooth wouldn't be of any use to me," said Nan, plucking up a little spirit. "You let me alone."

"None of your lip!" said the black-browed.

Nan started to run. The sea-serpent boy stuck out a foot and tripped her up. She fell her length on the tide-rippled sand. The others screamed with laughter.

"You won't hold your head so high now, I reckon," said the black-browed. "Strutting about here with your red scallops!"

Then someone exclaimed, "There's Blue Jack's boat coming in!" and away they all ran. The black cloud had dropped lower and every ruby pool was grey.

Nan picked herself up. Her dress was plastered with sand and her stockings were soiled. But she was free from her tormentors. Would these be her playmates in the future?

She must not cry...she must not! She climbed the rickety board steps that led up to Six-toed Jimmy's door. Like all the Harbour Mouth houses Six-toed Jimmy's was raised on blocks of wood to be out of the reach of any unusually high tide, and the space underneath it was filled with a medley of broken dishes, empty cans, old lobster traps, and all kinds of rubbish. The door was open and Nan looked into a kitchen the like of which she had never seen in her life. The bare floor was dirty, the ceiling was stained and smoked, the sink was full of dirty dishes. The remains of a meal were on the rickety old wooden table and horrid big black flies were swarming over it. A woman with an untidy mop of grayish hair was sitting on a rocker nursing a fat lump of a baby...a baby gray with dirt.

"*My sister*," thought Nan.

There was no sign of Cassie or Six-toed Jimmy, for which latter fact Nan felt grateful.

"Who are you and what do you want?" said the woman rather ungraciously.

She did not ask Nan in but Nan walked in. It was beginning to rain outside and a peal of thunder made the house shake. Nan knew she must say what she had come to say before her courage failed her, or she would turn and run from that dreadful house and that dreadful baby and those dreadful flies.

"I want to see Cassie, please," she said. "I have *something important* to tell her."

"Indeed, now!" said the woman. "It must be important, from the size of you. Well, Cass isn't home. Her dad took her to the Upper Glen for a ride and with this storm coming up there's no telling when they'll be back. Sit down."

Nan sat down on a broken chair. She had known the Harbour Mouth folks were poor but she had not known any of them were like this. Mrs. Tom Fitch in the Glen was poor but Mrs. Tom Fitch's house was as neat and tidy as Ingleside. Of course, everyone knew that Six-toed Jimmy drank up everything he made. And this was to be her home henceforth!

"Anyhow, I'll try to clean it up," thought Nan forlornly. But her heart was like lead. The flame of high self-sacrifice which had lured her on had gone out.

"What are you wanting to see Cass for?" asked Mrs. Six-toed curiously, as she wiped the baby's dirty face with a still dirtier apron. "If it's about that Sunday School concert she can't go and that's flat. She hasn't a decent rag. How can I get her any? I ask you."

"No, it's not about the concert," said Nan drearily. She might as well tell Mrs. Thomas the whole story. She would have to know it anyhow. "I came to tell her...to tell her that...that she is me and I'm her!"

Perhaps Mrs. Six-toed might be forgiven for not thinking this very lucid.

"You must be cracked," she said. "Whatever on earth do you mean?"

Nan lifted her head. The worst was now over.

"I mean that Cassie and I were born the same night and... and...the nurse changed us because she had a spite at Mother, and...and...Cassie ought to be living at Ingleside...and having advantages."

This last phrase was one she had heard her Sunday School teacher use but Nan thought it made a dignified ending to a very lame speech.

Mrs. Six-toed stared at her.

"Am I crazy or are you? What you've been saying doesn't make any sense. Whoever told you such a rigmarole?"

"Dovie Johnson."

Mrs. Six-toed threw back her tousled head and laughed. She might be dirty and draggled but she had an attractive laugh. "I might have knowed it. I've been washing for her aunt all summer and that kid is a pill! My, doesn't she think it smart to fool people! Well, little Miss What's-your-name, you'd better not be believing all Dovie's yarns or she'll lead you a merry dance."

"Do you mean it isn't true?" gasped Nan.

"Not very likely. Good glory, you must be pretty green to fall for anything like that. Cass must be a good year older than you. Who on earth are you, anyhow?"

"I'm Nan Blythe." Oh, beautiful thought! She *was* Nan Blythe!

"Nan Blythe! One of the Ingleside twins! Why, I remember the night you were born. I happened to call at Ingleside on an errand. I wasn't married to Six-toed then...more's the pity I ever was...and Cass's mother was living and healthy, with Cass beginning to walk. You look like your dad's mother...she was there that night, too, proud as Punch over her twin granddaughters. And to think you'd no more sense than to believe a crazy yarn like that."

"I'm in the habit of believing people," said Nan, rising with a slight stateliness of manner, but too deliriously happy to want to snub Mrs. Six-toed very sharply.

"Well, it's a habit you'd better get out of in this kind of a world," said Mrs. Six-toed cynically. "And quit running round with kids who like to fool people. Sit down, child. You can't go home till this shower's over. It's pouring rain and dark as a stack of black cats. Why, she's gone...the child's gone!"

Nan was already blotted out in the downpour. Nothing but the wild exultation born of Mrs. Six-toed's assurances could have carried her home through that storm. The wind buffeted her, the rain streamed upon her, the appalling thunderclaps made her think the world had burst open. Only the incessant icy-blue glare of the lightning showed her the road. Again and again she slipped and fell. But at last she reeled, dripping, into the hall at Ingleside.

Mother ran and caught her in her arms.

"Darling, what a fright you have given us! Oh, where have you been?"

"I only hope Jem and Walter won't catch their deaths out in that rain searching for you," said Susan, the sharpness of strain in her voice.

Nan had almost had the breath battered out of her. She could only gasp, as she felt Mother's arms enfolding her:

"Oh, Mother, I'm me...really me. I'm not Cassie Thomas and I'll never be anybody but me again."

"The poor pet is delirious," said Susan. "She must have et something that disagreed with her."

Anne bathed Nan and put her to bed before she would let her talk. Then she heard the whole story.

"Oh, Mummy, am I really your child?"

"Of course, darling. How could you think anything else?"

"I didn't ever think Dovie would tell me a story...not *Dovie.* Mummy, can you believe *anybody*? Jen Penny told Di awful stories..."

"They are only two girls out of all the little girls you know, dear. None of your other playmates has ever told you what wasn't true. There *are* people in the world like that, grown-ups as well as children. When you are a little older you will be better able to 'tell the gold from the tinsel.'"

"Mummy, I wish Walter and Jem and Di needn't know what a silly I was."

"They needn't. Di went to Lowbridge with Daddy, and the boys need only know you went too far down the Harbour Road and were caught in the storm. You were foolish to believe Dovie but you were a very fine brave little girl to go and offer what you thought her rightful place to poor little Cassie Thomas. Mother is proud of you."

The storm was over. The moon was looking down on a cool happy world.

"Oh, I'm so glad I'm *me*!" was Nan's last thought as she fell on sleep.

Gilbert and Anne came in later to look on the little sleeping faces that were so sweetly close to each other. Diana slept with the corners of her firm little mouth tucked in but Nan had gone to sleep smiling. Gilbert had heard the story and was so angry that it was well for Dovie Johnson that she was a good thirty miles away from him. But Anne was feeling conscience-stricken.

"I should have found out what was troubling her. But I've been too much taken up with other things this week...things that really mattered nothing compared to a child's unhappiness. Think of what the poor darling has suffered."

She stooped repentantly, gloatingly over them. They were still hers...wholly hers, to mother and love and protect. They still came to her with every love and grief of their little hearts. For a few years longer they would be hers...and then? Anne shivered. Motherhood was very sweet...but very terrible.

"I wonder what life holds for them," she whispered.

"At least, let's hope and trust they'll each get as good a husband as their mother got," said Gilbert teasingly.

32

"So the Ladies' Aid is going to have their quilting at Ingleside," said the doctor. "Bring out all your lordly dishes, Susan, and provide several brooms to sweep up the fragments of reputations afterwards."

Susan smiled wanly, as a woman tolerant of a man's lack of all understanding of vital things, but she did not feel like smiling... at least, until everything concerning the Aid supper had been settled.

"Hot chicken pie," she went about murmuring, "mashed potatoes and creamed peas for the main course. And it will be such a good chance to use your new lace tablecloth, Mrs. Dr. dear. Such a thing has never been seen in the Glen and I am confident it will make a sensation. I am looking forward to Annabel Clow's face when she sees it. And will you be using your blue and silver basket for the flowers?"

"Yes, full of pansies and yellow-green ferns from the maple grove. And I want you to put those three magnificent pink geraniums of yours somewhere around...in the living-room if we quilt there or on the balustrade of the verandah if it's warm enough to work out there. I'm glad we have so many flowers left. The garden has never been so beautiful as it has been this summer, Susan. But then I say that every autumn, don't I?"

There were many things to be settled. Who should sit by whom...it would never do, for instance, to have Mrs. Simon Millison sit beside Mrs. William McCreery, for they never spoke to each other because of some obscure old feud dating back to schooldays. Then there was the question of whom to invite...for it was the hostess' privilege to ask a few guests apart from the members of the Aid.

"I'm going to have Mrs. Best and Mrs. Campbell," said Anne.

Susan looked doubtful.

"They are newcomers, Mrs. Dr. dear,"...much as she might have said, "They are crocodiles."

"The doctor and I were newcomers once, Susan."

"But the doctor's uncle was here for years before that. Nobody knows anything about these Bests and Campbells. But it is your house, Mrs. Dr. dear, and whom am I to object to anyone you wish to have? I remember one quilting at Mrs. Carter Flagg's many years ago when Mrs. Flagg invited a strange woman. She came in *wincey*, Mrs. Dr. dear...said she didn't think a Ladies' Aid worth dressing up for! At least there will be no fear of that with Mrs. Campbell. She is very dressy...though *I* could never see myself wearing hydrangea blue to church."

Anne could not either, but she dared not smile.

"I thought that dress was lovely with Mrs. Campbell's silver hair, Susan. And by the way, she wants your recipe for spiced gooseberry relish. She says she had some of it at the Harvest Home supper and it was delicious."

"Oh, well, Mrs. Dr. dear, it is not everyone who can make spiced gooseberry..." and no more disapproval was expressed of hydrangea blue dresses. Mrs. Campbell might henceforth appear in the costume of a Fiji Islander if she chose and Susan would find excuses for it.

The young months had grown old but autumn was still remembering summer and the quilting day was more like June than October. Every member of the Ladies' Aid who could possibly come came, looking forward pleasurably to a good dish of gossip and an Ingleside supper, besides, possibly, seeing some sweet new thing in fashions since the doctor's wife had recently been to town.

Susan, unbowed by the culinary cares that were heaped upon her, stalked about, showing the ladies to the guest-room, serene in the knowledge that not one of them possessed an apron trimmed with crochet lace five inches deep made from Number One Hundred thread. Susan had captured first prize at the Charlottetown Exhibition the week before with that lace. She and Rebecca Dew had trysted there and made a day of it, and Susan had come home that night the proudest woman in Prince Edward Island.

Susan's face was perfectly controlled but her thoughts were her own, sometimes spiced with a trifle of mild malice.

"Celia Reese is here, looking for something to laugh at as usual. Well, she will not find it at our supper table and that you may tie to. Myra Murray in red velvet...a little too sumptuous for a quilting in my opinion but I am not denying she looks well in it. At least it is not wincey. Agatha Drew...and her glasses tied on with a string as usual. Sarah Taylor...it may be her last quilting... she has got a terrible heart, the doctor says, but the spirit of her! Mrs. Donald Reese...thank the Good Lord she didn't bring Mary Anna with her but no doubt we will hear plenty. Jane Burr from the Upper Glen. She isn't a member of the Aid. Well, I shall count the spoons after supper and that you may tie to. That family were all light-fingered. Candace Crawford...she doesn't often trouble an Aid meeting but a quilting is a good place to show off her pretty hands and her diamond ring. Emma Pollock with her petticoat showing below her dress, of course...a pretty woman but flimsy-minded like all that tribe. Tillie MacAllister, don't you go and upset the jelly on the tablecloth like you did at Mrs. Palmer's quilting. Martha Crothers, you will have a decent meal for once. It is too bad your husband could not have come too...I hear he has to live on nuts or something like that. Mrs. Elder Baxter...I hear the elder has scared Harold Reese away from Mina at last. Harold always had a wishbone in place of a backbone and faint heart never won fair lady as the Good Book says. Well, we have enough for two quilts and some over to thread needles."

The quilts were set up on the broad verandah and everyone was busy with fingers and tongues. Anne and Susan were deep in preparations for supper in the kitchen, and Walter, who had been kept home from school that day because of a slight sore throat, was squatted on the verandah steps, screened from view of the quilters by a curtain of vines. He always liked to listen to older people talking. They said such surprising, mysterious things... things you could think over afterwards and weave into the very stuff of drama, things that reflected the colours and shadows, the comedies and tragedies, the jests and the sorrows, of every Four Winds clan.

Of all the women present Walter liked Mrs. Myra Murray best, with her easy infectious laugh and the jolly little wrinkles round her eyes. She could tell the simplest story and make it seem dramatic and vital; she gladdened life wherever she went; and she did look so pretty in her cherry-red velvet, with the smooth ripples in her black hair, and the little red drops in her ears. Mrs. Tom Chubb, who was thin as a needle, he liked least...perhaps because he had once heard her calling him "a sickly child." He thought Mrs. Allan Milgrave looked just like a sleek grey hen and that Mrs. Grant Clow was like nothing so much as a barrel on legs. Young Mrs. David Ransome, with her taffy-coloured hair, was very handsome, "too handsome for a farm," Susan had said when Dave married her. The young bride, Mrs. Morton MacDougall, looked like a sleepy white poppy. Edith Bailey, the Glen dressmaker, with her misty silvery curls and humorous black eyes, didn't look as if she should be "an old maid." He liked Mrs. Meade, the oldest woman there, who had gentle, tolerant eyes and listened far more than she talked, and he did not like Celia Reese, with her sly amused look as if she were laughing at everybody.

The quilters had not really started talking yet...they were discussing the weather and deciding whether to quilt in fans or diamonds, so Walter was thinking of the beauty of the ripened day, the big lawn with its magnificent trees, and the world that looked as if some great kind Being had put golden arms about it. The tinted leaves were drifting slowly down but the knightly hollyhocks were still gay against the brick wall and the poplars wove sorcery of aspen along the path to the barn. Walter was so absorbed in the loveliness around him that the quilting conversation was in full swing before he was recalled to consciousness of it by Mrs. Simon Millison's pronouncement.

"That clan were noted for their sensational funerals. Will any of you who were there ever forget what happened at Peter Kirk's funeral?"

Walter pricked up his ears. This sounded interesting. But much to his disappointment Mrs. Simon did not go on to tell what had happened. Everybody must either have been at the funeral or heard the story.

("But why are they all looking so uncomfortable about it?")

"There is no doubt that everything Clara Wilson said about Peter was true, but he is in his grave, poor man, so let us leave him there," said Mrs. Tom Chubb self-righteously...as if somebody had proposed exhuming him.

"Mary Anna is always saying such clever things," said Mrs. Donald Reese. "Do you know what she said the other day when we were starting to Margaret Hollister's funeral? 'Ma,' she said, 'will there be any ice-cream at the funeral?'"

A few women exchanged furtive amused smiles. Most of them ignored Mrs. Donald. It was really the only thing to do when she began dragging Mary Anna into the conversation as she invariably did, in season and out of season. If you gave her the least encouragement she was maddening. "Do you know what Mary Anna said?" was a standing catchword in the Glen.

"Talking of funerals," said Celia Reese, "there was a queer one in Mowbray Narrows when I was a girl. Stanton Lane had gone out West and word came back that he had died. His folks wired to have the body sent home, so it was, but Wallace MacAllister, the undertaker, advised them against opening the casket. The funeral had just got off to a good start when in walked Stanton Lane himself, hale and hearty. It was never found out who the corpse really was."

"What did they do with him?" queried Agatha Drew.

"Oh, they buried him. Wallace said it couldn't be put off. But you couldn't rightly call it a funeral with everyone so happy over Stanton's return. Mr. Dawson changed the last hymn from 'Take Comfort, Christians,' to 'Sometimes a Light Surprises,' but most people thought he'd better have left well enough alone."

"Do you know what Mary Anna said to me the other day? She said, 'Ma, do the ministers know *everything*?'"

"Mr. Dawson always lost his head in a crisis," said Jane Burr. "The Upper Glen was part of his charge then and I remember one Sunday he dismissed the congregation and then remembered that the collection hadn't been taken up. So what does he do but grab a collection plate and run round the yard with it. To be sure," added Jane, "people gave that day who never gave before or after. They didn't like to refuse the minister. But it was hardly dignified of him."

"What I had against Mr. Dawson," said Miss Cornelia, "was the unmerciful length of his prayers at a funeral. It actually came to such a pass that people said they envied the corpse. He surpassed himself at Letty Grant's funeral. I saw her mother was on the point of fainting so I gave him a good poke in the back with my umbrella and told him he'd prayed long enough."

"He buried my poor Jarvis," said Mrs. George Carr, tears dropping down. She always cried when she spoke of her husband although he had been dead for twenty years.

"His brother was a minister, too," said Christine Marsh. "He was in the Glen when I was a girl. We had a concert in the hall one night and as he was one of the speakers he was sitting on the platform. He was as nervous as his brother and he kept fidgeting his chair further and further back and all at once he went, chair and all, clean over the edge on the bank of flowers and house-plants we had arranged around the base. All that could be seen of him was his feet sticking up above the platform. Somehow, it always spoiled his preaching for me after that. His feet were *so* big."

"The Lane funeral might have been a disappointment," said Emma Pollock, "but at least it was better than not having any funeral at all. You remember the Cromwell mix-up?"

There was a chorus of reminiscent laughter. "Let us hear the story," said Mrs. Campbell. "Remember, Mrs. Pollock, I'm a stranger here and all the family sagas are quite unknown to me."

Emma didn't know what "sagas" meant but she loved to tell a story.

"Abner Cromwell lived over near Lowbridge on one of the biggest farms in that district and he was an M.P.P. in those days. He was one of the biggest frogs in the Tory puddle and acquainted with everybody of any importance on the Island. He was married to Julie Flagg, whose mother was a Reese and her grandmother was a Clow so they were connected with almost every family in Four Winds as well. One day a notice came out in the *Daily Enterprise*... Mr. Abner Cromwell had died suddenly at Lowbridge and his funeral would be held at two o'clock the next afternoon. Somehow the Abner Cromwells missed seeing the notice...and of course there were no rural telephones in those days. The next morning Abner left for Halifax to attend a Liberal convention. At two o'clock people began arriving for the funeral, coming early to get a good seat, thinking there'd be such a crowd on account of Abner being such a prominent man. And a crowd there was, believe you me. For miles around the roads were just a string of buggies and people kept pouring in till about three.

Mrs. Abner was just about crazy trying to make them believe her husband wasn't dead. Some wouldn't believe her at first. She said to me in tears that they seemed to think she'd made away with the corpse. And when they were convinced they acted as if they thought Abner ought to be dead. And they tramped all over the lawn flower-beds she was so proud of. Any number of distant relations arrived, too, expecting supper and beds for the night and she hadn't much cooked...Julie was never very forehanded, that has to be admitted. When Abner arrived home two days afterwards he found her in bed with nervous prostration and she was months getting over it. She didn't eat a thing for six weeks... well, hardly anything. I heard she said if there really had been a funeral she couldn't have been more upset. But I never believed she really did say it."

"You can't be sure," said Mrs. William MacCreery. "People do say such awful things. When they're upset the truth pops out. Julie's sister Clarice actually went and sang in the choir as usual the first Sunday after her husband was buried."

"Not even a husband's funeral could damp Clarice down long," said Agatha Drew. "There was nothing *solid* about her. Always dancing and singing."

"*I* used to dance and sing...on the shore, where nobody heard me," said Myra Murray.

"Ah, but you've grown wiser since then," said Agatha.

"No-o-o, foolisher," said Myra Murray slowly. "Too foolish now to dance along the shore."

"At first," said Emma, not to be cheated out of a complete story, "they thought the notice had been put in for a joke... because Abner had lost his election a few days before...but it turned out it was for an Amasa Cromwell, living away in the back woods the other side of Lowbridge...no relation at all. He had really died. But it was a long time before people forgave Abner the disappointment, if they ever did."

"Well, it *was* a little inconvenient driving all that distance, right in planting time, too, and finding you had your journey for your pains," said Mrs. Tom Chubb defensively.

"And people like funerals as a rule," said Mrs. Donald Reese with spirit. "We're all like children, I guess. I took Mary Anna to her uncle Gordon's funeral and she enjoyed it so. 'Ma, couldn't we dig him up and have the fun of burying him over again?' she said."

They *did* laugh at this...everybody except Mrs. Elder Baxter, who primmed up her long thin face and jabbed the quilt mercilessly. Nothing was sacred nowadays. Everyone laughed at everything. But she, an elder's wife, was not going to countenance any laughter connected with a funeral.

"Speaking of Abner, do you remember the obituary his brother John wrote for *his* wife?" asked Mrs. Allan Milgrave. "It started out with, 'God, for reasons best known to Himself, has been pleased to take my beautiful bride and leave my cousin William's ugly wife alive.' Shall I ever forget the fuss it made!"

"How did such a thing ever come to be printed at all?" asked Mrs. Best.

"Why, he was managing editor of the *Enterprise* then. He worshipped his wife...Bertha Morris, she was...and he hated Mrs. William Cromwell because she hadn't wanted him to marry Bertha. She thought Bertha too flighty."

"But she was pretty," said Elizabeth Kirk.

"The prettiest thing I ever saw in my life," agreed Mrs. Milgrave. "Good looks ran in the Morrises. But fickle...fickle as a breeze. Nobody ever knew how she came to stay in one mind long enough to marry John. They say her mother kept her up to the notch. Bertha was in love with Fred Reese but he was notorious for flirting. 'A bird in the hand is worth two in the bush,' Mrs. Morris told her."

"I've heard that proverb all my life," said Myra Murray, "and

I wonder if it's true. Perhaps the birds in the bush could *sing* and the one in the hand couldn't."

Nobody knew just what to say but Mrs. Tom Chubb said it anyhow.

"You're always so whimsical, Myra."

"Do you know what Mary Anna said to me the other day?" said Mrs. Donald. "She said, 'Ma, what will I do if nobody ever asks me to marry him?'"

"*Us* old maids could answer that, couldn't we?" asked Celia Reese, giving Edith Bailey a nudge with her elbow. Celia disliked Edith because Edith was still rather pretty and not entirely out of the running.

"Gertrude Cromwell *was* ugly," said Mrs. Grant Clow. "She had a figure like a slat. But a great housekeeper. She washed every curtain she owned every month and if Bertha washed hers once a year it was as much as ever. And her window-shades were *always* crooked. Gertrude said it just gave her the shivers to drive past John Cromwell's house. And yet John Cromwell worshipped Bertha and William just put up with Gertrude. Men *are* strange. They say William overslept on his wedding morning and dressed in such a tearing hurry he got to the church with old shoes and odd socks on."

"Well, that was better than Oliver Random," giggled Mrs. George Carr. "*He* forgot to have a wedding suit made and his old Sunday suit was simply impossible. It had been *patched.* So he borrowed his brother's best suit. It only fitted him here and there."

"And at least William and Gertrude did get married," said Mrs. Simon. "Her sister Caroline *didn't.* She and Ronny Drew quarrelled over what minister they'd have marry them and never got married at all. Ronny was so mad he went and married Edna Stone before he'd time to cool off. Caroline went to the wedding. She held her head high but her face was like death."

"But she held her tongue at least," said Sarah Taylor. "Philippa Abbey didn't. When Jim Mowbray jilted her she went to his wedding and said the bitterest things out loud all through the ceremony. They were all Anglicans, of course," concluded Sarah Taylor, as if that accounted for any vagaries.

"Did she really go to the reception afterwards wearing all the jewelry Jim had given her while they were engaged?" asked Celia Reese.

"No, she didn't! I don't know how such stories get around, I'm sure. You'd think some people never did anything but repeat gossip. I daresay Jim Mowbray lived to wish he'd stuck to Philippa. His wife kept him down good and solid...though he always had a riotous time in her absence."

"The only time I ever saw Jim Mowbray was the night the junebugs nearly stampeded the congregation at the anniversary service in Lowbridge," said Christine Crawford. "And what the junebugs left undone Jim Mowbray contributed. It was a hot night and they had all the windows open. The junebugs just poured in and blundered about in hundreds. They picked up eighty-seven dead bugs on the choir platform the next morning. Some of the women got hysterical when the bugs flew too near their faces. Just across the aisles from me the new minister's wife was sitting...Mrs. Peter Loring. She had on a big lace hat with willow plumes..."

"She was always considered far too dressy and extravagant for a minister's wife," interpolated Mrs. Elder Baxter.

"'Watch me flick that bug off Mrs. Preacher's hat,' I heard Jim Mowbray whisper...he was sitting right behind her. He leaned forward and aimed a blow at the bug...missed it, but side-swiped the hat and sent it skittering down the aisle clean to the communion railing. Jim almost had a conniption. When the minister saw his wife's hat come sailing through the air he lost his place in his sermon, couldn't find it again and gave up in despair. The choir sang the last hymn, dabbing at junebugs all the time. Jim went down and brought the hat back to Mrs. Loring. He expected a calling down, for she was said to be high-spirited. But she just stuck it on her pretty yellow head again and laughed at him. 'If you hadn't done that,' she said, 'Peter would have gone on for another twenty minutes and we'd all have been stark staring mad.' Of course, it was nice of her not to be angry but people thought it wasn't just the thing for her to say of her husband."

"But you must remember how she was born," said Martha Crothers.

"Why, *how*?"

"She was Bessy Talbot from up west. Her father's house caught fire one night and in all the fuss and upheaval Bessy was born...*out in the garden...* under the stars."

"How romantic!" said Myra Murray.

"Romantic! I call it barely *respectable*."

"But think of being born under the stars!" said Myra dreamily. "Why, she ought to have been a child of the stars...sparkling...beautiful...brave...true...with a twinkle in her eyes."

"She was all that," said Martha, "whether the stars were accountable for it or not. And a hard time she had in Lowbridge where they thought a minister's wife should be all prunes and prisms. Why, one of the elders caught her dancing around her baby's cradle one day and he told her she ought not to rejoice over her son until she found out if he was *elected* or not."

"Talking of babies, do you know what Mary Anna said the other day, 'Ma,' she said, 'do *queens* have babies?'"

"That must have been Alexander Wilson," said Mrs. Allan. "A born crab if ever there was one. He wouldn't allow his family to speak a word at meal-times, I've heard. As for laughing...there never was any done in *his* house."

"Think of a house without laughter!" said Myra. "Why, it's...*sacrilegious*."

"Alexander used to take spells when he wouldn't speak to his wife for three days at a time," continued Mrs. Allan. "It was such a relief to her," she added.

"Alexander Wilson was a good honest business man at least," said Mrs. Grant Clow stiffly. The said Alexander was her fourth cousin and the Wilsons were clannish. "He left forty thousand dollars when he died."

"Such a pity he had to *leave* it," said Celia Reese.

"His brother Jeffry didn't leave a cent," said Mrs. Clow. "He was the ne'er-do-well of that family, I must admit. Goodness knows *he* did enough laughing. Spent everything he earned... hail-fellow-well-met with everyone...and died penniless. What did *he* get out of life with all his flinging about and laughing?"

"Not much perhaps," said Myra, "but think of all he put into it. He was always *giving*...cheer, sympathy, friendliness, even money. He was rich in friends at least and Alexander never had a friend in his life."

"Jeff's friends didn't bury him," retorted Mrs. Allan. "Alexander had to do that...and put up a real fine tombstone for him, too. It cost a hundred dollars."

"But when Jeff asked him for a loan of one hundred to pay for an operation that might have saved his life, didn't Alexander refuse it?" asked Celia Drew.

"Come, come, we're getting too uncharitable," protested Mrs. Carr. "After all, we don't live in a world of forget-me-nots and daisies and everyone has some faults."

"Lem Anderson is marrying Dorothy Clark today," said Mrs. Millison, thinking it was high time the conversation took a more cheerful line. "And it isn't a year since he swore he would blow out his brains if Jane Elliott wouldn't marry him."

"Young men do say such odd things," said Mrs. Chubb. "They've kept it very close...it never leaked out till three weeks ago that they were engaged. I was talking to his mother last week and she never hinted at a wedding so soon. I am not sure that I care much for a woman who can be such a Spinx."

"*I* am surprised at Dorothy Clark taking him," said Agatha Drew. "I thought last spring that she and Frank Clow were going to make a match of it."

"*I* heard Dorothy say that Frank was the best match but she really couldn't abide the thought of seeing that nose sticking out over the sheet every morning when she woke up."

Mrs. Elder Baxter gave a spinsterish shudder and refused to join in the laughter.

"You shouldn't say such things before a young girl like Edith," said Celia, winking around the quilt.

"Is Ada Clark engaged yet?" asked Emma Pollock.

"No, not exactly," said Mrs. Milison. "Just hopeful. But she'll land him yet. Those girls all have a knack of picking husbands. Her sister Pauline married the best farm over the harbour."

"Pauline is pretty but she is full of silly notions as ever," said Mrs. Milgrave. "Sometimes I think she'll never learn any sense."

"Oh, yes, she will," said Myra Murray. "Some day she will have children of her own and she will learn wisdom from them... as you and I did."

"Where are Lem and Dorothy going to live?" asked Mrs. Meade.

"Oh, Lem has bought a farm at the Upper Glen. The old Carey place, you know, where poor Mrs. Roger Carey murdered her husband."

"Murdered her husband!"

"Oh, I'm not saying he didn't deserve it, but everybody thought she went a little too far. Yes—weed-killer in his teacup... or was it his soup? Everybody knew it but nothing was ever done about it. The spool, please, Celia."

"But do you mean to say, Mrs. Millison, that she was never tried...or punished?" gasped Mrs. Campbell.

"Well, nobody wanted to get a neighbour into a scrape like that. The Careys were well connected in the Upper Glen. Besides, she was driven to desperation. Of course nobody approves of murder as a habit but if ever a man deserved to be murdered Roger Carey did. She went to the States and married again. She's been dead for years. Her second outlived her. It all happened when I was a girl. They used to say Roger Carey's ghost *walked*."

"Surely nobody believes in ghosts in this enlightened age," said Mrs. Baxter.

"Why aren't we to believe in ghosts?" demanded Tillie MacAllister. "Ghosts are interesting. I *know* a man who was haunted by a ghost that always laughed at him...sneering like. It used to make him so mad. The scissors, please, Mrs. MacDougall."

The little bride had to be asked for the scissors twice and handed them over blushing deeply. She was not yet used to being called Mrs. MacDougall.

"The old Truax house over harbour was haunted for years... raps and knocks all over the place...a most mysterious thing," said Christine Crawford.

"All the Truaxes had bad stomachs," said Mrs. Baxter.

"Of course if you don't believe in ghosts they can't happen," said Mrs. MacAllister sulkily. "But my sister worked in a house in Nova Scotia that was haunted by chuckles of laughter."

"What a jolly ghost!" said Myra. "I shouldn't mind that."

"Likely it was owls," said the determinedly sceptical Mrs. Baxter.

"*My* mother seen angels around her deathbed," said Agatha Drew with an air of plaintive triumph.

"Angels ain't ghosts," said Mrs. Baxter.

"Speaking of mothers, how is your Uncle Parker, Tillie?" asked Mrs. Chubb.

"Very poorly by spells. We don't know what is going to come of it. It's holding us all up...about our winter clothes, I mean. But I said to my sister the other day when we were talking it over, 'We'd better get black dresses anyhow,' I said, 'and then it's no matter what happens.'"

"Do you know what Mary Anna said the other day? She said, 'Ma, I'm going to stop asking God to make my hair curly. I've asked Him every night for a week and He hasn't done a thing.'"

"I've been asking Him something for twenty years," bitterly said Mrs. Bruce Duncan, who had not spoken before or lifted her dark eyes from the quilt. She was noted for her beautiful quilting...perhaps because she was never diverted by gossip from setting each stitch precisely where it should be.

A brief hush fell over the circle. They could all guess what she had asked for...but it was not a thing to be discussed at a quilting. Mrs. Duncan did not speak again.

"Is it true that May Flagg and Billy Carter have broken up and that he is going with one of the over-harbour MacDougalls?" asked Martha Crothers after a decent interval.

"Yes. Nobody knows what happened though."

"It's sad...what little things break off matches sometimes," said Candace Crawford. "Take Dick Pratt and Lilian MacAllister...he was just starting to propose to her at a picnic when his nose began to bleed. He had to go to the brook...and he met a strange girl there who lent him her handkerchief. He fell in love and they were married in two weeks' time."

"Did you hear what happened to Big Jim MacAllister last Saturday night in Milt Cooper's store at the Harbour Head?" asked Mrs. Simon, thinking it time somebody introduced a more cheerful topic than ghosts and jiltings. "He had got into the habit of setting on the stove all summer. But Saturday night was cold and Milt had lit a fire. So when poor Big Jim sat down... well, he scorched his..."

Mrs. Simon would not say what he had scorched but she patted a portion of her anatomy silently.

"His bottom," said Walter gravely, poking his head through the creeper screen. He honestly thought that Mrs. Simon could not remember the right word.

An appalled silence descended on the quilters. Had Walter Blythe been there all the time? Everyone was raking her recollection of the tales told to recall if any of them had been too terribly unfit for the ears of youth. Mrs. Dr. Blythe was said to be so fussy about what her children heard. Before their paralyzed tongues recovered Anne had come out and asked them to come to supper.

"Just ten minutes more, Mrs. Blythe. We'll have both quilts finished then," said Elizabeth Kirk.

The quilts were finished, taken out, shaken, held up and admired.

"I wonder who'll sleep under them," said Myra Murray.

"Perhaps a new mother will hold her first baby under one of them," said Anne.

"Or little children cuddle under them on a cold prairie night," said Miss Cornelia unexpectedly.

"Or some poor old rheumatic body be cosier for them," said Mrs. Meade.

"I hope nobody *dies* under them," said Mrs. Baxter sadly.

"Do you know what Mary Anna said before I came?" said Mrs. Donald as they filed into the dining-room. "She said, 'Ma, don't forget you must eat *everything* on your plate.'"

Whereupon they all sat down and ate and drank to the glory of God, for they had done a good afternoon's work and there was very little malice in most of them, after all.

After supper they went home. Jane Burr walked as far as the village with Mrs. Simon Millison.

"I must remember all the fixings to tell ma," said Jane

wistfully, not knowing that Susan was counting the spoons. "She never gets out since she's bed-rid but she loves to hear about things. That table will be a real treat to her."

"It was just like a picture you'd seen in a magazine," agreed Mrs. Simon with a sigh. "I can cook as good a supper as anyone, if I do say it, but I can't fix up a table with a single *prestige* of style. As for that young Walter, I could spank *his* bottom with a relish. Such a turn as he gave me!"

"And I suppose Ingleside is strewn with dead characters?" the doctor was saying.

"I wasn't quilting," said Anne, "so I didn't hear what was said."

"You never do, dearie," said Miss Cornelia, who had lingered to help Susan bind the quilts. "When *you* are at the quilt they never let themselves go. They think you don't approve of gossip."

"It all depends on the kind," said Anne.

"Well, nobody really said anything too terrible today. Most of the people they talked about were dead...or ought to be," said Miss Cornelia, recalling the story of Abner Cromwell's abortive funeral with a grin. "Only Mrs. Millison had to drag in that gruesome old murder story again about Madge Carey and her husband. I remember it all. There wasn't a vestige of proof that Madge did it...except that a cat died after eating some of the soup. The animal had been sick for a week. If you ask me, Roger Carey died of appendicitis...though of course nobody knew they had appendixes then."

"And indeed I think it is a great pity they ever found out," said Susan. "The spoons are all intact, Mrs. Dr. dear, and nothing happened to the tablecloth."

"Well, I must be getting home," said Miss Cornelia. "I'll send you up some spare-ribs next week when Marshall kills the pig."

Walter was again sitting on the steps with eyes full of dreams. Dusk had fallen. Where, he wondered, had it fallen from? Did some great spirit with bat-like wings pour it all over the world from a purple jar? The moon was rising and three wind-twisted old spruces looked like three lean, hump-backed old witches hobbling up a hill against it. Was that a little faun with furry ears crouching in the shadows? Suppose he opened the door in the brick wall *now,* wouldn't he step, not into the well-known garden but into some strange land of faery, where princesses were waking from enchanted sleeps, where perhaps he might find and follow Echo as he so often longed to do? One dared not speak. Something would vanish if one did.

"Darling," said Mother coming out, "you mustn't sit here any longer. It is getting cold. Remember your throat."

The spoken word *had* broken the spell. Some magic light had gone. The lawn was still a beautiful place but it was no longer fairyland. Walter got up.

"Mother, will you tell me what happened at Peter Kirk's funeral?"

Anne thought for a moment...then shivered.

"Not now, dear. Perhaps...sometime..."

33

Anne, alone in her room...for Gilbert had been called out...sat down at her window for a few minutes of communion with the tenderness of the night and of enjoyment of the eerie charm of her moonlit room. Say what you will, thought Anne, there is always something a little strange about a moonlit room. Its whole personality is changed. It is not so friendly...so human. It is remote and aloof and wrapped up in itself. Almost it regards you as an intruder.

She was a little tired after her busy day and everything was so beautifully quiet now...the children asleep, Ingleside restored to order. There was no sound in the house except a faint rhythmic thumping from the kitchen where Susan was setting her bread.

But through the open window came the sounds of the night, every one of which Anne knew and loved. Low laughter drifted up from the harbour on the still air. Someone was singing down in the Glen and it sounded like the haunting notes of some song heard a long ago. There were silvery moonlight paths over the water but Ingleside was hooded in shadow. The trees were whispering "dark sayings of old" and an owl was hooting in Rainbow Valley.

"What a happy summer this has been," thought Anne...and then recalled with a little pang something she had heard Aunt Highland Kitty of the Upper Glen say once..."the same summer will never be coming twice."

Never quite the same. Another summer would come...but the children would be a little older and Rilla would be going to school..."and I'll have no baby left," thought Anne sadly. Jem was twelve now and there was already talk of "the Entrance"... Jem who but yesterday had been a wee baby in the old House of Dreams. Walter was shooting up and that very morning she had heard Nan teasing Di about some "boy" in school; and Di had actually blushed and tossed her red head. Well, that was life. Gladness and pain...hope and fear...and change. Always change! You could not help it. You had to let the old go and take the new to your heart...learn to love *it* and then let *it* go in turn. Spring, lovely as it was, must yield to summer and summer lose itself in autumn. The birth...the bridal...the death...

Anne suddenly thought of Walter asking to be told what had happened at Peter Kirk's funeral. She had not thought of it for years, but she had not forgotten it. Nobody who had been there, she felt sure, had forgotten it or ever would. Sitting there in the moonlit dusk she recalled it all.

It had been in November...the first November they had spent at Ingleside...following a week of Indian summer days. The Kirks lived at Mowbray Narrows but came to the Glen church and Gilbert was their doctor; so he and Anne both went to the funeral.

It had been, she remembered, a mild, calm, pearl-grey day. All around them had been the lonely brown-and-purple landscape of November, with patches of sunlight here and there on upland and slope where the sun shone through a rift in the clouds. "Kirkwynd" was so near the shore that a breath of salt wind blew through the grim firs behind it. It was a big, prosperous-looking house but Anne always thought that the gable of the L looked exactly like a long, narrow, spiteful face.

Anne paused to speak to a little knot of women on the stiff flowerless lawn. They were all good hardworking souls to whom a funeral was a not unpleasant excitement.

"I forgot to bring a handkerchief," Mrs. Bryan Blake was saying plaintively. "Whatever will I do when I cry?"

"Why will you have to cry?" bluntly asked her sister-in-law, Camilla Blake. Camilla had no use for women who cried too easily. "Peter Kirk is no relation to you and you never liked him."

"I think it is *proper* to cry at a funeral," said Mrs. Blake stiffly. "It shows *feeling* when a neighbour has been summoned to his long home."

"If nobody cries at Peter's funeral except those who liked him there won't be many wet eyes," said Mrs. Curtis Rodd dryly. "That is the truth and why mince it? He was a pious old humbug and I know it if nobody else does. *Who* is that coming at the little gate? Don't ...*don't* tell me it's Clara Wilson."

"It *is*," whispered Mrs. Bryan incredulously.

"Well, you know after Peter's first wife died she told him she would never enter his house again until she came to his funeral and she's kept her word," said Camilla Blake. "She's a sister of Peter's first wife,"...in an explanatory aside to Anne, who looked curiously at Clara Wilson as she swept past them, unseeing, her smouldering topaz eyes staring straight ahead. She was a thin slip of a woman with a dark-browed, tragic face and black hair under one of the absurd bonnets elderly women still wore...a thing of feathers and "bugles" with a skimpy nose veil. She looked at and spoke to no one, as her long black taffeta skirt swished over the grass and up the verandah steps.

"There's Jed Clinton at the door, putting on his funeral face," said Camilla sarcastically. "He's evidently thinking it is time we went in. It's always been his boast that at *his* funerals everything goes according to schedule. He's never forgiven Winnie Clow for fainting *before* the sermon. It wouldn't have been so bad afterwards. Well, nobody is likely to faint at *this* funeral. Olivia isn't the fainting kind."

"Jed Clinton...the Lowbridge undertaker," said Mrs. Reese. "Why didn't they have the Glen man?"

"Who? Carter Flagg? Why, woman dear, Peter and him have been at daggers drawn all their lives. Carter wanted Amy Wilson, you know."

"A good many wanted her," said Camilla. "She was a very pretty girl, with her coppery red hair and inky black eyes. Though people thought Clara the handsomer of the two then. It's odd she never married. There's the minister at last...and the Rev. Mr. Owen of Lowbridge with him. Of course he is Olivia's cousin. All right except that he puts too many 'Oh's' in his prayers. We'd better go in or Jed will have a conniption."

Anne paused to look at Peter Kirk on her way to a chair. She had never liked him. "He has a cruel face," she thought, the first time she had ever seen him. Handsome, yes...but with cold steely eyes even then becoming pouchy, and the thin pinched merciless mouth of a miser. He was known to be selfish and arrogant in his dealings with his fellow-men in spite of his profession of piety and his unctuous prayers. "Always feels his importance," she had heard someone say once. Yet, on the whole, he had been respected and looked up to.

He was as arrogant in his death as in his life and there was something about the too-long fingers clasped over his still breast that made Anne shudder. She thought of a woman's heart being held in them and glanced at Olivia Kirk, sitting opposite to her in her mourning. Olivia was a tall, fair, handsome woman with large blue eyes... "no ugly woman for me," Peter Kirk had said once...and her face was composed and expressionless. There was no apparent trace of tears...but, then, Olivia had been a Random and the Randoms were not emotional. At least she sat decorously and the most heartbroken widow in the world could not have worn heavier weeds.

The air was cloyed with the perfume of the flowers that banked the coffin...for Peter Kirk, who had never known flowers existed. His lodge had sent a wreath, the church had sent one, the Conservative Association had sent one, the school trustees had sent one, the Cheese Board had sent one. His one, long-alienated son had sent nothing, but the Kirk clan at large had sent a huge anchor of white roses with "Harbour At Last" in red rosebuds across it, and there was one from Olivia herself...a pillow of calla-lilies. Camilla Blake's face twitched as she looked at it and Anne remembered that she had once heard Camilla say that she had been at Kirkwynd soon after Peter's second marriage when Peter had fired out of the window a potted calla-lily which the bride had brought with her. He wasn't, so he said, going to have his house cluttered up with weeds.

Olivia had apparently taken it very coolly and there had been no more calla-lilies at Kirkwynd. Could it be possible that

Olivia...but Anne looked at Mrs. Kirk's placid face and dismissed the suspicion. After all, it was generally the florist who suggested the flowers.

The choir sang "Death like a narrow sea divides that heavenly land from ours" and Anne caught Camilla's eye and knew they were both wondering just how Peter Kirk would fit into that heavenly land. Anne could almost hear Camilla saying, "Fancy Peter Kirk with a harp and halo if you dare."

The Rev. Mr. Owen read a chapter and prayed, with many "Oh's" and many entreaties that sorrowing hearts might be comforted. The Glen minister gave an address which many privately considered entirely too fulsome, even allowing for the fact that you had to say something good of the dead. To hear Peter Kirk called an affectionate father and a tender husband, a kind neighbour and an earnest Christian was, they felt, a misuse of language. Camilla took refuge behind her handkerchief, *not* to shed tears, and Stephen Macdonald cleared his throat once or twice. Mrs. Bryan must have borrowed a handkerchief from someone, for she was weeping into it, but Olivia's down-dropped blue eyes remained tearless.

Jed Clinton drew a breath of relief. All had gone beautifully. Another hymn...the customary parade for a last look at "the remains"...and another successful funeral would be added to his long list.

There was a slight disturbance in a corner of the large room and Clara Wilson made her way through the maze of chairs to the table beside the casket. She turned there and faced the assembly. Her absurd bonnet had slipped a trifle to one side and a loose end of heavy black hair had escaped from its coil and hung down on her shoulder. But nobody thought Clara Wilson looked absurd. Her long sallow face was flushed, her haunted tragic eyes were flaming. She was a woman possessed. Bitterness, like some gnawing incurable disease, seemed to pervade her being.

"You have listened to a pack of lies...you people who have come here 'to pay your respects'...or glut your curiosity, whichever it was. Now I shall tell you the truth about Peter Kirk. *I* am no hypocrite...I never feared him living and I do not fear him now that he is dead. Nobody has ever dared to tell the truth about him to his face but it is going to be told now...here at his funeral where he has been called a good husband and a kind neighbour. A good husband! He married my sister Amy...my beautiful sister, Amy. You all know how sweet and lovely she was. He made her life a misery to her. He tortured and humiliated her...he *liked* to do it. Oh, he went to church regularly...and made long prayers...and paid his debts. But he was a tyrant and a bully...his very dog ran when he heard him coming.

"I told Amy she would repent marrying him. I helped her make her wedding dress...I'd rather have made her shroud. She was wild about him then, poor thing, but she hadn't been his wife a week before she knew what he was. His mother had been a slave and he expected his wife to be one. 'There will be no arguments in *my* household,' he told her. She hadn't the spirit to argue...her heart was broken. Oh, I know what she went through, my poor pretty darling. He crossed her in everything. She couldn't have a flower-garden...she couldn't even have a kitten...I gave her one and he drowned it. She had to account to him for every cent she spent. Did ever any of you see her in a decent stitch of clothes? He would fault her for wearing her best hat if it looked like rain. Rain couldn't hurt any hat *she* had, poor soul. Her that loved pretty clothes! He was always sneering at her people. He never laughed in his life...did any of you ever hear him really laugh? He smiled...oh yes, he always smiled, calmly and sweetly when he was doing the most maddening things. He smiled when he told her after her little baby was born dead that she might as well have died, too, if she couldn't have anything but dead brats. She died after ten years of it...and I was glad she had escaped him. I told him then I'd never enter his house again till I came to his funeral. Some of you heard me. I've kept my word and now I've come and told the truth about him. It *is* the truth...*You* know it"... she pointed fiercely at Stephen Macdonald..."*You* know it"... the long finger darted at Camilla Blake..."*You* know it"...Olivia Kirk did not move a muscle..."*You* know it"...the poor minister himself felt as if that finger stabbed completely through him. "I cried at Peter Kirk's wedding but I told him I'd laugh at his funeral. And I am going to do it."

She swished furiously about and bent over the casket. Wrongs that had festered for years had been avenged. She had wreaked her hatred at last. Her whole body vibrated with triumph and satisfaction as she looked down at the cold quiet face of a dead man. Everybody listened for the burst of vindictive laughter. It did not come. Clara Wilson's angry face suddenly changed... twisted...crumpled up like a child's. Clara was...crying.

She turned, with the tears streaming down her ravaged cheeks, to leave the room. But Olivia Kirk rose before her and laid a hand on her arm. For a moment the two women looked at each other. The room was engulfed in a silence that seemed like a personal presence.

"Thank you, Clara Wilson," said Olivia Kirk. Her face was as inscrutable as ever but there was an undertone in her calm, even voice that made Anne shudder. She felt as if a pit had suddenly opened before her eyes. Clara Wilson might hate Peter Kirk, alive and dead, but Anne felt that her hatred was a pale thing compared to Olivia Kirk's.

Clara went out, weeping, passing an infuriated Jed with a spoiled funeral on his hands. The minister, who had intended to announce for a last hymn, "Asleep in Jesus," thought better of it and simply pronounced a tremulous benediction. Jed did not make the usual announcement that friends and relatives might now take a parting look at "the remains." The only decent thing to do, he felt, was to shut down the cover of the casket at once and bury Peter Kirk out of sight as soon as possible.

Anne drew a long breath as she went down the verandah steps. How lovely the cold fresh air was after that stifling, perfumed room where two women's bitterness had been as their torment.

The afternoon had grown colder and greyer. Little groups here and there on the lawn were discussing the affair with muted voices. Clara Wilson could still be seen crossing a sere pasture field on her way home.

"Well, didn't that beat all?" said Nelson dazedly.

"Shocking...shocking!" said Elder Baxter.

"Why didn't some of us stop her?" demanded Henry Reese.

"Because you all wanted to hear what she had to say," retorted Camilla.

"It wasn't...decorous," said Uncle Sandy MacDougall. He had got hold of a word that pleased him and rolled it under his tongue. "Not decorous. A funeral should be decorous whatever else it may be...decorous."

"Gosh, ain't life funny?" said Augustus Palmer.

"I mind when Peter and Amy began keeping company," mused old James Porter. "I was courting my woman that same winter. Clara was a fine-looking bit of goods then. And what a cherry pie she could make!"

"She was always a bitter-tongued girl," said Boyce Warren. "I suspected there'd be dynamite of some kind when I saw her coming but I didn't dream it would take that form. And Olivia! Would you have thought it? Weemen *are* a queer lot."

"It will make quite a story for the rest of our lives," said Camilla. "After all, I suppose if things like this never happened history would be dull stuff."

A demoralized Jed had got his pall-bearers rounded up and the casket carried out. As the hearse drove down the lane, followed by the slow-moving procession of buggies, a dog was heard howling heartbrokenly in the barn. Perhaps, after all, one living creature mourned Peter Kirk.

Stephen Macdonald joined Anne as she waited for Gilbert. He was a tall Upper Glen man with the head of an old Roman emperor. Anne had always liked him.

"Smells like snow," he said. "It always seems to me that November is a *homesick* time. Does it ever strike you that way, Mrs. Blythe?"

"Yes. The year is looking back sadly to her lost spring."

"Spring...spring! Mrs. Blythe, I'm getting old. I find myself imagining that the seasons are changing. Winter isn't what it was...I don't recognize summer...and spring...there are *no* springs now. At least, that's how we feel when folks we used to know don't come back to share them with us. Poor Clara Wilson now... what did you think of it all?"

"Oh, it was heartbreaking. Such hatred..."

"Ye-e-e-s. You see, she was in love with Peter herself long ago...terribly in love. Clara was the handsomest girl in Mowbray Narrows then...little dark curls all round her cream-white face... but Amy was a laughing, lilting thing. Peter dropped Clara and took up with Amy. It's strange the way we're made, Mrs. Blythe."

There was an eerie stir in the wind-torn firs behind Kirkwynd; far away a snow-squall whitened over a hill where a row of lombardies stabbed the grey sky. Everybody was hurrying to get away before it reached Mowbray Narrows.

"Have I any right to be so happy when other women are so miserable?" Anne wondered to herself as they drove home, remembering Olivia Kirk's eyes as she thanked Clara Wilson.

Anne got up from her window. It was nearly twelve years ago now. Clara Wilson was dead and Olivia Kirk had gone to the coast where she had married again. She had been much younger than Peter.

"Time is kinder than we think," thought Anne. "It's a dreadful mistake to cherish bitterness for years...hugging it to our hearts like a treasure. But I think the story of what happened at Peter Kirk's funeral is one which Walter must never know. It was certainly no story for children."

34

Rilla sat on the verandah steps at Ingleside with one knee crossed over the other...such adorable little fat brown knees!...very busy being unhappy. And if anyone asks why a petted little puss should be unhappy that inquirer must have forgotten her own childhood when things that were the merest trifles to grownups were dark and dreadful tragedies to her. Rilla was lost in deeps of despair because Susan had told her she was going to bake one of her silver-and-gold cakes for the Orphanage social that evening and she, Rilla, must carry it to the church in the afternoon.

Don't ask me why Rilla felt she would rather die than carry a cake through the village to the Glen St. Mary Presbyterian church. Tots get odd notions into their little pates at times and somehow Rilla had got it into hers that it was a shameful and humiliating thing to be seen carrying a cake anywhere. Perhaps it was because, one day when she was only five, she had met old Tillie Pake carrying a cake down the street with all the little village boys yelping at her heels and making fun of her. Old Tillie lived down at the Harbour Mouth and was a very dirty ragged old woman.

"Old Tillie Pake
Up and stole a cake
And it give her stomach-ache,"

chanted the boys.

To be classed with Tillie Pake was something Rilla just could not bear. The idea had become lodged in her mind that you just "couldn't be a lady" and carry cakes about. So this was why she sat disconsolately on the steps and the dear little mouth, with one front tooth missing, was without its usual smile. Instead of looking as if she understood what daffodils were thinking about or as if she shared with the golden rose a secret they alone knew, she looked like one crushed forever. Even her big hazel eyes that almost shut up when she laughed, were mournful and tormented, instead of being the usual pools of allurement. "It's the fairies that have touched your eyes," Aunt Kitty MacAllister told her once. Her father vowed she was born a charmer and had smiled at Dr. Parker half an hour after she was born. Rilla could, as yet, talk better with her eyes than her tongue, for she had a decided lisp. But she would grow out of that...she was growing fast. Last year Daddy had measured her by a rosebush; this year it was the phlox; soon it would be the hollyhocks and she would be going to school. Rilla had been very happy and very well-contented with herself until this terrible announcement of Susan's. Really, Rilla told the sky indignantly, Susan had no sense of shame. To be sure, Rilla pronounced it "thenth of thame" but the lovely soft-blue sky looked as if it understood.

Mummy and Daddy had gone to Charlottetown that morning and all the other children were in school, so Rilla and Susan were alone at Ingleside. Ordinarily Rilla would have been delighted under such circumstances. She was never lonely; she would have been glad to sit there on the steps or on her own particular mossy green stone in Rainbow Valley, with a fairy kitten or two for company, and spin fancies about everything she saw...the corner of the lawn that looked like a merry little land of butterflies...the poppies floating over the garden...that great fluffy cloud all alone in the sky...the big bumblebees booming over the nasturtiums...the honeysuckle that hung down to touch her red-brown curls with a yellow finger...the wind that blew... where did it blow to?...Cock Robin, who was back again and was strutting importantly along the railing of the verandah, wondering why Rilla would not play with him...Rilla who could think of nothing but the terrible fact that she must carry a cake...a *cake*...through the village to the church for the old social they were getting up for the orphans. Rilla was dimly aware that the Orphanage was at Lowbridge and that poor little children lived there who had no fathers or mothers. She felt terribly sorry for them. But not even for the orphanest of orphans was small Rilla Blythe willing to be seen in public *carrying a cake.*

Perhaps if it rained she wouldn't have to go. It didn't *look* like rain but Rilla clasped her hands together...there was a dimple at the root of every finger...and said earnestly:

"Plethe, dear God, make it rain hard. Make it rain pitchforkth. Or elth..." Rilla thought of another saving possibility, "make Thusanth cake burn...burn to a crithp."

Alas, when dinner time came the cake, done to a turn, filled and iced, was sitting triumphantly on the kitchen table. It was a favourite cake of Rilla's..."Gold-and-silver cake" did sound so *luxuriant...*but she felt that never again would she be able to eat a mouthful of it.

Still...wasn't that thunder rolling over the low hills across the harbour? Perhaps God had heard her prayer...perhaps there would be an earthquake before it was time to go. Couldn't she take a pain in her stomach if worst came to worst? No. Rilla shuddered. That would mean castor-oil. Better the earthquake!

The rest of the children did not notice that Rilla, sitting in her own dear chair, with the saucy white duck worked in crewels on the back, was very quiet. Thelfith pigth! If Mummy had been home *she* would have noticed it. Mummy had seen right away how troubled she was that dreadful day when Dad's picture had come out in the *Enterprise.* Rilla was crying bitterly in bed when Mummy came in and found out that Rilla thought it was only murderers that had their pictures in the papers. It had not taken Mummy long to put *that* to rights. Would Mummy like to see *her* daughter carrying cake through the Glen like old Tillie Pake?

Rilla found it hard to eat any dinner, though Susan had put down her own lovely blue plate with the wreath of rosebuds on it that Aunt Rachel Lynde had sent her on her last birthday and which she was generally allowed to have only on Sundays. Blue plateth and rothbudth! When you had to do such a shameful thing! Still, the fruit puffs Susan had made for dessert *were* nice.

"Thuthan, can't Nan and Di take the cake after thchool?" she pleaded.

"Di is going home from school with Jessie Reese and Nan has a bone in her leg," said Susan, under the impression that she was being joky. "Besides it would be too late. The committee wants all the cakes in by three so they can cut them up and arrange the tables before they go home to have their suppers. Why in the world don't you want to go, Roly-poly? You always think it is such fun to go for the mail."

Rilla *was* a bit of a roly-poly but she hated to be called that.

"I don't want to hurt my feelingth" she explained stiffly.

Susan laughed. Rilla was beginning to say things that made the family laugh. She never could understand why they laughed because she was always in earnest. Only Mummy never laughed; she hadn't laughed even when she found out that Rilla thought Daddy was a murderer.

"The social is to make money for poor little boys and girls who haven't any kind fathers or mothers," explained Susan...as if she was a baby who didn't understand!

"I'm next thing to an orphan," said Rilla. "I've only got one father and mother."

Susan just laughed again. *Nobody* understood.

"You know your mother *promised* the committee that cake, pet. I have not time to take it myself and it *must* go. So put on your blue gingham and toddle off."

"My doll hath been tooken ill," said Rilla desperately. "I mutht put her to bed and thtay with her. Maybe itth ammonia."

"Your doll will do very well till you get back. You can go and come in half an hour," was Susan's heartless response.

There was no hope. Even God had failed her...there wasn't a sign of rain. Rilla, too near tears to protest any further, went up and put on her new smocked organdy and her Sunday hat, trimmed with daisies. Perhaps if she looked *respectable* people wouldn't think she was like old Tillie Pake.

"I think my fathe itth clean if you will kindly look behind my earth," she told Susan with great stateliness.

She was afraid Susan might scold her for putting on her best dress and hat. But Susan merely inspected her ears, handed her a basket containing the cake, told her to mind her pretty manners and for goodness' sake not to stop to talk to every cat she met.

Rilla made a rebellious "face" at Gog and Magog and marched away. Susan looked after her tenderly.

"Fancy our baby being old enough to carry a cake all alone to the church," she thought, half proudly, half sorrowfully, as she went back to work, blissfully unaware of the torture she was inflicting on a small mite she would have given her life for.

Rilla had not felt so mortified since the time she had fallen asleep in church and tumbled off the seat. Ordinarily she loved going down to the village; there were so many interesting things to see: but today Mrs. Carter Flagg's fascinating clothesline, with all those lovely quilts on it, did not win a glance from Rilla, and the new cast-iron deer Mr. Augustus Palmer had set up in his yard left her cold. She had never passed it before without wishing they could have one like it on the lawn at Ingleside. But what were cast-iron deer now? Hot sunshine poured along the street like a river and *everybody* was out. Two girls went by, whispering to each other. Was it about *her*? She imagined what they might be saying. A man driving along the road stared at her. He was really wondering if that could be the Blythe baby and by George, what a little beauty she was! But Rilla felt that his eyes pierced the basket and saw the cake. And when Annie Drew drove by with her father Rilla was sure she was laughing at her. Annie Drew was ten and a very big girl in Rilla's eyes.

Then there was a whole crowd of boys and girls on Russell's corner. *She had to walk past them.* It was dreadful to feel that their eyes were all looking at her and then at each other. She marched by, so proudly desperate that they all thought she was stuck-up and had to be brought down a peg or two. *They'd* show that kitten-faced thing! A regular hoity-toity like all those Ingleside girls! Just because they lived up at the big house!

Millie Flagg strutted along behind her, imitating her walk and scuffing up clouds of dust over them both.

"Where's the basket going with the child?" shouted "Slicky" Drew.

"There's a smudge on your nose, Jam-face," jeered Bill Palmer.

"Cat got your tongue?" said Sarah Warren.

"Snippet!" sneered Beenie Bentley.

"Keep on your side of the road or I'll make you eat a junebug," big Sam Flagg stopped gnawing a raw carrot long enough to say.

"Look at her blushing," giggled Mamie Taylor.

"Bet you're taking a cake to the Presbyterian church," said Charlie Warren. "Half dough like all Susan Baker's cakes."

Pride would not let Rilla cry, but there was a limit to what one could bear. After all, an Ingleside cake...

"The next time any of you are thick I'll tell my father not to give you any medithine," she said defiantly.

Then she stared in dismay. That couldn't be Kenneth Ford coming around the corner of the Harbour road! It couldn't be! It was!

It was not to be borne. Ken and Walter were pals and Rilla thought in her small heart that Ken was the nicest, handsomest boy in the whole world. He seldom took much notice of her... though once he had given her a chocolate duck. And one unforgettable day he had sat down beside her on a mossy stone in Rainbow Valley and told her the story of the Three Bears and the Little House in the Wood. But she was content to worship afar. And now this wonderful being had caught her *carrying a cake!*

"'Lo, Roly-poly! Heat's something fierce, isn't it? Hope I'll get a slice of that cake tonight."

So he knew it was a cake! Everybody knew it!

Rilla was through the village and thought the worst was over when the worst happened. She looked down a side-road and saw her Sunday School teacher, Miss Emmy Parker, coming along it. Miss Emmy Parker was still quite a distance away but Rilla knew her by her dress...that frilled organdy dress of pale green with clusters of little white flowers all over it...the "cherry blossom dress," Rilla secretly called it. Miss Emmy had it on in Sunday School last Sunday and Rilla had thought it the sweetest dress she had ever seen. But then Miss Emmy always wore such pretty dresses...sometimes lacy and frilly, sometimes with the whisper of silk about them.

Rilla worshipped Miss Emmy. She was so pretty and dainty, with her white, white skin and her brown, brown eyes and her sad, sweet smile...sad, another small girl had whispered to Rilla one day, because the man she was going to marry had died. She was so glad she was in Miss Emmy's class. She would have hated to be in Miss Florrie Flagg's class...Florrie Flagg was *ugly* and Rilla couldn't bear an ugly teacher.

When Rilla met Miss Emmy away from Sunday School and Miss Emmy smiled and spoke to her it was one of the high moments of life for Rilla. Only to be nodded to on the street by Miss Emmy gave a strange, sudden lift of the heart and when Miss Emmy had invited all her class to a soap-bubble party, where they made the bubbles red with strawberry juice, Rilla had all but died of sheer bliss.

But to meet Miss Emmy, carrying a cake, was just not to be endured and Rilla was not going to endure it. Besides, Miss Emmy was going to get up a dialogue for the next Sunday School concert and Rilla was cherishing secret hopes of being asked to take the fairy's part in it...a fairy in scarlet with a little peaked green hat. But there would be no use in hoping for that if Miss Emmy saw her *carrying a cake.*

Miss Emmy was not going to see her! Rilla was standing on the little bridge crossing the brook, which was quite deep and creek-like just there. She snatched the cake out of the basket and hurled it into the brook where the alders met over a dark pool. The cake hurtled through the branches and sank with a plop and a gurgle. Rilla felt a wild spasm of relief and freedom and *escape*, as she turned to meet Miss Emmy, who, she now saw, was carrying a big bulgy brown paper parcel.

Miss Emmy smiled down at her, from beneath a little green hat with a tiny orange feather in it.

"Oh, you're beautiful, teacher...beautiful," gasped Rilla adoringly.

Miss Emmy smiled again. Even when your heart is broken... and Miss Emmy truly believed hers was...it is not unpleasant to be given such a sincere compliment.

"It's the new hat, I expect, dear. Fine feathers, you know. I suppose"...glancing at the empty basket..."you've been taking your cake up for the social. What a pity you're not going instead of coming. I'm taking mine...such a big, gooey chocolate cake."

Rilla gazed up piteously, unable to utter a word. Miss Emmy was *carrying a cake,* therefore, it could not be a disgraceful thing to carry a cake. And she...oh, what had she done? She had thrown Susan's lovely gold-and-silver cake into the brook...and she had lost the chance of walking up to the church with Miss Emmy, *both* carrying cakes!

After Miss Emmy had gone on Rilla went home with her dreadful secret. She buried herself in Rainbow Valley until supper time, when again nobody noticed that she was very quiet. She was terribly afraid Susan would ask to whom she had given the cake but there were no awkward questions. After supper the others went to play in Rainbow Valley but Rilla sat alone on the steps until the sun went down and the sky was all a windy gold behind Ingleside and the lights sprang up in the village below. Always Rilla liked to watch them blooming out, here and there, all over the Glen, but tonight she was interested in nothing. She had never been so unhappy in her life. She just didn't see how she could live. The evening deepened to purple and she was still more unhappy. A most delectable odour of maple sugar buns drifted out to her...Susan had waited for the evening coolness to do the family baking...but maple sugar buns, like all else, were just vanity. Miserably she climbed the stairs and went to bed under the new, pink-flowered spread she had once been so proud of. But she could not sleep. She was still haunted by the ghost of the cake she had drowned. Mother had promised the committee that cake...what would they think of Mother for not sending it? And it would have been the prettiest cake there! The wind had such a lonely sound tonight. It was reproaching her. It was saying, "Silly...silly...silly," over and over again.

"What is keeping you awake, pet?" said Susan, coming in with a maple sugar bun.

"Oh, Thuthan, I'm...I'm jutht tired of being *me.*"

Susan looked troubled. Come to think of it, the child had looked tired at supper.

"And of course the doctor's away. Doctors' families die and shoemakers' wives go barefoot," she thought. Then aloud:

"I am going to see if you have a temperature, my pet."

"No, no, Thuthan. It'th jutht...I've done thomething dreadful, Thuthan...Thatan made me do it...no, no, he didn't, Thuthan...I did it mythelf, I...I threw the cake into the creek."

"Land of hope and glory!" said Susan blankly. "Whatever made you do that?"

"Do what?" It was Mother, home from town. Susan retreated gladly, thankful that Mrs. Doctor had the situation in hand. Rilla sobbed out the whole story.

"Darling, I don't understand. *Why* did you think it was such a dreadful thing to take a cake to the church?"

"I thought it wath jutht like old Tillie Pake, Mummy. And I've dithgrathed you! Oh, Mummy, if you'll forgive me I'll never be naughty again...and I'll tell the committee you *did* thend a cake..."

"Never mind the committee, darling. They would have more than enough cakes...they always do. It's not likely anyone would notice we didn't send one. We just won't talk of this to anybody. But always after this, Bertha Marilla Blythe, remember the fact that neither Susan nor Mother would ever ask you to do anything disgraceful."

Life was sweet again. Daddy came to the door to say, "Goodnight, Kittenkin," and Susan slipped in to say they were going to have a chicken pie for dinner tomorrow.

"With lotth of gravy, Thuthan?"

"Lashings of it."

"And may I have a *brown* egg for breakfath, Thuthan. I don't detherve it..."

"You shall have two brown eggs if you want them. And now you *must* eat your bun and go to sleep, little pet."

Rilla ate her bun but before she went to sleep she slipped out of bed and knelt down. Very earnestly she said:

"Dear God, pleathe make me a good and obedient child alwayth, no matter what I'm told to do. And bleth dear Mith Emmy and all the poor orphanth."

35

The Ingleside children played together and walked together and had all kinds of adventures together; and each of them, in addition to this, had his and her own inner life of dream and fancy. Especially Nan, who from the very first had fashioned secret drama for herself out of everything she heard or saw or read and sojourned in realms of wonder and romance quite unsuspected in her household circle. At first she wove patterns of pixy dances and elves in haunted valleys and dryads in birch trees. She and the great willow at the gate had whispered secrets and the old empty Bailey house at the upper end of Rainbow Valley was the ruin of a haunted tower. For weeks she might be a king's daughter imprisoned in a lonely castle by the sea...for months she was a nurse in a leper colony in India or some land "far, far away." "Far, far away" had always been words of magic to Nan...like faint music over a windy hill.

As she grew older she built up her drama about the real people she saw in her little life. Especially the people in church. Nan liked to look at the people in church because everyone was so nicely dressed. It was almost miraculous. They looked so different from what they did on week days.

The quiet respectable occupants of the various family pews would have been amazed and perhaps a little horrified if they had known the romances the demure, brown-eyed maiden in the Ingleside pew was concocting about them. Black-browed, kind-hearted Annetta Millison would have been thunderstruck to know that Nan Blythe pictured her as a kidnapper of children, boiling them alive to make potions that would keep her young forever. Nan pictured this so vividly that she was half frightened to death when she met Annetta Millison once in a twilight lane astir with the golden whisper of buttercups. She was positively unable to reply to Annetta's friendly greeting and Annetta reflected that Nan Blythe was really getting to be a proud and saucy little puss and needed a bit of training in good manners. Pale Mrs. Rod Palmer never dreamed that she had poisoned someone and was dying of remorse. Elder Gordon MacAllister of the solemn face had no notion that a curse had been put on him at birth by a witch, the result being that he could never smile. Dark-moustached Fraser Palmer of a blameless life little knew that when Nan Blythe looked at him she was thinking, "I am sure that man has committed a dark and desperate deed. He looks as if he had some dreadful secret on his conscience." And Archibald Fyfe had no suspicion that when Nan Blythe saw him coming she was busy making up a rhyme as a reply to any remark he might make because he was never to be spoken to except in rhyme. He never did speak to her, being exceedingly afraid of children, but Nan got no end of fun out of desperately and quickly inventing a rhyme.

> "*I'm very well, thank you, Mr. Fyfe,*
> *How are you yourself and your wife?*"

or,

"Yes, it is a very fine day,
Just the right kind for making hay."

There is no knowing what Mrs. Morton Kirk would have said if she had been told that Nan Blythe would never come to her house...supposing she had ever been invited...because there was a *red footprint* on her doorstep; and her sister-in-law, placid, kind, unsought Elizabeth Kirk, did not dream she was an old maid because her lover had dropped dead at the altar just before the wedding ceremony.

It was all very amusing and interesting and Nan never lost her way between fact and fiction until she became possessed with the Lady with the Mysterious Eyes.

It is no use asking how dreams grow. Nan herself could never have told you how it came about. It started with the GLOOMY HOUSE...Nan saw it always just like that, spelled in capitals. She liked to spin her romances about places as well as people and the GLOOMY HOUSE was the only place around, except the old Bailey house, which lent itself to romance. Nan had never seen the HOUSE itself...she only knew that it was there, behind a thick dark spruce on the Lowbridge side-road, and had been vacant from time immemorial,—so Susan said. Nan didn't know what time immemorial was but it was a most fascinating phrase, just suited to gloomy houses.

Nan always ran madly past the lane that led up to the GLOOMY HOUSE when she went along the side-road to visit her chum, Dora Clow. It was a long dark tree-arched lane with thick grass growing between its ruts and ferns waist-high under the spruces. There was a long grey maple bough near the tumbledown gate that looked exactly like a crooked old arm reaching down to encircle her. Nan never knew when it might reach a wee bit further and grab her. It gave her such a thrill to escape it.

One day Nan, to her astonishment, heard Susan saying that Thomasine Fair had come to live in the GLOOMY HOUSE... or, as Susan unromantically phrased it, the old MacAllister place.

"She will find it rather lonely, I should imagine," Mother had said. "It's so out-of-the-way."

"She will not mind that," said Susan. "She never goes anywhere, not even to church. Has not gone anywhere for years... though they say she walks in her garden at night. Well, well, to think what she has come to...her that was so handsome and such a terrible flirt. The hearts she broke in her day! And look at her now! Well, it is a warning and that you may tie to."

Just to whom it was a warning Susan did not explain and nothing more was said, for nobody at Ingleside was very much interested in Thomasine Fair. But Nan, who had grown a little tired of all her old dream lives and was agog for something new, seized on Thomasine Fair in the GLOOMY HOUSE. Bit by bit, day after day, night after night...one could believe *anything* at night...she built up a legend about her until the whole thing flowered out unrecognisably and became a dearer dream to Nan than any she had hitherto known. Nothing before had ever seemed so entrancing, so *real,* as this vision of the Lady with the Mysterious Eyes. Great black velvet eyes...*hollow* eyes...*haunted* eyes...filled with remorse for the hearts she had broken. *Wicked* eyes...anyone who broke hearts and never went to church must be wicked. Wicked people were so interesting. The Lady was burying herself from the world as a penance for her crimes.

Could she be a princess? No, princesses were too scarce in P. E. Island. But she was tall, slim, remote, icily beautiful like a princess, with long jet-black hair in two thick braids over her shoulders, right to her feet. She would have a clear-cut ivory face, a beautiful Grecian nose, like the nose of Mother's Artemis of the Silver Bow, and white lovely hands which she would wring as she walked in the garden at night, waiting for the one true lover she had disdained and learned too late to love...you perceive how the legend was growing?...while her long black velvet skirts trailed over the grass. She would wear a golden girdle and great pearl earrings in her ears and she must live her life of shadow and mystery until the lover came to set her free. Then she would repent of her old wickedness and heartlessness and hold out her beautiful hands to him and bend her proud head in submission at last. They would sit by the fountain...there was a fountain by this time...and pledge their vows anew and she would follow him, "over the hills and faraway, beyond their utmost purple rim," just as the Sleeping Princess did in the poem Mother read to her one night from the old volume of Tennyson Father had given her long, long ago. But the lover of the Mysterious Eyed gave her jewels beyond all compare.

The GLOOMY HOUSE would be beautifully furnished, of course, and there would be secret rooms and staircases, and the Lady with the Mysterious Eyes would sleep on a bed made of mother-of-pearl under a canopy of purple velvet. She would be attended by a greyhound...a brace of them...a whole retinue of them...and she would always be listening...listening...listening... for the music of a very far-off harp. But she could not hear it as long as she was wicked until her lover came and forgave her... and there you were.

Of course is sounds very foolish. Dreams do sound so foolish when they are put into cold brutal words. Ten-year-old Nan never put hers into words...she only lived them. This dream of the wicked Lady with the Mysterious Eyes became as real to her as the life that went on around her. It took possession of her. For two years now it had been part of her...she had somehow come, in some strange way, to believe it. Not for worlds would she have told anyone, not even Mother, about it. It was her own peculiar treasure, her inalienable secret, without which she could no longer imagine life going on. She would rather steal off by herself to dream of the Lady with the Mysterious Eyes than play in Rainbow Valley.

Anne noticed this tendency and worried a little over it. Nan was getting too much that way. Gilbert wanted to send her up to Avonlea for a visit, but Nan, for the first time, pleaded passionately not to be sent. She didn't want to leave home, she said piteously. To herself she said she would just die if she had to go so far away from the strange sad lovely Lady with the Mysterious Eyes. True, the Mysterious Eyed never went out anywhere. But she *might* go out some day and if she, Nan, were away she would miss seeing her. How wonderful it would be to get just a glimpse of her! Why, the very road along which she passed would be forever romantic. The day on which it happened would be different from all other days. She would make a ring around it in the calendar. Nan had got to the point when she greatly desired to see her just once. She knew quite well that much she had imagined about her was nothing but imagination. But she hadn't the slightest doubt that Thomasine Fair was young and lovely and wicked and alluring...Nan was by this time absolutely certain she had heard Susan say so...and as long as she was that, Nan could go on imagining things about her forever.

Nan could hardly believe her ears when Susan said to her one morning:

"There is a parcel I want to send up to Thomasine Fair at the old MacAllister place. Your father brought it out from town last night. Will you run up with it this afternoon, pet?"

Just like that! Nan caught her breath. *Would* she? Did dreams really come true in such fashion? She would see the GLOOMY HOUSE...she would see her beautiful wicked Lady with the Mysterious Eyes. Actually see her...perhaps hear her speak... perhaps...oh, bliss!...touch her slender white hand. As for the greyhounds and the fountain and so forth, Nan knew she had only imagined them but surely the reality would be equally wonderful.

Nan watched the clock all the forenoon, seeing the time draw slowly...oh, so slowly...nearer and nearer. When a thundercloud rolled up ominously and rain began to fall she could hardly keep the tears back.

"I don't see *how* God could let it rain today," she whispered rebelliously.

But the shower was soon over and the sun shone again. Nan could eat hardly any dinner for excitement.

"Mummy, may I wear my yellow dress?"

"Why do you want to dress up like that to call on a neighbour, child?"

A neighbour! But of course Mother didn't understand... couldn't understand.

"*Please,* Mummy."

"Very well," said Anne. The yellow dress would be outgrown very soon. May as well let Nan get the good of it.

Nan's legs were fairly trembling as she set off, the precious small parcel in her hand. She took a short-cut through Rainbow Valley, up the hill, to the side-road. The raindrops were still lying on the nasturtium leaves like great pearls; there was a delicious freshness in the air; the bees were buzzing in the white clover that edged the brook; slim blue dragonflies were glittering over the water...devil's-darning-needles, Susan called them; in the hill pasture the daisies nodded to her...swayed to her...waved to her... laughed to her, with cool gold-and-silver laughter. Everything was so lovely and she was going to see the Wicked Lady with the Mysterious Eyes. What would the Lady say to her? And was it *quite* safe to go to see her? Suppose you stayed a few minutes with her and found that a hundred years had gone by, as in the story she and Walter had read last week?

36

Nan felt a queer tickly sensation in her spine as she turned into the lane. Did the dead maple bough move? No, she had escaped it...she was past. Aha, old witch, you didn't catch *Me!* She was walking up the lane of which the mud and the ruts had no power to blight her anticipation. Just a few steps more...the GLOOMY HOUSE was before her, amid and behind those dark dripping trees. She was going to see it at last! She shivered a little...and did not know that it was because of a secret unadmitted fear of losing her dream. Which is always, for youth or maturity or age, a catastrophe.

She pushed her way through a gap in a wild growth of young spruces that was choking up the end of the lane. Her eyes were shut; could she dare to open them? For a moment sheer terror possessed her and for two pins she would have turned and run. After all...the Lady *was* wicked. Who knew what she might do to you? She might even be a Witch. How was it that it had never occurred to her before that the Wicked Lady might be a Witch?

Then she resolutely opened her eyes and stared piteously.

Was *this* the GLOOMY HOUSE...the dark, stately, towered and turreted mansion of her dreams? This!

It was a big house, once white, now a muddy gray. Here and there, broken shutters, once green, were swinging loose. The front steps were broken. A forlorn glassed-in porch had most of its panes shattered. The scrolled trimming around the verandah was broken. Why, it was only a tired old house worn out with living!

Nan looked about desperately. There was no fountain...no garden...well, nothing you could really call a garden. The space in front of the house, surrounded by a ragged paling, was full of weeds and knee-high tangled grass. A lank pig rooted beyond the paling. Burdocks grew along the mid-walk. Straggly clumps of golden-glow were in the corners, but there *was* one splendid clump of militant tiger-lilies and, just by the worn steps, a gay bed of marigolds.

Nan went slowly up the walk to the marigold bed. The GLOOMY HOUSE was gone forever. But the Lady with the Mysterious Eyes remained. Surely *she* was real...she must be! *What* had Susan really said about her so long ago?

"Laws-a-mercy, ye nearly scared the liver out of me!" said a rather mumbly though friendly voice.

Nan looked at the figure that had suddenly risen up from beside the marigold bed. *Who was it?* It could *not* be...Nan refused to believe that *this* was Thomasine Fair. It would be just too terrible!

"Why," thought Nan, heartsick with disappointment, "she... she's *old!*"

Thomasine Fair, if Thomasine Fair it was...and she knew now it was Thomasine Fair...was certainly old. And fat! She looked like the feather-bed with the string tied round its middle to which angular Susan was always comparing stout ladies. She was barefooted, wore a green dress that had faded yellowish, and a man's old felt hat on her sparse, sandy-grey hair. Her face was round as an O, ruddy and wrinkled, with a snub nose. Her eyes were a faded blue, surrounded by great, jolly-looking crow's-feet.

Oh, my Lady...my charming, Wicked Lady with the Mysterious Eyes, where are you? What has become of you? You *did* exist!

"Well now, and what nice little girl are you?" asked Thomasine Fair.

Nan clutched after her manners.

"I'm...I'm Nan Blythe. I came up to bring you this."

Thomasine pounced on the parcel joyfully.

"Well, if I ain't glad to get my specks back!" she said. "I've missed 'em turrible for reading the almanack on Sundays. And you're one of the Blythe girls? What pretty hair you've got! I've always wanted to see some of you. I've heered your ma was bringing you up scientific. Do you like it?"

"Like...what?" Oh, wicked, charming Lady, *you* did not read the almanack on Sundays. Nor did you talk of "ma's."

"Why, bein' brought up scientific."

"I like the way I'm being brought up," said Nan, trying to smile and barely succeeding.

"Well, your ma is a real fine woman. She's holding her own. I declare the first time I saw her at Libby Taylor's funeral I thought she was a bride, she looked so happy. I always think when I see your ma come into a room that everyone perks up as if they expected something to happen. The new fashions set her, too. Most of us just ain't made to wear 'em. But come in and set a while...I'm glad to see someone...it gets kinder lonesome by spells. I can't afford a telephone. Flowers is company...did ye ever see finer merrygolds? And I've got a cat."

Nan wanted to flee to the uttermost parts of the earth, but she felt it would never do to hurt the old lady's feelings by refusing to go in. Thomasine, her petticoat showing below her skirt, led the way up the sagging steps into a room which was evidently kitchen and living-room combined. It was scrupulously clean and gay with thrifty house plants. The air was full of the pleasant fragrance of newly cooked bread.

"Set here," said Thomasine kindly, pushing forward a rocker with a gay patched cushion. "I'll move that callow-lily out of your way. Wait till I get my lower plate in. I look funny with it out, don't I? But it hurts me a mite. There, I'll talk clearer now."

A spotted cat, uttering all kinds of fancy meows, came forward to greet them. Oh, for the greyhounds of a vanished dream!

"That cat's a fine ratter," said Thomasine. "This place is overrun with rats. But it keeps the rain out and I got sick of living round with relations. Couldn't call my soul my own. Ordered round as if I was dirt. Jim's wife was the worst. Complained because I was making faces at the moon one night. Well, what if I was? Did it hurt the moon? Says I, 'I ain't going to be a pincushion any longer.' So I come here on my own and here I'll stay as long as I have use of my legs. Now, what'll you have? Can I make you an onion sandwich?"

"No...no, thank you."

"They're fine when you have a cold. I've been having one... notice how hoarse I am? But I just tie a piece of red flannel with turpentine and goose-grease on it round my throat when I go to bed. Nothing better."

Red flannel and goose-grease! Not to speak of turpentine!

"If you won't have a sandwich...sure you won't?...I'll see what's in the cooky box."

The cookies...cut in the shape of roosters and ducks...were surprisingly good and fairly melted in your mouth. Mrs. Fair beamed at Nan out of her round faded eyes.

"Now you'll like me, won't you? I like to have little girls like me."

"I'll try," gasped Nan, who at that moment was hating poor Thomasine Fair as we can hate only those who destroy our illusions.

"I've got some little grandchildren of my own out West, you know."

Grandchildren!

"I'll show you their pictures. Pretty, ain't they? That's poor dear Poppa's picture up there. Twenty years since he died."

Poor dear Poppa's picture was a large "crayon" of a bearded man with a curly fringe of white hair surrounding a bald head.

Oh, lover disdained!

"He was a good husband though he was bald at thirty," said Mrs. Fair fondly. "My, but I had the pick of the beaus when I was a girl. I'm old now but I had a fine time when I was young. The beaus on Sunday nights! Trying to sit each other out! And me holding up my head as haughty as any queen! Poppa was among them from the start but at first I hadn't nothing to say to him. I liked 'em a bit more dashing. There was Andrew Metcalf now...I was as near as no matter running away with him. But I knew 'twould be unlucky. Don't you ever run away. It *is* unlucky and don't let anyone ever tell you different."

"I...I won't...indeed I won't."

"In the end I married Poppa. His patience gin out at last and he give me twenty-four hours to take him or leave him. My pa wanted me to settle down. He got nervous when Jim Hewitt drowned himself because I wouldn't have him. Poppa and I were real happy when we got used to each other. He said I suited him because I didn't do too much thinking. Poppa held women weren't made for thinking. He said it made 'em dried-up and unnatteral. Baked beans disagreed with him turrible and he had spells of lumbago but my balmagilia balsam always straightened that out. There was a specialist in town said he could cure him permanent but Poppa always said if you got into the hands of them specialists they'd never let you out again...never. I miss him to feed the pig. He was real fond of pork. I never eat a bit of bacon but I think of him. That picture opposite Poppa is Queen Victoria. Sometimes I say to her, 'If they stripped all them lace and jewels off you, my dear, I doubt if you'd be any better-looking than I am."

Before she let Nan go she insisted on her taking a bag of peppermints, a pink glass slipper for holding flowers, and a glass of gooseberry jelly.

"That's for your ma. I've always had good luck with my gooseberry jelly. I'm coming down to Ingleside some day. I want to see them chiney dogs of yours. Tell Susan Baker I'm much obliged for that mess of turnip greens she sent me in the spring."

Turnip greens!

"I 'lowed I'd thank her at Jacob Warren's funeral but she got away too quick. I like to take my time at funerals. There hasn't been one for a month. I always think it's a dull old time when there's no funerals going. There's always a fine lot of funerals over Lowbridge way. It don't seem fair. Come again and see me, won't you? You've got something about you...'loving favour is better than silver and gold,' the Good Book says and I guess it's right."

She smiled very pleasantly at Nan...she *had* a sweet smile. In it you saw the pretty Thomasine of long ago. Nan managed another smile herself. Her eyes were stinging. She *must* get away before she cried outright.

"Nice, well-behaved leetle creetur," mused old Thomasine Fair, looking out of her window after Nan. "Hasn't got her ma's gift of gab but maybe none the worse of that. Most of the kids today think they're smart when they're just being sassy. That little thing's visit has kind of made me feel young again."

Thomasine sighed and went out to finish cutting her marigolds and hoeing up some of the burdocks.

"Thank goodness, I've kept limber," she reflected.

Nan went back to Ingleside the poorer by a lost dream. A dell full of daisies could not lure her...singing water called to her in vain. She wanted to get home and shut herself away from human eyes. Two girls she met giggled after they passed her. Were they laughing at her? How everybody would laugh if they knew! Silly little Nan Blythe who had spun a romance of cobweb fancies about a pale queen of mystery and found instead poor Poppa's widow and peppermints.

Peppermints!

Nan would not cry. Big girls of ten must not cry. But she felt indescribably dreary. Something precious and beautiful was gone...lost...a secret store of joy which, so she believed, could never be hers again. She found Ingleside filled with the delicious smell of spice cookies but she did not go into the kitchen to coax some out of Susan. At supper her appetite was noticeably poor, even though she read castor-oil in Susan's eye. Anne had noticed that Nan had been very quiet ever since her return from the old MacAllister place...Nan, who sang literally from daylight to dark and after. Had the long walk on a hot day been too much for the child?

"Why that anguished expression, daughter?" she asked casually, when she went into the twins' room at dusk with fresh towels and found Nan curled up on the window-seat, instead of being down stalking tigers in Equatorial jungles with the others in Rainbow Valley.

Nan hadn't meant to tell *anybody* that she had been so silly. But somehow things told themselves to Mother.

"Oh, Mother, is *everything* in life a disappointment?"

"Not everything, dear. Would you like to tell me what disappointed you today?"

"Oh, Mummy, Thomasine Fair is...is *good!* And her nose turns up!"

"But why," asked Anne in honest bewilderment, "should you care whether her nose turns up or down?"

It all came out then. Anne listened with her usual serious face, praying that she be not betrayed into a stifled shriek of laughter. She remembered the child she had been at old Green Gables. She remembered the Haunted Wood and two small girls who had been terribly frightened by their own pretending thereof. And she knew the dreadful bitterness of losing a dream.

"You musn't take the vanishing of your fancies so much to heart, dear."

"I can't help it," said Nan despairingly. "If I had my life to live over again I'd never imagine *anything.* And I never will again."

"My foolish dear...my *dear* foolish dear, don't say that. An imagination is a wonderful thing to have...but like every gift we must possess it and not let it possess us. You take your imaginings a wee bit too seriously. Oh, it's delightful...I know that rapture. But you must learn to keep on this side of the borderline between the real and the unreal. *Then* the power to escape at will into a beautiful world of your own will help you amazingly through the hard places of life. I can always solve a problem more easily after I've had a voyage or two to the Islands of Enchantment."

Nan felt her self-respect coming back to her with these words of comfort and wisdom. Mother did not think it so silly after all. And no doubt there was somewhere in the world a Wicked Beautiful Lady with Mysterious Eyes, even if she did not live in the GLOOMY HOUSE...which, now that Nan came to think of it, was not such a bad place after all, with its orange marigolds and its friendly spotted cat and its geraniums and poor dear Poppa's picture. It was really rather a jolly place and perhaps some day she would go and see Thomasine Fair again and get some more of those nice cookies. She did not hate Thomasine any longer.

"What a nice mother you are!" she sighed, in the shelter and sanctuary of those beloved arms.

A violet-grey dusk was coming over the hill. The summer night darkened about them...a night of velvet and whispers. A star came out over the big apple tree. When Mrs. Marshall Elliott came and Mother had to go down Nan was happy again. Mother had said she was going to repaper their room with a lovely buttercup-yellow paper and get a new cedar chest for her and Di to keep things in. Only it would not be a cedar chest. It would be an enchanted treasure chest which could not be opened unless certain mystic words were pronounced. One word the Witch of the Snow might whisper to you, the cold and lovely white Witch of the Snow. A wind might tell you another, as it passed you...a sad grey wind that mourned. Sooner or later you would find all the words and open the chest, to find it filled with pearls and rubies and diamonds galore. Wasn't galore a nice word?

Oh, the old magic had not gone. The world was still full of it.

37

"Can I be your dearest friend this year?" asked Delilah Green, during that afternoon recess.

Delilah had very round, dark-blue eyes, sleek sugar-brown curls, a small rosy mouth, and a thrilling voice with a little quaver in it. Diana Blythe responded to the charm of that voice instantly.

It was known in the Glen school that Diana Blythe was rather at loose ends for a chum. For two years she and Pauline Reese had been cronies but Pauline's family had moved away and Diana felt very lonely. Pauline had been a good sort. To be sure, she was quite lacking in the mystic charm that the now almost forgotten Jenny Penny had possessed but she was practical, full of fun, *sensible.* That last was Susan's adjective and was the highest praise Susan could bestow. She had been entirely satisfied with Pauline as a friend for Diana.

Diana looked at Delilah doubtfully, then glanced across the playground at Laura Carr, who was also a new girl. Laura and she had spent the forenoon recess together and had found each other very agreeable. But Laura was rather plain, with freckles and unmanageable sandy hair. She had none of Delilah Green's beauty and not a spark of her allure.

Delilah understood Diana's look and a hurt expression crept over her face; her blue eyes seemed ready to brim with tears.

"If you love *her* you can't love *me.* Choose between us," said Delilah, holding out her hands dramatically. Her voice was more thrilling than ever...it positively sent a creep along Diana's spine. She put her hands in Delilah's and they looked at each other solemnly, feeling dedicated and sealed. At least, Diana felt that way.

"You'll love me *forever,* won't you?" asked Delilah passionately.

"Forever," vowed Diana with equal passion.

Delilah slipped her arms around Diana's waist and they walked down to the brook together. The rest of the Fourth class understood that an alliance had been concluded. Laura Carr gave a tiny sigh. She had liked Diana Blythe very much. But she knew she could not compete with Delilah.

"I'm *so* glad you're going to let me love you," Delilah was saying. "I'm so very affectionate...I just can't help loving people. *Please* be kind to me, Diana. I am a child of sorrow. I was put under a curse at birth. Nobody...*nobody* loves me."

Delilah somehow contrived to put ages of loneliness and loveliness into that "nobody." Diana tightened her clasp.

"You'll never have to say that after this, Delilah. I will always love you."

"World without end?"

"World without end," answered Diana. They kissed each other, as in a rite. Two boys on the fence whooped derisively, but who cared?

"You'll like me ever so much better than Laura Carr," said Delilah. "Now that we're dear friends I can tell you what I wouldn't have *dreamed* of telling you if you had picked her. *She is deceitful.* Dreadfully deceitful. She pretends to be your friend to your face and behind your back she makes fun of you and says the *meanest* things. A girl I know went to school with her at Mowbray's Narrows and she told me. You've had a narrow escape. *I'm* so different from that...I am as true as gold, Diana."

"I'm sure you are. But what did you mean by saying you were a child of sorrow, Delilah?"

Delilah's eyes seemed to expand until they were absolutely enormous.

"I have a *stepmother*," she whispered.

"A stepmother?"

"When your mother dies and your father marries again *she* is a stepmother," said Delilah, with still more thrills in her voice.

"Now you know it all, Diana. If you knew the way I am treated! But I never complain. I suffer in silence."

If Delilah really suffered in silence it might be wondered where Diana got all the information she showered on the Ingleside folks during the next few weeks. She was in the throes of a wild passion of adoration and sympathy for and with sorrow-laden, persecuted Delilah, and she had to talk about her to anyone who would listen.

"I suppose this new infatuation will run its course in due time," said Anne. "Who is this Delilah, Susan? I don't want the children to be little snobs...but after our experience with Jenny Penny..."

"The Greens are very respectable, Mrs. Dr. dear. They are well-known at Lowbridge. They moved into the old Hunter place this summer. Mrs. Green is the second wife and has two children of her own. I do not know much about her but she seems to have a slow, kind, easy way with her. I can hardly believe she uses Delilah as Di says."

"Don't put too much credence in everything Delilah tells you," Anne warned Diana. "She may be prone to exaggerate a little. Remember Jenny Penny..."

"Why, Mother, Delilah isn't a single bit like Jenny Penny," said Di indignantly. "Not one bit. She is *scrupulously* truthful. If you only saw her, Mother, you'd know she couldn't tell a lie. They all pick on her at home because she is so *different.* And she has *such* an affectionate nature. She has been persecuted from her birth. Her stepmother *hates* her. It just breaks my heart to hear of her sufferings. Why, Mother, she doesn't get enough to eat, truly she doesn't. She never knows what it is not to be hungry. Mother, they send her to bed without any supper lots of times and she cries herself to sleep. Did *you* ever cry because you were hungry, Mother?"

"Often," said Mother.

Diana stared at her mother, all the wind taken out of the sails of her rhetorical question.

"I was often very hungry before I came to Green Gables—at the orphanage...and before. I've never cared to talk of those days."

"Well, you ought to be able to understand Delilah, then," said Di, rallying her confused wits. "When she is *so* hungry she just sits down and imagines things to eat. Just *think* of her imagining things to eat!"

"You and Nan do enough of that yourselves," said Anne. But Di would not listen.

"Her sufferings are not only physical but *spiritual.* Why, she wants to be a missionary, Mother...to consecrate her life...and they *all laugh at her.*"

"Very heartless of them," agreed Anne. But something in her voice made Di suspicious.

"Mother, *why* will you be so sceptical?" she demanded reproachfully.

"For the second time," smiled Mother, "I must remind you of Jenny Penny. You believed in her, too."

"I was only a *child* then and it was easy to fool me," said Diana in her stateliest manner. She felt that Mother was not her usual sympathetic and understanding self in regard to Delilah Green. After that Diana talked only to Susan about her, since Nan merely nodded when Delilah's name was mentioned. "Just jealousy," thought Diana sadly.

Not that Susan was so markedly sympathetic either. But Diana just had to talk to somebody about Delilah and Susan's derision did not hurt like Mother's. You wouldn't expect Susan to understand fully. But Mother had been a girl...Mother had loved Aunt Diana...Mother had such a tender heart. How was it that the account of poor darling Delilah's ill-treatment left her so cold?

"Maybe she's a little jealous, too, because I love Delilah so much," reflected Diana sagely. "They say mothers do get like that. Kind of *possessive*."

"It makes my blood boil to hear of the way her stepmother treats Delilah," Di told Susan. "She is a *martyr,* Susan. She never has anything but a little porridge for breakfast and supper...a very little bit of porridge. And she isn't allowed sugar on the porridge. Susan, I've given up taking sugar on mine because it made me feel *guilty.*"

"Oh, so that's why. Well, sugar has gone up a cent, so maybe it is just as well."

Diana vowed she wouldn't tell Susan anything more about Delilah, but next evening she was so indignant she couldn't help herself.

"Susan, Delilah's mother chased her last night with a *red-hot teakettle.* Think of it, Susan. Of course Delilah says she doesn't do that very often...only when she is *greatly exasperated.* Mostly she just locks Delilah in a dark garret...a *haunted* garret. The ghosts that poor child has seen, Susan! It can't be healthy for her. The last time they shut her in the garret she saw the *weirdest* little black creature sitting on the spinning-wheel, *humming.*"

"What kind of a creature," asked Susan gravely. She was beginning to enjoy Delilah's tribulations and Di's italics, and she and Mrs. Dr. laughed over them in secret.

"I don't know...it was just a *creature.* It almost drove her to suicide. I am really afraid she will be driven to it yet. You know, Susan, she had an uncle who committed suicide *twice.*"

"Was not once enough?" asked Susan heartlessly.

Di went off in a huff, but next day she had to come back with another tale of woe.

"Delilah has never had a doll, Susan. She did so hope she would get one in her stocking last Christmas. And what do you think she found instead, Susan? A *switch!* They whip her almost every day, you know. Think of that poor child being whipped, Susan."

"I was whipped several times when I was young and I am none the worse of it now," said Susan, who would have done goodness knows what if anyone had ever tried to whip an Ingleside child.

"When I told Delilah about our Christmas trees, she wept, Susan. She never had a Christmas tree. But she is bound she is going to have one this year. She had found an old umbrella with nothing but the ribs and she is going to set it in a pail and decorate it for a Christmas tree. Isn't that *pathetic,* Susan?"

"Are there not plenty of young spruces handy? The back of the old Hunter place has practically gone spruce of late years," said Susan. "I do wish that girl was called anything but Delilah. Such a name for a Christian child!"

"Why, it is in the Bible, Susan. Delilah is very proud of her Bible name. Today in school, Susan, I told Delilah we were going to have chicken for dinner tomorrow and she said...what do you think she said, Susan?"

"I am sure I could never guess," said Susan emphatically. "And you have no business to be talking in school."

"Oh, we don't. Delilah says we must never break any of the rules. Her standards are very high. We write each other letters in our scribblers and exchange them. Well, Delilah said, 'Could you bring me a bone, Diana?' It brought tears to my eye. I'm going to take her a bone...with a lot of meat on it. Delilah *needs* good food. She has to work like a slave...a *slave,* Susan. She has to do all the housework...well, nearly all anyway. And if it isn't done right she is *savagely shaken...* or made to eat in the kitchen *with the servants.*"

"The Greens have only one little French hired boy."

"Well, she has to eat with him. And he sits in his sockfeet and eats in his shirtsleeves. Delilah says she doesn't mind those things now when she has me to love her. She has no one to love her but me, Susan?"

"Awful!" said Susan, with great gravity of countenance.

"Delilah says if she had a million dollars she'd give it all to me, Susan. Of course I wouldn't take it but it shows how good her heart is."

"It is as easy to give away a million as a hundred if you have not got either," was as far as Susan would go.

38

Diana was overjoyed. After all, Mother wasn't jealous...Mother wasn't possessive...Mother did understand.

Mother and Father were going up to Avonlea for the week-end and Mother had told her she could ask Delilah Green to spend Saturday and Saturday night at Ingleside.

"I saw Delilah at the Sunday School picnic," Anne told Susan. "She is a pretty, lady-like little thing...though of course she *must* exaggerate. Perhaps her stepmother *is* a little hard on her...and I've heard her father is rather dour and strict. She probably has some grievances and likes to dramatize them by way of getting sympathy."

Susan was a bit dubious.

"But at least anyone living in Laura Green's house will be clean," she reflected. Fine-tooth combs did not enter into this question.

Diana was full of plans for Delilah's entertainment.

"Can we have a roast chicken, Susan...with lots of stuffing?

And *pie.* You don't know how that poor child longs to taste pie. They never have pies...her stepmother is too mean."

Susan was very nice about it. Jem and Nan had gone to Avonlea and Walter was down at the House of Dreams with Kenneth Ford. There was nothing to cast a shadow on Delilah's visit and it certainly seemed to go off very well. Delilah arrived Saturday morning very nicely dressed in pink muslin...at least the stepmother seemed to do her well in the matter of clothes. And she had, as Susan saw at a glance, irreproachable ears and nails.

"This is *the* day of my life," she said solemnly to Diana. "My, what a grand house this is! And them's the china dogs! Oh, they're wonderful!"

Everything was wonderful. Delilah worked the poor word to death. She helped Diana set the table for dinner and picked the little glass basket full of pink sweetpeas for a centrepiece.

"Oh, you don't know how I love to do something just because I *like* to do it," she told Diana. "Isn't there anything else I can do, *please?*"

"You can crack the nuts for the cake I'm going to make this afternoon," said Susan, who was herself falling under the spell of Delilah's beauty and voice. After all, perhaps Laura Green *was* a Tartar. You couldn't always go by what people seemed like in public. Delilah's plate was heaped with chicken and stuffing and gravy and she got a second piece of pie without hinting for it.

"I've often wondered what it would be like to have all you could eat for once. It is a wonderful sensation," she told Diana as they left the table.

They had a gay afternoon. Susan had given Diana a box of candy and Diana shared it with Delilah. Delilah admired one of Di's dolls and Di gave it to her. They cleaned out the pansy bed and dug up a few stray dandelions that had invaded the lawn. They helped Susan polish the silver and assisted her to get supper. Delilah was so efficient and tidy that Susan capitulated completely. Only two things marred the afternoon...Delilah contrived to spatter her dress with ink and she lost her pearl bead necklace. But Susan took the ink out nicely...some of the colour coming out too...with salts of lemon and Delilah said it didn't matter about the necklace. *Nothing* mattered except that she was at Ingleside with her dearest Diana.

"Aren't we going to sleep in the spare-room bed?" asked Diana when bedtime came. "We always put company in the spare-room, Susan."

"Your Aunt Diana is coming with your father and mother tomorrow night," said Susan. "The spare-room has been made up for her. You can have the Shrimp on your own bed and you couldn't have him in the spare-room."

"My, but your sheets smell nice!" said Delilah as they snuggled down.

"Susan always boils them with orris root," said Diana.

Delilah sighed.

"I wonder if you know what a lucky girl you are, Diana. If *I* had a home like you...but it's my lot in life. I just have to bear it."

Susan, on her nightly round of the house before retiring, came in and told them to stop chattering and go to sleep. She gave them two maple sugar buns apiece.

"I can never forget your kindness, Miss Baker," said Delilah, her voice quivering with emotion. Susan went to her bed reflecting that a nicer-mannered, more appealing little girl she had never seen. Certainly she had misjudged Delilah Green. Though at that moment it occurred to Susan that, for a child who never got enough to eat, the bones of the said Delilah Green were very well covered!

Delilah went home the next afternoon and Mother and Father and Aunt Diana came at night. On Monday the bolt fell from the proverbial blue. Diana, returning to school at the noon hour, caught her own name as she entered the school porch. Inside the schoolroom Delilah Green was the centre of a group of curious girls.

"I was *so* disappointed in Ingleside. After the way Di has bragged about her house I expected a *mansion.* Of course it's big enough, but some of the furniture is shabby. The chairs want to be recovered the *worst* way."

"Did you see the china dogs?" asked Bessy Palmer.

"They're nothing wonderful. They haven't even got hair. I told Diana right on the spot I was disappointed."

Diana was standing "rooted to the ground"...or at least to the porch floor. She did not think about eavesdropping...she was simply too dumfounded to move.

"I'm sorry for Diana," went on Delilah. "The way her parents neglect their family is something scandalous. Her mother is an awful gadabout. The way she goes off and leaves them young ones is terrible with only that old Susan to look after them... and she's half cracked. She'll land them all in the poorhouse yet. The waste that goes on in her kitchen you wouldn't believe. The doctor's wife is too gay and lazy to cook even when she is home, so Susan has it all her own way. She was going to give us our meals *in the kitchen* but I just up and said to her, 'Am I company or am I not?' Susan said if I gave her any sass she'd shut me up in the back closet. I said, 'You don't dare to,' and she didn't. 'You can overcrow the Ingleside children, Susan Baker, but you can't overcrow *me*,' I said to her. Oh, I tell you I stood up to Susan. I wouldn't let her give Rilla soothing-syrup. 'Don't you know it's poison to children?' I said.

"She took it out on me at meals though. The mean little helpings she gives you! There was chicken but I only got the Pope's nose and nobody even asked me to take the second piece of pie. But Susan would have let me sleep in the spare-room though and Di wouldn't hear to it...just out of pure meanness.

She's so jealous. But still I'm sorry for her. She told me Nan pinches her *something scandalous.* Her arms are black and blue. We slept in her room and a mangy old tomcat was lying on the foot of the bed all night. It wasn't *haygeenic* and I told Di so. And my pearl necklace *disappeared.* Of course I'm not saying Susan took it. I believe she's *honest...* but it's funny. And Shirley threw an ink-bottle at me. It ruined my dress but I don't care. Ma'll have to get me a new one. Well, anyhow, I dug all the dandelions out of their lawn for them and polished up the silver. You should have seen it. I don't know *when* it has been cleaned before. I tell you Susan takes it easy when the doctor's wife's away. I let her see I saw through her. 'Why don't you ever wash the potato pot, Susan?' I asked her. You should of seen her face. Look at my new ring, girls. A boy I know at Lowbridge give it to me."

"Why, I've seen Diana Blythe wearing that ring often," said Peggy MacAllister contemptuously.

"And I don't believe one single word you've been saying about Ingleside, Delilah Green," said Laura Carr.

Before Delilah could reply Diana, who had recovered her powers of locomotion and speech, dashed into the schoolroom.

"Judas!" she said. Afterwards she thought repentantly that it had not been a very ladylike thing to say. But she had been stung to the heart and when your feelings are all stirred up you can't pick and choose your words.

"I ain't Judas!" muttered Delilah, flushing, probably for the first time in her life.

"You are! There isn't one spark of sincerity in you! Don't you ever speak to me again as long as you live!"

Diana rushed out of the schoolhouse and ran home. She couldn't stay in school that afternoon...she just couldn't! The Ingleside front door was banged as it had never been banged before.

"Darling, what is the matter?" asked Anne, interrupted in her kitchen conference with Susan by a weeping daughter who flung herself stormily against the maternal shoulder.

The whole story was sobbed out, somewhat disjointedly.

"I've been hurt in all my *finer feelings,* Mother. And I'll never believe in anyone again!"

"My dear, all your friends won't be like this. Pauline wasn't."

"This is *twice,*" said Diana bitterly, still smarting under the sense of betrayal and loss. "There isn't going to be any third time."

"I'm sorry Di has lost her faith in humanity," said Anne rather ruefully, when Di had gone upstairs. "This is a real tragedy for her. She *has* been unlucky in some of her chums. Jenny Penny...and now Delilah Green. The trouble is Di always falls for the girls who can tell interesting stories. And Delilah's martyr pose was very alluring."

"If you ask me, Mrs. Dr. dear, that Green child is a perfect minx," said Susan, all the more implacably because she had been so neatly fooled herself by Delilah's eyes and manners. "The idea of her calling our cats mangy! I am not saying that there are not such things as tomcats, Mrs. Dr. dear, but little girls should not talk of them. I am no lover of cats, but the Shrimp is seven years old and should at least be *respected.* And as for my potato pot..."

But Susan really couldn't express her feelings about the potato pot.

In her own room Di was reflecting that perhaps it was not too late to be "best friends" with Laura Carr after all. Laura was *true,* even if she wasn't very exciting. Di sighed. Some colour *had* gone out of life with her belief in Delilah's piteous lot.

39

A bitter east wind was snarling around Ingleside like a shrewish old woman. It was one of those chill, drizzly, late August days that take the heart out of you, one of those days when everything goes wrong...what in old Avonlea days had been called "a Jonah day." The new pup Gilbert had brought home for the boys had gnawed the enamel off the dining table leg... Susan had found that the moths had been having a Roman holiday in the blanket closet...Nan's new kitten had ruined the choicest fern...Jem and Bertie Shakespeare had been making the most abominable racket in the garret all the afternoon with tin pails for drums...Anne herself had broken a painted glass lampshade. But somehow it had done her good just to hear it smash! Rilla had had earache and Shirley had a mysterious rash on his neck, which worried Anne but at which Gilbert only glanced casually and said in an absent-minded voice that he didn't think it meant anything. Of course it didn't mean anything to *him!* Shirley was only his own son! And it didn't matter to him either that he had invited the Trents to dinner one evening last week and forgotten to tell Anne until they arrived. She and Susan had had an extra busy day and had planned a pick-up supper. And Mrs. Trent with the reputation of being Charlottetown's smartest hostess! *Where* were Walter's stockings with the black tops and the blue toes? "Do you think, Walter, that you could *just for once* put a thing where it belongs? Nan, I *don't* know where the Seven Seas are. For mercy's sake, stop asking questions! I don't wonder they poisoned Socrates. They *ought* to have."

Walter and Nan stared. Never had they heard their mother speak in such a tone before. Walter's look annoyed Anne still more.

"Diana, is it necessary to be forever reminding you not to twist your legs around the piano stool? Shirley, if you haven't got that new magazine all sticky with jam! And perhaps *somebody* would be kind enough to tell me where the prisms of the hanging lamp have gone!"

Nobody could tell her...Susan having unhooked them and taken them out to wash them...and Anne whisked herself upstairs to escape from the grieved eyes of her children. In her own room she paced up and down feverishly. *What* was the matter with her? Was she turning into one of those peevish creatures who had no patience with anybody? Everything annoyed her these days. A little mannerism of Gilbert's she had never minded before got on her nerves. She was sick-and-tired of never-ending, monotonous duties...sick-and-tired of catering to her family's whims. Once everything she did for her house and household gave her delight. Now she did not seem to care what she did. She felt all the time like a creature in a nightmare, trying to overtake someone with fettered feet.

The worst of it all was that Gilbert never noticed that there was any change in her. He was busy night and day and seemed to care for nothing but his work. The only thing he had said at dinner that day had been "Pass the mustard, please."

"*I* can talk to the chairs and table, of course," thought Anne bitterly. "We're just getting to be a sort of *habit* with each other... nothing else. He never noticed that I had on a new dress last night. And it's so long since he called me 'Anne-girl' that I've forgotten when. Well, I suppose all marriages come to this in the end. Probably most women go through this. He just takes me for granted. His work is the only thing that means anything to him now. *Where* is my handkerchief?"

Anne got her handkerchief and sat down in her chair to torture herself luxuriantly. Gilbert didn't love her any more. When he kissed her he kissed her absently...just "habit." All the glamour was gone. Old jokes they had laughed together over came up in recollection, charged with tragedy now. How could she ever have thought them funny? Monty Turner who kissed his wife systematically once a week...made a memorandum to remind him. *("Would any wife want such kisses?")* Curtis Ames who met his wife in a new bonnet and didn't know her. Mrs. Clancy Dare who had said, "I don't care an awful lot about my husband but I'd miss him if he wasn't round." *("I suppose Gilbert would miss me if I weren't around! Has it come to that with us?")* Nat Elliott who told his wife after ten years of marriage, "if you must know I'm just tired of being married." *("And we've been married fifteen years!")* Well, perhaps all men were like that. Probably Miss Cornelia would say that they were. After a time they were hard to hold. *("If my husband has to be 'held' I don't want to hold him.")* But there was Mrs. Theodore Clow who had said proudly at a Ladies' Aid, "We've been married twenty years and my husband loves me as much as he did on our wedding day." But perhaps she was deceiving herself or only "keeping face." And she looked every day of her age and more. *("I wonder if I am beginning to look old.")*

For the first time her years felt like a weight. She went to the mirror and looked at herself critically. There *were* some tiny crow's-feet around her eyes but they were only visible in a strong light. Her chin lines were yet unblurred. She had always been pale. Her hair was thick and wavy without a grey thread. But did anybody *really* like red hair? Her nose was still definitely good. Anne patted it as a friend, recalling certain moments of life when her nose was all that carried her through. But Gilbert just took her nose for granted now. It might be crooked or pug, for all it mattered to him. Likely he had forgotten that she *had* a nose. Like Mrs. Dare, he might miss it if it wasn't there.

"Well, I must go and see to Rilla and Shirley," thought Anne drearily. "At least, *they* need me still, poor darlings. What made me so snappish with them? Oh, I suppose they're all saying behind my back, 'How cranky poor Mother is getting!'"

It continued to rain and the wind continued to wail. The fantasia of tin pans in the garret had stopped but the ceaseless chirping of a solitary cricket in the living-room nearly drove her mad. The noon mail brought her two letters. One was from Marilla... but Anne sighed as she folded it up. Marilla's handwriting was getting so frail and shaky. The other letter was from Mrs. Barrett Fowler of Charlottetown whom Anne knew very slightly. And Mrs. Barrett Fowler wanted Dr. and Mrs. Blythe to dine with her next Tuesday night at seven o'clock "to meet your old friend, Mrs. Andrew Dawson of Winnipeg, *nee* Christine Stuart."

Anne dropped the letter. A flood of old memories poured over her...some of them decidedly unpleasant. Christine Stuart of Redmond...the girl to whom people had once said Gilbert was engaged...the girl of whom she had once been so bitterly jealous...yes, she admitted it now, twenty years after...she *had* been jealous...she had hated Christine Stuart. She had not thought of Christine for years but she remembered her distinctly. A tall, ivory-white girl with great dark-blue eyes and blue-black masses of hair. And a certain air of distinction. But with a long nose... yes, definitely a long nose. Handsome...oh, you couldn't deny that Christine had been very handsome. She remembered hearing many years ago that Christine had "married well" and gone West.

Gilbert came in for a hurried bite of supper...there was an epidemic of measles in the Upper Glen...and Anne silently handed him Mrs. Fowler's letter.

"Christine Stuart! Of course we'll go. I'd like to see her for old sake's sake," he said, with the first appearance of admiration he had shown for weeks. "Poor girl, she has had her own troubles. She lost her husband four years ago, you know."

Anne didn't know. And how came Gilbert to know? Why had he never told her? And had he forgotten that next Tuesday was the anniversary of their own wedding day? A day on which they had never accepted any invitation but went off on a little bat of their own. Well, *she* wouldn't remind him. He could see his Christine if he wanted to. What had a girl at Redmond once said to her darkly, "There was a good deal more between Gilbert and Christine than you ever knew, Anne." She had merely laughed at it at the time...Claire Hallett was a spiteful thing. But perhaps there *had* been something in it. Anne suddenly remembered, with a little chill of the spirit, that not long after her marriage she had found a small photograph of Christine in an old pocketbook of Gilbert's. Gilbert had seemed quite indifferent and said he'd wondered where that old snap had got to. But...was it one of those unimportant things that are significant of things tremendously important? Was it possible...had Gilbert ever loved Christine? Was she, Anne, only a second choice? The consolation prize?

"Surely I'm not...jealous," thought Anne, trying to laugh. It was all very ridiculous. What more natural than that Gilbert should like the idea of meeting an old Redmond friend? What more natural than that a busy man, married for fifteen years, should forget times and seasons and days and months? Anne wrote to Mrs. Fowler, accepting her invitation...and then put in the three days before Tuesday hoping desperately that somebody in the Upper Glen would start having a baby Tuesday afternoon about half past five.

40

The hoped-for baby arrived too soon. Gilbert was sent for at nine Monday night. Anne wept herself to sleep and wakened at three. It used to be delicious to wake in the night...to lie and look out of her window at the night's enfolding loveliness...to hear Gilbert's regular breathing beside her...to think of the children across the hall and the beautiful new day that was coming. But now! Anne was still awake when the dawn, clear and green as fluor-spar, was in the eastern sky and Gilbert came home at last. "Twins," he said hollowly as he flung himself into bed and was asleep in a minute. Twins, indeed! The dawn of the fifteenth anniversary of your wedding day and all your husband could say to you was "Twins." He didn't even remember it *was* an anniversary.

Gilbert apparently didn't remember it any better when he came down at eleven. For the first time he did not mention it; for the first time he had no gift for her. Very well, *he* shouldn't get his gift either. She had had ready for weeks...a silver-handled pocket-knife with the date on one side and his initials on the other. Of course he must buy it from her with a cent, lest it cut their love. But since he had forgotten she would forget too, with a vengeance.

Gilbert seemed in a sort of daze all day. He hardly spoke to anyone and moped about the library. Was he lost in glamourous anticipation of seeing his Christine again? Probably he had been hankering after her all these years in the back of his mind. Anne knew quite well this idea was absolutely unreasonable but when was jealousy ever reasonable? It was no use trying to be philosophical. Philosophy had no effect on her mood.

They were going to town on the five-o'clock train. "Can we come in and watch you dreth, Mummy?" asked Rilla.

"Oh, if you want to," said Anne...then pulled herself up sharply. Why, her voice was getting querulous. "Come along, darling," she added repentantly.

Rilla had no greater delight than watching Mummy dress. But even Rilla thought Mummy was not getting much fun out of it that night.

Anne took some thought as to what dress she should wear. Not that it mattered, she told herself bitterly, what she put on. Gilbert never noticed now. The mirror was no longer her friend... she looked pale and tired...and *unwanted*. But she must not look too countrified and *passé* before Christine. *("I won't have her sorry for me.")* Was it to be her new apple-green net over a slip with rosebuds in it? Or her cream silk gauze with its Eton jacket of Cluny lace? She tried both of them on and decided on the net. She experimented with several hair-do's and concluded that the new drooping pompadour was very becoming.

"Oh, Mummy, you look beautiful!" gasped Rilla in round-eyed admiration.

Well, children and fools were supposed to tell the truth. Had not Rebecca Dew once told her that she was "comparatively beautiful"? As for Gilbert, he used to pay her compliments in the past but when had he given utterance to one of late months? Anne could not recall a single one.

Gilbert passed through on his way to his dressing closet and said not a word about her new dress. Anne stood for a moment burning with resentment; then she petulantly tore off the dress and flung it on the bed. She would wear her old black...a thin affair that was considered extremely "smart" in Four Winds circles but which Gilbert had never liked. What should she wear on her neck? Jem's beads, though treasured for years, had long since crumbled. She really hadn't a decent necklace. Well...she got out the little box containing the pink enamel heart Gilbert had given her at Redmond. She seldom wore it now...after all, pink didn't go well with her red hair...but she would put it on tonight. Would Gilbert notice it? There, she was ready. Why wasn't Gilbert? What was keeping him? Oh, no doubt he was shaving *very* carefully! She tapped sharply on the door.

"Gilbert, we're going to miss the train if you don't hurry."

"You sound school-teacherish," said Gilbert, coming out. "Anything wrong with your metatarsals?"

Oh, he could make a joke of it, could he? She would not let herself think how well he looked in his tails. After all, the modern fashions of men's clothes were really ridiculous. Entirely lacking in glamour. How gorgeous it must have been in "the spacious days of Great Elizabeth" when men could wear white satin doublets and cloaks of crimson velvet and lace ruffs! Yet they were not effeminate. They were the most wonderful and adventurous men the world had ever seen.

"Well, come along if you're in such a hurry," said Gilbert absently. He was always absent now when he spoke to her. She was just a part of the furniture...yes, just a piece of furniture!

Jem drove them to the station. Susan and Miss Cornelia... who had come up to ask Susan if they could depend on her as usual for scalloped potatoes for the church supper...looked after them admiringly.

"Anne is holding her own," said Miss Cornelia.

"She is," agreed Susan, "though I have sometimes thought these past few weeks that her liver needed stirring up a bit. But she keeps her looks. And the doctor has got the same nice flat stomach he always had."

"An ideal couple," said Miss Cornelia.

The ideal couple said nothing in particular very beautifully all the way to town. Of course Gilbert was too profoundly stirred over the prospect of seeing his old love to talk to his wife! Anne sneezed. She began to be afraid she was taking a cold in the head. How ghastly it would be to sniffle all through dinner under the eyes of Mrs. Andrew Dawson, *nee* Christine Stuart! A spot on her lip stung...probably a horrible cold-sore was coming on it. Did Juliet ever sneeze? Fancy Portia with chilblains! Or Argive Helen hiccoughing! Or Cleopatra with corns!

When Anne came downstairs in the Barrett Fowler residence she stumbled over the bear's head on the rug in the hall, staggered through the drawing-room door and across the wilderness of overstuffed furniture and gilt fandangoes Mrs. Barrett Fowler called her drawing-room, and fell on the chesterfield, fortunately landing right side up. She looked about in dismay for Christine, then thankfully realized that Christine had not yet put in an appearance. How awful it would have been had she been sitting there amusedly watching Gilbert Blythe's wife make such a drunken entrance! Gilbert hadn't even asked if she were hurt. He was already deep in conversation with Dr. Fowler and some unknown Dr. Murray, who hailed from New Brunswick and was the author of a notable monograph on tropical diseases which was making a stir in medical circles. But Anne noticed that when Christine came downstairs, heralded by a sniff of heliotrope, the monograph was promptly forgotten. Gilbert stood up with a very evident light of interest in his eyes.

Christine stood for an impressive moment in the doorway. No falling over bears' heads for her. Christine, Anne remembered, had of old that habit of pausing in the doorway to show herself off. And no doubt she regarded this as an excellent chance to show Gilbert what he had lost.

She wore a gown of purple velvet with long flowing sleeves, lined with gold, and a fish-tail train lined with gold lace. A gold bandeau encircled the still dark wings of her hair. A long, thin gold chain, starred with diamonds, hung from her neck. Anne instantly felt frumpy, provincial, unfinished, dowdy, and six months behind the fashion. She wished she had not put on that silly enamel heart.

There was no question that Christine was as handsome as ever. A bit too sleek and well-preserved, perhaps...yes, considerably stouter. Her nose had assuredly not grown any shorter and her chin was definitely middle-aged. Standing in the doorway like that, you saw that her feet were...substantial. And wasn't her air of distinction getting a little shopworn? But her cheeks were still like smooth ivory and her great dark-blue eyes still looked out brilliantly from under that intriguing parallel crease that had been considered so fascinating at Redmond. Yes, Mrs. Andrew Dawson was a very handsome woman...and did not at all convey the impression that her heart had been wholly buried in the said Andrew Dawson's grave.

Christine took possession of the whole room the moment she entered it. Anne felt as if she were not in the picture at all. But she sat up erectly. Christine should not see any middle-aged sag. She would go into battle with all flags flying. Her grey eyes turned exceedingly green and a faint flush coloured her oval cheek. *("Remember you have a nose!")* Dr. Murray, who had not noticed her particularly before, thought in some surprise that Blythe had a very uncommon-looking wife. That posturing Mrs. Dawson looked positively commonplace beside her.

"Why, Gilbert Blythe, you're as handsome as ever," Christine was saying archly...Christine *arch!*... "It's so nice to find you haven't changed."

("She talks with the same old drawl. How I always hated that velvet voice of hers!")

"When I look at you," said Gilbert, "time ceases to have any meaning at all. Where did you learn the secret of immortal youth?"

Christine laughed.

("Isn't her laughter a little tinny?")

"You could always pay a pretty compliment, Gilbert. You know"...with an arch glance around the circle... "Dr. Blythe was an old flame of mine in those days he is pretending to think were of yesterday. And Anne Shirley! You haven't changed as much as I've been told...though I don't think I'd have known you if we'd just happened to meet on the street. Your hair is a *little* darker than it used to be, isn't it? Isn't it *divine* to meet again like this? I was so afraid your lumbago wouldn't let you come."

"*My* lumbago!"

"Why, yes; aren't you subject to it? I thought you were..."

"I must have got things twisted," said Mrs. Fowler apologetically. "Somebody told me you were down with a very severe attack of lumbago..."

"That is Mrs. Dr. Parker of Lowbridge. I have never had lumbago in my life," said Anne in a flat voice.

"How very nice that you haven't got it," said Christine, with something faintly insolent in her tone. "It's *such* a wretched thing. I have an aunt who is a perfect martyr to it."

Her air seemed to relegate Anne to the generation of aunts. Anne managed a smile with her lips, not her eyes. If she could only think of something clever to say! She knew that at three o'clock that night she would probably think of a brilliant retort she might have made but that did not help her now.

"They tell me you have seven children," said Christine, speaking to Anne but looking at Gilbert.

"Only six living," said Anne, wincing. Even yet she could never think of little white Joyce without pain.

"*What* a family!" said Christine.

Instantly it seemed a disgraceful and absurd thing to have a large family.

"You, I think, have none," said Anne.

"I never cared for children, you know." Christine shrugged her remarkably fine shoulders but her voice was a little hard. "I'm afraid I'm not the maternal type. I really never thought that it was woman's sole mission to bring children into an already overcrowded world."

They went in to dinner then. Gilbert took Christine, Dr. Murray took Mrs. Fowler, and Dr. Fowler, a rotund little man, who could not talk to anybody except another doctor, took Anne.

Anne felt that the room was rather stifling. There was a mysterious sickly scent in it. Probably Mrs. Fowler had been burning incense. The menu was good and Anne went through the motions of eating without any appetite and smiled until she felt she was beginning to look like a Cheshire cat. She could not keep her eyes off Christine, who was smiling at Gilbert continuously. Her teeth were beautiful...almost too beautiful. They looked like a toothpaste advertisement. Christine made very effective play with her hands as she talked. She had lovely hands...rather large, though.

She was talking to Gilbert about rhythmic speeds for living. What on earth did she mean? Did she know, herself? Then they switched to the Passion Play.

"Have you ever been to Oberammergau?" Christine asked Anne.

When she knew perfectly well Anne hadn't! Why did the simplest question sound insolent when Christine asked it?

"Of course a family ties you down terribly," said Christine. "Oh, whom do you think I saw last month when I was in Halifax? That little friend of yours...the one who married the ugly minister...what *was* his name?"

"Jonas Blake," said Anne. "Philippa Gordon married him. And I never thought he was ugly."

"*Didn't* you? Of course tastes differ. Well, anyway I met them. *Poor* Philippa!"

Christine's use of "poor" was very effective.

"Why poor?" asked Anne. "I think she and Jonas have been very happy."

"Happy! My dear, if you could see the place they live in! A wretched little fishing village where it was an excitement if the pigs broke into the garden! I was told that the Jonas-man had had a good church in Kingsport and had given it up because he thought it his 'duty' to go to the fishermen who 'needed' him. I have no use for such fanatics. 'How *can* you live in such an isolated, out-of-the-way place as this?' I asked Philippa. Do you know what she said?"

Christine threw out her beringed hands expressively.

"Perhaps what I would say of Glen St. Mary," said Anne. "That it was the only place in the world to live in."

"Fancy you being contented there," smiled Christine. *("That terrible mouthful of teeth!")* "Do you really never feel that you want a broader life? You used to be quite ambitious, if I remember aright. Didn't you write some rather clever little things when you were at Redmond? A bit fantastic and whimsical, of course, but still..."

"I wrote them for the people who still believe in fairyland. There is a surprising lot of them, you know, and they like to get news from that country."

"And you've quite given it up?"

"Not altogether...but I'm writing living epistles now," said Anne, thinking of Jem and Co.

Christine stared, not recognizing the quotation. What did Anne Shirley mean? But then, of course, she had been noted at Redmond for her mysterious speeches. She had kept her looks astonishingly but probably she was one of those women who got married and stopped thinking. Poor Gilbert! She had hooked him before he came to Redmond. He had never had the least chance to escape her.

"Does anybody ever eat philopenas now?" asked Dr. Murray, who had just cracked a twin almond. Christine turned to Gilbert.

"Do you remember that philopena *we* ate once?" she asked. *("Did a significant look pass between them?")*

"Do you suppose I could forget it?" asked Gilbert.

They plunged into a spate of "do-you-remembers," while Anne stared at the picture of fish and oranges hanging over the sideboard. She had never thought that Gilbert and Christine had had so many memories in common. "Do you remember our picnic up the Arm?...Do you remember the night we went to the negro church?...Do you remember the night we went to the masquerade?...you were a Spanish lady in a black velvet dress with a lace mantilla and fan."

Gilbert apparently remembered them all in detail. But he had forgotten his wedding anniversary!

When they went back to the drawing-room Christine glanced out of the window at an eastern sky that was showing pale silver behind the dark poplars.

"Gilbert, let us take a stroll in the garden. I want to learn again the meaning of moonrise in September."

("Does moonrise mean anything in September that it doesn't mean in any other month? And what does she mean by 'again.' Did she ever learn it before...with him?")

Out they went. Anne felt that she had been very neatly and sweetly brushed aside. She sat down on a chair that commanded a view of the garden...though she would not admit even to herself that she selected it for that reason. She could see Christine and Gilbert walking down the path. What were they saying to each other? Christine seemed to be doing most of the talking. Perhaps Gilbert was too dumb with emotion to speak. Was he smiling out there in the moonrise over memories in which she had no share? She recalled nights she and Gilbert had walked in moonlit gardens of Avonlea. Had *he* forgotten?

Christine was looking up at the sky. Of course she knew she was showing off that fine, full white throat of hers when she lifted her face like that. Did ever a moon take so long in rising?

Other guests were dropping in when they finally came back. There was talk, laughter, music. Christine sang...very well. She had always been "musical." She sang *at* Gilbert..."the dear dead days beyond recall." Gilbert leaned back in an easy-chair and was uncommonly silent. Was he looking back wistfully to those dear dead days? Was he picturing what his life would have been if he had married Christine? *("I've always known what Gilbert was thinking of before. My head is beginning to ache. If we don't get away soon I'll be throwing up my head and howling. Thank heaven our train leaves early.")*

When Anne came downstairs Christine was standing in the porch with Gilbert. She reached up and picked a leaf from his shoulder; the gesture was like a caress.

"Are you really well, Gilbert? You look frightfully tired. I *know* you're overdoing it."

A wave of horror swept over Annie. Gilbert *did* look tired... frightfully tired...and she hadn't seen it until Christine pointed it out! Never would she forget the humiliation of that moment. *("I've been taking Gilbert too much for granted and blaming him for doing the same thing.")*

Christine turned to her.

"It's been so nice to meet you again, Anne. Quite like old times."

"Quite," said Anne.

"But I've just been telling Gilbert he looked a little tired. You ought to take better care of him, Anne. There was a time, you know, when I really had quite a fancy for this husband of yours. I believe he really was the nicest beau I ever had. But you must forgive me since I didn't take him from you."

Anne froze up again.

"Perhaps he is pitying himself that you didn't," she said, with a certain "queenishness" not unknown to Christine in Redmond days, as she stepped into Dr. Fowler's carriage for the drive to the station.

"You dear funny thing!" said Christine, with a shrug of her

beautiful shoulders. She was looking after them as if something amused her hugely.

41

"Had a nice evening?" asked Gilbert, more absently than ever as he helped her on the train.

"Oh, lovely," said Anne...who felt that she had, in Jane Welsh Carlyle's splendid phrase, "spent the evening under a harrow."

"What made you do your hair that way?" said Gilbert still absently.

"It's the new fashion."

"Well, it doesn't suit you. It may be all right for some hair but not for yours."

"Oh, it is too bad my hair is red," said Anne icily.

Gilbert thought he was wise in dropping a dangerous subject. Anne, he reflected, had always been a bit sensitive about her hair. He was too tired to talk, anyway. He leaned his head back on the car seat and shut his eyes. For the first time Anne noticed little glints of grey in the hair above his ears. But she hardened her heart.

They walked silently home from the Glen station by the short-cut to Ingleside. The air was filled with the breath of spruce and spice fern. The moon was shining over dew-wet fields. They passed an old deserted house with sad and broken windows that had once danced with light. "Just like my life," thought Anne. Everything seemed to have for her some dreary meaning now. The dim white moth that fluttered past them on the lawn was, she thought sadly, like a ghost of faded love. Then she caught her foot in a croquet hoop and nearly fell headlong into a clump of phlox. What on earth did the children mean by leaving it there? She would tell them what she thought about it tomorrow!

Gilbert only said, "O-o-o-ps!" and steadied her with a hand. Would he have been so casual about it if it had been Christine who had tripped while they were puzzling out the meaning of moonrises?

Gilbert rushed off to his office the moment they were inside the house and Anne went silently up to their room, where the moonlight was lying on the floor, still and silver and cold. She went to the open window and looked out. It was evidently the Carter Flaggs' dog's night to howl and he was putting his heart into it. The lombardy leaves glistened like silver in the moonlight. The house about her seemed whispering tonight... whispering sinisterly, as if it were no longer her friend.

Anne felt sick and cold and empty. The gold of life had turned to withered leaves. Nothing had any meaning any longer. Everything seemed remote and unreal.

Far down the tide was keeping its world-old tryst with the shore. She could...now that Norman Douglas had cut down his spruce bush...see her little House of Dreams. How happy they had been there...when it was enough just to be together in their own home, with their visions, their caresses, their silences! All the colour of the morning in their lives...Gilbert looking at her with that smile in his eyes he kept for her alone...finding every day a new way of saying, "I love you"...sharing laughter as they shared sorrow.

And now...Gilbert had grown tired of her. Men had always been like that...always would be. She had thought Gilbert was an exception but now she knew the truth. And how was she going to adjust her life to it?

"There are the children, of course," she thought dully. "I must go on living for them. And nobody must know...*nobody.* I will not be pitied."

What was that? Somebody was coming up the stairs, three steps at a time, as Gilbert used to do long ago in the House of Dreams...as he had not done for a long time now. It couldn't be Gilbert...it was!

He burst into the room...he flung a little packet on the table...he caught Anne by the waist and waltzed her round and round the room like a crazy schoolboy, coming to rest at last breathlessly in a silver pool of moonlight.

"I was right, Anne...thank God, I was right! Mrs. Garrow is going to be all right...the specialist has said so."

"Mrs. Garrow? Gilbert, have you gone crazy?"

"Didn't I tell you? Surely I told you...well, I suppose it's been such a sore subject I just couldn't talk of it. I've been worried to death about it for the past two weeks...couldn't think of anything else, waking or sleeping. Mrs. Garrow lives in Lowbridge and was Parker's patient. He asked me in for a consultation...I diagnosed her case differently from him...we almost fought...I was sure I was right...I insisted there was a chance...we sent her to Montreal...Parker said she'd never come back alive...her husband was ready to shoot me on sight. When she was gone I went to bits...perhaps I *was* mistaken...perhaps I'd tortured her needlessly. I found the letter in my office when I went in...I was *right*...they've operated...she has an excellent chance of living. Anne girl, I could jump over the moon! I've shed twenty years."

Anne had either to laugh or cry...so she began to laugh. It was lovely to be able to laugh again...lovely to feel like laughing. Everything was suddenly all right.

"I suppose that is why you forgot this was our anniversary?" she taunted him.

Gilbert released her long enough to pounce on the little packet he had dropped on the table.

"I didn't forget it. Two weeks ago I sent to Toronto for this. And it didn't come till tonight. I felt so small this morning when I hadn't a thing to give you that I didn't mention the day...

thought you'd forgotten it, too...hoped you had. When I went into the office there was my present along with Parker's letter. See how you like it."

It was a little diamond pendant. Even in the moonlight it sparkled like a living thing.

"Gilbert...and I..."

"Try it on. I wish it had come this morning...then you'd have had something to wear to the dinner besides that old enamel heart. Though it *did* look rather nice snuggling in that pretty white hollow in your throat, darling. Why didn't you leave on that green dress, Anne? I liked it...it reminded me of that dress with the rosebuds on it you used to wear at Redmond."

("So he had noticed the dress! So he still remembered the old Redmond one he had admired so much!")

Anne felt like a released bird...she was flying again. Gilbert's arms were around her...his eyes were looking into hers in the moonlight.

"You *do* love me, Gilbert? I'm not just a habit with you? You haven't *said* you loved me for so long."

"My dear, dear love! I didn't think you needed words to know that. I couldn't live without you. Always you give me strength. There's a verse somewhere in the Bible that is meant for you...'She will do him good and not evil all the days of her life.'"

Life which had seemed so grey and foolish a few moments before was golden and rose and splendidly rainbowed again. The diamond pendant slipped to the floor, unheeded for the moment. It was beautiful...but there were so many things lovelier...confidence and peace and delightful work...laughter and kindness...that old *safe* feeling of a sure love.

"Oh, if we could keep this moment for ever, Gilbert!"

"We're going to have some moments. It's time we had a second honeymoon. Anne, there's going to be a big medical congress in London next February. We're going to it...and after it we'll see a bit of the Old World. There's a holiday coming to us. We'll be nothing but lovers again...it will be just like being married over again. You haven't been like yourself for a long time. *("So he had noticed.")* You're tired and overworked...you need a change. *("You too, dearest. I've been so horribly blind.")* I'm not going to have it cast up to me that doctors' wives never get a pill. We'll come back rested and fresh, with our sense of humour completely restored. Well, try your pendant on and let's get to bed. I'm half dead for sleep...haven't had a decent night's sleep for weeks, what with twins and worry over Mrs. Garrow."

"What on earth were you and Christine talking about so long in the garden tonight?" asked Anne, peacocking before the mirror with her diamonds.

Gilbert yawned.

"Oh, I don't know. Christine just gabbled on. But here is one fact she presented me with. A flea can jump two hundred times its own length. Did you know that, Anne?"

("They were talking of fleas when I was writhing with jealousy. What an idiot I've been!")

"How on earth did you come to be talking of fleas?"

"I can't remember...perhaps it was Dobermann pinschers suggested it."

"Dobermann pinschers! *What* are Dobermann pinschers?"

"A new kind of dog. Christine seems to be a dog connoisseur. I was so obsessed with Mrs. Garrow that I didn't pay much attention to what she was saying. Now and then I caught a word about complexes and repressions...that new psychology that's coming up...and art...and gout and politics...and frogs."

"Frogs!"

"Some experiments a Winnipeg research man is making. Christine was never very entertaining, but she's a worse bore than ever. And malicious! She never used to be malicious."

"What did she say that was so malicious?" asked Anne innocently.

"Didn't you notice? Oh, I suppose you wouldn't catch on... you're so free from that sort of thing yourself. Well, it doesn't matter. That laugh of hers got on my nerves a bit. And she's got fat. Thank goodness, you haven't got fat, Anne-girl."

"Oh, I don't think she is so very fat," said Anne charitably. "And she certainly is a very handsome woman."

"So-so. But her face has got hard...she's the same age as you but she looks ten years older."

"And you talking to her about immortal youth!"

Gilbert grinned guiltily.

"One has to say something civil. Civilization can't exist without a *little* hypocrisy. Oh, well, Christine isn't a bad old scout, even if she doesn't belong to the race of Joseph. It's not her fault that the pinch of salt was left out of her. What's this?"

"My anniversary remembrance for you. And I want a cent for it...I'm not taking any risks. Such tortures as I've endured this evening! I was eaten up with jealousy of Christine."

Gilbert looked genuinely astonished. It had never occurred to him that Anne could be jealous of anybody.

"Why, Anne-girl, I never thought you had it in you."

"Oh, but I have. Why, years ago I was madly jealous of your correspondence with Ruby Gillis."

"*Did* I ever correspond with Ruby Gillis? I'd forgotten. Poor Ruby! But what about Roy Gardner? The pot mustn't call the kettle black."

"Roy Gardner? Philippa wrote me not long ago that she'd seen him and he'd got positively corpulent. Gilbert, Dr. Murray may be a very eminent man in his profession but he looks just like a lath and Dr. Fowler looked like a doughnut. You looked so handsome...and *finished...* beside them."

"Oh, thanks...thanks. That's something like a wife should say. By way of returning the compliment I thought you looked unusually well tonight, Anne, in spite of that dress. You had a little colour and your eyes were gorgeous. Ah-h-h, that's good! No place like bed when you're all in. There's another verse in the Bible...queer how those old verses you learn in Sunday School come back to you through life!...'I will lay me down in peace and sleep.' In peace...and sleep...goo'night."

Gilbert was asleep almost before he finished the word. Dearest tired Gilbert! Babies might come and babies might go but none should disturb his rest that night. The telephone might ring its head off.

Anne was not sleepy. She was too happy to sleep just yet. She moved softly about the room, putting things away, braiding her hair, looking like a beloved woman. Finally she slipped on a negligee and went across the hall to the boys' room. Walter and Jem in their bed and Shirley in his cot were all sound asleep. The Shrimp, who had outlived generations of pert kittens and become a family habit, was curled up at Shirley's feet. Jem had fallen asleep while reading "The Life Book of Captain Jim"...it was open on the spread. Why, how *long* Jem looked lying under the bedclothes! He would soon be grown up. What a sturdy reliable little chap he was! Walter was smiling in his sleep as someone who knew a charming secret. The moon was shining on his pillow through the bars of the leaded window...casting the shadow of a clearly defined cross on the wall above his head. In long after years Annie was to remember that and wonder if it were an omen of Courcelette...of a cross-marked grave "somewhere in France." But tonight it was only a shadow...nothing more. The rash had quite gone from Shirley's neck. Gilbert had been right. He was always right.

Nan and Diana and Rilla were in the next room...Diana with darling little damp red curls all over her head and one little sunburned hand under her cheek, and Nan with long fans of lashes brushing hers. The eyes behind those blue-veined lids were hazel like her father's. And Rilla was sleeping on her stomach. Anne turned her right side up but her buttoned eyes never opened.

They were all growing so fast. In just a few short years they would be all young men and women...youth tiptoe...expectant...a-star with its sweet wild dreams...little ships sailing out of safe harbour to unknown ports. The boys would go away to their life work and the girls...ah, the mist-veiled forms of beautiful brides might be seen coming down the old stairs at Ingleside. But they would be still hers for a few years yet...hers to love and guide...to sing the songs that so many mothers had sung. Hers... and Gilbert's.

She went out and down the hall to the oriel window. All her suspicions and jealousies and resentments had gone where old moons go. She felt confident and gay and blithe.

"Blythe! I feel Blythe," she said, laughing at the foolish little pun. "I feel exactly as I did that morning Pacifique told me Gilbert had 'got de turn.'"

Below her was the mystery and loveliness of a garden at night. The far-away hills, dusted with moonlight, were a poem. Before many months she would be seeing moonlight on the far dim hills of Scotland...over Melrose...over ruined Kenilworth... over the church by the Avon where Shakespeare slept...perhaps even over the Colosseum...over the Acropolis...over sorrowful rivers flowing by dead empires.

The night was cool; soon the sharper, cooler nights of autumn would come; then the deep snow...the deep white snow...the deep cold snow of winter...nights wild with wind and storm. But who would care? There would be the magic of firelight in gracious rooms...hadn't Gilbert spoken not long ago of apple logs he was getting to burn in the fireplace? They would glorify the grey days that were bound to come. What would matter drifted snow and biting wind when love burned clear and bright, with spring beyond? And all the little sweetnesses of life sprinkling the road.

She turned away from the window. In her white gown, with her hair in its two long braids, she looked like the Anne of

Green Gables days...of Redmond days...of the House of Dreams days. That inward glow was still shining through her. Through the open doorway came the soft sound of children breathing. Gilbert, who seldom snored, was indubitably snoring now. Anne grinned. She thought of something Christine had said. Poor childless Christine, shooting her little arrows of mockery.

"What a family!" Anne repeated exultantly.

Also available in the L. M. Montgomery Kindred Classics series:

Anne of Green Gables & Anne of Avonlea
978-1-77471-262-7

Anne of the Island & Anne of Windy Poplars
978-1-77471-429-4